EMBERSTONE'S FLAME

CRYSTAL BUCHANAN

EmberStone's Flame

Copyright © 2025 by Crystal Buchanan.

MILTON & HUGO L.L.C.
4407 Park Ave., Suite 5
Union City, NJ 07087, USA

Website: *www. miltonandhugo.com*
Hotline: *1- 888-778-0033*
Email: *info@miltonandhugo.com*

Ordering Information:
Quantity sales. Special discounts are granted to corporations, associations, and other organizations. For more information on these discounts, please reach out to the publisher using the contact information provided above.

Library of Congress Control Number: 2025910070
ISBN-13:   979-8-89285-569-3   [Paperback Edition]
                979-8-89285-570-9   [Hardback Edition]
                979-8-89285-571-6   [Digital Edition]

Rev. date: 05/29/2025

CONTENTS

DEDICATION

This book is dedicated to readers who find comfort in the shadows who embrace the darkness and who appreciate the captivating dance between love and destruction. It is for those who crave stories that delve deep into the complexities of morally ambiguous characters revealing their struggles and triumphs. These narratives explore the fascinating pull of forbidden desires where passion intertwines with danger creating a potent mix of emotion and intrigue. It invites those drawn to intense battles fought not only with swords and fire but also with hearts and souls illustrating the profound conflicts that arise within. This journey through the depths of human experience promises to resonate with anyone who understands that light and dark are often entwined in unexpected ways.

To the lovers of dark fantasy romance, who understand the allure of a villain's charm and the bittersweet agony of a love born amidst chaos and bloodshed, this story stands as a testament to your unwavering passion for the unconventional. It celebrates narratives that defy simple categorization and characters who challenge our perceptions of good and evil.

This dedication is also for readers who deeply value the intricate blending of action and emotion where intense physical combat seamlessly intertwines with emotionally charged encounters that leave a lasting imprint on the soul. It is for those who appreciate the beauty found in the broken moments recognizing the strength that often lies in vulnerability. These readers understand the enduring power of connections forged in adversity where challenges bring people together and reveal their true selves. They celebrate the complexities of human experience embracing the highs and lows and finding meaning in the struggles that shape our lives reminding us that love and resilience can emerge even from chaos.

This book is for anyone who has felt the sting of betrayal, the burning desire for vengeance, and the intoxicating embrace of a love that transcends boundaries and defies logic. It is for those seeking not just a story but an experience of a journey into the heart of darkness, where passions burn bright and the lines between right and wrong blur into an enticing tapestry of desire and destruction. May this tale ignite your imagination, stir your emotions, and leave you breathlessly anticipating what lies beyond the final page. For it is in the shadows, where the most intense loves are found, that the truest stories reside. May this one find its way into your heart and stay there, burning long after you've turned the last page. This is a story of love, loss, and the fires that forge our souls. It is a story for you.

CHAPTER

ONE

Whispering Boneyard

T he razor-edged Kethani wind howled a mournful dirge, whipping through the skeletal remains of what was once my home, Oakhaven. Embers, like dying stars in the perpetually twilight sky of the Ashfall, flickered amidst the charred wood and crumbling grey stone, the remnants of the once proud Hearthstone architecture. I gasped, the atmosphere heavy with the smell of smoke, acrid and metallic, the lingering breath of the Drakon's fire. A coppery tang, unnatural and sickening, clung to my throat, a bitter taste mirroring the agony in my heart. Nineteen years old, and all I had left were ashes, the acrid scent clinging to my clothes like a shroud, and the ghosts of screams, the screams of my family, their faces twisted in terror, forever etched in my memory echoing in the wind, a constant, chilling chorus. My lungs burned with each ragged breath, the air thin and choked with ash, each inhalation a physical torment. I could still feel the heat radiating from the ground, a phantom touch of the inferno, the Drakon's inferno that had consumed everything.

The ground itself was cracked and blackened, the very earth seared and scarred. Even the resilient Kethani earth, known for its enduring strength, showed Drakon's power. I closed my eyes, the screams still ringing in my ears, a symphony of terror I couldn't escape, punctuated by the relentless screech of the Ashfall wind whistling through the broken window frames. The once vibrant blue of the Skystone River now choked with ash and debris, was barely visible beyond the ruined

1

fields. My fingers, raw and bleeding, clutched the charred remains of my mother's embroidered shawl, the only tangible piece of my past that survived. The Drakon had taken everything, but not my will to survive. Not yet.

Two years. Two years after the Obsidian Covenant, those obsidian-skinned devils from the Shattered Peaks descended upon Oakhaven, their shadow falling like a shroud of death around me. Their arrival wasn't heralded by trumpets or a thunderous roar but by a creeping silence, broken only by the unsettling whisper of the wind whistling through the newly fractured earth. The earth trembled not just from their demonic legions but from the very fabric of reality warping under their influence. Their laughter, a chilling counterpoint to the screams I heard, echoed with the guttural rasp of something ancient and malevolent, a sound that still haunts my dreams. I remember the searing heat of the hellfire, not the fiery orange of mortal flames, but an unholy, violet fire that smelled of brimstone and decaying flesh. It licked at my skin, branding me with scars that ran deeper than I ever Thought Possible, scars that pulse with phantom pain. The sickening crunch of bone, so many bones underfoot, the ground slick with blood and a viscous, obsidian ichor that the demons dripped from their jagged, obsidian weapons. The terrified eyes of my parents, wide and pleading, were consumed by shadows that coalesced from the very air itself, not simple darkness, but a palpable entity, a ravenous hunger given form. Their last breaths were snatched away by something that felt less like death and more like a deliberate, agonizing erasure.

The Obsidian Covenant didn't merely kill; they unmade. The air itself felt different afterward, heavy with the lingering scent of sulphur and despair, the taste of ash clinging to the back of my throat. Even the sun seemed dimmer, its light choked by the lingering darkness of the Covenant's passage. The whispers still linger in the ruins of Oakhaven, whispers of forgotten gods and broken pacts, of a power so ancient and corrupt it threatens to unravel the very world. I can still feel the heat, the fear, the overwhelming despair. The memories, raw and visceral, claw at me still, fueling the inferno of rage that burns within my very soul, a rage that is tempered only by the icy determination to avenge my people, to cleanse this world of the Obsidian Covenant's vile taint. It's a fire I can't extinguish but one I will wield.

I wasn't just a survivor; I was a Flame elemental, my very essence woven from the Whisperwind Fire, a volatile, sentient flame that pulsed deep within the heart of Mount Cinder Fang. This inherent power, once a source of wonder and a mark of my lineage, the last of the Cinderkin, now felt like a cruel mockery, a constant reminder of my failure to protect those I loved. The Whisperwind Fire within me pulsed, a throbbing echo of my grief, my fury, a tempestuous rage that mirrored the volcanic heart of my ancestral home. Its heat radiated from my skin, not as a gentle warmth, but as a scorching inferno, a tangible manifestation of my burning resentment, capable of igniting dry brush a league away. The flames felt like a brand, a searing reminder of the night the Shadow Blight consumed my village, its obsidian tendrils choking the life from the earth, leaving only ash and the ghosts of screams in their wake. I tasted ash and bitterness, the metallic tang of my sorrow, but also the acrid scent of the Blight, a lingering horror that clung to my senses, a phantom pain sharper than any physical wound.

My very being was a paradox: I was the last spark of a dying race, forged in the fires of Mount Cinder Fang, yet burdened by its destruction. The obsidian shards embedded in my skin, fragments from the Blight's attack, pulsed faintly with a dark energy that mirrored the fire's inferno, a constant, chilling reminder of my defeat. I could still feel the tremors of the mountain's grief, a low hum resonating through my bones, a shared sorrow that bound me to the ravaged land. The once fertile plains around Cinder Fang were now barren wastelands, scarred by the Blight's passage, a desolate testament to the power I had failed to control. My vengeance was not merely a personal quest; it was a duty to my ancestors, to the fallen Cinderkin, and to the ravaged land itself. The Whisperwind Fire demanded retribution.

The Covenant's attack wasn't random. I knew, somehow, a gut feeling sharpened by years spent studying their grim history etched in the petrified wood of the Whispering Boneyard that it had been meticulously planned, brutally efficient. They hadn't just destroyed Oakhaven; they'd obliterated it with a precision that suggested knowledge far beyond simple conquest. Oakhaven, nestled in the emerald valley between the Whisperwind Mountains and the petrified forest, wasn't just a village; it was a nexus of the old ways, a repository of forgotten crafts. The artisans, famed for their intricate clockwork automatons powered by captured sunstones, and the farmers, who cultivated strains of luminescent wheat that sustained our valley through the long winters, were more than villagers; they were guardians of fragile equilibrium. Their mastery of the arcane arts passed down through generations, was a threat the Covenant couldn't tolerate.

They hadn't just used fire; the air itself had crackled with malevolent energy, a corrupted magic that twisted the very fabric of reality. The ground, once fertile and vibrant, was now a choked wasteland, poisoned by their unholy sorcery. I saw the villagers, their faces contorted in silent screams, not merely reduced to smouldering corpses, but transformed into grotesque parodies of their former selves, their bodies warped and twisted into monstrous forms by the Covenant's dark magic. Their screams, I realized, weren't just sounds; they were whispers clinging to the poisoned air, a haunting chorus of agony that followed me through the ravaged landscape. The crackling flames weren't just fire; they were fueled by a demonic essence, dancing like mocking spirits, each flickering a cruel reminder of the lives extinguished.

I fought, desperate, fueled by adrenaline and the raw, primal instinct to survive, but also by a burning rage born of betrayal. The Covenant, sworn protectors of the Elder Pact, had violated every sacred oath, every tenet of their purported faith. Their claws, I discovered, weren't just demonic; they were tipped with shards of obsidian harvested from the forbidden heart of the Whisperwind Mountains, each strike carrying a debilitating curse. The chilling touch of death wasn't just a fleeting sensation; it was the cold embrace of the Obsidian Blight, a creeping corruption that threatened to consume not only my body but my very soul. I survived, barely, escaping through a hidden passage known only to the village elder, a tunnel that led into the labyrinthine tunnels beneath the petrified forest. But the cost... the cost was terrible. I carry it with me, a constant, burning weight, the chilling memory of Oakhaven's destruction, and the knowledge that the Covenant will stop at nothing to claim all that remains of the old ways, and with it, the very essence of our world.

I clutched a small, obsidian shard in my hand, its surface cool and smooth against my burning skin. The obsidian itself was unlike any I'd ever seen deeper black than night, seeming to absorb rather than reflect the meagre light filtering through the ravaged remains of Oakhaven. It was a fragment of the Covenant's sigil, a grim reminder of the demonic forces that had shattered my life. The sigil itself, as I remembered it from the village elder's whispered warnings, was a swirling vortex of crimson and black, a representation of the abyss from which the Covenant drew its power. This shard, however, was only obsidian, hinting at a ritualistic shattering, a deliberate destruction perhaps meant to obscure the true nature of their power.

It was the only thing I had salvaged from the carnage, a tangible link to the perpetrators of my village's destruction. The air still tasted of sulphur and ash, a phantom smell clinging to the tattered remnants of my once peaceful home. The bodies, mostly ash and bone now, lay scattered amidst the twisted, blackened timbers of what were once homes. Even the river, usually a silver ribbon through the valley, ran sluggish and black, choked with debris and something…else. Something that slithered beneath the surface glimpsed in the briefest moments. This shard wasn't just a memento; it was a burning promise, a testament to my unwavering dedication to revenge. My fingers traced the cryptic clue, a fragment of a map etched into its surface, not merely lines, but symbols, arcane glyphs that spoke of twisted geography, places known only to those who dabbled in forbidden knowledge.

The map hinted at a path to one of the Covenant's most powerful demons, Malkor, a being I believed played a crucial role in Oakhaven's destruction. He was a Lord of the Burning Mire, a fetid swamp to the west, a place shunned even by the most hardened hunters, whispered to be the gateway to the Abyss itself. The very air above the Mire was said to hum with malevolent energy, distorting the sun's light into an eerie, blood-red glow. I would find him. I would make him pay. The shard felt warm now, pulsing faintly in my hand, a grim compass guiding me toward my vengeance.

The map, etched with runes that burned with infernal light only when exposed to the specific alchemical flame of a dried, crushed Nightshade bloom, had been painstakingly deciphered over months.

Months spent hunched over the brittle parchment in the dimly lit Scriptorium of the Order of the Silver Flame, the air thick with the scent of aging vellum and the faint, metallic tang of dragon's blood ink. My fingers, calloused from years of painstaking research, traced the glyphs, a language older than the mountains, a dialect of the fallen angels, understood only by a handful of initiates within the Covenant. It led me, not to a place on any known cartography, but to a person, a demon known as Malkor, a twisted creature whose dark power was whispered of in hushed tones even among the Covenant's elite, the Circle of Ash. Malkor's name, however, wasn't simply written; it appeared on the fragment as if branded there with molten infernal metal, the runes themselves seeming to writhe with malevolent energy that even the protective sigils woven into the parchment struggled to contain. I saw it and felt a chill run down my spine that had nothing to do with the Scriptorium's perpetually frigid temperature. Its very existence spoke volumes, not just of the level of devastation he'd caused, but of the methods used. The whispered tales spoke of corrupted landscapes, of rivers turned to molten glass, of armies annihilated not by brute force, but by the insidious twisting of their very souls.

The very core of his being, it was said, was an inferno of rage and cruelty fueled by a forbidden pact with a primordial entity known only as the Devourer. He was the key, I realized, the key that could unlock the truth behind the massacre at Oakhaven, the systematic slaughter of my family, their souls consumed, leaving behind only the blackened husks of their once vibrant lives. He was the key to my vengeance, a vengeance that had consumed me for the past five years, driving me deeper and deeper into the forbidden lore of the Covenant. The Order, once a refuge, now felt like a cage, its rules and restrictions suffocating my desperate need for justice. But Malkor's location was only the first step; finding him would be the true test.

The journey to find Malkor was fraught with peril. My heart hammered against my ribs with each step through the Ashen Wastes, the land scarred not only by demonic influence but by the lingering aftershocks of the Cataclysm, a cataclysmic event centuries past that had shattered the world and birthed the very demons Malkor now commanded. The atmosphere, heavy with the odour of sulphur and death, a smell that clung to me like a shroud, was further tainted by the acrid tang of petrified blood, a constant reminder of the countless lives consumed by this cursed realm. I saw grotesque creatures, warped by demonic influence, their forms twisted mockeries of nature's beauty; the Kryll, with their iridescent, chitinous carapaces and razor-sharp mandibles; the Ashwalkers, skeletal monstrosities dragging themselves across the landscape, their bodies perpetually aflame; and the Grotesques, shifting, amorphous beings whose forms shifted and changed with alarming speed, defying any easy description. Their very existence was a chilling testament to Malkor's power, a twisted reflection of his corrupted essence. I fought my way through hordes of lesser demons, my flames, drawn from the last embers of the Sunstone, a relic from a time before the Cataclysm, a desperate dance of destruction, a whirlwind born of fury and fear.

My weapon, a sword made from the heart of a dying star, made a sad sound as it cut through the flesh of demons. Each swing felt like it carried the sadness of many souls who had suffered under the harsh rule of darkness. With every swing of the shiny blade I felt their pain mix with mine giving me the strength to keep going. I depended on my quick movements and my deep understanding of this cursed land which I gained from years of being a Shadow Walker. I navigated through dangerous terrain with surprising ease. I learned this skill out of necessity and to survive. I saw the hardened rivers of lava winding through this empty land. The lava which was once hot and flowing now felt dangerous and solid. The canyons around me were filled with shaky tectonic plates making it risky for anyone who wasn't careful. As I walked on the shifting sands I felt like I was walking on a hidden danger. There were deep holes beneath me waiting to catch anyone who wasn't careful. I knew each of these dangers well. I moved through them with a skill that felt like second nature as if I was dancing with death itself.

Every time I faced the strange creatures in this world it made me stronger. Each time I escaped death I learned something important. I narrowly escaped Kryll's deadly jaws which made me realize just how close I was to danger. Then I had to jump across a deep gap that suddenly appeared under me pushing my limits and instincts to the test.

The path wound through the Whisperwind Peaks, a jagged, unforgiving range where the wind howled like a banshee and the snow fell perpetually, clinging to the obsidian cliffs like the icy grip of despair. Each step was a battle against the elements, against the treacherous, frost-covered terrain, and the gnawing emptiness in my gut. The air itself seemed to carry the scent of death, a bitter blend of charred wood and frozen blood, a constant, suffocating reminder of Oakhaven's demise. It had been a village of vibrant life, nestled in the sun-drenched valley below, its laughter now replaced by the mournful cry of ravens circling the skeletal remains of homes. Malkor, the obsidian sorcerer, had unleashed a storm of shadow and fire, leaving behind only ashes and sorrow.

The stench of ash clung to my threadbare cloak, once the emerald glory of Oakhaven, now a ragged shroud the colour of despair. Its rough wool scraped against my skin, a constant, agonizing reminder of my ruin. The silver oak leaf, my sister Elara's cursed gift, bit into my flesh, a frigid weight against my chest, a tangible link to the inferno that stole everything. I could taste the metallic tang of blood, mine, perhaps, mingling with hers, a phantom echo of the screams that still clawed at the edges of my sanity.

Elara's smile, a sunburst against the encroaching darkness, haunted my memory, a cruel mockery of the life she'd had, snatched away in a heartbeat. I felt the phantom warmth of her hand in mine, the ghostly pressure of her embrace, before the flames consumed her, leaving only the bitter taste of ash and regret. Her image, along with the ravaged faces of my parents, and my friends, their eyes wide with terror, their skin blistered and blackened, seared themselves onto the back of my eyelids, a horrifying carousel of loss. Each ghostly visage stoked the fire in my gut, a burning coal of vengeance that threatened to consume me as thoroughly as Malkor's hellfire had consumed them. This rage, this incandescent fury, would be my salvation. It would be Malkor's damnation.

The whispering voices of doubt were not just figments of my imagination; they were echoes of Malkor's dark magic, slithering into my mind, trying to break my spirit, to make me abandon my quest. But the fire within me, a burning ember of vengeance nurtured by years of grief and fueled by the memories of Oakhaven's joyous festivals and the warmth of hearth fires, refused to be extinguished. It burned hotter than any blizzard, brighter than any shadow. I would find Malkor, in his obsidian tower, high atop the jagged peaks, and I would make him pay for what he had done. I would avenge Oakhaven.

My training, rigorous and unforgiving, had prepared me for the brutality of this quest. It wasn't just the physical conditioning, the gruelling dawn-to-dusk drills in the Obsidian Fields, the bone-jarring climbs up the razor-edged peaks of the Whispering Mountains, the weeks spent enduring the hallucinatory heat of the Scarlet Sands. No, it was the mental fortitude, forged in the crucible of the Order of the Silent Fang. We learned to control our breathing, to still our minds amidst chaos, to anticipate the enemy's move before they even conceived of it. We learned to read the subtle shifts in the wind, and the tremor of the earth not just through heightened senses, but through a deep, almost mystical connection to the very land itself. This connection fostered through generations of ritual and meditation in the heart of the Whispering Caves, was as much a weapon as any blade.

I possessed skills that made me more than just a survivor; I was a warrior, a force of nature honed by the harsh realities of the Broken Lands. My twin blades, Whisper and Fang, danced in my hands like extensions of my own will, forged from the heart of a fallen star and imbued with the spirits of long-dead warriors. I moved like a wraith, silent and deadly, my movements precise and economical, a testament to years spent mastering the art of shadow walking, a technique passed down through the generations of my family, a lineage of assassins sworn to protect the ancient secrets of the Sunken City. My senses were heightened, enabling me to detect the slightest tremor in the ground, the faintest shift in the air, the subtle scent of fear or treachery. Even the whispers of the wind carried secrets to my trained ears, the rustle of leaves revealing a hidden patrol, the sigh of the wind forecasting a shift in the weather, potentially life-threatening in these unforgiving lands.

Years spent honing my abilities in the unforgiving wilderness, the treacherous swamps of the Black Mire, and the frost-choked valleys of the Frozen Peaks had transformed me into a predator, capable of both brutal efficiency and cunning strategy. But it wasn't just survival

I mastered; I learned to thrive, to read the land like a map, to use its very elements, the shadows, the wind, and the earth itself to my advantage. My quest was not just a test of strength, but a test of my will, my cunning, and my unwavering connection to the ancient power that flowed through my veins, a power both a blessing and a curse in the Broken Lands.

The demon-infested lands weren't simply a geographically defined region; they were a blighted scar upon the face of Aetheros, a continent fractured by a cataclysmic war between the angelic Host and the infernal legions centuries past. The very air hummed with malevolent energy, a palpable corruption that seeped into the bones and twisted the landscape. Twisted, skeletal trees clawed at the perpetually twilight sky, their branches adorned with the desiccated corpses of long-dead creatures. Rivers ran black, their waters thick with a viscous ichor that reeked of sulphur and decay. The demonic presence wasn't just felt; it was seen, in the grotesque, shifting shadows that danced at the periphery of vision, in the unsettling whispers carried on the wind, and in the horrifying creatures that stalked the ravaged land: hulking, obsidian golems animated by dark magic, wraiths with eyes burning like embers, and the occasional glimpse of something far, far worse, something that lurked in the deepest chasms, its true form veiled in impenetrable darkness.

My vampiric curse, a consequence of the attack by the Crimson Hand, a notorious cult dedicated to Malkor, the fallen god of shadows, was inextricably linked to this corrupted land. The demonic energy amplified my thirst, feeding the darkness within me like a starved beast. The hunger wasn't merely for blood; it was a craving for the very essence of life, a desire to consume the light from the world and leave only ashes in its wake. My memories, once a source of strength, were now a torment, each vivid image a searing brand that fueled both my rage and the insidious whispers of the darkness. They promised oblivion, a release from the unending pain, a reunion with the family lost to the Crimson Hand's brutal savagery.

My only allies in this desolate wasteland were the remnants of the Silver Order, a clandestine group of vampire hunters sworn to eradicate the Crimson Hand and contain the spread of demonic influence. Their methods were as ruthless as the enemy they faced, but their commitment to the light, however faint, offered a flicker of hope amid the encroaching darkness. I carried a relic gifted to me by their leader, a shard of obsidian blessed by a long-dead paladin, its cool touch a constant reminder of my vow, a shield against the encroaching abyss. But the obsidian's power waned with every passing day, its protective glow dimming as my humanity flickered. The battle was not only against the darkness within but also against the ever-present threat of the demonic hordes, each encountering a desperate gamble for survival, a dance with death upon the razor's edge.

The obsidian shard, a searing brand against my flesh, pulsed with a malevolent heat that mirrored the fire in my soul. It guided me, a treacherous compass through the blighted wastes, a landscape sculpted by the Covenant's depravity, a monument to their infernal triumph. Twisted, skeletal trees clawed at the sky, their gnarled branches like skeletal fingers reaching for my life. Jagged rocks, slick with a viscous, oily slime, crushed underfoot, the sound a hateful symphony in the oppressive silence. The air itself was a living thing, a miasma thick enough to taste, a fetid blend of decay and brimstone that choked my lungs and coated my tongue with the bitter ash of a thousand deaths. Despair, cold and absolute, pressed down, a crushing weight on my already burdened spirit.

The years I spent with the Order changed me and shaped me into a highly effective weapon. I didn't move like a ghost but with the quickness of a hungry wolf a spirit made from darkness and revenge. My senses honed by constant training and years of fighting shouted warnings: I could hear the soft movement of a snake sliding through the plants; I smelled the sharp scent of sulfur like a warning that something evil was coming; and I felt the deep rumbling heartbeat of a monster a strong pulse that shook my bones and warned me of danger. This wasn't just about staying alive; it was a painful struggle against death. It showed how determined I was and how much I hated the Covenant. That anger pushed me with every heartbeat, every step and every breath I took. *"I will not let myself down."*

My journey was a relentless, agonizing gauntlet. The raw, slick rock tore at my hands, leaving bleeding furrows that burned with every nerve-jangling grip as I wrestled my way through treacherous ravines. Sheer cliffs clawed at the sky, the wind a howling banshee screaming in my ears, a physical assault mirroring the terror that gnawed at my soul. The icy rivers choked with the rotting debris of a broken world, stole the feeling from my legs, the numb chill seeping into my very bones.

I wasn't merely evading patrols; I was dodging nightmares given flesh. Grotesque, mutated things, twisted mockeries of life, their flesh a festering canvas of the Covenant's depravity. Their very presence was a miasma of evil, a palpable stench of decay and demonic power that clawed at my sanity. These weren't just beasts; they were the whispers of hell made manifest, each corrupted sinew a testament to their unspeakable experiments. I saw the flicker of unholy intelligence in their vacant eyes, a chilling understanding of their monstrous existence.

The fight was not merely survival; it was a holy war waged in my soul. My flames, born of desperate defiance and righteous fury, erupted, a searing counterpoint to the chilling dread. They consumed those corrupted things, their flesh sizzling and popping like grotesque firecrackers, the stench of burning flesh and sulphur thick enough to choke on, a bitter perfume clinging to my clothes long after they were reduced to ash. Even the heat of the inferno was a meagre shield against the icy terror that threatened to consume me. Their death, however, offered a fleeting comfort, a fragile victory in a landscape of unending horror. I was not merely surviving; I was fighting for the memory of a world that no longer existed, a fight etched not only into my body but into the very core of my being.

The memory claws at me still, a visceral nightmare etched into my very soul. Those Grolak... hulking monstrosities, their claws like obsidian shards, their bark-like hide slick with the ichor of a thousand fallen foes. They weren't just an ambush; it was a maelstrom of snapping jaws and razor-edged fury, a tide of muscle and malice that crashed down in that cursed canyon. The air itself thrummed with their feral roars, a symphony of death that scraped raw the inside of my skull.

I fought like a cornered demon, a whirlwind of searing flame and desperate evasion. Each flicker of my pyre was a prayer, each incinerated Grolak a fleeting respite from the suffocating pressure. The stench of burning hair and singed flesh, my own and theirs choked me. I tasted blood, metallic and sharp, and the acrid bite of smoke burned the back of my throat.

Fear, cold and clammy, slicked my skin even as the heat of my power threatened to blister me alive. But fear breeds cunning. Their mindless savagery was their undoing. I lured them, a dance with death, into the heart of my trap, a fissure in the rock face, waiting to swallow them whole. Then, I unleashed the inferno. Not just fire, but raw, unbridled rage. The heat was a physical entity, a living thing that roared and clawed as it consumed them, its incandescent breath searing my very being. I felt the power surge through me, a terrifying, exhilarating force that threatened to consume me as readily as it consumed them.

The silence that followed was deafening, broken only by the crackle of dying embers and the frantic pounding of my own heart. The canyon, once a tomb of impending doom, now reeked of charred flesh and the bitter tang of victory hard won. The lingering heat on my skin, a brand of fire and fury, is a testament to my survival. But the memory remains, a searing brand far deeper than any physical wound, a constant reminder of the darkness I faced and the terrible power I wield, a power that could just as easily destroy me as save me.

Each mile devoured, the beast within me swelled, a ravenous tide threatening to breach the frail dam of my will. The darkness wasn't just a gnawing hunger; it was a physical violation, icy claws tearing at my insides, the metallic tang of blood already staining my tongue in anticipation. Its whispers weren't promises, they were commands, a guttural symphony of oblivion promising to drown the screaming echoes of my memories, the charred timbers of Oakhaven, the acrid stench of smoke still clinging to my nostrils, the ghostly warmth of my loved ones' lifeless hands clutched in mine.

I fought it, yes, but the fight was a desperate, bloody ballet against myself. My purpose, once a beacon, flickered, threatened by the seductive weight of despair. Their faces, their smiles, haunted me not as comforting images, but as accusing spectres, their lost light mocking my inability to truly avenge them. This wasn't grief; it was a festering wound, a constant, searing agony that pulsed with a rhythm matching the beast's own predatory heart.

The taste of blood wasn't just a phantom sensation; it was a visceral memory, a crimson tide surging in my mouth, hot and metallic, staining my very being. Oblivion wasn't a release; it was a siren's song, a velvet-throated promise of an endless night where I could finally succumb, finally rest, beneath the weight of my curse. But vengeance, incandescent and brutal, still burned brighter, a wildfire consuming the shadows of my self-destruction, fueling the desperate, terrifying struggle.

The night felt like a cold hungry monster trying to grab me but in the thick darkness between the old trees I discovered a temporary safe place. The strong smell of wood smoke hit my nose hard as the fire crackled and reached out toward the wet ground. It reminded me of the anger that was eating away at me inside. I felt its warmth a weak shield against the cold feelings of sadness. It gave me a little comfort in a world filled with darkness.

Here, amidst the crackling embers, the ghosts of my losses rose, their icy fingers tracing the scars etched onto my very being, a tapestry woven from betrayal and bloodshed. Each fallen ember was a memory, a searing brand upon my heart. Yet, from the ashes of devastation, I had forged something... resilient. A strength born not of hope, but of unrelenting fury. The fragile balance teetered on a knife's edge, the vengeance that pulsed in my veins, a venomous serpent coiled tight, threatening to consume me whole.

Malkor. The name scraped across my soul like obsidian shards, a taste of rust and bile, not just ash and blood. The stench of him, a metallic reek clinging to the very air I breathed, preceded his presence. Finding him wasn't a need; it was a visceral compulsion, a hunt driven by a thirst for vengeance so ravenous it consumed even the screaming, clawing terror of my inner demons. These weren't mere demons; they were twisted reflections of myself, born of the atrocities I'd witnessed, and the choices I'd made. This internal war, a brutal, unending siege against the festering darkness that mirrored the carnage I unleashed upon the world, was a battle fought in the echoing chambers of my fractured mind. My sanity, a fragile thing already, was a single, sputtering ember, threatened not by a hurricane, but by a malevolent storm of despair and regret, each guest a fresh memory, a brutal reminder of my failures, my compromises. The taste of defeat? It was already coating my tongue, a metallic film foreshadowing the utter annihilation I felt creeping towards me. The hunt was a race against that annihilation, a desperate gamble against the encroaching void that Malkor's very existence threatened to plunge me into.

The obsidian shard bit into my palm, its icy surface a stark contrast to the sweat slicking my skin. Runes, wicked whispers carved into the black glass, pulsed with a malevolent light that mirrored the fire in my gut. This wasn't just a map; it was a curse, a roadmap to the abyss, guiding me not merely to a demon, but to the festering wound at my soul's core, the memory of screaming villagers, the stench of burning flesh, a phantom pain that clawed at my throat. Each footfall echoed in the oppressive silence, a drumbeat of dread. The air grew thick, a suffocating blanket woven from the shadows themselves. The forest reeked of decay, a symphony of rotting leaves and damp earth, a smell that clung to me, mirroring the rot within. Fear, cold and sharp as shattered bone, pierced me, a constant companion.

This wasn't vengeance. Vengeance was a cheap thrill. This was an excavation, a brutal unearthing of my monstrous capacity for suffering. The weight of it pressed down, not merely on my shoulders, but on my very soul, crushing me under the unbearable weight of memory and regret, a burden far exceeding any physical chain. I was drowning in it, each breath a desperate gasp in the suffocating darkness of my past. And yet, with every horrifying step, a flicker of something else ignited within me: not hope, not exactly, but a perverse, furious energy, a cold fire that burned hotter than any demon's hellfire. It fueled my steps, a twisted promise of self-destruction and, perhaps, salvation.

The wind, a rasping, acrid breath of decay, clawed at my cloak as I stumbled through the skeletal remains of a Kingdom. The stench of rot and desperation clung to everything, a thick, suffocating blanket woven from the sighs of the dying. I met their eyes, the eyes of scavengers, hollowed by hunger, glittering with a primal fear that mirrored my own. Some offered scraps, a crust of blackened bread, a sip of brackish water, their generosity a fragile bloom in this wasteland of despair. Their kindness is a chilling reminder of the humanity still flickering in the heart of darkness. Others... others were vultures, their smiles as sharp as broken glass, their eyes burning with the cold fire of avarice. I felt the prickle of their gaze on my skin, sensed the subtle shift in their weight, the tightening of their grip on the rusted blades hidden beneath their rags. Their hunger wasn't just for food.

The taste of ash was perpetual on my tongue, a constant reminder of the devastation. The rasp of their voices, a chorus of desperation and malice, grated against my eardrums. I learned to read the twitch of a muscle, the flicker of a shadow, the subtle dilation of a pupil. Each encounter was a gamble, a dance on the razor's edge between life and death. My instincts, honed by the relentless pressure of survival, screamed warnings I couldn't afford to ignore. This wasn't merely strength that kept me alive; it was a cold, calculating cunning, a ruthlessly pragmatic caution forged in the crucible of this blighted world. Trust was a luxury I could no longer afford. Survival here was a brutal, solitary art.

The world ripped itself apart. One moment, the sun-bleached bones of a wasteland glared under a merciless sky; the next, a claustrophobic green hell choked me, the air thick with the stench of rotting vegetation and damp earth. It wasn't just a change of scenery; it was a visceral assault. A shift felt not just in my bones, but in the very marrow of my being, a taste of metallic tang on my tongue. The rain wasn't a downpour, it was a deluge, a liquid hammer beating me into submission, each drop an icy shard piercing my skin. Nights weren't cold; they were the icy grip of death, stealing my breath, leaving me shivering, a broken thing huddled against the unforgiving earth, the taste of fear bitter on my tongue. The threat of ambush wasn't a gnawing; it was a razor-edged terror, a constant whisper in the wind, the rustle of leaves a prelude to screams.

My tough experiences shaped my training and it was the only thing that kept me from falling into darkness. I rely not only on my skills but also on my instincts. I've developed a smooth way of moving that lets me glide through the shadows like a ghost. My willpower wasn't enough. It felt like a hot piece of coal in my stomach pushing me to fight hard just to survive. My experience wasn't just a trip; it felt like I was being constantly tested. Every step I took was a tough victory against the heavy burden of the Covenant and the harsh nature that seemed to enjoy my pain. My body didn't just hurt; it felt like a war zone. Every muscle was yelling in pain showing how much it had been through. My spirit wasn't tired; it felt like a broken mirror showing my hurt soul. The pain of loss felt heavy on me like a cage I couldn't escape.

But I pressed on. Oakhaven's ashes fueled my rage, a white-hot fire burning away the despair. But it was more than vengeance; it was a desperate struggle against the darkness that had taken root in my soul, a gnawing, insidious evil that promised oblivion and whispered sweet lies of surrender. This darkness...it tasted like blood and regret, and it was winning. But I would not yield. Not yet.

Malkor's lair pulsed. Not a gentle thrum, but a sickening, visceral beat that hammered against my ribs, a malignant heartbeat echoing in my skull. The air didn't just crackle; it screamed, a high-pitched shriek that vibrated in my teeth, tasting ozone and brimstone. The ground wasn't trembling. It convulsed, a writhing beast beneath my boots, threatening to swallow me whole. Malkor's power wasn't just felt; it was a physical blow, a crushing weight that bent my knees, stole the breath from my lungs, a palpable darkness pressing against my soul, threatening to snuff out the flickering ember of my will.

The abyss gaped, a maw of churning shadows that mirrored not just my turmoil, but the festering rot at my soul's core. The stench of decay, acrid and ancient, clawed at my nostrils, a physical manifestation of Malkor's power, a psychic rape, dredging up forgotten horrors that writhed like venomous serpents in my gut. I tasted the metallic tang of fear, the coppery edge of blood already blooming on my cracked lips.

My struggle wasn't merely physical; it was a visceral, agonizing rending of my being. Malkor's insidious whispers, a seductive siren song laced with the promise of oblivion, gnawed at the fragile remnants of my will. He offered power, yes, but it was the power of annihilation, a seductive embrace that promised the sweet release of utter darkness. I felt the chilling caress of his influence, a phantom touch that sent icy tendrils down my spine, leaving me trembling with a potent cocktail of terror and forbidden longing.

The internal screams, a cacophony of fractured selves, amplified the external threat until it roared, a monstrous symphony of despair that clawed at my very soul, the stench of its decay thick in the air, a bitter taste of ash on my tongue. I wasn't merely vulnerable; I was a shattered vase, shards of my being scattered across a precipice so steep, so black, that the wind itself moaned a lament for my impending fall. The abyss wasn't merely profound; it was a maw of infinite hunger, its gravity a physical weight crushing the air from my lungs, silencing even the desperate rasp of a strangled breath. This darkness wasn't approaching; it pulsed within me, a malignant heartbeat echoing the ancient, seductive whispers of oblivion, a language etched in the very bone of the earth, promising release in a voice both alluring and terrifying, a serpent coiled around my heart, its scales slick with the cold sweat of surrender.

The final step cracked under my boots, the sound of a brittle echo in the cavernous maw of my damnation. Years. A hunt etched onto my soul, a relentless pursuit that had clawed me to this precipice, the air thick with the coppery tang of blood and the acrid stench of sulfur. Vengeance, once a white-hot inferno that seared my very being, now flickered, a pathetic spark threatened by Malkor's breath, a glacial wind that sliced through me, stealing the warmth from my bones, leaving only the icy grip of despair. Each rasping breath tasted of ash and regret, a testament to the price exacted. But the embers still glowed, deep within, with a defiant pulse against the encroaching void. To extinguish them would be to surrender, to become the very shadow I hunted, to drown in the abyss of Malkor's triumph. My body screamed, a symphony of agony, but the will remained, a jagged shard of defiance piercing the encroaching darkness. I would not break. I would not yield. I would conquer. This was my oath, my curse, my salvation.

CHAPTER

TWO

Serpent's Shadows

The air crackled with an electric anticipation, a tangible tension vibrating within me like the distant rumble of an approaching storm. Before me loomed Malkor, the elusive figure spoken of in hushed whispers, shrouded in a cloak of shadow. A rancid stench of sulphur and decay curled around him like a sinister fog, tainting the atmosphere with its foreboding presence. He defied the monstrous image my mind had conjured; instead, he possessed a chilling elegance that was both captivating and terrifying. His features were sharp and angular, almost sculptural in their precision, while his eyes blazed with a fierce, unholy light that cleaved through the suffocating darkness.

He was less a beast and more a cunning predator, exuding an unsettling grace as he shifted imperceptibly, poised as if ready to spring forth. My hand tightened around the obsidian shard, its cool, smooth surface contrasting starkly with the heat radiating from my own anxious body. A tremor of fear coursed through my veins, yet beneath that tremor surged a defiant fire—was it bravery or sheer desperation that fueled my resolve? I squared my shoulders, steeling myself against the rising tide of dread that threatened to drown me as I confronted this embodiment of my darkest nightmares.

The truth was, I hadn't actively sought this confrontation. My entire life had been devoted to the Order, upholding its sacred laws and its unwavering commitment to justice. Yet here I stood, teetering on the brink of violating every tenet I had ever sworn to uphold. Malkor offered a sinister bargain, a twisted pact that could save my village, but it came at the cost of my very soul. He demanded the lifeblood of a sacred creature, an innocent being I had vowed to protect, a creature whose purity mirrored my own dwindling faith in the righteousness of my cause.

The obsidian shard felt heavier in my grasp, a leaden weight that mirrored the burden gnawing at my conscience. My heart raced against my ribs, not only with fear but with the nauseating realization of the betrayal looming before me. The defiance I had felt moments before crumbled, leaving behind a festering self-loathing. This confrontation was not merely with Malkor; it was a confrontation with the monster I was becoming. To save my people, I would have to embody the very evil I had dedicated my life to combat.

This was it—the moment I had dreaded and yet, paradoxically, walked willingly toward, fully aware that I might never absolve myself from the choice I was about to make. The silence stretched, palpable and suffocating, broken only by the frantic, traitorous rhythm of my heart, a condemnation echoing in the stillness around me. Perhaps failure would not mean death; perhaps it would manifest as a living hell, haunting me with the knowledge that I had consciously chosen darkness.

I launched myself forward, a whirlwind of fire and fury. My flames erupted, engulfing Malkor in a searing inferno. He met my assault with a chilling indifference, his laughter echoing like the crack of doom as he conjured a wall of obsidian, deflecting my attack. The force of the collision sent me reeling back, the impact jarring my very being. I stumbled, my breath ragged, the taste of blood already blooming on my tongue. My vampiric hunger gnawed at me, a relentless tide threatening to overwhelm me, but it was the other hunger that truly terrified me. The hunger for power, the hunger that had driven me to this very fight, a hunger that whispered promises of dominance, even at the cost of everything I held dear.

This wasn't only about Malkor; it was about showing everyone including myself that I could be strong. I wanted to silence the doubts that kept bothering me, the thoughts that told me I was just a weak person pretending to be a hero. I saw the shiny obsidian wall standing in front of me blocking my path to my dreams. To defeat Malkor I realized that it would take more than just anger and power; it would require a real sacrifice. I gave up part of my humanity.

Malkor's laughter spurred me on, a cruel symphony to the turmoil within. I saw a glimmer of weakness in his defences, a chink in the obsidian. To exploit it, to strike the killing blow, meant channelling a forbidden power, a dark magic I'd sworn never to touch, a magic that would twist my very essence, corrupting the very soul I was fighting to protect. The choice clawed at me, a vile beast tearing at my conscience. Did I want victory so desperately that I was willing to pay such a hideous price? The answer, a chilling whisper in the back of my mind, was a sickening yes. With a guttural scream, a scream born of desperation and self-loathing, I unleashed the forbidden magic, feeling the darkness consume me even as I shattered Malkor's defences. My victory felt hollow, ash in my mouth, the taste of blood and betrayal mingling on my tongue. I had won, but at what cost? The cost, I knew, would haunt me long after the echoes of Malkor's laughter faded into silence.

Malkor's blur of motion was a lethal dance, his obsidian claws shredding my defences. Agony, amplified by a gnawing, forbidden hunger, twisted me. The seductive whisper of Malkor's power, a venomous temptation, coiled within. My flames flared, fueled by terror and rage, yet tainted by a desperate, shameful hope that surrender might quell the consuming need. A taste... just a taste.

I fought back with desperate ferocity, each swing of my sword a testament to my refusal to yield, a refusal that felt less and less certain with every passing moment. My training, my oaths, the lives I'd sworn to protect, all felt like flimsy shields against the encroaching darkness within. He was stronger, faster, more skilled. I could feel myself being overpowered, his strength an immense, crushing weight against my dwindling power, and a deeper, more insidious weight: the weight of my failing resolve.

Then, a crack in my defences. A glancing blow, but enough to send me reeling. Malkor pressed his advantage, and at that moment, faced with the certain prospect of death, I saw a flicker of his power, a hint of its terrible allure, and my hand instinctively reached for a forbidden technique, a dark art I had vowed never to use, a power that would consume me, but might, just might, save me. The choice was a poisoned chalice, a betrayal of everything I believed in, but the hunger screamed louder than my conscience. I used it. The searing power flowed through me, momentarily repelling Malkor, but leaving me shivering with a cold dread far worse than the physical pain. Victory felt like defeat, a pyrrhic triumph stained with the blood of my broken principles. I had won this battle, but at what cost?

The battle raged, a furious exchange of blows right in the heart of that demonic lair. The ground trembled beneath my feet, the air thick with the stench of brimstone and burning flesh, it was almost unbearable. I was completely outmatched, my energy dwindling, my body screaming in protest. Each blow landed like a hammer blow, each one chipping away not only at my strength but at the fragile remnants of my faith. I'd sworn an oath, a sacred vow to never take a life, to find another way, a path of redemption even for the damned. But Malkor... he was a plague, a blight upon creation, and his cruelty echoed in the screams of the souls trapped within this infernal prison.

My strength failed, the very air seemed to press down, suffocating me. Just as I felt the final crushing blow coming, I saw it, an opportunity, a brief lapse in Malkor's guard. But it wasn't just a strike I saw; it was a chance to use the forbidden spell, the one my master had warned against, the one that tapped into a dark power I'd always vehemently rejected. It was a power that tasted of despair, that felt like selling my very soul.

The choice ripped through me. To fail meant the countless souls trapped here would suffer eternally. To succeed meant violating everything I believed in, staining my soul with darkness I feared I could never cleanse. There was no other option, no escape from this terrible dilemma. With a choked sob, a silent prayer for forgiveness on my lips, I unleashed it, a torrent of fire fueled by forbidden magic, a fiery embrace that I hoped would be Malkor's last. Even as the flames consumed him, I felt the searing weight of my transgression, the cold dread of the irreversible choice I had made. The victory felt hollow, tainted by the price I'd paid, a price far greater than the cost of the battle itself.

But it wasn't enough.

Malkor emerged from the flames, unscathed, a cruel smile playing on his lips. He raised his hand, and a bolt of pure demonic energy struck me, sending me flying through the air. I slammed against a jagged rock, the impact tearing through my flesh, shattering my bones. A scream tore from my throat, not just of pain, but of betrayal. The searing agony was a physical manifestation of the far greater pain gnawing at my soul.

This wasn't just Malkor's victory; it was my failure. For years, I'd sworn an oath to protect the innocent, to uphold justice, and to never compromise my ideals. But the whispers had started months ago, whispers of a power that could save my dying sister, a power Malkor alone possessed. I'd initially dismissed them as the ravings of desperation, a traitorous thought creeping into the sacred garden of my convictions.

Now, lying broken and bleeding, the whispers screamed louder than the agony in my bones. I'd sought him out, desperately hoping for a miracle, a chance to save her, even if it meant bending my moral code. A desperate prayer for a miracle had been answered with a demonic bargain, and I'd almost accepted it. Almost. The vision of my sister, pale and frail, flashed before my eyes, fueling a terrible internal conflict. Was saving her worth the price of my soul?

A maelstrom of pain and colour exploded Malkor's twisted face, a stark reminder of my near betrayal. His triumph wasn't just physical; it was the crushing of my spirit. The agony of failure, of almost surrendering my values, resonated far louder than my broken bones. Regret, deeper than any physical wound, consumed me. My body shattered, my soul fractured by a choice not yet made. Could I still resist, even now, broken and lost in the abyss? Malkor's jeering grin, the final image seared into my memory, mocked my defeat. Not darkness itself, but the bitter taste of broken vows—sworn on my mother's grave—to never wield his forbidden magic. Desperation had driven me to trade a piece of my soul, a fleeting victory bought at an immeasurable cost. My betrayal, not Malkor's victory, was the true torment. The surrounding void was a chilling testament to a forever-tainted soul.

I awoke to suffocating darkness and the clammy grip of decay. A nauseating stench filled the air, yet beneath it, a perversely alluring fragrance both repelled and enthralled. This primal urge, this desperate need, warred with my ingrained sense of justice. Pain wracked my battered body, a symphony of agony on a rough stone slab, but I lived, barely. The intoxicating scent intensified, a siren call promising oblivion and power. My training fought a losing battle against the encroaching desperation.

I knew, with chilling certainty, that the source of the fragrance, whatever it was, was responsible for my injuries. A part of me, the righteous part, the part that swore an oath to protect the innocent, yearned to escape, to find help, to expose this evil. But another part, a darker, hungrier part, whispered insidious lies: survival. This was my only chance. To survive, I would have to do what I vowed I'd never do—make a pact with this darkness, this…thing.

The choice was clear, and yet agonizingly unbearable. It meant betraying everything I believed in, compromising my soul for a chance at life. And even if I surrendered to this…temptation…would it even save me? The failure of that possibility alone was a torment I couldn't bear to contemplate. Yet the alternative—certain, agonizing death— was far worse. The scent drew me in, despite my desperate internal resistance, and I knew, with cold dread, that I was about to make a choice I would regret for the rest of my—if I had a rest—life.

A figure emerged from the shadows, tall and imposing, his form outlined by the flickering light of a nearby brazier. My breath hitched, he was a demon, and that much was horrifyingly clear. His features were sharp and angular, his eyes like chips of obsidian, burning into me. I felt the weight of his presence, a crushing force that pressed down, suffocating yet strangely captivating. Fear clawed at my throat, but I couldn't look away. He moved with an unsettling grace, each step precise and deliberate, and I felt a primal instinct to flee battling with a morbid fascination. My heart hammered against my ribs.

"You're awake," he said, his voice a low, melodious rumble that sent shivers down my spine. I could feel his eyes on me strong and powerful like a leader watching over its target. I heard words in a language I didn't know but somehow I got what they meant. The tone didn't feel kind or mean to me; it just felt... Sure! Just let me know the original text you want me to rewrite and I'll be happy to help. A deep chill settled over me even stronger than just feeling cold. My heart was pounding in my chest.

I felt his gaze on me, intense and unsettling like he was seeing right through me. He approached slowly, and I braced myself. He knelt, his touch feather-light as he examined my wounds. A jolt, a mix of pain and pleasure, shot through me as his fingers brushed my skin, leaving me breathless. His touch, surprisingly gentle, careful, almost tender, was a stark contrast to the intensity of his stare. I couldn't help but shiver, a strange combination of fear and...something else.

"Malkor underestimated you," he continued, his voice laced with a strange mixture of respect and amusement. *"But his power is still formidable. You are lucky to be alive."*

"Who... who are you?" I whispered my voice barely a rasp. My question felt impossibly fragile, hanging in the air between us.

"Linx," he replied, his name echoing in the silence like a death knell. "I owe Malkor a debt. He spared my life, and he chose to leave you in my care unfortunately. Consider this payment... a twisted form of repayment." His eyes bore into mine, searching, probing. I felt the intensity of his gaze, a hunger there, but not the same bloodlust I'd encountered before. This was different, deeper, more primal. I could feel my breath catch in my throat; a shiver ran down my spine. It felt... ancient. I wondered what he saw in me.

He had mended my wounds, an astonishing feat of demonic magic that defied all reason and understanding. His healing was both potent and swift, an intoxicating force surging through my veins like wildfire. I felt strength flooding back into my muscles, the dull ache and searing pain retreating into the shadows, yet an unsettling sense of violation lingered like a dark cloud over my thoughts. It was utterly terrifying. I felt...used as if I were a mere vessel for his power. A deep, chilling unease coiled tightly in my gut, a stark contrast to the physical relief washing over me. I knew, with a certainty that chilled me to the bone, that this so-called "gift" came with a horrifying price.

Linx rose, his eyes still fixed on me. *"Your body is still weak, but you'll recover. The debt... it will be settled."*

His words hung heavy in the air, filled with unspoken implications. A cold dread settled in my stomach as he asserted his dominance, draining me of power and leaving me vulnerable. The healing was not a gift but a binding contract sealed in blood and pain; I felt it deep within me. This was more than a physical debt; he had taken something from me, a piece of my soul. The darkness within me pulsed in sync with the terrifying darkness in his eyes, igniting a primal fear.

The air crackled with an unspoken challenge, a battle of wills fought not with weapons but with penetrating gazes. I knew this was just the beginning, a dangerous encounter that would irrevocably alter my quest for vengeance. Escaping Linx's clutches wasn't merely about physical strength; it felt like a test of my will and spirit, under the relentless pressure of an unforeseen, powerful threat. The embers of vengeance still burned within me, but now dimmed by fear and uncertainty. A new and terrifying battle had begun, not only against the Obsidian Covenant but against Linx, the enigmatic demon who held my fate in his hands. The stakes? Everything.

The flickering brazier light, a malevolent eye in the gloom of the cavern, cast long, dancing shadows that writhed and twisted around us like living things. Linx remained motionless, a statue carved from the very darkness itself, his obsidian eyes burning with an inner fire that seemed to consume the meagre light. The silence stretched, an agonizing expanse punctuated only by the crackle of the flames and the frantic, irregular thump of my own heart. It wasn't just the silence; it was the quality of the silence, thick and heavy, pregnant with unspoken menace. I could almost taste it, a metallic tang on my tongue, the taste of fear and impending doom.

His gaze pierced through me like icy fingers tracing my soul, revealing every insecurity, every flaw. I wanted to scream, to escape, but I was paralyzed by the raw power radiating from him. The air vibrated with contained energy, and the room felt like a cage, its walls pressing down under the weight of his presence. My breath hitched, a ragged gasp caught in fear's grip, while sweat beaded on my forehead, cold against my skin. The air changed, sharp and metallic, like the scent of blood. This was no mere man; this was something ancient and terrifyingly beyond my comprehension.

I tried to shift, seeking relief from the throbbing ache in my broken ribs, but a low growl rumbled in Linx's chest, silencing me. It vibrated through the floor, a manifestation of his displeasure. Though I was physically free, I felt trapped by an invisible force emanating from him, a pressure that made it hard to breathe. It wasn't just his brute power; it was a psychological control that chilled me to the core, eroding my will with slow, deliberate precision. He methodically stripped away my defences, each word and shift of his posture chipping at my resolve. My carefully constructed self-assurance felt like sand slipping through my fingers, vanishing under his relentless gaze. Panic clawed at my mind like a frantic bird in a cage built of fear and control. I sensed my spirit weakening, and with sickening certainty, I knew I was losing.

His movements, fluid and graceful, belied the brutal precision of his healing. Clad in indigo robes, he moved like a wraith, his shadow a living serpent. Reflected on the obsidian floor, his image shimmered, both substantial and ghostly. A chilling dread seized me; the air crackled with his potent energy.

He stopped before me again, his gaze piercing through me like a hawk's. The heavy silence pressed down, a palpable weight stealing the air from my lungs. It was a void, broken only by the relentless drip of water from above, each drop amplifying my frayed nerves. My heart pounded against my ribs, a frantic drumbeat in the oppressive quiet. The air was sharp and metallic, thick with a strange energy surrounding him. My muscles tensed, caught between fear and fascination; he was a storm contained within a man, a terrifying yet beautiful paradox.

Finally, he spoke, his voice a low, silken caress laced with chilling control. *"Malkor's debt is paid,"* he declared, the words hanging like a sharpened blade, a causal assertion of his dominance. The silence that followed amplified the unspoken threat simmering beneath the surface, pressing down on those who dared to breathe. His dark eyes swept across the gathered figures, instilling a chilling awareness of their insignificance. *"But my desires are yet to be satisfied,"* he continued, each word a deliberate drawl that hinted at vast, uncharted ambition. A subtle shift in his posture revealed the terrible power he held, a power destined to unleash suffering on anyone in his way. His desires were anything but benign.

He didn't explicitly state his desires, but I understood. It wasn't just physical; a palpable heat radiated from him, with a predatory glint in his eyes that hinted at something more sinister. He wanted to control me completely, dismantling my independence and reducing me to a mere extension of his will. It wasn't just about lust but a deeper hunger for dominion. A cold dread settled in my bones, not from physical violence, but from the threat of losing my identity, of becoming a shadow of my former self, serving his twisted desires. I gasped, caught between fear and a futile hope, knowing he intended not just domination, but annihilation—transforming my spirit into a puppet dancing to his tune, while I remained powerless to resist.

His knees crunched on the grit, his fingers pressing hard, a deliberate violation. Calloused fingers scraped my jaw, raising goosebumps, a primal fear, not just a shiver. I flinched, but his probing touch continued, a ruthless examination, a subtle pressure chipping away at my defences. He sought weakness, his silent threat as suffocating as his touch. Breath caught, a silent scream trapped as dust motes danced, indifferent witnesses to the power struggle. The acrid scent of earth and metal heightened my terror. Frozen, I felt like prey under his unwavering gaze.

"*You fought bravely,*" he conceded, his voice carrying a strange mix of admiration and disdain. The words hung heavily in the air, filled with unspoken implications. His sharp, assessing gaze lingered on the scorched earth around them, a testament to the ferocity of the recent battle. "*Your fire… it is impressive—a rare and powerful force, even for a flame elemental. But it is raw and untamed,*" he continued, a subtle tremor in his voice betraying a hint of what seemed to be envy.

He pointed at the charred remains of a once mighty oak. "*Look at this. The power, the intensity… breathtaking. But you've squandered it. You unleashed a wildfire when you needed precision. Such uncontrolled fury can destroy your enemies, but it risks everything else too.*" He paused, his expression firm. "*A true master of flame would have channelled that power, danced with the flames rather than being consumed by them.*" Moving closer, he added, "*I see your potential, but it means nothing without discipline. I can teach you to harness that fire, to make it yours. But it will require dedication and obedience.*"

He paused, his eyes narrowing slightly as a flicker of intensity ignited within them. The dim light cast shadows across his angular features, emphasizing the resolve etched in his expression. "*I can refine it,*" he stated, his voice steady and low, resonating with an undercurrent of authority. "*I can make it stronger,*" he continued, the weight of his promise hanging in the air like a palpable force. *"I can make you stronger."* The words emerged as an enticing offer, yet they held an unwavering command that suggested there was little room for refusal—an invitation laced with the urgency of necessity.

The air crackled with tense energy, charged with unspoken desires and a simmering threat that made my skin crawl. This was no raw menace of lesser demons; it was insidious, a chilling charm masking a master puppeteer's intent. I felt the strings tightening, each tug a violation of my will. His unsettling touch cauterized my wounds but left me profoundly altered, opening a deeper vulnerability—emotional and spiritual. My fears and secrets lay bare before him, his cold gaze exploiting weaknesses with chilling efficiency. This was no simple predator/prey dynamic; it was a perverse dance of power, and I was losing. The air tasted of iron and something ancient, his power clinging to me like a shroud. My heart raced, a frantic beat against the heavy silence, as I tasted fear—metallic and bitter—before the terrible unknown.

I felt Linx watching me while I explored the cave. My red hair shone in the flickering light of the torch he was holding. I will do whatever it takes to make sure I get out of this situation alive.

"Blaze" he called his voice resonating in the cavernous space of the cave walls relaying his words back to me as if echoing in response. *"Come here"* he urged, his tone filled with urgency beckoning me to approach him without hesitation.

When I shifted my gaze to him our eyes locked in an intense moment with his piercing gaze beating mine to the finish. I felt the weight of the connection between us compelling me to act. I had no option but to plaster an expression of innocence on my face masking the truth that lay beneath. *"What is it?"* I asked, trying to sound genuinely curious despite knowing his direct question and the implications it carried for both of us in that charged moment.

I felt a sharp feeling of fear in the air like static electricity. It clung to my skin making me uneasy. The smell of metal mixed with his strong cologne creating a sickening odor that almost overwhelmed me. As he took each of his three quick steps toward me I felt more and more uncomfortable. With every step I had a strong feeling that something bad was about to happen. I noticed him coming towards me moving like a predator. His arms reached out and it felt like he was casting a cold sharp shadow over me like a snake getting ready to attack. As I looked up his huge figure blocked the little light around us making everything feel heavy and scary. I struggled to breathe and I felt like my sense of safety was slipping away. Every slow breath I let out felt wrong like I was doing something I shouldn't. I could really feel the danger coming from him especially with the harsh words floating around us like a dark cloud that was about to explode.

"You know" he growled, his voice rumbling deep from within, dragging out each word to deliver violence-filled promises that echoed ominously. As he clasped my face in his grip any thoughts of apologies or pleas for mercy were far from my grasp. *"My patience?"* he hissed *"A wretched serpent that finally encloses around its tail. Not a second more."* The finality in his tone was chilling, leaving me frozen in a moment that felt like an eternity.

As if his words weren't enough to send shivers down my spine my heart raced uncontrollably each beat echoing in my ears. The tension in the air was palpable wrapping around me like a heavy blanket. *"What are you going to do?"* I stuttered my voice barely above a whisper so quietly that it made my next words feel like a gentle breeze, fleeting and almost ethereal. I held my breath waiting for his response, dread mingling with curiosity.

I felt a creepy smile spread across his lips with the corners hidden in shadow making him seem like he was made of darkness itself. His fingers were freezing but incredibly strong as they held my chin tightly making me look into his eyes. That moment felt exciting and scary all at once. The smell of his cologne was strong and deep mixed with something wild and natural. It filled my nose and surrounded me like a thick fog. The scent felt heavy just like the tightness in my chest and my heart raced because he was so close. *"Whatever I want"* he breathed his words, a low growl that resonated against my skin, vibrating through me like a warning bell. It was a promise and a threat all at once leaving me teetering on the edge of fear and desire.

Suddenly his mouth came down hard on mine like an overwhelming force. His lips pressed against mine, taking away my breath and making it hard to catch my breath. I found myself gasping for anything—anything at all—except for him. I tasted something bitter and metallic about him. It was a strange mix of strength and an intense need to control that sparked a fire deep inside me. His touch was far from gentle; it felt like a strong claim marking me as his in a way that sent chills down my spine. I knew I should fight against it and step back from the storm he was creating. But I couldn't help feeling drawn to him and a part of me secretly wanted the wild chaos he offered. Every moment felt like a risky game and I found myself caught up in the exciting yet scary chaos of it all.

I let out a deep groan, a sound that came from deep inside me as he kissed me with a passion that felt both strong and possessive. A strong statement lit a fire inside me that I didn't even know was there waiting to come out. I felt a strong wild energy rushing through me waking up feelings that had been asleep for a long time. The smell around me was amazing. It was a strong mix of rich leather and a deep natural scent that wrapped around me like a thick fog filling my senses with a warm feeling of wanting. The smell was so different from the fast beating of my heart which I could hear in my ears like a drum beating hard. My body was reacting to him in ways I never expected.

His touch felt like an invasion to me. It was both exciting and scary like a sudden strike that broke down the walls I had worked so hard to build around myself. Every time his fingers brushed against my skin I felt shivers run down my back waking up every nerve in a wonderful way. As his hands moved gently over my skin they quickly ripped through the fabric like it was just a thin wall blocking his strong feelings. The fabric slipped off and I felt completely open both in my body and my feelings as he looked at me with strong intensity.

Every moment felt electric with a strong tension that surrounded us. It drew me deeper into a new place filled with passion and desire. I felt the heat coming from his body, a warmth that was very different from the cool air around us. I felt drawn in like something powerful was pulling me closer and I just couldn't resist it. My mind raced with a mix of thoughts and feelings. I felt fear, excitement and vulnerability all fighting for attention. It was like a chaotic dance that left me breathless.

His lips felt like a strong storm, powerful and unbreakable but there was a gentle side to how he kissed me. It was as if he was uncovering the true nature of who I am. With each kiss he took off the layers of my protective shell showing the real me underneath—a woman who wanted this moment and the freedom that came with it. I gave myself to him leaning into his touch and wanting more as a warm fire filled my body.

In that amazing moment everything around us disappeared and it felt like it was just me and you wrapped up in a strong hug. Time didn't matter anymore as I got completely lost in the other person. It felt like our souls came together in a powerful burst of longing and connection. I felt pure happiness at that moment. It was a quick taste of freedom and nothing else was important except the bond we had. As we flew higher caught up in our excitement I realized that this was only the start of a journey that would take us to amazing places we had only dreamed about.

I leaned toward him filled with an urgency that was almost desperate while his rough and unyielding fingers traced the contours of my form exploring every curve with a hunger that made my breath hitch in my throat. I let out a strangled gasp when his hands enveloped my breasts, the sensation overwhelming. The way his thumbs rubbed against my already sensitive nipples sent waves of intense pleasure mixed with fear coursing through my body leaving me breathless and yearning for more.

His flavour lingered on my tongue, a reminder of the sensation he brought the electric charge that sparked between us. The immense strength of his determination tied me to him in a manner that was as exhilarating as it was frightening a thrilling dance on the edge of surrender. I was caught in a whirlwind of emotions torn between the intoxicating allure of his dominance and the raw vulnerability that it evoked within me. In that moment I was entirely lost in a tumultuous sea of desire and fear, a testament to the powerful connection we shared.

"*This is going to be exciting* "he whispered, his tone heavy with desire and filled with unexpressed feelings. The anticipation hung in the air between them electric and palpable as if they were standing on the brink of something extraordinary, something unforgettable.

I leaned back, pressing my body into him, sensing the heat emanating from him like a comforting embrace. The gentle textile of his shirt glided over my skin amplifying my sensitivity to the narrow space separating us as if the fabric itself was a bridge connecting our two worlds. I was quiet, my breathing even but light as I took in the charged atmosphere that enveloped us dense and tangible like a thick fog infused with unspoken emotions. The soft glow of the dim light enveloped us in shadows creating an intimate cocoon where every subtle movement felt magnified and conversation seemed pointless and almost unnecessary. We were suspended in this moment, each heartbeat echoing in the silence allowing the unexpressed tension to linger between us, thickening the air with possibilities that danced just beyond the reach of words.

He laughed lightly a sound that danced in the air as his hand slid down to gently grasp the slick heat between my legs sending shivers of excitement coursing through me. *"Will you remain where you are or will you oppose me?"* he inquired a mischievous sparkle flickering in his gaze as his fingers flirted at the edge of my doorway—both inviting and provoking in equal measure. The atmosphere thickened with unspoken tension every second stretching out like an eternity as I weighed my response. I found myself caught in a web of conflicting emotions torn between the allure of compliance and the thrilling desire to challenge the curiosity he had so skillfully ignited within me. It was a tantalizing dance of power and submission and I could feel the pulse of anticipation growing stronger urging me to make a choice that could shift the dynamics between us forever. The moment felt electrically charged with possibilities that lay just beyond the threshold of my decision.

*"I... I can't bring myself to move "*I murmured my voice barely above a whisper filled with longing. My body yearned for him as if it possessed a will of its own pulling me closer despite the chaos swirling in my mind. It was an overwhelming desire, a magnetic force I couldn't resist.

Without any hesitation, he quickly secured me with his powerful hands lifting me with surprising ease. The cave wall was cool and moist as it pressed against my back causing an involuntary shiver to run down my spine. The contrast between the chill of the stone and the warmth of his body was electric, heightening my senses. Without thinking I instinctively encircled his waist with my legs feeling the heat of his body seep through the layers of our clothing like a slow-burning fire. The distant torch cast a flickering glow around us illuminating the contours of his face and revealing a captivating blend of resolve and intensity in his eyes. He pulled me closer and I could feel the undeniable pressure of his firm erection against my entrance igniting a rush of desire within me. The air was thick with tension, each heartbeat echoing the unspoken longing that hung between us.

With my back pressed firmly against the cold unyielding wall of the cave he would lower his hands both moving toward the belt of his pants using the pressure of the wall to keep me pinned up against him. My hands clenched tightly around his neck feeling the warmth of his skin beneath my fingertips. That moment felt like an eternity stretching out years of unspoken desires and hidden passion between us enveloping us in a world that existed solely for the two of us. Suddenly a loud clunk echoed throughout the cave reverberating off the stone walls as I heard his belt buckle hit the ground with a resounding thud. My gaze dropped instinctively taking in the sight of his pants now around his ankles and I let out a breath I didn't realize I was holding. The air felt charged with anticipation thick with the electric energy of the moment. I took a deep breath trying to steady myself as I absorbed the reality of what was happening, my heart racing with a mix of excitement and nervousness.

"Don't you want this?" " he inquired, his tone husky and rich with anticipation. His words lingered in the air charged with a promise of what was to come and I found myself captivated by his raw magnetic energy teetering on the edge of surrender to the moment that beckoned us both.

I gasped as he pushed inside me a rush of sensation coursing through my body. I shouted, gripping his shoulders tightly, feeling the strain that lay within each muscle just below his skin. His skin felt warm against the cool air that enveloped us a stark contrast that heightened my awareness of every moment. I could feel his heartbeat accelerating beneath my fingers, a rhythmic reminder of the vibrant bond we shared in that intimate space. With each thrust, he moved into me with an intensity and speed that left me breathless drawing me deeper into an abyss of pleasure. The cave around us echoed with the noise of our bodies colliding the sound mingling harmoniously with my soft moans and his deep grunts creating a symphony of passion. It was as if time stood still and in that sacred moment we were the only two beings in existence lost in the depths of our desire.

He extended his hand toward us, and his fingers discovered my clit. I inhaled sharply while he circled the area feeling my climax rise swiftly within me, a potent surge of desire that took my breath away consuming my thoughts entirely.

"Linx " I breathed out my body tightening in a delicious crescendo as I reached my peak, every sensation amplifying wrapping around me like an electric embrace overwhelming yet exhilarating.

With a low groan that resonated through the air, he became increasingly erratic in his thrusts, his movements driven by a desperate need for release as he pursued his climax. The tension hung thick around us and with a final deep grunt he finally surrendered releasing himself within me flooding us both with an overwhelming sense of connection.

For a brief moment, we held on to that hug, our bodies intertwined as we regained our breath. The gentle heat of our bodies met one another creating a subtle rhythm of heartbeats that echoed in the stillness surrounding us. In that intimate embrace, time seemed to stand still and the outside world faded into a distant memory. The way our chests rose and fell in perfect harmony made it feel like we were dancing to an unspoken melody while everything else around us blurred into insignificance. It was as if we existed in a bubble of our own making where nothing could intrude upon the warmth and connection we shared.

The delicate aroma of my fragrance hung in the air blending seamlessly with the refreshing evening atmosphere forming a warm bubble that connected us in those brief moments. Each inhalation was a reminder of our closeness, a fragrant testament to our shared experience. As he gradually eased away from me I felt a bittersweet pang at the loss of his warmth against my skin. He gently placed me down and I couldn't help but notice the remnants of our recent encounter. A soft sensation coursed down my thighs, a lingering reminder of the passion we had just shared. These fleeting moments filled with tenderness and connection would remain etched in my memory, a beautiful snapshot of our time together.

I hesitated searching my mind carefully trying to find the appropriate word that would perfectly convey my thoughts.

With a sly grin, he wrapped his arms around me pulling me closer as if to shield me from the world around us. *"Only the start,"* he said playfully, his eyes glinting with mischief. *"Be thankful I was tender with you for your first experience "* he remarked softly, his voice a warm caress. Before I could respond he leaned in pressing his lips against mine in another passionate kiss that sent shivers down my spine igniting a fire within me that I had never known before.

He walked towards a shadowed alcove, his movements deliberate and purposeful. A fountain loomed ahead, its basin filled with a dark, glistening liquid that resembled blood, pooling ominously at the bottom. *"You are mine now, Blaze,"* he stated, his voice low and firm, devoid of any emotion that wasn't absolute control. *"For the time being, at least. Consider this a temporary... arrangement."* The crimson liquid bubbled slightly, casting an eerie glow that illuminated his sharp features, reflecting the intensity of the moment.

He returned a rough-hewn wooden bowl cradling a crimson liquid that pulsed with an inner light, a malevolent heartbeat. The light shifted, a blood-red spectrum only a creature of darkness could truly appreciate. Unnatural heat warped the air, a tangible wave preceding him, sending a shiver of anticipation down my spine. The scent, pure, metallic blood, thick and ancient, a primal blend of life and death, hit me. My fangs throbbed, my vampiric instincts a roaring hunger, not just physical, but a craving for power, for the life force within. My breath constricted, my body vibrated with the need, a cellular yearning for the intoxicating, deadly elixir. The world shrunk to the pulsing bowl, promising oblivion.

"Drink," he commanded, his voice barely a whisper. *"It will strengthen you. It will help you to endure what is to come."*

This wasn't mere blood; it was demonic essence, a nightmare brew, viscous and malevolent, pulsing with unnatural life. It wasn't enhancement, but a binding pact etched into my soul, a chilling certainty gripping me. The air throbbed with his power, the liquid a brutal tide of dark magic, not persuasion, but insidious mind control—refusal impossible. The metallic, acrid taste, like a forged blade, was strangely alluring, a horrifying sweetness masking surrender. He was ensnaring me, each drop a violation, tightening his grip on my will. My control crumbled, my thoughts clouded by his parasitic influence, shaping my desires. Fear, a crushing weight, couldn't quell the seductive power, the intoxicating promise of dominion. But the price was my soul, already slipping away.

I hesitated for only a moment, the internal battle between my will and my primal needs raging within me like a storm at sea. The hunger wasn't a simple emptiness; it was a visceral, agonizing pain, a gnawing beast clawing at my insides, threatening to tear me apart from the inside out. My stomach clenched, a knot of desperation tightening with each passing second. The air itself felt thick and heavy with the scent of my desperation. My vision swam slightly, the edges blurring as weakness threatened to overwhelm me. With a sigh of resignation, more a weary acceptance than a true surrender, I reached for the offered bowl. My hand trembled, not just from weakness, but from a deep-seated fear that resonated in the very marrow of my bones. The polished wood felt strangely cold against my clammy skin.

I lifted the bowl, the rich aroma assaulting my senses, a complex blend of savoury spices and something else... something subtly sweet and almost unnervingly alluring. The first spoonful was a revelation. It was warm, intensely flavorful, a symphony of tastes that danced across my tongue, a heady elixir that promised oblivion from the torment of hunger. A wave of pure, unadulterated energy surged through my veins, a revitalizing flood that chased away the icy tendrils of weakness. My limbs felt stronger, my vision sharpened, and a fiery warmth bloomed in my chest, rekindling the embers of my vitality. It was intoxicating, a potent brew that mended my fractured body with breathtaking speed.

But with that surging strength came the chilling realization of my predicament. It wasn't just the physical rejuvenation; it was the insidious feeling of dependency, a subtle shift in the very fabric of my being. The awareness of his control was no longer a whisper; it was a palpable presence, a weight settling upon my shoulders, binding me with invisible chains forged in something darker than steel. I could feel it, a tightening, a subtle adjustment in the unseen mechanisms that now dictated my existence. The delicious warmth of the broth was tainted by the icy grip of fear, the intoxicating flavour replaced by the bitter taste of submission. The power he'd given me was a gilded cage, and I was already beginning to learn the rules of my confinement.

Days blurred into a relentless cycle of gruelling training. Linx, a master manipulator, exploited my weaknesses with chilling precision, pushing me past exhaustion. His brutal methods—endless repetitions, curt dismissals, and a cold assessment—systematically chipped away at my confidence and self-worth. His subtle, sadistic manipulations aimed to break my resistance, replacing my autonomy with unwavering obedience. Sleep offered no escape from the crushing weight of his expectations and the nightmares of his relentless gaze. I became a puppet, my will eroded, my sanity questioned, and my very self dissolved under his control.

My physical training was as brutal as my emotional conditioning. He pushed my body to the brink of exhaustion, refining my abilities with relentless exercises that left my muscles screaming in protest. We started before dawn, the pre-sunrise chill biting at my skin as I endured punishing routines: gruelling sprints across uneven terrain, weighted callisthenics that tested my limits, and brutal hand-to-hand combat drills that left me bruised and bleeding. The air hung thick with the scent of sweat and exertion, a testament to the relentless effort. I felt the burn, the ache, the sheer agony, a deep, bone-jarring pain that settled in my muscles and joints long after the sessions ended. Yet I pushed on, driven by a fierce determination and the knowledge that surrender was not an option. He wasn't merely building my physical strength; he was forging an unbreakable will.

He forged my monstrous appetite into a weapon. It wasn't suppression, but mastery: a delicate balance between surrender and defiance. Through sensory deprivation and calculated exposure to blood's allure, he honed my awareness, teaching me to channel the ravenous hunger, transforming its agonizing thirst into potent, controllable energy—sharpening my senses and fueling my resolve.

The struggle was constant, a relentless battle waged within me, a war between the primal beast and the disciplined warrior I was becoming. Sleep offered little respite; nightmares plagued me, visions of unchecked hunger and the devastation it could inflict. But even in those dark moments, I clung to the training, to the progress I was making. I saw glimmers of victory, moments where I stood defiant against the insatiable cravings, moments where I proved to myself, and him, that

I could master the darkness within. I was winning, inch by agonizing inch, but the fight was far from over. The path ahead remained arduous, but I was prepared to walk it.

Beyond the physical abuse, I felt him chipping away at my mental fortitude, subtly undermining my sense of self. He'd whisper observations, sometimes subtle, sometimes brutally blunt, about my vulnerabilities, my weaknesses, and my dependence on his supposed care. I felt him playing on my deepest insecurities, my most crippling fears, exploiting them to reinforce his suffocating control. I could feel myself shrinking, my spirit wilting under the constant barrage of his insidious manipulations. The words, even the unspoken implications, burrowed into my mind, poisoning my thoughts, and twisting my perception of myself. I started to doubt everything, questioning my sanity, my judgment, my very worth.

His words were like carefully placed stones, gradually building a wall of psychological control. He never resorted to outright force or cruelty, yet he exerted a pressure that was just as effective, even more insidious. He manipulated me with a chilling grace, an almost artistic precision. I felt him twisting my perceptions, a slow, insidious tightening that made me question my sanity and judgment. Doubt gnawed at me, a relentless worm eating away at my certainty. I wasn't sure anymore what was real and what was a product of his mind games; the lines blurred, then vanished entirely. It was terrifying, this erosion of myself.

My relationship with him was a twisted dance, a game of dominance and submission where I was perpetually on the verge of breaking, of succumbing to his complete control. I felt him meticulously dismantling my defences, leaving me vulnerable and utterly dependent on him. The raw, violent training sessions left me bruised and battered, yet intertwined with those were moments of chilling intimacy. He would brush my skin, his touch sending shocks of both pain and pleasure through me, a terrifying paradox I couldn't understand. I felt myself losing myself, dissolving into the terrifying power he held over me. The fear was a constant companion, a cold hand clutching my heart, yet strangely, there was also something else... a twisted, forbidden fascination that kept me trapped.

One night, as we stood in the dimly lit chamber, his gaze cutting like a blade, he stated simply, *"Your vengeance will be mine to claim."* I felt a chill crawl down my spine; the words held no gentleness, only a profound and disturbing assertion of ownership. It was a chilling revelation, and I knew then that his intentions were far from altruistic. My fight for freedom wouldn't just be against the Obsidian Covenant; it would be a battle against him as well. The embers of my vengeance burned fiercely within me, but now they flickered under the heavy weight of Linx's dominion. I realized then that the battle for my soul had become far more complex than merely defeating the Covenant. Defeating Linx, a far more terrifying adversary than any demon I'd faced, was now my paramount concern.

The opportunity clawed its way into existence under a sky choked with black, spitting rain. A storm, a physical manifestation of the maelstrom tearing through my very soul, raged outside. The wind, a banshee's shriek amplified a thousandfold, clawed at the ancient stones of Linx's fortress, a deafening roar that swallowed my every move. Adrenaline, a venomous serpent, coiled in my veins, its icy bite a stark contrast to the fear that gnawed at the fragile edges of my sanity. Linx, the viper, basked in his self-deceived power, lulled into a stupor by the very poison he'd brewed. He hadn't seen the embers of my defiance, not the slow burn, the simmering rage that had been quietly forging itself into a weapon in the crucible of his cruelty. I moved like a phantom, the cold, slick stone a chilling caress against my skin, each breath a prayer, each step a gamble on the precipice of oblivion. The metallic tang of blood, my own, a scratch from the unforgiving stone, filled my nostrils. The air, thick with the scent of rain and fear, choked me. Then, I saw it: the unguarded gate, a maw yawning in the heart of his defences. This was it. My retribution. My chance to tear down the edifice of his tyranny, stone by agonizing stone.

Jagged ice ripped my soles. Yet, I moved like a ghost through the suffocating darkness, Linx's brutal training—years of agonizing drills—forged me into a weapon, honed not on steel, but suffering. Each breath was a rasp, the air thick with mildew and decay. The claustrophobic labyrinth pressed in, each footstep a blow to my sanity. My senses screamed—the metallic tang of blood, a constant reminder of my monstrous nature. This hunger wasn't a beast, but a hellhound, its breath hot on my throat. Control was a terrifying dance with oblivion; to yield was to unleash the inner storm. This wasn't life, but a defiant struggle against death.

The suffocating armoury, a tomb of rusted iron, throbbed with the wicked hum of countless blades. Each weapon, a twisted mockery of art, pulsed with palpable evil; I tasted the lingering bloodlust. Linx, his face a grim testament to brutal wars, clutched his obsidian arsenal, a horrifying collection mirroring his dark past. My gaze locked onto a uniquely curved obsidian scimitar, its oily surface writhing with demonic energy. The blade's unholy aura, a stench of brimstone, scorched my soul. It was more than a weapon; it was a conduit of forbidden power, igniting a primal hunger I never knew I possessed. Its siren song of annihilation threatened to consume me, but I fought the horrifying allure, my resistance a fragile bulwark against its seductive evil.

A jolt, raw adrenaline flooding my veins, and I snatched the blade. Ice-cold steel bit into my palm, the familiar heft a perverse comfort after weeks of brutal, bone-jarring training. It was familiar, yes, the weight, a ghost of countless drills, the feel of a second skin against my calloused grip. But this... this was different. Sharper. Hungrier. The polished surface vibrated with a low thrum, a pulse of raw, untamed power that mirrored the savage beat of my own heart, a power that tasted of blood and whispered promises of vengeance. The scent of oiled leather and whetstone clung to it, a heady aroma that spoke of countless deaths, and countless victories. This wasn't just a weapon; it was an extension of my soul, sharpened to a razor's edge by years of simmering rage.

My escape wasn't stealth; it was a maelstrom of carnage. I erupted from the shadows, a screaming banshee of rage, the wicked curve of my blade, a silver streak in the epileptic flicker of the torches. The stench of ozone and burnt flesh filled my nostrils as Linx met my assault. He wasn't just fighting; he was a fury incarnate, a storm of demonic energy that slammed into me with the force of a collapsing mountain. The impact ripped through me, a white hot searing pain blossoming across my arm, the metallic tang of blood thick on my tongue. I roared, a primal scream tearing from my throat, the taste of blood a bitter sacrament as I clawed my way back to my feet.

This wasn't a duel; it was a cataclysm. Each clash of steel shrieked, a death knell echoing through the suffocating, ancient chambers of the fortress. I felt the bone-jarring impact of his blows, the icy kiss of his power freezing my very soul. But fear was a luxury I couldn't afford. Adrenaline, a molten river coursing through my veins, fueled every desperate parry, every frenzied lunge. My lungs burned, a furnace of agony; my muscles screamed, taut strings threatening to snap. The air itself crackled with the raw power of our hate, a palpable thing that choked me, yet I would not, could not, yield. Escape wasn't just a goal; it was the only breath left in my ravaged lungs, the only prayer left on my blistered lips. It was life itself.

The air crackled, a venomous hiss of raw magic that tasted like ozone and scorched earth. Each strike was a cataclysmic collision—my searing, emerald flames, a maelstrom of incandescent fury, impacting Linx's obsidian darkness with the force of a collapsing star. The stench of burning flesh, both mine and his, filled my nostrils. This wasn't just a fight for freedom; it was a desperate, visceral struggle to excise the parasitic demon that had twisted my very soul. Linx, a creature of insidious charm and brutal power, had meticulously disassembled me, piece by agonizing piece, leaving me a fractured ruin of my former self. His control was a suffocating weight, a venomous serpent coiled around my heart, its icy scales scraping against my ribs with every laboured breath.

The metallic tang of my blood filled my mouth—a bitter, coppery tide—as I roared, a primal scream tearing from my throat. The pain, a white-hot brand searing my muscles, fueled my rage, a burning inferno that mirrored the tempest of fire I wielded. Each blow I landed echoed like a death knell—a tiny, agonizing fissure in the suffocating grip of Linx's dominion. I could feel him, a malignant presence, a writhing vortex of shadows and malice within my very marrow, fighting with a ferocity that mirrored my own. His whispers, insidious and seductive, slithered through my mind, promising power, oblivion, and release. But I would not succumb. I would not be his puppet. I would shatter his hold, claw my way back from the precipice of annihilation, and reclaim not just my body, but the very essence of my being. I would survive.

The fight was a relentless maelstrom of agony. Each bone-jarring impact—a thunderclap against my flesh—ignited a searing brand across my skin. The coppery tang of blood filled my mouth, a metallic tide rising with every ragged gasp for air. Bruises, blossoming like obscene flowers, bloomed across my body, each a testament to Linx's brutal efficiency. My muscles screamed, not just with pain, but with the terrifying knowledge that they were failing, fibres snapping under the strain. This wasn't just a fight; it was a slow, agonizing crucifixion.

Linx, a predator in human form, his eyes glittering with cold calculation, savoured my suffering. His power wasn't just physical; it was a psychic assault, a relentless probing of my weaknesses, a meticulous dismantling of my defences. His taunts whispered like venomous snakes, slithered into my mind, each word a poisoned dart aimed at my crumbling resolve. I could feel him, a suffocating presence, a weight pressing down on my soul, twisting my doubts into monstrous, crippling fears. He knew me, intimately, exploiting every fear, every insecurity, turning my strength against me. His strategy wasn't just combat; it was psychological warfare, a brutal game of attrition designed to break me before my body gave way.

The air itself tasted of fear and blood, thick and cloying. My vision swam, blurring at the edges, the arena a kaleidoscope of pain and impending defeat. With each brutal blow, my resolve fractured, splintering under the onslaught. But even as despair threatened to swallow me whole, a feral, primal rage ignited within, a flickering ember of defiance against the encroaching darkness. I would not yield. Not yet. This fight... wasn't just about survival; it was about proving to myself, to him, that I was more than the sum of my vulnerabilities. That I was unbreakable.

My inner inferno mirrored the raging fire in my soul. Defiance, a molten core, fueled a fury beyond Linx's magic. Years of enslavement ignited a primal rage, each blow a scream against his lingering control. Sweat, blood, and the stench of his magic fueled my blinding, desperate fight. Fear, a coiled serpent, sharpened my resolve. Every strike was a prayer for freedom, a visceral rejection of his power. I would not break. I would be free.

My breath hitched, a ragged gasp stolen from the storm itself, as I launched myself, a desperate, feral thing, at him. The clash of steel shrieked in my ears, a deafening clang that echoed the chaos in my soul. My blade found its mark, a searing, agonizing rip through his flesh, the coppery tang of blood filling my nostrils. His grunt of pain, a guttural animal sound, was music to my ears. No hesitation. No second thought. I ripped free, the stolen weapon a burning weight in my hand, and plunged into the maelstrom of the night.

The wind, a clawing beast, tore at my cloak, the icy rain a brutal lash against my skin. Each drop was a tiny hammer blow, driving home the desperate reality of my situation. The taste of blood, my own, I realized with chilling certainty, mingling with what rain filled my mouth, metallic and sharp. My heart hammered a frantic rhythm against my ribs, a desperate drumbeat against the howling wind. Fear, raw and primal, gnawed at my composure, but it was a fear I would not surrender to. Escape. Survival. These weren't just words, they were the fierce, burning prayer that fueled my every ragged breath. Behind me, his roar, a venomous promise of revenge, was swallowed by the storm, a final, bitter taste on my tongue. But I ran on, the darkness my only sanctuary, my only hope.

The grove choked me with the stench of damp earth and decaying leaves, a fetid counterpoint to the coppery tang of my blood, still blooming on my lip. My body, a shattered ruin, crashed to the unforgiving ground far from the cursed fortress. Each shuddering breath sent splinters of pain through me, a brutal, agonizing orchestra of broken bones and pulsing bruises. The darkness, them, still clawed at the edges of my mind, their insatiable hunger, a phantom pressure against my skull, a taste of ash and despair on my tongue. Weakness, a crushing weight, pinned me to the earth. My limbs, leaden anchors dragging me towards oblivion.

Freedom erupted, a wild torrent shattering years of bondage. It tasted like life giving rain after a desolate drought, and smelled like the first breath of pure air after suffocating captivity. Hard-won through sacrifice, it blazed within me, a defiant spirit refusing subjugation. This fire, a resilience reborn, ensured my liberation.

The escape ripped me apart, leaving a landscape of raw, throbbing flesh and a soul shredded beyond repair. The physical wounds, a tapestry of ragged scars tracing the map of Linx's cruelty, were merely the surface. Beneath, a festering infection gnawed at my spirit, a poison more insidious than any blade. His manipulations, the subtle whispers, the chilling gaslighting, and the calculated erosion of my very being, had carved fissures deep into my soul, leaving me hollowed out, a ghost of my former self. The metallic tang of blood still lingered in my memory, a phantom taste bitter on my tongue.

Even now, free from his physical grasp, I feel the phantom pressure of his hand, a ghost's touch on my throat, choking the breath from my lungs. The world assaults me, a sudden clang of metal, a whispered word in the shadows, each sound a thunderclap that sends my heart into a frantic, suffocating gallop. A cold dread, a relentless, icy hand, grips my chest, its fingers tightening with every tremor of fear. The scent of his cologne, a cloying sweetness that clings to the air, still haunts my dreams, a suffocating shroud of memory.

Rebuilding is a Herculean task, a Sisyphean struggle against the relentless weight of trauma. Each step forward is a battle, a gruelling climb up a mountain of shattered trust and self-loathing. But even as despair threatens to engulf me, a flicker of defiance remains, a tiny ember refusing to be extinguished. I will not be defined by Linx's cruelty. I will reclaim my life, one agonizing, victorious inch at a time. I will rise.

The wind howled a banshee wail, clawing at the flimsy shelter, mirroring the tempest raging within me. Rain lashed against my skin, each icy drop a searing brand echoing the brutal imprint Linx had left. His scent, a cloying blend of leather and something feral, something wrong, still clung to my memory, a phantom touch igniting the raw nerve endings where his cruelty had carved its mark. He'd been more than a teacher; he was a sculptor of pain, a perverse artist moulding me from the clay of my vulnerabilities. The taste of fear, metallic and bitter, lingered on my tongue, a constant reminder of the calculated humiliation, the deliberate dismantling of my defences.

He'd tempered my abilities in the furnace of my suffering, shaping my reflexes into lethal tools. His icy gaze, a haunting intelligence, pursued me even in sleep. His touch, a phantom torment, simultaneously shattered and fortified me. The scars, physical and spiritual, a tapestry of betrayal and agonizing self-knowledge, marked my soul. Though stronger, a predator born of his sadistic training, I carry the burden of his cruelty. My victory is bitter, my triumph hollow; I'm a testament to his brutality, his name a chilling echo in my mind.

My enhanced vampiric cravings, a consequence of Linx's blood, threatened to consume me. This potent power, while exhilarating, fueled a monstrous hunger, twisting my reflection into something alien. I was stronger, yet far more dangerous; a volatile paradox demanding control before the beast within devoured me.

The curved blade, a demonic relic from his arsenal, haunted my thoughts. Its power promised amplified strength, but at what price? Would it intensify my vampiric nature, or offer control? Escape was a victory, but the Obsidian Covenant loomed. Linx's wounds, both physical and emotional, fueled my burning vengeance. My quest: revenge and self-mastery, even if it cost my life.

CHAPTER

THREE

Whispers of the wind

The mud, slick as a butcher's slab, sucked at my boots, each step a betrayal. Rain, a relentless icy hammer, lashed my face, blurring the already indistinct shapes of the towering trees. The reek of rot, damp earth, decaying leaves, something else... something feral, warred with the metallic tang of my blood, thick and cloying on my lips. Each ragged gasp tore at my shredded ribs, a searing brand of agony that blossomed with every shuddering breath. This physical torment, however, was a mere prelude to the gnawing horror that consumed me from within.

It wasn't just hunger; it felt like a black hole in my gut, a ravenous beast clawing to be unleashed. A primal, visceral scream echoed in my bones, a thirst not for water, but for something more. My veins pulsed, not with blood, but with a desperate need—a second, frantic heartbeat that hammered a relentless rhythm of deprivation against my ribs. This wasn't merely about survival; it was a degrading struggle against a pang of hunger that threatened to unravel my very soul, leaving only the hollow shell of a man—a vessel for this monstrous, consuming need. I knew, with chilling certainty, what it wanted.

It began with a whisper, a sandpaper rasp across my tongue, a gnawing emptiness in my gut that pulsed like a second heart. But the whisper roared. A searing agony exploded in my chest, a molten fist clenching around my ribs, the pain blossoming outward, a venomous vine crawling through my limbs, leaving me boneless, shuddering, a puppet on broken strings. The world fractured into a kaleidoscope of blurry crimson and sickly yellow, my ears ringing with the phantom scream of my starved cells. The metallic tang of blood wasn't a phantom; it was a physical presence, a perverse perfume clinging to the air, mocking my desperate inhalation, taunting me with its impossible sweetness, a cruel siren song in this desolate wasteland of craving. My skin crawled, each pore screaming its silent agony. This wasn't hunger; this was a primal, visceral need, a hunger that clawed at my soul, threatening to unravel me from the inside out. I was drowning in it, consumed by it, a prisoner in the iron grip of my insatiable desire.

My fingers, slick with a film of sweat, crawled toward the soil, the dampness clinging to them like a lover's embrace. The reek of fecund earth, a brutal, primal perfume, warred with the metallic tang of blood, a whisper, a promise, a heartbeat barely muffled beneath the surface. A shudder, visceral and raw, ripped through me; a desperate, animal yearning to claw its way up from the pit of my gut. I recoiled, my hand scorched not by fire, but by the searing knowledge of what it craved. Linx's fate, a bloated husk, eyes vacant, his humanity devoured by the very thing that now gnawed at my soul, haunted me. His surrender was a siren's call, a tempting oblivion I couldn't afford.

This hunger, this monstrous thing within, pulsed with a life of its own, a ravening beast tearing at the fragile bars of my self-control. It wasn't a mere desire; it was a fundamental shift in being, a twisting of my very essence towards the abyss. The taste of it, the memory of it, lingered on my tongue, a phantom touch, a forbidden pleasure that promised an unending feast, an erasure of the self. But I would not become him. I would not succumb to the seductive, whispering darkness. I would choke it, wrestle it, tear it from my being with my bare hands until my last ragged breath was a defiant scream against the unending night.

The coppery tang of blood, thick and hot, scorched my tongue, a phantom taste that slammed into me, a visceral punch to the gut. I could still feel the power, a brutal tide surging through my veins, a delirious, terrifying ecstasy that left me gasping for air. Those moments... the black oblivion, the consuming hunger momentarily quenched, but at what unimaginable cost? They weren't glimpses; they were ravages, tearing away at my sanity, revealing a monster beneath, a creature of pure, savage instinct, a reflection of something ancient and abhorrent, devoid of empathy, of remorse, of everything human. The stench of it still clung to me, a cloying miasma of fear and primal need.

My own heart hammered against my ribs, a frantic drumbeat against the encroaching silence of that darker self. I fought it, claws scrabbling at the fragile remnants of my soul, the desperate, suffocating terror of utter annihilation a constant companion. It wasn't just darkness; it was a void, a gaping maw promising oblivion, threatening to swallow me whole, leaving behind only a hollow shell, a testament to the beast that had claimed my humanity.

The rain, a torrential deluge, flayed my skin, each icy drop a searing brand against the fire still burning within. It wasn't cleansing; it was a mocking baptism, washing over the filth of my soul, yet failing to extinguish the inferno of my memories. The acrid stench of smoke, wood smoke, flesh, and something indescribably foul, clung to me, a phantom limb of the massacre. I squeezed my eyes shut, but the village blazed behind my lids, not in flickering flames, but in the searing white-hot glare of a thousand suns. The screams... God, the screams. They weren't just sounds; they were shards of glass driven into my skull, each one a splintered echo of my own broken heart, a symphony of agony conducted by the devil himself.

The taste of blood, mine, theirs, metallic and coppery, coated my tongue, a bitter reminder of the crimson tide that stained the earth, a macabre tapestry woven with the lives of my kin. The hunger... it gnawed, a ravenous beast within, fueled by the ashes of my past, by the vengeful whispers of the dead. This wasn't just pain; it was a slow, agonizing vivisection, each memory a scalpel slicing deeper into the very core of my being. And the desire... the burning need for retribution, for annihilation, choked me, a desperate, gasping inhalation of poisoned air. There would be no end to this torment, only the bitter, agonizing sweet release of... vengeance.

Days bled into nights, a crimson tide staining the endless twilight. The hunger wasn't a companion; it was a ravenous beast, its claws tearing at my insides, its hot breath scorching my lungs. The reek of decay, a miasma clinging to the damp earth, mingled with the coppery tang of my desperation. I stalked the pathetic creatures, a twitching rabbit, a bird whose frantic beating heart I felt thudding against my palm before its lifeblood, meagre as it was, stained my fingers. Each drop was a bitter mockery, a thin crimson trickle against the firestorm raging in my throat. The screams, muffled and swallowed by the oppressive silence of the wilderness, haunted me more than any howl of a predator. Their tiny lives, extinguished in my desperate grasp, were a testament to my own slow, agonizing demise. This wasn't sustenance; it was ritual sacrifice at the altar of my own insatiable need.

The moral compass, once a guiding star, now spun wildly, a fractured piece of glass reflecting the grotesque parody of survival. I, once a woman of principle, was reduced to a creature driven by instinct, a predator stripped bare of any pretense of humanity. The cold, slickness of blood on my skin wasn't just crimson; it was the stain of my soul, a searing brand marking my descent into this primal abyss. The taste, metallic and acrid, burned a path down my throat, leaving only the gnawing emptiness behind.

Loneliness, a physical entity, pressed against me, a suffocating weight amplified by the whispering wind through the skeletal branches of the dead trees. I saw my reflection in the murky water, a gaunt stranger, eyes hollowed out by starvation, hands stained a horrifying shade of scarlet, a testament to the monstrous metamorphosis unfolding within. With each passing moonless night, I questioned not just my humanity, but my very essence, wondering if the beast within would completely obliterate the fragile embers of the woman I once was, leaving behind only a husk, driven by a hunger that knew no end.

The war inside me was a visceral maelstrom, a screaming battle between the desperate need to live and the sickening urge to survive. The metallic tang of blood, a phantom taste on my tongue, mocked my abstinence. To feed was to surrender another piece of my soul, to let the vampiric curse etch deeper into my very marrow, its icy tendrils already gripping my heart.

The hunger wasn't a gnawing; it was a searing brand, a white-hot iron pressed against my ribs, each pulse a hammer blow. My bones ached with it, a deep, resonating thrum that vibrated through my teeth. To deny this monstrous craving was to invite oblivion, a slow, agonizing decay into a husk, a puppet animated not by strings, but by the vile, pulsing instinct that was rapidly becoming my only master. I felt the opposing forces tearing at my very essence—a brutal tug of war between the flickering ember of my will and the insatiable, ravenous beast that roared for release. The scent of blood, sharp and metallic, haunted every breath, a cruel siren's call whispering promises of oblivion and ecstasy in the same breath. This was no mere conflict; it was a slow, agonizing crucifixion of self, each moment a hammer blow to the spirit.

The cave maw yawned, a festering wound in the earth, its entrance a curtain of snarling vines and skeletal branches clawing at the suffocating twilight. The meagre shelter it offered was a cruel joke; a damp, earthy stink clinging to my ragged clothes, the air thick with the scent of decay and something else... something feral. Rest? A pathetic fantasy. Hunger, a ravenous beast, gnawed at my insides, its teeth sinking into my very soul. My body, a traitorous vessel, shuddered with tremors that rattled my bones like dice in a death rattle. Sleep brought no solace, only a crimson tide of nightmares, a relentless, visceral replay of the carnage that had brought me here. Each dream was a fresh wound, the taste of blood metallic on my tongue even in waking moments.

The cave's damp chill seeped into my marrow, a glacial grip that rivalled the gnawing emptiness in my gut. It wasn't just hunger; it was a hollowness that echoed the vast, terrifying void opening up inside me. A desperate, primal scream clawed at my throat, choked by the desperate need for... something. Anything. To quell this burning, this consuming pressure behind my eyes, threatening to shatter my skull. My attempts to curl into a fetal position were met with the agonizing rebellion of my ravaged muscles; each spasm a fresh torment. My breath hitched, a ragged gasp against the vice of my ribs. Every pulse hammered a brutal reminder of my mortality, each beat a countdown to oblivion. I was not merely hungry; I was unravelling. This wasn't survival; it was a slow, agonizing descent into something... else.

The wicked curve of the blade scavenged from Linx's unholy armory, burned a phantom image onto my retinas. Its demonic hum vibrated through my very bones, a tangible thrumming that promised oblivion and power in equal measure. The stench of Sulfur and something ancient, something wrong, clung to the memory, a cloying perfume masking the metallic tang of blood. My suffering, a gnawing, ravenous beast within, clawed at my sanity, urging me to grasp this forbidden succour.

But the hesitation was a physical thing, a lead weight anchoring me to the precipice. This wasn't just a dangerous path; it was a greased slope plunging into the black heart of hell. The power it whispered was a siren's kiss, a seductive poison that could bloat my already monstrous vampiric nature, transforming me into something beyond redemption, something beyond me. I could feel it, the seductive caress of its dark energy, a chilling caress that promised not strength, but annihilation.

The fear, raw and visceral, was a fist clenching around my heart, squeezing the breath from my lungs. It warred with a desperate, feverish lust for the power it offered, a gnawing hunger that echoed the insatiable emptiness within. The cold sweat slicked my skin, a stark contrast to the heat of the demonic energy pulsing in my veins, a treacherous tide threatening to drown me in its unholy depths. The risk wasn't abstract; it was a physical manifestation of my deepest dread, a chilling premonition etched into the very marrow of my being. I knew, with the chilling certainty of impending doom, what I risked losing. And what I craved.

The weight of the decision crushed me, a vice tightening around my chest, each breath a battle. Survival screamed in my ears, a primal, desperate shriek, while the icy tendrils of fear, the fear of becoming it, coiled around my soul. The line between man and monster wasn't a blur; it was a jagged chasm, and I teetered precariously on its edge, the stench of decay, a sickeningly sweet metallic tang, already clinging to my tongue. The hunger wasn't gnawing; it was a ravenous beast within, its claws tearing at my insides, a symphony of agonizing pain punctuated by the maddening whispers of surrender.

I was a cage of bone and sinew, imprisoned not only by my body but also by a cursed inheritance—a legacy of darkness etched into my very being. Each heartbeat felt like a hammer blow against the fragile walls of my humanity, a desperate defence against the encroaching tide of monstrous hunger. It wasn't merely a craving; it was a possession, a violation, a corruption seeping into my marrow, twisting my thoughts and distorting my very essence.

The darkness wasn't a threat; it was a lover, seductive and deadly, whispering promises of power, of oblivion. I felt its icy breath on my neck, saw its reflection in the haunted depths of my own eyes, and tasted its bitter triumph on my lips. It wasn't just a promise; it was a certainty, a chilling premonition of my inevitable transformation, a metamorphosis into the very thing that haunted my waking hours and stained my nightmares with a crimson, unforgiving hue. The taste of blood, not just imagined, but real, a horrifying taste of the future, a future I fought with every fibre of my being, but a future that seemed, with every passing moment, less a possibility and more an inescapable destiny.

The hunger clawed at my insides, a ravenous beast tearing at my flesh, its icy breath chilling me to the bone. The emptiness wasn't just physical; it was a desolate wasteland echoing with the rasping whispers of exhaustion, a gnawing hollowness that stole my strength, leaving me trembling, exposed, and utterly vulnerable. It was a grotesque parody of survival, a constant, bitter reminder of Linx's twisted handiwork, a branding iron searing my soul. His face, a mask of glacial indifference, burned behind my eyelids, those eyes, twin chips of obsidian, glittering with predatory hunger, haunted my every waking moment.

His methods had been a brutal ballet of pain and precision, each lesson a scar etched onto my very being. He'd pushed me, relentlessly, to the precipice of oblivion, honing my skills with the cold efficiency of a surgeon dissecting a corpse. I felt the phantom sting of his touch, the ghost of his power still clinging to me, a vile residue of his control. He'd used the very essence of my strength, the skills he had forged, to bind me, to shackle my will, to reduce me to a puppet dancing to his cruel tune.

That sickening power... it would never touch me again. The vow ripped through me, a wildfire consuming the remnants of my fear. No more. I would not be his instrument, his plaything. I would break free from his insidious grasp, claim my destiny, rise above the ashes of his manipulation, and forge my own, unshakeable will. My own master. I would be my own master.

The rain wasn't merely falling; it was a brutal assault, each icy drop a searing brand etching the loneliness into my very bones. The forest, a claustrophobic maw of black, choked the breath from my lungs, its oppressive weight mirroring the gaping void that had become my soul. My stomach screamed, not merely hunger, but the gnawing, feral hunger of the beast that was consuming me from the inside out; a monster born not of myth, but of this desolate, godforsaken place. The transformation, a slow, agonizing metamorphosis, was a feast for the darkness, and I, its helpless, delectable prey. With each second, a fragment of my humanity chipped away, a precious shard lost to the encroaching abyss. I tasted despair, a bitter metallic tang on my tongue, and felt the chilling breath of oblivion on my neck. Yet, a spark flickered a defiant member of defiance—a stubborn refusal to surrender that mirrored the fierce pride that once defined me, before the forest, before this. It was a thread, thin as a spider's silk, connecting me to something more than this encroaching night, and I clutched it with the desperation of a drowning man.

I knew the Obsidian Covenant was still out there, hunting me. But my immediate enemy was within me, the relentless vampiric hunger that threatened to consume me, to obliterate the last vestiges of my humanity. I had escaped Linx, but had I truly escaped my inner demons? I had to find a way, a way to survive, a way to control this monstrous appetite that threatened to drown me in darkness. My vengeance on the Obsidian Covenant remained my primary goal, but first, I had to confront the far greater threat within my being. The path ahead was dark and fraught with danger, but I would not surrender. Not yet. My journey for revenge would continue. But before I could face my external enemy, I had to conquer the darkness that threatened to devour me from the inside. The fight for survival was only just beginning. I could feel it, a cold, gnawing fear coupled with the burning, insatiable need. I had to find a way to reconcile these warring parts of myself. This was my fight and my fight alone.

The skeletal fingers of the ancient trees twisted like the limbs of some drowned god clawed at the bruised, blood-red twilight. Their gnarled surfaces, slick with relentless rain, scraped against my skin like the rasp of a thousand tiny knives. The icy needles of the downpour weren't just piercing my flesh; they were driving shards of frozen despair into my very soul. With each drop, a tiny hammer blows against my already shattered will. The reek of wet earth and decaying things, the stench of a thousand forgotten deaths, filled my nostrils, a nauseating counterpoint to the metallic tang of blood welling from a fresh gash on my arm.

The forest floor, a sucking, fetid bog, clung to my boots with the tenacity of a drowning man. Each agonizing pull was a physical manifestation of the despair gripping my heart, the mud weighing me down, mirroring the crushing weight of my circumstances. My muscles, screaming in protest, felt like they were tearing themselves apart, fibre by fibre, each spasm a tiny death. But the hunger... the hunger was a separate entity, a ravenous beast dwelling within my gut, its cold breath icy against my insides. It wasn't just a physical ache; it was a gnawing emptiness, a black hole threatening to devour my very being, to swallow me whole and leave behind only the echo of my despair. The taste of my fear coated my tongue, bitter and metallic.

I stumbled forward, a broken marionette dragged along by invisible strings of desperation. The hunger clawed at my sanity, whispering insidious promises of oblivion, a seductive escape from this agonizing torment. But a flicker of defiance, a stubborn ember in the ashes of my hope, refused to be extinguished. I had to survive. I had to find something. Anything. Before the darkness consumed me completely before hunger claimed its victory and silenced the ragged whisper of my resolve forever.

The world fractured into a kaleidoscope of swirling crimson and black. My knees buckled, the impact jarring loose a fresh torrent of blood; its metallic shriek filled my ears, a gruesome counterpoint to the ragged rasp of my breath. The damp earth tasted of iron and decay, clinging to my cracked lips like a shroud. Each heartbeat hammered a brutal rhythm against my ribs, a frantic drumbeat of impending doom. This wasn't just weakness; it was oblivion creeping in, icy fingers clutching at my soul. I was less than a shadow, a ghost teetering on the precipice of nothingness, my existence a flickering candle flame threatened by a gale-force wind. The thirst, oh God, the thirst, it wasn't just physical; it was a gnawing emptiness that echoed the desolate cavern of my heart, a hunger for something... more than mere survival. It was a primal scream trapped within, a desperate plea for solace in this blood-soaked wasteland. I had to find it. I had to. Or become the very darkness that surrounded me.

Rain lashed my face, a brutal, icy assault. Through the sheets of water, a flicker, no, a pulsating flicker, caught my eye. A dark shape, hunched and malevolent, not just brooding, but seething, a silhouette etched against the greasy blackness of the storm. My heart didn't just hammer; it throbbed, a frantic drum against my ribs, each beat a desperate plea. The stench of ozone and wet earth fought with the coppery tang of blood, a phantom scent that sharpened my terror.

He emerged from the shadows, impossibly slow, a colossus wreathed in the storm itself. Not merely tall and imposing, but a monstrosity, a being sculpted from a nightmare, his presence a palpable chill that sunk its claws into my very bones, freezing my blood.

Nausea wasn't a wave; it was a tidal surge, threatening to drown me in icy dread. His cloak was less a garment than a shroud of absolute darkness, the hood a cowl of shadows concealing features I couldn't even imagine. But even veiled, his power was a crushing weight, a suffocating pressure that stole the air from my lungs, a vice around my chest, crushing the life from me. The very air vibrated with it, a low hum of malevolent energy that resonated deep within my soul.

Caspian the enigmatic Whispering Wind demon is a figure of legend whose name resonates throughout the realm. Everyone knows who he is and the immense power he possesses captivating all with his ethereal presence.

The growl ripped from his chest, a seismic tremor that fractured the very earth beneath me. Dust, tasting of iron and ancient death, sprayed my face as the ground bucked and heaved, a physical manifestation of his incandescent rage. The sound wasn't just a growl; it was a guttural shriek of pure, unadulterated hatred, a sonic assault that clawed at my eardrums and vibrated through my teeth. The fleeting warmth, the almost imperceptible flicker of...something akin to kindness... in his cryptic blood offer, was obliterated. This was no mere rejection; it was a venomous curse, a branding iron pressed against my soul, searing a wound far deeper than any blade could inflict. The stench of ozone and decay filled my nostrils, mirroring the chilling despair that iced my veins. My heart hammered against my ribs, a frantic drumbeat against the encroaching silence of utter terror. This wasn't just dread; it was the paralyzing grip of absolute, bone-deep certainty. I hadn't just made a mistake. I had invited damnation.

"You should be dead," Caspian's voice, a rasping whisper like nails on a coffin, clawed its way into my skull, drowning out the torrential drumming of the rain. The stench of wet earth and decaying leaves filled my nostrils, a grim perfume mirroring the suffocating weight of his centuries, a crushing burden of ages pressing down on my chest, each breath a battle against his legacy. The echoes of his countless battles weren't just a chilling resonance in my bones; they vibrated through my very marrow, a symphony of death played on the strings of my soul. His words, icy daggers dipped in the venom of a thousand lost hopes, tore through me, each syllable a searing brand. The taste of fear, metallic and bitter, coated my tongue. *"A pathetic spark,"* he hissed, the word spitting from his lips like venom, *"a flickering fly in a hurricane, destined for oblivion."* His eyes, twin pools of glacial fury reflecting the storm, held me captive. There was something else there too, buried beneath the frost, a flicker of something broken, something almost… regretful. But the icy certainty of his intent remained. He meant to extinguish me, not merely kill me, but to utterly erase me from existence.

He advanced, a predator unsheathing its claws. The air itself thickened, a cloying miasma clinging to my skin, each molecule vibrating with the raw, malevolent power radiating from him. The pressure on my chest wasn't just atmospheric; it was the crushing weight of his contempt, a physical force that stole the breath from my lungs, leaving me gasping, a desperate fish hauled from the water. His hood fell back, revealing eyes, twin chips of obsidian polished to a glacial sheen, reflecting nothing but the bleak, endless void within. They weren't just cold; they burned with a glacial fire, an icy inferno that seared my very soul.

The scent of ozone and decay, the stench of his dark essence, filled my nostrils, a bitter counterpoint to the metallic tang of blood blooming in my mouth. Gone was any flicker of the compassion I'd deluded myself into seeing; replaced by a hatred so profound, so absolute, it tasted like ash and bitterness on my tongue. This wasn't disgust; it was annihilation, a silent promise of exquisite torment whispered in the chilling silence between us. His gaze was a tangible thing, a weapon aimed at the very core of my being, stripping me bare, and exposing the tremor of fear that rattled my bones.

My stomach gnawed, a ravenous beast clawing at my insides, each pang a searing brand. The metallic tang of blood, my own, I suspected, filled my mouth, a bitter counterpoint to the phantom taste of roasted meat that mocked my emptiness. His shadow loomed, a suffocating blanket of menace woven from the flickering torchlight. I could smell the leather of his boots, sharp and acrid, a scent that spoke of violence and long nights. The tremor in my legs wasn't just from hunger; it was a primal fear, a seismic shudder threatening to shatter the brittle facade I presented. But I wouldn't break. He wouldn't see the terror that clawed at my throat, the icy grip of panic on my heart. I stood defiant, a statue carved from bone and will, my eyes burning with a cold fury that masked the agonizing emptiness within. Let him see only the storm in my gaze, not the hurricane raging inside.

"I will not be broken," I rasped, the words a guttural growl clawing its way from my throat, a defiant shriek swallowed by the tempest's roar. The taste of iron, my blood, a metallic tang coating my tongue, was a perverse sacrament. It was a promise, a venomous oath whispered to the echoing chambers of my soul, a pledge less to him, and more to the fractured, defiant ghost of myself. The storm raged outside, mirroring the maelstrom within. My muscles coiled, tense as taut wires, each fibre screaming in protest, yet refusing to yield. This wasn't mere strength; it was a primal, incandescent rage, born in the crucible of unimaginable pain, forged in the fires of relentless, suffocating despair. It was the desperate thrashing of a wounded beast, cornered, bleeding, but refusing, absolutely refusing, to submit. This wasn't just a stand. It was a primal scream against annihilation. This was war.

Caspian's laughter clawed at the silence of the ancient forest, a rasping, feral sound that scraped against the bark of the skeletal trees and chilled the very marrow of the bones. The reek of pine and decaying leaves hung heavy in the air, a cloying sweetness mingling with the metallic tang of blood, his blood, perhaps. *"Oh, you're far from extinguished,"* he hissed, the words slithering out like venomous snakes, each syllable a deliberate torment. His eyes, chips of obsidian in a face etched by cruelties both inflicted and endured, gleamed with a predatory delight. *"Weakened? Broken? Those are but the appetizers, my dear. The main course is utter vulnerability. Feel the earth tremble beneath you, feel the very fabric of your existence unravelling. This… this is only the beginning of your end."*

The stench of blood, metallic and thick, clung to the air, a perverse perfume. I circled a slow, deliberate waltz of death, my gaze raking over her. Not just wounds, crimson rivers carved into her flesh, each ragged gash a testament to her futile fight. I saw the fading defiance in her eyes, the raw terror blooming in their depths, a bloom more intoxicating than any flower. My breath hitched, not from exertion, but from the heady scent of her fear, a feral tang that pricked my nostrils and set my teeth on edge. The floorboards groaned beneath my weight, a counterpoint to the frantic thump of her heart, a rhythm I could almost feel vibrating through the very soles of my boots. This wasn't a hunt; it was a ritual, a dark communion. I savoured the power, the absolute control, the knowledge that her life hung precariously on my whim. My fingers itched to trace the brutal map of her suffering, to feel the yielding softness beneath the ravaged skin. The slow, deliberate arc of my circle tightened, the coils of my obsession tightening with it. She was broken, yes, but not yet extinguished. And that, my dear, was the most exquisite part of all.

"Linx's plaything," he hissed, the word a venomous spray, tasting of bile and dust on his tongue. The air itself seemed to crackle with the raw contempt radiating from him; a palpable heat pressed against my skin, mirroring the burning humiliation in my gut. His eyes, chips of obsidian flecked with cruel amusement, bored into me, dissecting my very soul. The scent of his disdain, sharp, metallic, like ozone after a lightning strike, filled my nostrils. To be so easily shattered, a delicate porcelain doll under his contemptuous gaze, the fragments of my pride scattering like shattered glass. He savoured the moment, this slow, deliberate crashing of my spirit, a perverse pleasure etched onto his lips in a cruel, almost beautiful smile. The creature he spoke of, myself, a pathetic thing, a weakness he found both exhilarating and utterly contemptible.

My body recoiled, a microscopic tremor barely concealing the seismic shift within. Linx. The very sound, a jagged shard of obsidian scraping across my soul, reopened a wound festering with years of betrayal. The stench of it, a bitter blend of regret and ash, filled my nostrils, choking the breath from my lungs. My heart, a trapped bird frantic against its cage of ribs, hammered a brutal tattoo against my skin. Caspian, that viper, wouldn't see me flinch. He wouldn't have the cruel pleasure of witnessing my agony, the raw, exposed nerve of my vulnerability. My teeth ground together, a vicious rasp in the suffocating silence, the forced calm of a brittle mask barely clinging to my face. The ghost of his laughter, a cruel mockery, echoed in my ears, a phantom touch chilling my skin even as the searing heat of his betrayal branded itself onto my memory. The loss... a black hole consumes.

The silence stretched, a taut, unbearable thing between us. The rain continued its relentless assault, blurring the edges of the forest into an indistinct, watery canvas. Caspian's gaze, though still cold, held a flicker of something else—a grudging respect, perhaps, or something darker, more akin to fascination. He shifted his weight, the rustle of his dark cloak a whisper in the storm.

"*The Obsidian Covenant,*" he finally said, his voice low and gravelly, each word carefully chosen. "*They are a blight upon this world, a festering wound that needs to be cauterized.*"

My hunger, a constant gnawing presence, nodded slowly. The words felt like a cold stone settling in my gut, a confirmation of what I already knew, a shared understanding that hung heavy between us despite our mutual animosity. Caspian, even he, a demon, couldn't deny the Covenant's cruelty. I felt a grim satisfaction in that shared acknowledgment, a tiny flicker of something akin to kinship in the bleak landscape of our hatred. The weight of it, the brutal reality of their actions, pressed down on me. I could almost taste the ash and blood.

"*I seek vengeance,*" I stated, my voice raw with grief and rage, "*for what they did to my village. I saw it, you see, the burning homes, the screams... I felt the ground tremble beneath my feet, not just from the explosions, but from the terror that ripped through everything. I lost everything that day. And I will not rest until I have made them pay for what they took from me, for what they took from us.*"

"Vengeance," he repeated, the word tasting like ash on his tongue. *"A dangerous path. One often paved with blood and regret."*

He didn't offer platitudes or empty reassurances. He understood the consuming nature of vengeance, the all-encompassing need for retribution. He had walked that path himself, countless times.

"I have information " he continued his gaze fixed intently on the swirling vortex of rain outside. *"I possess crucial intelligence about the Covenant's movements, their strategies and future plans. This knowledge could change everything for us so we must act wisely and swiftly on it."*

I raised an eyebrow. This was unexpected. Why would he help me? The reasons, I suspected, were as complex and twisted as the path that I'd travelled to reach this uneasy truce. I felt a knot of unease tighten in my stomach. What did he want in return? I couldn't shake the feeling that I was walking into a trap, a carefully laid snare disguised as an olive branch.

"What do you want in return?" I asked, my voice tight with suspicion. I knew, I knew there was no such thing as a gift, especially not from a demon like Caspian. A cold dread snaked through me; I could practically taste the bitter tang of betrayal. My heart hammered against my ribs, a frantic drumbeat against the silence. I waited, every nerve ending screaming for his answer, bracing myself for whatever vile bargain he'd offer.

Caspian let out a low chuckle, the sound chilling in the damp air. *"Nothing so simple,"* he replied, his eyes glinting with an unnerving intelligence. *"Cooperation. Assistance. Let's just say... a mutually beneficial arrangement."*

He didn't elaborate, leaving the specifics vague, shrouded in the mystery that clung to him like a second skin. But I understood the underlying implication: an alliance, fragile and potentially explosive, forged in the fires of shared hatred and mutual need. I felt a shiver run down my spine, a prickle of apprehension mixed with a strange, unsettling thrill. It was a dangerous game, this alliance, and I knew, instinctively, that I was playing with fire. The weight of it settled on my shoulders, heavy and inescapable.

The journey back toward the relative safety of the Whispering Wind's hidden sanctuary was fraught with peril. The forest, alive with the rustling of unseen creatures and the ominous creak of ancient trees, felt oppressive, a suffocating blanket of darkness and looming danger. Caspian, though initially reluctant, acted as a guide, his knowledge of the forest's hidden paths proving invaluable. His movements were silent, almost ghostly, his presence a shadow that moved effortlessly through the tangled undergrowth.

My legs burned, each step a monumental effort. Hunger gnawed at me, a hollow ache that stole my strength, leaving me weak and unsteady as I tried to match Caspian's stride. The thirst... that vampiric thirst clawed at me, a relentless, agonizing pulse that mirrored my desperate vulnerability. It was a torment, a constant reminder of the danger I was in. I hated relying on Caspian, my pride screaming against the necessity, but I had no choice. I simply couldn't do it alone.

Several times, we were forced to fight. Covenant patrols, small groups of demons and corrupted human soldiers ambushed us from the shadows. Caspian's combat style was brutal, efficient, and utterly ruthless. He moved with a terrifying grace, his blades flashing like lightning in the gloom, leaving behind a trail of carnage and death. I, despite my weakened state, fought with the ferocity of a cornered animal.

My fire magic, though limited by my gnawing hunger, still held a devastating power; I could feel the heat sear my own throat as I unleashed each blast. I saw them fight, their combined skills a whirlwind of motion, a dance of death. Their coordinated attacks proved formidable, and I watched, a grim satisfaction growing inside me, as they overcame the Covenant's forces with bloody efficiency. I tasted the metallic tang of blood in the air, my blood mingling with the enemy's. It was a victory, hard-won and brutal, but a victory nonetheless.

Between the skirmishes, an uneasy silence descended. I avoided their eyes, noticing their interactions were brief and functional, each word carefully chosen, each movement measured and controlled. The air crackled with unspoken tension, I felt it acutely, a mixture of distrust, grudging respect, and a simmering undercurrent of something more potent, something darker that pricked my skin and made my muscles tense.

As we neared the sanctuary, the forest thinned, giving way to a rocky outcrop. I felt a shiver, not entirely from the cold. In the distance, shrouded in mist, lay a cluster of ancient stone buildings, almost swallowed by the encroaching darkness. I could feel it then, a strange energy humming in the air, a powerful magical current that was both alluring and menacing. It sent a thrill down my spine, a prickling sensation on my skin. I gripped my staff tighter, my heart pounding a rhythm against my ribs.

"*This is it,*" Caspian said, his voice a mere breath in the cold night air. "*The Whispering Wind's Sanctuary. But remember, trust is a luxury we cannot afford.*"

The sanctuary was a maze of winding corridors and hidden chambers, each room a dizzying swirl of different magics. I could practically taste the air, thick with the scent of ancient herbs and something else, something darker, more primal, the metallic tang of blood and the raw thrum of power. It made my skin prickle. Caspian led me through the labyrinthine passages, his movements so fluid and assured he seemed a silent ghost gliding through the shadows. I struggled to keep up, my heart hammering a frantic rhythm against my ribs. He finally stopped before a large, imposing oak door, its surface etched with strange symbols that pulsed with a faint, inner light, a light that seemed to call to me and filled me with a strange, unsettling anticipation.

He turned to me, his expression unreadable. "*We'll see what the others think of our... alliance,*" he said, his voice low. I felt a chill run down my spine. This was it. My stomach clenched. "*This is where your... usefulness will be tested,*" he continued, and I knew, with a certainty that settled like a stone in my gut, that this was far more dangerous than I'd anticipated. I wondered, with a sudden surge of fear, if I was truly up to the task.

He pushed open the door, revealing a large chamber, lit by flickering torches that cast long, dancing shadows on the rough-hewn stone walls. Around a long, heavy oak table sat several figures, cloaked and hooded, their faces hidden in shadow. The air was thick with an almost palpable tension, a palpable sense of anticipation and unease. Weak and hungry, I felt a shiver run down my spine. This wasn't simply a meeting; it was a judgment, I knew it in my gut. My future, my alliance with Caspian, hung precariously in the balance. I could feel the weight of it pressing down on me, a suffocating burden. My heart hammered against my ribs. I wanted to run, to escape the intensity of it all, but I was trapped, frozen in place by the sheer terror of the unknown.

Caspian led me into the chamber, and I felt every eye in the place fall on us. The silence was absolute, a thick, suffocating blanket broken only by the crackling torches and the frantic thump thump thump of my own heart. I knew, with a chilling certainty that sent a shiver down my spine, that the real game was only just beginning. This alliance, fragile and fraught with such palpable danger, felt like a gamble, a desperate, reckless play for survival against a common enemy that loomed far larger than even our internal conflicts. The darkness of the forest, I realized, had been nothing but a prelude, a mere taste, of the storm that awaited us within the sanctuary of the Whispering Wind. The whispers of the wind, once subtle and almost comforting, had become a deafening roar in my ears.

CHAPTER

FOUR

A Dance with Darkness

T he air in the sanctuary hung heavy, filled with a suffocating mix of ancient herbs and an acrid, metallic scent that clawed at the back of my throat—a coppery tang that threatened to make me retch. It was the stench of blood, both old and shockingly fresh, a testament to the brutal rituals and secret sacrifices that had stained these shadowed walls for centuries. A sharp, icy chill snaked down my spine, lodging itself in the marrow of my bones. My breath hitched in my chest, a ragged gasp caught in the thick, fetid air.

Around the massive oak table, hooded figures sat in eerie stillness, their features engulfed by the swirling gloom cast by the flickering torchlight. Shadows twisted and writhed, creating an illusion that masked any semblance of humanity hidden beneath the heavy, tattered cloth. My heart raced wildly, a frantic drumbeat echoing the escalating dread coiling in my chest. Each figure radiated a palpable aura of power, electric energy that crackled in the air, raising goosebumps on my skin and making the fine hairs on my arms stand on end.

The oppressive silence hung heavy, suffocating, pierced only by the ragged rhythm of my breathing and the ominous drip, drip, drip of some viscous liquid from an unseen source, each drop a reminder of the foreboding atmosphere. I felt hopelessly trapped, out of my depth, a trespasser in a realm where darkness reigned supreme, where the very air seemed to throb with malevolence as if it conspired against me.

Caspian, his customary aloofness shattered by tension so palpable it crackled in the air like static electricity, guided me to a place before the rough-hewn table. He remained silent, his gaze locked on the shadowy figures huddled around it, their faces obscured by the flickering torchlight, their expressions impenetrable, a mask of enigmatic stillness. The silence stretched, a taut, unbearable membrane, punctuated only by the erratic crackle of the torches, a rhythm mimicking the frantic drumbeat of my own heart. Their scrutiny was a physical weight, pressing down on me, suffocating, crushing the breath from my lungs. I felt utterly exposed, a naked nerve laid bare to their judgment, a pawn in a game whose rules remained frustratingly obscure. A sheen of cold sweat slicked my skin; my breath hitched, and a ragged gasp trapped in my throat. My hands clenched into fists, dug into the rough-hewn wood of the table, the coarse grain offering scant comfort against the icy dread that threatened to engulf me. The urge to speak, to demand answers, clawed at me, but the words were strangled in my throat, choked by a rising tide of fear.

Their silence was a verdict, a damning indictment, and I stood paralyzed, a statue carved from apprehension, awaiting the inevitable judgment. The very air throbbed with unspoken accusations, each one a hammer blow against my fragile sense of self, reducing me to insignificance beneath the weight of their immense, chilling power.

A towering figure, broader and more imposing than his cloaked companions, stepped away from the shadowy cluster. The fabric of his hood, as dark as a raven's wing, seemed to drink in the scant light that dared enter the chamber, shrouding him in an almost palpable gloom. When he finally broke the heavy silence, his voice emerged not just as a sound but as a force of nature—a deep, resonant tremor that vibrated through the very stones beneath their feet and thundered in the chests of those who stood before him. The air crackled with an electric energy, charged by the sheer power of his words. *"Caspian,"* his voice boomed, each syllable reverberating with the weight of ages past, *"explain... this alliance."*

Caspian's gaze flickered toward me, a fleeting acknowledgement so brief it felt almost dismissive, before snapping back to the speaker with an intensity that made my skin prickle. A sharp, insistent unease coursed down my spine, his gaze not merely assessing but a cold appraisal—wary and subtly distrustful, like a predator sizing up its prey before making the kill.

"This is Blaze," he intoned, his voice a low, controlled rumble that reverberated in the taut silence surrounding us. Though his words were ostensibly directed at the small gathering around him, they felt like a keenly aimed arrow precisely intended for me, a subtle branding that left its mark. *"A flame elemental. She possesses... unique abilities."* He paused deliberately, allowing the silence to stretch taut, thick with unspoken implications that coiled in the air like a miasma, clinging to the edges of our collective unease.

My fingers tightened around the worn leather strap of my bag, the rough texture providing a fleeting comfort against the rising tide of apprehension that churned within me. The atmosphere was thick, charged with a tension almost as tangible as the anticipation that crackled in the air. What secrets did he hint at, concealed within those carefully chosen words? What were these *"unique abilities,"* and why did their mere mention elicit such a heavy, unsettling hesitation from him—and the others? The uncertainty gnawed at me like a ravenous beast, a cold dread settling in the pit of my stomach, leaving an indelible mark of worry that echoed in the depths of my mind.

"Unique abilities?" the taller figure questioned, a hint of skepticism lacing their words. *"What abilities, precisely?"*

Caspian's gaze, glacial and unwavering, returned to mine, sending a fresh tremor of unease spiralling down my spine. For a fleeting instant, a flicker of genuine concern—a nearly imperceptible crack in his meticulously forged mask of icy detachment—washed over his features. It vanished in the blink of an eye, swiftly replaced by the familiar, chilling intensity that constricted my breath and sent a leaden weight plummeting into the pit of my stomach. When he spoke, each word was meticulously chosen, deliberate, like precious gems being carefully set in a gilded casing: *"Her power is considerable, but her control... is... fragile."*

The unspoken words hung in the air between us, thick and suffocating, creating a palpable silence that was far more revealing than any confession could ever be. He had refrained from naming my vampiric curse directly, yet the implication loomed like a poisoned arrow, piercing through the delicate veil of his cryptic pronouncements. The instability he alluded to wasn't merely a threat to others; it was a ticking time bomb within me, a dangerous fragility pressing down, a suffocating weight of unspoken dread that I could feel coiling tighter with every breath.

The silence returned, a suffocating blanket woven from the rhythmic rasp of countless breaths. My stomach clenched, a knot of hunger warring with a deeper, chilling apprehension. Their gazes weren't merely staring; they were physical weights, pressing down, probing, dissecting me with the cold precision of scalpels. I felt exposed, utterly vulnerable, my very soul laid bare under the harsh glare of their judgment. Sweat beaded on my skin, a slick, unwelcome film betraying my mounting terror. Panic, a wild animal, clawed at my throat, its icy talons digging deep. Yet, I remained rigid, a statue carved from fear and desperate self-control. The air itself thickened a palpable miasma of unspoken condemnation, of centuries of accumulated power and suspicion.

Then, with a sickening, gut-wrenching realization, the enormity of Caspian's gamble crashed over me. He had brought me, a nobody, an insignificant flicker of rebellion, into the obsidian heart of Whispering Wind, a shadowy cabal, a clandestine organization operating beyond the already morally ambiguous boundaries of demon society, a place where the rules were unwritten and the consequences unthinkable. I was utterly, terrifyingly alone, a solitary member of defiance threatened by a tempest of ancient, unknowable power, a single spark poised to be extinguished in a sea of fathomless darkness.

Finally, another hooded figure emerged from the shadows, their voice an eerie, high-pitched shriek that pierced the still air like a hawk circling its unsuspecting prey. The words fell from their lips, sharp as shards of ice, slicing through the hushed tension in the dimly lit chamber. *"And what tangible value does she hold for us, Caspian?"* they demanded, their tone laced with an unsettling urgency. *"We are not mere philanthropists dispensing favours to the needy. We seek demonstrable results—a clear return on our... investment."* The flickering candlelight illuminated the edges of their hood, revealing only the glint of hungry eyes, as the weight of their expectation settled heavily in the room.

I snapped my attention to the hooded man standing across the dimly lit room, my heart racing as a surge of adrenaline coursed through me. My eyes narrowed, locking onto his shadowy figure, and I felt my fangs slide dangerously close to the surface, nearly peeking out from behind my tightly pressed lips. The air was thick with tension, and the faint scent of damp earth and something metallic filled my nostrils, sharpening my senses further.

Caspian's response to the man came swiftly, his voice a smooth, velvety counterpoint to the other man's abrasive tone. *"Zayn, Her combat prowess is undeniable; she moves like a tempest, a whirlwind of lethal efficiency that leaves her adversaries reeling. Each precise strike is a testament to her years of rigorous training, honed under the watchful eyes of seasoned warriors. Beyond her physical abilities, she possesses a sharp intelligence that is crucial to our success against the Obsidian Covenant—insight that could dismantle their meticulously crafted defences and expose their vulnerabilities."*

He let the implications linger in the air, the silence thick with unvoiced thoughts, before he continued, his tone shifting subtly, with an underlying steeliness that betrayed the urgency of his message. *"Furthermore, her capacity for... adaptation... borders on the preternatural. She's like a chameleon, skillfully shifting her approach to meet any challenge, whether it's navigating treacherous politics or engaging in fierce combat. An asset so uniquely valuable that attempting to replace her would be not just impractical but a grave tactical error, one that could cost us dearly in the escalating conflict ahead."*

The conversation unfolded like a viper's dance, a sinuous ballet of veiled threats and honeyed promises. I was the central figure, was simultaneously the prize and the pawn in this high-stakes negotiation. Caspian, my unlikely champion, wove a tapestry of words, portraying me as a volatile but invaluable asset. He meticulously sculpted my image, showcasing my formidable strengths while subtly obscuring my weaknesses, a masterclass in strategic deflection. His carefully chosen phrases, however, revealed fissures in his carefully constructed facade, hinting at a far-reaching, Machiavellian scheme that extended far beyond the immediate, brutal pressure of the Obsidian Covenant's looming shadow. The air crackled with unspoken tensions, each word a carefully calibrated pressure point in a silent war of wills.

The debate, a relentless tide of rhetoric, crashed over me, each wave a fresh assault on my dwindling reserves. My hunger wasn't merely a pang; it was a ravenous beast gnawing at my insides, a desperate, primal ache that threatened to shatter my composure. I fought to maintain a facade of strength, a carefully constructed mask concealing the growing weakness within. My vision blurred, the edges of the room swimming in a hazy distortion. The cacophony of voices, once sharp and distinct, faded into a dull, oppressive drone, a relentless buzzing in my ears. My body trembled, not with cold, but with a desperate, internal fire, a scorching need for blood pulsed through my veins, a raw, visceral craving that clawed at my sanity, threatening to break free.

My skin prickled, a crawling sensation that spread from my fingertips to my toes. Muscles spasmed, jerking uncontrollably beneath my increasingly strained control. The sweat slicked my palms; my breath hitched in ragged gasps.

I was teetering on the precipice, the fragile edges of my self-control threatening to crumble completely. The room spun, the faces of the debaters morphing into indistinct blurs. I was losing control, not just of my hunger, but of myself. Biting the inside of my bottom lip with my fang I felt my blood swell up in my mouth.

Caspian effortlessly pulled me out of the room, his grip firm yet reassuring. He cast a brief, assessing glance at the people seated around the table before declaring, *"She's staying with me."* His voice held a possessive weight, laced with an intensity that brooked no argument. As if reading the silent scream my eyes moved with a blur of motion that defied both gravity and belief. I watched, rooted to the spot, my breath catching in my throat, as the glint of his dagger flashed, followed by a swift, precise incision across his forearm. Crimson blossomed almost instantaneously, a horrifying yet strangely mesmerizing spectacle; the rich, viscous fluid welling like a dark ruby, reflecting the flickering torchlight. He offered his arm, the sharp edges of the wound stark against the pale skin, a grotesque yet strangely beautiful offering.

The gesture was a stark inversion of his usual icy reserve, a seismic shift in his demeanour that left me breathless. My heart, a frantic drum against my ribs, threatened to shatter. It was a reckless, almost suicidal act of bravery, a bold, silent testament to his unexpected, profound investment in my survival, a silent, blood red promise etched into the very fabric of his being, a promise that resonated with chilling intensity in the pit of my stomach.

The gesture hung in the air, a tangible thing, silencing the hushed murmurs that had rippled through the chamber like a disturbed pond. Their initial expressions of disapproval, a tapestry of furrowed brows and pursed lips, froze into masks of stunned disbelief as they watched Caspian while the door still hung open. His act, a flagrant breach of their ancient, inviolable code, a brazen act of defiance that clawed at the very fabric of their order, sent a jolt of icy fear through me, a tremor that resonated deep in my bones. It was a reckless gamble, a perilous dance on the precipice of ruin, yet in that electrifying moment, the truth blazed forth, incandescent and undeniable: his allegiance, his unwavering loyalty, belonged not to them, but to me. A surge of triumphant exhilaration coursed through my veins, a heady cocktail laced with the bitter sting of apprehension. They knew. He had dared to show them, to flaunt his defiance in their faces, and the consequences, however glorious or terrifying, were now irrevocably unleashed.

A tremor, barely perceptible, ran through me before the overwhelming urge conquered my hesitation. The scent of his blood, a heady perfume of sweet iron and something deeper, more primal, assaulted my senses, a siren song that drowned out all reason. My fangs, aching with a hunger that bordered on agony, throbbed against my lips. I accepted his offered arm, the heat of his skin a searing contrast to the icy fire that pulsed through my veins. With a sharp intake of breath, I sank my teeth into his flesh, the initial resistance yielding to a desperate, almost frantic, plunge.

It wasn't just hunger; it was an urgent, primal yearning that transcended the mere physical. It was a craving that resonated from a deep, instinctual core, tapping into something ancient within me. The taste, a complex symphony of robust copper, deep earthy musk, and an enigmatic, intoxicating sweetness, flooded my palate, overwhelming my senses in a breathtaking wave of pure sensation. Each note danced vividly, painting a rich tapestry of flavour that spiralled through my very being, igniting a feral desire that was impossible to ignore.

Caspian remained perfectly still, his face a mask of impassivity that hid whatever emotions might roil beneath. Yet, in that stillness, I sensed a profound acceptance and arousal, a surrender that resonated with my desperate hunger. The flow of his lifeblood, warm and vibrant against my fangs, wasn't just sustenance; it was a current, connecting us on a level far deeper than the physical. This wasn't a transaction; it was an offering, a silent oath sworn in the shared intimacy of blood and breath.

A pact forged not merely in whispered promises but in the irrefutable bond of a primal act that transcended language—an act painted in the vivid strokes of vulnerability and shared risk, a delicate entanglement of fates sealed in the shadows that enveloped us. This moment was far more than a simple feeding; it was a sacred communion where souls intertwined in an unbreakable tapestry of trust.

With a certainty that resonated deep within the marrow of my bones, I felt the weight of significance in every heartbeat, every breath. I understood in that instant that the choices we had made would ripple through our lives, altering our destinies in ways we couldn't yet fully comprehend. This was the threshold of transformation, and I knew with unwavering conviction that nothing would ever be the same again.

The blood, thick and vibrant crimson, pulsed through my veins like a molten river, pushing back the encroaching darkness that had threatened to claim me as its own. Each swallow was a desperate act of reclamation, a fierce battle fought against the creeping paralysis. My hunger, a gnawing emptiness that had stretched into an eternity, finally receded, leaving behind a trembling body flooded with raw, untamed energy. The metallic tang exploded on my tongue, an overwhelmingly rich flavour that transcended mere taste; it was a visceral experience, a surge of untamed power coursing through my very being.

When I at last raised my head I found myself mere inches away from Caspian's face, our eyes locked in a gaze that transcended the limitations of space and time. It was as if the world around us had faded into a mere backdrop leaving only the two of us suspended in a moment that felt eternal. A dizzying vortex of emotions swirled within me—an overwhelming relief at having survived what felt like an insurmountable challenge the intoxicating exhilaration of victory that pulsed through my veins and a tender vulnerability that washed over me so profound and utterly unexpected that it stole my breath away. This emotional storm was far too intricate and too multifaceted for any mere words to truly encompass.

I felt the feather-light brush of his breath against my skin, a gentle caress that ignited a spark within me. The warmth of his nearness was a stark and glorious contrast to the bone-deep chill that had held me captive just moments before. The icy grip of death which had loomed so closely loosened its relentless hold replaced by the vibrant life-affirming heat of his presence that enveloped me like a soft embrace. It was at that moment that I felt his hand firmly clasping my hip, his claw-like fingers pressing into my skin with a rough intensity that sent shivers cascading down my spine. This sensation was a curious blend of pleasure and discomfort as if his demonic grip was both possessive and primal leaving a lingering impression—an indelible reminder of his dark otherworldly nature.

In that fleeting instant surrounded by the remnants of despair and the promise of newfound hope, I realized that I was teetering on the precipice of something transformative. The universe had conspired to bring us together in this moment and I knew deep down that nothing would ever be the same again.

With my thirst finally slaked, an unnerving serenity descended. The energy surging from Caspian's blood was unlike any sustenance I'd ever known; it transcended mere nourishment. It was a connection, raw, potent, volatile, a dark, pulsing cord that tethered her to me, this cursed, ancient being, in a bond far exceeding any simple exchange of life force. I felt it: a thrumming, intoxicating power, a tide of obsidian energy flowing between us, a visceral, electric hum that vibrated in my very bones. This was no mere meal; it was a claim, a branding, a searing mark of possession, a declaration etched in the very fabric of existence itself. The taste of his blood lingered, a metallic tang interwoven with the chilling certainty of his subjugation. My triumph was absolute, chilling in its completeness.

The meeting continued after he pulled me back into the room, Caspian's blood dripping from the corner of my mouth, but a palpable shift in the dynamics crackled through the air. Gone was the weakness, the desperation that had clung to me like a shroud. I stood tall, my very posture a silent assertion of my rightful place within this precarious alliance. Caspian's actions, however, rendered any pretense of subtlety brutally obsolete. He wasn't merely offering information; he was offering his unwavering protection, a pledge sealed not in ink but in the unspoken promise of his life, should the need arise. The subtle whispers of wind that had earlier hinted at change now roared like a full-blown storm, its chaotic fury a stark contrast to the unwavering calm at its epicentre, Caspian and I, standing shoulder to shoulder, our alliance forged not just in blood, but in a mutual understanding far transcending any battlefield triumph.

This was it, the true game, a brutal ballet of power and trust, its opening notes echoing through the very stones of the room. The Obsidian Covenant, once a significant milestone, now appeared as merely a single, insignificant tessera in a far larger, infinitely more dangerous mosaic. And I, unwittingly perhaps, stood squarely in its heart. My fate, irrevocably entwined with Caspian's, became a breathtaking, terrifying pas de deux, a dance of passion and peril, performed under the ever-present, chilling shadow of death. Whispering Wind, once perceived as a sanctuary, now revealed itself as yet another battlefield, a deceptively serene arena where our true struggle would be fought, not with swords and shields, but with the far more potent weapons of loyalty, betrayal, and unwavering ambition. I knew it, felt it resonating deep within the marrow of my bones; this was only the beginning.

The days blend together, a maelstrom of shadows and whispers. Clandestine rendezvous, punctuated by the metallic tang of blood and the acrid bite of fear, spiralled into missions that clawed at my sanity. The Obsidian Covenant's lair, that glacial tomb, its echoing silence, a constant pressure against my eardrums, the taste of terror still thick on my tongue haunted my every waking moment. I was a wreck, a shattered vessel clinging to Caspian's unwavering strength. His intimate knowledge of the Covenant, a viper's nest of secrets, was my only lifeline; without him, I was adrift in a sea of lethal betrayals.

His strategies were not merely sharp, they were surgical strikes, anticipating my thoughts, and preempting my moves with chilling accuracy. The way he moved, a phantom in the darkness, a predator in its element, sent shivers down my spine. I craved the answers to his uncanny prescience, but he remained an enigma, his instructions delivered in a low, gravelly voice that vibrates with unspoken power. Yet, beneath that commanding tone, a subtle shift, a tremor of something warmer... a flicker of... concern?

It was a poison in my veins, that concern. A discordant note in the symphony of death we conducted. His unexpected gentleness, a stark contrast to the brutal reality of our fight, was a terrifying puzzle. It unnerved me, this fragile tenderness in the face of such overwhelming darkness. It was a warmth against my skin, a phantom touch that sent tremors through me, as alien and compelling as the icy grip of fear that held us both captive in this desperate, desperate dance with death.

The training was a brutal baptism. Caspian, a predator in human skin, relentlessly drove me to the precipice. His methods were merciless, a calculated dismantling of my self-imposed limitations. Each searing blast of untamed flame, each agonizing near miss, was a testament to his iron will and my desperate struggle for control. The scent of ozone and singed flesh clung to the air, a bitter perfume to the agony. His touch, a branding iron disguised as correction, ignited fire not just in my magic, but in my very core. A jolt, raw and electric, would course through me at his lightest graze, a stark counterpoint to the glacial hardness of his gaze, his words like shards of ice chipping away at my resolve.

He was a storm incarnate, a captivating whirlwind of raw power, dark charisma, and simmering menace. The air crackled with his presence, a palpable tension that tasted like copper and ozone on my tongue, a feeling that resonated in the very marrow of my bones. His eyes, the colour of a winter storm, held a depth that both terrified and enthralled me; they saw past the surface, the trembling vulnerability hidden beneath my carefully constructed defences. The scent of his iron, wood smoke, and something primal, untamed haunted my senses, a constant, intoxicating reminder of his proximity.

The sexual tension wasn't just an undercurrent; it was a raging torrent threatening to breach the dam of our strained partnership. It thrummed between us a silent desperate language spoken in stolen glances lingering rough touches and the unspoken acknowledgment of a volatile attraction that defied logic and reason. Every muscle in my body was taut, every nerve screaming in anticipation of the next explosive moment that seemed imminent. I felt as if I were teetering on the edge of a precipice caught between the burning inferno of his relentless training and the seductive allure of his very presence. Each interaction was laced with electricity, an undeniable pull that drew me closer even as I fought to maintain my composure. I was trapped suspended in a dizzying dance of desire, a prisoner in a gilded cage of my own making where every heartbeat echoed with the promise of what could be. The lines between professional and personal blurred into a haze of longing creating a tension so thick it was almost tangible leaving me breathless and yearning for a resolution that felt just out of reach yet tantalizingly close.

Sweat sting my eyes, the taste of blood metallic on my tongue, a phantom echo of the brutal training I just endured. Alone, I stood in the sanctuary's hidden armoury, a vault of forgotten power. The air was thick, a suffocating brew of stale incense, aged leather, and the acrid tang of blood centuries old, perhaps, staining the very stones. Each polished blade, each gleaming surface, seemed to write faintly in the flickering torch light, a silent, predatory dance. The drip, drip, drip of water from some unseen spring was a morbid metronome, beating time against the frantic drum of my own heart, a savage tattoo of fear and exhilaration.

My fingers, slick with sweat, traced the sinuous curves of the demon blade's hilt, the cold steel biting into my skin. It wasn't just cold; it was dead cold, a chill that seeped into my bones, a resonance that vibrated not just in my hand, but deep within my soul a forgotten memory clawing its way to the surface, a scream from a life not my own. A primal terror, raw and visceral, clenched my chest. Who had wielded this thing before me? What unspeakable horrors had it tasted? The weight, a crushing burden, settled in my hand yet, simultaneously, it felt like a key, unlocking some dormant power within me, a terrifying potential that both thrilled and repulsed. This wasn't merely a weapon; it was an extension of something ancient, something malevolent... something alive. The pull was irresistible, a dark siren song whispering promises of power beyond comprehension, a power I both craved and dreaded with equal, terrifying intensity. I knew, with a certainty that chilled me to

the marrow, that yielding to its call could damn me forever. And yet...
I couldn't look away.

Caspian materialized in the doorway a predator framed against the dying light, his silhouette a jagged promise of violence that sent a shiver racing down my spine. The silence that had enveloped the room shattered in an instant replaced by a visceral hum that vibrated deep within my bones—a physical manifestation of his fierce presence. His gaze, a glacial burn dissected my face with unnerving precision, stripping away every layer of pretense that I had carefully constructed over the years. I felt the tremor in my hands, the frantic flutter of my pulse against my ribs—a frantic drumbeat echoing through the suffocating stillness that hung in the air. It was as if time itself had stopped and in that moment I knew he wasn't just looking; he was truly seeing me probing for the secrets I had buried deep within the shadows of my mind, secrets I hadn't even known existed until the searing intensity of his scrutiny brought them to the surface. The air crackled with tension thick with unspoken threat, the metallic tang of blood lingering like a phantom in my nostrils. He stood there a dark figure in the dying light and I couldn't shake the feeling that he wanted to devour me whole to unravel the very fabric of my being and expose the raw vulnerable core that I had fought so hard to protect. In that charged moment I understood the dangerous allure of his presence, a magnetism that both terrified and captivated me.

My red hair fell over my shoulders like a flowing waterfall of fire standing out against the cold hard walls of the armory. I scanned the room with my yellow eyes sharp like a hawk's. Then I spotted Caspian. His blond hair looked like it was glowing under the bright fluorescent lights. My blue eyes sparkled with mischief as I leaned against a rack of medieval weapons. I felt strong and relaxed like a predator ready to spring into action.

"You know, Blaze," Caspian began, his voice a low rumble that seemed to vibrate through the very air of the room, "for a vampire who's supposed to be in tune with her desires, you're doing a shit job of admitting what you really want."

I narrowed my eyes feeling my fangs show a little from under my upper lip as I tried to stay calm. So what is it that I am supposed to want? I shot back my voice full of both annoyance and curiosity.

Caspian pushed off from the doorframe, his movements fluid and deliberate as he closed the distance between us. *"You want me to fuck you,"* he said bluntly, his eyes locked onto mine, daring me to deny it.

I rolled my eyes but I could feel my cheeks getting warm giving away how I really felt. I think you're out of touch with reality demons. *"I really don't want to be intimate with you. Sure! Please provide the text you would like me to rewrite from the first-person perspective."*

Caspian chuckled, the sound sending an unwelcome shiver down my spine. *"Liar,"* he whispered, his breath hot against my ear. "Your body tells a different story."

Before I could respond I felt Caspian's fingers on my throat gently tilting my head to show the soft skin of my neck. His touch felt powerful, sending waves of excitement through my body. I could feel myself getting excited even though I was trying to deny it.

"Tell me Blaze, "Caspian murmured, his lips ghosting over my pulse, sending shivers down my spine. *"Do you get this wet when you're truly not interested?* "His voice was low and filled with an intoxicating mix of curiosity and desire. As his hand slid down my chest his fingers deftly unbuttoning my shirt I felt a rush of anticipation. He revealed the swell of my breasts yet his touch was teasing tantalizingly close but never quite reaching the places I ached for him to explore. Each brush of his fingertips ignited a fire within me leaving me breathless caught between longing and restraint craving more of his deliberate tantalizing dance.

"Fuck you," I let out a hiss my body tense as I tried hard not to press up against him.

"Soon," Caspian promised, his hand moving lower, tracing the delicate hem of my pants before slipping smoothly underneath the fabric. His fingers danced playfully along the waistband of my panties teasing the sensitive skin beneath with a gentle feather-light touch. Each movement sent shivers of anticipation coursing through me igniting a spark of desire that I could no longer ignore. "But first, I want to hear you admit it."

My breath caught as his fingers lightly brushed against my clit and that small touch sent waves of pleasure through my body. *"Admit what?"* I managed to choke out my pride, a stubborn flame refusing to be extinguished, flickering defiantly in the face of adversity even as I struggled to keep it under control.

"That you want this," Caspian said, his fingers dipping lower to gather some of my wetness before circling my clit once more teasingly coaxing me closer to the edge of ecstasy igniting a fire within me that I could no longer resist. "That you want me."

My control was slipping away as my hips subtly rocked against his hand instinctively seeking more friction and pleasure lost in the intoxicating sensations flooding through my body. *"I... I don't—"*

Caspian cut me off with a kiss that was fierce and demanding, his tongue boldly invading my mouth as his fingers continued their maddening dance along my skin. I kissed him back with equal fervor pouring all my longing and desire into the moment. My hands fisted tightly in his shirt feeling the warmth of his body against mine as I fought to keep from begging for more. The world around us faded away leaving only the intensity of our connection and the heat of our shared passion.

Abruptly Caspian pulled away his fingers retreating from my panties leaving me gasping and frustrated with a wave of longing crashing over me. "Not yet " he said, his voice low and teasing a wicked grin spreading across his face as he took in my flushed cheeks and swollen lips which betrayed my desire. The tension in the air thickened and my heart raced with anticipation caught between his playful teasing and the urgent need that surged within me. *"I want you to feel this ache, this need, until you can't deny it any longer."*

My heart pounded fiercely in my chest, my body screaming for a long-awaited release. *"You bastard "* I growled my voice low and filled with rage, my eyes flashing with both anger and unfulfilled desire. I could feel the tension building an electric charge coursing through me demanding satisfaction.

Caspian merely laughed, stepping back to admire the picture I had created—disheveled yearning and undeniably wanting each brushstroke capturing the raw emotion that pulsed through the scene. "Think about this the next time you try to tell yourself you don't want me,"He said nothing more, his gaze taking over me with a mixture of intrigue and intensity. "*The Obsidian Covenant*," he breathed, each syllable dripping with a chilling certainty of impending catastrophe, "*they're plotting something immense. Something... unnatural.*"

A wave of icy dread surged through me as my legs for some reason clenched together, a paralyzing fear that stung like the bitter taste of ash and despair. The words slithered around me like a venomous serpent, wrapping tightly and leaving behind a chilling certainty: whatever malevolence the Covenant concocted was not just looming; it was ready to engulf us all in its suffocating darkness.

My head snapped around, his eyes locking onto mine like predatory birds. "*Different how?*" I rasped, the word a mere breath against the sudden, suffocating thickness of the air. The taste of copper—my blood, perhaps?—tingled on my tongue. I shouldn't, I knew I shouldn't trust the viper coiled at my feet, but a strange, chilling calm settled over me, a bone-deep stillness that silenced the frantic drum of my heart. It wasn't peace; it was something far more sinister, a resonance vibrating between us, a dark mirror reflecting the shadowed corners of my soul. His gaze, cold and fathomless as a glacial lake, promised oblivion, and yet... I felt a perverse pull, a dangerous allure in that icy abyss. This unsettling harmony, this treacherous comfort, was a siren song, a prelude to the storm I knew raged beneath his deceptively placid surface—a storm that mirrored and threatened to consume, my own.

"*It's not villages anymore,*" Caspian hissed the words in a venomous whisper that slithered into my ears. His breath, hot and carrying the metallic tang of blood mingled with the unsettling sweetness of crushed lilies, washed over me. A primal fear, cold and sharp as shattered glass, pierced my calm. His nearness, a suffocating pressure against my skin, was both repellent and utterly intoxicating. The predatory glint in his eyes, the subtle tremor in his powerful hands, it all spoke of a man wrestling with a burden far heavier than any crown.

"*They're going for the heart,*" he rasped, his voice a gravelly caress against the edge of panic. The rough wool of his tunic scraped against my arm as I unconsciously leaned closer, drawn in by the magnetic pull of his desperation. The flickering candlelight glinted off the steel of his belt buckle, a cold counterpoint to the fevered intensity in his gaze.

"The pillars of power are crumbling," he ground out, each syllable laced with the bitter taste of ash and betrayal. The chilling implications slammed into me like a physical blow. Not just villages, the very foundations of our world were under siege. My heart hammered a frantic rhythm against my ribs, a frantic drumbeat against the suffocating silence that followed. Feeling his hands snake around my waist as if wanting my body right up against his. This wasn't a skirmish; it was a war for survival, and the horrifying truth, the sheer, brutal scale of it, left me reeling, a nauseating dread twisting in the pit of my stomach.

"And you think I can help?" I snarled, the words a raw, guttural rasp. The implications slammed into me, a physical blow, a leviathan of responsibility, a monstrous weight of expectation. My pulse hammered a frantic tattoo against my ribs, a frantic drumbeat echoing the tremor in my hands. The thrill was a wildfire, a delicious, terrifying inferno consuming me, the sheer, audacious possibility of it, of rising from the ashes, of carving my mark on the very fabric of existence. But the terror? That was a venomous serpent coiled tight in my gut, its icy fangs already sinking into my flesh. A cold sweat slicked my skin, the taste of fear metallic on my tongue, the air thick and suffocating in my lungs. Doubt, a chilling whisper, clawed at the edges of my exhilaration, a parasitic vine strangling the burgeoning bloom of hope. What if I failed? What if I was nothing more than a pathetic charlatan, exposed and humiliated beneath the unforgiving glare of the spotlight? The stakes were too high; the abyss yawned beneath my feet.

Caspian's nod was a tremor, a seismic shift in the suffocating stillness of the room. His eyes, twin chips of obsidian burning with a cold fire, locked onto me. The scent of ozone and old leather, the metallic tang of blood barely masked by his expensive cologne, hung heavy in the air. *"You, Blaze,"* Caspian rasped, the words like gravel grinding against bone, *"are the earthquakes in their meticulously planned city. The wildfire that consumes their careful designs. They underestimated your raw, untamed power once. The taste of that mistake still burns in their mouths. But they've learned."* His voice dropped, a low growl rumbling in his chest, the scent of impending violence sharpening the air. *"They've rebuilt stronger, their ranks tighter, their strategy honed to a razor's edge. This isn't a game anymore, Blaze. This is a war. And we must be ready to bleed for every inch of ground."*

The stench of blood and brine clung to us, a grim perfume to the desperate pact we forged. We were shattered fragments, jagged edges scraping against each other, a brutal, necessary fit. I felt it, a raw, visceral clinging, a desperate hunger in the air between us. Caspian's enigmatic mask, usually impenetrable, cracked under the pressure. I saw the vulnerability not just in the etched lines of his face but felt it in the tremor of his hand as he gripped mine, and tasted the metallic tang of fear on his breath. His eyes, usually cold pools of shadowed secrets, now held a flickering inferno of weariness, a burning exhaustion that mirrored my own. I didn't just ache with his burden; I carried it, the weight of his past sins pressing down on me, a suffocating blanket woven from guilt and regret. The dance in his soul, loyalty and betrayal intertwined in a deadly waltz, was no longer a detached observation; it was a fever dream I was drowning in, a desperate, consuming struggle to decipher the labyrinth of his heart, to understand the man who had become my anchor in this storm-tossed sea, to possess the truth hidden within those haunted eyes.

The crimson and gold bled across the bruised sky, a dying sunset mirroring the violence simmering beneath our feet. We perched on the skeletal remains of that forgotten building, the wind a razor edged caress against skin raw with adrenaline. Below, the city sprawled, a festering wound, a labyrinth of shadowed alleys reeking of desperation and decay. The stench of stale beer and something far more sinister, something metallic and coppery, clawed at my nostrils. I could taste the grit of it on my tongue.

He shifted beside me, the weight of his silence heavy as the city's secrets. His eyes, the colour of a storm-wracked sea, held a cold fire that mirrored the dangerous glint of the switchblade nestled in his belt. He wasn't just a partner; he was a storm cloud made flesh, beautiful and terrifying in equal measure. A man who'd seen too much, and tasted the bitter ash of betrayal more than once. My breath hitched; fear, sharp and icy, pierced the exhilaration. This wasn't just a job; this was a gamble with our very souls, played out against the backdrop of a city that devoured hope and spat out despair. The wind howled, a mournful dirge for the lives lost and the ones we were about to claim.

"Why the fuck are you helping me?" "I spoke the words, breaking the heavy silence like a sharp piece of glass. The question didn't just sit in my mind; it grew and turned into a nasty snake curled up in my stomach, its skin shiny with the sweat of my unshared worries. I felt a sharp taste of fear in my mouth reminding me how vulnerable I really was. I could feel my hands shaking showing the chaos inside my heart. I felt a growing sense of uncertainty with shadows moving eerily in the corners of my eyes. All of this built up to my urgent and desperate call for help. My voice which usually felt smooth and strong now sounded rough and worn. It showed how much chaos I felt inside.

My soul had been shaped by constant betrayal and had grown tough from always having to fight to survive. My struggle left me with scars but it also made me a strong fighter in a world that hasn't been kind to me. I could feel the air around me was thick and heavy filled with unspoken truths that seemed to hang in the atmosphere because of his mysterious presence. I felt like a moth attracted to a bright light standing on the edge of a high cliff where I couldn't tell if I was about to be saved or if I was making a big mistake. I wanted to understand why he was being so kind to me when I didn't expect it. In a world where I couldn't trust anyone, the idea of someone trying to connect with me felt strange and uncomfortable.

The silence stretched, a taut membrane threatening to burst. Caspian's gaze, a glacial spear, remained locked on the horizon, the salt spray stinging my face as the wind whipped my hair. Anticipation clawed at my throat, a raw, visceral thing, the silence itself vibrating with unspoken power. When he finally spoke, his voice, a rasping tremor against the roar of the sea, sent a chill down my spine. I leaned in, the scent of brine and ozone sharp in my nostrils, my heart a frantic drum against my ribs. *"Let's just say our desire to see the Obsidian Covenant shattered... is shared. And perhaps... something far more profound."*

His words hung, poisoned darts in the suffocating air. The weight of them pressed down, crushing, leaving me breathless. He turned, his eyes, pools of shadowed obsidian reflecting a storm of unknown intensity, holding mine captive. I was drowning in them, unable to break free, the taste of fear bitter on my tongue. *"Something more..."* echoed in my mind, a promise and a threat entwined. A delicious, terrifying tremor, a potent cocktail of exhilaration and dread, convulsed me, leaving me trembling, exposed, utterly at his mercy. What dark, intoxicating depths did that *"something more"* conceal?

I felt the air crackle around us buzzing with a strong energy. It was like a silent scream showing the deep feelings we both had but didn't say out loud. I felt a deep need inside me like a fire that burned right through the masks I showed to everyone else. I dressed in soft velvet danced a dangerous waltz with him who wore smooth silk like a snake. We moved carefully on the sharp edge knowing that one wrong step could lead to trouble. Every time I stole a glance I knew I was taking a big risk. Each word I whispered felt like a sharp dart ready to hurt. The smell of my perfume wrapped around him like a second skin. It was strong and risky, always reminding us of the delicate situation we were in. I felt betrayal like ash and blood in my mouth. The memory of my hand felt like a mark burned into my soul. In the middle of their wild game I noticed something delicate breaking through the hard concrete: a trust that felt as fragile as glass and as powerful as poison. It was like a brave flower standing out in a garden full of sharp thorns. My trust formed in the face of possible disaster became my most powerful weapon and my prettiest lie.

The pact wasn't forged in the fires of camaraderie but in the icy grip of necessity. A shared enemy, a beast with teeth of shadow and claws of steel, had driven them together, two wolves, snarling, yet chained by a single, taut leash of survival. The air crackled with unspoken tension, thick as the blood spilled on the battlefield, a scent of iron and fear clinging to their shared skin. His eyes, glacial blue flecked with the fury of a winter storm, met hers, obsidian pools reflecting a chilling calculation. Each felt the phantom weight of the other's blade, a constant, chilling reminder of their precarious alliance. They were shields, yes, but shields that could just as easily become weapons, poised to strike with the venomous grace of vipers. The taste of betrayal lingered on their tongues, a bitter counterpoint to the metallic tang of blood, a constant threat whispering promises of ruin in the back of their minds. Their bond was a tapestry woven from suspicion, shadowed by the cold certainty that one wrong move, one flicker of weakness, would unravel it all, leaving them bleeding into the dust.

Time hemorrhaged, each day a crimson stain bleeding into the next. The stench of sweat and blood, a constant companion, clung to my clothes, my skin, my very soul. Battles weren't fought; they were clawed from the jaws of oblivion. Near-death experiences weren't close calls; they were icy fingers scrabbling at my throat, leaving me gasping for air, the metallic tang of fear coating my tongue. Caspian, a predator in human skin, honed my skills with a cold precision that chilled me to the bone. Each lesson was a dance with death, each sparring match a brutal ballet of steel and fury. The impact of his blows resonated not just physically, but in the icy certainty of his gaze, a gaze that saw through me, knew me better than I knew myself.

He peeled back the silken layers of Whispering Wind, revealing a viper's nest of ambition and treachery. Their machinations slithered through my mind, a venomous cocktail of intrigue and betrayal, leaving me breathless, utterly captivated, and consumed by a paralyzing dread. The silken whispers of their conspiracies filled my ears, a constant, insidious hum against the backdrop of my pounding heart. His involvement wasn't subtle; it was a palpable force, a shadow stretching long and dark across the land. I saw it in the glacial glint of his eyes, in the ghost of a smile that never quite reached them, in the lethal grace of his movements, a phantom power that hummed beneath the surface, as dangerous as it was alluring.

My admiration warped into a sickening fascination, a gnawing unease twisting in my gut like a venomous serpent coiling tighter with each passing moment. The weight of his secrets pressed down on me as heavy as a tombstone suffocating in its intensity. I was left with a chilling question echoing in the silence like a haunting refrain: how deep did the blood run? How far would he go to protect the darkness that lurked within him? This unsettling curiosity clawed at my mind intertwining with a sense of foreboding that threatened to engulf me. I could feel the shadows drawing closer whispering secrets I was not yet ready to hear.

My reason shrieked, a banshee wail in the echoing chambers of my skull, yet I found myself trusting him. Trusting his judgment, a chilling paradox considering the coppery tang of his blood, still ghosting my tongue, a metallic sweetness that clung like a curse. It was my lifeline, a vile, intoxicating elixir that staved off the ravenous hunger clawing at my soul, the beast within me yearning to break free. Each draught was a branding iron, searing a connection so profound, so viscerally intimate, it defied logic, defied explanation. The heat bloomed within me, a wildfire spreading through starved veins, forging a bond that felt both terrifying and exquisitely right.

This was a dance with death, a grotesque tango spun on the precipice of oblivion. Predator and prey, master and slave, the roles blurred, shifted, with each stolen, desperate sip. His gaze, a fathomless abyss of dark allure, pierced the flimsy veil of my control, and with every pulse of his blood thrumming through my veins, I felt myself surrendering, falling into the chasm he had carved within my being. The fear was a physical entity, a cold hand gripping my heart, yet it was entwined with a need so desperate, so primal, it eclipsed all reason, all sanity. He was a viper, seductive and deadly, and I, the fool, willingly drank from his venomous kiss.

The flickering candlelight cast long shadows across Caspian's face, etching the harsh lines of his jaw, and the haunted depths of his eyes. In those stolen moments of quiet, the air itself thrummed with the unspoken weight of his confessions. His voice, a low growl that vibrated in my chest, painted pictures of betrayal, the acrid sting of it on his tongue, the icy grip of fear on his heart. He spoke of his demonic nature, not as a detached observation, but as a ravenous beast caged within, its claws scraping against bone, its breath hot on his skin. I tasted the bitterness of his struggle and felt the tremor in his hands as he described his desperate attempts to subdue it, a battle waged in the blackest corners of his soul.

His past unfurled before me, a tapestry woven with shadows and whispers; a chilling saga of loss that left a metallic tang in my mouth, the phantom scent of blood and decay clinging to the air. He was a paradox, a creature of darkness sculpted with heartbreaking beauty. Beneath the glacial surface, the hardened shell built to protect a shattered heart pulsed a raw, terrifying vulnerability. It was a dangerous game we played, this intimate exchange of darkness; a dance on the precipice of oblivion. I saw myself reflected in the tormented depths of his gaze, a mirror to my shadowed self, my own suppressed demons. The stories were not merely words; they were searing brands upon my soul, each syllable a searing touch, a raw nerve exposed. He offered a piece of his fractured soul, and in that offering, I found a desperate need, a burning compulsion, to bear my own.

The acrid stench of burning flesh still clung to my memory, a phantom smell mingling with the phantom heat that seared my skin, the pyre of my village, a landscape etched into my soul. I didn't just confess the pain; I vomited it forth, raw and bleeding, a torrent of ash and agony. This cursed existence, this vampiric hunger gnawing at my very essence, clawed at me, a beast within a cage of bone and muscle. The bitter bile of vengeance, a serpent coiled in my gut, pulsed with a life of its own; its insatiable thirst was a constant, agonizing pressure against my ribs. I laid bare the festering wound of my heart, a chasm of rage and despair, exposing the very core of my being.

And in Caspian's eyes, I saw the reflection of my tormented abyss, a shared darkness illuminated by a flickering, desperate hope. It wasn't just understanding that bloomed between us, it was a twisted, thorny vine of empathy, taking root in the poisoned soil of our shared trauma. This connection, a feral, untamed thing, transcended purpose; it was a pact forged in the fires of hell, a bond forged in blood and bone, far stronger than any loyalty sworn on a battlefield.

Our relationship was a viper coiled around my heart, its venom a cocktail of incandescent passion and brutal violence. I tasted the metallic tang of blood and felt the ragged rasp of each breath tearing through my lungs, a physical manifestation of the chaos that consumed us. The bone-deep ache wasn't just physical; it was the echo of every cruel word, every desperate caress, every shattering blow. Yet, even in the suffocating darkness, something else pulsed, a perverse, intoxicating bond, forged not just in shared blood, but in the very marrow of our suffering. It was a reckless dance with the devil, a gamble played with the chips of our souls. I saw it mirrored in Caspian's eyes, that same frantic, desperate hunger, that wild, reckless pull toward the abyss. We were tethered, two damaged souls lashed together by an invisible chain forged in the fires of our shared torment.

His touch, when it came, was a branding iron, leaving scars both physical and emotional. His silence was a suffocating blanket woven from shadows and unspoken threats. The air crackled between us, charged with a volatile energy that tasted like ash and ozone. Our alliance wasn't a balance; it was a knife edge, a precipice we danced upon, each step a gamble between incandescent love, venomous hate, and the primal, desperate will to survive. The question wasn't could this twisted bond survive, but whether would it consume us both. It was a gnawing beast, feeding on my hope, its claws of fear tearing at my insides, leaving trails of icy dread in their wake. Even as the storm raged, even as the thunder threatened to shatter everything, I clung to that treacherous hope, a fragile lifeline in a sea of despair.

CHAPTER

FIVE

Crimson Tides

The obsidian fortress, a malevolent monolith, tore at the bruised, violet sky, its jagged towers like the skeletal claws of some gargantuan beast, raking the gathering storm. Rain, a frigid, brutal assault, flayed the cobbled pathway, transforming it into a treacherous river of mud slick with, yes, definitely, fresh blood. The coppery tang stung my nostrils, a brutal counterpoint to the cloying stench of decay that clung to the very air. But it was the other scent, a metallic aridity that burned the back of my throat, that truly chilled me to the bone. It screamed of dark sorcery, of power so vile it tasted of ash and shattered souls. This wasn't merely impending doom; this was doom's arrival, its shadow already stretching long and cold across my heart.

My hand instinctively went to the hilt of my blade, the worn leather cool against my palm, a meagre comfort against the palpable dread that coiled in my gut, a viper ready to strike. They were waiting for me, I knew it, those things lurking within those black, malevolent walls. And they smelled of death, of power, of something ancient and utterly inhuman.

The wind screamed, a banshee wail clawing at my cloak, spitting icy rain in my face. Caspian, a wraith beside me, felt less like a man and more like a predator, his presence a tangible weight against the storm's fury. My heart, a trapped bird, beat a frantic tattoo against my ribs, each thud a counterpoint to the thunder that rolled across the jagged peaks.

His unnerving calm, a glacial stillness radiating from him, was a stark, brutal contrast to the inferno of fear and adrenaline that consumed me. This wasn't just a culmination; it was the venomous apex of weeks spent gnawing at the edges of the Obsidian Covenant's power, weeks fueled by sweat, blood, and stolen moments, kisses that tasted of salt spray, impending doom, and the bittersweet poison of forbidden desire. His hand, calloused but gentle, brushed mine. I felt the ghost of his touch even through the thick gloves, a spark in the darkness.

The weight of it all pressed down, not just expectation, but the crushing weight of consequences. Our chance. Caspian and I, two shadows against a monstrous empire. To strike at their obsidian heart, to shatter their carefully crafted world… It was a gamble that could buy us freedom or send us to a grave carved in the storm-lashed rock. The cold steel of my blade bit into my palm, a familiar, agonizing comfort against the tremors that shook my hand. This wasn't just a mission; it was a symphony of vengeance, a desperate prayer painted in blood and whispered in the wind. This was our war. And tonight, we fought.

The plan, my plan, a viper coiled around the Covenant's heart, pulsed with a terrifying elegance. Caspian's brute force was the venom, my deception the fangs. The stench of decay clinging to the alleyways, a reeking testament to the Covenant's casual cruelty, clawed at my nostrils as we moved. My traitorous heart hammered a frantic rhythm against my ribs, a counterpoint to the scrape of steel on stone, the whisper of our footfalls. I knew the Covenant's labyrinth-like the lines etched onto my soul, a betrayal etched deeper with each breath. This route, my route, bypassed the heavily guarded gates, a path forged in shadows and the bitter taste of compromise.

We were phantoms, yes, but phantoms with teeth. The icy grip of fear, a familiar companion, tightened around my throat. Each precise movement was a gamble, a dance with death under the flickering gaslight. My fire magic, once a raging inferno that threatened to consume me, was now a caged beast, its power a raw, throbbing pulse beneath my skin. The heat scorched my lungs, each controlled burst a searing kiss of destruction; a whisper of the inferno that slumbered within. My blood sang with the anticipation of carnage, each flicker of flame a prelude to the symphony of screams that would soon fill the night. The thrill wasn't merely excitement; it was a dark, delicious hunger.

The reek of decay and damp earth clung to the air, a miasma mirroring the dread twisting in my gut. We slipped past patrols, a phantom dance of misdirection and illusion, borrowed power, purchased with a debt to some nameless ghoul in the Whispering Wind's festering heart. My muscles screamed, a symphony of fear conducted by a frantic heartbeat. Each breath rasped in my throat, a strangled counterpoint to the ever-present hum of adrenaline.

Caspian. His eyes, the colour of a winter storm, held a chilling preternatural awareness. He didn't just anticipate the obstacles; he felt them before they materialized, a precognitive tremor running through his lean frame. The ghost of his touch, a feather-light pressure on my arm, sent a white-hot brand searing through me, a brutal reminder of the fragile thread binding our lives together, a thread easily snapped.

The weight of their scrutiny was palpable, a physical pressure on my back, the cold breath of unseen eyes. Even the illusions, shimmering mirages born of forbidden magic, felt thin, fragile veils against their relentless gaze. Terror, a venomous serpent, coiled around my heart, squeezing the air from my lungs. The clammy grip of fear threatened to suffocate me, but I held on, a desperate swimmer clinging to a splintered raft.

Caspian's hand, a branding iron against my skin, was not just a command; it was a promise, a poisoned chalice of reassurance laced with the bitter taste of our shared doom. Each touch was a stark confession of the abyss we teetered over, an unspoken acknowledgement that one false step would send us tumbling into the endless night.

The obsidian walls loomed, each jagged stone a tooth in a monstrous maw, and with every foot closer, the oppressive magic clawed at me, a physical violation. The air itself thickened, a rancid, metallic tang stinging my nostrils, a miasma of despair so potent it tasted like ash and regret on my tongue. Dread wasn't just a feeling; it was a living entity, a venomous serpent coiling around my heart, squeezing the breath from my lungs, each tightening coil a crushing weight on my chest, mirroring the crushing weight of the betrayal that had brought me here. The wind, a banshee's wail, tore at my cloak, whispering secrets of the horrors within, secrets that resonated with the bitter, gnawing emptiness that had become my constant companion.

My own shadow stretched long and distorted a grotesque mockery of my former self, a haunting testament to the darkness that had begun to bloom within me feeding voraciously on the fractured remnants of my once-vibrant hope. The cold seeped deep into my bones, chilling me to the core but it was nothing compared to the icy terror that gripped me, a primal scream trapped within my throat, a desperate silent plea against the encroaching abyss that threatened to consume me whole. Each heartbeat echoed in the stillness a reminder of the life that once pulsed with fervor now stifled by despair. This fortress looming ominously around me was more than just stone and magic; it was a cruel mirror reflecting the shattered landscape of my soul, a landscape littered with the debris of lost dreams and silent cries. In that moment I realized that the true battle lay not just outside these walls but within as I grappled with the shadows that sought to claim me.

The rain, a torrential, blinding curtain, barely revealed the fissure, their unholy entry. Caspian, his eyes burning with a malevolent, inner light that mirrored the storm's fury, fumbled the key. It was bone, intricately carved with symbols that seemed to writhe beneath his touch, a key that whispered of ages long past and deals made with powers best left undisturbed. With a guttural rasp, a sound like grinding stone and tormented souls, he forced the passage open.

The air inside hit Caspian like a physical blow, a suffocating weight of damp earth, the metallic tang of blood, and that cloying sweetness, a sickening perfume of decay, of things long dead and violently resurrected. It clung to the back of his throat, a vile caress. The passage was a tomb, a claustrophobic crawl space barely wide enough for his broad shoulders, the rough-hewn stone scratching at his skin. Terror, cold and sharp, pricked at his senses, a counterpoint to the grim satisfaction that pulsed in his demonic heart. He knew the risks, the price, but the prize... the prize justified the descent into this fetid hell. This was no mere fortress; it was a cage, and he held the key to its most terrible secrets.

They moved in silence, their senses heightened, every footstep measured. The storm howled a banshee wail, its fury a mocking echo of the tempest in my soul. Each thunderclap was a hammer blow against my ribs, a brutal counterpoint to the frantic, trapped bird rhythm of my heart. The passage yawned beneath me, a black maw swallowing me whole, dragging me down into the fetid gut of the earth. The air, thick with the stench of rot and damp clay, choked me. It clung to my lungs, a slimy, suffocating shroud. I tasted the metallic tang of terror on my tongue, the grit of pulverized rock grinding between my teeth. The darkness wasn't just a lack of light; it was a sentient entity, a suffocating weight pressing down, crushing the breath from my body, stealing the very air from my screaming lungs. This wasn't fear; it was a primal, gut-wrenching terror, a cold, clawing hand seizing my heart and squeezing until I saw stars. My lifeblood turned to ice; my resolve shattered into a million trembling fragments.

The interior of the fortress was a horrifying spectacle of Gothic architecture and depraved artistry. Massive stone chambers were adorned with grotesque carvings, depicting scenes of torture and sacrifice. The air was thick with the stench of blood and decay, the flickering torchlight revealing disturbing murals depicting the Covenant's twisted rituals. A nauseating sweetness, like overripe fruit decaying in the sun, clung to the air around them. Their unsettling realism wasn't just visual; it was a physical assault. The faintest tremor ran through the floorboards beneath my feet, a silent pulse echoing the frantic hammering of my own heart. Their eyes, impossibly lifelike, seemed to bore into my soul, glinting with a cruel intelligence that transcended mere craftsmanship.

A primal scream choked in my throat, a desperate, wordless protest against the grotesque perfection of their forms. The metallic tang of blood, or something disturbingly similar, filled my mouth, a phantom taste mirroring the icy dread that gripped me. My breath caught a ragged gasp in the suffocating silence. I wanted to flee, to tear my gaze away from their horrifying perfection, but an unseen force held me captive, a morbid fascination warring with the gut-wrenching terror that threatened to shatter me. My skin wasn't just crawling; it felt as though a thousand insects were gnawing beneath the surface, each bite a tiny echo of the larger horror I witnessed. This wasn't mere realism; it was a violation, a profane mockery of life itself, and the unbearable weight of it threatened to crush me.

I felt the artifact thrum with a dark energy that shook me to my core. A sharp taste of ozone filled my mouth as I sensed its power. It wasn't just power for me; it felt like a loud fierce hunger inside. It was both beautiful and scary, able to wipe out entire worlds or put them back together with a god's rough touch. Caspian's warning kept replaying in my head like a harsh whisper mixing with the sound of the artifact. He said *"The Covenant's ritual won't just break the realms, I believe it will tear apart the very core of what makes life meaningful. I saw his haunted eyes with deep lines from a life spent chasing shadows."* I understood the danger. I saw the cracks he talked about rough gaps in reality that released strange monsters from worlds we can't even understand. Caspian wasn't just someone who was afraid; his deep desperation sparked a bold courage in me. I felt a strong urge to stand up against the coming disaster. I needed to stop them. I realized this wasn't just a mission; it felt like a risky chance to avoid being forgotten.

They navigated the fortress's treacherous corridors, their movements silent and deadly. They bypassed more patrols, the tension ratcheting up with each step. The weight of a thousand souls crushed me, their silent screams a physical pressure against my chest. The air, thick with the metallic tang of fear and the cloying sweetness of impending doom, clogged my lungs. My heart, a trapped bird beating against its cage of ribs, threatened to shatter the fragile silence. Each ragged breath tasted of ash and despair. The cold sweat slicked my skin, a chilling betrayal in the stifling heat of the moment. This wasn't just responsibility; it was a suffocating, inescapable burden, the weight of their lives, their hopes, and their futures, all resting on the razor's edge of my decision.

The fear wasn't a mere knot; it was a venomous serpent coiled tight in my gut, its fangs poised to strike. But I wouldn't yield. Not to the paralysis of terror, not to the seductive whisper of failure. I'd stared into the abyss, smelled the putrid breath of annihilation, and I wouldn't flinch. My resolve, forged in the fires of countless sleepless nights and the ghosts of decisions past, hardened my gaze. This wasn't about me. This was about them. Their lives, their futures, the future of everything I held dear, hung precariously on this single, agonizing choice. The ticking clock wasn't just a sound, it was the relentless drumming of fate, a macabre rhythm accompanying my desperate dance with destiny. I had to be more than strong; I had to be unbreakable. For them. Their survival, their liberation, would be my redemption.

Their journey led them through chambers filled with chained prisoners, their whimpers and cries a constant reminder of the Covenant's cruelty. Rage, a molten core erupting in my chest, threatened to shatter my ribs and spill its incandescent fury across the floor. The heat wasn't just a feeling; it was a physical force, a searing brand that seared my insides, the metallic tang of blood blooming on my tongue. My vision blurred, a crimson haze overlaying the world, the sharp scent of ozone stinging my nostrils. Caspian's touch, a brutal counterpoint to the internal explosion, was a vice on my arms, his fingers digging into my flesh, a desperate anchor against the maelstrom. His voice, a gravelly whisper barely audible above the roar in my ears, was a pathetically inadequate balm. *"Focus,"* he rasped, the word tasting like ash in my mouth. The larger picture? Control? Efficiency? Those were the concerns of a sane man, and sanity was a distant star, swallowed by the supernova of my wrath. The fire wasn't raging; it was consuming, a wildfire devouring my reason, leaving only the primal urge to obliterate. And in that obliteration, a perverse, terrifying clarity bloomed: the sweet, terrible promise of release.

At last, the chamber yawned before them a gaping maw of shadow at the very black heart of the fortress. It seemed to beckon with a sinister allure its depths concealing untold horrors. The air didn't merely crackle; it screamed—a high-pitched whine that pierced the silence scraping against their eardrums and vibrating painfully in their teeth. Each breath they took was filled with an acrid stench metallic and sickeningly sweet reminiscent of decaying lilies that clung to their throats and choked them. My pulse hammered a frantic rhythm against my ribs, an anxious counterpoint to the artifact's throbbing malevolence that loomed before us. It pulsed like a heartbeat of pure unadulterated evil resonating deep in my bones echoing a dreadful promise of despair and darkness. Every instinct screamed at me to flee yet an inexplicable force kept me rooted to the spot drawn as if by an invisible thread to the very source of this malevolent energy.

This wasn't just an artifact; it was an abomination. A grotesque mockery of creation, welded from bone bleached white as a skull, metal warped and twisted as if by some infernal agony, and obsidian so black it seemed to devour light itself. The darkness it radiated wasn't just absence; it was a palpable presence, a suffocating weight that pressed down, stealing the breath from my lungs, squeezing the hope from my soul. I saw Elias, his usually sharp eyes wide with a terror that mirrored my own, yet a grim determination etched on his face. Even Anya, always the stoic one, trembled, her hand instinctively reaching for the hilt of her blade, a blade that felt as useless as a child's toy against… this thing. The fear was visceral, primal, a cold dread that clawed its way into our very beings. We were intruders in a place where we did not belong, facing an ancient evil that could snuff out our existence like a candle flame.

The stench of ozone and decay clawed at their throats, a bitter counterpoint to the metallic tang of blood blooming on the cobblestones. But they weren't alone. A tremor, low and guttural, vibrated through the ancient stones beneath their feet, a promise of something vast and unseen, something that tasted of ash and whispered of annihilation. His eyes, the colour of a bruised plum, flickered to hers, a silent acknowledgment of the primal terror that twisted their guts. Hers, hardened by a lifetime of betrayals and shadowed desires, held only a cold, calculating gleam. This wasn't just a presence; it was a malevolent consciousness, a thing that coiled in the darkness, hungry for their souls.

The Covenant's elite guard, a legion of grotesque demons and corrupted humans surrounded them, their eyes burning with hatred and dark energy. A fierce battle erupted, a clash of magic and steel, of flame and shadow. The fire, mine, erupted, a maelstrom of incandescent fury that ripped through their ranks with a scream of heat and searing light. The stench of burning flesh choked me, the taste of ash acrid on my tongue, the roar a physical blow against my eardrums. My face felt like it was melting, the power of a molten river coursing through my veins, a terrifying, exhilarating agony. I saw their eyes, wide with terror and disbelief, before the flames claimed them, their screams swallowed by the inferno.

Caspian, a predator unleashed, moved like a phantom through the carnage. Each strike, a ballet of brutal grace, was a death sentence. The air itself vibrated with the malevolent energy he exuded, a palpable aura of demonic power that tasted of Sulfur and despair and felt like icy claws raking down my spine. He was a masterpiece of controlled savagery, his chilling calm a mask for the unholy might he commanded. My admiration was a bitter thing, laced with a dread so profound it felt like physical pain. This wasn't just power; it was something ancient, something wicked, something... hungry.

The air crackled, not just with magic, but with the palpable presence of something far beyond human comprehension. A chilling certainty, cold as the grave, settled in my bones. We weren't facing an army; we were facing oblivion.

The battle roared a maelstrom of fire and blood, the stench of ozone and burnt flesh thick in the air. My muscles screamed, not just a protest, but a raw, agonizing shriek, each fibre a wire snapping under unbearable tension. The drain on my magic felt like icy tendrils creeping into my very soul, a chilling paralysis threatening to steal my strength, but the terror only sharpened my focus. Rage, a white-hot inferno, seared my insides, fueled by the phantom heat of the flames that had consumed my home, the echoes of my people's screams a constant, bone-jarring dirge in my ears. Their faces, twisted in agony, burned into my mind, I would avenge them, I swore it, even if it cost me everything.

Beside me, Caspian, his face a mask of grim determination etched against the backdrop of flickering flames, fought with the ferocious grace of a cornered wolf. He was more than a protector; he was a bastion of unwavering resolve, a titan against the relentless, snarling horde. I saw the blow land, a sickening thud that ripped through the cacophony, the crimson bloom staining his cloak like a malevolent flower. Even as pain contorted his features, his stance remains unshaken, his sword a silver blur, each strike precise and deadly, a testament to the years of brutal training. He didn't need words; the shared tremor of our breaths, the fierce glint in his eye, spoke volumes. We would stand, or we would fall, together. There was no other option. The taste of blood, my own or his, I couldn't tell, filled my mouth, a metallic tang that only intensified my grim purpose. We would not yield.

A maelstrom of steel and shattered bone, that's all I remember of the fight. The air, thick with the stench of Sulfur and sweat, clawed at my lungs as I tore through the demonic horde. My hands, slick with the ichor of fallen friends, trembled, a pathetic tremor against the throbbing pulse of adrenaline. Then, the artifact. Cold, slick obsidian, humming with a power that vibrated in my very bones, a resonance that tasted like ash and fear on my tongue. I snatched it, the weight of millennia crushing my grip, just as Caspian's roar ripped through the cacophony.

He moved like a phantom, a whirlwind of blade flash and guttural cries, a desperate dance with a demon whose eyes burned with the cold fire of hell itself. The creature's claws ripped through his defences; I saw the crimson bloom across his ribs, a brutal slash that seemed to tear through me as well. The coppery tang of his blood filled my nostrils, a brutal counterpoint to the artifact's chilling hum. It wasn't just his blood; it was the echo of his sacrifice, the raw, visceral testament to loyalty that burned hotter than any hellfire. This wasn't some simple bond; this was a tethering, a dark, intoxicating fusion. Fear, yes, a cold dread that gnawed at the edges of my sanity. But interwoven with it, was a terrifying, exhilarating desire, a desperate hunger for him, for the wild, untamed strength that pulsed in every fibre of his being.

And beneath it all, a crushing weight of respect, a bone-deep understanding of his unwavering commitment, a commitment that had just cost him dearly. The artifact's weight in my hands became unbearable, a physical manifestation of the guilt that choked me, a bitter taste of responsibility for his bleeding wounds. The world spun, the stench of blood and brimstone a suffocating blanket around my horrified heart.

The air, thick with the stench of sweat and fear, clawed at their lungs as they bolted. Each footfall echoed a thunderclap in the claustrophobic maze of the fortress, a death knell answered by the relentless clang of Covenant boots behind them. Seraphina, her emerald eyes blazing with primal terror and steely resolve, scrambled over a fallen stone, the rough edges biting into her already bleeding palm. Behind her, Kaelen, his usually wry smile twisted in grim determination, hurled a jagged shard of rock, silencing one pursuer with a sickening crunch that sent a wave of nausea through Seraphina.

Their escape wasn't just a flight; it was a symphony of desperation, the rasp of their breaths, the frantic thud of their hearts, the metallic tang of blood mingling with the dust. They were a whirlwind of calculated chaos, a ballet of death played out in flickering torchlight and the chilling whisper of blades. The final burst from the fortress gates, a desperate leap into the teeth of a tempest that tore at their clothes and lashed their faces with rain, only intensified the raw, visceral agony of their freedom. The storm itself seemed to howl a mournful dirge for those left behind, a testament to their audacious gamble and the price they might yet pay for their survival.

The rain, a brutal, icy fist, hammered us as we slithered through the mud, each step a betrayal of our aching bodies. Finally, the fetid reek of the hidden grotto, our sanctuary, our desperate gamble, hit me, a sickly sweet relief against the stench of the storm. My muscles screamed a chorus of agony, and the chill of the soaked earth seeped into my very marrow. But it was the sight of Caspian, his face ashen, a single, ragged breath hitching in his chest, that truly stole my breath. I lowered him gently, the rough-hewn stone a cold comfort beneath him. His eyes, usually blazing with the fire of a rebellious spirit, were now dull pools reflecting the flickering torchlight, haunted eyes that mirrored the shadows clinging to my soul.

His wound, a crimson stain blooming across his chest, pulsed faintly under my touch, a haunting reminder of the battle he had fought. The metallic tang of blood filled my nostrils a stark contrast to the damp earthy smell of our refuge where nature seemed to wrap us in a cocoon of false safety. A primal fear raw and visceral coiled in my gut as I watched him struggle. This wasn't just exhaustion; it was the bone-deep weariness of a soul tested to its limits and pushed beyond what should have been bearable. This wasn't merely relief; it was the fragile terrified hope clinging to the edge of a precipice teetering between despair and the flickering possibility of survival. Each shallow breath he took echoed the fragility of life itself making me acutely aware of how quickly everything could change. In that moment time stood still and all that mattered was the tenuous thread that bound us to hope and the fight that lay ahead.

He gazed at me, a silent plea in those haunted eyes, a burden shared between us, heavy as the guilt that clung to me like the mud plastered to my clothes. The weight of our actions, the blood spilled, the lives jeopardized... it pressed down, suffocating, a suffocating blanket of fear and responsibility, a dark secret we now shared in the heart of this damp, echoing cavern. The shiver that ran down my spine was no longer just cold; it was the icy breath of dread whispering promises of unforeseen consequences. Caspian's fate, and perhaps my own, hung precariously in the balance.

The coppery tang of his blood filled my nostrils, a sickeningly sweet perfume clinging to the air thick with the reek of scorched earth and ozone. My knees dug into the rough-hewn stone as I pressed against his side, the ragged tear in his flesh a gaping maw, pulsing with a life I wasn't sure I could keep. Victory? It tasted like ash in my mouth, a bitter aftertaste to the adrenaline that still shrieked in my veins, a frantic drumbeat against my ribs. Their near death, his near death, was a physical thing, a cold weight crushing my lungs, stealing the very breath from my body. But beneath the terror, a deeper chill snaked through me, the icy grip of understanding. He, a creature of shadow and fire, my saviour, my damnation, our bond pulsed with dark, chaotic energy that was both thrilled and terrified.

The blood on my hands, warm and slick, was a perverse baptism. Each sticky smear is a testament to the carnage, a grim tally of our success. Success? This wasn't triumph; it was a pyrrhic victory, the first step on a long, blood-soaked march toward a vengeance as brutal and unforgiving as the demon himself. The path stretched before me, a desolate wasteland under a sky choked with the smoke of our battles. And him? He was a labyrinth of contradictions, a storm of contradictions. Our relationship wasn't complicated; it was a war zone, a silent battle waged in glances and unspoken desires, a constant teetering on the precipice of annihilation. And I, the fool, was armed only with a fragile heart and a desperate hope, a hope as doomed as a moth drawn to a flame.

The Whisperwind Mountains howled, a banshee wail echoing the tempest tearing at the cave's mouth. This sanctuary, a claustrophobic maw carved into the very heart of the earth, offered no solace. Rain, a furious, icy onslaught, blasted against the entrance, a cruel percussion to the frantic hammering of my own heart, a drum solo of dread. Caspian's wound, a crimson chasm across his gut, pulsed with a sickening rhythm, staining the rough stone floor of a macabre canvas. The metallic tang of his blood filled the air, thick and cloying, mingling with the damp, earthy scent of the cave. My own body, a battlefield of bruises and searing aches, screamed in protest with every strained movement. Each trembling attempt to stanch the torrent of his lifeblood felt futile, a desperate dance against the reaper's scythe.

The silence was a taut wire, stretched to its breaking point, humming with a raw, primal fear. The drip, drip, drip of water was a mocking metronome marking the slow, agonizing beat of Caspian's ragged breaths, each gasping a wrenching rasp against my pounding ears. The cold, a malevolent entity, wormed its way into my bones, a stark contrast to the feverish heat of my panic. Each of Caspian's breaths stole a piece of my soul, each ragged inhale a desperate plea echoing my own silent, anguished prayer. God, let him live. Let him live, or damn this wretched, unforgiving world and take me with him. The weight of his fate, the weight of my failure, pressed down, threatening to crush me beneath its icy grip.

His face, a chalky white against the infernal crimson of his usual skin, felt like a punch to the gut. The air itself seemed to crackle with the absence of his usual, vibrant malevolence. Gone were the sharp angles of his demonic features, replaced by a gaunt fragility that made my breath catch. His eyes, usually burning coals, were dull embers, shadowed hollows that spoke of pain so profound it resonated in my bones. The scent of Sulfur, always thick around him, was replaced by something else...a faint, metallic tang, like blood mixed with ozone.

That vulnerability...it was a grotesque mockery of his power, a horrifying dissonance that ripped through me. This wasn't the imperious demon who commanded legions, who wielded shadows like weapons. This was...something broken. And the sight of it ignited a maelstrom within me. Gratitude for his...survival? A frantic, desperate concern clawed at my throat, a raw, visceral fear for this creature who had once terrified me. And then...tenderness. A shameful, terrifying bloom of tenderness so potent it felt like a betrayal, a dangerous current pulling me towards the precipice of something I couldn't comprehend, something both exhilarating and utterly terrifying. The taste of ash and fear filled my mouth, the tremor in my hands a mirror of the chaos raging in my soul.

"It's... abyssal," Caspian croaked, his voice a grating whisper that scraped against the raw edges of my nerves. The flickering candlelight glinted off the sweat beading on his forehead, highlighting the stark hollows beneath his eyes, eyes that burned with a feverish, unsettling light. The stench of ozone and something else... something metallic and sickeningly sweet, clung to the air around him, a physical manifestation of the terror he carried. A tremor, visceral and bone-deep, shook me. The icy tendrils of dread weren't just creeping; they were clawing their way into my heart, squeezing the air from my lungs.

His confession, when it came, was a death rattle, each syllable a poisoned dart. *"I... I failed to fathom their depravity,"* he rasped, his voice cracking under the crushing weight of his guilt. The admission wasn't just failure; it was a guttural scream of despair. My breath caught a strangled gasp in my throat. I hadn't needed his words. I'd felt the chilling truth seep into my soul long before, tasted it on the bitter tang of fear that coated my tongue, smelled it in the acrid reek of their dark magic, and felt the phantom touch of their corrupted power on my skin. His slumped posture was a broken monument to his shattered pride, the defeat etched into every line of his ravaged face a brutal testament to the unspeakable horrors he had witnessed. The weight of it pressed down on me, suffocating.

His gaze met mine, a glacial challenge that sparked a fire in my gut. My own eyes burned, not just with anger, but with the raw, acrid sting of betrayal. The metallic tang of blood still coated my tongue; the phantom ache in my shoulder was a constant, throbbing reminder. *"Underestimated?"* I snarled the word with a venomous hiss. *"They nearly ripped us apart. Felt the Covenant blades graze my skin, tasted the fear, the metallic reek of their scorched flesh clinging to the air."*

My voice, thick with unshed fury, dropped to a low growl. *"And it wasn't just the Covenant scum. There was... something else, lurking in the periphery, a presence that chilled me to the bone. A slick, unnatural movement in the shadows, too fast for human eyes, too alien for any Covenant I'd ever faced. The air itself crackled with its malevolence; I could taste the dread, bitter, metallic, like licking a freshly forged blade. It wasn't just fear, it was... knowing. Knowing that something ancient and profoundly wrong had watched us, tasted our fear, and found it... delicious. Even now, the memory claws at me, an icy tendril wrapped around my heart, squeezing the life out of my composure."*

Darkness clawed at the cave mouth, a sudden, suffocating presence. Caspian's breath hitched, a rasp in the heavy air, mirroring the icy grip that clenched my gut. The scent of ozone, sharp and metallic, filled my nostrils as a figure materialized—Lyra, bathed in the malevolent glare of the storm. Her usually vibrant aura, the one that had always felt like a warm hearth in the heart of the chilling wilderness, was extinguished. Gone was the playful glint in her eyes, replaced by a predatory stillness that made the hairs on my arms stand on end. A low growl, primal and guttural, rumbled in my chest, fear, raw and visceral.

This wasn't the Lyra who shared whispered strategies around crackling fires, the Lyra whose laughter had once chased away the shadows of doubt. This was something... else. Her face, etched with a cruel understanding I couldn't fathom, was a mask of lethal calm. The familiar warmth of her presence was replaced by an unsettling chill, a radiating coldness that seeped into my bones. My hand, slick with a cold sweat, tightened around the hilt of my sword; the familiar weight offered little comfort. Her eyes—deep pools of obsidian, devoid of any light—bored into me, promising oblivion. The air crackled with an unspoken threat, a palpable tension that screamed of betrayal, a betrayal that reeked of blood and whispered secrets. My heart hammered a frantic rhythm against my ribs, a desperate drumbeat against the encroaching darkness that Lyra, my supposed ally, seemed to embody.

Lyra's shadow stretched long and skeletal across the blood-slicked stones, the flickering torchlight catching the wicked curve of the dagger nestled against her thigh, a predator poised to strike. The scent of iron, sharp and coppery, clung to the air, mingling with the cloying sweetness of decay from the nearby charnel house. Her voice, a silken whisper edged with steel, slithered into the silence. *"Well, well,"* she purred, a predatory gleam in her eyes that held the cold wisdom of a thousand nights spent in the company of shadows. *"Look what the scavenging dogs dragged in. Two broken wings, fluttering feebly in the face of their inevitable end."* The contempt in her tone was a tangible thing, a palpable force that pressed down on her victims, a suffocating blanket woven from years of calculated cruelty and unwavering ambition.

My hand, slick with a cold sweat that betrayed my composure, clamped around the hilt of my dagger. The familiar, brutal weight of the steel, a perverse comfort in this charnel house of impending doom, pressed into my palm, a chilling promise against the throbbing pulse in my temple. Caspian, a ravaged landscape of blood and grit, let out a guttural growl, a raw, primal sound that vibrated through the very floorboards beneath my feet. The stench of iron, sharp and acrid, filled my nostrils, a grim counterpoint to the metallic tang of my fear. My breath hitched, a strangled sob in my chest, each inhale a burning agony. The silence before the storm wasn't quiet; it was a tangible thing, thick with the ozone crackle of anticipation, each hair on my arms standing on end, screaming in a symphony of dread. This wasn't just fear; it was the chilling premonition of a fate carved in bone and shadow.

"Lyra " I hissed the name, each syllable dripping with venom, a whisper that tasted of ash and betrayal on my tongue. The air around me crackled with unspoken fury, a palpable energy that I could almost taste—metallic and bitter like a storm brewing on the horizon. "What. Is. The meaning of this grotesque display? Explain yourself! " My eyes burned with a fierce intensity and I felt it—the icy dread clawing at my soul, a violation so profound it left me reeling and disoriented. I could hardly comprehend the depths of my betrayal, the sense of loss wrapping around me like a vice. The scent of fear lingered in the atmosphere mingling with something else—something rotten and far more sinister—clinging to the air like a shroud suffocating and relentless. I stood there trembling, caught in a web of confusion and rage desperate for answers yet aware that the truth would cut deeper than any blade. The moment stretched taut and heavy as I awaited her response, heart pounding in my chest.

Lyra's laughter clawed at the air, a rasping, guttural sound that scraped against the damp cave walls, bouncing back in a chilling symphony of echoes. The stale, earthy scent of the cavern mingled with the metallic tang of her bloodlust, a perfume only she could appreciate. "Meaning?" she hissed, her voice a venomous whisper that slithered through the oppressive silence. Emerald eyes, flecked with cruel amusement, burned into whatever unfortunate soul dared to question her. "Darling," she purred, the word dripping with condescension as thick as the cave's dripping water, *"the meaning is as clear as the glint of avarice in your own pathetic eyes. The artifact... is mine."* The final word hung in the air, heavy with a possessive fury that promised brutal consequences to anyone foolish enough to disagree.

The revelation slammed into me, a physical impact that ripped the breath from my lungs. Betrayal. It wasn't just a cold fist; it was a vice, crushing my ribs, the metallic tang of blood blooming on my tongue as the air thinned to razor blades. Lyra. I'd bared my soul to her, shared the taste of fear clinging to my sweat after our last desperate gambit, the phantom ache in my leg a constant reminder of our shared near death. We'd tasted victory together, the bitter metallic tang of blood and sweat a communion, the prize gleaming like a siren's call. Now, those same eyes that had mirrored my terror reflected a predatory gleam, a polished obsidian reflecting the cold fire of ambition I'd never glimpsed, never suspected. She was ready to slit our throats, our throats, for the thing we'd clawed for from the jaws of oblivion, our sanity shredded in the process.

Nausea, thick and cloying, rose in my throat, choking off the scream building in my chest. The rage was a white-hot inferno, scorching my insides, threatening to consume me. But beneath the flames, a deeper, blacker ice spread, freezing my very marrow. This wasn't just a fight; it was a primal struggle for survival, a desperate dance with death orchestrated by someone I thought I knew, someone whose smile had once been my anchor in the storm. The chilling certainty of her intent, the glint of steel in her gaze, solidified the horrifying truth: I was staring into the abyss, and the abyss was wearing Lyra's face.

Lyra's dagger, a sliver of obsidian in the sickly yellow lamplight, screamed towards me. My heart, a frantic drum against my ribs, hammered a rhythm of pure terror. Flame erupted from my fingertips, a desperate, searing bloom against the encroaching darkness. The heat blasted my face, a searing kiss of agony, as the cave exploded in a maelstrom of fire. The roar was deafening, a primal shriek drowning out even the frantic beat of my blood. Smoke choked me, thick and acrid, the metallic tang of burning flesh clinging to the back of my throat, a taste of primal horror that clawed at my gut. Caspian's grunt, a guttural, pained animal sound, tore through the inferno. But even wounded, even bleeding, he fought with the savage grace of a cornered beast, his demonic power a churning vortex of shadow and raw, untamed energy.

The combined might of our assault, even with Caspian's crippling wounds, slammed into Lyra. But she was a whirlwind of death, a viper coiled and striking. Her movements, deceptively swift and brutal, held a cold, calculated precision that chilled me to the bone. Each strike was a testament to her ruthless skill; a dance of death played out in the flickering firelight. The coppery tang of blood filled my mouth, my own, I feared, as I stumbled, my arms screaming in protest, bone-deep exhaustion warring with a desperate need to survive. Her eyes glimpsed in that hellish glow, held nothing but cold, unwavering intent, a chilling reflection of the darkness she embodied. This wasn't just a fight; it was a war waged in the heart of the earth, and Lyra was a merciless, terrifying goddess of carnage.

The fight was a butchering, a claustrophobic waltz with death in that suffocating cave. My flames, desperate gasps of fire against the encroaching dark, collided with Lyra's vile magic, a maelstrom of raw power that vibrated through my very bones, the stench of ozone and burning flesh thick in the air. The ground buckled beneath us, a tremor in the earth mirroring the frantic hammering of my heart. Each pulse was a thunderclap in my ears, drowned out only by Lyra's chilling laughter, a sound like ice cracking on a frozen lake. Caspian, a whirlwind of furious motion, was a shield of muscle and bone against Lyra's onslaught, his grunts swallowed by the roaring chaos, replaced by the metallic tang of blood in my mouth. I saw him take a blow meant for me and felt the shudder of his body as he absorbed the impact, the sickening crunch echoing in the confined space.

His desperate, almost feral determination was fueled by a love that was both fierce and utterly terrifying in its intensity. Lyra, a predator draped in shadows, anticipated our every move with terrifying preternatural grace. Each of her strikes was a poisoned dart, aimed not just to kill, but to break, to shatter. I felt the glacial chill of her intent, the icy kiss of death, a constant pressure against my throat, the taste of fear acrid on my tongue. The air itself seemed to scream.

A fleeting lull, a breath stolen from the maelstrom of battle. Lyra's eyes, usually blazing with cold fury, flickered; a calculated distraction.

Caspian seized the instant, his blade a silver comet, finding its mark. The impact sent Lyra staggering, a jarring crack echoing in the silent space between heartbeats. But in that reeling moment, she revealed the abyss that yawned within her, a betrayal so profound it tasted of ash and brimstone.

From the folds of her silken gown, she produced it: a minuscule vial, no larger than a hummingbird's egg, cradling a liquid that pulsed with an unnatural, iridescent light. The scent, acrid, metallic, and sickeningly sweet, filled Caspian's nostrils, a harbinger of the horror to come. With the grace of a viper, she flung the contents.

The liquid hit Caspian with a sizzling hiss, a vile emerald smoke erupting violently as it devoured his skin leaving a trail of agony in its wake. The scream that ripped from his throat was primal a raw and unfiltered sound stripped bare of all humanity echoing through the chaos like a tortured symphony heard over the din of clashing steel and the anguished cries of his comrades. His muscles contorted grotesquely twisting into a horrifying parody of human form as if the very essence of pain had taken physical shape. Each spasm felt like a cruel mockery of life, a reminder of the torment that consumed him amidst the relentless battle surrounding him.

His skin, a canvas of vibrant, sickening green, pulsed with the demonic energy consuming him. Eyes, once bright with defiance, rolled back, revealing the whites, suffused with an unholy light. This was no mere poison; this was a soul-rending curse, a vile concoction brewed in the heart of some forgotten hell.

It wasn't merely breaking his body; it was shattering his will, twisting his very essence into something monstrous, a puppet dancing on strings of infernal power, his spirit a captive in a cage of writhing, corrupted flesh. Lyra watched her expression with a mask of chilling satisfaction, a predatory gleam in her eyes that betrayed a mind both brilliant and utterly depraved.

The shriek tore through me, a physical wound mirroring the one that blossomed across Lyra's chest. Crimson blossomed, staining the obsidian floor, a grotesque counterpoint to the sterile, metallic tang of Covenant blood. My lover, my ally, felled not by the enemy's blade, but by a betrayal so intimate, so personal, it tasted of ash and betrayal on my tongue. A gut-wrenching sob choked me, a silent scream swallowed by the roaring inferno that erupted within. Fury, raw and incandescent, seared my senses, blinding me to everything but the searing injustice of it.

My flames, usually a controlled dance of power, became a frantic, desperate maelstrom. With each blast, a guttural roar escaped my lips, a testament to the agony twisting my soul. They weren't just fired anymore; they were my anguish made manifest, each pulse a burning echo of Lyra's dying breath against my ear. Her scent, lavender and iron, clung to the air, a phantom touch that fueled my furious assault.

But Lyra, the brilliant strategist, the woman who knew me better than I knew myself, had foreseen this. She'd anticipated my blind rage, the very mechanism of my destruction. I fought with the cold precision of a predator, a honed instinct honed through years of bloodshed. The familiar numbness settled, a chilling calm that allowed me to channel the adrenaline into a deadly ballet. Each calculated strike, each perfectly placed parry, felt like a sacrilege, a violation of the sacred bond we had forged in blood and shared secrets. It was a cold, clinical dissection of our love; a brutal autopsy of our shared past. The battle was a maelstrom of steel and fire, a symphony of agony and despair.

The enemy, a familiar face twisted by malice and deceit, moved with a chilling familiarity, exploiting every vulnerability, every tremor of grief that betrayed my carefully constructed facade. Each blow landed like a poisoned kiss, a personal insult etched into my very being. The taste of blood, my own, hers, his, filled my mouth, a bitter testament to the brutal price of betrayal. My heart, a shattered ruin, pulsed only with the rhythm of vengeance.

Finally, exhausted and wounded, I was forced to retreat, leaving Caspian writhing in agony under Lyra's control. I watched, helpless, as Lyra, clutching the artifact, vanished into the storm, leaving me alone in the cave with my grievously wounded lover. The weight of her betrayal crushed me; I felt it physically, a leaden weight in my chest. I had failed.

The success of their mission, the artifact, all of it was lost, but the loss of Caspian, the corruption of our bond, was the real devastation. The rain hammered down, I could feel it on my skin, washing away the blood and mingling with the tears that streamed down my face.

My victory was bitter, their triumph tainted by her treachery. I knew, deep in my gut, that this fight wasn't over; it had just shifted to a new, more personal, and terrifying level. The shadows of the cave seemed to deepen, mirroring the darkness that had consumed me. I felt the weight of my failures, the crushing weight of my inability to protect him, settling upon me like a shroud; Lyra's betrayal, a wound far deeper than any physical injury I'd sustained.

As I cradled Caspian's broken body, I felt the cold seeping into my bones, and I knew this was only the beginning of a new, far more treacherous battle, a battle fought not only against a powerful enemy but against the insidious corruption that had poisoned Lyra's soul, and, in turn, poisoned ours. The crimson tides of her betrayal had swept over us, leaving a trail of destruction in their wake. I would fight. I had to fight. The fight to reclaim Caspian and our future, our shattered future, was far from over. The darkness that had enveloped us felt absolute, a suffocating blanket. But I would endure. This long, arduous struggle filled with despair and agony, would be fueled by the bitter taste of vengeance, a vengeance I would taste only when I had reclaimed what was mine.

CHAPTER

SIX

Whispered Vengeance

T he faintest sliver of dawn, a bruised purple bleeding into a
hesitant rose, painted the cave entrance. Caspian's breathing,
though still shallow, had at last found a rhythm, a fragile,
fluttering regularity. The iridescent poison, a malevolent stain that had
pulsed with venomous light only hours before, had receded, leaving
his skin a disturbingly pale shade, like alabaster sculpted by frost, its
surface faintly veined with the lingering imprint of its passage. He was
alive, a tenuous fact clinging to him like a wisp of morning mist. The
air itself seemed to hold its breath, the silence thick with the unspoken
knowledge of his precarious state; a fragile butterfly, indeed, poised on
the razor's edge of oblivion, its wings dusted with the chilling power of
death. The silence was punctuated only by the drip, drip, drip of water
from unseen stalactites, each drop echoing the precarious rhythm of
his heartbeat.

I sat beside him, my hand clasped tight in his, the rough texture of
his skin a stark contrast to the smooth coolness of the cave walls. His
touch, faint as a butterfly's wing, yet somehow profoundly comforting,
was a fragile warmth against the icy bite that seeped into my very
marrow. A tremor, a barely perceptible vibration, ran through his hand,
a silent symphony of his inner struggle, a testament to the battle still
raging within him. His near-death experience echoed in my heart,
a raw, visceral ache that resonated with the shuddering breaths still
escaping my lips.

Releasing a breath of anger simmered within me as I finally confessed my deepest feelings. "If you wake up completely and heal I'll admit it... I want you. Please. " The weight of my words hung in the air heavy with unspoken longing. A tear warm and bittersweet rolled down my cheek, a testament to my vulnerability and hope.

The terror of losing him was a cold fist squeezing my chest, but even more profound was the chilling revelation of our shared fragility, our intertwined vulnerability laid bare. It was a painful mirroring, a haunting reflection of the trauma that had etched itself onto our souls, leaving its indelible scars, a shared tapestry woven from sorrow and resilience. The weight of it pressed down, a crushing, inescapable burden, heavy as the ancient stones surrounding us. The silence hummed with unspoken understanding, a silent pact forged in the crucible of near death, binding us together in a shared sorrow and an unwavering, fragile hope.

A searing wave of memory crashed over me, a tidal surge of fire, screams, and the stench of burning flesh, the Obsidian Covenant's brutal assault on my village. The horrific tableau replayed with agonizing clarity: my family, trapped within a fiery cage, their desperate silhouettes writhing against the incandescent backdrop. The image seared itself onto my retinas, a brand of unimaginable loss. The heat, a phantom pyre, enveloped me, a suffocating blanket of terror that stole my breath. I felt the lick of flames on my skin, an illusion so vivid it brought tears to my eyes. The crackling inferno echoed in my ears, the acrid smoke a phantom fist crushing my chest. A strangled gasp tore from my lips; the pain was raw, visceral, and a fresh wound reopened after years of festering. My heart, a frantic drum against my ribs, threatened to burst from its cage. Cold sweat slicked my skin, my hands trembling with the force of the remembered trauma. It wasn't a memory; it was a relieved nightmare, all too real, all too present, the agony as sharp as shattered glass.

The secret gnawed at me, a festering wound I'd kept hidden, buried deep within the suffocating silence of my soul. The villagers' deaths, my villagers, slaughtered like sheep, were not merely a tragedy; they were a gaping chasm, a void that had swallowed me whole. The silence was a prison, its walls constructed of guilt and unanswered screams. It clawed at me, a relentless, suffocating weight that pressed down on my chest, stealing the air from my lungs. My only respite, my only solace, was found in the searing heat of the flames, a burning rage that consumed me utterly, fueling my relentless, obsessive hunt for vengeance. I lived for it, breathed it, felt its pulsing rhythm thrumming through my veins, a feverish beat that echoed the frantic hammering of my own heart.

Every nerve ending vibrated with a raw, unyielding thirst for retribution. I was a wraith, a shadow, driven only by the anguished whispers of the departed, their faces haunting my every waking moment. But now, as I sat beside Caspian, his lifeblood ebbing away, the dam holding back the torrent of my grief finally shattered. The floodgates opened, unleashing a deluge of sorrow that threatened to drown me.

A sob, raw and guttural, tore from my throat, a sound swallowed and amplified by the cavernous emptiness. Tears, hot and acrid, carved fiery trails down my cheeks, each drop a searing testament to the pain. The memories, once faint whispers at the edge of consciousness, now crashed over me with brutal, unforgiving clarity, a crushing weight that stole the air from my lungs. I saw it again, the stark, primal terror reflected in my mother's eyes, wide and pleading, a silent scream trapped behind the glassy film of fear.

The agonizing screams of my little brother echoed in my ears, sharp and piercing, clawing at the back of my throat, a sound that would forever haunt the chambers of my heart. The paralysis returned, a leaden cloak settling upon my limbs, suffocating me with the gut-wrenching helplessness I had felt as the inferno devoured everything, home, family, life itself, leaving behind only ashes and the smoking ruins of my world.

The stench of smoke, thick and choking, filled my nostrils; the searing heat licked at my skin; the roar of the flames reverberated through my very bones. It wasn't just a memory; it was a living, breathing nightmare, inescapable, a relentless tide pulling me under. The images, their faces contorted in silent, agonizing terror, played on repeat in the dark theatre of my mind, a horrific film I was forced to watch again and again, forever trapped within its burning frame.

Caspian stirred, his eyelids fluttering like the wings of a trapped bird, finally lifting to reveal eyes clouded with the fog of unconsciousness. A flicker of recognition, faint as a dying ember, sparked within their depths before being almost immediately swallowed by confusion. A jolt, raw and visceral, shot through me, a wave of relief so potent it threatened to send me reeling. His fingers tightened around mine, his grip surprisingly firm, a stark contrast to the fragility I'd feared. The warmth of his skin, a comforting solidity against my own, banished the icy grip of terror that had held me captive.

Tears streamed down my face, uncontrolled, unrestrained rivers of emotion carving paths through the landscape of my grief. The raw, unfiltered pain etched itself onto my features, a brutally honest reflection of the agonizing fear that had threatened to consume me when I believed I had lost him forever. He saw my tears, I knew it; the understanding dawned slowly in his eyes, a fragile, hesitant sunrise pushing through the lingering darkness of his near-death experience. A single, whispered sigh escaped his lips, a fragile testament to his return.

"Blaze... I told you... you wanted me" he whispered his voice rough and strained as if wrestling with emotions he could barely contain though lets out a slight chuckle.

The rough stone of his shoulder dug into my cheek as I wept, racking sobs tearing from my throat. My confession poured forth, a torrent of grief and guilt, a dam of unspoken horrors finally breached. The massacre replayed in vivid detail, the incandescent glare of the flames, licking at thatched roofs and human flesh; the screams, a cacophony of terror that still clawed at my eardrums. I relived the searing heat, the smell of burning flesh clinging to my memory like a shroud. The faces of my family, twisted in agony, were seared into my mind, their silent screams a relentless symphony of despair.

Even now, two years later, I could feel the phantom heat on my skin, the hunger gnawing at my insides, a physical manifestation of the consuming hatred that had become my constant companion. That relentless pursuit, that brutal hunt, had driven me relentlessly, a desperate, solitary chase that had led me here, to this bleak cave, to this desperate gamble for survival, to him. Each detail, each horrific memory, each agonizing moment was laid bare, until my voice was a ragged whisper, my body trembling with exhaustion, the dam finally emptied, the pain finally, agonizingly released, leaving behind only a hollow ache and the chilling silence of aftermath.

Caspian listened patiently, his hand a warm, unwavering weight in mine. The gentle pressure, a comforting anchor in the tempest of my emotions, soothed the frantic beating of my heart. He didn't interrupt the torrent of my grief, didn't offer hollow platitudes that would have felt like salt in a gaping wound. His silence was a balm, a profound respect for the depth of my sorrow. He simply held me, a steadfast presence against the storm, allowing the tears to flow freely, a cathartic release I hadn't permitted myself until this moment. Each sob was a weight lifted, each tear a drop of pain relinquished.

I felt him absorbing my anguish, not just hearing my words, but truly feeling the raw, aching emptiness that clawed at my soul. His understanding wasn't merely empathy; it was a shared kinship forged in the crucible of loss. In the depths of his compassionate gaze, I saw a reflection of my sorrow, a mirrored pain that transcended the need for spoken words. The subtle tremor in his jaw, the faint shadow clinging to the edges of his eyes, these silent gestures spoke volumes. Lyra's betrayal, my brush with death; these trials had cracked open the wellspring of his long-suppressed grief, bringing him closer to a pain he'd kept carefully locked away. He understood her pain, the betrayal, the loss, in a way that no one else ever could, a profound understanding born of shared suffering.

When the torrent of emotion finally subsided, leaving me breathless and spent, I felt Caspian's thumb, feather-light, brush away the stray tears tracing glistening paths down my cheeks. His touch wasn't merely gentle; it was reverent, a sacred act of silent understanding that bridged the chasm between us. It was an empathy so profound, so deeply felt, it transcended the harrowing experiences we'd shared, the scars that still pulsed beneath the surface. I leaned into the warmth of his touch, a small beacon against the lingering tremor that ran through me like a subterranean river. My breath caught in my throat, a ragged sob barely contained. In that hushed, intimate moment, the weight of the world lifted; I felt, unequivocally, utterly safe.

"I... I didn't know," he murmured, his voice a ragged whisper choked with unshed tears. The confession hung heavy in the air, a fragile thing dwarfed by the enormity of her sorrow. "I'm so sorry," he repeated, the words catching in his throat, feeling like pebbles scraping against raw nerves. His apology felt pathetically insufficient, a single flickering match against the inferno of her pain, a futile attempt to illuminate the vast, desolate landscape she had just revealed. The silence that followed was a crushing weight, amplifying the inadequacy of his words and the depth of his regret.

"It doesn't matter," I breathed, the words lost in the vast emptiness of the room, swallowed by the suffocating silence. A tremor ran through me, a physical manifestation of the hollowness that echoed in my chest. *"It's just... it's always been there. A constant, insidious presence, a shadow that stretches long and dark, clinging to me like a second skin, no matter how frantically I try to outrun it. I've clawed at it, fought it, begged it to leave. I've thrown myself into work, into relationships, into oblivion itself, trying to outrun the relentless pursuit of this... this thing. But it's woven into the very core of my being, an inextricable thread, a dark stitch in the tapestry of my soul, one I can never, ever unravel."*

He pulled me closer, his arms a haven around me, a hug both fiercely protective and deeply comforting. I melted against him, the warmth of his body a sunbeam cutting through the lingering chill of the air. His embrace wasn't just safe; it was sanctuary, a bulwark against the storm that still raged, a tempest mirrored in the turmoil within us. I inhaled his scent, a familiar balm, a grounding anchor, and at that moment, the world stilled, its chaos momentarily muted.

In the dark cave I smelled something strong that stirred deep inside me. I could feel the wet walls of the cave and the excitement made my skin tingle. I was inside feeling excited about what was about to happen. I noticed him looking at me with my bright red hair and sharp yellow eyes as I lay next to Caspian. My blond hair spread out on the cool ground shining like spun gold. My body shaped by who I am showed the strong energy that flowed inside me.

I looked up to meet Caspian's blue eyes and we shared a quiet moment of understanding without saying a word. My lips opened and the words hung between them like an exciting promise. "I want you" I said softly, my eyes glowing red with my strong desire for blood.

Caspian's response was a low throaty chuckle that reverberated off the ancient stone walls filling the air with a tension that was almost palpable. "It took you long enough to say that to me but I'm going to make you beg for it my spark " he growled his voice a gravelly purr that sent delightful shivers racing down my spine. The promise in his tone was intoxicating, igniting a fire deep within me. In one fluid motion he flipped me onto my back a swift and powerful movement that caught me entirely off guard eliciting a gasp from my parted lips. My heart raced each beat echoing the thrill of the moment. The world around us faded away leaving just the two of us suspended in a charged atmosphere of desire and anticipation where nothing else mattered but the connection we shared.

He stood over me, his eyes scanning my body with a look that made me feel like he was trying to eat me alive. I felt his fingers moving slowly down my chest teasing me as he circled around but never actually touched my nipples. It drove me crazy and I could feel my body reacting to his playful challenge. "Let's see how much you really want this, " he said with a teasing smile.

I moved around under him, my hips pushing up as a quiet request for more. Caspian smiled slyly as he slowly removed my clothes, uncovering my smooth skin little by little. He touched me gently almost like he was being careful as he felt the shape of my body. Each gentle stroke made the strong feelings inside me grow even more.

As my shirt fell away revealing my skin to the warm air Caspian dipped his head with a teasing intensity tracing the delicate outline of my navel with his tongue. His hands warm and skilled continued their slow descent igniting a fire within me that I could no longer ignore. My breath hitch caught in my throat as he reached the waistband of my pants. With a surprising deftness his fingers expertly undid the clasp the soft sound echoing in the charged atmosphere. He then began to slide the garment down my legs, his movements deliberate and tantalizing leaving me completely exposed to his hungry gaze, a mix of desire and anticipation swirling between us.

The cool air of the cave kissed my bare skin, refreshing yet unable to compete with the intense heat that blazed between us. My body arched involuntarily as Caspian's mouth traced the same path his hands had taken moments before his lips leaving a trail of fire in their wake igniting every nerve ending within me. I tangled my fingers in his hair feeling the silky strands slip between my fingers as I pulled him closer.

The urgency of my desire surged as I urged him to satisfy the deep ache that throbbed within me an insatiable craving that demanded to be fulfilled. The cavern echoed with our soft breaths and muffled whispers as we lost ourselves in this moment wrapped in each other's warmth where the outside world faded away into oblivion.

Caspian's laughter vibrated against my skin, a sound that was both infuriating and arousing, stirring a heat deep within me. "Patience my spark " he chided playfully, his breath hot and tantalizing against my inner thigh sending shivers coursing through my body. He pressed a lingering teasing kiss to the sensitive flesh, his fangs grazing my skin ever so lightly threatening to break the surface and awaken a primal response. The tension in the air crackled and I could feel the world around us fade away leaving only the intoxicating connection between us a magnetic pull I could not resist.

My control snapped entirely. With a feral growl that echoed with raw intensity I flipped their positions pinning Caspian firmly beneath me. My eyes blazed with a fierce predatory light as she straddled him, our bodies a tangle of desire and power. My hair cascaded around us like a curtain of flame creating an almost otherworldly aura that enveloped us in our heated moment. "Fuck patience " I hissed my voice low and charged with urgency as I felt my own fangs elongating in response to her arousal a primal instinct awakening deep within me demanding to be unleashed.

Before Caspian could react I leaned down sinking my teeth into the tender flesh of his neck with a primal urgency. The taste of his blood rich and potent exploded on my tongue a heady mix of sweetness and sin that sent shivers of delight coursing through me. Caspian groaned softly, his body arching beneath mine as he surrendered to the intensity of the moment, a tantalizing blend of fear and ecstasy. It was as if time itself had frozen leaving only the two of us in this intoxicating dance of passion and surrender igniting a fire within that was both thrilling and dangerous.

The metallic tang of blood mingled intoxicatingly with the scent of their arousal creating a potent elixir that drove them both to the brink of madness. It was a heady mix that both thrilled and terrified them igniting an insatiable hunger deep within. I released my firm hold on his neck savoring the taste of him as I licked the wound closed my tongue dancing over his skin. Slowly I moved lower my mouth leaving a wet heated path down his chest tracing every contour every heartbeat as desire enveloped us pulling us deeper into an abyss of passion and longing.

Caspian's hands found their way into my hair guiding me southward without uttering a single word. His silent command ignited a spark within me and I needed no further encouragement to follow his lead. With a sense of urgency I deftly freed him from the constraints of his pants, his cock springing free hard and eager for my attention. The heat of the moment enveloped us both, heightening the anticipation that hung in the air. I wrapped my hand around the base, my fingers barely meeting as I stroked him gently yet firmly eliciting a guttural moan from deep within his chest. The sound reverberated in my ears fueling my desire and urging me to continue this intimate exploration of our shared passion.

I felt a mischievous spark in my eye as I took him in my mouth. My tongue danced around the tip before I went deeper wrapping my lips around him tightly. I felt Caspian push his hips forward getting deeper into my mouth. *"Fuck Blaze "* I said feeling my grip on my emotions slipping away.

I hummed in approval the vibrations sending delightful jolts of pleasure coursing through Caspian's body. I sucked harder my mouth enveloping him while my hand twisted around the base of his cock creating a rhythm that intensified our shared ecstasy. His muscles tensed the tension in his body coiling like a tightly wound spring as he teetered on the edge of release lost in the sensations that surged through him. Each movement was deliberately igniting a fire between us that was impossible to ignore drawing us closer to an inevitable climax that would leave us both breathless.

Sensing his impending climax I decided to release him with a soft pop, a delicate string of saliva stretching between my lips and the tip of his cock. I looked up at him, my eyes gleaming with a playful mischief that hinted at the thrill of what was to come. "Not yet " I purred my voice thick with desire and teasing seduction as I savored the moment relishing the power I held. The heat between us crackled and I could feel his anticipation growing promising even more delicious sensations ahead.

Caspian growled low, his demon side clawing fiercely to the surface, a primal force barely contained within him. With a swift motion he flipped us once again, his powerful body covering mine like an unyielding blanket of steel radiating both heat and intensity. "You're going to be the death of me woman " he muttered in his voice a mix of frustration and desire as he positioned himself at my entrance. I could feel the tension crackling in the air, an electric pulse between us igniting the moment.

The shared vulnerability, the raw ache of our losses, the chilling brush of terror that had almost consumed us, forged a bond stronger than steel. It was a connection forged not in dominance or submission, but in the crucible of shared darkness, a resilience born from the ashes of despair. Our relationship had transcended the tangled, volatile threads of sexual tension and uneasy alliance. It was something far more profound, a tapestry woven with the complex hues of shared trauma, a deep and abiding understanding born from the fires of our shared suffering. It was a love forged in the heart of the storm.

A profound silence descended, heavy and expectant, punctuated only by the relentless drip...drip...drip of water echoing through the cavern. The nascent dawn seeped into the cave, painting the rough-hewn walls with elongated shadows that writhed and pulsed like phantoms. This wasn't a silence born of defeat; it was a shared sanctuary, a silent testament etched in the understanding that flickered in his eyes, a mirrored reflection of our shared wounds. We had stared into the abyss of death, felt the venomous sting of betrayal, and endured pain so profound it threatened to shatter us. Yet, in the crucible of those horrors, forged together in the fires of our shared trauma, I discovered a wellspring of strength I never knew existed, a resilience tempered into unyielding steel. It was a resilience that pulsed with the promise of a future, a future where our love, though scarred and battle-worn, would stand defiant against the encroaching darkness of the Obsidian Covenant, against the myriad threats that perpetually clawed at the edges of our world. I met his gaze, and in the depths of his eyes, I saw not just shared survival, but the unwavering certainty that together, we would conquer.

The crimson tide of betrayal had receded, leaving behind not merely a new understanding, but a profound, almost sacred bond, a love forged in the white-hot crucible of our shared agony. It blossomed within me, a warmth that spread like wildfire, chasing away the lingering frost of the aftermath. The journey ahead remained treacherous, a perilous path winding through shadowed valleys and over treacherous peaks; the Obsidian Covenant, a malevolent force, still held a commanding advantage. Yet, as I gazed into Caspian's eyes, eyes that mirrored the storm within my soul, I saw not fear, but a fierce, unwavering resolve. A determination is as bright and sharp as obsidian itself, yet tempered by the incandescent glow of our newfound love. We would face the coming tempest, not merely as comrades in arms against a common foe, but as two souls inextricably entwined, our love a beacon burning fiercely against the encroaching darkness, a love that transcended the harsh realities of our dark and dangerous worlds, a love that defied even death itself.

The fight for survival raged, a brutal ballet of flickering torchlight and desperate shadows, but now it was a dance we would share, our hands clasped tight, our love a defiant beacon against the encroaching, suffocating night. The spectre of the past, a chilling presence, still lingered at the edges of our vision, but I knew it would no longer hold us captive. It was now a foundation, a testament to the unyielding strength of our shared spirit, the crucible in which a love forged in fire had been tempered. This love, born from the ashes of our suffering, defied the very darkness that had sought to claim us, a defiant bloom in a desolate landscape. I felt the healing begin, a slow, steady dawn breaking through the storm within, a gentle mending of the fractured pieces of my soul. But even as hope kindled within, I knew the war was far from over. The shadows still stretched long, their menace palpable. We would fight, together, our love, our shield, our shared strength, our weapon.

The silence stretched, thick and heavy with unspoken emotions, a tangible presence pressing down on me like a physical weight. It felt less like an absence of sound and more like a suffocating blanket woven from anxiety, regret, and the lingering scent of fear. The only sound was the rhythmic drip, drip, drip of water from the cave ceiling, each drop echoing unnervingly loud in the oppressive stillness, a stark counterpoint to the erratic thump, thump, thump of my own heart, a frantic drumbeat against my ribs. Caspian's hand, still warm despite his near-death experience, rested in mine, the residual heat a fragile comfort against the damp chill of the cave. His fingers, long and slender, intertwined with mine, a comforting pressure that anchored me to the present, a lifeline in this suffocating darkness.

I looked at him, his face pale and etched with exhaustion, his normally vibrant hazel eyes now dark and shadowed, his gaze searching, intense, and deeply unsettling. A shiver, born less of cold and more of a primal fear, ran down my spine. The lingering effects of the Nightshade poison were evident, a faint tremor still ran through his hand, a subtle vibration against my palm, a stark reminder of his fragility. But his eyes, oh, his eyes held a strength that belied his weakened state; a steely determination that shone even through the exhaustion, a flicker of defiance in the face of death itself.

He opened his mouth to speak, his lips moving slightly, forming silent words, then closed it again, a fleeting flicker of hesitation crossing his face, a shadow of doubt momentarily eclipsing the unwavering strength I'd seen just moments before. A single bead of sweat traced a path down his temple, glinting in the faint light filtering from the cave entrance. I held my breath, waiting, the silence pressing in, my unspoken fears, of loss, of failure, of the uncertain future, mirroring his, a silent conversation weaving between us, as heavy and suffocating as the air itself.

Finally, he spoke, his voice a low murmur barely audible above the relentless drip, drip, drip of water echoing in the cavernous space. The words seemed to catch in his throat, each syllable a painful effort. He shifted his weight, the damp stone cold against his back, and ran a trembling hand through his already dishevelled hair. His eyes, usually bright and mischievous, were shadowed and filled with a profound weariness. He cleared his throat, a rattling sound like dry leaves skittering across the pavement. Then, leaning closer, his breath misting slightly in the cool air, he whispered, *"There's something... something I need to tell you. Something I should have told you a long time ago… something that will… change everything."*

My heart quickened, a frantic drumbeat against my ribs. The air, thick with unspoken words and the scent of old books and pipe tobacco from his study, felt suddenly suffocating. I'd laid myself bare, a vulnerable landscape of past betrayals and self-doubt spread out before him. I'd confessed the things I'd hidden from everyone, even myself, the stammering insecurities, the crushing weight of guilt over a youthful indiscretion, the lingering phantom pain of a lost love. But he remained an enigma, a sculpted statue in the dim light, his face impassive, his gaze distant, though his eyes, the colour of a stormy sea, held a flicker of something…unreadable. His silence wasn't merely quiet; it was a wall, a fortress built of granite and shadows, impenetrable. His reluctance, his almost painful hesitation to reciprocate, wasn't just intriguing; it was a barbed hook, snagging my curiosity and pulling me deeper into this unsettling intimacy.

A cold knot of apprehension, slick with dread, tightened in my stomach, a vice around my breath. A tremor, not just of nerves, but of something deeper, a primal fear of rejection, ran through me, shaking my very core. I squeezed his hand, the pressure a silent, desperate invitation, a plea etched into the fragile contact. My fingers dug into his, searching for a connection, a response, anything beyond the chilling stillness. The skin beneath my touch was unexpectedly warm, a surprising counterpoint to the glacial distance in his eyes. More than understanding, I ached for connection, for a reciprocal vulnerability, a shared space beyond the barriers we'd both erected. I craved a glimpse beyond the wall, a fragile bridge across the chasm between us.

"My… my past isn't as straightforward as I've let on " he began his voice trembling slightly as he spoke. His gaze dropped to our intertwined hands, the rough texture of his calloused skin a stark contrast to my soft delicate ones. A blush faint as a whisper crept up my neck, a mixture of embarrassment and intrigue flaring within me. He squeezed my hand gently, a silent apology radiating from the pressure of his grip. *"I… I wasn't always with the Whispering Wind "* he repeated the words catching in his throat like a bitter pill that stuck stubbornly refusing to go down easily. He swallowed hard the muscles in his jaw working visibly as he

wrestled with the unspoken weight of his confession, the burden of his past pressing heavily upon him.

He traced the line of my palm with his thumb, his touch hesitant and almost afraid as if he was unsure of how I would respond to the truth he was about to unveil. *"Before... before I found my place amongst them I was... adrift. A wanderer, a shadow clinging to the edges of society "* he continued his voice barely above a whisper filled with a heavy sense of loss. *"I lived a life of... necessity driven by desperation and a longing for survival. Let's just say I made choices I deeply regret—choices that forced me to flee to reinvent myself. "* The words hung in the air between us heavy with the weight of his revelations.

"The Whispering Wind... they offered me a sanctuary, a chance to rebuild to atone for the things I had done " he said, his eyes flickering up to meet mine filled with a mixture of shame and a desperate plea for understanding. I could see the turmoil within him, the struggle between the man he had been and the man he was trying to become. *"It's a story I haven't been ready to share but... you deserve the truth. "* His voice trailed off leaving an echo of vulnerability that resonated deeply within me.

In that moment I realized he was not just revealing the shadows of his past; he was entrusting me with a piece of his soul. The air felt charged with unspoken emotions and I could feel the gravity of his honesty drawing us closer. This was more than a confession; it was an invitation to understand him to see him not just as a member of the Whispering Wind but as a complex individual shaped by the trials he had endured. I took a deep breath ready to embrace the depth of his truth knowing that it was a pivotal moment for us both.

My eyebrows rose, a barely perceptible twitch betraying my surprise. I knew he was a demon, a creature of immense power whose very presence radiated a palpable chill, a frost that seeped into the marrow of my bones. But the specifics of his millennia-long existence remained frustratingly elusive, locked away in the shadowy recesses of his ancient, obsidian heart. I'd sensed it, of course, the raw, untamed energy thrumming beneath his deceptively calm exterior, a power that felt both terrifying and strangely compelling. The Whispering Wind, the clandestine organization he'd claimed allegiance to, was equally shrouded in enigma. For years, I'd stalked their movements from the shadows, a silent observer meticulously piecing together fragments of their machinations, yet their true motives remained maddeningly obscure, a puzzle with pieces deliberately misplaced. Even now, after countless hours spent deciphering cryptic messages and interpreting barely perceptible shifts in their operational patterns, I could only speculate about their ultimate goals.

Our alliance, forged in the crucible of a shared, desperate need, felt less like a partnership and more like a precarious balancing act on a razor's edge, a tense equilibrium built upon a foundation of mistrust, held together only by begrudging respect born of mutual necessity and a healthy dose of fear. But this confession... this admission he'd just uttered, sent a fresh wave of icy dread washing over me. It was a chilling revelation, a glimpse into a darkness far deeper, far more sinister than I could have ever conceived. It wasn't simply the details of his past; it was the implications, the horrifying possibilities hinted at beneath the surface of his words that truly unsettled me. A knot of icy apprehension tightened in my gut, a premonition of the coming storm, a certainty that this was merely the opening act in a far greater, far more terrifying tragedy.

The air hung thick and heavy with unspoken things, the scent of wood smoke and damp earth clinging to the twilight. I watched him, silhouetted against the dying light, his shoulders slumped but his jaw clenched tight. He took a shuddering breath, the kind that comes from the bottom of your lungs, a desperate attempt to fill the void within. His eyes, the colour of a stormy sea, locked with mine, and I saw it then, a kaleidoscope of emotions swirling within their depths. Vulnerability, raw and aching, was undeniable; it painted itself across his face in the faint tremor of his lower lip and the subtle quiver in his hands. But intertwined with that vulnerability, a stubborn thread of defiance, a refusal to break, a defiant spark that flickered in the stormy grey of his eyes. He cleared his throat, the sound rough and strained, a physical manifestation of the internal struggle playing out within him. *"Before... before Lyra,"* he finally managed the name itself, a fragile thing, catching on the jagged edges of his raw emotion, a whispered prayer on his lips. A beat of silence stretched between us, pregnant with unspoken history. *"I served the Obsidian Covenant."* The words hung in the air, heavy as the impending storm clouds gathered on the horizon. The name itself felt like a cold weight in my chest, a promise of darkness and secrets yet to be revealed.

The words hung in the air, heavy with the unspoken accusations and the chilling weight of their meaning. *"Seraphina,"* Caspian had said, his voice barely a whisper, yet somehow carrying the force of a shout, *"I was a Shadowbinder."* The syllables, each one a poisoned dart, settled in my stomach, a leaden weight pressing down on my diaphragm, stealing my breath. The revelation hit me with the brutal force of a physical blow, a fist slamming into my solar plexus. I gasped, a ragged, involuntary sound, reeling from the impact as if I'd been thrown against a wall. My knees threatened to buckle; I gripped the edge of the rough-hewn table to steady myself.

Caspian, my reluctant ally, the man whose life I had saved from the collapsing mineshaft just weeks ago, the man whose quiet intensity had begun to thaw my guarded heart... he was a Shadowbinder. A member of the very organization I had dedicated the last five years of my life to dismantling, a ruthless cabal of assassins and sorcerers known for their brutal efficiency and absolute loyalty to their shadowy master. My blood ran cold, a frigid tide replacing the warmth that had, foolishly, begun to bloom within me. The crimson tides of betrayal surged within me, a sickening blend of shock, a white-hot, incandescent rage that threatened to consume me, and a chilling, bone-deep sense of betrayal so profound it felt like an icy hand gripping my heart.

It wasn't just the betrayal itself; it was the shattering of my carefully constructed worldview. Every shared moment, every glance, every hesitant smile, all tainted, rendered suspect. The trust I had foolishly placed in him, the vulnerability I'd allowed myself to feel in his presence, now felt like a cruel joke, a naïve folly that had left me exposed and bleeding. A tremor, violent and uncontrollable, ran through me; this betrayal threatened to shatter not just my mission, but everything I thought I knew about loyalty, about friendship, about the very nature of good and evil. The carefully constructed world I had built around myself crumbled, leaving me standing on the precipice of something vast and terrifying.

"You... you were one of them?" I whispered, the words catching in my throat like a fishbone, the sound barely audible above the frantic thump thump thumping of my own heart. Disbelief, cold and suffocating, wasn't just a fist clenching my heart; it was an icy vice, squeezing the air from my lungs. The ornate, gilded frame of the portrait behind Elias seemed to shimmer and distort, blurring the edges of the already fading image of the stern-faced man within. Resentment, sharp and bitter as crushed glass, tasted like ash and lye in my mouth, a burning, corrosive sensation that spread from my tongue to the back of my throat. It wasn't just resentment; it was betrayal, a cold, festering wound ripped open after years of carefully stitched-up healing. The tremor that ran through me wasn't just a physical manifestation of shock; it was a full-body convulsion, a shudder that started in my toes and climbed, icy fingers of fear, all the way to the crown of my head. My knees threatened to buckle, and I instinctively reached out, my fingers finding purchase on the cold, smooth surface of the ancient oak table beside me. The polished wood felt strangely comforting against the overwhelming tide of nausea and horror that threatened to pull me under.

Caspian nodded, his jaw clenched so tight the muscles bunched visibly beneath his tanned skin. The faintest tremor ran through his broad shoulders, a barely perceptible ripple beneath the crisp, dark fabric of his tailored jacket. *"Yes,"* he rasped, the single word a low, guttural sound. *"I was... a high-ranking lieutenant in the Obsidian Hand. My responsibilities encompassed deep infiltration of rival syndicates, often posing as a legitimate businessman, sometimes a low-level operative, always adapting. Gathering intelligence was paramount, financial records, coded communications, and even whispered gossip in dimly lit taverns. Eliminating threats... that involved everything from discreet poisonings to... more... direct methods. I was... effective,"* he repeated, the word hanging heavy in the air, laced with a chilling self-awareness.

His voice, once steady, was now strained, a fragile thread against the backdrop of his imposing frame. He paused, his gaze drifting to a distant point, his eyes losing focus, reflecting a turmoil far deeper than the surface suggested. *"I believed in their cause,"* he finally admitted, a flicker of something akin to pain briefly illuminating his harsh features. *"At least at first. They promised power, the kind that could rewrite history, an influence that reached the highest echelons of society... and revenge. Revenge against the Crimson Dynasty, who had... decimated my family. They painted a vivid picture; a world sculpted by our will, free from the tyranny of those who had wronged us. A world where the Obsidian Hand reigned supreme. For a time, I believed it was a righteous path."*

He spoke his voice a low growl that vibrated with barely controlled fury, of a deep-seated resentment towards the celestial beings, the Luminians, their shimmering wings a constant mockery of his broken spirit. This hatred, he explained, wasn't born overnight, but had festered for centuries, a malignant growth fueled by perceived injustice and systematic oppression. The Luminians, with their effortless grace and godlike power, had promised the Covenant dominion over the cosmos, a golden age of prosperity and influence. But those promises, etched in shimmering celestial script upon ancient tablets, proved to be hollow lies.

He recounted tales of resource exploitation, of entire star systems subjugated and their populations enslaved, all for the Luminians' insatiable hunger for power. He spoke of betrayals not just by the Luminians, but within the Obsidian Covenant itself—subtle machinations, backstabbing alliances, and the cold, calculated maneuvering of those who sought to climb the ranks through any means necessary.

He spoke of Lyra, his former lover, a woman whose beauty was a breathtaking tapestry of starlight and shadow, a deceptive façade concealing a heart as black and cold as the void between galaxies. Her eyes, once pools of molten gold reflecting his adoration, now seemed to hold the distant, uncaring glint of distant nebulae. Lyra, he confessed, had been the catalyst for his defection, the final shattering blow in a series of devastating betrayals. Their relationship, once a passionate inferno, had ended not with a fiery explosion, but a slow, agonizing freeze. Her ambition, a chilling, calculated climb for power within the Covenant, had culminated in her betrayal; she'd orchestrated his downfall, framing him for a crime he didn't commit.

The revelation had been a brutal awakening, stripping him bare and leaving him exposed to the harsh realities of the Obsidian Covenant. The Covenant's inherent cruelty, once a distant, uncomfortable truth, had become starkly clear. He described the ritualistic sacrifices, the casual disregard for sentient life, the insidious whispers of forbidden knowledge and dark magic that permeated their ranks. The power they wielded, once alluring and seductive, now felt like a suffocating weight, a poisonous embrace. He'd been deeply entrenched, hopelessly entangled in their web of deceit and ambition, before he finally saw the truth—too late to save himself completely, but not too late to break free.

He described the Covenant's operations with chilling precision, detailing the logistical nightmare of their interstellar fleet, and the perfectly synchronized movements of their warships, each a brutal testament to their advanced technology. He spoke of the terrifying efficiency of their ground forces, the relentless, coordinated assaults that left entire planets in smouldering ruins. Their control wasn't maintained through brute force alone, though that certainly played a part; he described the sophisticated propaganda campaigns, the subtle manipulations of local populations, turning brother against brother, fostering fear and obedience through carefully targeted information warfare.

He recounted the horrors he'd witnessed firsthand: the plasma-scorched bodies of civilians lining the streets of a once vibrant city, the screams echoing in his memory even now; the ritualistic sacrifices he'd been forced to observe, the chillingly calm expressions of the Covenant's religious leaders as they oversaw the butchering. He detailed the specific orders he'd followed, the cold, clinical instructions relayed through encrypted channels, demanding the extermination of resistance pockets, the systematic cleansing of entire populations deemed undesirable. Each order was a weight on his conscience. He painted a portrait not just of a terrifying organization, but of a terrifying ideology, a cold, calculating ambition for galactic domination fueled by a warped, fanatical religious fervour that justified any cruelty, any atrocity. Their thirst for power was a boundless ocean, swallowing everything in its path. His words weren't just gruesome; they were a visceral assault, the stench of burnt flesh and the metallic tang of blood clinging to every syllable.

As he spoke, a low, gravelly voice that seemed to vibrate in the very air around us, I found myself strangely captivated. My initial anger, a righteous fire that had burned so fiercely just moments before, began to dwindle, replaced by a chilling fascination that sent a shiver down my spine. He wasn't just recounting a series of past events; I felt the raw, visceral weight of his experiences pressing against me, a palpable darkness that mirrored the shadowed corners of my soul, a darkness I usually kept carefully hidden. He wasn't simply confessing to crimes, the stark, brutal details of which painted a horrifying tableau before my eyes, I saw him exposing the brutal, unvarnished reality of the world we inhabited, a world far grimmer and more unforgiving than the sanitized version I'd always believed in. A world where morality, I realized with a sickening lurch in my stomach, wasn't a given, a comfortable principle to uphold, but a luxury, a privilege afforded only to the few fortunate enough to exist outside its harsh, unforgiving landscape.

He wasn't simply seeking forgiveness, a hollow plea for absolution. I understood, with a clarity that both terrified and strangely exhilarated me, that he was seeking something far deeper, far more profound: understanding. He craved an acknowledgment of the intricate web of circumstances, the agonizing choices, and the relentless pressures that had driven him to the precipice of what society deemed irredeemable. A strange, unsettling pull emanated from him, a sense of shared experience, a dark kinship forged in the crucible of shared suffering, despite the horrifying nature of his confession. My heart pounded a frantic rhythm against my ribs, a wild drumbeat accompanying his words; my breath hitched in my throat, and a strangled gasp caught between the rising tide of my emotions. My eyes were locked on his, mesmerized, unable to tear myself away from the vortex of his confession, a confession that felt less like a legal deposition and more like a desperate, intimate unveiling of a soul laid bare.

The air in the dimly lit cell hung heavy with the scent of mildew and despair. He spoke in a low, gravelly voice, each word a carefully chosen stone in a confession that chipped away at the veneer of my own carefully constructed morality. He detailed the raid on the village of Oakhaven, as not a mere massacre, but a calculated act of terror, the systematic targeting of women and children, and the deliberate burning of homes. He described the chilling efficiency of his squad, their practiced movements, and the cold precision of their weaponry. He wasn't boasting; his tone was flat, almost clinical as if recounting a particularly gruesome surgical procedure. Then came the story of the ambush at the Silver River crossing, the betrayal of Allied forces, and the subsequent slaughter. With each horrific anecdote, the lines blurred. He wasn't simply a monster, but a man caught in a relentless current, swept along by forces beyond his control.

I saw it in the way his eyes flickered, a fleeting expression of fear, followed by a steely resolve. He hadn't been a mindless puppet, but a pragmatist, a survivor in a brutal world where loyalty was a luxury and morality a dangerous weakness. His ruthlessness was mirrored in my past, a chilling echo of the choices I'd made, and the compromises I'd accepted in my relentless pursuit of vengeance. The ambition that fueled him, the desperate need to escape the poverty and hopelessness of his upbringing, was a twisted reflection of my climb to power, a journey paved with the broken bodies and shattered lives of my enemies.

His confession wasn't just a chronicle of atrocities; it was a portrait of systemic corruption, a stark depiction of a world where the lines between right and wrong were deliberately obfuscated. He spoke of promises broken, of orders given and rescinded in a heartbeat, of a network of deceit so complex and vast it seemed inescapable. He'd been a pawn, just like me. Manipulated by those in power, used and discarded when no longer useful, left to face the consequences alone. His haunted eyes, the deeply etched lines around his mouth, were a roadmap of betrayal, broken trust, and unspoken grief. They reflected not just his past, but mine as well, and in that shared experience, in the brutal symmetry of our fates, I found a perverse kinship, a chilling understanding that transcended the chasm of our crimes. The world that forged him was the same world that shaped me, a world that demanded retribution, a world that echoed in the hollow chambers of my own vengeful heart.

As he spoke of the betrayal, the pain in his voice was palpable, a raw agony that sliced through me. I felt it, a physical ache mirroring his own. He revealed a vulnerability I hadn't expected, a crack in the carefully constructed façade of ruthless efficiency I'd always seen. He shared stories, each one a blow to the Obsidian Covenant's image, exposing flaws that I could, I knew I could, exploit in my quest for revenge. The details he gave me felt like weapons being placed directly into my hands.

His revelations weren't just a confession; they were a gift, a key to unlocking the secrets of the Obsidian Covenant, and, more importantly, a window into his soul. He had revealed his vulnerabilities, not as weakness, but as strength, a testament to his ability to confront his past, acknowledge his mistakes, and strive for something better.

When he finally finished speaking a long silence enveloped us, falling like a heavy blanket between our souls broken only by the gentle drip of water echoing in the stillness. The dawn light had fully arrived casting soft beams that painted the cave walls in warm hues of orange and gold illuminating the shadows that danced around us. The air around us hummed with unspoken emotions—regret understanding and an unsettling intimacy that lingered just out of reach making it difficult to know what to say next or how to bridge the distance that had grown between us.

I reached out, my fingers trembling slightly as I traced the lines of his face. The faint scars, etched into his skin like a roadmap of hardship, felt rough beneath my fingertips. I lingered there, my touch hesitant, almost afraid to disturb the fragile peace I sensed. I saw the pain in his eyes, a deep, familiar ache that mirrored something within myself. The weight of his past was palpable, a heavy cloak he seemed to wear, yet even then, I saw it—a flicker of hope, a tiny spark of redemption burning stubbornly in the depths of those haunted eyes. It gave me a fragile, hesitant hope in return.

"So, you're my enemy," I whispered, the words catching in my throat like shards of ice. The single flickering torchlight cast long, dancing shadows across the rough-hewn stone walls of the chamber, highlighting the unsettlingly calm expression on his face. He was Lysander, the man responsible for the death of my brother, the architect of the siege that had ravaged my homeland, the very embodiment of everything I hated. Yet, here he was, his gloved hands meticulously working on the complex mechanism before him, a mechanism that, if I understood correctly, was the key to unlocking the very prison I was currently trapped in.

A shiver, cold and sharp as a winter's wind, ran down my spine, raising gooseflesh on my arms. The air hung heavy with the scent of damp stone and something else… something metallic, faintly coppery, that sent a fresh wave of nausea rolling through me. I couldn't believe what I was seeing, what I was hearing. My ears felt like they were playing tricks on me; surely this was some elaborate hallucination, a cruel twist of fate conjured from my exhaustion and despair. The rhythmic click click click of the mechanism seemed to mock my disbelief, each sound driving the knot of confusion tightening in my stomach into a painful, suffocating coil. My breath hitched in my chest. Was this a trap? A ploy? Or… could it be something else entirely? The possibility, however improbable, sent a tremor of something akin to hope, fragile and flickering like the torchlight itself, through my despair.

He looked at me, his gaze deep and earnest. I felt a shiver run down my spine under the weight of his stare. *"I am trying to atone,"* he said, his voice low and sincere. The words hung in the air, heavy with unspoken regret. I saw the pain etched on his face, a mirror to the turmoil I felt myself. *"What I did... I cannot undo it,"* he continued, his voice catching slightly. But I could see the desperate hope in his eyes. *"But I can try to make amends. And the destruction of the Obsidian Covenant... that is my chance,"* he finished, the words almost a plea. I wondered if he truly believed in this chance for redemption. I wondered if I believed it too.

He didn't seek absolution; he sought to change the future, to right the wrongs of his past, to find a semblance of peace. His redemption wasn't about escaping the consequences of his actions, but about confronting them, fighting against them, and using his past knowledge and skills to ensure that no one else would suffer the same fate. Their shared vulnerability, their shared pain, and their shared past had forged a bond stronger than any allegiance, any oath, or any contract.

I saw it then, clear as day. They were two sides of the same coin, I realized, both scarred by the violence of the Obsidian Covenant. I felt a chill run down my spine remembering it, the brutality of it all. Both were driven by a thirst for vengeance, I knew, a thirst I understood intimately. But I also saw something more, something beyond the anger: a yearning for a future where their shared scars didn't define them, but instead fueled their determination to fight for a better world, a world I desperately wanted to help them build.

I leaned in, pressing a soft kiss against his lips. It wasn't a kiss of passion, not yet; it felt like a kiss of understanding, a kiss of alliance, a seal on a bond forged in the crucible of our shared trauma and mutual betrayal. I felt the weight of it, the unspoken promise. The crimson tides of the past had receded, but I could still feel the currents of our future, intertwined and powerful, flowing ever onward. My heart beat a little faster, a quiet rhythm echoing the pulse of our new, fragile connection. I knew, with a certainty that settled deep in my bones, that this was only the beginning.

CHAPTER

SEVEN

Shadows of Doubt

The kiss, a viper's strike disguised as a butterfly's wing, left a burning brand of dread, the metallic tang of fear coating my tongue. Caspian's confession—a serpent coiled in honeyed words—hung heavy in the suffocating air, a miasma thick enough to taste, acrid and bitter, poisoning the very marrow of our shared moment. The scent of his betrayal clung to me, a phantom limb of his touch, a grotesque parody of intimacy. Days bled into nights, a crimson tide of lost time, each drop a scream swallowed whole.

Our alliance, a gilded cage of necessity, groaned under the crushing weight of the abyss between us; a chasm carved not merely from doubt and suspicion, but from the raw, festering wound of his treachery, a wound that pulsed with a poisonous rhythm mirroring the frantic beat of my own heart. The very air vibrated with the unspoken accusations, a silent scream echoing in the hollow chambers of my soul. His eyes, once pools of captivating allure, now held the cold, glittering malice of a predator, leaving me stripped bare, exposed to the chilling wind of his deceit.

My senses screamed, overloaded. The metallic tang of blood, his blood, I imagined, filled my mouth, a coppery film clinging to my tongue. The ghost of his touch, a brand seared onto my skin, ignited a wildfire of icy terror that pulsed through me, a living thing. Each ragged breath he stole was a venomous hiss in the suffocating silence, a death knell echoing the frantic, thunderous drumbeat of my heart against my ribs. Caspian. The viper I'd mistaken for a prince. His eyes, once pools of captivating enigma, now burned with a glacial malice that froze my very soul. They were the eyes of a predator, calculating, ancient, utterly devoid of the man I'd loved, or so I'd pathetically believed.

His smile, a rictus of pure, predatory pleasure, was a razor blade, slicing through the fragile veil of my sanity. Each carefully chosen word was a poisoned dart, aimed straight at my heart. My stomach convulsed, a maelstrom of bile and bone-deep fear, twisting with every infinitesimal change in his expression, every flicker of the savage glee lurking beneath the surface of that deceptively charming facade. The air itself crackled with the raw, lethal energy radiating from him, a palpable threat that coiled around me, constricting, suffocating.

Years of shared peril, forged in the crucible of survival, had built a fragile trust, a gossamer thread now stretched taut, ready to snap at the slightest breeze. This wasn't mere unease; it was a venomous tendril of suspicion, coiling around my heart, whispering insidious doubts, and seductive lies that clawed at the edges of my sanity. My breath caught, a strangled gasp in my throat, as I peered into the abyss of his eyes, searching for the truth, for some lingering ember of the man I loved, or the cold, hard glint of the traitor he had become. The hunt was on, and the prey was far closer than I'd ever imagined.

The coppery tang of my blood, thick and metallic on my tongue, was a meagre reprieve from the ravenous hunger clawing at my insides. It burned a path down my throat, leaving a gritty residue that tasted of rust and terror. His touch, feather-light on the ragged gashes, felt like the caress of death itself, glacial, inhuman, the polished marble of a tomb pressing against my quivering flesh. Each painstaking application of my crimson stain was a deliberate torment, a slow, agonizing ritual performed for his eyes alone, a macabre ballet in the flickering candlelight. The scent of it, acrid and sharp, filled the suffocating air.

His eyes, usually blazing infernos, were now twin glacial pools, reflecting a storm of such terrifying intensity it threatened to shatter the very air around us. I tasted his fear, a bitter, acrid undercurrent to the metallic sweetness of my blood, a rancid aftertaste that clung to my palate like a venomous curse. It wasn't mere caution I saw in their depths, but something far more sinister, a calculated cruelty cloaked in the flimsy veil of solicitous concern. His concern was a lie, a venomous serpent coiled within a heart of obsidian. The air crackled with the unspoken threat, the weight of his deception pressing down on me, heavy as a shroud. He wasn't healing me; he was savouring my pain.

The very air crackled with unspoken tension. His movements, though precise, lacked the fluidity of genuine compassion. They were precise, efficient, almost mechanical, a stark contrast to the vibrant chaos that usually consumed him. This manufactured kindness, this suffocating politeness, was a cage, its bars forged from his chilling control. It wasn't his touch that unnerved me, it was the chilling absence of anything genuine beneath it, a void as vast and terrifying as the eternal night itself. The performance was exquisite, but the emptiness behind it left me shivering, a predator left exposed to the predatory nature of his intentions.

The fire roared, a hungry beast gnawing at the night, its orange fangs licking at the encroaching darkness. The heat scorched my face, a counterpoint to the icy dread creeping into my bones. Caspian, his eyes—the colour of a stormy sea—held mine with a chilling intensity. The scent of wood smoke and something else, something feral and unsettling, clung to the air. My voice, a ragged whisper against the crackling inferno, barely carried the weight of the question that had festered within me like a malignant growth. *"Why,"* I rasped, each word a physical blow, *"are you helping me, Caspian?"* The silence that followed was a suffocating entity, pressing down on me, heavier than any mountain.

My heart, a frantic drum solo against my ribs, threatened to shatter the cage of bone. The knot in my stomach tightened, a venomous serpent constricting my breath, stealing the air in ragged gasps. The silence stretched, a taut wire humming with the anticipation of his answer, a truth far more treacherous and terrifying than any shadowed, viper-infested jungle. The metallic tang of fear wasn't just a taste; it was the acrid stench of dread burning in my throat, a bitter premonition clinging to the back of my tongue like a venomous kiss. This wasn't mere aid; this was a meticulously crafted game orchestrated by a master puppeteer, his eyes gleaming with a cold intelligence that chilled me to the marrow. I, a pawn in his intricate, lethal design, felt the icy grip of his power, a suffocating weight pressing down, crushing the last vestiges of my hope. His smile, when it finally came, would be the prelude to my doom, a chilling masterpiece of calculated cruelty.

His gaze bored into me, a glacial, impenetrable wall. The firelight, a malevolent dancer, licked across his sharp features, its flickering shadows revealing a face sculpted from granite and shadowed secrets. A cold dread, icy fingers clutching my heart, replaced the earlier unease. The scent of wood smoke, usually comforting, now felt acrid, mirroring the bitterness in his words. *"Because the Obsidian Covenant must be destroyed,"* he rasped, each syllable a deliberate hammer blow against the silence. His voice, a low growl rumbling from deep within his chest, sent shivers down my spine. *"Their methods...are an abomination against everything sacred."*

I leaned in, drawn in despite the warning bells screaming in my head, the frantic thudding of my pulse a frantic counterpoint to the crackling fire. The knot in my stomach tightened into a fist of pure terror. This wasn't just apprehension; this was primal fear, a gut-wrenching certainty that I was playing with forces far beyond my comprehension. His words, thick with unspoken horrors, hung heavy in the air, suffocating me. The taste of ash and fear filled my mouth. I'd stumbled into something ancient, something evil...and I had no idea how to escape.

His words, each syllable a meticulously crafted shard of ice, pierced me. The glacial chill wasn't a trickle; it was a torrent, a frozen river surging through my veins, freezing my blood in its icy grip. His answer, a polished lie shimmering with the deceptive gleam of a serpent's scale, lacked the incandescent fury that usually burned in his eyes, a firestorm that had always captivated me, enslaved me. Now, only the suffocating black hole of his deceit remained, a void deeper and colder than the abyss itself, sucking the very air from my lungs. The metallic tang of fear wasn't just a taste; it was a corrosive acid, burning its way down my throat, mingling with the bile of betrayal, the bitter ashes of a love consumed by treachery.

His cologne, once a comforting, earthy musk that spoke of nights and stolen kisses, now reeked of death, a cloying shroud clinging to the air, thick and suffocating, a poisonous miasma clinging to the memory of what we were. The ghost of his touch lingered, a phantom limb of agony, a stark reminder of the man he used to be, a man I could never reclaim from the icy clutches of this devastating betrayal. His gaze, once molten gold, now held the chilling gleam of a predator, calculating, devoid of warmth. This was not the man I loved; this was a stranger in familiar clothing, a master of disguise, and his performance was flawless, utterly terrifying.

His voice, a practiced baritone, resonated with a chilling detachment, each syllable a carefully placed stone in a wall designed to keep me out. The rehearsed cadence, the subtly forced inflection—it grated on my nerves, a discordant symphony playing against the frantic drumbeat of my heart. This wasn't the man I knew, the man whose soul I believed I'd glimpsed, the man whose laughter had once echoed with the thunder of a summer storm. This was a stranger, a meticulously crafted imitation, wearing his skin like a borrowed mask. And the unsettling truth, the chilling realization that clawed at my mind, was this: I had no idea who he truly was. The wrongness of it all, a suffocating pressure in my chest, threatened to crack me open.

"Unacceptable?" I spat the word a venomous shard in the silence. My voice, a raw rasp, betrayed the icy fury clawing at my throat. You were one of them. The confession hung between us, thick and suffocating like the stench of burnt flesh that still clung to my nostrils, a phantom smell from the hellscape I'd witnessed. 'Unacceptable'? The word tasted like ash and bile in my mouth, a pathetic whimper against the symphony of screams that echoed in my skull. My stomach roiled, not just with nausea, but with a primal, burning rage that threatened to consume me. The images weren't just seared into my memory; they were branded onto my soul, each detail a searing brand, a grotesque tapestry woven from the threads of their depravity, the glint of steel, the stifled cries, the chilling indifference in their eyes. I felt the cold sweat slicking my palms, the tremor in my hands a physical manifestation of the horror that threatened to unravel me. You, you, a viper in human skin, dared to pronounce such a flimsy judgment on the abyss you helped create?

His jaw, a granite cliff against the storm of their accusations, didn't twitch. The air hung thick with the stench of betrayal, the metallic tang of blood still clinging to the memory of his deeds. *"I have seen the error,"* he rasped, each syllable a drop of venom in the suffocating silence. His eyes, twin chips of obsidian, burned into them, unwavering, unflinching. The taste of ash and regret coated his tongue, a bitter counterpoint to the icy certainty in his voice. *"I have felt the true depravity of their cause, the chilling emptiness at its core, the putrid stench of its hypocrisy. The icy grip of fear in the hearts of those they claimed to save."* He paused, the silence a physical weight, before adding, with a chilling calmness that sent a fresh wave of dread through the room, *"My past, a tapestry woven with shadows, does not, cannot, diminish the fire of my redemption."*

His words, precise and cold as surgical steel, sliced through the air, yet left me ravenous for something more, something real. The scent of lilies, usually so calming, turned acrid in my nostrils, a bitter counterpoint to the carefully constructed calm in his eyes. I yearned for a tremor of guilt, a crack in the icy façade, a single tear to betray the monster I sensed lurking beneath. But there was nothing. Only the polished surface reflected my desperate hope like a mocking mirror.

His confession dripped from his lips, a casual boast, the nonchalant recounting of a prized kill. But the hunt he described wasn't of deer; it was a life's work sculpted from the blackest obsidian, a macabre masterpiece embroidered with the screams of his victims. The taste of ash wasn't just in my mouth; it choked me, a bitter grit clinging to the back of my throat, mirroring the cinders of his soul. Crimson wasn't merely a stain; it was a living tapestry woven into the very fabric of his being, a horrifying fresco seared onto my retinas, the stench of coppery blood thick enough to gag on. His touch, even across the room, felt like ice-cold steel, the chilling weight of his past pressing down with the force of a collapsing tomb. How could I, a woman who prized mercy above all, possibly share a breath, a moment, with this predator? This thing, whose charisma was merely a gilded cage surrounding a savage heart, whose every smile was a razor's edge, whose very presence exuded the nauseating stench of death itself? The monster was charming, undeniably so, but the rot at his core pulsed beneath the polished veneer; I saw it, I smelled it, I tasted the horrifying truth in every word, every glance, every breath he stole.

The weight of it wasn't just a blanket; it was a crushing tomb, burying me beneath the cold, hard earth of his undeniable atrocities. The phantom touch of her blood spilled on the stones of his past, felt like ice against my skin. My own heart, a trapped bird beating against its cage, screamed the question: Was forgiveness even possible? Could I, would I, ever truly look past the horrors he had inflicted, the lives he had extinguished, the darkness that clung to him like a second skin? The answer, a chilling whisper in the echoing chambers of my soul, eluded me.

The air hung thick and acrid, a miasma of unspoken fury clinging to the silence that stretched between them like a taut wire. Each day was a slow, agonizing crawl across a landscape of shattered trust, the silence punctuated only by the scrape of a chair, the brittle snap of a twig underfoot, sounds magnified a thousandfold in the oppressive stillness. Her eyes, usually pools of molten gold, were now chips of glacial ice, reflecting the cold dawn light that painted the room in shades of betrayal. His touch, once a brand, a searing pleasure, was now a phantom limb, the memory of its heat a cruel mockery of the icy chasm that separated them.

The scent of jasmine, their perfume of stolen moments, now reeked of deceit, each delicate bloom a sharp, accusing finger. Beneath the veneer of polite civility, a war raged, a silent, brutal battle waged with barely concealed threats, the weight of unspoken accusations pressing down like a physical force, crushing the last vestiges of their fragile truce. The raw, animalistic hunger that had once sparked between them was now a festering wound, a constant, throbbing reminder of the precarious balance, the volatile power, and the catastrophic failure of their dangerous game.

The air thickened, a miasma of suspicion clinging to him like cheap perfume. I dissected him, a vivisection of subtle movements: the almost imperceptible jerk of his left eyelid, the way his Adam's apple bobbed a fraction too high with each carefully chosen word. The metallic tang of blood, my own, a taste of fear, filled my mouth as I replayed his every utterance. His past, once a tapestry woven with intriguing threads, now unravelled before me, revealing the rotten core beneath. Each *"kind"* gesture was a viper's strike, venom seeping into my trust; every syllable was a poisoned dart aimed at my heart. His voice, a silken caress before, now grated against my raw nerves, a discordant violin screeching a symphony of deceit.

The Covenant's secrets, once a beacon guiding me through the treacherous darkness, now felt like a spider's silk, impossibly intricate and deadly. I could almost feel the strands wrapping around me, tightening, suffocating. The chill wasn't just a creeping dread; it was an icy hand gripping my soul, squeezing the life from me. He wasn't just playing me; he was conducting a macabre orchestra, and I, the unwitting soloist, was playing my final, desperate movement. My mind screamed, a cacophony of betrayal and terror. I was trapped. And I knew, with chilling certainty, the game was far from over.

A cold sweat slicked my palms as the gnawing unease, a viper coiled in my gut, propelled me. The whispers of the Whispering Wind, once a comforting murmur, now grated like nails on a chalkboard, each breath a ragged rasp fueled by the chilling certainty of betrayal. The air itself felt thick with suspicion, a miasma clinging to the shadowed corners of our clandestine gatherings, the scent of fear, sharp and metallic, a constant companion. Their secrecy, a suffocating blanket woven from lies and half-truths, mirrored the Obsidian Covenant's impenetrable darkness. Every word tasted like ash in my mouth; each carefully chosen syllable was a gamble, a potential death knell.

My investigation became an obsession, a feverish plunge into the Covenant's murky depths, driven by a thirst for the truth that clawed at my throat. I unearthed his past connections, whispers, rumours, and half-remembered faces in dimly lit taverns, each encountering a heart-stopping risk. The taste of cheap wine and the reek of stale tobacco clung to the information I gleaned, a bitter reminder of the danger. Each clandestine meeting hammered a frantic rhythm against my ribs; the press of bodies, the rasp of hushed voices, the ever-present chill of potential discovery, a knife twisting in my gut. My eyes burned with exhaustion, my muscles coiled tight with fear, each shadow a potential assassin, each glance a potential betrayal.

The taste of their polished lies was ash and bile in my mouth, a serpent's venom coiling around my tongue. Each carefully chosen word, a slick caress against my ears, felt like a spider's leg skittering across my skin. I didn't want their gilded half-truths; I needed the raw, bleeding truth, the kind that would claw at my throat, the kind that smelled of decay and tasted of blood. The Whispering Wind, with its façade of serene beauty, a suffocating perfume of lilies masking the stench of its rotten core, was a festering wound upon the world. Its lies had poisoned my soul, a creeping paralysis that chilled me to the bone, and the only cure was the scalding fire of the truth. I would tear through the carefully constructed illusion, brick by agonizing brick, I would rip the silken mask from its face, even if it meant shattering the very foundations of reality, even if it meant drowning in the torrent of its dark secrets. I would have the truth, and it would be mine, even if it killed me.

The air in the study hung thick with the scent of stale coffee and the brittle parchment of ancient documents. My lamp cast long, skeletal shadows across the papers, each one a potential clue in Caspian's elaborate game. Then, it hit me, a searing flash of insight, hot and sharp as a brand. A discrepancy, microscopic in size, yet titanic in its implications. In his meticulously crafted tale of escape from the Covenant's iron grip, a single detail, a seemingly insignificant shift in location, screamed a lie. The taste of bile rose in my throat; a cold dread, slick and greasy, coated my tongue.

Caspian, that viper, so charming, so believable, his carefully constructed facade threatened to shatter. The subtle shift, a street, a building, easily overlooked by the casual observer, yet a chasm of deception to a mind like mine, honed by years spent deciphering the whispers between lines. My fingers, slick with sweat, traced the offending words. The feel of the rough paper, almost a physical manifestation of the shattering truth, sent shivers down my spine. This wasn't just an error; this was a deliberate omission, a calculated deception designed to mask the horror he'd truly experienced, or, God forbid, perpetrated. The smug certainty of his escape narrative curdled into a venomous bitterness in my gut. I had him.

The silken threads of her carefully constructed life, once so vibrant, now snapped with the sickening crackle of a thousand breaking bones. A bitter perfume, the scent of decay and crushed lilies filled the air, a tangible manifestation of her unravelling. The taste of ash coated her tongue, a grim premonition of the exquisite agony to come. It wouldn't be a mere unravelling; it would be a meticulously orchestrated symphony of ruin, each discordant note a deliberate strike against her very soul, a testament to her ruthless ambition and the venomous betrayals she'd so expertly woven. She savoured the anticipation, a perverse delight blooming in the shadowed corners of her heart, as the world around her, once so meticulously controlled, descended into glorious, chaotic splendour.

His story, so eloquently recounted, had painted a picture of a desperate escape, but this small detail cast a shadow of doubt, suggesting a more deliberate, perhaps even orchestrated departure. The realization sent a cold wave of fear washing over me. My heart hammered against my ribs. Had he been lying all along? I felt a sickening twist in my gut. Was his betrayal not a thing of the past, but a calculated maneuver in the present, designed to manipulate me? The thought chilled me to the bone. I questioned everything I thought I knew. Every word, every gesture he'd made, now seemed suspect, tainted by this new, horrifying possibility.

The question clawed at me, a venomous serpent coiled in my gut poisoning the already fragile air between us. His sleeping form, a gilded statue bathed in the cruel moonlight, mocked my torment, a stark reminder of the chasm that lay between us. That blond hair, usually a beacon of sun-kissed warmth, now felt like a silken shroud draped over a secret too heavy to bear. As the moonlight streamed through the window it became a treacherous spotlight revealing the sharp angles of his jaw and the jagged scar—a crimson brand across his brow—a mark of some past violence that mirrored the chaos and violence tearing through my soul. He breathed a shallow, almost imperceptible sigh, his peace a vile insult to the turmoil raging within me, a stark contrast to the tempest that brewed in my heart. The deception hung in the air like a noxious fog, a bitter metallic tang on my tongue that coated every thought and tainted every memory. It was as if the very essence of our relationship had warped into something unrecognizable, a fragile facade that could shatter at the slightest touch. I felt the weight of my choices crashing down on me and the question loomed larger and darker as the night deepened, demanding an answer that I was terrified to confront.

My heart hammered against my ribs, a frantic bird trapped in a cage of bone. A suffocating dread, cold as grave dirt, squeezed the air from my lungs, leaving me gasping for breath. The sweat-slicked my skin, a clammy, chilling film. Fool, I hissed internally, the self-loathing a burning acid in my veins. This wasn't some naïve misunderstanding; it was a calculated betrayal, a deliberate wound inflicted by a hand I'd once trusted implicitly. The weight of it crushed me, a mountain of despair pressing down on my chest, threatening to shatter my very being. How could I breathe, how could I live, shrouded in this suffocating uncertainty? The truth, a phantom limb, throbbed with a desperate, agonizing need.

Dawn bled a sickly yellow through the blinds, illuminating the dust motes dancing in the suffocating air. My heart, a trapped bird, beat a frantic tattoo against my ribs. His face, usually a mask of carefully cultivated charm, was pale, almost translucent, the shadows in his eyes betraying a flicker of something... fear? Or was it merely practiced indifference? The unspoken accusation hung between us, thick and acrid, a miasma brewed from years of shared secrets, of carefully constructed lies now crumbling to dust. The taste of bile rose in my throat; the sweat-slicked my palms, cold and clammy.

He didn't deny it. The lie, a viper coiled in his heart, slithered out in a carefully chosen cascade of words. Each syllable, a poisoned dart, found its mark. This wasn't just a discrepancy; it was a meticulously crafted tapestry of deception, a whole new layer of his carefully curated persona, unveiled with the chilling grace of a predator. The scent of his expensive cologne, usually so comforting, now felt like a suffocating shroud. A glacial dread, sharp and precise as shattered ice, pierced me to the core. The words burrowed into me, each one a fresh wound, bleeding into the festering chasm of betrayal. His infuriating calm, a polished veneer over a core of ruthless calculation, only fueled the inferno of rage that threatened to consume me. My teeth ground together, the pressure a physical manifestation of my suppressed fury. I wanted to shatter the fragile peace of the room, to unleash the storm that raged within, but instead, I clamped down, forcing myself to remain a statue, to absorb the full, sickening weight of his treachery. The silence that followed felt heavier than any scream.

My jaw clenched, a vice of agony mirroring the crushing weight in my chest. His confession wasn't an apology; it was a venomous spit, a cold, calculated evisceration. The metallic tang of blood filled my mouth, a phantom taste of the wounds he'd inflicted. I listened, each syllable a razor blade slicing through my gut, the knot tightening until it felt like a fist squeezing my heart. He detailed his manipulations, a chilling litany of subtle, insidious betrayals, each one a calculated strike, precise as a surgeon's scalpel. He spoke of them as if describing a masterpiece, a grand strategy unfolding across a chessboard littered with the shattered remnants of lives. He savoured the words, a cruel artist painting a self-portrait in shades of moral bankruptcy; a ruthless, breathtaking dance of loyalty and betrayal, a dizzying blur of grey in his self-serving, morally bankrupt universe. He'd used me, a pawn in his twisted game, leveraging my rage, twisting my thirst for vengeance into the very fuel that drove his ambition. The sickening realization slammed into me like a physical blow, a gut-wrenching betrayal layered upon the festering wounds of countless others. His words weren't just a confession; they were a grotesque unveiling, revealing the chilling truth: he was a predator, a sociopathic maestro of manipulation, his only compass a ruthless pursuit of self-preservation. My pain? My suffering? Irrelevant. Mere collateral damage in his horrifying, beautiful game of survival.

His words, a viper's hiss laced with ice, struck me not just as betrayal, but as a calculated evisceration, a surgical incision into the very core of my trust. The venom wasn't just a burning cold; it was a creeping paralysis, a chilling frost that seized my breath and turned my blood into glacial shards. The blow wasn't just to my gut; it shattered my ribs, splintered my soul, left me gasping for air, the taste of ash and iron blooming on my tongue. But the worst part wasn't the pain, the agony that threatened to consume me. It was the knowledge that I had allowed this to happen. I, who prided myself on my unwavering loyalty, my unshakeable moral compass, had been blind, naïve, a fool.

He'd hinted at it before, subtle whispers of discontent, but I'd dismissed them, blinded by my own need to believe in him, in us. Now, the truth clawed at me, a beast I'd kept caged with wishful thinking. My belief in justice, in the inherent goodness of people, a bedrock of my existence, crumbled under the weight of his treachery. The rage, hot, warred with a chilling sense of responsibility. Had I been too trusting? Too soft? Has my compassion become a weapon used against me?

He wanted something from me, I knew it. Something I swore I would never give. Something that violated everything I stood for. But the alternative...the thought of allowing him to inflict further damage, to hurt others because of my stubborn refusal, was unbearable. The image of his satisfaction, the smug triumph in his eyes, haunted me, twisting the knife already plunged deep within. The choice was a poisoned chalice: comply and betray every principle I held dear, or refuse and watch the suffering of innocent people.

My hands trembled uncontrollably, each finger quivering as if trying to escape the weight of the moment. My breath hitched painfully in my throat a frantic gasp that echoed the turmoil brewing inside me. This wasn't just a betrayal; it was a test—a dark and terrible trial designed to break me to expose the very fragility of my spirit. And in this harrowing moment—gasping for breath tasting the acrid bitterness of ash and the metallic tang of iron—I knew with a sickening certainty that I was failing. I felt as though I was teetering on the edge of a precipice peering into an abyss that threatened to swallow me whole. I was about to make a choice I would regret for the rest of my life: a decision that would carve itself into the fabric of my being, staining my soul with darkness as profound as the icy venom that had already taken root within my heart. This was not merely a moment of weakness; it was a pivotal juncture that would shape my destiny and define who I would become. Each heartbeat echoed the weight of my impending choice and as panic surged through me I realized that the path ahead was fraught with peril. Would I succumb to despair allowing the shadows to claim me or would I find the strength to fight against the tide of darkness threatening to engulf my very soul?

But in the maelstrom of rage, a nauseating clarity bloomed, a sickening sweetness of understanding. The sickening lurch in my stomach wasn't just a physical reaction; it was the earth cracking open beneath my feet, revealing the abyss of my naivete. He wasn't merely dangerous; he was a predator cloaked in silk, a master puppeteer pulling strings I hadn't even known existed. His complexity wasn't just intriguing; it was a terrifying symphony of brilliance and depravity, a mesmerizing dance on the precipice of chaos.

The audacity, the sheer, breathtaking audacity of his actions... it was a poisoned chalice, the bitter draught both horrifying and intoxicating. The horror clawed at my throat, a physical constriction, while a perverse fascination, a morbid curiosity, coiled around my heart, tightening its grip with each ragged breath. Against every fibre of my being, against the screaming protest of my shattered trust, I found myself inexorably drawn to the viper's nest, to the heart of the storm that was him. I was enthralled, terrified, and utterly, hopelessly consumed.

The revelation slammed into me, a physical blow shattering the already precarious trust. The air itself went cold, leaving behind a gaping maw of distrust where the warmth of intimacy had bloomed. I felt it, a sickening rending, like bone cracking, spreading through the meticulously crafted edifice of our relationship. The scent of betrayal, sharp and acrid, filled my nostrils as the ground dissolved beneath my feet. But even as the dust of our shattered world choked me, a fierce, exhilarating current surged through my veins. This wasn't an ending; it was a cataclysmic birth, a birth screaming with the raw power of a paradigm shift. The scales weren't merely tipped; they were pulverized, the roles inverted with brutal finality.

Caspian, his true nature a viper coiled in my heart, had become something far more than a simple adversary. His ruthlessness, a chilling masterpiece of calculated cruelty, was a grotesque reflection of my burgeoning ambition. He was a twisted mirror, a foe and, in some perverse, terrifying alliance, my key. The danger wasn't some abstract notion; it pressed against me, a tangible weight, a suffocating pressure against my chest. I could taste the metallic tang of fear, but the heady rush of potential dominance, of orchestrating his downfall, ignited a fire in my belly, scorching away any lingering doubt.

The game, I realized with a predatory clarity, had only just begun. And I, forever altered by his treachery, was not merely ready to play, I was ravenous.

The wind howled a mournful dirge across the desolate plains, mirroring the tempest raging within me. The landscape was as barren as my soul felt, a stark expanse of grey rock and withered scrub, the sky a bruised purple mirroring the darkness that clung to me like a shroud. I had admitted my manipulations, my calculated betrayals, and laid bare the cold, hard truth of my self-serving nature. My eyes blazed with a dangerous mixture of anger and something akin to…fascination, as I watched him. Then, I retreated into a simmering silence, leaving him to grapple alone with the consequences of his confession, the weight of it pressing down on him as heavily as the oppressive sky pressed down on the land.

The remorse wasn't a tidal wave, crashing over me and leaving wreckage in its wake. It was a subtle tremor, a barely perceptible shift in the tectonic plates of my carefully constructed self. Regret? I'd scoffed at the notion for years. My life, a brutal tapestry woven from deceit and the hard-won threads of survival, had taught me that sentimentality was a weakness, a crippling vulnerability I couldn't allow myself. Yet, as I watched the firelight paint his eyes with fleeting, shifting hues, embers glowing in the depths of their dark pools, a flicker ignited within me. It wasn't simply disappointment; it was something colder, sharper, more akin to… a desolate understanding. The carefully constructed walls of my cynicism, brick by agonizing brick, seemed to crumble under the weight of this unexpected emotion, leaving me exposed to a raw and unfamiliar landscape of the heart.

It wasn't the disappointment of a betrayed lover; I was not and never would be, that to him. It was my disappointment, the bitter taste of a master strategist witnessing a crucial element in my plan faltering. I had calculated every move, every betrayal, every carefully constructed lie. He'd manipulated me, using my thirst for revenge, my burning hatred for the Obsidian Covenant, as a tool in his own game of survival. But he hadn't accounted for my resilience, my unexpected capacity for both ruthless pragmatism and a surprising depth of emotion. I felt the sting of his failure, a personal affront to my meticulously crafted scheme. It was my victory that slipped through his fingers, and the knowledge of that near triumph only intensified the frustration.

My role, as he saw it, was simple: a pawn in his game against the Obsidian Covenant. He'd use me to infiltrate them, gain their confidence, then betray them from the inside. He'd planned for risks, of course, factored them into his cold calculations. Self-preservation was his only real concern. But he hadn't accounted for me. I wasn't a predictable tool; I was fiercely independent, and my suspicions grew with every passing day. My relentless digging, my pursuit of the truth, threatened to unravel everything he'd so carefully constructed. I felt the weight of his plan pressing down on me, a suffocating burden. And I knew, with a chilling certainty, that I couldn't let him succeed.

The forced confession was a performance, a meticulously orchestrated display. I watched him, his hand trembling slightly as he peeled back the layers of his elaborate deceit, revealing the festering corruption beneath. It wasn't the gnawing of guilt that fueled his actions, not remorse, I knew that with a chilling certainty. This was a calculated move, born of stark necessity. He needed to regain the upper hand, to subtly, yet forcefully, reposition himself in our power dynamic, to ensure my continued usefulness. More than usefulness, though. Now that I possessed the truth, I had become a far more dangerous asset, a volatile element he desperately needed to manage. His eyes, glittering with a fear that even his carefully constructed lies couldn't entirely mask, betrayed the fragile foundation of his control. The tremor in his voice, a barely perceptible crack in his carefully crafted facade, spoke volumes more than his words ever could. He was playing a desperate game, and the stakes, for both of us, had just risen exponentially.

The silence stretched between us, thick and heavy, a suffocating weight pressing down. I felt it, the unspoken accusations, the simmering threat of violence hanging in the air like a palpable thing. I knew he knew I was capable of killing him. I saw the fear tighten his chest, and a strange, perverse thrill, a sliver of dark satisfaction, laced through my apprehension. My capacity for violence... it terrified him, yes, but a part of me saw the seduction in that fear too. It was a power I felt keenly, a raw, dangerous energy that hummed beneath my skin.

The moral dilemma gnawing at me wasn't about loyalty to him; it was about my survival. I needed him. I needed his strength, his unwavering hatred for the Covenant, and his ability to infiltrate their ranks. Betraying me now would be suicidal for him. Not only would he lose a powerful ally, but he'd also lose the leverage he needed to navigate the treacherous currents of his clandestine world. I knew it. I felt it in the way he hesitated, in the tremor of his hand when he spoke my name. The fear in his eyes was a mirror of my own. We were bound together, each dependent on the other, a precarious balance teetering on the edge of a knife.

A biting wind sharp as shattered glass lashed at him with relentless ferocity whipping his blond hair into a frenzied halo around a face etched with weariness and lined with the shadows of countless sleepless nights. He stood there a solitary figure against the backdrop of a desolate expanse, a monochrome canvas of grey rock and wind-ravaged earth stretching endlessly to a horizon as bleak as his own troubled soul. Each gust of wind felt like a reminder of the battles he had fought both outside and within the cold air biting at his skin like the betrayals he had endured. The Whispering Wind once his comrades in arms were now mere phantoms in his mind, their voices reduced to eerie echoes that haunted his thoughts. Their whispered betrayals and ruthless climb for power reverberated in the howling gale an unending symphony of regret and treachery that clawed at his sanity.

As he gazed into the distance he recalled the Obsidian Covenant, a group whose very name struck fear into the hearts of those who knew of their cold ambition. Their obsidian eyes gleamed with a chilling intensity reflecting the darkness that resided not just within them but also within himself. The thought of their atrocities pressed down on him like a heavy shroud, a burden more suffocating than any physical chain could ever be. He had witnessed horrors that would turn the strongest stomach and had committed acts that would haunt him for the rest of his days. Each moment of violence each split-second decision made in the heat of conflict left a searing brand upon his conscience that refused to fade.

In those moments of reflection, he found himself grappling with the concepts of right and wrong—those once-clear distinctions that now seemed like childish concepts afforded to those who had never walked the razor's edge of survival. For him, the line dividing good from evil had become a phantom, a shimmering mirage dancing just out of reach in the scorching desert of his existence. The only compass guiding him was self-preservation, a primal instinct that overshadowed any moral compass he might have once possessed.

The world around him was unforgiving a brutal reminder that in this harsh reality, survival was the only true morality. Each day was a battle not just against external forces but against the relentless tide of doubt and guilt that threatened to engulf him. He was a soldier yes but more than that he was a survivor forged in the crucible of conflict and shaped by the flames of betrayal. He could not afford the luxury of remorse; it would only serve to weigh him down further dragging him into the abyss he so desperately sought to escape.

With a deep breath, he steeled himself against the biting wind. He would not let his past define him. The horizon stretched before him a cold and empty promise but within that emptiness lay the potential for new beginnings for forging a path that while fraught with peril might also lead to redemption. The journey ahead would not be easy but it was a journey he had to undertake if only to reclaim the fragments of his shattered soul.

I tasted betrayal and it felt bitter and sharp like metal stuck to the top of my mouth. It matched the emptiness I felt inside. Loyalty means sticking by someone or something no matter what. I believe in being loyal to my friends and family. When I promise to support them I really mean it. I think being loyal helps build strong relationships and shows that I care about the people in my life. It's important to stand by them in good times and bad and to never give up on them. I always thought of it as a silly story, a secret that I never believed in. I've laughed at it since I can remember but that memory is filled with the terrible smell of being left behind. I only felt the intense hunger to survive a strong and rough instinct that was as sharp as a snake's fang. I built my life from the tough cold ground showing how determined I am to succeed. I felt like a wildfire inside with my eyes glowing with a heat that seemed to burn the air around me. I felt a strong desire for revenge that surged within me like a powerful energy pushing against my own walls of doubt and skepticism. My touch wasn't soft or weak at all. I felt a strong shake like an earthquake that broke apart everything I had carefully built. It revealed the scared and fragile part of me that I usually kept hidden deep inside. I felt a mix of fear and excitement as my carefully built walls started to break down. This feeling of being vulnerable was new to me like tasting blood and ash in my mouth. It was so strange that I thought it might completely tear me apart.

The wind made a sad loud sound matching the storm of feelings he was experiencing inside. He had chosen his way a long time ago, a dangerous route built on lies and cleverness. Self-preservation, a harsh and unforgiving goal, had been his main focus. But now a doubt as sharp as broken glass cut through his carefully built calm. Could he really control me, a woman with a strong spirit that could burn through even the toughest defenses? Could he manage my emotions and handle my unpredictable nature without getting caught up in my chaos and being overwhelmed by the fire he tried to manage? He worried that the answer was very uncertain, just one wrong move away from disappearing completely.

He shifted his weight causing the rough ground to shake and send a jolt up my back. This feeling was a harsh contrast to the smooth comfort of my usual black seat. Azazel created in the core of a fading star and shaped by the voices of the cursed sensed a shaking. This was not a physical tremor but a disturbance deep within his spirit. This small feeling of doubt, this big change you created in his carefully built defenses was something terrible. The smell of his fear was strong and sharp, making my nose tingle. It tasted bitter like burnt ash in my mouth. I noticed a small crack in the strong walls of his personality. This weakness glowed with a strange unhealthy light and it seemed ready to break the calm and cool image he had built around himself. "It wasn't only disturbing; it was a breach." "What is this... humanity?" It was a painful spot in the complete darkness, a strange twist on the strength I desired. Still seeing it sparked a flame inside me, a strong curiosity that overshadowed my long-held dislike.

His gaze, a brand, seared my profile, the firelight carving shadows deep enough to swallow a soul. The heat wasn't just on my face; it was a visceral furnace, mirroring the inferno of rage that gnawed at my insides, tasting of ash and bitter triumph. I saw it then, a feral gleam in my own eyes, a predatory excitement that chilled me to the bone, colder than the steel blade I'd dreamt of holding against his throat. He'd underestimated me, the fool, and the satisfaction was a venomous sweetness, a dark bloom in the pit of my stomach. That underestimation? It wasn't a mistake; it was an invitation. He'd unwittingly unleashed something primal, something far more terrifying, far more intoxicating, than any danger I'd ever known. His games of manipulation? Pathetic. The rules, my dear, had been rewritten in blood. The power shift wasn't subtle; it was a seismic tremor, ripping through the earth beneath our feet. This wasn't just a game anymore; it was a war, and I, my love, was about to unleash hell.

CHAPTER

EIGHT

Vengeance Unleashed

The air crackled, a venomous hiss in the suffocating silence, a taut wire humming with the potential for catastrophic snapping. Caspian, his composure a meticulously crafted mask barely concealing the tremor in his jaw, felt the prickle of unease blooms into a full blown, icy terror. I tasted it too, the metallic tang of blood, not physical, but the coppery reek of impending carnage, thick and cloying in my mouth, coating my tongue like a perverse sacrament. My gut churned, a frozen knot of dread radiating outward, chilling me to the bone. My silence wasn't merely dangerous; it was a predator stalking him, a coiled viper poised to strike. He thought he held the power, the anticipation of a visible tremor in his rigidly controlled posture. Fool.

This wasn't some petty game; this was a symphony of destruction composed in the chambers of my heart, each note a meticulously planned act of violence. My thoughts weren't racing; they were a precision guided missile, locked onto its target. The possibilities weren't just lethal; they were exquisite, a breathtaking tapestry woven from pain and retribution. The scent of ozone, the smell of electricity just before the storm breaks, filled the space between us, a tangible manifestation of the raw power I held, the power I was about to unleash. My smile widened, slow and deliberate, a predatory grin revealing teeth sharpened by years of simmering rage. He was about to learn what true silence meant, the deafening silence of oblivion.

From the suffocating darkness, he crawled. Malkor. The very name tasted like ash and blood on Caspian's tongue, a bitter premonition of the carnage to come. No mere hulking behemoth, he was a monument to depravity, a grotesque parody of power sculpted from the nightmare itself. His obsidian skin, polished to a mirror sheen that reflected the flickering torch light in fragmented, malevolent gleams, seemed to drink the very light from the air. The stench of Sulfur and decay, thick and cloying, rolled off him in waves, a physical manifestation of his unholy essence.

His eyes, burning coals of hate that bored into Caspian's soul, held the cold fire of a thousand dying stars. They weren't just looking; they were consuming, stripping away his defences, leaving him raw and vulnerable. Strapped to his back, two obsidian blades, wickedly curved and pulsing with dark energy that hummed like a thousand tormented souls, promised a death both swift and excruciating. The air itself crackled with the anticipation of their first taste of flesh.

Malkor's smirk wasn't just cruel; it was a deliberate, agonizing caress of contempt, a silent testament to his utter dominance. It spoke volumes, of massacres witnessed, of souls crushed beneath his heel, of power so absolute it bordered on cosmic indifference. Caspian, hardened by years of brutal warfare, felt a chill crawl down his spine, a primal fear that transcended mere physical threat. This wasn't just a battle; it was an intrusion into the very fabric of reality, a confrontation with an evil so profound it threatened to unravel the world itself. The weight of Malkor's presence pressed down, a suffocating blanket of dread woven from the shadows and the whispers of the damned. Caspian knew, with a certainty that chilled him to the bone, that this fight would define his legacy, or end it.

"Well, well," Malkor's voice, a volcanic tremor that rattled my teeth and tasted of ash and blood filled the cavern. The air itself seemed to crackle with the raw, feral energy radiating from him. A shiver, icy and sharp as shattered glass, stabbed down my spine. "The Whispering Wind's pathetic little plaything dares to show its face." His gaze, a predatory sun burning through the gloom, sliced from Caspian, his face a mask of grim determination, to me, stripping away my defences with its malevolent intensity. The stench of his rank breath, a miasma of decay

and power, washed over me, choking the air from my lungs. My heart hammered a frantic tattoo against my ribs, a drumbeat of pure terror. *"And he brings...a toy."*

The hilt of my sword bit into my palm, the cold steel a meagre comfort against the rising tide of dread. My knuckles, bone white against the darkening metal, were slick with a sweat that tasted like fear itself. His words hung in the air, thick and poisonous, each syllable a venomous barb aimed directly at my soul. Caspian's hand, calloused and strong, rested lightly on mine; a silent promise, a desperate hope in the face of unimaginable horror. This wasn't a game; it was a ritual sacrifice, and Malkor was the high priest of annihilation.

Caspian's hand, a predator poised, tightened fractionally on the dagger's hilt. The obsidian gleam of the blade, cold against his skin, was a stark contrast to the sweat slicking my palms, a betrayal of the icy calm he radiated. His eyes, twin chips of glacial ice, locked with Malkor's, betraying nothing. But Malkor, the brute, saw me. He sensed the tempest brewing within me, the raw fury that tasted like bile and scorched my throat.

My knuckles bone white against the crimson stain blossoming beneath my fingernails screamed in silent protest, a vivid reminder of the violence I had just unleashed. The metallic tang of blood, a grim offering to the simmering rage coursing through my veins, filled my mouth with a bitter taste that only fueled my growing fury. My vision narrowed, honing in on Malkor's sneering face, a grotesque parody of composure that twisted my insides. His smug expression was a challenge, a taunt that ignited an even deeper fire within me. Each ragged breath felt like fire in my lungs, the heat burning its way to my throat making it difficult to contain the primal instinct to lash out further. The world around me faded leaving only the pulsating rhythm of my heart and the growing desire for retribution. I could feel the weight of the moment pressing down on me a heavy shroud of tension as I prepared to confront the monster before me. In that instant, I was both alive and consumed teetering on the edge of fury and resolve.

The heat radiating from me was palpable, an inferno threatening to erupt and engulf us all. My body trembled, not from fear, but from the sheer, unadulterated desire to obliterate him. To feel the satisfying crunch of bone beneath my fist. I fought the urge to unleash the storm, the primal scream trapped in my chest threatened to tear me apart. Caspian's stillness was a mask, a performance. Mine was a cage, built of iron will and sheer, terrifying self-control. The muscles in my jaw locked tight enough to shatter, throbbed with the agony of restraint. The silence stretched, thick and suffocating, a volatile mix of impending violence and barely contained chaos.

The air, thick with the scent of incense and ozone, crackled with unspoken threats. My voice, a honed obsidian blade itself, sliced through the silence. *"I'm here for the Obsidian Grimoire,"* I said, each syllable a deliberate drop of venom. The words hung heavy, tasting of ash and old magic. My eyes, twin chips of glacial ice, locked onto theirs. *"And you,"* I hissed, the word a venomous whisper that slithered into the marrow of their bones, *"are in our fucking way."* The subtle tremor in my hand, barely perceptible beneath the weight of the ancient dagger at my hip, betrayed the barely contained fury simmering beneath my controlled exterior. A lifetime of betrayal and bloodshed pulsed in my veins, a dark tide threatening to overwhelm the fragile calm I projected. This wasn't just about a book; it was about survival, about reclaiming what was rightfully mine, even if it meant wading through rivers of blood to get it.

Malkor's laughter clawed at the air, a rasping, obsidian sound that scraped against Caspian's teeth and chilled him to the bone. The wind, a mournful howl echoing Malkor's mirth, whipped icy tendrils around them, carrying the scent of frozen earth and something else… something acrid and metallic, like blood newly spilled on rusted iron. *"The Grimoire?"* Malkor sneered his eyes, twin chips of glacial quartz, boring into Caspian. *"Such a pathetically naïve notion. You think you can simply stroll into the heart of our dominion and claim what is rightfully ours?"* His hand, a gnarled claw adorned with rings of tarnished silver, swept across the desolate, bone-strewn landscape. The very ground seemed to shudder beneath his gaze, a tremor that resonated deep within Caspian's chest, mirroring the primal fear that coiled in his gut. *"This blighted land, this very power…it is woven into our very being. It is our birthright. You are but an insect daring to trespass on the throne of a god."*

The battle erupted, a maelstrom of screaming metal and searing heat that choked the very air. My senses overloaded, the stench of burnt flesh and ozone stinging my nostrils, the shriek of tearing steel a discordant symphony against the roar of the flames. I was the eye of that storm, a whirlwind of fury, my heart a frantic drum against my ribs. Each swing of my blade was a prayer and a curse, a desperate invocation of power both terrifying and exhilarating. The fire within me, a malevolent spirit unleashed, roared in answer. It wasn't just fire; it was raw, untamed chaos, a searing torrent that blistered the air, singed my hair, and left the metallic tang of blood on my tongue, my blood, a crimson sacrifice painting the already hellish landscape.

The pain? A fleeting whisper compared to the feral scream of adrenaline ripping through my veins. I moved with a predator's grace, honed by years of shadowed training, each strike a calculated caress of death. The heat, the searing kiss of the inferno, was no longer a threat but a perverse comfort, mirroring the burning rage that consumed me. It was a rage born not just of battle, but of betrayal, of loss, of the ghosts that clawed at my soul, fueling each desperate parry, each desperate thrust. The ground bucked beneath the cataclysmic clash of steel, the very earth shuddering under the weight of my unleashed power, a power dark and ancient. This was no mere fight; it was a primal dance with oblivion, and I would waltz with death itself until only one remained standing. Victory or death. There was no other option. No other choice.

Caspian wasn't fighting; he was dismantling Malkor. The air itself crackled with the anticipation of each precise movement, a whisper of steel, a ghost of motion. The stench of sweat and blood, thick and cloying, clung to him, a brutal perfume of his deadly ballet. His eyes, twin chips of glacial ice, never left Malkor, assessing, calculating. Years spent slithering through the underbelly of the world had honed him to a lethal instrument, every muscle coiled, every sinew singing a deadly song. This wasn't just a dance of death; it was a symphony of attrition, each economical strike a carefully placed note, a rasping whisper against the monstrous bellow of Malkor's power.

The glint of his dagger, a venomous serpent's tongue, blurred into a silver shriek, each thrust aimed not to spill blood, but to drain it, to sap Malkor's strength, to unravel the very fabric of his terrifying might. He knew a direct assault would be suicide, a pathetic moth fluttering against a supernova. No, Malkor's downfall would be slow, agonizing, a meticulously crafted masterpiece of controlled destruction, orchestrated for my intervention. The weight of that responsibility, the cold certainty of my impending strike, pressed down on me with the icy grip of fate. His calculated savagery was a chilling testament to his cunning, a horrifying beauty that both thrilled and terrified me.

Malkor, the obsidian-skinned behemoth, was anything but a fool. My fire, a torrent meant to incinerate, he met with a contemptuous sneer and the brutal, earth-shattering force of his blows. With each swing of his blades, obsidian shards singing a death knell through the air ripped through the very fabric of my defences. The near misses weren't just heat; they were searing brands, branding the memory of his power onto my flesh. The metallic tang of blood filled my mouth, my own, undoubtedly, a bitter counterpoint to the acrid stench of ozone clinging to the air after each parry. Caspian's desperate strikes were deflected with a casual grace that mocked our efforts, his massive frame moving with a fluidity that defied physics, a predator's grace honed by centuries of slaughter. The clang of our blades, a deafening symphony of destruction, resonated deep within my bones, drowning out the roar of my flames, reducing them to pathetic whispers against his monstrous laughter. That laughter, a guttural, echoing roar that vibrated in my very skull, a symphony of pure, unadulterated malice, a terrifying promise of the oblivion he intended to deliver, threatened to shatter my sanity, to tear my soul apart. His eyes, twin pools of molten darkness, gleamed with a savage joy, the hungry delight of a butcher surveying his prize. I was not merely fighting a man; I was facing a force of nature, a demon-given flesh, and his amusement was a chilling prelude to my demise.

The fight was a maelstrom, a brutal ballet of death played out under a sky the colour of a bruised plum. My breath rasped, a ragged sound swallowed by the howling wind that whipped across the cracked earth, tasting of dust and blood, my blood, the coppery tang a searing fire on my tongue. Each of Malkor's blows landed not merely with bone-jarring force, but with the sickening crunch of shattered bone, the raw, visceral impact echoing in my skull. My muscles screamed, not in protest, but in agony, a symphony of tearing fibres and grinding joints, the exhaustion of a leaden shroud suffocating me. I saw it mirrored in Malkor's eyes, a cold, feral triumph reflected in the obsidian gleam of his dust-caked blade, the grim reflection a mockery of my fading strength. The scent of sweat, iron, and the acrid stench of fear filled my nostrils; even the ravaged landscape seemed to pulse with malevolent energy.

Caspian's eyes, usually alight with a reckless spark, were narrowed to slits, two chips of flint in a face carved by years of brutal survival. The urgency wasn't just radiating from him, it was a palpable force, a desperate plea etched into the very lines of his grim, determined features; I could feel the weight of his unspoken words: he must act, or we both die here. And with the chilling certainty of death's icy grip, I knew he was right.

A feral scream ripped from Caspian's throat as he hurled himself at Malkor, a human projectile aimed for the demon's blind side, a hairline fracture in the obsidian fortress of its defences. The air thrummed with the stench of brimstone and the coppery tang of Malkor's blood, a scent Caspian savoured even as the demon's shadow, vast and suffocating, fell upon him. His muscles screamed in protest, every fibre strained to its breaking point, yet he moved like a wraith, a blur of motion too fast for mortal eyes. The demon's downward slash whistled past, a wind of death that singed Caspian's cheek; he felt the heat of it, the raw, terrifying power before he slithered under the follow-up blow, a viper striking into Malkor's exposed flank.

The dagger, blessed by ancient rites and honed to razor sharpness, found its mark. Malkor's roar was a seismic event, a volcanic eruption of pain, shock, and incandescent rage that rattled Caspian's very bones. The ground trembled under the force of it. The demon's eyes, burning pits of hellfire, locked onto Caspian, its gaze searing his soul. But it was enough. A fleeting moment snatched from the jaws of eternity, but enough. Caspian knew, with a certainty that chilled him to the marrow, that this stolen breath was all he had.

Every fibre of my being screamed in defiance as I funnelled the last vestiges of my power, a searing white-hot agony, into a single, annihilating point. My vision tunnelled, the world dissolving into a crimson haze focused solely on Malkor's grotesque visage. The energy throbbed, a monstrous heart beating within me, each pulse a white-hot brand etching itself onto my soul. The air itself shrieked, a cacophony of crackling ozone and the stench of burnt ozone filled my nostrils.

Then, I unleashed it, a raw, incandescent torrent that tore through the suffocating silence, a scream of pure, untamed power.

I watched, breath stolen, as the blast slammed into Malkor, a blinding eruption of light and heat that seared the very fabric of reality. The concussion slammed against my ears, a deafening roar that echoed in the marrow of my bones. The taste of blood, metallic and coppery, filled my mouth as the power ripped from me, leaving me hollowed out, a spent husk. But exhilaration, sharp and raw, pierced the bone-deep weariness. I had done it.

The blast struck Malkor squarely in the obsidian chest, a wave of searing heat that ripped through his hide, the smell of burning Sulfur and scorched flesh assaulting my senses. He staggered his monstrous form momentarily flickering, a grotesque distortion in the ravaged landscape. His power, the chilling aura that had suffocated the very air, faltered, weakened. A tremor of fear, barely perceptible beneath his brutal façade, flickered in his eyes.

Caspian, a viper sensing the slightest crack in his prey's armour, saw the opportunity, a glint of savage triumph in his merciless eyes. With a guttural roar, he plunged his dagger, the honed steel finding its mark with sickening precision. The agonizing shriek that tore from Malkor's throat was a symphony of pain and defeat. The demon king, once a force of unimaginable terror, crumpled to his knees, his body convulsing in a paroxysm of agony, his reign of fear finally and irrevocably broken. The lingering heat of the blast still radiated from his charred remains.

The air hung thick and cloying, tasting of ozone and blood. Not dead, not yet, but broken. My power, the very essence of me, was a spent ember, a flickering flame threatening to snuff out altogether. Each ragged breath tore at my lungs, a searing agony that echoed the tremors racking my body. The rock, rough against my sweat-slicked skin, offered scant comfort. My muscles screamed, a symphony of pain conducted by exhaustion.

Caspian loomed, his shadow stretching long and menacing across the ravaged landscape. His face, normally a mask of cold calculation, was etched with something deeper: a predatory satisfaction barely masked by feigned concern. The glint in his eyes, however, betrayed him, the cold gleam of a hunter who knew he'd only wounded the beast, not killed it. This was just a reprieve, a fleeting moment before the storm broke again. The Obsidian Covenant... the very name tasted like ash in my mouth, a bitter reminder of their limitless power and insatiable hunger for dominance. Malkor, a mere pawn in their grand scheme, served as a brutal executioner wielding death and despair with ruthless efficiency amidst a legion of demons. Their reach extended into every shadowed corner of existence infiltrating the hearts and minds of the unsuspecting. With every whisper of their name, their influence spread like a creeping darkness, an all-consuming void that threatened to swallow the world whole. Hope felt like a distant memory overshadowed by the suffocating dread they brought forth leaving only despair in their wake.

The Grimoire... It pulsed in my mind, a heartbeat of pure malevolent magic. Obtaining it had just transitioned from a desperate gamble to a suicide mission. The price of failure... that price was etched into the very fabric of reality, a chilling promise whispered on the wind. We were far from safe. Far from over. The fight had just truly begun.

The air hung thick, a miasma of ozone and blood, acrid and choking. Shattered obsidian, like the teeth of some monstrous beast, crushed underfoot. The scorched earth steamed, a testament to the infernal heat of Malkor's fury, the very ground scarred and weeping. My boots, caked in the viscous residue of his defeat, sunk into the churned soil. He lay there, a colossus fallen, his obsidian hide cracked and smoking, each fissure a jagged wound spewing not blood, but something far more sinister, something that shimmered with malevolent energy. The agony contorting his monstrous frame was palpable, a silent scream resonating in the ravaged landscape.

Caspian, his breath ragged, felt a grim satisfaction, a chilling certainty. Malkor would rise again, this much I knew; the very air crackled with the anticipation of his return. But this pyrrhic victory, bought with the sweat and blood of our sacrifice, had purchased something more valuable than mere survival; it had bought us time. Time to hunt him, to finish what we had started before that infernal power could reignite before that shadow could once more consume the land. We would not allow him to recover. Not this time.

Exhaustion clawed at me, a brutal hand squeezing the air from my lungs, yet a savage exhilaration roared in defiance. Adrenaline, a venomous cocktail of bone-deep weariness and savage triumph, pulsed in my veins, a frantic drumbeat against the ribs of my cage. I had faced him, the behemoth, the creature of shadow and nightmare, and I had broken him. Every fibre of my being, every cursed drop of this ancient, unholy blood, had screamed in protest, had fought to the brink of oblivion, and yet... I had won.

But in that victory, a chilling dread, a serpent of ice, coiled around my heart. The taste of power, the raw, brutal ecstasy of annihilation, clung to me, a sickening sweetness coating my tongue. The metallic tang of blood, still warm on my lips, was overshadowed by the bitter, gnawing hunger, a bottomless pit of insatiable thirst that clawed at my very soul. The weight of it, the monstrous weight of my vampiric curse, crushed me, a suffocating blanket of darkness whispering insidious promises of oblivion, of an unending, seductive sleep. The Obsidian Grimoire, the instrument of my victory, felt insignificant, a mere trinket compared to the terrifying reality of my nature. This wasn't a triumph. This was damnation. The phantom scent of burning flesh and ozone still clung to my clothes, a grim reminder of the carnage. The taste of ash and the screech of tortured metal echoed in the silence.

My reflection, a distorted parody of humanity, stared back from the obsidian surface of a shattered mirror—the eyes, ancient and burning, reflecting the bottomless abyss within. The fear wasn't of another battle, another foe. The terror was me. The terror was the monstrous truth of my existence, a truth more potent, more terrifying than any army of shadows, any hellish horde I might ever face. This... this was my true enemy.

Caspian examined Malkor's body, his eyes scanning for any sign of weakness, any chink in his armour that they could exploit. He wanted to end this now, permanently. But the demon's resilience surprised even him. It would require more than a simple dagger thrust; they needed a more decisive blow, a way to permanently neutralize the demon, not merely incapacitate him. His mind raced, assessing their situation, and calculating their next move.

The wind howled around us, a mournful dirge that echoed my grim reality. We had won a battle, but I knew the war was far from over. The Obsidian Covenant was vast and powerful, and our quest for the

Grimoire had only just begun. I felt the road ahead was fraught with danger, each step forward leading us deeper into the heart of darkness. The shadows of doubt, the whispers of fear, haunted me, reminding me of the cost of our defiance and the fragility of our alliance. Yet, despite it all, I felt a strange bond forming between us, forged in the crucible of battle, bound by a shared purpose and a mutual understanding of the darkness we both inhabited.

Our connection, as dangerous as it was, felt like my only lifeline in this treacherous landscape of betrayal and blood. The game continued, the stakes higher than ever before, the future uncertain and filled with grim possibilities. But I knew this: we would face the darkness together, our hands stained with blood, our souls intertwined in a dance of shadows and fire. I felt it in my bones, a grim determination, a fierce loyalty to those beside me. I wouldn't falter. We wouldn't.

The silence that followed Malkor's defeat was heavy, pregnant with unspoken anxieties. The adrenaline that had fueled their fight ebbed away, leaving behind a bone-deep weariness. I leaned against the rough-hewn rock, the warmth of the stone a stark contrast to the chilling emptiness I felt inside. My breath hitched in my chest, a ragged sound lost in the vastness of the landscape. I shivered, though it wasn't entirely from the cold. The silence pressed down on me, heavy and suffocating. I closed my eyes, trying to find some solace, some flicker of warmth within myself to match the stone against my back, but found only a hollow ache. I tasted dust on my lips, the grit a bitter reminder of my isolation. The victory felt hollow, a fleeting respite in an endless war. The taste of Malkor's blood, inadvertently consumed during the melee, lingered on her tongue, a bitter reminder of the insatiable hunger that gnawed at my soul.

Caspian knelt beside me, his gaze searching mine, a silent conversation passing between us. He didn't speak of the battle, of our shared triumph, or even of Malkor's continued, albeit weakened, threat. Instead, he focused on me, the tremor in my hand, the haunted look in my eyes, the subtle shifts in my demeanour. I felt his understanding, a mirroring of the darkness that consumed me. He knew, as I did, that our alliance, forged in the heat of that terrible battle, needed more than a shared enemy to survive. It needed a foundation of trust, however precarious, a trust I felt, tentatively, beginning to build between us.

"*The Grimoire* " Caspian finally said his voice low and measured, breaking the silence that had stretched taut between them like a tightly wound string. The weight of his words hung in the air heavy with significance. "*It's still our objective* " he continued his gaze unwavering as if willing the others to grasp the gravity of their situation. "*But we need to renegotiate our terms.* "There was a sense of urgency in his tone, a recognition that their previous agreements might no longer suffice in the face of the challenges ahead. Turning to his companions he could see the flicker of concern in their eyes mirroring his own thoughts. They were at a crossroads and the path forward would require careful consideration and mutual understanding to ensure their success.

I nodded slowly, my gaze fixed on the ground. The word 'renegotiate' hit me like a physical blow, a painful truth resonating in my chest. Their current arrangement, born of necessity and mutual desperation, felt like walking on eggshells. I owed him, not only for his timely intervention in that brutal fight, the memory still seared into my mind, but also for the countless times his blood had kept me alive, had quenched the endless, burning thirst that consumed me. A debt that weighed heavier with each sunrise, each sunset. And yet... he was a demon, a member of the shadowy Whispering Wind, a creature I should, logically, fear and despise with every fibre of my being. Instead... I felt it, a pull, a magnetic force drawing me to him, a dangerous attraction that defied everything I knew, everything I believed. It terrified me, this feeling, this connection.

"*We both know Malkor isn't the end,*" I replied, my voice rough, like the wind scraping across bare rock. "*I feel it in my bones, the Obsidian Covenant's vastness, its power stretching further than we can see. This... alliance of ours... needs to be stronger, and more defined. I won't let us fail.*"

Caspian inclined his head, a flicker of approval in his dark eyes. I saw it, that spark of understanding. He understood my need for clarity, for a structure to hold against the chaos that threatened to consume us both. I, too, needed more than simply a temporary pact; the feeling was mutual, a silent acknowledgment passing between us. I felt a dangerous attraction to him, a primal pull that resonated deep within my being, a heat mirroring his own, a yearning that clashed violently with my ingrained distrust. His ancient soul, I sensed, mirrored my wariness, a battle between this powerful, unexpected connection and the deep-seated prejudices we both carried.

"I won't lie to you, Blaze," Caspian said, his voice a low murmur that carried the weight of centuries. *"My allegiance is first and foremost to the Whispering Wind. But the Covenant... they are a threat to us all. And your knowledge of their inner workings, your... single-minded pursuit of vengeance... It's invaluable."*

He paused, allowing his words to hang in the air, heavy with unspoken meaning. The air crackled with a charged energy that was as much sexual as it was strategic. Their bodies, still trembling from the exertion of battle, stood close, their auras intertwining like tendrils of smoke.

"In return for your assistance, and your continued cooperation in obtaining the Grimoire," Caspian continued, his voice deepening with the intensity of his gaze, *"I will ensure your safety, to the best of my ability. I will provide you with the blood you require to control your... condition. And I will share the information gathered by the Whispering Wind concerning the Obsidian Covenant, giving you the advantage you need."*

I studied him, my eyes searching his face for deception, for the slightest flicker of a lie. I found nothing. Only raw power, carefully controlled, and a chilling pragmatism that sent a shiver down my spine. The harsh reality of our situation pressed down on me, leaving little room for sentimentality, for any romantic notions of love and loyalty. I felt the weight of it, a crushing burden. It was a brutal bargain, I knew, one that gnawed at my conscience, but it was a bargain nonetheless, a desperate gamble that offered a glimmer of hope amid our seemingly hopeless struggle. I clung to that hope, a fragile thing as if my very life depended on it.

"And what about you?" I finally asked, my voice soft, almost a whisper. I felt a tremor of nervousness in my chest as the words left my lips. What do I gain from this... this new arrangement? The question hung in the air between us, heavy and unspoken. I desperately wanted to know his motivation, to understand what he hoped to achieve. My reasons felt shaky and uncertain even to me.

Caspian smiled, a slow, predatory curve of his lips that sent a shiver down my spine. I felt a prickle of unease, a cold dread creeping up my neck. My breath hitched; I couldn't look away from that smile, from the way his eyes gleamed. I knew, instinctively, that something dangerous was about to happen. My heart hammered against my ribs, a frantic drumbeat in the sudden silence. *"The Obsidian Grimoire, of course. But also,"* he paused, his gaze intense, *"the pleasure of watching you wield your power. Of seeing you dance with the flames, of feeling the heat of your vengeance. There is... a certain thrill, in observing such ferocious beauty."*

His words were devoid of romantic overtones. They were, instead, a frank assessment of the situation, an acknowledgment of the primal attraction that simmered between them. I knew he wasn't speaking of love, not in the traditional sense. It was something darker, more raw, more potent. A primal something that vibrated in the air between us. And despite my reluctance, a reluctance that clawed at me, I found myself strangely drawn to that intensity. It was a dangerous pull, a moth to a flame, and even as I recoiled, I couldn't tear my gaze away. I felt a shiver, not of fear exactly, but of something akin to awe, mixed with a terrifying sense of anticipation.

"And what if I fail?" I questioned, my voice a low murmur barely audible above my racing heart. *"What if I can't get the Grimoire? What if my efforts are all for nothing? The thought of that failure... It terrifies me."*

Caspian chuckled, a low rumble in his chest that vibrated through the floor and up into my very bones. *"Failure is not an option, Blaze. And should it become so... Well, let's just say I'll find other ways to ensure you repay your debt."* His hand reached out, and I flinched, barely perceptible, even to myself, before his fingers brushed against my cheek. His touch felt like a spark lighting a fire inside me. It was both frightening and exciting, filled with equal parts fear and a strong risky desire. I caught my breath. My face turned red, a warmth that matched the fire inside me.

Their renegotiated alliance wasn't sealed with a handshake or a formal oath. Instead, it was forged in the raw, dangerous energy that crackled between them—a volatile blend of mutual need, shared desperation, and a chilling, undeniable attraction. They understood the precarious nature of their partnership, its vulnerability to betrayal and its inherent dangers. The very essence of their alliance danced on the edge of a knife, a perilous dance where the lines between dominance and submission, love and hate, blurred into a chaotic, electrifying union.

The Obsidian Grimoire remained the main objective but the situation had changed. The fight was no longer just about getting revenge; it now involved the complicated and risky feelings growing between them. Doubts were still there but in those doubts something new was forming—a connection that was strong and surprising like the fire in my heart and the struggle in Caspian's soul. They moved forward together deep into the darkness engaged in a dangerous balance between light and dark.

The days that followed were a blur of frantic activity. I felt the pressure mounting with each passing hour. Caspian, using the Whispering Wind's network, fed me information about the Obsidian Covenant: their structure, key players, hidden sanctuaries, everything. He painted a vivid picture of their informants, their secret routes, and their weaknesses. I, in turn, shared my knowledge, my firsthand experience of their brutality, and their relentless thirst for power. I could feel the chill of their pursuit still, a constant shadow in my memory. We worked together, our skills a perfect fit, a lethal partnership forged in necessity and fueled by our shared desire for revenge. I found myself pouring over maps and plans with him, countless hours spent discussing strategy, plotting our next moves, and dissecting our opponents' strengths and weaknesses. I felt the weight of our shared purpose, intensifying the bond between us, a connection both thrilling and terrifying. It was a dangerous dance, but one I was willing to lead.

My nightly encounters with Caspian, initially born from my desperate need for his blood, evolved into something far more complex than I could have ever imagined. The intimacy was never gentle; it was always a raw, untamed reflection of our natures, a physical manifestation of our strange alliance. Our bodies became a battleground, a charged entanglement of power and submission, where dominance and desire clashed. I, despite the inherent risk, found a perverse comfort in Caspian's control, a strange solace in surrendering to his power. His touch, though often harsh, was undeniably intoxicating, a spark that ignited flames within me that even my flame elemental abilities couldn't contain. I felt the heat bloom across my skin, a searing brand of his possession.

I saw it in his eyes too, despite his outward stoicism, the pull of my spirit, the fierce, untamed fire that burned so brightly within me. He discovered that my vulnerability, the vulnerability I only showed him, was a hidden wellspring of strength, a testament to my resilience in the face of unimaginable horrors. Our shared darkness became a strange and powerful bond, a testament to the dangerous attraction we both felt, a connection forged in blood and desire, one I couldn't, and wouldn't, deny.

My relationship with him was a fragile tapestry woven from threads of mutual respect, underlying resentment, and a complex sexual dynamic that bordered on obsession. We were both morally grey, bound together by the darkness we shared. I knew the possibility of betrayal was always present, a constant undercurrent pulsing beneath our shared purpose. The game continued, the stakes increasing with each passing day, our destinies intertwined in a perilous dance of vengeance, desire, and the looming shadow of the Obsidian Covenant. Our partnership was a paradox, a testament to our shared darkness, an alliance founded on a mutual understanding of our flaws and our inherent wickedness, where passion and hatred danced together in an intricate, terrifying ballet. I felt it all acutely; the pull of his darkness, the thrill of our shared danger, the ever-present fear that one wrong move would shatter everything. I knew, deep down, that I was as culpable as he was, as wicked, as driven by the same shadows.

The rhythmic clang of the blacksmith's hammer, usually a comforting sound, grated on my nerves. I sat hunched in the shadows of the tavern, the rough-hewn wooden table digging into my arms. My shoulders ached; I hadn't slept properly in days. Caspian had insisted on this meeting, this supposedly inconspicuous gathering in a remote village bordering the Obsidian Covenant's territory. I shifted uncomfortably, the rough fabric of my cloak scratching against my skin. The air hung heavy with the scent of wood smoke and stale ale, a far cry from the sterile, almost clinical scent of the Covenant's obsidian fortresses, a scent I knew all too well. My hand instinctively went to the hilt of my dagger, hidden beneath my cloak. He'd been unusually quiet, his usual predatory grace replaced by a brooding intensity that sent shivers down my spine. I wondered what he was hiding, what dark secret lay behind those usually bright, calculating eyes. A knot of apprehension tightened in my stomach. I needed to know what he wanted.

It wasn't the silence that unnerved me; it was the subtle shift in his demeanour, a change so profound that I felt the ground beneath my feet shifting. Caspian, the enigmatic demon, the master strategist, was troubled. And that troubled me far more than any impending battle with the Covenant. I felt a cold dread creep into my bones, a deeper fear than the usual pre-battle anxiety. His usual calm, his almost arrogant confidence, was gone, replaced by something…unsettling. I watched him, trying to decipher the unspoken fear in his eyes, a fear that mirrored, and yet somehow surpassed, my own.

He finally spoke, his voice a low rasp that cut through the tavern's murmur. *"There's something you need to know, Blaze. Something they haven't told you, something they've kept hidden, even from Malkor."*

I leaned forward, my senses sharpening, the elemental fire simmering beneath my skin making me practically vibrate. *"What is it?"* I whispered, my voice a mere breath. The tension in the room thickened, a palpable, suffocating weight pressing down on me. It felt like I couldn't breathe. Even the boisterous laughter from the other patrons felt distant, muffled, a muted hum in the sudden, heavy silence that had fallen. My heart hammered against my ribs, a frantic drumbeat against the oppressive quiet. I felt a prickle of unease crawling up my spine. What was happening? My eyes darted around the room, searching for an explanation, for any clue as to what was causing this unsettling shift in the atmosphere.

Caspian hesitated, his gaze fixed on the flickering candlelight. He took a slow, deliberate sip from his tankard, the liquid amber catching the light. He placed it down, the sound echoing in the sudden silence.

"The Obsidian Covenant," he began, his voice dropping to an almost inaudible murmur, *"isn't what it seems."*

I paused, letting the weight of his words hang heavy in the air. A cold dread crept into my heart, a chilling premonition that overshadowed even my burning desire for vengeance. This was far more profound than I'd ever imagined. The organization I had dedicated my life to destroying, I felt it in my bones, a sickening certainty, was more complex, more insidious, than I could have ever conceived.

"*They are not merely a band of power hungry demons,*" Caspian continued, his voice regaining its strength, but laced with an unsettling gravity. "*They are a cult, Blaze. A twisted, ancient cult dedicated to a forgotten entity, a being of unimaginable power, a being who craves… awakening.*"

The words hung in the air, heavy with implications that sent a shiver of fear down my spine. I felt a cold dread bloom in my chest. An ancient entity? An awakening? The scope of the threat dwarfed my initial understanding. My quest for vengeance, once a singular, focused path, now seemed hopelessly inadequate. I had been fighting a shadow, a mere pawn in a far greater, far more sinister game. I realized, with a sickening lurch in my stomach, how small, how insignificant my actions had been. My carefully constructed plans crumbled to dust. My anger felt… childish, almost. The sheer scale of it all pressed down on me, crushing the breath from my lungs.

"*This entity,*" Caspian continued, "*feeds on chaos, on the suffering of others. The Obsidian Covenant's actions, their brutality… it's all a ritual, a sacrifice to appease this being. Their ultimate goal isn't merely conquest or domination. It's something far more insidious, something that would plunge the world into eternal darkness.*"

He described the entity, its nature, its power, and its insatiable hunger, in chilling detail. The words painted a terrifying picture, a reality far darker and more terrifying than the burning hatred she felt for the Covenant. The scale of the threat was staggering, extending beyond simple vengeance. This was a fight for the very survival of the world, a battle against an ancient, malevolent entity far more powerful than any demon she had ever faced.

The implications were staggering. I felt it, a cold dread gripping my heart. Their strategy, their entire approach… it all needed a complete overhaul, and I knew I was the one who had to lead the charge. My singular focus on vengeance, the burning rage that had fueled me for so long, was now drastically inadequate. I could feel the shift, a sickening realization dawning in my gut. The Obsidian Grimoire, once my primary objective, the thing I'd obsessed over, was now just a secondary tool in a far larger battle, a battle far beyond my initial understanding.

171

This wasn't about personal retribution anymore; the weight of it settled heavily on my shoulders. This fight... was about the survival of all, and I was at the center of it.

"*The Grimoire,*" Caspian continued, his gaze piercing, "*it's a key, Blaze. A key to unlock... something far more terrifying than you can imagine. It's not just a weapon; it's a catalyst.*"

He explained that the Grimoire wasn't just a book of spells and rituals; it contained knowledge of the entity's weaknesses, its vulnerabilities, and the means to thwart its awakening. Their initial objective hadn't changed; obtaining the Grimoire remained paramount, but its importance had multiplied exponentially. It was no longer just a tool for revenge; it was now the key to survival.

The revelation reshaped their alliance. The precarious balance of power between them shifted. Their shared danger deepened, intertwining their fates more profoundly and terrifyingly. The sexual tension that had simmered between them intensified, fueled by their shared peril and the weight of their responsibility. Their nights together became even more intense, their bodies a battlefield where passion and fear intertwined, their connection a precarious dance between power and vulnerability. The blood Caspian offered wasn't just sustenance; it was a binding agent, a physical manifestation of their precarious alliance.

My heart hammered against my ribs. Their fight, our fight, against the Obsidian Covenant was no longer about revenge. It was a desperate, gut-wrenching struggle for survival, a race against time I felt pounding in my ears. The urgency choked me; the stakes felt like a physical weight, crushing me under their impossible height. Every swing of my sword, every whispered word, felt like it carried the world's fate on my shoulders. My internal conflict raged; my thirst for vengeance, once a burning flame, was now a tiny spark lost in a wildfire of a far greater, more terrifying struggle. It demanded everything from me, more than I ever thought I possessed, more than I could ever have imagined bearing. The doubts I'd harboured before? They were insignificant now, swallowed whole by a darkness far greater, a darkness that threatened not only my life but the very existence of everything I knew.

The days that followed were a blur of frantic activity. Their days were spent gathering intelligence, utilizing the extensive network of the Whispering Wind to uncover the cult's secrets, their hidden sanctuaries, and the rituals they performed. Nights were spent in a desperate, urgent pursuit of the Grimoire, the weight of the world resting heavily upon their shoulders. The line between their shared mission and their passionate entanglement blurred further. Their love, if it could be called that, was a dangerous fire, a volatile mixture of passion and desperation.

Caspian, in his usual enigmatic way, remained both a source of strength and an enigma to me. His actions remained shrouded in secrecy, leaving me to guess at his motives, but his dedication to our shared cause was undeniable. I felt it in the way he held himself, in the quiet intensity of his gaze. I, in turn, found a newfound strength, a grim determination born from the sheer gravity of the situation. The weight of the world pressed down on me, a crushing burden, but I refused to yield. I was no longer driven by vengeance alone, though the embers of that still glowed within me, but by the urgent, terrifying necessity to protect the world, our world, from this ancient evil. I could feel the cold breath of it on my neck, and it fueled my resolve.

The path ahead was fraught with peril, riddled with unseen dangers and unforeseen obstacles. But Caspian and I, bound together by a precarious alliance fueled by both necessity and a dangerous attraction, pressed on. I moved like a shadow through the night, every action calculated, every step measured. My destiny, intertwined with his, felt like a weight, a responsibility that pressed down on me with every beat of my heart. The revelation had changed everything, I felt it in the tremors of my fear, transforming our conflict into a desperate struggle against a cosmic horror, a fight for existence itself. The shadows of doubt still lingered, a cold knot in my stomach, but now, they were overshadowed by the looming terror of an awakening that threatened to consume us all. I could feel it, a creeping dread that snaked its way into my bones.

NINE

The Heart of Darkness

A colossal obsidian fortress, a monolith that devoured moonlight, dominated the landscape. Its jagged silhouette, a serrated wound against the starless void, spoke of the malevolent force it imprisoned. Caspian, his customary elegance supplanted by rigid control, preceded us, his movements as ethereal and silent as a phantom's glide. I followed, a simmering furnace of apprehension burning within, my senses acutely attuned to the oppressive atmosphere. A palpable, suffocating aura of dread hung heavy in the air, a chilling shroud that pressed down upon us with unbearable weight.

Instead of a violent breach, their penetration was a subtle ballet of subterfuge. Caspian, leveraging his intimate understanding of the Covenant's infrastructure, expertly steered them through clandestine routes and overlooked areas; their advance was a silent testament to their mastery of covert operations. He possessed an unsettling intimacy with the fortress, as though its very foundations confided their secrets to him. My elemental perception, interwoven with his infernal intuition, charted the intricate pathways; my fiery aura, was a vigilant protector against the ever-present threat of ambush.

The deeper we penetrated the labyrinthine tunnels beneath the Obsidian Citadel, the more unsettling the atmosphere became. The silence wasn't empty; it was a tangible weight, pressing down on me, heavy with the echoes of whispered incantations in a language that felt like ice against my tongue. I tasted the cloying, metallic scent of burnt offerings, not of flesh, but something far more ancient and unsettling; a scent that clung to the very fabric of the tunnels, a perfume of decay and dark magic that I couldn't shake.

The air grew colder, not a simple decrease in temperature, but an unnatural chill that seeped into my bones, emanating from the obsidian walls themselves. I stared at my reflection in their mirror like a sheen, a grotesque parody staring back at me. These walls pulsed faintly with a cold inner light, a sickly, bioluminescent glow that seemed to leach vitality from me, draining my very strength. I felt a growing unease, a primal fear clawing at my insides.

I passed chambers where the arcane symbols weren't merely carvings, but three-dimensional constructs of solidified shadow, pulsating softly with their own internal light. These cryptic glyphs, etched in a language older than recorded history, spoke not only of forgotten rituals and unholy alliances but hinted at a cosmology utterly alien to my own; a tapestry of forgotten gods and monstrous entities whose very existence defied my comprehension. Strange, unsettling images flickered at the edges of my vision, not fleeting glimpses, but persistent, shimmering hallucinations; grotesque figures engaged in acts of unspeakable cruelty, their forms shifting and twisting, their actions echoing with primal savagery that resonated deep within my subconscious. These weren't merely visions, but psychic echoes, fragments of my memories, nightmares made manifest from the very essence of the place.

The ground beneath my feet was uneven, occasionally yielding with a sickening squelch underfoot, revealing glimpses of a viscous, iridescent slime that seemed to writhe with an independent sentience. The air itself hummed with a low, resonant frequency, a vibration that resonated within my very bones, a discordant symphony of decay and oblivion. The deeper I went, the more certain I became: this was no mere tomb, but a living prison, a festering wound on the fabric of reality.

I moved through the heart of the fortress, a maze of twisting tunnels and hidden chambers. Each step I took brought me closer to the horrifying truth. My heart pounded in my chest, a frantic drumbeat against the echoing silence. The air grew colder and heavier, the very stones seeming to press in on me. Caspian's movements were precise, his every action betraying a deep familiarity with this infernal place, a knowledge that both fascinated and unsettled me. He seemed to anticipate every turn, every obstacle, his presence was both a comfort and a constant reminder of the danger they faced.

Caspian's hand, a sudden, arresting gesture, cut off my words. A distant drone, a subtle thrumming barely audible at first, rippled through the very earth beneath us. This ethereal vibration intensified, swelling into a cataclysmic crescendo that vibrated within my ribcage, a sound pregnant with primordial power, radiating an aura of wicked antiquity. My pulse hammered a frantic tattoo against the escalating hum, a deafening counterpoint to the mounting terror. A chilling dread, icy and incisive, gripped me. The ground shuddered, a palpable testament to the encroaching horror.

Driven by a rhythmic thrum, their pulses hammered against their ribs, senses stretched taut against the suffocating gloom. The drone swelled, guiding them into a colossal cavern that dwarfed all previous chambers. There, within a spectral luminescence, a monolithic obsidian altar dominated the space, its surface a labyrinth of glyphs that pulsed and contorted with sinister life.

A throng of Pact fiends encircled the altar, their guttural litany a chilling symphony weaving a spell that pierced my soul. Their synchronized movements, a ghastly ballet of subservience and immolation, pulsed with an eerie rhythm. The acrid scent of spilled blood hung heavy in the air as they writhed in torment, their agonized cries stifled by the awesome, radiating force of the altar.

Nausea was so profound it threatened to split my skull and clawed at me as I saw it, the heart. A malevolent crystal, the size of a man's fist, pulsing deep within the altar's obsidian core. Not a gentle thrum, but a sickening, crackling beat, a percussive rhythm that vibrated through the very stones beneath my feet, a brutal counterpoint to the screams echoing around me. The air itself throbbed with its foul energy, a stench of ozone and something ancient, something wrong, clinging to the back of my throat. Its light, a sickly, emerald luminescence, was not just illumination; it was a revelation, burning away the flimsy veil of normalcy.

This wasn't some crazed cult; this was a thing of unimaginable age, a titan of darkness unbound, its power a palpable weight pressing down, crushing the very air from my lungs. The icy dread that gripped me wasn't fear; it was the awestruck terror of witnessing an ancient evil, one that predated humanity, flexing its horrifying might. My own insignificance, my utter vulnerability in the face of such cosmic horror, was a truth etched into my very soul by that ghastly, pulsating light.

A searing revelation hit me like a hammer blow: the Obsidian Covenant was not merely a demonic cabal lusting for power; it served as a horrifying gateway, a dark and twisted channel for an ancient malevolent entity that had long been imprisoned in the shadows of time. The chilling concept of this entity sent shivers down my spine for it was no longer just a figment of imagination or a tale spun from the minds of fearful souls. Caspian's whispered warnings about this being were no mere myth; they were rooted in a grim reality that I could no longer dismiss. The very fabric of our world trembled at the thought of its dreadful resurrection which was now ominously at hand. The Covenant's insidious rituals were not just acts of desperation; they were the key to unleashing a force that could plunge our realm into chaos. I felt the weight of impending doom as if the very air around me vibrated with the dark anticipation of what was to come.

Caspian, his eyes slits of glacial blue in the flickering torchlight, hissed the words, *"The Heart of Malzahar. It's thrumming... I can feel it, a vile pulse against my own."* The stench of ozone and decay, a cloying sweetness overlaid with the reek of ancient death, filled his nostrils; the air itself vibrated with a low, guttural hum that resonated deep in his bones. Terror, raw and visceral, clawed at him, a cold hand gripping his heart while a perverse fascination, a morbid curiosity, held him captive. This wasn't mere awe; it was the crushing weight of cosmic horror, the terrifying revelation of a power beyond human comprehension. Their petty squabbles, their centuries-long sectarian war... child's play compared to the cataclysm they'd unleashed. This wasn't some simple demon; this was a primordial entity, a titan of eldritch darkness, awakening from a slumber older than time itself, and Caspian, the hunted, the haunted, the man who'd stumbled upon its prison... he held the key. The weight of that knowledge, the burden of that power, threatened to shatter him.

Fear and morbid curiosity warred within me as we observed the ceremony's grim progress. A cacophony of demonic incantations swelled, the chamber's atmosphere thickening with a dreadful, escalating power. The obsidian core throbbed with escalating luminescence, its light a malevolent beacon. An oppressive aura of imminent catastrophe hung heavy in the air, tangible and suffocating.

A piercing, unearthly wail cleaved the air, instantly triggering a frenzied retreat. Demons, their features twisted in abject horror, recoiled in disarray. The obsidian core throbbed wildly, its luminescence sputtered, failing, then extinguished in a void of unnatural blackness. An oppressive, stifling quietude settled, punctuated only by Caspian's and my own ragged gasps, a testament to the harrowing ordeal.

The ceremony's collapse only amplified the impending doom. Through the Heart of Malzahar, the Covenant's wellspring of might lay fractured, its malevolent master persisted, its ascension postponed but not prevented. This revelation irrevocably altered their purpose; their quest for retribution morphed into a frantic struggle against cosmic annihilation.

Caspian, the master tactician, quietly devised a strategy, his intellect already mapping their next assault. My own terror, though profound, yielded to a steely resolve. The thirst for retribution paled beside the urgent need for existence, a struggle against archaic wickedness poised to shroud the world in perpetual night. Their fragile pact, now indissoluble, was cemented in the furnace of shared danger, a frenzied race to avert utter annihilation. The simmering attraction between them, ever-present, was eclipsed by the grim focus in their gaze, a common objective eclipsing personal yearnings. They had glimpsed the abyss, yet the true conflict remained.

A whirlwind of frenetic investigation consumed the ensuing days. Deep within the fortress's labyrinthine depths, they unearthed archaic scrolls and enigmatic divinations, revealing the entity's shadowy genesis and its sinister intentions. Hidden vaults, choked with ghastly relics, bore chilling witness to the cult's age-old devotion to the malevolent Malazar. Their relentless pursuit unveiled the entity's chinks in its formidable defences, its vulnerabilities—subtle fissures in its seemingly impenetrable power. The horrifying revelations they acquired were a dreadful burden, yet amidst the terror, a fragile ember of hope ignited—a possibility of defiance.

I found Caspian's deep knowledge of demon texts really helpful. His understanding opened my eyes to the great power of the entity we were dealing with. I used my control over the elements to break through the fortress's dangerous defenses. My bright flames burned away the leftover dark magic from the Covenant. My connection with them was strong. Together we formed a powerful team because we faced danger and fought hard for our survival. During the night I felt a strong closeness with the other person. We held each other tightly searching for comfort and a way to let go of our worries. I found it hard to tell the difference between their passionate hug and their bigger goal. The blood Caspian gave me meant more than just staying alive; it showed our risky agreement and confirmed how our fates were connected.

A concealed route, a clandestine tunnel, opened before them, plunging them into the fortress's forgotten depths. This was a place of primordial might, emanating a baleful aura that menaced to engulf their very beings. With trepidation, their senses sharpened, they proceeded, each footstep deliberate, each action precisely choreographed. The air vibrated with potent energy; the very stones throbbed with an age-old, sinister power.

In the chamber's shadowed depths, they discovered it—not the obsidian shard previously glimpsed, but Malazar's very soul. A maelstrom of impenetrable darkness, it throbbed with an eon old might, a terrifying spectacle that dwarfed their previous comprehension of the entity's wickedness. Yet, within this horrifying abyss of power, a flicker of hope ignited: the potential to weaponize its dreadful essence, to turn its formidable strength against the malevolent source itself.

Desperate, yet daring, their strategy was their sole lifeline. Piecemeal, the intricate scheme unfolded. Caspian, leveraging his formidable network and expertise, would forge alliances with influential factions, amassing a formidable army for the climactic confrontation. Simultaneously, I would dedicate myself to refining my abilities, steeling myself for the inevitable clash with the sinister being.

From the wreckage of shared suffering bloomed an improbable union, their bond forged in the crucible of existential threat. Their love, a tempestuous dance of dominance and fragility, burned with the perilous intensity of desperate hope and profound admiration. Intertwined destinies, they were two halves of a fractured whole, their future inextricably linked to the world's survival. Facing the imminent cataclysm, the crushing weight of global fate settled upon them, a burden they shouldered with resolute silence and a burgeoning affection born of adversity.

The air crackled, a suffocating blanket woven from ozone's metallic tang and the stench of raw terror. My lungs burned, each ragged breath a desperate fight against the weight pressing down, a weight far heavier than the Heart of Malazar's stolen power now pulsing like a malevolent heart within my very being. The prickling on my neck wasn't a mere sensation; it was a brand, searing agony etched by icy claws across my skin, heralding a doom I knew instinctively. The earth's tremor was a guttural groan, a dying beast's last convulsion; the wind's whisper, a venomous hiss spitting promises of oblivion. This wasn't foreboding; it was the icy grip of certain death, a visceral understanding that the abyss itself had opened its maw and was already swallowing me whole. Before I could even scream, a voice, slick as viper's venom and cold as a grave, slithered into my skull, its very essence a violation, a mockery of my will.

"Blaze " rasped the word, a searing brand that marked not just my skin but also my very soul. It felt like a phantom touch igniting nerves that screamed in agony setting my entire being ablaze with a torment that transcended the physical. The taste that lingered in my mouth wasn't merely ash and iron; it was a visceral concoction, the metallic tang of blood intertwined with the acrid bite of shattered bone remnants of a violence that left its imprint not only on the ground but deep within me. Ozone and burnt sugar? No, that descriptor seemed far too simplistic an inadequate attempt to encapsulate the horror that enveloped me. The scent was far more sinister—it was the fetid stench of incinerated flesh a sickly sweetness that clung to the air mingling with the reek of sulfur and ozone creating a foul perfume of annihilation crafted by a malevolent deity bent on my destruction.

Its voice, a guttural tremor that reverberated through the very architecture of my being, was not merely an expression of malice; it was a cacophony, a symphony of contempt that assaulted my senses with each note. Each syllable was a calculated hammer blow against the fragile edifice of my sanity designed to pulverize me into oblivion. I felt every syllable resonate within me each sound mirroring the chaos that had become my existence. The voice I realized with a shudder held the echoes of ages long past a cruel and knowing laughter that emanated from the very depths of the abyss. It was as if this entity had witnessed the rise and fall of empires and the suffering of countless souls and now chose to turn its gaze upon me.

It purred the sound of a caress only a viper could deliver its promise slick with venom and fraught with the allure of exquisite unrelenting pain. *"Fate "* it hissed the syllables dripping with the ichor of a thousand broken dreams, the weight of despair woven into every word. *"That twisted sadistic omnipotent jester has chosen you. This... exquisite game of cruelty... is your exquisite torment. "* Each word was a dagger piercing the fragile veil of hope that I had managed to cling to in this bleak existence.

I could almost envision Fate, a grotesque figure cloaked in shadows lurking just beyond the edges of my perception relishing in the torment it had orchestrated. This was not mere chance; it was a meticulously crafted design, a cruel joke played out on the stage of my life. The very notion sent chills racing down my spine and as I stood there paralyzed by the weight of its malevolence I felt the ground beneath me shift an unsettling tremor that mirrored the chaos within my heart. Each heartbeat echoed like a war drum, a reminder of my own fragility in the face of such overwhelming darkness.

In that moment I understood that this was not just a battle against an external force; it was a struggle for my very essence, an attempt to reclaim the pieces of myself that had been scattered by the ruthless winds of fate. I had to resist to fight back against the tide of despair that threatened to swallow me whole. The realization ignited a flicker of defiance within me, a spark that fought against the encroaching shadows. I was not merely a pawn in its game; I was the architect of my own destiny even if the odds were painfully stacked against me.

As the voice continued its taunts I felt the weight of its contempt pressing down but I also felt the stirrings of something deeper something primal. The urge to survive and to rise from the ashes of my despair ignited a fire within me that could not be extinguished. It was a defiance born not from arrogance but from the understanding that I had the power to shape my own narrative. This being with its malicious intent had underestimated the resilience of the human spirit and in that underestimation lay my strength.

"Exquisite torment" it repeated as if savouring the words but I could sense the tremor in its voice, the flicker of uncertainty beneath the surface. Perhaps my struggle and my refusal to be broken was an unpredictable variable in its cruel equation. I would not be merely a victim of fate's whims; I would rise even if it meant clawing through the very depths of this hell. I would confront the darkness and challenge the malevolence that sought to consume me and in doing so I would reclaim my existence, my identity and my very soul.

Linx.

He erupted from the shadows, not merely appearing, but becoming, his form a violent bloom of darkness coalescing into terrifying solidity. The stench of ozone and burnt earth stung my nostrils as his obsidian eyes, twin pools of molten night, fixed upon me with a hunger that chilled me to the bone. The cavern, our accidental sanctuary, shrunk to a suffocating tomb. The rough-hewn stone pressed against my skin, a cold, unforgiving weight mirroring the dread that clenched my heart.

This wasn't the same creature. This was something... amplified. A raw, brutal power pulsed from him, a tangible thrumming that vibrated in my teeth and resonates deep within my chest cavity. The air itself crackled with it, malevolent magic so potent it tasted like ash and fear on my tongue. His chest, a canvas of fresh, weeping wounds, a testament to battles fought not just for survival, but for something far more desperate, far more... personal. Each ragged scar seemed to writhe, to pulse with the same ferocious energy that radiated from him.

Gone was his languid grace, replaced by a coiled, lethal energy, a predator poised to spring. His anger wasn't just simmering, it was a raging inferno, burning bright in the darkness of his eyes, a terrifying reflection of the despair that clawed at the edges of his formidable power. He wasn't just desperate; he was broken, and his brokenness was a weapon more terrifying than any blade. The silence screamed.

Caspian erupted beside me unleashing a searing blast of raw power that slammed against Linx's suffocating darkness with an explosive force. The air itself screamed in a high-pitched whine that vibrated in my teeth creating a tangible pressure that built in my chest as the two demons locked eyes in a deadly standoff. Their mutual hatred was not simply felt; it was a visceral almost metallic sensation that lingered on my tongue, a coppery tang mingled with the acrid scent of blood and brimstone. I could smell the ozone crackling in the atmosphere, a telltale sign of the impending chaos while I felt the heat radiating from Caspian's fury scorching my skin, an intense warmth that was both exhilarating and terrifying. In stark contrast, the icy chill of Linx's malevolence penetrated deeper, freezing the marrow in my bones and causing shivers to race down my spine.

Linx stood before us a creature sculpted from shadows and cruel amusement, his eyes burning with a glacial fire that pierced through the darkness like a cruel beacon. He was a predator relishing the fear emanating from everyone around him, especially me. On the other hand, Caspian was a tempestuous whirlwind of chaotic energy his face contorted into a mask of simmering rage. Every muscle in his body was coiled a caged beast yearning for release ready to unleash havoc at any moment. I found myself standing between these two titanic forces feeling like a pathetic wisp of smoke, a trembling reed caught in the torrent of their ancient and bitter feud. The weight of their conflict loomed over me, a suffocating presence that threatened to shatter my very essence. My life felt like a flickering candle flame struggling to survive amidst the hurricane of their hatred each flicker a reminder of my fragility in the face of such overwhelming darkness.

"*Linx,*" Caspian's voice, a gravelly shriek that clawed at the air, sliced through the fetid miasma of blood and rot, a reeking perfume clinging to him like a shroud woven from nightmares. The ozone, acrid and metallic, burned Linx's nostrils, the stench of a near-death he'd narrowly escaped, a lingering echo of his own mortality. Caspian's eyes, twin pits of obsidian flecked with predatory gold, bored into Linx's very being, cold and calculating, promising an eternity of torment. A low growl vibrated in his chest, a prelude to the storm brewing within.

"*Last time,*" he hissed, the word a physical impact, a sonic hammer blow that shattered the fragile calm, each syllable a poisoned dart aimed at Linx's heart. The taste of fear, bitter and metallic, flooded Linx's mouth. *"Was a... mercy."* The word dripped with venomous sarcasm, laced with the chilling awareness of his own power. *"This time... this time,"* Caspian's voice cracked, not with weakness, but with the exquisite anticipation of a predator savouring its kill, *"I will sculpt your suffering. I will draw it out until every fibre of your being screams for release... a release I will deny."*

His grip, bone white against the worn leather of his gauntlet, pulsed with a barely contained fury, a seismic tremor beneath a deceptively calm exterior. The air itself seemed to crackle with the raw, untamed energy he exuded; the scent of ozone intensified, mingling with the coppery tang of blood and the sickly sweet stench of decay, forming a suffocating aura of impending doom. This wasn't merely violence; it was a meticulously planned symphony of destruction, orchestrated by a mind as sharp and ruthless as a shattered obsidian shard. Caspian was a masterpiece of controlled chaos, a predator who revelled not just in the kill, but in the exquisite artistry of the hunt.

Linx's laughter clawed its way from his throat, a rasping, guttural sound that scraped against the cavern's ancient stones, bouncing off unseen stalactites like the death knell of a thousand hopes. The air itself seemed to vibrate with the malice echoing in his voice. *"And risk losing such a... priceless toy?"* His gaze, cold and predatory as a winter wolf, snaked across my face, a possessive touch that branded my skin with icy fire. The scent of ozone and something feral, something distinctly Linx, hung heavy in the air around him. *"Caspian,"* he hissed, the word dripping with venom, *"I don't merely have unfinished business with her. I have a score to settle, a debt to be repaid in blood. And believe me, the interest has compounded exponentially."*

"Debt settled," Caspian hissed the word in a venomous whisper that slithered through the air thick with the coppery tang of blood and the cloying sweetness of lilies, her lilies. His hand, a predator's claw, tightened on the cold steel of his sword hilt; the motion, a phantom caress, promised swift and brutal justice. The glint of moonlight on the blade mirrored the chilling gleam in his eyes, eyes that held the cold weight of a thousand betrayals and the simmering heat of a barely contained rage. *"She's mine, and if you think I will let you lay another finger on her again you're sadly mistaken"* he ground out, each syllable a hammer

blow against the silence, the possessive pronoun a declaration of war, a branding iron searing its mark on the very soul of his enemy. The air crackled with unspoken threats, the promise of retribution humming in the silence between them, a discordant symphony only the dead could truly appreciate.

"*Doubt it?*" Linx's sneer twisted the predatory smile into something feral. The air crackled with the unspoken threat as he closed the distance, his gaze a physical weight, branding me with its intensity. The scent of him, ozone and something dark, primal, filled my nostrils, a suffocating perfume of danger. Her lips still bear the ghost of my blood, don't they? The metallic tang, the faint coppery sweetness lingering like a curse? His fingers, long and sharp as a predator's claws, grazed my cheek, the touch igniting a firestorm of revulsion and a terrifying, forbidden pleasure. A shudder, raw and visceral, ripped through me. *"I feel it, the connection. The thrumming pulse, a subterranean tremor resonating between our very souls. It's not a question of belief, darling. It's a primal truth. It's ours, and she's mine."* The final word hung in the air, heavy with possessive obsession, and laced with a chilling certainty that left me breathless and terrified.

Ice splintered in my veins. The memory of Linx, his possession, wasn't a flood; it was a tidal wave, crashing over me, dragging me down into the black, suffocating depths of that violation. The metallic tang of blood filled my mouth, a phantom taste mirroring the bitter, coiling shame that choked me. Rage wasn't an ember; it was a wildfire, scorching my insides, threatening to consume me entirely. His touch… the ghost of it still lingered, a phantom pressure against my skin, raising gooseflesh even now. It wasn't simply unpleasant; it was a venomous caress, a perverse symphony of agony and… something else. A sickening, forbidden echo of intimacy that twisted my stomach with a nauseating familiarity, a perverse resonance that defied logic and reason, a horrifying whisper of connection in the heart of the deepest defilement. The monster had left its mark, not just on my body, but on my very soul.

"*Leave her alone* " Caspian hissed the words escaping his lips like a venomous rasp that clawed at the air thick with the metallic tang of blood and the cloying sweetness of impending violence. His eyes the colour of a storm-wracked sea glittered with a chilling intensity, a simmering rage that threatened to boil over and consume everything in its path. The tremor in his hands barely perceptible beneath the finely woven silk of his sleeve betrayed the barely contained fury that pulsed beneath his aristocratic facade. He was a predator wounded but not broken and the warning in his gaze was as sharp and lethal as a viper's strike.

This moment was charged with an electric tension, the atmosphere crackling with unspoken threats and unyielding resolve. Each heartbeat echoed like a drum marking the countdown to a confrontation that loomed just beyond the veil of civility. The shadows danced around him as if they too were drawn to his ferocity whispering secrets of battles fought and won. Caspian stood his ground unwilling to yield a fortress of quiet strength amidst the chaos. This wasn't merely a request; it was a promise etched in the cold hard steel of his soul. The weight of his conviction hung heavily in the air challenging any who dared to cross the line he had drawn. He would protect her no matter the cost and in that moment the world around him faded leaving only the fiery determination that blazed in his heart.

"No," Linx snarled, the raw hunger in his glacial eyes burning a hole through me. The scent of ozone and something feral, musk and blood, clung to him like a second skin. "Need?" he spat, the word a venomous whisper that slithered down my spine, raising gooseflesh on my arms. "Need is a weak word. I crave her. This... this pathetic pretense is over. I intend to possess her. To break her, to mould her, to make her mine in a way that leaves no doubt, no escape. And the taste of her surrender... that will be the sweetest nectar."

The air crackled, a tangible pressure pressed against my eardrums, a vile taste of ozone coating my tongue. It wasn't just tension; it was the raw, feral energy of two titans locked in a silent, brutal war, their hatred a palpable force that threatened to shatter my very soul. I could feel their power, one, a burning, searing inferno; the other, a chilling, glacial void, grinding against each other, cosmic friction tearing at the fabric of reality itself. Then he moved. Linx, a predator cloaked in shadow, a whisper of muscle and malice, a phantom closing the distance with the grace of a wraith and the speed of a viper. Before my mind could even scream a warning, the stench of his foul breath, copper and decay, filled my nostrils. His teeth, yellowed fangs honed to razor sharpness, flashed in the gloom, aimed not just at my neck, but at the very lifeblood coursing through my veins. His intent was not merely to kill; it was to annihilate.

Caspian wasn't merely faster; he was a blur, a wraith in the flickering torchlight. The air itself crackled with the anticipation of his movement, a metallic tang of blood already staining the stale air before the steel even sang. His blade honed to a razor's edge, whispered a death knell, a silent scream of polished obsidian, before finding its mark. The impact resonated in Linx's chest, a sickening thud that echoed in Caspian's ears, a brutal percussion against the backdrop of Linx's strangled gasp. Lynx's eyes, wide with a horrifying mix of disbelief and the dawning comprehension of his own mortality, stared blankly at the blade protruding from his heart. The coppery reek of his lifeblood, thick and cloying, filled Caspian's nostrils as the weight of his act settled upon him, a cold, heavy mantle of grim satisfaction mixed with a bitter undercurrent of regret. He'd expected defiance, a desperate struggle, but Linx's collapse had been devoid of grace, a stark reminder of the swift, brutal end Caspian had so efficiently delivered.

The silence wasn't merely absence; it was a physical violation, a clawed fist crushing the air from my lungs, leaving me gasping for breath in a vacuum of stark terror. My ears screamed, a discordant symphony against the frantic, traitorous drum of my heart, a frantic tattoo against the ribs that felt like they might shatter. Linx... a broken doll, his form a grotesque parody of life, sprawled amidst the carnage. Caspian's strike, a blur of motion still seared into my very soul, a bone-deep ice that froze my blood and constricted my breath.

The stench... God, the stench! Brimstone, raw and sulphurous, a demonic perfume clinging to the reeking copper tang of Linx's spilled lifeblood. It was a living thing, a malevolent entity in itself, thick and suffocating, a palpable presence that vibrated with the lingering chaos of the spell, a raw, untamed power that hummed with the aftershock of annihilation. The air itself tasted of death, metallic and acrid, a grim testament to Caspian's ruthless efficiency, a brutal efficiency that mirrored the icy calculation I'd always sensed, hidden beneath his charming facade. This... this wasn't just a battle; it was a ritual sacrifice, and I, the horrified witness, was left drowning in its foul, lingering essence.

Caspian's ragged breath, a harsh rasp against the suffocating stillness, was the only sound. He loomed over Linx, a silhouette etched against the fading light, the obsidian blade still slick with ichor, dripping with the lifeblood of the fallen demon. The tremor in his hand, barely perceptible, betrayed the violence he'd just committed. Those eyes, usually glittering with a dangerous, almost playful brilliance, were now bottomless pools of something dark and primal. A horrifying, beautiful grief wrestled with a chilling, cold satisfaction, a tempest of raw emotion that both terrified and enthralled me. It was a glimpse into the brutal, magnificent heart hidden beneath the polished veneer of the man I thought I knew, a glimpse that promised both oblivion and ecstasy.

"He wouldn't. Stop," Caspian rasped, the words catching in his throat like blood. The metallic tang of his sheathed sword filled the air, a stark counterpoint to the coppery taste of fear still clinging to my tongue. His muscles, coiled tight as a viper about to strike, vibrated with barely contained rage. The chill of the dungeon air seemed to intensify around him, a palpable dread clinging to the damp stone walls. *"He meant to brand you. To claim you, body and soul, for eternity."* His gaze, a glacial storm of shadowed grey, pierced me. A lifetime of unspoken battles, of victories hard won and losses etched onto his soul, flickered across his face, a glimpse into the abyss from which he'd clawed his way back. *"I couldn't. Let him defile what is sacred to me."* The tremor in his voice, barely audible, revealed a depth of feeling far more terrifying than any overt threat.

My eyes, magnets drawn to the abyss of Caspian's gaze, locked. Disbelief, a physical force, choked the breath from my lungs, a vice around my windpipe. The air hung thick and acrid, a miasma of burnt sulfur and the sickeningly sweet metallic tang of Linx's pulverized flesh. The stench, a brutal symphony of death, clawed at my nostrils, a grotesque reminder of the carnage. Gone. Linx, that monstrous thing, whose infernal touch still seared phantom fire across my skin, whose very presence had been a soul-crushing weight, a suffocating shadow, dead. And Caspian... Caspian, that enigma cloaked in shadows deeper than any grave, the architect of my torment, the one who'd danced with my nightmares and whispered promises of oblivion... my saviour? Again. The irony burned hotter than any sulfurous pyre, leaving bitter ash in its wake. A saviour who had also played a part in this... this atrocity. His face, a mask of chilling stillness, revealed nothing, yet somehow everything. His silence roared louder than any battle cry. The weight of his gaze, of his responsibility, pressed down on me, a suffocating burden almost as heavy as Linx's absence.

The silence screamed loudly in the air around us. It wasn't the tranquil quiet of peace; rather it was the deafening roar of a thousand unspoken questions, each one a razor blade slicing through the fragile calm that enveloped us. This shared near-death experience, this grotesque baptism of blood, had forged an alliance as delicate as spun glass yet paradoxically strangely stronger than anything we had known before. The murder—the shocking and unexpected demise of Linx at Caspian's hand—hung heavily between us like a volatile catalyst igniting emotions we had long buried. The weight of our unshared burdens pressed down demanding acknowledgment. In that moment we were bound together by a darkness that threatened to consume us yet it also sparked an unbreakable bond that would forever alter our fates.

His eyes, pools of molten obsidian reflecting the flickering torchlight, held a darkness that mirrored my own. But beneath that shadowed depth, I saw something else... something that chilled me to the bone and ignited a wildfire in my gut. The sexual tension wasn't just there; it pulsed, a raw, feral energy that thrummed between us like a second heartbeat, a discordant symphony of desire and dread. It was the heat of a furnace against my skin, the taste of blood and ash on my tongue, the phantom weight of his touch lingering, a cruel and exquisite torment. Our connection, born in the crucible of our first encounter, was no longer a simmering ember. It was a raging inferno, threatening to consume us both. The Obsidian Covenant's threat was a distant hum compared to the explosive potential of this... this us.

An eerie quiet descended upon the cavern. The immediate peril had vanished, yet a profound unease lingered, a palpable weight of consequence pressing down on them. A deep sigh of relief warred with an unsettling weariness and the gnawing sting of culpability.

Linx's demise, a savage act of necessity, cast a long shadow. The silence pulsed with the residue of battle, a haunting resonance of their brutal deed, a stark testament to their own inner demons. The world's destiny remained precarious, a menacing spectre eclipsing all else. Yet, in this aftermath of violence and hard-won victory, a peculiar intimacy blossomed between me and Caspian—a shared comprehension forged in the crucible of bloodshed, a mutual acknowledgment of their shared fragility and the treacherous path they trod. Their future was veiled in enigma, their connection precarious and fragile, but the bond between them, solidified by this horrific ordeal, was irrefutable. The abyss had struck again, but I and Caspian emerged, transformed, our alliance irrevocably altered. The conflict was far from concluded.

A precarious hush reigned in the cavern, instantly vulnerable. Linx's demise cast a heavy pall, a tangible burden suffocating the motionless air. Caspian returned his blade to its scabbard; the sharp metallic snap resonated harshly in the suffocating quiet. He faced me, his features an enigma, a façade of suppressed rage overlaid with… exhaustion, a profound, bone-deep weariness.

A grim urgency resonated in his raspy whisper echoing the weight of impending danger. *"We must depart immediately* "he urged, his eyes scanning the shadows as if they could materialize threats. *"The Obsidian Covenant's awareness of his disappearance will trigger an immediate and relentless pursuit. Time is not on our side and every second we delay increases the peril we face."*

Stunned, I registered a delayed assent. The brutal savagery of the event left a foul acidity on my tongue. Though the death had been swift, almost a kindness, the deed itself remained a palpable chasm between them, a silent condemnation. The shared culpability of their blood-soaked bond pressed down, a crushing weight far exceeding any physical strain. My gaze dropped to my hands; I was astonished by their faint tremor. The lingering spectre of Linx's invasive touch, a chilling defilement, continued to fester beneath my skin, an unwelcome phantom.

Caspian's eyes mirrored my own, a fleeting shadow of profound anguish momentarily eclipsing his countenance. His hand extended, fingertips lightly grazing mine—a tacit understanding of our shared

190

ordeal, a connection forged in the fires of brutality. The contact, surprisingly soothing, anchored me to the immediate moment, a powerful counterpoint to the internal tempest raging within.

Caspian's voice, firm and resolute, declared, *"Our survival hinges on arriving at Malazar's core ahead of them. It's our sole opportunity."*

Malazar's core: a globe of obsidian, thrumming with malevolent energy, fueled the Covenant's might. A reckless, self destructive maneuver, it remained their solitary lifeline. Toppling the Covenant's architect—the monster who razed her village, the one whose infernal legacy was a daily, agonizing battle against her bloodlust—this was a quest forged in the crucible of fiery retribution.

Their journey was fraught with peril. They navigated treacherous pathways, their movements swift and silent, each step a calculated risk. The fortress walls echoed with unseen movements, the air thick with the malevolent presence of the Covenant. They encountered patrols, and skirmishes erupting in quick, brutal bursts of violence. Caspian fought with the ruthless efficiency of a seasoned warrior, his movements a blur of shadows and steel, his demonic power a force to be reckoned with. Exhaustion clung to me like a shroud, internal chaos a tempest in my soul, yet I fought with a ferocious resolve born of vengeance. My power, a raging inferno, consumed my foes with terrifying efficiency. Years of relentless training had sharpened my skills; my control, once fallible, was now absolute, surgically precise. The incandescent fury simmering within me became a weapon of unimaginable destruction. My vampiric nature, a persistent, gnawing hunger, was subdued only by an agonizing act of self-mastery, a necessary, brutal discipline.

An unspoken discord vibrated between them, a constant, menacing hum beneath their lethal game. Their brutal proximity, the fleeting glimpses of shared fragility within the maelstrom, unexpectedly intertwined their fates, forging a paradoxical bond of intense, precarious closeness. Bound by absolute trust, their actions became one, a seamless, balletic slaughter executed in the abyss.

Caspian's gaze held a watchful distance, his countenance betraying minimal emotion. He spoke sparingly, his movements precise and swift. But amidst the chaos, in the lulls between harrowing confrontations, subtle cracks appeared in his stoic facade. A fleeting caress, a shared glance pregnant with unspoken meaning, a silent concordance that transcended mere communication, these ephemeral moments, easily disregarded as pragmatic necessities, ignited like embers of warmth in the frigid core of their perilous pact.

The journey to the Covenant leader's sanctum was an ordeal, demanding both mastery and fortitude. A chilling aura, thick with suffocating foreboding, descended upon them. They navigated the labyrinthine, dimly lit passages, past inert sentinels, their perceptions sharpened, every fibre vibrating with tension. As they neared the chamber, an oppressive force, a palpable burden, pressed down, crushing their spirits. The oppressive quiet was almost a physical presence, pierced only by the thunderous pulse of their own fear.

A vast, echoing chamber yawned before them, its heart a colossal obsidian throne. Upon this dark eminence sat the Covenant's leader—a behemoth cloaked in shadows, radiating an oppressive weight of authority. His very being pulsed with a malignant energy, a tangible menace that choked the air. Surrounding him, a legion of Covenant soldiers stood vigilant, their eyes blazing with fervent devotion, their lethal arms gleaming ominously under the feeble illumination.

On the precipice of a seemingly impossible task, Caspian and I stood defiant. The weight of insurmountable adversity pressed down, but we remained steadfast, our eyes fixed on the Covenant's tyrannical leader, our determination unshakeable. This was the final reckoning. The crucible of destiny awaited.

A tempest of fire and steel erupted, a frenzied dance of carnage. My pyromantic onslaught was a precise, annihilating torrent. Caspian, a whirlwind of demonic fury, fought with savage abandon, his powers cleaving through the Covenant ranks with terrifying elegance. Together, they were a vortex of destruction, their combined might be an overwhelming spectacle. But the Covenant legions were a relentless tide, their assault unwavering. Caspian and I, battered and exhausted, our powers waning, were driven to the brink.

The Covenant's leader, a malevolent force at the battle's epicentre, remained unshaken. Infernal energy, unleashed in relentless surges, fractured the earth, a cataclysmic tremor convulsing the very ground. Overwhelmed by the sheer, terrifying might, Caspian, with an act of selfless courage, interposed himself, as a bulwark against the annihilating assault. He absorbed the full fury of the demonic explosion, his form collapsing under its devastating weight.

Caspian's agonizing collapse was a horrifying spectacle. A tempest of fury, untamed and ferocious, consumed me, igniting my latent abilities. With every fibre of my being, I unleashed a torrent of power; my fiery essence blazed with unprecedented intensity. I battled with the ferocity of a whirlwind, shattering the Covenant's ranks, and carving a desperate pathway to reach Caspian.

A wave of agonizing power surged through me as I finally reached Caspian, my hands trembling as I cupped his head, his hair slick with sweat and blood. The crimson bloom on his lips was a horrifying blossom, a stark contrast to the ghostly pallor of his skin. His eyes, usually so bright, were clouded with pain, yet a faint, heartbreaking smile flickered across his lips. The whisper that escaped him, barely audible above the frantic thump of my own heart, tore at my soul. *"Worth it,"* he breathed, the words catching in his throat, each syllable a testament to his unbearable sacrifice. Tears blurred my vision, the taste of despair bitter on my tongue as I felt the life draining from him, leaving me with a crushing emptiness in its wake.

The final battle was a desperate, heart-wrenching act of defiance. My grief, a raw, bleeding wound in my chest, fueled a rage that burned hotter than any dragon's breath. It was a power that surged through me, a terrifying, exhilarating force that transcended even my own understanding, a power born of utter devastation and fueled by a love so profound it shattered the very chains of despair.

The leader, his power diminished by Caspian's selfless, agonizing sacrifice, a sacrifice I could still feel echoing in the marrow of my bones, found himself utterly outmatched. In a whirlwind of searing flame and untamed magic, I brought him down, each striking a hammer blow against the mountain of my sorrow. With the leader of the Obsidian Covenant vanquished, I tasted a bitter victory, a triumph stained with the blood of my village, a pyrrhic win bought with the life of my dearest Caspian. The silence that followed was deafening, filled only with the phantom echo of his laughter, a ghost of a smile that would haunt my dreams forever.

The silence clawed at my ears, a physical pressure crushing my chest, heavier than the mountains of corpses surrounding me. The reek of blood, coppery and acrid, stung my nostrils, mingling with the metallic tang of fear still clinging to the air. Broken Covenant bodies, limbs twisted at unnatural angles, littered the ground like discarded toys, their vacant eyes staring up at a sky that mocked our victory with its cold indifference. My fingers, numb with the icy chill of death, traced the jagged line of Caspian's shattered cheekbone. Tears, freezing instantly on my skin, felt like tiny shards of ice against the burning agony in my soul. His death wasn't a sacrifice; it was a brutal, agonizing theft, a violation that left a chasm in my very being, a wound that burned with a searing, unholy fire.

This pyrrhic triumph tasted like ash and bile. The cheers of the others were muted, distant, drowned out by the roaring tempest in my head, a maelstrom of grief and rage. Their gamble had paid off, but the price... God, the unspeakable price! The victory was a hollow shell, echoing with the screams of the fallen, each whisper a searing brand on my memory. A suffocating wave of despair threatened to pull me under, to drag me down into the suffocating darkness that clung to us all, a darkness woven from the threads of loss, stained crimson with the blood of our shared nightmare.

Caspian my beloved Caspian whose eyes were usually sparkling with mischief and warmth were now glazed and still devoid of the light that once defined him. He was the brilliant strategist, the reckless warrior, the man who had held my heart in his calloused hands, reduced to this... this broken husk of his former self. How could this be? We had stared into the abyss together and it had stared back leaving an indelible mark on our souls that felt both haunting and forever etched in our memories. The world that had once been vibrant and full of promise had now transformed into a wasteland mirroring the overwhelming emptiness that gnawed at my gut. It was a relentless gnawing pain that threatened to consume me whole, leaving me gasping for breath in the suffocating silence. Every moment without the man I loved felt like a dagger to my heart, a reminder of what we had lost and what I feared we might never regain. The weight of despair hung heavily around us binding us to this desolate reality.

This victory, this bitter, blood-soaked triumph, felt like a curse, a constant, agonizing reminder of what we had lost, of the love that had been stolen from me, leaving behind only a hollow ache and the crushing weight of unimaginable sorrow. Our intertwined fates, forged in the hellfire of battle, were irrevocably, devastatingly scarred. The crimson stain on my hands, Caspian's blood, would forever be a testament to the terrible, utterly devastating cost of our victory.

CHAPTER

TEN

Embers of Sacrifice

A malevolent thrum, a palpable pulse of wickedness, resonated through the obsidian throne chamber, vibrating deep within my very being. God, what is this? It feels... ancient, a sickness at the heart of the world itself. The Covenant's chief, a colossal figure shrouded in darkness, lifted a hand, talons extended. He's... enjoying this. Savouring our fear. From him unleashed a geyser of sinister power, a virulent torrent of hatred that crashed against Caspian and me. Caspian! I hope he's alright... We were flung against the merciless stone, its surface fracturing and disintegrating under the brutal force. My bones are screaming! This is... far beyond anything I've ever faced. The atmosphere crackled with potent energy; reality itself seemed to unravel at the seams. Is this... death? Or something worse? No, I won't succumb. I can't. Not now. Not like this. I have to protect Caspian... I have to find a way to fight back... but how...?

Caspian's body slammed against the jagged edges of the shattered pillar, the impact of a brutal percussion echoing in his skull. The taste of blood, metallic and thick, coated his tongue as a guttural scream, ripped from his very soul, tore through the silence. He heaved himself up, each muscle screaming in protest, a symphony of agony that clawed at his mind. The icy fire in his eyes, usually a glacial storm threatening to consume all in its path, was now a dull, agonizing ember, choked by the suffocating weight of pain. His vision swam with crimson, the fractured stone a grotesque blur against the throbbing in his temples. With a trembling hand, he sheathed his blade—a concession to mortality that felt like a branding iron upon his pride.

This was no mere conflict; it was a maelstrom of violence that had carved its way through his very being, leaving a trail of crimson destruction in its wake. The infernal power he wielded, once a seamless extension of his will, now felt like a crushing burden, a leaden weight anchoring him to the precipice of oblivion. Each ragged breath was a reminder of his mortality, a stark contrast to the godlike strength he was accustomed to. The world tilted, a dizzying carousel of pain and the stark, inescapable reality of his near demise. His arrogance, his unshakeable composure, lay shattered beneath a mountain of his own blood.

A tempest of rage possessed me. My incandescent hair, a fiery halo, framed the fury in my eyes as I unleashed a cataclysm of flame. A searing inferno, born of vengeance and despair, incinerated the Covenant soldiers, leaving only dust in their wake. My assault was brutal, instinctual, a desperate dance of destruction driven by the need to shield Caspian, to obliterate the memory of my ravaged village, to finally vanquish the shadows that had clung to my soul. Each eruption of fire was a raw, agonized shriek, reflecting the maelstrom within. The vampiric craving clawed at the edges of my self-control, a relentless torment I fiercely battled to subdue. My formidable power, once a crushing weight, now flowed through me, a honed instrument of death wielded with breathtaking lethality.

Undeterred, the Covenant's chieftains chuckled—a rasping, gravelly sound that reverberated through the echoing expanse of the Obsidian Chasm. The chasm, a scar upon the face of Xylos, was said to be the birthplace of the Shadow Blight, a malevolent energy that pulsed with a sickly, violet luminescence. His arms, adorned with jagged obsidian bracers pulsating with the same blight, ascended once more. Each upward thrust unleashed fresh surges of malevolent energy, each wave more ferocious than its predecessor, cracking the very fabric of reality itself.

The air crackled with the scent of ozone and brimstone, a familiar aroma to those who had witnessed the Covenant's dark rituals before. The earth beneath them, already riddled with fissures glowing with the Shadow Blight, shuddered, fractured, and then catastrophically collapsed, not into simple darkness, but into a maelstrom of swirling shadows and chaotic energy. They plunged into an abyss of impenetrable darkness, where even the Blight's violet glow was swallowed whole, into a realm of utter hopelessness known only as the Nethervoid, a place from which legends claimed no one ever returned. The screams of the falling chieftains were swallowed by the abyss, leaving only the echoing rasp of the dying wind and the ever-present hum of the Shadow Blight.

The air detonated, a supernova of sound and searing heat that ripped the very fabric of reality. My ears rang, a deafening symphony of destruction, while the stench of ozone and burning flesh choked me. Caspian, a ruin sculpted from shattered bone and torn muscle, flung himself before the blast, a human sacrifice to the inferno. His body, a canvas of crimson blossoming across ravaged skin, crumpled like a discarded doll. The taste of his blood, metallic, coppery, sickeningly sweet, filled the air, a grim testament to the unimaginable force that had struck him. Each convulsion shuddered through him, a brutal tremor that mirrored the seismic upheaval within my own soul. The agony was a physical thing, a claw tearing at my gut, a vice squeezing my heart.

But even as he lay broken, a defiant spark ignited in his eyes, a molten gold burning against the encroaching black. He rose, not with grace, but with a terrifying, agonizing slowness, each movement a testament to sheer, brutal will. His gaze, a searing brand, pierced the chaos, locking onto mine with an intensity that stole my breath. *"Run, Blaze,"* he rasped, his voice a broken whisper, a gravelly sigh against the howling maelstrom. His breath hitched a ragged, desperate gasp, each syllable a precious fragment of his dwindling strength. *"Escape. Live."* The words hung in the air, heavy with the weight of his sacrifice, a cruel, beautiful burden I could scarcely bear.

Flee? The very thought scraped against my soul like shattered glass, a raw and jagged sensation that left me reeling. Caspian's lifeblood pulsed weakly a crimson rhythm against the stark white of the snow, each beating a hammer blow against the granite of my resolve reverberating through my very core. To abandon him? To leave him to the merciless clutches of the Covenant's viper Malkor whose laughter echoed in my ears like the crack of a whip sharp and unforgiving? His eyes cold and calculating held the chilling gleam of obsidian reflecting a darkness that chilled me to the marrow. The thought was unthinkable—no it was a blasphemy against everything I believed in everything I held sacred. To turn my back now would be a betrayal that would etch itself into my very bones an indelible mark of shame and cowardice. I could not allow fear to dictate my actions nor could I permit the weight of despair to smother the flickering flame of hope that still resided within me.

My rage wasn't a mere surge; it was a volcanic eruption, molten fury choking me, searing my lungs with its incandescent breath. The air itself tasted of ash and blood. This wasn't just survival; it was a primal scream against the encroaching darkness, a desperate, clawing fight for the only man who'd ever shown me the fragile, incandescent beauty of compassion amidst the suffocating despair of this frozen hell. Caspian, with his haunted eyes that mirrored the vast, unforgiving landscape, and a spirit that burned with a stubborn, defiant flame even as his body faltered. He was the lighthouse in my unending storm, the single flickering candle in a tomb of ice. And I would tear down Malkor's empire, stone by agonizing stone, to keep that flame alive.

The coppery reek, thick and suffocating, clawed at my throat, a metallic shriek mirroring the ragged rasps tearing from his chest. His skin, the parchment hue of forgotten centuries, felt like crumbling bone beneath my shaking fingers; ice clinging to the fragile pulse thrumming faintly beneath. Each shuddering breath was a desperate, choked defiance against the encroaching abyss, a black tide I would fight to the death to keep from claiming him. My fear tasted like rust and ash on my tongue, a bitter metallic tang, but it was drowned in a burning, volcanic rage, a primal scream against the cold, skeletal fingers of death reaching for him. He wasn't just a man; he was a tempest of contradictions, a wildfire of defiance burning in the heart of a storm. His soul, etched with scars that mirrored my own, a map of battles fought and lost, pulsed with a stubborn, defiant light. He was everything I clung to, everything I'd risked everything for. And I wouldn't let him fade, not to this cold, grasping oblivion. Not without tearing the very fabric of existence apart to save him. I would not let him die.

A roar, a guttural scream ripped from the scorched landscape of my soul, echoed the cataclysm within. I surged, a human volcano erupting, the air itself shimmering with the heat of my incandescent rage. The taste of ash and blood filled my mouth; the stench of burning flesh and ozone stung my nostrils. Every fibre of my being, every last dying ember of my power, fueled the inferno that consumed me. My flames, once disciplined, now pulsed with a desperate, crimson madness, a chaotic dance of annihilation. Precision was a forgotten luxury; strategy, a laughable weakness. This wasn't a fight; it was a primal scream rendered in fire and fury. Each blow landed not with calculated lethality, but with the blind, unhinged power of a cornered beast. I was a maelstrom of destruction, a hurricane of burning hatred, a tempest of agony unleashed upon this world. The earth trembled beneath my onslaught, the air itself cracked and wept under the pressure of my wrath. They would remember me not as a warrior, but as the very embodiment of their undoing. The lingering scent of my carnage, a bitter perfume of devastation, would forever stain their memory.

Blood roared in my ears, a crimson tide drowning out the screams of the Covenant. My muscles, screaming in protest, obeyed the primal fury that possessed me. The stench of burnt flesh and ozone filled my nostrils, a sickeningly sweet perfume to the carnage I wrought. Each swing of my blade was a thunderbolt, a searing white hot arc that cleaved through their ranks. Their shields, once a wall of impassive defiance, shattered like cheap glass under the weight of my rage; their desperate cries were swallowed by the inferno I had become. I tasted the metallic tang of blood, my mixing with theirs, a bitter sacrament to my brutal dance. Caspian's face, pale and ravaged, flashed before my eyes, a desperate plea etched into his features. That image, that burning need, fueled me; the darkness that had been my constant companion for years recoiled before the incandescent white heat of my protective rage. It wasn't merely a light; it was a supernova igniting within me, consuming the shadows, leaving only the single-minded purpose of reaching him, of saving him from the abyss. My heart, a frantic drum against my ribs, hammered out a rhythm of desperate hope, a terrifying counterpoint to the symphony of death surrounding me.

The stench of salt and decay hung heavy in the air as I reached Caspian, his body a stark, shivering monument on the blood-soaked sand. My knees buckled, the gritty ground scraping against my skin as

I knelt, cradling his ravaged head in my calloused hands. His skin was slick with a clammy sweat that chilled me to the bone, and it felt like polished marble, impossibly cold. Each ragged gasp tore at the silence, a rasping sound that echoed the hollow ache in my chest. His eyes, glazed with a film of death's encroaching frost, flickered up to meet mine, eyes that had once held the wild glint of a storm, now mirroring the desolate, grey expanse of the sea.

Pain, a raw, physical agony, warred with a strange, unsettling peace in their depths. A heartbreaking, almost obscene serenity. *"Worth it,"* he breathed, the words ghosting from his lips, a breath barely strong enough to rustle the stray strands of his blood-matted hair. A cruel, twisted smile, a rictus of defiance against the encroaching darkness, played on his lips. The taste of salt and the coppery tang of blood filled my mouth, mirroring the bitter, unshed tears welling in my own eyes. This wasn't just a death; it was a sacrifice etched onto his very being, a testament to a soul both broken and gloriously, tragically, whole.

The acrid bite of cordite filled my nostrils, a metallic tang clinging to the hot, scalding tears that traced rivers down my soot-stained cheeks. His eyes, the colour of a storm-wracked sea, locked onto mine, a terrifyingly calm blue amidst the swirling chaos. My own heart, a trapped bird beating against its cage of ribs, splintered under the unbearable weight of his sacrifice. This wasn't just an ending; it was a brutal, final punctuation mark etched in blood and fire. I felt the ragged rasp of his breath against the silence, each exhale a whispered goodbye, each inhale a desperate, failing struggle against the encroaching dark. He was a broken statue, carved from courage and sculpted by unimaginable pain, his life force seeping away like sand through ravaged fingers. He had given everything, his spirit, his strength, his very soul, not for some abstract ideal, but for me, a debt I could never repay, a burden I would carry to my grave. The scent of his blood, sharp and coppery, mingled with the stench of death, branding the moment onto my soul. His gaze, even now, held a fierce, unwavering love, a love that burned brighter than any inferno, even as his body succumbed to the cold embrace of oblivion.

His death—a searing brand on my soul—ignited a furnace within. Not just anger, no. This is... deeper. It's everything I ever felt for him, twisted and weaponized. The raw, animal rage that had clawed at my throat twisted, sharpened, into a diamond-hard resolve. He took everything. Everything. And now... now I take back. Power, viscous and incandescent, flooded my veins, a molten tide that slammed against the Covenant leader, throwing him back as if he were a child's toy. Good. Let him feel the fear. Let him know what it means to face the storm you unleashed. He staggered, his eyes, usually cold and calculating, widening with a terror I savoured.

That look... that's what I wanted. That's the price of his actions. The tide had turned, yes, but it was a tsunami of my grief, a maelstrom of my burning will to live, to avenge. Live? I will live, and I will make sure his name is whispered in fear for generations to come. My breath hitched, and a ragged sob caught in the throat of a scream. Don't break now. He wouldn't want you to break. Then, fueled by the phantom weight of his hand on my shoulder, the echoing rasp of his dying breath still ringing in my ears, I unleashed it, the final, obliterating wave. This is for you. This is for us. This is... justice.

The chamber didn't merely roar; it shrieked. The air itself cracked and splintered under the onslaught of my flame magic, a maelstrom of searing heat that tasted of ash and brimstone on my tongue. The heat blistered my skin, yet I felt nothing but the exquisite agony of retribution as the firestorm consumed him, his screams swallowed by the inferno. When the flames finally subsided, leaving only the acrid stench of Sulfur clinging to the scorched stone, a chilling silence descended. Only the faint, almost imperceptible whisper of his final, defeated gasp remained. The ashes, fine and grey, swirled like the ghosts of his ambition in the dying embers.

The battle ceased, not with a whisper, but a gut-wrenching, bone-jarring silence that clawed at my ears, a void where the screams and clang of steel had been. The acrid stench of burnt flesh and ozone hung heavy in the air, a suffocating shroud clinging to my lungs. I crumpled beside Caspian, the cobbles biting into my knees. Victory? It felt like a lead weight crushing my chest, a hollow mockery ringing in my ears. His hand, still warm with the ghost of life, grew frigid in mine, the chilling reality of his absence settling like ice in my veins. Each stolen breath was a searing reminder of the price. His sacrifice, a crimson tapestry woven with agony and courage, had toppled the Obsidian Covenant and avenged the charred remains of my home, a place that now existed only as ash and bitter memory in my soul. But the pyrrhic triumph tasted like ash, leaving behind only the bitter, desolate landscape of my grief. He, my Caspian, the fire in my heart, the anchor of my soul, was gone, and with him, everything I held dear. The victory was a poisoned chalice, leaving me bereft, a hollow shell echoing with the ghosts of what could have been.

The world fractured into a kaleidoscope of blood red and gunmetal grey blurring at the edges of my vision. The screams, once a deafening roar, now rasped like a dying beast in my ears, a phantom pain in my skull mirroring the ache in my chest. His hand was still imprinted on my skin like a brand, a searing ghost of warmth against the creeping chill that threatened to consume me. Gone. He's gone. The taste of iron, metallic and coppery, clung to my tongue, a bitter reminder. His death wouldn't be meaningless. No. I'd make sure of it.

His strength, a molten fire branding my veins, refused to die. The phantom heat of his sacrifice seared my chest, a jagged scar that pulsed with a raw, agonizing rhythm, the frantic beat of a heart ripped open, its ragged edges still smoking. It wasn't just a memory; it was the phantom touch of his lips on mine, the taste of blood and ash lingering on my tongue, the ghost of his scent, sandalwood and ozone, clinging to my skin. Our madness, a desperate, incandescent dance on the precipice of oblivion, had been a supernova, yes, but one that left behind not just embers, but a black hole in my soul, a gravity well pulling me into an endless vortex of grief and rage. This wasn't vengeance, not merely retribution. This was the hurricane-force wrath of a soul shattered, a storm born of love so breathtakingly beautiful, so brutally destructive, that it etched itself into the very fabric of my being. It was the screaming echo of us, a testament to the exquisite, agonizing torment of our incandescent, self-immolating passion.

The darkness wasn't just an absence of light; it was a clawing entity, thick as tar and heavy as a tombstone on my chest, choking the breath from my lungs. A chasm yawned before me, a fetid maw reeking of grave dirt and the metallic tang of blood, a stench that clung to the ragged edges of shattered hope and the pulverized remnants of lives brutally extinguished. They'd driven a stake through its heart, yes, but the beast still throbbed, its shadow a malignant blight across the desecrated earth, a landscape etched with the scars of its fury. I would confront it. Alone? Perhaps. But never truly, utterly alone. His essence, a wildfire burning in my soul, was inextricably bound to mine, a phantom limb fused to my very being. I felt the icy ghost of his touch, the phantom kiss branding my skin with the searing memory of his lips, a brand I would carry to my grave. I would keep him with me, a sacred vow etched in the marrow of my bones. Each ragged breath, each frantic heartbeat, a defiant hymn to our forbidden love, a burning oath whispered on the gale force winds of the approaching apocalypse. Forget him? Never. Yield? My very soul would shatter before I succumbed.

The air enveloped me in a greasy suffocating shroud thick with the stench of burnt flesh and ozone that clawed at my throat. The acrid tang lingered in the back of my mouth a metallic scream that echoed on my tongue—the taste of death itself hot and coppery. Dust fine as pulverized bone danced mockingly in the skeletal shafts of light that struggled to penetrate the shattered obsidian remnants of the once-magnificent throne room. Silence reigned supreme but not the gentle hush of slumber; rather it was a suffocating palpable void, a tangible pressure that crushed the breath from my lungs. It felt as though an invisible force bore down upon me a weight so immense it threatened to shatter my ribs with its relentless grip. My gasps came out ragged and shallow, the only sound reverberating in this tomb of broken marble, each breath a desperate strangled plea against the oppressive stillness that surrounded me. Every inhalation felt like a battle, each exhalation a surrender to the overwhelming despair of the scene before me. In that desolate space where echoes of the past lingered like ghosts, I was left alone with my thoughts and the haunting remnants of what had once been a place of power and glory now reduced to a haunting memory.

Caspian's weight, a dead weight of lead and despair, dragged me down. His hand, cold as gravestone, a death grip that felt strangely intimate, clung to mine, his icy fingers digging into my flesh. Each frantic heartbeat, a thunderous drum against the oppressive quiet, echoed the terror that gnawed at my soul. His stillness, his lifelessness, a damning accusation of my failure. The overwhelming guilt, a suffocating tide, threatened to drown me more surely than the miasma. I had failed him. Again. The bitter taste of ash and regret coated my tongue, mingling with the metallic tang of blood, his blood, my blood, smeared across my hands, a testament to our shared failure.

This victory... This putrid triumph choked me, a taste of ash and bile, acrid and bitter on my tongue. The Obsidian Covenant, their shattered husk of a leader, a charred monument to my wrath, lay amidst the pyre. A mountain of corpses, a grotesque monument sculpted in agony and screaming flesh, fueled the inferno. Their screams, a symphony of terror, still clawed at the ragged edges of my sanity. I had won, yes. But the cost... Christ, the unspeakable cost.

Caspian's vacant eyes, twin pools of lifeless obsidian reflecting the hellfire that consumed us both, stared into the abyss, a mirror to the void gnawing at my soul. His stillness, a crushing weight, a physical burden on my chest, pressed down, heavy as the guilt that clung to me, thick and suffocating as the smoke still clung to my throat. The stench of charred flesh, a miasma of death and decay, permeated my being; a branding iron searing its image into the very marrow of my bones, a gruesome, indelible testament to this hollow, blood-soaked victory. The feel of his cold, stiff hand in mine, moments before... a phantom touch that burned with an icy fire. His last breath, a rasping whisper against my ear, a silent curse echoing the screams of the fallen. This victory? It's a festering wound, a poisoned chalice I'll forever clink against the bitter teeth of my own damnation.

Caspian's weight, a suffocating tombstone of a man, crushed the breath from me. His corpse, a leaden sack reeking of damp earth and the coppery tang of his own blood pinned me to the cold, unforgiving ground. The lingering warmth of his skin, obscene against mine, felt like a branding iron searing a memory into my flesh, a horrifying smoothness that mocked the brutal violence that had ended him. The iron stench, thick and metallic, clawed at my throat, a brutal symphony of death echoing the crimson tide that had drained from him, leaving behind only this... this grotesque parody of the man he was.

His eyes, those twin embers that once burned with a furious, incandescent brilliance, a chaotic beauty that both terrified and enthralled me, were now dull, lifeless orbs reflecting the fractured moonlight, a pathetic imitation of the stars they mirrored in life. That smile, a cruel, mocking rictus frozen on his lips, felt less like a brand and more like a psychic scar, a festering wound in my soul. It was a testament to the savage, desperate hope that had fueled him, a wildfire I had personally stamped out with my own two hands, leaving only ashes and the bitter taste of regret. The dust motes dancing in the moonlight seemed to mock me, each one a tiny, accusing spectre of his vibrant life, now stolen, and the weight of that theft pressed down on me, heavier than his lifeless body. The emptiness, the echoing silence of his absence, screamed louder than any lament.

Caspian. The name itself tasted like burnt iron and ash on my tongue, a bitter echo of the inferno that had consumed him. His eyes, even in death, haunted me, twin pools of molten gold reflecting the hellfire he'd wrestled with, the demons he'd slain. He'd smelled of wood smoke and ozone, a scent now permanently etched into my memory, a phantom perfume clinging to the ragged edges of my sanity. He'd defied the very fabric of existence, a tapestry woven from defiance and shadowed power, his sacrifice a pyre blazing brighter than a thousand suns. Not a mere libation; a flaying, a gutting of his very soul, offered to that ravenous, obsidian god of vengeance, Malkor's patron, a monstrous entity whose hunger gnawed at the very foundations of reality.

My village, a festering wound on the face of the earth owed its very existence to his obliteration to the agonizing screams that still echoed vividly in my ears haunting my every thought. Yet I the wretch he had fought so fiercely for the one he had entrusted with the fruits of his suffering and sacrifice had betrayed him in the most unimaginable way. This was not merely a simple failure or a momentary lapse in judgment; it was a betrayal so profound so deeply laced with cowardice and self-serving deceit that the very air itself seemed to recoil from its stench. Each day I found myself surrounded by reminders of his legacy, the very foundations of our village steeped in his memory. And with every passing moment, the weight of my treachery bore down on me a relentless reminder that I had squandered the trust and hope he had placed in me leaving nothing but a void in my heart where redemption should have thrived.

His death, a brutal masterpiece of carnage, a symphony of shattering bone and spilled viscera, played on an endless loop in my mind. The victory, a hollow shell, crumbled to dust between my fingers, leaving only the acrid taste of regret and the suffocating weight of his sacrifice. His blood, Malkor's crimson curse, stained not just my soul, but the very marrow of my being, a permanent, searing brand that would fester and bloom with every passing heartbeat. The agony wasn't just physical; it was the slow, agonizing unravelling of my soul, each thread snapping with the sickening crunch of bone, leaving me a broken husk, a testament to my unforgivable failure.

My fingers, ghosting over the harsh line of his jaw, snagged on the stubborn stubble, a phantom touch, a cruel mockery of warmth. The rasp of it against my skin was a physical echo of the grief that ripped through me, a raw, visceral wound. He'd been my shield, my shadow, my... everything. The incandescent heat of our connection, forged in the white-hot furnace of shared peril, now left only a chilling emptiness. It had been a burning rope, binding us together, a torment and a salvation all at once. His scent, the sharp tang of wood smoke and something wild, uniquely him, still clung to my skin, a cruel reminder. We'd started as wary wolves, eyes locked in a dance of mistrust and simmering, desperate hunger. That hunger had bloomed into something ferocious, something breathtaking, something I only truly grasped now that the silence was deafening, the world a hollow shell without his presence. The bitter taste of loss coated my tongue, a metallic tang that mirrored the agony clawing at my soul.

The darkness, a clawing, icy hand, still clung, but it's vampiric hunger was a whisper compared to the gut-wrenching emptiness. Empty. Like a well that's been pumped dry, leaving only the gritty sediment of despair. The rage, a searing brand across my soul, had been a wildfire, consuming all, but now it was ash, a bitter taste on my tongue. Ash...is that all I am now? Reduced to this...this hollow shell? My profound loss—it wasn't just a shadow; it was a gaping maw in the fabric of reality, swallowing the light. Light... I remember the light. Warmth. Laughter. Was it all a dream? A cruel, fleeting dream? The silence screams louder than any roar ever could. It mocks me. It whispers that it's permanent. That this...this abyss...is my home now. And the worst part? The quiet acceptance creeps in, a chilling, insidious tendril wrapping around my heart. Is this…giving up? No. It's…resignation. A weary surrender to the inevitable. But even resignation has a bitter aftertaste, doesn't it? A slow, agonizing drip of despair.

The fire within, once a blazing inferno that fueled my every strike against the demonic hordes, felt like embers choked by suffocating grief. The heat was gone, replaced by a chilling hollowness, the mocking echo of power now useless against the final, inescapable darkness that had claimed him. The scent of his blood, still faint in the air, a phantom touch, only deepened the torment. I'd tasted the blood of a thousand demons and felt their life force drain into me, yet this… this absence, this silence… It was a wound that would never heal. I had shattered the skull of a demon lord and felt his ichor splatter across my armour, but I couldn't save Elias. My anchor, my storm-battered refuge, snatched away, leaving me adrift in a sea of despair. He was the reason the fire had burned so fiercely, the heart beating within the rage. Now, the heart was still. The fire was dead.

A shudder, deep and visceral, pulsed through the fractured earth, a guttural groan resonating in my very marrow. The stone beneath me heaved, fissures like a morbid web spreading across the floor. The already unstable chasm was succumbing to its weight, a slow, agonizing disintegration. Escape was paramount; I had to flee this sepulchre of despair before it consumed me. Yet, the prospect of abandoning Caspian, leaving his lifeless form to the merciless crush of the collapsing cavern, was agonizing. I would not allow him to be swallowed by the encroaching dust and debris; his fate would not be oblivion.

A white-hot spike of adrenaline, a feral torrent of power, ripped through me, forcing my arms to heaven Caspian's weight—a dead weight, chillingly cold against my sweat-slicked skin. The reek of blood, thick and metallic, filled my nostrils, mingling with the acrid tang of smoke and the coppery taste of my own terror on my tongue. My muscles, screaming in a chorus of agony, threatened to tear under the crushing burden. Each fibre burned with the searing knowledge of his stillness, the finality of it a cruel, physical blow. Instinct, a raw, untamed beast within, clawed at the reins of my reason; every strained breath, every agonizing step, precise, desperate defiance of the chaos that gnawed at my soul.

The ground, a treacherous tapestry of splintered wood and pulverized stone, grated against my knees as I navigated the ravaged landscape, each movement a gamble against the imminent, crushing weight of oblivion. The air itself vibrated with the unspoken promise of further devastation, a tangible pressure on my chest, a suffocating premonition of what lay ahead. My heart hammered a frantic tattoo against my ribs, a frantic drumbeat against the silence of death that clung to Caspian like a shroud.

A hairline fracture, a venomous scar across the ancient stone, snaked into the darkness, a forgotten exit I'd noted in the death throes of our initial assault on the throne room. The stench of mildew and decay, thick as a shroud, clung to the air, a chilling whisper against my skin. This wasn't just a passage; it was a knife edge of dread, a gauntlet thrown down by the very stones themselves. My only hope is a desperate, bloody prayer against the suffocating weight of our doom. My heart, a frantic drum against my ribs, urged me onward. The distant gleam, a malevolent eye in the abyss, pulsed with a sickly promise. Fear, cold and sharp, clawed at my throat, yet a harder, colder thing, a grim determination forged in the fires of countless betrayals and near deaths, propelled me into the maw of the earth. I would not succumb. Not here. Not now.

The rasping of my breath, a counterpoint to the screech of wind-whipped rock, mirrored the agony in my soul. Each step was a crucifixion, my boots sinking into the treacherous screen, the weight of Caspian's absence a physical vice around my chest, crushing the air from my lungs. The taste of grit and blood, my own, I was sure, coated my tongue, a bitter reminder of this infernal pilgrimage. My grief, a tangible thing, clawed at my throat, a monstrous shadow lengthening with each agonizing mile. But I would not yield. Caspian, my brilliant, reckless Caspian, deserved more than this desolate expanse. His sacrifice, a wound that ripped through my very being, demanded a sacred atonement. I would not rest until his body, defiled by this cursed mountain, lay consecrated, his spirit finally at peace, a final, agonizing offering laid at the altar of his memory. This, my torment, was my penance. My obsessive, burning purpose.

The air hung thick and fetid, a suffocating blanket clinging to my skin as I finally stumbled into the hidden passage. The tunnel, a black maw reeking of damp earth and something ancient, something wrong, squeezed the breath from my lungs. Each ragged gasp scraped against raw ribs. Exhaustion, a crushing weight, threatened to drag me under; my vision swam with dizzying blacks and grays. My legs, leaden and trembling, threatened to give way. The taste of dust and despair coated my tongue. Then, I fell, the rough stone a brutal caress against my cheek. But even as the world tilted, a tidal wave of relief crashed over me, drowning the agony. I had escaped the crumbling, mausoleum-like throne room, its whispers of death still echoing in my ears. I had secured Caspian's remains, his broken, precious body, a burden and a victory clutched tight against my soul. The stench of decay clung to him, a bitter reminder of the price of freedom. But it was a scent I would bear, a testament to my defiance, to my impossible triumph.

The wasteland clawed at me as I stumbled from the suffocating darkness. Ice, not wind, lashed at my face, each shard a tiny, agonizing death. The taste of it was metallic, a coppery tang mingling with the bitter reek of ozone clinging to the bruised, plum-black sky. Above, the dying light bled across the shattered obsidian peaks of what had once been the Obsidian Covenant's fortress, a monument now to a butchery so complete, that it echoed in the very marrow of my bones. The silence wasn't calm; it was a suffocating pressure, a monstrous weight pressing down, heavy with the ghosts of screams and the reeking, acrid stench of shattered lives. My own ragged breath hitched in my throat, a desperate gasp in the face of this...this annihilation. The world, remade in fire and shadow, felt like a tomb waiting to swallow me whole. The crushing weight of my failure, the failure of us, settled onto my shoulders, a burden heavier than any mountain.

The victory tasted like ash. A metallic tang coated my tongue, the phantom echo of blood still clinging to the air, thick and cloying. No triumphant roar escaped my lips, only a ragged breath that rasped against the ravaged landscape of my soul. The hollowness within me wasn't simply a void; it was a chasm, a gaping maw that swallowed the light, leaving only the bitter chill of a winter's night clinging to my bones. My heart, once a fiery forge, was now a cold, dead cinder, each beating a hammer blow against the cage of my ribs. The screams of the fallen, a symphony of agony, still clawed at the edges of my mind, a torment sharper than any blade.

They'd called it retribution for this pyrrhic triumph that seemed to shimmer with illusory glory. But the blood staining my hands—the blood of those I loved and held dear—was a crimson tide that surged forth a relentless wave that would forever drown the fragile embers of my fleeting joy. This wasn't a victory; it was annihilation, a hollow shell of triumph that echoed with despair. A victory forged in the fires of hell a descent I had willingly embraced leaving behind the ashes of everything I had ever cherished and held close to my heart. The cost of this so-called victory? Unbearable and insurmountable. The weight of my actions crushed me beneath it, a titan of sorrow pressing down grinding me inexorably into the dust from which I had once drawn strength and hope. Each breath I took was heavy with remorse, a reminder that in seeking retribution I had lost far more than I could ever reclaim.

Uncertainty shrouded the future, a path veiled in ambiguity lay before me. The global order had fractured, its equilibrium shattered beyond repair. Unforeseen perils loomed, and formidable obstacles awaited. Yet, I would confront them, fueled not just by my pyromantic abilities, but by the incandescent memory of Caspian, his fortitude, his ultimate offering, forever etched in my soul. His legacy, a sacred trust, demanded I persevere, ensuring his sacrifice would not be in vain, his death a catalyst for lasting victory.

The victory tasted like ash and blood, a bitter grit clinging to my tongue, a phantom echo of Caspian's final, agonizing breath rasping in my ears. This hollow triumph bought with a price too steep to bear, felt like a fist clenched around my heart, squeezing the air from my lungs. The sorrow, a monstrous weight, threatened to crush me beneath its obsidian claws, to drag me down into the mire of despair where even the faintest glimmer of light was extinguished. But from the ruins of my soul, scorched and scarred, a fierce fire ignited.

Caspian's face, etched in the memory of my soul, a ghostly vision shimmering behind my eyelids, fueled this inferno. His hand, strong and warm in mine only moments before the shattering blow, was now a spectral presence, guiding my every move. His loss—a wound that ripped through my very being, leaving a jagged, bleeding chasm—would not define me. It would forget me. The darkness, a palpable entity, pressed against me, a suffocating shroud woven from the whispers of doubt and the chilling breath of grief.

The glacial fingers clawed at my flesh, a venomous kiss of frost that stole the breath from my lungs. The reek of his death, a symphony of rot and brine, choked me, a miasma clinging to the wind like a shroud. But I would not break. I would not yield to the suffocating darkness that threatened to consume me. Alone, I stood at the precipice of oblivion, yet Caspian's spirit, a phantom limb thrumming with forbidden power, pulsed within me. His love, a white-hot brand seared into my very being, burned brighter than a thousand dying stars, defying the endless night. His sacrifice, a jagged scar across my soul, a testament to a love both fierce and agonizing, would not be meaningless. It would be my strength, my weapon, my vengeance.

This pyrrhic victory, a bitter, metallic tang of ash coating my tongue, the acrid stench of smoke still clinging to my clothes, would be the bedrock of something monstrously magnificent. His death, a gaping wound in my soul, a phantom limb that throbbed with a constant, agonizing ache, would fuel the forge of my vengeance. I would build a world worthy of him, a world sculpted from the raw, searing agony of loss, a testament forged in the white-hot crucible of my grief. His sacrifice, a scream swallowed by the void, would become a defiant, echoing roar that shattered the complacent silence of that suffocating darkness. A world where his light, though snuffed out like a candle in a gale, would burn eternally within me, a furious, incandescent inferno against the encroaching night. A blazing, unflinching beacon that would guide me, consume me, and ultimately, consume them all.

CHAPTER

ELEVEN

Broken Bonds

T he silence that followed the final, earth-shattering explosion was deafening. Not the peaceful quiet of a forest clearing, but a heavy, oppressive silence, pregnant with the lingering scent of burnt ozone and the metallic tang of blood. God, that smell...it's clinging to everything. To me. To him. Caspian lay cradled in my arms, his body still warm but his breathing shallow, erratic. So shallow. Each breath... a tiny, fragile thing. The triumphant roar that had once echoed through the cavern was replaced by the chilling whisper of impending death. This... this isn't right. It shouldn't end like this. His chest rose and fell with agonizing slowness, each breath a struggle against the unseen forces that were slowly draining the life from him. I can feel it, the life ebbing away. Like sand through my fingers. And there's nothing... There is nothing I can do to stop it. Damn it, damn it all to hell!

A wave of nausea washed over me, the metallic tang of blood suddenly overwhelming. Is this what it feels like? To watch someone die? To be powerless... My fingers tightened around his still-warm form, a desperate, futile attempt to hold on to something, anything, in the face of the encroaching void. No... no, please... don't let this be the end. Not like this.

Agony ripped through me, a screaming symphony of shattered bone and shredded flesh. The stench of my own blood, metallic and acrid, filled my nostrils as each ragged breath sent spasms of pain jolting through my ruined body. My magic, once a blazing inferno that could scorch the heavens, was a dying ember, flickering pathetically against the encroaching darkness. It felt like a ravenous beast gnawing at my very soul, a vile mockery of the power that once flowed through me. The vampiric hunger, a constant, gnawing companion since the Obsidian Covenant's brutal betrayal, was a mere whisper compared to the cataclysm within. This wasn't just pain; it was the shattering of my spirit, a profound grief so immense it threatened to tear me asunder, to unravel the very fabric of my existence. The taste of ash and despair coated my tongue, mirroring the desolate wasteland that had become my inner world. This wasn't just death; it was annihilation.

My fingertips, ghosting the exquisite line of his jaw, lingered on the stark angles of his cheekbones, now alarmingly pallid. The intense, almost feral gleam that usually blazed in his eyes was extinguished, their fiery depths clouded, reduced to a bleak, ash grey. Even in death, a haunting, almost spectral beauty clung to him, a cruel jest against my grief. The vivid scarlet of his blood, staining my hands, offered a stark counterpoint to the chilling coolness of his skin. His blond hair, once impeccably groomed, lay in disarray, dark tendrils plastered to his brow, matted with the grim residue of his final struggle.

The earth ripped a scream from my gut, a seismic howl that resonated not just in my bones, but in the very soul of me. Dust, the acrid scent of pulverized stone and something else... something ancient and foul, choked my lungs. The cavern's heart, once a throbbing pulse of obsidian power, expelled its final breath, a groan that felt like the dying gasp of a titan, a sound that clawed at the edges of sanity. Fractures, like venomous veins, throbbed crimson with molten rock, spreading across the floor in a grotesque parody of life, consuming the ravaged throne room. The obsidian shards, once gleaming with the power of the Covenant, now lay scattered, mocking the memory of their obscene might. My own hand, stained crimson, trembled, not from fear, but from the unbearable weight of what I'd done.

This... victory, choked with the bitter tang of dust and the metallic reek of blood, felt like a funeral pyre built upon the ruins of my own soul. The echoes of their annihilation, a symphony of shattered stone and dying breaths, haunted me, a testament not to my power, but to the terrible price of my ambition. The taste of ash was nothing compared to the gnawing emptiness in my heart, a void carved by a sacrifice that would forever stain my memories.

Caspian's inert weight, a crushing burden in my arms, was a stark testament to my inadequacy. I had not safeguarded him; I'd been unable to deflect the encroaching shadows that had engulfed their existence. My oath—to avenge my ravaged village, to obliterate the Obsidian Covenant—had cost me everything; it had claimed the one soul truly precious to me. Images assaulted me—shared perils faced side by side, tentative explorations of affection, the fierce, consuming love that had flared between us amid the carnage. Their bond, forged in mutual suspicion and a smouldering attraction, had grown into something extraordinary, something I'd only grasped in its devastating absence.

Clawing terror choked me, a vice around my throat. The cave wasn't just collapsing; it was exploding inwards, a monstrous groan of fracturing rock that vibrated through my bones, tasting of dust and the metallic tang of fear. Entombment wasn't a threat, it was a certainty, a suffocating weight pressing down on us both. But desertion? A betrayal as cold and unforgiving as the stone itself. Not yet. His sacrifice, the reckless, beautiful madness of offering himself to appease the ravenous beast within me, ignited a fury within, a white-hot blaze that incinerated my self-preservation. I had to save him. Not just a life, but this life, this fragile, exquisite shell holding the soul I'd come to crave, a soul that sang a melody so exquisite it eclipsed even the gnawing emptiness in my own cursed heart. The scent of his blood, still lingering on my tongue, was a promise, a torment, a desperate prayer. I would not fail him.

My muscles screamed, a symphony of agony conducted by the devil himself, as I heaved him upward. Each fibre burned, a searing brand, a testament to the impossible weight I bore. The stench, a gut-wrenching blend of decay and pulverized earth clawed at my throat, a suffocating vice threatening to collapse my lungs. His limp body, heavier than any mountain, pressed against me, a chilling reminder of his utter dependence, a dependence that gnawed at my soul. Abandonment? The thought was a viper coiled in my gut, its venom coursing through my veins, spurring me onward.

The ground, treacherous and unforgiving, groaned a death rattle beneath each agonizing step. Loose scree skittered underfoot, threatening to send us both tumbling into the abyss. My vision blurred, a kaleidoscope of sweat and dust, gritty and bitter on my tongue. Tears, hot and stinging, mixed with the grime caked onto my face, a grotesque mask of my suffering. But surrender was not an option. Not when the bitter taste of betrayal still clung to my palate, a more potent poison than any miasma. Not when the ghost of his trust, fragile as spun glass, demanded I carry on, carry him to...to what? I didn't know. But I would. I had to.

A barely perceptible cleft, a fracture in the unforgiving rock, presented itself—a desperate avenue of retreat I'd dimly registered on our descent. This perilous, claustrophobic channel, choked with shadows, offered my sole hope of survival as the cavern threatened to implode. I slithered through, the abrasive stone grating cruelly against my flesh, my agony a mere trifle in the face of certain death. Caspian's lifeless weight, a crushing reminder of my hard-won triumph, pressed upon me, a sombre testament to the brutal price of victory.

The tunnel choked me, a tomb of suffocating darkness pressing in from all sides. Each step, a grinding agony against the slick, slime-coated rock, felt like dragging a mountain. The air, thick and fetid with the stench of damp earth and something ancient and vile, clawed at my lungs, stealing the breath from my screaming body. Phantasmal eyes, twin points of incandescent green, burned into the blackness ahead, the imagined claws of some hellish predator tearing at my very soul, a visceral, gut-wrenching terror. The taste of fear, metallic and acrid, coated my tongue.

But Caspian's near death, his shattered, trusting gaze seared into my memory, fueled a fury that burned hotter than any hellfire. His sacrifice, a crimson stain on the cold stone of this cursed passage, wouldn't be in vain. Not while I still drew breath, not while this gnawing, desperate hope remained. I would reach the end of this abyss, if it killed me, and damn the consequences. I moved, a driven automaton, fueled by vengeance and a grief so profound it threatened to shatter my very being.

Finally, I collapsed into the suffocating darkness of a hidden alcove, a tomb carved into the groaning heart of the ancient stones. The air bit at my lungs, a glacial fist clenching around my ribs, the silence a crushing weight compared to the screaming chaos I'd left behind. My body, a broken vessel, betrayed me, each shudder a fresh wave of the horror I'd barely escaped. The damp stone chilled me to the bone, a stark contrast to the sweat still clinging to my skin, a grim testament to my frantic flight. My escape? A pyrrhic victory, the metallic tang of blood, my own, or another's, I couldn't tell, a bitter mockery of triumph coating my tongue. The hollowness echoing within me was far deeper than the cavern itself, a chasm of fear and exhaustion threatening to swallow me whole.

A barren expanse unfolded, a stark testament to the war's brutal passage. The twilight sky, bruised plum and ominous, clawed at my skin with its icy breath. A profound stillness hung in the air, suffocating, laden with grief's unbearable burden. The Obsidian Covenant's subjugation had been secured yet at a price beyond comprehension. Caspian's absence hollowed the world, plunging it into an abyss of unending night.

The weight of comprehension slammed into me, a physical blow that stole the air from my lungs, leaving only the bitter taste of ash and betrayal. My village was avenged, yes, the crimson stain on the earth was finally dry, but at what monstrous price? His light, the only beacon piercing the suffocating darkness of my grief, was snuffed out, brutal, agonizing darkness that clawed at the edges of my sanity, the scent of wood smoke and death clinging to it like a shroud. The path ahead, a jagged scar across a ravaged landscape, the wind a mournful keening through the skeletal remains of our homes, promised only more pain.

Yet, to yield to the despair that gnawed at my soul, to let the icy tendrils of hopelessness wrap around my heart... that was a betrayal I would not commit. He, with his eyes the colour of a storm-wracked sea and a laugh that once chased away shadows, wouldn't have it. I would etch his memory into my very being, a living testament to his courage. I would become the embodiment of his indomitable spirit, a wildfire consuming the darkness, relentlessly pursuing the fight for the world he died defending, a world stained with the blood of innocents, a world that now owed him a debt only vengeance could repay.

Caspian's face, peaceful in its finality, held a subtle, almost mischievous grin. A profound sorrow washed over me, yet his ultimate offering would not be in vain. I vowed to champion his cause, his memory a radiant star illuminating the pervasive gloom. Though darkness still clung to the world, a renewed purpose ignited within me, forged in the fires of grief and anguish. From the wreckage of this pyrrhic triumph, I would emerge, resolute and unshakeable. I would confront tomorrow, not in solitude, but with Caspian's indomitable spirit as my steadfast companion. The struggle, I knew, was far from over.

The wind, a razor-edged blade, tore at my cloak, icy fingers clawing at my exposed skin as I carried Caspian's lifeless weight across the ravaged landscape. The aftermath of the battle was a panorama of devastation; the Obsidian Covenant's once-impregnable fortress, a monument to dark power, lay shattered and smoking, a grim tableau of their pyrrhic victory. Twisted metal shrieked a mournful song against the mournful howl of the wind, and the air hung thick with the stench of blood and burnt timber. My triumph felt hollow, a bitter parody of victory, the sweetness of revenge long since swallowed by the overwhelming tide of grief. Caspian's stillness in my arms was a leaden weight, a constant, agonizing reminder of the terrible cost, not merely of the battle, but of the friendship, the loyalty, and the shared dreams now reduced to ashes in the wind. Each ragged breath I drew felt like a shard of glass in my lungs, mirroring the jagged fracture in my soul.

I found a sheltered cave, a small sanctuary carved from the very rock itself, and gently laid him down on a bed of moss as soft as a newborn's breath. The meagre light filtering through the cave mouth painted his face in a chiaroscuro of shadow and illumination, a stark contrast between his almost unearthly beauty and the grim finality of death. His lips, slightly parted in a sigh that seemed to linger on the air, held a serene expression, a mask of peace that belied the chilling pallor of his skin, the subtle bluish tinge beneath his translucent eyelids hinting at the icy grip of the end. The silence of the cave, broken only by the occasional drip of water, amplified the profound stillness of his repose, a stillness that felt both heavy and exquisitely fragile.

I ran my fingers along the smooth curve of his cheek, tracing the line of his jaw, the sharp angles of his bone structure, now chillingly still, devoid of the vibrant life that had once animated him. A profound sense of loss washed over me, a grief so immense it threatened to crack my very being. The memories of their encounters, vivid and agonizing, flooded my consciousness: the initial, prickly hostility, a battlefield of words and wary glances that had slowly given way to a simmering tension. This tension, a potent, volatile brew, had gradually morphed into something deeper, more complex, a connection forged in the crucible of shared adversity. I recalled the perilous missions they'd undertaken together, the grudging respect that bloomed amidst the chaos, a fragile flower pushing through concrete. Then there was the passion, explosive and undeniable, a wildfire ignited in the heart of the storm; a desperate, beautiful defiance against the crushing weight of their circumstances. Each of these moments, once vibrant and real, now felt impossibly precious, irretrievably lost, shards of a shattered masterpiece. The silence in the room amplified the enormity of my sorrow, a deafening testament to the absence that echoed in my soul.

Our alliance, a precarious edifice built on shifting sands of mutual mistrust and a simmering, unspoken desire, had been repeatedly tested, strained to the very brink of collapse by the relentless, unforgiving demands of our mission. The trust we'd forged, fragile as a butterfly's wing, had felt real, palpable, a fragile bloom in a desert of suspicion. Now, doubt, cold and insidious, coiled around my heart, suffocating the embers of belief. Had Caspian's allegiance been genuine, a selfless act of sacrifice born of shared purpose? Or had his aid been a meticulously crafted performance, a puppet show of feigned camaraderie, a calculated manipulation designed to achieve an end I couldn't even begin to fathom? The subtle shifts in his gaze, the carefully chosen words, the almost imperceptible hesitations—they now played back in my mind like a damning indictment, each a tiny tremor foreshadowing the potential chasm of betrayal that yawned between us.

Doubt, a venomous serpent, coiled icy tendrils around my heart, its scales shimmering with the cold gleam of betrayal. His final act, the reckless, extravagant outpouring of his lifeblood, the very essence of his being, offered to shield me from her vampiric hunger, was it a testament to genuine, selfless love? Or a masterpiece of manipulation, a carefully orchestrated performance designed to bind me to him forever? The question gnawed at me, a relentless torment that overshadowed even the crushing weight of my grief. His sacrifice, so profoundly moving on the surface, felt tainted, a desperate gambit for posthumous control, a cruel twist of the knife that pierced the fragile tapestry of my sorrow. The very air around me seemed to vibrate with the chilling possibility, the suspicion of a bitter poison that seeped into my bones, twisting the sweet memory of his love into something acrid and suspect. Was I truly free, or merely a puppet dancing on the strings of his even in death dominion? The uncertainty was a torment far worse than any physical pain.

Days bled into weeks, each indistinguishable from the last. The cave became my prison, my sanctuary, a damp, echoing tomb where I kept vigil over Caspian's lifeless form. I couldn't bring myself to abandon him, not yet. A morbid intimacy bloomed in that confined space; a strange solace, born of grief, clung to me like the clinging dampness of the cave walls. His stillness, the chilling pallor of his skin, held a perverse comfort. I spoke to him constantly, a relentless monologue pouring from my lips. I relived the brutal battle, painting vivid word pictures of the carnage, the screams, the stench of blood and fear. I bared my soul, confessing my deepest fears, of failure, of abandonment, of the gnawing uncertainty that shadowed my future.

My doubts, once whispered anxieties, now roared like a caged beast within me. Anger, hot and corrosive, gnawed at my insides, a festering wound mirroring the one in my heart. And then came the confession, the unspoken truth that festered beneath the surface of my grief: the chilling suspicion that our alliance, forged in necessity and sealed in blood, had been nothing more than a calculated power play, a cynical dance of ambition where I had been as much a pawn as he. Had he been using me? Or had I been no better than he, equally driven by self-interest, equally blind to the true cost of our shared ambition? The question hung unanswered, heavy and suffocating in the still, cold air of the cave.

The oppressive silence of the cave pressed in, broken only by the relentless drip, drip, drip of water from the cavern ceiling, a metronome counting down the agonizing seconds, a monotonous rhythm that mirrored the hollow ache in my chest. The air hung heavy, thick with the scent of damp earth and something else, something faintly familiar that only amplified the phantom touch of his hand lingering on my skin. Memories, vivid and brutal, assaulted my senses: the intoxicating scent of his cologne, a heady mix of sandalwood and something dark and masculine; the feel of his lips, a searing brand on my soul; the raw, untamed fire of our passion, a conflagration that now felt like ashes in my mouth. Sleep offered no respite; instead, I replayed our conversations, dissecting each syllable, each subtle inflection, each pregnant pause, searching desperately for a hidden meaning, a subtle shift in tone, any shred of evidence that might explain the inexplicable, the shattering betrayal that had left me adrift in this desolate cavern of my own making. Even the echoing drips seemed to mock my desperate search, each one a tiny hammer blow against the fragile remains of my hope.

The candlelight, a frantic, sputtering thing, threw jagged shadows that writhed and pulsed like living things. Caspian's reek, wood smoke thick as a shroud, overlaid by the acrid tang of blood, a metallic whisper that clawed at the back of my throat, hung heavy in the air. His discarded cloak, a dark, whispering thing that seemed to hold its breath, lay sprawled on the table, a macabre tapestry. A seam, barely a breath's width, a scar upon its shadowed surface, betrayed a secret. My fingers, slick with a cold sweat, traced its phantom line, each tremor a rebellion against the icy dread that gripped me. With a gasp, a choked prayer caught in my throat, I pressed.

Within the dimly lit confines of the ancient chest nestled amongst the soft velvety lining lay a slim leather-bound scroll that seemed to pulse with an energy all its own. Unfurling it with agonizing slowness each movement felt like an intrusion into a world long forgotten. I found myself staring at a series of cryptic symbols, a chilling tapestry of arcane markings etched in a spidery script that appeared to writhe under the flickering candlelight. An icy tendril of fear snaked up my spine leaving a trail of gooseflesh in its wake as if the very essence of the scroll was alive and aware of my presence. My heart raced a frantic drum against my ribs threatening to shatter the fragile silence of the room. In that moment I felt the weight of history pressing down upon me urging me to decipher its secrets or risk being consumed by the shadows that lurked just beyond my sight.

Each painstakingly deciphered symbol revealed a fragment of a horrifying truth, a chilling mosaic assembling itself before my eyes. The coded messages spoke not of mere treachery, but of a vast, sprawling conspiracy, a betrayal that dwarfed any I could have previously conceived. Its tendrils, I realized with a sickening lurch, reached into the highest echelons of power, threatening to unravel the very fabric of our world.

Caspian's entanglement with Whispering Wind, the shadowy organization he'd vehemently denounced, ran far deeper than I'd ever imagined. The intercepted messages revealed not mere collaboration, but a secret alliance forged in the darkest corners of the underworld, a pact with the infamous Obsidian Covenant. This revelation wasn't merely a crack in the already precarious edifice of my trust; it was a catastrophic collapse, leaving me reeling amidst the rubble of shattered faith. The betrayal felt visceral, a cruel twist of the knife that exposed the insidious manipulation I'd been so blind to. I was adrift, utterly alone in a sea of deception, the bitter taste of betrayal clinging to the back of my throat.

The rage that ignited within me was a wildfire, consuming all reason and threatening to incinerate the fragile remnants of my grief. The man I had foolishly placed on a pedestal, the man who'd sworn oaths of loyalty, risking his life for mine, the man I was terrifyingly close to loving, he was a viper, a venomous liar, a traitor whose deceit stung with the icy venom of betrayal. This wasn't just a breach of trust; it was a shattering of my very soul, a seismic event that ripped apart the carefully constructed foundation of my world. The weight of his treachery pressed down upon me, a crushing, suffocating burden that added to the already unbearable heaviness of my loss, a weight threatening to drag me beneath the waves of despair. Each breath was a struggle, each heartbeat a painful reminder of the man he pretended to be, the man I would never know.

The biting wind, a physical manifestation of my despair, whipped around me, a stark counterpoint to the still-smouldering embers of the Obsidian Covenant's pyre. Alone, utterly alone, I stood in the desolate wilderness, the skeletal remains of trees clawing at the bruised twilight sky. The ghost of Caspian, his laughter echoing faintly in the mournful howl of the wind, was a constant, agonizing companion. His betrayal, the final, crushing blow after the shattering loss of our village, felt heavier than the pack I carried, a leaden weight pressing down on my soul. The victory, the hard-won triumph over the Obsidian Covenant, had felt like a pyrrhic one even then, a fleeting moment of triumph swallowed whole by the encroaching darkness.

I had avenged my village, yes, but the cost was unbearable. Caspian was gone, ripped from my life, taking with him not only the vibrant love we shared but also the fragile shoots of hope and trust I'd painstakingly nurtured. The world, once vibrant with possibilities, now felt barren, mirroring the bleak landscape that surrounded me. My heart, a shattered mosaic of grief and betrayal, ached with a loneliness so profound it threatened to consume me entirely.

My future stretched before me, a bleak and uncertain landscape shrouded in the icy grip of betrayal. The path ahead, a treacherous precipice strewn with peril, was one I had to navigate alone. My only companions were the flicker of my magic, the sharpness of my wit, and a resilience forged in the fires of heartbreak. This world, I knew now, was a brutal arena where survival was a daily struggle, and trust, a fragile, shimmering jewel rarer and more valuable than life itself. The weight of the deception pressed upon me, a crushing burden augmenting my grief; a leaden cloak clinging to my soul. Memories, once cherished treasures, were now tarnished, their vibrant hues dulled by the bitter poison of treachery. The passionate fire of our shared past now smouldered, choked by the acrid smoke of betrayal, leaving behind only ashes and a searing emptiness. The very air tasted of loss, a constant reminder of the shattered trust and the agonizing price of innocence.

Caspian's sacrifice, once a beacon of selfless love illuminating my world, now cast a long, chilling shadow. What I'd perceived as an act of devotion was revealed as a calculated maneuver, a final, desperate assertion of control in a game whose scope dwarfed my comprehension. The agonizing realization struck me with the force of a physical blow: I had been a pawn, a mere piece in a chess match played on a board far grander than I could have ever conceived. I had been used, my trust meticulously manipulated, my affections cynically played upon, and ultimately, betrayed by the very person who had begun to weave a fragile, intoxicating spell around my heart. The cold, hard truth, a bitter pill to swallow, left me reeling, the sweetness of nascent love replaced by the acrid taste of disillusionment and betrayal.

The battle was won, a pyrrhic victory etched in the blood-soaked earth. But the war, a relentless tide of shadow and sorrow, had only just begun. A chilling certainty, cold as a winter's grave, settled upon me: my fight would not be solely against the Obsidian Covenant, their malevolent power and tangible darkness, but against the insidious spectres of shattered trust, the ghosts of betrayal whispering insidious doubts in the echoing chambers of my heart. Vengeance, once a blazing inferno consuming my every thought, was now interwoven with a deeper struggle, a desperate, agonizing battle against the insidious poison of treachery, a frantic fight to salvage the fragments of my faith in humanity, or rather, the horrifying absence of it in those I once considered allies.

I would face the future alone... Alone? Again? The thought tasted like bitter ash in my mouth. A solitary figure silhouetted against the encroaching darkness... Is this really my life now? A perpetual twilight? But I would not be broken. No. Not this time. I've been broken before, but I've mended. I will mend again. From the ashes of despair, I would rise, stronger... Stronger than what? Stronger than the memories that claw at me in the night? Stronger than the doubt that whispers insidious lies? More resolute... Resolute in what? In facing the unknown? In accepting the inevitable loneliness? And infinitely more cautious... Cautiousness is good. Cautiousness keeps you alive. But will it also keep me from living?

The oppressive darkness that clung to me like a shroud... It feels like a physical weight, pressing down, suffocating... would not consume me; It won't. I won't let it. it would instead forge me anew... Forge me into what? A weapon? A shield? Something... hardened. hardening my resolve into an unbreakable shield... A shield against what? Against the pain? Against the fear? Against the inevitable heartbreak? driving me onward toward a future shrouded in uncertainty... Uncertainty is all I've ever known, isn't it? yet undeniably perilous... Perilous, yes. But also... potentially... liberating? Is that even possible?

The journey ahead promised to be a gruelling odyssey, a relentless march through treacherous landscapes both physical and emotional. But I would not falter. I would not yield. I would survive. I would endure. And I would avenge not only the innocent souls lost in the burning ruins of my village but also the shattered remnants of my spirit, the wounds inflicted by those I once held dear. My vengeance would be a testament to my resilience, a beacon burning bright in the encroaching night.

The coded messages weren't merely a revelation of Caspian's deception; they were a harrowing exposé of his soul, a chilling glimpse into the tormented past that had warped his actions and driven him to such desperate measures. As I painstakingly deciphered the cryptic symbols, a harrowing narrative unfolded, a tragic tale of betrayal so profound it had etched itself onto his very being, a story woven from threads of manipulation, agonizing self-doubt, and increasingly frantic attempts at redemption. Caspian, it transpired, had been far more than a pawn in a larger game; he was a master manipulator, a cunning double agent operating at the very heart of Whispering Wind, subtly, almost invisibly, sabotaging their operations from within. His alliance with me, his seemingly selfless sacrifices, acts that had initially seemed born of unwavering loyalty, were all meticulously orchestrated components of a brilliantly conceived plan, a daring gambit designed to cripple the Obsidian Covenant from the inside, a plan born of vengeance and a desperate yearning for absolution.

The weight of his past pressed down on him like a physical burden. The damning messages weren't just words on a screen; they were echoes of a life he desperately wanted to bury, a life spent as a fervent devotee of the Obsidian Covenant, a brutal organization whose methods were synonymous with unimaginable suffering. He'd meticulously documented his atrocities, unspeakable acts of cruelty, horrors perpetrated in the name of a twisted loyalty that now clawed at his conscience, poisoning his sleep and driving him to a relentless, agonizing pursuit of atonement. His metamorphosis from ruthless enforcer to clandestine saboteur wasn't a sudden, dramatic break; it was a slow, agonizing crawl through a landscape of self-loathing, a tortuous journey toward self-redemption, each step stained with the blood of his past. The very air he breathed seemed thick with the ghosts of his victims.

The fragmented messages, scrawled in hurried hands across scavenged scraps of parchment and hastily keyed into malfunctioning datapads, chronicled a harrowing descent into despair. Each entry, a testament to the corrosive effects of guilt, revealed a growing disgust with the Covenant's brutal efficiency, a sickening realization of the monstrous ideals he had once fervently embraced. He had seen, up close and personal, the grotesque aftermath of his actions, the vacant stares of the innocent, the chilling silence where laughter once echoed, the lingering stench of death clinging to the ravaged landscapes he had helped to create.

The heartless warrior he once was lay shattered, a husk replaced by a soul consumed by remorse. Guilt, a relentless, gnawing beast, had taken root in his heart, its venomous tendrils slowly, inexorably, eating away at his very being, leaving behind only a hollow shell of the man he used to be. His desperate attempts at atonement were meticulously documented: clandestine acts of sabotage, carefully planned to cripple the Covenant's war machine without causing undue suspicion; subtle acts of subversion, like whispers of dissent sown among the ranks; covert operations to shield innocents from the organization's wrath, to minimize the carnage, a silent, solitary war waged from within the very heart of the enemy. Each entry was a desperate plea for absolution, a fragile hope clinging to the tattered edges of his fractured soul.

The messages laid bare the festering roots of his hatred, revealing a depth far beyond simple factional conflict. It wasn't merely opposition; it was a poisoned wellspring fed by a past transgression, a personal failing that gnawed at his conscience, and mine. His past life as an Obsidian Covenant enforcer wasn't just a detail; it was the smoking gun. He had been instrumental, a key player, in the brutal, systematic destruction of my village, a horrifying event that etched itself onto my soul, a brand that fueled my relentless pursuit of justice. The memory, dredged up by his confessions, struck me anew with the force of a physical blow, a gut-wrenching cocktail of profound sadness and incandescent rage. The man who, with twisted, self-serving intentions, had attempted to offer me aid, was the same man who had played a crucial, devastating role in the annihilation of everything I held dear. The revelation was a brutal, agonizing unravelling of a complex tapestry woven from threads of guilt, betrayal, and the desperate, elusive hope of redemption. The weight of it pressed down, suffocating.

He sought redemption not in grand, sweeping pronouncements, but in the quiet, precise choreography of defiance. His sabotage was surgical, targeting key operations with an almost artistic precision, crippling the enemy while minimizing collateral damage. He fed vital intelligence to the resistance, whispers in the dark that guided their strategies, ensuring victories that spared innocent lives. Each act, each carefully crafted coded message, was a confession, a desperate plea etched in the language of subversion. He was a man fractured by his past, his loyalties a constantly shifting kaleidoscope, his motivations veiled in a labyrinth of deceit. The path he walked was morally ambiguous, a twilight zone where shadows danced with a conscience. His methods, at times undeniably dubious, were nonetheless imbued with a palpable yearning for atonement, a silent scream for absolution whispered in every carefully placed line of code, every cryptic symbol painstakingly drawn. The very air around him crackled with the tension between his dark history and his burning desire to atone.

I found a twisted, almost perverse empathy within Caspian's messages, a reflection of my tormented soul. His internal struggle mirrored mine with unsettling accuracy: both of us wrestling with the crushing weight of past actions, the suffocating burden of guilt and the seductive whisper of vengeance. We both clawed for redemption, though our paths diverged wildly, our methods as different as night and day. My anger, initially a white-hot inferno fueled by grief and the bitter sting of betrayal, began to cool, replaced by a chilling, unsettling understanding. Caspian's attempts at amends, however clumsy and flawed, revealed the intricate tapestry of his character, a testament to the brutal internal battles he waged against his demons. The sheer desperation in his efforts, the raw vulnerability peeking through the cracks of his hardened exterior, forced me to confront the horrifying possibility that we were, in essence, two sides of the same broken coin.

His plan, a Machiavellian tapestry woven from ambition and desperation, was intricate and lethally dangerous. It demanded a series of balletic maneuvers, each step a calculated risk, requiring not only cunning manipulation but an unwavering, almost fanatical commitment. The stakes were astronomical; failure wasn't simply an option—it was a death sentence, not just for him, but for countless others caught in the web he had spun. He had played a perilous game of deception, a high-stakes gamble on a treacherous landscape riddled with betrayals and shifting alliances, forever teetering precariously on a razor's edge between the ghosts of his past and the uncertain future he craved. The messages weren't merely admissions of guilt; they were a raw, unflinching confession, a desperate plea for understanding and forgiveness, a testament to the often overlooked human capacity for profound change, for wrenching self-redemption even in the face of unimaginable consequences.

The coded messages, however, offered only fragmented glimpses into Caspian's actions, leaving behind a frustrating trail of gaps, inconsistencies, and tantalizing hints that hinted at a far more elaborate and sinister plot. This conspiracy, a venomous serpent coiled around the Obsidian Covenant and Whispering Wind, extended far beyond their immediate sphere of influence, its tendrils reaching into the deepest shadows of their world. Caspian's involvement transcended mere participation; his actions were inextricably interwoven with a tapestry of ancient prophecies, long-forgotten alliances, and forces of such terrifying power that they threatened to unravel the very fabric of reality, leaving behind a chaotic void where their world once stood. The implications were staggering, hinting at a conflict of cosmic proportions, a battle for the very soul of their existence.

The revelation hung in the air, a suffocating weight of ambiguity. Caspian, the man I loved, the man I believed I was losing, he was a liar, a traitor, the very betrayal a dagger twisting in my heart. Yet, the truth was far more intricate, a tapestry woven with threads of darkness and light. He had been a protector, a silent guardian, risking everything to stem the tide of bloodshed, a sacrifice that echoed in the hollow chambers of my soul. I remembered the genuine kindness in his eyes, the fleeting moments of tenderness, the quiet acts of care that had blossomed even amidst the poisonous bloom of his deception. These memories, once cherished, now felt tainted, yet their authenticity remained undeniable. He was a complex enigma, a mesmerizing blend of good and evil, light and shadow, his actions a haunting paradox that defied easy judgment. My grief, once a simple ache, now throbbed with a strange, almost painful understanding, a recognition of his multifaceted nature that left me reeling, lost in the labyrinth of his truth.

In his final, selfless act, the crimson tide of his lifeblood spilled forth, a sacrifice not for glory or absolution in the eyes of the world, but a profound act of redemption forged in the crucible of his soul. This wasn't merely self-sacrifice; it was a transcendence, a shattering of the chains of his past, a testament to the dormant capacity for selfless, unadulterated love he held within. His love for me, a fierce, unorthodox flame, burning bright even amidst the shadows of his past, had become the catalyst, the relentless engine driving his desperate, agonizing pursuit of atonement. His actions weren't a cold calculation, a means to a predetermined end; they were a visceral outpouring of love, a desperate plea for forgiveness whispered in the language of sacrifice, a fervent hope to amend the fractured tapestry of his past and weave a future where love, finally, could bloom unhindered.

The rough cave walls pressed in, cold and damp against my skin. Caspian's stillness beside me was a stark contrast to the storm that had raged within me only hours ago. He looks so... peaceful now, I thought, tracing the line of his jaw with a trembling finger. The coded messages, meticulously deciphered, lay scattered around us like fallen leaves, fragments of a life I'd only glimpsed, a life far more intricate and shadowed than I'd ever imagined. My Caspian, the man I thought I knew... was he even a man I truly knew at all?

The anger, that white-hot fury, had begun to recede, leaving behind a hollow ache. He'd hurt me so badly. How can I...? Sadness, a heavy, suffocating blanket, settled over me. This crushing weight... it's almost unbearable. But woven through the sadness was something else... understanding. Understanding? But he betrayed me! He lied! A dawning realization of the burdens he carried, the impossible choices he'd made. Impossible choices? What right does he have to make choices that ruined my life? He wasn't just a spy, a double agent. No, he was more than that... but how can I even think that? He was a man wrestling with his demons, fighting for something he believed in, even if it meant sacrificing everything. Fighting for something? What could possibly be worth all this pain? What could justify... everything? A flicker of respect, fragile as a newborn flame, ignited within me. Respect? Is this even possible? Am I losing my mind? This feels wrong, so terribly wrong. Like I'm betraying myself, betraying everything I thought I knew. It felt almost... traitorous. Respect for the man who had inflicted such pain. But... maybe there's more to this than I ever knew. Maybe... just maybe... I can start to understand.

His journey wasn't over. Not even with the coppery tang of his own blood staining the snow, the icy grip of death a mere whisper away, Caspian's story clawed its way onward. I tasted it, the bitter ash of betrayal in the cryptic, blood-smeared messages, the metallic scent of fear clinging to the enemies he'd carved a path through, the suffocating weight of his unfinished business, now a leaden shroud pressing down on my chest. His fight? It was mine, a poisoned chalice thrust into my trembling hand. The thought lodged itself deep, a shard of ice boring into my gut, its chill spreading through my veins like a creeping paralysis. But from that frozen core, something else ignited a white-hot rage, a burning resolve sharper than any blade, hotter than dragonfire, blooming in defiance of the encroaching darkness. This wasn't just inheritance; it was a damnation I would embrace.

The betrayal, the sharp, stinging wound of his deception, still throbbed. But it was no longer the dominant force. It was counterpointed by something else, something larger: acceptance. A grim, hard won acceptance that love and loss were not mutually exclusive, that the complexities of the human heart defied simple definitions. Redemption, his pursuit of it, and now, mine, became the North Star guiding me through this darkness.

The battle ahead clawed at me, a jagged, icy precipice promising oblivion. The stench of blood, still clinging to the cave walls like a shroud, haunted my nostrils, a gruesome testament to Caspian's final, agonizing breath. His sacrifice wasn't a silent echo; it was a scream trapped in my bones, a raw, throbbing pulse against the suffocating stillness. The taste of ash and despair coated my tongue, a bitter reminder of the world he'd failed to save, a world I now swore to avenge. His courage, a phantom limb, ached with its absence but fueled my fury, a white-hot inferno burning in my gut. This wasn't mere justice I craved; it was retribution, a storm of righteous wrath to shatter the complacency of those who dared to profit from his death. For Caspian, whose haunted eyes still burned into my memory, yes. But more for myself, for the broken shard of my own soul that mirrored the shattered world he'd left behind. This fight wasn't for a world worth saving; it was for the creation of one.

CHAPTER

TWELVE

Whispering Shadows of Love

The candle flame bucked, a dying gasp, casting Caspian's face in a grotesque chiaroscuro. His skull, bleached bone beneath the flickering light, seemed to grin at me, a predatory smile twisting his lips, a macabre mockery of peace. The scent of old parchment and something else, something acrid and metallic, clung to him, a perfume of death. My fingers, trembling, dared to trace the harsh line of his jaw. The stubble, coarse as granite, rasped against my skin, a phantom's kiss that ignited a fire of fear and a perverse fascination. His eyes, though closed, held a terrifying stillness, the icy gleam of a predator's gaze lingering in their depths, promising a slow, exquisite torment. The cold seeped into my bones, a chilling echo of the emptiness that radiated from him, a void that both horrified and strangely drew me in.

The coded messages lay scattered, a macabre mosaic of torn paper whispering secrets in the stale air. The scent of aged parchment and dust, thick and cloying, clung to my throat, a bitter counterpoint to the metallic tang of fear coiling in my gut. Each fragment, brittle as a dead man's bone, felt like it might crumble to ash beneath my shaking fingers. My heart hammered a frantic rhythm against my ribs, a desperate drumbeat against the oppressive silence. I snatched one up, the ink a greasy smear under the flickering candlelight, a grotesque parody of life itself. The symbol, a jagged, obsidian glyph, wasn't just unfamiliar; it clawed its way into my soul, a searing brand. It wasn't the guilt I expected that choked me, no, it was something far more treacherous, far more devastating: a love so dark, so incandescently poisonous, it threatened to consume me whole.

A strangled sob tore from my throat, a raw, animal sound. The acrid scent of beeswax filled my nostrils as I etched another symbol onto the parchment, a jagged line, a heart impaled, not merely pierced, by a blade dripping with obsidian shadows. My breath caught a frantic bird trapped in my ribs. The candlelight, a malevolent flicker, pulsed like a diseased heart, mirroring the storm raging within me, a frenzied, agonizing ballet of sorrow and memories that clawed at my sanity. The rough texture of the parchment scraped against my skin, a physical manifestation of the brutal wounds festering within. Each stroke of the quill was a fresh stab, reopening old scars, each drop of ink a bead of bitter regret. The silence screamed louder than any tempest.

The room squeezed, a suffocating weight on my chest. The air, thick and cloying, reeked of beeswax, a sweetness that curdled in my throat, overridden by the metallic tang, copper, blood, and the coppery taste of fear itself rising in the back of my mouth. My skin prickled; the cold, damp stone floor seemed to radiate a chill that seeped into my bones, a glacial whisper against the oppressive heat of the air. Each breath rasped, a struggle against the unseen pressure, the silence punctuated only by the frantic drumming of my own heart, a frantic tattoo against the suffocating stillness. This wasn't just a room; it was a tomb, breathing secrets, and I was trapped within its suffocating embrace, a prisoner of its ancient, shadowed heart.

The brittle paper, smelling faintly of dust and despair, cut into my palm. Etched there, a single word, Forgive…, seared itself onto my soul like a brand. It wasn't a question, no, not a question at all. It was a razor-edged command, a ghost's shriek clawing its way from the suffocating earth, a desperate plea laced with the bitter tang of regret and the coppery scent of old blood. The word vibrated a physical thing, throbbing in the echoing silence, a silence broken only by the ragged, frantic beat of my own heart, a frantic drum against the ribs of my cage. This wasn't just a storm within; it was a cataclysm, a maelstrom of guilt and grief threatening to tear me asunder. The weight of it, the crushing, unbearable weight, pressed down a tombstone on my chest.

Their ghost, I knew, wouldn't find rest until I granted this... this brutal, agonizing mercy.

His death—a sacrifice to the ravenous beast gnawing at my soul, a beast that tasted of iron and ash and the chilling breath of the grave— left a void so absolute it sucked the very light from the world. It wasn't a clean break, no gentle release. Instead, it was a savage tearing a jagged rip through my very being leaving me hemorrhaging grief and drowning in a churning sea of guilt, the bitter taste of betrayal clinging to my tongue like a curse. The stench of his blood still phantom sharp in my nostrils mingled with the acrid reek of the burning pyre where they'd tossed his body—a pyre that mirrored the flames consuming me from the inside out. Each flicker of that fire echoed the torment within a relentless reminder of the life extinguished too soon. I could almost hear his laughter in the crackling embers, a ghostly sound that twisted the knife of my sorrow deeper. My heart, once a vibrant vessel of love and dreams, now lay in shambles, a desolate landscape littered with memories too painful to bear. The world around me faded into a desaturated blur each color muted by the weight of my despair. I wandered through the remnants of our shared moments grasping at shadows desperately seeking solace in a reality that felt irrevocably altered forever shadowed by his absence.

The weight of his past—his hand in the crimson stain of my village, a revelation that clawed its way from his dying lips, scorching my soul—twisted the knife of my sorrow. Each ragged breath was a lament, each heartbeat a drumbeat of self-recrimination. It wasn't simply the loss of a lover; it was the annihilation of a fragile hope, the shattering of a potential alliance with a man as labyrinthine and dangerous as a shadowed alleyway. I'd glimpsed the brilliant, terrifying depths of his soul, a kaleidoscope of darkness and cunning, only to have it ripped from my grasp, leaving me with nothing but shattered pieces of truth I'll never fully comprehend, and the crushing, inescapable burden of my terrible responsibility, the weight of a thousand silent screams echoing in the emptiness he left behind. His eyes, even in death, haunted me with their unspoken secrets, a final, chilling accusation.

The Obsidian Covenant, my sworn enemies, remained at large, their insidious machinations a creeping shadow threatening to consume the world. For two years, a white-hot thirst for vengeance had been my sole compass, driving every action, and hardening every decision. But Caspian's sacrifice, a searing brand on my soul, had irrevocably altered my perspective. Vengeance, I now understood, wasn't the simplistic balm I'd craved; it was a treacherous labyrinth of moral ambiguities, unforeseen consequences, and the chilling possibility of catastrophic collateral damage. The weight of countless lives, potentially sacrificed on the altar of my wrath, pressed down upon me, a crushing burden far heavier than any sword. The fire of retribution still burned, but it was now tempered by a chilling awareness of the price of revenge. Caspian's memory, a constant echo in the silent chambers of my heart, urged me toward a different path, one demanding a far more intricate and perilous strategy than the straightforward pursuit of bloodshed.

The thought of the Whispering Wind, Caspian's former organization, the very people he'd betrayed to save me, clawed at my conscience. Their methods were ethically dubious, at best; their operations were cloaked in secrecy so profound it felt like a suffocating weight. Yet, I'd developed a grudging admiration for Caspian, for his audacious subterfuge, his quiet acts of rebellion that chipped away at the organization's monolithic power from within. His death had ripped a gaping hole in their structure, a weakness the Covenant, with their merciless efficiency, would undoubtedly exploit. The choice pressed upon me with agonizing clarity: continue my relentless, blood-soaked pursuit of vengeance against the Covenant, or forge an uneasy alliance with the morally ambiguous Whispering Wind, an organization whose methods were as perilous as the enemy they opposed. The air itself felt thick with the weight of this decision, a suffocating blend of grief, betrayal, and the chilling prospect of what lay ahead, whichever path I chose.

The choice felt like swallowing a poisoned chalice, the bitter draught chilling me to the bone. Joining the Whispering Wind meant potentially allying with individuals as treacherous and unpredictable as the Covenant itself, shadows cloaked in deceit, masters of manipulation whose smiles held the sting of a viper. Their methods were as abhorrent as their aims, and the very thought sent a shiver down my spine. Yet, to remain alone, to confront the Covenant's relentless onslaught without an ally, felt like facing a hurricane armed with nothing but a sputtering candle flame. Their power was a crushing weight, a well-oiled machine of ruthless efficiency; their organization, a terrifying web of influence that stretched across the land. I, a lone flame elemental, fueled by a burning thirst for vengeance and haunted by a heart ripped asunder, was a single spark against their inferno. The weight of my decision pressed down, each option promising a different kind of ruin.

The wind, a sibilant whisper weaving through the skeletal branches of the ancient trees, carried Caspian's voice, a phantom echo of his last, coded words, resonating now not just in my ears, but deep within the marrow of my bones. He had gambled everything on me, wagered his very life for a sliver of redemption, a desperate hope for absolution. His sacrifice, a stark, brutal testament to his unwavering loyalty, burned in my heart, a searing brand I could not, would not, ignore. To let his sacrifice be in vain was unthinkable, a betrayal of the trust he'd placed in me, a desecration of the memory of his noble heart. I would honour his legacy, continuing the fight, not merely for vengeance, a hollow and insufficient response to the enormity of his loss, but for a world reborn, a world where such self-sacrificing heroism wasn't born of necessity, a world where the likes of Caspian could find peace, not in the cold embrace of death, but in the radiant warmth of true, lasting redemption. A world worthy of his memory.

Days bled into nights, a relentless crimson tide staining the fabric of my existence. The weight of my decision pressed down, a physical burden crushing the breath from my lungs. I wandered through a desolate landscape, a wasteland mirroring the desolation in my heart. The echoes of battle, the screams of the dying, the clang of steel, these were not merely sounds; they were phantom limbs, wraiths clinging to my consciousness. I retraced our steps, Caspian and I, revisiting the hallowed ground where we'd fought side by side. Each battlefield became a shrine to our shared victories, a bittersweet tapestry woven from threads of triumph and terror.

I relived the intense moments of vulnerability, the fleeting glances that spoke volumes, the unspoken trust that had blossomed amidst the carnage like a fragile flower pushing through cracked earth. Each memory, once a source of strength, was now a sharp, searing stab of pain, a constant, agonizing reminder of my irreplaceable loss, a phantom limb that throbbed with the absence of his presence. The wind whispered his name through the skeletal trees, a mournful lament echoing the emptiness that gnawed at my soul.

I sought solace in the heart of the inferno, my pyrokinetic power a volatile balm, as much a source of comfort as it was a tormenting reflection of my inner turmoil. The fire danced and writhed, a chaotic mirror to the tempest raging within me; its flickering flames mirrored the uncertainty that veiled my judgment, a shroud of doubt woven from ash and smoke. The pull of vengeance, a scorching brand upon my soul, clawed at me, a burning desire to inflict the same devastation upon those who had razed my village to the ground, leaving only embers and ghosts in their wake. Yet, the spectral memory of Caspian's sacrifice, a chilling whisper of selflessness against the roar of my rage, urged me toward a different path, a treacherous, tenuous alliance, fraught with peril, but perhaps the only path to true justice, to a future free from the suffocating ash of the past.

The coded messages yielded far more than Caspian's murky past; they unveiled a clandestine network, a hidden alliance of rebels waging a desperate insurgency against the Covenant from its very heart. This was a group whose methods were as shrouded in secrecy as Caspian's own, their morality a shifting, treacherous landscape as dark and complex as the shadowed alleys where they operated. These weren't paragons of virtue; their hands, like Caspian's, were undoubtedly stained. But they fought against a greater evil, a monolithic tyranny that threatened to extinguish them all, a leviathan whose tendrils already reached for me. The choice was stark, brutal: risk a precarious alliance with the very organization that had once inflicted such profound harm, or continue my lonely struggle against impossible odds, a David facing a Goliath armed with an arsenal of unimaginable power.

The choice wasn't a simple black-and-white affair; it was a swirling vortex of greys, a labyrinthine maze of moral ambiguities that threatened to consume me. I weighed the potential consequences, each possibility a chilling weight on my soul. An alliance with the enigmatic Whispering Wind, a serpentine entity whose whispers promised power but reeked of betrayal, could lead to insidious manipulation, a slow, agonizing erosion of my autonomy, and ultimately, even greater suffering than I already endured. Yet, to continue this perilous journey alone, to stubbornly cling to independence, meant almost certain death, a brutal end that would render Caspian's courageous sacrifice utterly meaningless, his memory a bitter monument to my folly. The air itself seemed thick with the weight of my indecision, each breath a laboured struggle against the crushing pressure of fate.

The cryptic symbols of Caspian's last message swam before my eyes, not a lament etched in despair, but a beacon of hope, a testament to a future where their world cast off the suffocating, tyrannical yoke of the Obsidian Covenant. It pulsed with a love that defied even the cold embrace of death, a love that ignited within me the courage to confront the agonizing choice before me, a choice that would not only carve the path of my destiny but shape the very fate of countless others. The crushing weight of responsibility bore down, the lives of so many hanging precariously in the balance, a burden I felt pressed heavily upon my shoulders, a tangible weight threatening to crush me beneath its immense pressure.

With a heavy heart, but with a newfound determination, I made my decision. I wouldn't seek vengeance alone; I couldn't let Caspian's sacrifice be in vain. I knew I had to seek out the Whispering Wind, navigate their treacherous waters, and forge an uneasy alliance. I would use their knowledge and resources to fight the Obsidian Covenant from within. It was a risky gamble, I knew, a path filled with potential betrayals and unforeseen consequences. But it felt like the best chance of victory, the only chance. It was a path that offered a glimmer of a future free from the shadows of the past, a future where I could honour Caspian's memory, and perhaps, finally find some measure of peace.

My path ahead was fraught with danger, I could feel it in my bones, but my heart, though broken, was not defeated. I would carry Caspian's flame, his struggle for redemption, and I would fight for a future worthy of his sacrifice, a future where love and vengeance could somehow coexist in this dark, cruel world of ours. The journey would be long and perilous, but I would walk it, fueled by my love for him, the crushing weight of my loss, and an unwavering determination to create a world free from the Obsidian Covenant's dark reign. The fight had just begun, and I was ready.

The grit, vile and acrid, scraped my throat, a taste of ash and despair. Caspian, foolhardy Caspian, vanished into the Whispering Wind's maw, a churning, grey vortex that reeked of ozone and something ancient, something unholy. The wind, a tangible, icy hand, clawed at my face, its relentless pulse a physical blow against my ribs, mirroring the agonizing constriction in my chest. Each ragged breath felt like dragging shards of glass through my lungs. Fear, raw and suffocating, choked me. His last desperate cry, a strangled whimper swallowed by the storm, still echoed in the hollow chambers of my soul. This wasn't just grief; it was the icy grip of betrayal, the bitter taste of failure clinging to my tongue, heavier than the ash. I tasted his blood, or was it mine? Mingled with the metallic tang of fear. The world spun, a dizzying kaleidoscope of grey and terror, and I knew, with a certainty that chilled me to the bone, that Caspian was lost to me, lost forever to the insatiable hunger of the Whispering Wind.

No roar, no volcanic eruption of rage. Only a gaze, a molten weight pressing between us, the dying embers of a wildfire. His eyes, the bruised purple of a storm-wracked sky seconds before the deluge, held a glacial ocean of unshed grief. Each unspoken word was a jagged shard of ice, cutting through the suffocating silence. The air crackled, thick with the metallic tang of blood and the acrid bite of unshed tears, mine, mirroring his own. This silent pact, this fragile thread spun from the raw fibres of our shared despair, was a gossamer thing, easily snapped, a promise hanging by a hair above the abyss of oblivion. His hand, calloused and scarred, twitched, a ghost of the violence barely contained within him. The scent of wood smoke and something else, something primal and feral, clung to him like a shroud. This wasn't just a look; it was a battle fought and lost, a lifetime etched into the lines around his haunted eyes.

His silence was a physical thing, a weight pressing down as his eyes, twin embers burning with searing intensity, branded themselves onto my soul. The sorrow etched around his mouth wasn't just lines; it was a canyon carved by years of unshed tears, a landscape ravaged by grief, the bitter taste of which I could almost feel on my tongue. But even within that desolate wasteland, a flicker, a fragile, incandescent spark of defiance, a stubborn refusal to succumb to the darkness. It was the faintest scent of wood smoke in a blizzard, the ghost of a heartbeat beneath a mountain of despair, a single, tenacious wildflower pushing through cracked earth. That tiny ember, barely visible in the inferno of his pain, was enough to prevent the final, shattering collapse of my own world.

A scalding tear, a traitorous betrayal, carved a frigid furrow down my cheek, unnoticed in the maelstrom of grief. The wind, a venomous serpent hissing secrets only the dead understand, clawed at me, a physical manifestation of the emptiness he'd ripped from my soul. It wasn't silence; it was a vacuum, a suffocating absence that pressed against my eardrums, a pressure worse than any scream. Only the wraithlike sigh of the mist, a mournful keening, dared to break the oppressive stillness. The metallic tang of ash, acrid and bitter, coated my tongue, the gritty residue of a farewell that had shattered my very being, leaving me hollowed out, a vessel adrift on a sea of despair. The phantom pressure of his hand still lingered, a cruel mockery of the warmth he once provided. My heart, a shattered kaleidoscope of memories, reflected the bleak landscape of my future, a wasteland mirroring the desolation within.

The parting felt surreal. Two weeks ago, we were fighting side by side, our bodies intertwined in a desperate dance of survival against the Obsidian Covenant. I remember the sweat stinging my eyes, the metallic tang of blood in the air, and the fierce grip of his hand on mine. Now, the bond we forged in that crucible of battle felt tenuous, a fragile thing easily shattered by the winds of fate. I was left with the echoing silence of his absence, a void that seemed to swallow the light, leaving me adrift in the darkness. I felt a cold dread creep into my bones, a chilling loneliness that mirrored the desolate landscape surrounding me. His absence was a physical ache, a gaping wound in my soul. I kept replaying our last moments together, searching for a clue, a sign, anything that could explain this sudden, devastating emptiness.

Caspian's departure, a jagged shard tearing through the fabric of my soul, held not just inevitability, but a chilling finality. The reek of betrayal clung to the air even after he was gone, a phantom scent mingling with the bitter taste of ash on my tongue. His world, the Whispering Wind, a labyrinth of shadows and whispered oaths, demanded a silence so profound it felt like a physical weight crushing my chest. Even the incandescent fire of our love, a tempestuous ocean raging between us, couldn't breach the fortress of his secrecy. He was swallowed by that clandestine network, a viper's nest of intrigue and violence, forced back to his crucial, deadly dance with the Obsidian Covenant, a monstrous entity whose very name sent icy tendrils down my spine. His vanishing was a gut-wrenching blow, a sacrifice carved not just in sorrow, but in the searing pain of a thousand phantom touches. Essential, yes, for our survival. But oh, the agonizing price we pay for this desperate, bloody war. The taste of dust and blood, his blood lingers, a constant, bitter reminder of the cost of our shared fight for freedom.

Alone again, the weight of my mission pressed down a physical burden mirroring the crushing responsibility. Caspian's final instructions, a chilling litany etched into my memory, echoed in the oppressive silence: find the hidden rebellion cell within the Covenant, gather intel, and sow discord. The words tasted like ash in my mouth. Discord. It wasn't just about gathering information; it was about actively hurting people, people who, for all I knew, shared my own desperate yearning for freedom from the Covenant's iron grip.

My hand trembled as I traced the worn leather of my satchel feeling the weight of the small meticulously crafted poison vials nestled within. Each vial seemed to pulse with a life of its own, a constant reminder of the dark path I was being asked to tread. Caspian had insisted; a necessary evil he'd called a term that echoed in my mind like a haunting refrain. Yet this 'necessary evil' felt like a betrayal of everything I had ever held dear. My training instilled from childhood had emphasized honor integrity and selflessness as the pillars of a noble life. Now in this moment of uncertainty, I was being asked to become a viper to sink my fangs into the very fabric of my beliefs. To infiltrate, undermine, deceive and potentially condemn innocent lives all in the name of bolstering a rebellion I wasn't even sure I truly trusted. The weight of my choices pressed heavily upon me, each vial a symbol of the moral quagmire I found myself in torn between loyalty and conscience.

The faces of the Covenant's patrols, their unwavering loyalty chillingly displayed, flashed before my eyes. Were they truly the monsters Caspian painted them to be? Or were they simply desperate people clinging to a false hope, manipulated by a corrupt system? Could

I justify betraying them, even for the sake of a greater good that felt increasingly elusive? The choice gnawed at me, a relentless ache in my gut. The thought of failure, of Caspian's disappointment, spurred me onward, yet the prospect of success—of achieving my mission through treachery—filled me with a creeping dread, a sickening premonition of regret that clung to me like a shroud. I was already failing, even before I began; failing my own conscience, failing my own principles. The mission was becoming a slow, agonizing descent into the very darkness I was supposed to be fighting against.

A deceptively simple task, at least in its stark articulation; in reality, it felt like navigating a labyrinth of razor-sharp blades while blindfolded, every step a gamble against sudden, catastrophic failure. My journey demanded not only stealth, honed to an almost supernatural keenness but also a cunning so profound it bordered on the Machiavellian, a level of deception I'd previously considered abhorrent. Before Caspian, vengeance had been a wildfire, a raging inferno consuming all reason. Now, it was a carefully banked ember, glowing faintly beneath a controlled layer of ash—a potent fuel source, meticulously managed, providing the heat for a plan that demanded meticulous subtlety and unwavering patience. The air itself seemed thick with the weight of unspoken dangers, the scent of betrayal hanging heavy in the still air.

A biting wind whipped across the desolate landscape, stinging my exposed skin as I moved with a hunter's grace, each footstep deliberate, each breath measured. The memories of him, sharp and vivid as shards of obsidian, pierced the numbness that threatened to engulf me. They were phantom limbs, a constant, throbbing ache beneath the surface of my steely resolve. I relived the echoes of our laughter, the shared vulnerability that had blossomed in the crucible of war, a fragile flower pushing through the cracks of chaos. The intensity of our passion, a searing brand, was etched indelibly on my soul. Now, those memories were bittersweet, a poignant symphony of joy and loss.

Yet, their very pain fueled my relentless march forward, a potent elixir that sustained my strength, my purpose. His spectral presence clung to me, a phantom scent of blood and lavender, a jarring juxtaposition that mirrored the complexity of our bond. The ghostly impression of his touch lingered on my skin, a paradoxical comfort, a painful reminder of the profound connection we had forged, a connection that defied even the crushing weight of our ravaged world. It was a love forged in fire, tempered by loss, and etched into the very fabric of my being.

I spent days hunched over Caspian's encrypted messages, the flickering lamplight casting long shadows across the worn parchment. His code, a labyrinth of interwoven symbols and ciphers, yielded slowly to my relentless efforts. Each painstakingly decoded message was a shard of revelation, another fragment in the mosaic leading to the hidden cell within the impenetrable Covenant. The messages spoke not merely of betrayal, but of a web of deceit spun from the highest echelons of power; hidden alliances shifted like desert sands, their loyalties as fickle as the wind. A network of rebels, their faces obscured by shadow, worked from within the very heart of the Covenant, their carefully laid plans a testament to years of patient subterfuge. Caspian's infiltration was far more extensive than I'd ever imagined; he wasn't just an operative, but a phantom, deeply embedded within the Covenant's rigid structure, a double agent whose actions reverberated through the very foundations of their tyrannical regime, their consequences far-reaching and chillingly unpredictable. The weight of his trust, and the gravity of the secrets he'd entrusted to me, pressed down with the crushing force of a collapsing edifice.

As I delved deeper into the encrypted messages, the moral ambiguities of my mission crystallized with chilling clarity. Are these really the good guys? The propaganda painted such a rosy picture. The rebels, I discovered, were far from the pristine heroes of propaganda. Their methods were brutal, often verging on savagery; their motives were a tangled web of personal ambition woven with genuine, if flawed, idealism. Ambition... idealism... it's all so messy. Is there even a clean version of this conflict? Yet, the Obsidian Covenant, their shared enemy, loomed as an existential threat, a nihilistic force poised to unravel the very tapestry of existence. Existential threat... that's a strong word. But is it true? Or is this just fear-mongering, used to justify their actions?

My alliance with these morally compromised rebels wasn't a simple matter of choosing good over evil; it was a grim calculation, a desperate gamble on the lesser evil, a necessary compromise in a world where the lines between right and wrong had been brutally smeared beyond recognition. Lesser evil? Is that even a real thing? It feels more like choosing between two shades of darkness. The weight of this choice, this unavoidable descent into moral gray, pressed down on me with the crushing force of a collapsing star. Am I doing the right thing? Or am I just delaying the inevitable, becoming complicit in something far worse? This isn't the clean fight I was promised. This is... survival. Is that enough? God, I wish there was a better answer.

The ever-present pull of my vampiric urges clawed at me, a relentless tide threatening to drag me under. Caspian's blood had been a mere trickle against the raging inferno of my hunger, a fleeting balm that now left only the searing ache of its absence. A new source was paramount, a desperate necessity to quell the beast that clawed its way to the surface, threatening to shatter the fragile facade of control I'd so painstakingly constructed. The hunger was no longer a companion; it was a parasitic twin, a dark mirror reflecting not only the bleakness of my existence but the chilling depths of the Obsidian Covenant itself, its sinister shadow stretching long and malevolent across my soul. The fear wasn't a simple apprehension; it was a chilling dread, a venomous serpent coiled tight around my heart, a constant, agonizing reminder of the precarious balance I teetered upon, a balance easily shattered by the slightest slip, the merest flicker of weakness. The very air thrummed with the urgency of my need, a silent scream only I could hear, a desperate plea for respite from the insatiable hunger that threatened to consume me utterly.

My days were a relentless cycle of navigating treacherous, unforgiving terrain, jagged peaks clawing at the sky, another sunrise, another day closer to... what exactly? I still haven't figured that out. Sun-baked desserts shimmering with deceptive calm, that shimmering heat, it's almost hypnotic. I need to stay focused. One misstep and... and shadowed alleyways whispering secrets I couldn't afford to ignore. Secrets that could kill me, or save me. Probably kill me. Information gathering was a constant, perilous dance; each contact a gamble, this one's a known liar, but he might be the only lead I've got. Worth the risk? Probably not, but I don't have a choice. Each whispered word is a potential betrayal. Every breath I take is a risk. Am I being followed? Paranoia is a survival mechanism, but it's also a slow killer. I moved like a phantom, a ghost in the machine, they don't even know I exist, and I prefer to keep it that way. Maintaining a low profile that was as much a shield as it was a prison. This anonymity… It's a cage of my own making. But a necessary one. For now.

The nights clawed at me, a relentless beast. The stench of stale lamp oil choked the air, its flickering light painting grotesque, dancing shadows that writhed like phantoms across the maps, maps whose creases mirrored not only the fatigue etched deep into my face, but the twisting anxieties that gnawed at my soul. Each coded message, a venomous viper coiled on the parchment, hissed its secrets only under the relentless pressure of my feverish gaze. The ink, cold and slick beneath my trembling fingers, felt like the icy breath of death itself. Every deciphered fragment, a shard of glass tearing at the fragile tapestry of my sanity, added to the deadly puzzle, a mosaic of betrayal and murder. My next move, a gambit played against a ghost in the machine, demanded not just meticulous planning, but the cold, calculating precision of a surgeon dissecting a corpse. Sleep? A laughable, pathetic notion. A luxury I traded long ago, sacrificing rest for the incandescent, all-consuming pursuit of vengeance. The taste of it, bitter and metallic, was on my tongue, a constant reminder of the price I was willing to pay.

The Covenant's shadow was a palpable entity, a suffocating blanket of fear that permeated every aspect of my existence. Is this real? Or am I losing my mind? It feels so…real. Its tendrils, invisible yet inescapable, reached into every crevice, every shadow, every whispered conversation. They're watching. I know they are. Every rustle of leaves, every creak of the floorboards…it's them. The chilling certainty of being watched was a constant companion, a persistent hum beneath the surface of every waking moment. Breathe. Just breathe. Don't let them see you panic. The dread of discovery, a cold, clammy hand clutching at my heart, was a chilling prelude to each new dawn. Another day. Another chance they might find me. Will I even make it to sunset? The air itself crackled with unspoken threats, the silence punctuated by the ever-present whisper of impending doom. It's in the silence. That's where the fear lives. In the spaces between the sounds. Maybe if I made some noise…no, worse. They'll hear me. I need to escape. But where can I go? Is there anywhere safe? They know too much. How did they find out? What did I do? I should have been more careful…

The salt spray, a brutal baptism, flayed my eyes, a mockery of the tears choked back, bitter and unshed. The grey sea, a churning beast, mirrored the tempest in my soul, each monstrous wave a hammer blow against the ribs of my grief. Caspian's absence, a physical ache, a wound that refused to heal, throbbed with each sickening crash of the surf. My fingers, clumsy and trembling, sought the raised, livid moon of my scar, a brand seared into my flesh, a pact forged in the crucible of our desperate love, a constant, burning reminder of our shared transgression. I saw him then, a phantom etched against the jagged teeth of the mountains, a fleeting silhouette against a sky the colour of bruised plums, a sky bleeding into the encroaching night. His face, a mask of hard angles and shadowed depths, haunted the fading light, each line a testament to the brutal beauty, the agonizing sweetness of our doomed existence. The scent of brine and the metallic tang of blood, his blood, mine, clung to the air, a bitter perfume of loss and desperate longing. He was gone, but the taste of him, sharp and unforgettable, remained, a phantom kiss on my ravaged soul.

My finger, a trembling reed, traced the ghost of his lips in the sand, the coarse grains a physical torment against my skin, mirroring the raw ache in my heart. His laughter, a cruel mockery, clawed at the silence between the wind-ravaged dunes, a phantom echo that tasted of salt and regret. It was a sound born of arrogance, of a power he wielded over me, even now, absent. I recalled the searing brand of his kiss, a brutal violation disguised as intimacy. The rough stubble of his beard, a map of his ruthlessness, scraped against my flesh, leaving an imprint not just on my skin but on my soul, a violent bloom of pleasure and pain, a toxic flower I couldn't uproot. The taste of him, of him and the sea, lingered, bitter and inescapable. His ghost was a tangible presence, heavy with the weight of what he'd taken, and what he'd left behind, a desolate landscape mirroring the wasteland in my heart.

"*Caspian,*" I rasped, the name of a shard of ice lodged in my throat. The wind, a brutal, clawing hand, tore the word from my lips, leaving only the desolate, keening shriek of a gull, a harbinger of ill omen. My fingers, slick with a cold sweat, dug into the worn leather of the pouch. It felt heavier than a king's ransom, a leaden weight mirroring the crushing grief in my chest. Inside, the river stone, glacial, smooth as a serpent's skin, pressed against my palm, a chilling echo of his touch. Its icy surface burned. The phantom scent of woodsmoke and his sweat, acrid and clinging, was a suffocating shroud, dragging me back into the fetid darkness of that cave, our desperate, claustrophobic refuge from the storm that raged both within and without. The taste of ash and fear still lingered on my tongue, a bitter reminder of our desperate gamble. He had looked at me, then, with eyes that held the weight of a thousand betrayals, a thousand unspoken promises. A single, desperate, soul-wrenching look before the earth swallowed him whole.

The flickering candlelight cast long, skeletal shadows, twisting the familiar room into a grotesque parody of comfort. His eyes, the icy grey of a storm-wracked ocean, locked onto mine, a glacial grip that chilled me to the bone. The scent of wood smoke and something else, something feral and unsettling, clung to him like a shroud. *"We'll meet again,"* he breathed, the words a rasping whisper, swallowed almost instantly by the gale that clawed at the windows, a beast with teeth of ice. His touch, fleeting as it was, left a lingering brand of heat against my skin, a stark contrast to the bone-deep chill that settled in my soul. But the wind, a cruel, uncaring god, devoured his promise, leaving only the echoing emptiness of the storm-lashed night. That silence, thick and suffocating, pressed down on me, a physical weight crushing the fragile hope in my chest, leaving behind only the bitter taste of despair and the raw, agonizing burn of a love born under a sky of merciless stars. The gnawing emptiness wasn't just an ache; it was a ravenous hunger, a void threatening to consume me entirely.

The crushing weight of unspoken promises, Did I promise him anything? Or did I just let him believe...? No, I promised. I promised with every stolen glance, every shared breath under that infernal sky. The silent oaths whispered in stolen moments under a sky choked with smoke and ash, propelled me forward. Each cough of smoke was a reminder of his fragility, his vulnerability, the risk he took believing in me. The incandescent memories of our brief, incandescent time together, the shared intimacy, a fragile bloom amidst the battlefield's brutal bloom, the fierce camaraderie forged in the crucible of war, served as a lifeline in the tempestuous sea of uncertainty.

That shared laugh, under the rain…was it real? Or just a fleeting mirage in this hell? I had to succeed, not merely for vengeance, a bitter fruit I craved yet recoiled from, Vengeance? Is that even what I want? Or is it just a convenient justification for my grief? No, not grief, it's…a burning need for justice.…not simply for the fractured world I desperately fought to save, but for him, for the man who had gambled everything on my success, Everything? He risked everything for me. For a chance, a gamble…and I am the only card left in his hand. A man whose depth and complexity I was only beginning to fathom, There's so much more to him than I understand. A whole lifetime couldn't unravel his mysteries. a soul mirrored in the burning embers of my own. Our souls are intertwined… forged in the same fires, yet separate, burning with different kinds of light. Will we ever truly merge, or will this flame consume us both?

The path ahead was a treacherous labyrinth, a gauntlet of peril and betrayal, each step a gamble against oblivion. Can I really do this? Is this madness? No, it's… purpose. His purpose. Yet, the ember of hope that flickered in my heart burned with a fierce, unwavering intensity, mirroring the inferno that raged within my soul. That fire…it's fueled by rage and grief, but mostly…by his memory. I won't let it die. I would carry his memory, a sacred relic, his sacrifices, a debt I vowed to repay in blood and fire, a debt that feels heavier than mountains, sharper than any blade. His love, a guiding star in the darkest night, and continue our fight. Continue? I'll conquer. For him. Their war against the Covenant, a monstrous tide of darkness, was far from over; it was a battle for the very soul of existence. They took everything from me… but not my will. Not my spirit.

But I would face it, ready to embrace the shadows, to become the very darkness they fear, to wrestle with the demons that haunted the battlefield, demons both real and imagined, fueled by doubt and loss, but I'll fight through them, to fight for a future where love, fragile yet tenacious, could blossom even amidst the ashes of a shattered world. A future where we… we could have been. A future I will build. Our parting was a temporary eclipse, a cruel intermission in our epic. Just an intermission…it isn't the end. It can't be. Our fight, however, was eternal, a war waged across the ages, a battle for a love that transcended even death itself. His love…it's my shield, my sword, my very reason for breathing. It will guide me, even though hell itself.

THIRTEEN

Paths Diverge

The wind, a razor-edged blade, tore at my cloak, icy fingers clawing at the exposed skin beneath. Across the desolate plains, stretching endlessly before me like a frozen sea, the landscape mirrored the tempest raging within. Caspian's absence was a gnawing emptiness, a void that swallowed my resolve, a constant ache that no amount of rigorous self-discipline could staunch. Weeks I had spent meticulously tracing his cryptic instructions, my progress a slow, agonizing crawl towards the obsidian heart of the Covenant—a journey measured not in miles, but in mounting dread. Each step forward felt like sinking deeper into quicksand; the closer I approached, the more treacherous the terrain grew, the air itself seeming to thicken with menace. I stood now on the precipice, poised on the very edge of Willowshade's shadowed kingdom, the chilling breath of its mysteries already upon me. The air tasted of secrets and death.

The initial thrill of cracking Caspian's cipher, a heady rush of adrenaline and intellectual triumph, had evaporated like morning mist. A chilling reality had settled in its place: the rebellion wasn't the noble uprising it had seemed. Instead, it was a fractured mosaic of ambition, a kaleidoscope of conflicting desires vying for dominance. The cell, once perceived as a unified front of righteous warriors fighting for liberation, revealed itself to be a viper's nest of self-interest. Some members were fueled by a genuine, albeit naïve, altruism, their hearts burning with a desperate hope for freedom.

Others, however, were driven by a naked lust for power, their eyes fixed on the spoils of victory, regardless of the cost. And still, others, the most pitiable, were simply desperate, clinging to the rebellion as a lifeline in a sea of despair, their loyalty a fragile thing, bought with promises and fueled by fear. I found myself adrift in a treacherous labyrinth of deception, a labyrinth where every shadow whispered treachery, and trust was a currency too precious, too easily squandered, to be risked. My every move was fraught with peril, each alliance a gamble with potentially devastating consequences.

The road was a kaleidoscope of faces. I met hardened veterans, their features etched with the brutal map of countless battles, eyes that held the cold weight of witnessed horrors, and mouths that rarely smiled, save for a grim, knowing curve. Cunning spies, ghosts in the shadows, their whispers like slivers of ice in the chill night air, traded secrets as valuable as life itself, their words are carefully chosen, each syllable a calculated risk. And then there were the civilians, their faces a haunting mixture of desperation and flickering hope, clinging to the fragile promise of liberation like drowning men to a piece of driftwood. Each encounter was a high-stakes game of poker, a delicate dance on a razor's edge. I learned to reveal only the necessary fragments of truth, using carefully chosen words as shields, my secrets guarded as fiercely as a lioness protects her cubs. I honed my ability to decipher the subtext, to read the unspoken language of the eyes, the subtle tremor in a voice, the almost imperceptible shift in posture, clues that separated truth from carefully constructed lies. My survival hinged not just on logic and evidence, but on an almost preternatural instinct, a sixth sense sharpened by necessity and honed by years spent navigating this treacherous landscape.

My vampiric urges, once a manageable affliction, now clawed at me with the ferocity of a starving wolf. The constant hunger wasn't a mere gnawing; it was a volcanic eruption of need, a relentless predator that consumed me from the inside out, its icy breath chilling my very soul. The blood of small animals, a gruesome, desperate appeasement, offered only fleeting respite, a thin veil against the insatiable thirst. Each kill, a brutal act of necessity, left me coated in a film of guilt and self-loathing, the stench of decay clinging to me far longer than the metallic tang of blood. This self-hatred was not merely a burden; it was an iron crown, heavy and unforgiving, a constant, agonizing reminder of the monstrous darkness that festered within, threatening to overwhelm and consume me entirely. The world, once vibrant and full of light, now seemed to bleed into a perpetual twilight, mirroring the unending night that had become my existence.

I sought solace in the desolate grandeur of the unforgiving landscape, its vastness a balm to my fractured spirit. The silence of the plains, broken only by the whisper of wind through withered grasses, became my sanctuary, a refuge where I could confront the demons that clawed at my soul without the judgmental gaze of others. Hours bled into days as I meditated, striving to quell the untamed inferno that raged within me, a metaphorical fire mirroring the literal heat that shimmered off the parched earth. The struggle was a relentless tempest, each wave of self-doubt threatening to consume me. Exhaustion gnawed at my bones, yet I pushed onward, relentlessly testing the limits of my endurance, the tensile strength of my resolve, the fragile boundaries of my self-control. The landscape, harsh and unforgiving, became a mirror reflecting the turmoil within, each jagged peak and barren expanse a testament to the arduous journey of self-discovery I had undertaken.

One night, huddled around a meagre fire that cast long, dancing shadows against the immense, indifferent canvas of the star-strewn sky, I found myself lost in contemplation of my relationship with Caspian. It was a complex and multifaceted tapestry, woven with threads of incandescent passion, stark dominance, willing submission, and a deep, abiding mutual respect that ran deeper than mere affection. Our connection transcended the commonplace definitions of intimacy; it was a bond forged in the white-hot crucible of shared peril, a partnership built on a foundation of unwavering trust and an understanding that resonated far beyond the purely physical. Our sexual encounters were intense, brutal even, a tempestuous clash of wills that left us breathless and aching, yet interwoven with an undeniable tenderness, a fierce and unwavering affection that defied the harshness of our actions. It was a dance of power, a dangerous game of cat and mouse played out against the breathtaking, terrifying backdrop of life or death stakes, a constant awareness of mortality that only served to heighten the intensity of our connection. The crackling fire seemed to mirror the volatile yet undeniable passion that burned between us, a flickering reflection of the powerful, unpredictable force that bound our lives together.

I traced the jagged map of the scar on my arm, a pale, raised ridge etched into my skin, a brutal souvenir from one of our countless battles. The memory of his touch, a phantom warmth against my skin, lingered like the scent of wood smoke after a long-dead fire. His hand, calloused and strong, even in memory, sent a shiver of longing through me, a visceral ache that resonated deep in my bones. His absence was a constant, gnawing emptiness, a void that threatened to swallow me whole. But from that very emptiness, a paradoxical strength bloomed. Knowing he was out there, facing his demons, fighting his own relentless battles, fueled my resilience. It was a silent pact, forged in blood and shared sacrifice, a bond that even the vast distance couldn't sever. His struggle was my strength, his survival my hope.

The deeper I plunged into the Covenant's festering heart, the more their depravity gnawed at my soul. I witnessed their brutality not as a distant horror, but up close, a visceral tapestry woven from casual cruelty and sadistic glee inflicted upon those who dared to defy their iron will. Their power wasn't merely immense; it was a suffocating presence, a miasma of control that stretched its tendrils into every corner of the land, its insidious influence poisoning the very air I breathed. The rebellion, I understood with chilling clarity, was not merely a desperate gambit, but a suicide charge against an unstoppable juggernaut, a flickering candle against a hurricane. The moral ambiguity of my alliance was no longer a nagging doubt, but a crushing weight, a suffocating burden of guilt that pressed upon my chest, each beat of my heart a morbid echo of the atrocities I was complicit in opposing. The faces of the victims, their silent screams, haunted my waking hours and bled into my dreams, leaving me to question not only the righteousness of my cause but the very nature of my humanity.

I sought refuge within the crumbling ruin, a skeletal husk of what was once a grand edifice, now reduced to rubble and choking dust. The wind, a mournful sigh through shattered archways, whispered secrets only the stones could understand. Within its dilapidated walls, I discovered a hidden cache—a trove of the Covenant's documents: meticulously recorded accounts of unspeakable atrocities, chillingly detailed plans for future campaigns of conquest. These records, penned in elegant script yet stained with the grim realities they described, unveiled a conspiracy of staggering depth, revealing alliances that even the shrewd Caspian hadn't suspected. The enemy's tendrils, I realized with a sickening lurch, extended far beyond the battlefield, insinuating themselves into the very fabric of the land. The scope of the task before me had escalated, not merely to terrifying levels, but to a horrifying, almost unimaginable scale. The weight of this knowledge pressed down, a suffocating burden threatening to crush me beneath its immensity.

The intel I uncovered confirmed a chilling truth: the rebellion wasn't merely a struggle for survival; it was a desperate fight for the liberation of an entire region, choking under the Obsidian Covenant's iron fist. Their ambition transcended simple conquest; it was a terrifying perversion of power, a blasphemous bid to manipulate the very flow of elemental energies. They sought to unleash a cataclysm of unimaginable scale, a maelstrom of raw power that threatened to unravel the very fabric of existence. This revelation, a stark and terrifying dawn, ignited a fire within me, a chilling exhilaration that mingled with the sobering weight of responsibility. The urgency of my mission, and the critical need to dismantle the Covenant from within, solidified into an unbreakable resolve. The fate of countless worlds hung precariously in the balance, a burden I was now inextricably bound to bear.

Time bled from days into weeks, weeks melting into months. My body, a vessel pushed to the very brink of collapse, screamed its protest, yet my spirit, forged in the crucible of adversity, refused to yield. I honed my instincts until they were razor sharp, my resourcefulness a lifeline in the suffocating grip of desperation, my resolve an unwavering beacon in the encroaching darkness. I became more than a phantom; I was a ghost, a breath of air barely disturbing the stillness, a shadow slipping through the cracks of the Covenant's iron grip. My disguises were seamless, my deceptions masterful, my movements fluid and silent as I navigated the treacherous currents of their ranks, undetected, unseen. I was a chameleon, not merely adapting to my surroundings, but becoming them, a master of survival, my wits my only weapons, my cunning my most potent shield.

The hunger gnawed at me, a relentless, visceral reminder of my fragile mortality. God, how long has it been? Days? Weeks? Time's lost all meaning. It was a constant, gnawing presence, a phantom limb pain in my gut, twisting my insides with a desperate need. Just a little something... anything... to take the edge off. Please. I scavenged for alternatives, desperate measures to quell the overwhelming urge to consume, to devour. Those roots... They looked promising. They weren't. I tried roots, bitter and fibrous; I chewed on bark, tasting only dust and despair. Useless.

Useless. Why bother? These desperate attempts offered only fleeting reprieve, temporary illusions of satiety, ultimately failing to silence the primal scream within. It's mocking me. This hunger, this... this emptiness... it's winning. The hunger, this ancient, unyielding instinct, chipped away at my sanity, testing the very limits of my self-control, threatening to unravel me completely. Think... think rationally. Don't give in. Don't let it control you. Each failed attempt sharpened the desperation, intensifying the agonizing awareness of my body's relentless demand. It's getting stronger. I can feel it... consuming me from the inside out. My resolve, once a sturdy fortress, began to crumble under the ceaseless assault. It's... it's almost... too much. Maybe... just a little...

The air in the obsidian-walled corridor thrummed with a palpable tension, a silent symphony of anticipation, dread, and a chilling certainty. Each footfall echoed unnervingly loud in the oppressive silence, amplifying the frantic hammering of my heart. I was so close, a hair's breadth from the heart of the Obsidian Covenant, from the culmination of years spent chasing justice down a treacherous path. But proximity only sharpened the awareness of the lethal dangers that lurked, unseen shadows poised to strike. This final confrontation, this desperate gamble for retribution, demanded everything: every fibre of my being, every cunning tactic honed in the fires of adversity, every ounce of unwavering resolve. The stakes were not merely high; they were existential. Failure meant oblivion, not just for me, but for everything Caspian had fought, and died, for.

My journey had been a brutal crucible, forging me anew in its relentless heat. It had stripped away innocence, leaving behind something harder, sharper, more ruthless, something undeniably alive in a way I'd never known before. Caspian's memory, the ghost of his smile, the echo of his sacrifice, the unspoken promise etched in his dying gaze, burned as a fierce, unwavering fuel, propelling me forward. The solitary path I'd carved, a path strewn with the wreckage of my past and the shadows of countless close calls, had led me here. This was the culmination, the apex of a long, agonizing climb. But as I stood on the precipice, poised to confront the darkness, I knew, with chilling certainty, that it was only the beginning.

The flickering candlelight, a frail sentinel against the encroaching darkness, cast long, dancing shadows across Caspian's gaunt face, accentuating the sharp angles of his cheekbones and the deep, etched canyons around his eyes, a roadmap of hardship etched by time and sorrow. He sat hunched over a worn map, its parchment brittle and yellowed with age, the faded ink a ghostly testament to forgotten journeys. His calloused finger, thick with the grime of countless battles and betrayals, traced the lines with a hesitant touch, as if reluctant to disturb the sleeping memories held within.

The room, a cramped cell hewn into the very heart of the Whispering Wind's hidden fortress, was a stark, chilling space; rough-hewn stone walls breathed a damp chill, a stark contrast to the inferno of guilt and desperate hope that raged within him. His usual commanding presence, the confident bearing of a seasoned warrior, was utterly gone, replaced by a profound weariness that sagged his shoulders and weighed upon him like a physical shackle. The weight of his guilt, a palpable entity, pressed down, threatening to crush him beneath its crushing burden. Even the faintest whisper of the wind seemed to mock his despair, a chilling reminder of the choices that had led him here.

I found Caspian's deep knowledge of demon texts really helpful. His understanding opened my eyes to the great power of the entity we were dealing with. I used my control over the elements to break through the fortress's dangerous defenses. My bright flames burned away the leftover dark magic from the Covenant. My connection with them was strong. Together we formed a powerful team because we faced danger and fought hard for our survival. During the night I felt a strong closeness with the other person. We held each other tightly searching for comfort and a way to let go of our worries. I found it hard to tell the difference between their passionate hug and their bigger goal. The blood Caspian gave me meant more than just staying alive; it showed our risky agreement and confirmed how our fates were connected.

His redemption, he knew, wouldn't be a simple, whispered apology, a fleeting act of contrition. It would be a gruelling ascent, a relentless climb up a mountain forged from his past mistakes. He needed more than words; he needed action, a tangible, unwavering demonstration of his transformed heart. He had to prove, not just to Blaze, whose trust he'd shattered, but to the very core of his being, that his love wasn't a manipulative tool, a gilded cage, but a genuine, selfless force, capable of healing both himself and the wounds he had inflicted. The path ahead was arduous, fraught with peril, but the possibility of earning back Blaze's trust, of proving his worth, fueled his every step. His redemption was not a destination, but a continuous journey, a testament to his unwavering commitment to change.

The map, a brittle parchment crackling with the faint scent of Sulfur and death, depicted the treacherous labyrinth of the Obsidian Covenant's hidden fortress, a cyclopean structure carved into the very heart of a dead volcano, a place where countless demons had met their agonizing demise, their screams echoing still in the twisted, obsidian corridors. He knew its layout intimately; he'd not only helped design its defences but had personally overseen the construction, his own hands stained with the blood of sacrificed slaves and the sweat of demonic artisans. He'd once revelled in its oppressive power, in the chilling efficiency of its torture chambers, in its unparalleled capacity for inflicting unimaginable suffering. The glyphs etched into its walls, a perverse testament to dark rituals, still seared themselves onto his memory. Now, the very idea of entering its obsidian walls filled him with a visceral dread, a cold premonition of the horrors he might face, not just the demons it contained, but the ghosts of his past, the weight of his complicity in its creation, a burden heavier than any mountain. The map felt like a curse held in his trembling hand.

His mission was deceptively simple: infiltrate the impenetrable fortress of Xalzar and steal the Covenant's most prized possession, the Heart of Obsidian, a pulsating artifact of immense power, capable of

256

amplifying their demonic energies to apocalyptic levels. His plan was audacious, reckless even, a suicide run painted across the tapestry of night. But Caspian thrived on such risks; the adrenaline, the razor's edge of survival, was the only comfort he'd known since... well since everything went wrong. He needed to prove his worth, to transcend his past misdeeds, a tapestry woven from betrayal and blood, and earn something far greater than mere survival: Blaze's forgiveness. The weight of his failure pressed down on him, a crushing burden only the audacious gamble of this mission could hope to alleviate. He had to demonstrate his worthiness, to show Blaze that redemption, even at the cost of his life, was a price he was willing, no, eager, to pay.

His preparations were meticulous, bordering on obsessive. He didn't just study the layout of the obsidian fortress; he inhabited it in his mind, retracing each serpentine corridor in his memory until the route flowed through him like blood. He didn't merely practice his combat techniques; he pushed his body to the absolute brink of collapse, each strike honed to lethal precision, each parry a testament to years of unwavering discipline. He didn't simply seek ancient enchantments; he delved into forgotten grimoires, deciphering cryptic runes and whispering incantations under the pale light of a waning moon, desperate for any advantage against the impossible odds. The weight of his past failures pressed down on him, not as a mere burden, but as a suffocating shroud, each ghost of his mistakes a chilling reminder of the price of failure. The very air seemed thick with the unspoken dread of his impending mission, a silent testament to the monumental task ahead. He sharpened his blades until they gleamed with a deathly light, a reflection of the cold resolve hardening in his eyes.

He knew brute force was a fool's errand. Against the Covenant, with their legions of fiercely loyal, immensely powerful demons, only cunning would suffice. Stealth, the art of becoming a phantom, a whisper in the suffocating darkness, unseen and unheard, would be his only shield. He needed to move with the grace of a wraith, anticipating their every move, exploiting their blind spots, turning their strength against them. The prize was heavily guarded; a single misstep, a flicker of light, a breath misplaced, any lapse in his meticulous plan could be his last. The air crackled with the palpable threat of their power, a constant reminder of the razor's edge he walked.

His initial plan had been brutally simple: breach the impenetrable fortress, secure the Heart of the Covenant, and escape with his life. But as the meticulously crafted preparations progressed, his motivations deepened, transforming from a desperate bid for personal redemption into a complex tapestry of vengeance and defiance. He wasn't merely seeking absolution for his past transgressions; he yearned to cripple the Covenant, to pave a less bloody path for Blaze's righteous fury. He envisioned himself as more than just a deserter; he would become a saboteur, striking at the heart of the organization he had once blindly served, a poisoned dagger aimed at its very soul. The weight of his betrayal now fueled a burning desire to dismantle the machine he had helped build.

His journey into the heart of the obsidian fortress was a harrowing descent into the abyss. He navigated a labyrinth of treacherous corridors, their slick, black stone slick with unseen moisture, evading patrols of heavily armed demons whose eyes glowed with infernal fire. Each footstep echoed with unnerving clarity, each shadow a potential ambush. He deactivated magically enhanced traps, intricate mechanisms of razor-sharp blades, searing flames, and crushing weights, with the precision of a master surgeon, his movements fluid and deadly. He moved like a wraith, a ghost gliding through the suffocating darkness, his only light the faint glimmer of his enchanted blade.

Every breath was a calculated risk, each heartbeat a drum against the oppressive silence punctuated by the drip, drip, drip of viscous fluids from unseen sources. The air hung heavy with the stench of decay, a nauseating cocktail of blood, Sulfur, and something ancient and indescribably foul. The fortress itself was a monument to darkness, a testament to the Covenant's depravity, its very stones seeming to writhe with malevolent energy, a palpable evil that pressed in on him from all sides, threatening to crush his spirit as surely as any physical trap. The silence itself felt menacing, broken only by the occasional guttural growl from some unseen horror lurking in the shadows.

The clash with the Covenant's elite guard was a brutal, balletic dance of death played out under a flickering, hellish light. He fought with a savage grace born not just of desperation, but of a primal, cornered rage. His movements were a blur of controlled fury, each striking a precise, agonizing calculation designed to exploit weakness and inflict maximum, crippling damage. He melted into the shadows, becoming one with the darkness, a wraithlike figure who used the gloom as both shield and weapon. He snatched their energy swords, their plasma rifles, turning their advanced technology and brutal tactics against them with chilling efficiency, anticipating their maneuvers, twisting their strategies into instruments of his annihilation. He fought with the grim, unwavering resolve of a man facing not only imminent death but also the spectral horrors of his past, each swing of his blade a desperate attempt at expiation. The very air vibrated with the high-pitched whine of his weapon, a death song, a keening lament for the sins that haunted him, a requiem for the fallen, and a defiant roar against the encroaching darkness.

He reached the chamber, its oppressive silence broken only by the rhythmic thrum of the Heart of Obsidian. The massive stone pulsed with malevolent energy, its obsidian surface a swirling vortex of darkness that swallowed the meagre light of the flickering candles. These cast long, dancing shadows that writhed and contorted like phantoms, mimicking the chaotic power within the heart itself. The air crackled with arcane energy, a palpable tension that vibrated not just in the air, but in his very bones. The scent of ozone and brimstone hung heavy, a suffocating perfume of demonic power. He felt the weight of his responsibility, not merely a burden on his shoulders, but a crushing pressure upon his soul, his heart hammering against his ribs like a frantic bird trapped in a cage. Sweat beaded on his brow, a cold sheen reflecting the malevolent glow emanating from the Heart, a stark reminder of the terrible power—and the terrible price—that awaited.

The Guardian of the Heart, a hulking demon lord whose very presence radiated a palpable malice that chilled Caspian to the bone, stood before him. Jagged horns crowned his skull, a grotesque mockery of a crown, and eyes like burning coals fixed on Caspian with predatory intensity. The air crackled with malevolent energy, the ground trembling under the weight of the demon's power. The battle that followed was a maelstrom of incandescent fury and devastating destruction; a chaotic ballet of fire and steel. Each clash of their weapons sent shockwaves rippling through the very fabric of reality. Caspian fought not merely for his redemption, but for Blaze's future, for the chance to prove the purity of his love, to erase the bitter stain of doubt that shadowed their bond. The duel was a brutal dance of death, a desperate struggle for survival where every parry, every thrust, was a gamble with mortality.

The demon lord's power was a physical force, an immense, suffocating weight that pressed down on Caspian, testing his limits to their absolute breaking point. He felt his strength ebb, his will fracture, his very soul threatened with annihilation. But he fought on, driven by a force far stronger than his fear, a burning, incandescent desire for redemption that fueled his body and soul, a love for Blaze that ignited an unwavering resolve within him, defying death itself. The taste of blood mingled with the metallic tang of fear in his mouth, but his eyes blazed with defiance as he met the demon lord's infernal gaze.

Finally, with a desperate, lunging thrust that defied both gravity and his failing strength, Caspian plunged his sword deep into the demon lord's obsidian heart. The creature's death rattle was a deafening roar, a sonic earthquake that shook the very foundations of the shattered battlefield. Then, as quickly as it had begun, the monstrous form dissolved into a swirling vortex of black dust, leaving behind only the acrid stench of Sulfur and the echoing silence of its demise.

Caspian collapsed to his knees, his body wracked with exhaustion. Each shuddering breath hitched in his throat, a ragged gasp for air that mirrored the tempest raging within his soul. His armour, once gleaming, was now marred by scorch marks and rents, a testament to the brutal battle just fought. Sweat plastered his hair to his forehead, mingling with the grime of the fight. He'd stared into the abyss and wrestled back his darkness, emerging victorious, yet profoundly weary. The triumph felt bittersweet, a hard-won victory stained with the blood of a thousand battles, both internal and external. His redemption was far from complete; the weight of his past sins still pressed heavily upon him, a constant reminder of the treacherous journey ahead.

This victory, however, was a crucial step, a vital bridge towards earning Blaze's long-denied forgiveness. The price he'd paid was steep—scars both visible and hidden marked him deeply—and the road ahead promised even greater perils, a gauntlet of trials that would test his resolve to its very limits. But Caspian, his eyes burning with a newfound resolve, refused to falter. He would face the daunting challenges that lay before him, the arduous path paved with dangers both mortal and supernatural, head-on. He was no longer running from himself, from his past, from the shadow of his mistakes. He was finally confronting them, walking toward the light, one agonizing, determined step at a time.

He clutched the Heart, its obsidian surface pulsing with malevolent energy that throbbed in his very bones, a tangible trophy of his daring victory. Slipping from the fortress's iron grip, he melted back into the comforting embrace of the shadows, his old allies. His escape was a harrowing dance with death, each footfall a calculated risk on the knife edge of discovery. He'd gambled everything, and against all odds, he'd won. The stolen artifact, cold and heavy in his grasp, was more than a prize; it was a symbol of his unwavering commitment to atonement, a first payment on a debt of immeasurable weight. But this was only the beginning, a single, arduous step on a pilgrimage of redemption. The path ahead, fraught with peril and uncertainty, stretched before him, a stark testament to his ferocious determination to earn Blaze's trust and, even more elusive, her forgiveness. His redemption? Far, impossibly far, from complete.

The forest floor, slick with dampness, clung to my bare feet as I moved, the air heavy with the cloying sweetness of pine needles and the earthy musk of decaying leaves. For days, I'd stalked the Obsidian Covenant, my senses sharpened to an almost painful acuity, each rustle and snap a potential clue. The near-constant gnawing hunger, a brutal inheritance of my vampiric transformation, pulsed in my veins like a second, malevolent heartbeat, a relentless, unwelcome companion. Caspian's blood, a bitter necessity, had dulled the edge of the cravings, but they still returned, each time a terrifying wave threatening to drown me. The act of accepting his help, of relying on him, felt like a slow, agonizing surrender, a creeping erosion of the fiercely guarded independence I'd fought so hard to maintain. Yet the alternative — the horrifying prospect of succumbing to the insatiable hunger, of losing myself completely to the savage beast that slumbered within — was an abyss I couldn't fathom facing. The very thought sent a fresh wave of icy dread through me, a tremor that had nothing to do with the damp chill of the forest.

A sudden rustle in the undergrowth froze me rigid. My muscles coiled, a primal instinct driving my hand to the wickedly curved blade strapped to my thigh. The air, thick with the scent of damp earth and decaying leaves, held its breath. Then, a figure emerged from the shadows, a silhouette stark against the bruised purple of the fading light. It was Cascade, a woman whose name whispered of waterfalls and hidden depths. Cascade possessed a reputation as potent as the mountain herbs she used, famed not just for her uncanny ability to mend shattered bones and staunch bleeding wounds, but for her power to soothe the deeper, spiritual scars that war inflicted. Our previous encounter had been fleeting, a mere brush of hands and shared glances, yet her quiet strength—a calm defiance in the face of chaos—lingered in my memory like the lingering scent of pine after a storm. The memory, sharp and vivid, fueled a burgeoning hope in this desperate hour.

Cascades' eyes, usually a vibrant, cerulean blue that sparkled with warmth, were now veiled in a deep, unsettling shadow of worry. Her gaze, usually so inviting, held a palpable anxiety. *"Blaze,"* she breathed, the sound barely audible above the whisper of the wind, a fragile tremor in the stillness. *"I felt your presence... felt the echo of your pain. You're grievously wounded."*

A searing wave of anger—hot and brutal—crashed over me overwhelming my senses and leaving me gasping in its wake. It was the culmination of accumulated frustrations from the hunt, the sting of fresh wounds that pulsed with every heartbeat and the constant gnawing fear that had settled in the pit of my stomach igniting a furious blaze of aggression that I struggled to contain. I had meticulously avoided any confrontation desperate to shield the fragile remnants of my strength and avoid exposing the vulnerability that Caspian's aid—however well-intentioned—had cruelly laid bare. The memory of his help felt less like a lifeline and more like a brand searing my skin and marking me as weak and dependent. Each moment I recalled his assistance only fueled the simmering resentment that threatened to boil over leaving me consumed by a bitter rage that I could no longer ignore. *"I don't need your help! Get the fuck lost!* " I snapped my voice sharper than I had intended, laced with an edge of pain and frustration. I could feel the weight of my words hanging in the air, a stark reminder of my struggle to retain my independence in a world that seemed determined to undermine it. With every heartbeat, I wrestled with the tumultuous emotions surging within me desperate to reclaim my sense of self.

Cascade didn't flinch, her gaze unwavering as she assessed the damage. *"Pride won't heal this,"* she stated, her voice low and firm, the words carrying the weight of grim experience. *"The poison... It's unlike anything I've ever encountered. A truly vile concoction."* Her gloved hand, delicate yet purposeful, gestured to the deep gash marrying my arm, a grim souvenir from my last brutal encounter with the Covenant. I'd treated it, yes, but only superficially, a desperate measure to stanch the bleeding and ensure survival. Now, a dull, throbbing ache pulsed from the wound, its edges inflamed, a sickly, bruised purple darkening alarmingly at the margins. A creeping numbness threatened to spread from the wound's center, a chilling testament to the poison's insidious nature. The air itself seemed to crackle with a palpable sense of unease around the infected flesh.

Cascade's words, sharp and precise as shards of glass, pierced the armour I'd painstakingly constructed. The raw pain wasn't just emotional; it was a visceral, physical agony, a constant, throbbing ache mirroring the relentless battle against the demon that gnawed at my soul. The fight was exhausting, a Sisyphean struggle against the darkness within. Healing wasn't simply a matter of mending broken bones and closing wounds; it was a desperate need to excise the deep, festering scars left by Linx and Caspian, scars that ran far deeper than the skin, poisoning my very being. The memories, like phantom limbs, pulsed with searing intensity, a constant reminder of the horrors I'd endured.

Reluctantly, I allowed Cascade to examine my wounds. Her touch, feather-light yet firm, was a startling contrast to the brutal violence that had inflicted them. Each movement was precise, guided by an intuitive grace that spoke of years spent mastering the body's intricate tapestry of muscle, sinew, and bone. As she worked, her fingers, cool and deft, danced across my skin, tracing the ragged edges of the lacerations. A low, melodic hum, an ancient healing chant, vibrated from her lips, the words weaving a spell of soothing warmth that seemed to penetrate the very marrow of my bones. The magic wasn't a sudden, dramatic burst, but a gentle, persistent flow, a quiet river mending the torn flesh and knitting together the shattered edges of my spirit. It eased not only the physical pain, the throbbing ache and the searing heat but also the deeper, more insidious wounds, the gnawing anxiety, and the suffocating despair that had become my constant, unwelcome companions. With each murmured syllable, each careful touch, the shadows that had clung to me for so long began to recede, replaced by a tentative, fragile hope. The air itself seemed to lighten, charged with a potent energy that both healed and comforted.

The experience felt strangely intimate, a vulnerability I hadn't allowed myself to feel since the catastrophic fire that razed my village, leaving only ashes and the ghosts of memory. The acrid scent of smoke still clung to my thoughts, a constant reminder of the devastation. But Cascade's acceptance, her unwavering empathy, flowed over me like a gentle river, erasing the scorched earth of my trauma. It was a peace I hadn't known was possible, a quiet sanctuary built on the foundation of her kindness. The healing was more than just the meticulous mending of a physical wound; it was a balm for my bruised soul, a slow, deliberate soothing of the deep, festering scars that ran far deeper than flesh. Her presence, a warm ember in the desolate landscape of my heart, ignited a flickering hope where only despair had lived before.

Meanwhile, Caspian's journey careened through a maelstrom of unforeseen consequences. The theft of the Heart of Obsidian, a daring act of defiance, had not only secured the artifact but also unexpectedly illuminated him to a hidden faction. Deep within the treacherous labyrinth of the Whispering Wind, a cabal of dissenting demons, simmering with years of simmering resentment against their tyrannical leadership, had observed Caspian's transformation. They had witnessed his agonizing struggle for redemption, the stark contrast between his past actions and his present desperate attempts to atone. In Caspian, they saw not a traitor, but a potential champion, a figurehead around whom their rebellion could coalesce. His audacious theft of the Heart provided the perfect catalyst, the long-awaited opportunity to shatter the corrupt regime from within and seize control. The shadows whispered with the promise of an alliance forged in rebellion, a dangerous gamble with potentially devastating consequences.

A whisper of movement in the periphery, and then a figure materialized from the gloom, cloaked in shadows so deep they seemed to absorb the very light. The hood concealed the face entirely, leaving only the suggestion of eyes, gleaming faintly like embers in the darkness. A voice, low and resonant as the tolling of a distant bell, cut through the night's stillness. It possessed the chilling authority of ages, each syllable heavy with the weight of forgotten centuries, the power of untold secrets. *"Caspian,"* the voice purred, the name itself tasting of ash and regret. *"We know what you did. We know your intentions, and we are here to... rectify the situation."*

Caspian, his gaze narrowed with suspicion yet alight with a flicker of morbid curiosity, listened intently. The figure, cloaked in shadows yet radiating an unsettling power, unveiled the horrifying scope of the Whispering Wind's insidious corruption. Their manipulations weren't merely subtle machinations; they were a tapestry of deceit, woven with threads of betrayal that snaked far beyond Caspian's ill-fated involvement, ensnaring kingdoms and shattering lives in their wake. The weight of this revelation pressed down on him, a suffocating burden of responsibility. Then came the offer, stark and chilling in its implications: join their burgeoning rebellion, a desperate gambit to dismantle the organization from within, or face the inevitable, crushing consequences of their wrath, consequences that promised to be far more devastating than any he had yet imagined.

The proposal hung before him, a shimmering, double-edged blade. It offered a tantalizing path to redemption, a chance to cleanse the stain of his past sins by striking a devastating blow against the very heart of the Obsidian Covenant, the corrupt system that had moulded him into its instrument. But the allure of atonement was inextricably entwined with the chilling reality of rebellion. He would not only be defying the iron fist of the Covenant but also turning his back on the Whispering Wind, the brotherhood he once called his own, the men who had shared his blood and secrets. The risks were monumental, a precipice of potential ruin; failure meant not just defeat, but annihilation. This was a suicidal mission, a desperate gamble, yet the path to true redemption, however perilous, blazed before him with a stark and uncompromising clarity.

The decision gnawed at him, a relentless tide eroding the foundations of his resolve. He'd spent sleepless nights weighing the shimmering promise of redemption against the treacherous precipice of risk. The scales trembled, each pan burdened with the weight of his past: one side, the agonizingly slow climb towards atonement; the other, the seductive, yet ultimately ruinous, ease of his former life. His heart, a bruised and battered organ, ached with the burden of guilt, each beat a mournful drum urging him towards the daunting, yet necessary, path of amends. The alternative, to remain tethered to the manipulative web he'd woven, to continue the insidious dance of deception, was not merely undesirable; it was an unthinkable abyss, a descent into the bleakest depths of his own self-loathing.

Caspian, his heart a battlefield mirroring the one to come, accepted their offer. The weight of past betrayals pressed upon him, a burden he now wielded as a weapon in his quest for redemption. He pledged his allegiance to the rebellion, his former sins recast as leverage against the oppressive regime. The dissenting faction, a clandestine network of rebels operating in the shadows, showered him with resources, not just weapons and supplies, but crucial intelligence gleaned from the enemy's inner circle, and the unwavering support of hardened warriors who saw in him not a traitor, but a potential saviour. This unlikely alliance, forged in the crucible of shared desperation and a thirst for justice, would prove invaluable. They understood the fire that consumed him, the gnawing needs to atone, and their aims, the overthrow of tyranny and the establishment of a just society mirrored his own with chilling precision. The battle ahead loomed, a maelstrom of violence and uncertainty, but Caspian, armed with their support and driven by his burning desire for redemption, felt, for the first time in a long time, a flicker of hope.

Caspian and I discovered surprising friends in places we never expected. Our different journeys began to come together much like two rivers merging into a wild ocean. They both fought against the Obsidian Covenant, an evil group that threatened their world. However they had very different ways of fighting. I preferred a direct and aggressive attack while Caspian chose a sneakier approach focusing on getting in and undermining the enemy from within. These unexpected partnerships created during tough times were not just simple teamwork. They were complex connections built from a mix of shared struggles, a bit of mutual respect and the risk of serious betrayal. Amid the chaos love also grew making the already difficult situation even more complicated.

My struggles which used to feel so isolated now come together to create a complex story. My future used to be separate from theirs but now our paths are tightly connected. Our lives are mixed up in a complicated dance of being heroes and villains showing loyalty and betrayal and feeling hope and despair. I stood ready for a big showdown, a fight that would decide the future of the Obsidian Covenant and the land we fought for. This battle would also change me and Caspian, shaping our souls in the heat of the struggle. The new allies gave us more strength and brought in a new level of mystery. This changed the battlefield and made me think hard about what is right and wrong, who I can trust and what good and evil really mean. I realized that the fight had changed from being just my own struggle to becoming a battle for the heart and soul of our world.

CHAPTER

FOURTEEN

Blood Soaked Redemption

The weight of my choices wasn't just metaphorical; it was a physical vice, crushing the breath from my lungs, and bowing my spine until my ribs cracked under the pressure. Cascade's healing had plastered over the wounds, a grotesque mask over the ravaged landscape beneath. The gashes throbbed a phantom pain echoing the deeper, searing burns of Linx's touch. His touch, the memory of it, a branding iron searing my very soul, a relentless loop of icy fingers and the acrid stench of his power, a nightmare that clawed its way into my waking moments, its talons digging into my flesh. I'd offered myself, a desperate, gut-wrenching gamble, a trade made in the stygian abyss of despair, a soul bartered for a breath of survival. But the price... God, the price. It was a cataclysm, an unimaginable inferno consuming every fibre of my being.

The metallic tang of his dominance, a coppery stain on my tongue, haunted me, a phantom limb of his control, a constant, bitter reminder of my utter helplessness, my sickening, bone-deep weakness. Even the air itself reeked of him, thick, suffocating, a miasma of his power, a suffocating shroud weaving around me, whispering promises of his return in the darkness. His power... wasn't just a violation; it was a corruption, seeping into my very essence, leaving me hollowed, broken, and irrevocably changed.

Caspian's blood, a bitter draught that had slaked my thirst, now clung to me, a morbid reminder of the debt I owed. Each sunrise brought the weight of his assistance crashing down, a suffocating burden far exceeding the life it had saved. His help, invaluable though it was, had woven me into a tapestry of complex emotions, a dangerous entanglement of threads. I found myself inexplicably drawn to him, a perilous dance between attraction and repulsion, a desperate waltz of dependence and defiance. He was a demon, a creature sculpted from shadow and fueled by darkness, yet within the obsidian depths of his eyes, a flicker of something else ignited, a vulnerability, a fragile ember of remorse that mirrored the smouldering pain I kept carefully hidden within my own heart. I fought against this unsettling pull, fiercely clinging to the tattered remnants of my independence, but the feelings persisted, a relentless undertow beneath the tempestuous surface of my emotions, a constant, insidious whisper against the storm raging within.

The Obsidian Covenant's battle clawed at my soul, each sickening clang of steel a death rattle echoing in my skull, the coppery tang of blood a constant reminder of my precarious existence. The hunger, a ravenous beast gnawing at my insides, pulsed with a sickening rhythm, a throbbing counterpoint to the icy grip of fear that threatened to freeze my very blood. It was a war waged within, a brutal insurgency against the insidious whispers of my vampiric nature, a battle fought on the razor's edge of sanity. But I endured. Fueled by a rage so incandescent it seared my mind, a white-hot inferno of vengeance born from the ashes of my village—a landscape of charred bone and twisted metal seared onto my memory. The screams, the agonized screams of my family, still tore through my soul, a symphony of despair that reverberated through my very marrow. Sleep was a poisoned chalice, offering only visions of writhing bodies and the acrid stench of death. Rest was a betrayal, a luxury I couldn't afford. Vengeance was my oxygen, my unholy sacrament, my unwavering lodestar in this tempest of grief and insatiable hunger. It was the only thing preventing me from being utterly consumed, devoured whole by the echoing emptiness of the abyss, a darkness that mirrored the black hole where my heart used to beat.

The quiet strength I'd glimpsed in Cascade, a resilience etched subtly into her very being, offered a fleeting reprieve from the tempest raging within. Her acceptance, a balm so gentle yet so profound, had chipped away at the formidable emotional walls I'd painstakingly constructed, brick by agonizing brick. It was a moment of incandescent human connection, a fragile beacon piercing the suffocating darkness that had become my constant companion. But the solace was bittersweet; I knew my solitude remained a necessary armour, a shield forged in the fires of past hurts, protecting me from further vulnerability, from the risk of another shattering blow. The peace was temporary, a fragile butterfly resting on a thorny branch, its wings shimmering with the promise of flight, but always aware of the potential for a sudden, brutal storm.

Caspian, meanwhile, wrestled with demons that clawed at his soul, their icy fingers tightening around his heart. His alliance with the rebel faction, the Whispering Wind, was a gamble of desperate proportions, a treacherous tightrope walk towards redemption that felt increasingly elusive. He had betrayed his kin, a violation that echoed in the hollow chambers of his guilt, risking everything, his name, his future, the very fragments of his fractured self, for a chance to atone for a past steeped in shadows. The weight of his actions, the years spent weaving a tapestry of deception and manipulative whispers, crushed him beneath an unbearable burden. Each breath was a laboured struggle against the suffocating weight of his memories. He had walked a path paved with darkness, and the shadows clung to him like a shroud, their insidious temptations slithering into his mind, whispering promises of oblivion, a seductive escape from the torment of his conscience. The very air seemed thick with the stench of his past misdeeds, a constant, suffocating reminder of the man he had been, and the man he desperately yearned to become.

The stench of incense and decay, a cloying perfume of faith and rot, clung to the air as they approached. This rebel cell, shrouded in a secrecy thicker than midnight, offered him not a lifeline, but a baptism in fire, a chance to scour the venomous corruption that had eaten into his soul, leaving only a hollow shell of the man he once was. Their eyes, burning coals in the dim light, saw not a simple defector, but a weapon, a blade honed to lethal sharpness by years of simmering resentment. He, who had tasted the honeyed poison of the Whispering Wind's power, had seen the rot beneath its silken mask, the twitching, vulnerable heart beneath the flawless facade. Their trust, a fragile moth fluttering around a flickering candle flame, was a priceless jewel, easily shattered by the slightest tremor of doubt. The chilling weight of that trust pressed down on him, a suffocating burden. But it was this perilous gamble, this dance with the abyss, that ignited the dying embers of his soul. He would earn their trust, not with empty words, but with a symphony of bloodshed, a pyrotechnic display of vengeance forged in the crucible of his despair. The taste of ash and blood would be a testament to his loyalty.

The information they provided was invaluable, a meticulously detailed tapestry woven from threads of Obsidian Covenant machinations. It revealed their insidious plans, their clandestine alliances, a spiderweb of power stretching across continents, and their chilling, ultimate goals: a reign of terror that promised to extinguish the very light of hope. Caspian felt the crushing weight of these secrets, the burden of knowledge pressing down on him like a physical force. This was not merely information; it was a responsibility, a mantle he bore alone, the fate of countless lives resting solely on his shoulders. He knew that he must balance his burning thirst for revenge against the cold, calculating strategy demanded by this perilous game. The stakes were not merely high; they were astronomical, a precipice overlooking an abyss of unimaginable horrors. One misstep, one poorly considered action, could not only shatter the rebellion, leaving its embers to be ruthlessly stamped out but also condemn Caspian to a torment so profound, so utterly agonizing, that death itself would seem a blessed release.

The rebellion against the Whispering Wind wasn't a mere power struggle; it was a desperate battle for the organization's very soul. Years of insidious corruption had warped its noble purpose, twisting its ideals into grotesque parodies for the insatiable greed of its leaders. They had choked the life from its sacred mission, leaving behind only a hollow shell of its former glory. Caspian's involvement transcended personal vengeance. He fought not for retribution, but for restoration, a desperate bid to cleanse the festering wound of corruption and rekindle the flame of justice within the very system he'd once served, a system he now sought to redeem. The stakes were higher than any single life; this was a fight for the future of the Whispering Wind, a fight for its heart and its honour.

He found himself shoulder to shoulder with demons—former enemies, victims of the very system he'd once served. The shared crucible of rebellion forged an unexpected camaraderie, a brotherhood forged not in loyalty but in the shared scars of betrayal. They had seen the darkness at the heart of power, the insidious tendrils of manipulation twisting truth into grotesque parodies. Each had tasted the bitter ashes of deceit, each bore the wounds of a system designed to crush dissent. United now by a burning need to expose the truth, they were an unlikely alliance, bound not by blood or creed, but by the shared pain of oppression and the unwavering resolve to dismantle the corrupt edifice that had wronged them all. Their rebellion was a symphony of defiance, each notes a testament to their resilience, a discordant harmony born from the ashes of their past.

The rebellion was a tempest of danger, each heartbeat a gamble, each decision a precarious balancing act on the razor's edge. The Obsidian Covenant, a shadow lurking in the periphery, knew of Caspian's defiance. Their spies, like vipers in the grass, slithered through the rebel ranks, their venomous whispers weaving plots of demise. Caspian himself was a phantom, moving through the labyrinthine shadows, his senses honed to a razor's edge, each rustle of leaves, each whispered word, a potential harbinger of betrayal or death. The weight of command pressed upon him, a crushing burden of responsibility that stole the breath from his lungs. This relentless vigilance, this perpetual dance with fate, was a heady cocktail of exhilaration and bone-deep exhaustion, leaving him perpetually teetering on the precipice of collapse. The taste of fear was a constant companion, mingling with the adrenaline that pulsed through his veins, a bitter-sweet reminder of the stakes. Every breath he took was a testament to his defiance, a defiant act against the crushing weight of the Obsidian Covenant's might.

The dismantling of the Whispering Wind was a painstaking, internal battle mirrored by the turmoil in his soul. Each carefully removed component echoed the fracturing of his resolve, each precise movement a counterpoint to the chaotic surge of emotion he felt for Blaze. This was no mere repayment of a debt; it was a tangled web of obligation, burgeoning affection, and a primal attraction that threatened to unravel him completely. Their encounters crackled with a volatile energy, a dangerous dance on the precipice of something far greater than either of them could comprehend. The pull towards her was undeniable, a connection that defied his demonic essence, a stark contrast to the darkness that consumed him, a pure, white-hot intensity burning away the shadows. He was caught in a vice, the crushing weight of his vengeance pitted against the intoxicating, all-consuming pull of his feelings for Blaze, a conflict that threatened to tear him asunder.

The weight of his past pressed down on him, a crushing burden of memory and regret. Each whispered confession, each shadowed deed, clung to him like the clinging mist of a haunted moor. He couldn't outrun the spectral figures of his past, their accusations echoing in the silent chambers of his soul. Yet, he clung fiercely to the fragile hope of redemption, a flickering candle against the encroaching darkness. He had chosen this path, a treacherous ascent towards grace, a journey through a landscape of physical peril and emotional torment. Thorns of doubt snagged at his resolve, while the icy winds of self-loathing threatened to extinguish his flickering flame. His redemption wasn't merely a matter of defeating the Obsidian Covenant; it was inextricably bound to the brutal, ongoing battle for his soul, a war fought within the very marrow of his being. The success of one hinged entirely upon the other; failure in either arena meant utter annihilation.

My journey and Caspian's used to go in different directions like rivers cutting through their own valleys. Now they are coming together because we both really need it. At first my fight against the cruel Obsidian Covenant felt lonely. But soon I realized that my struggles were connected to others. Our fates became linked like threads in a tapestry as we faced the threat of war together. I didn't just fight to stay alive; I fought for justice that I had been denied for so long. I wanted to find a way to make things right even when it felt like it was out of reach. The upcoming battle was not just about fighting with swords and magic; it was a fierce struggle of beliefs and ideas. It felt like a storm that could take over our very souls. I found myself in a tough situation that pushed me to my limits. It made me question who I thought I was and helped me create a new version of myself. I came out of it changed forever.

My demons—the memories of my past failures, the missed chances that still echo in my mind and the heavy weight of things I can't forget—moved together in a dark rhythm with the growing threat of the Obsidian Covenant. I faced a cruel enemy that led to a fierce fight for my survival. I desperately struggled to find a little hope in a world filled with sadness and darkness. Every moment felt like it lasted forever as I dealt with my inner struggles. The memories of my challenges swirled around me like a storm trying to pull me down and drown my hope. My partnership felt as delicate as a spider's web stretched over a deep gap but it had a strong power. This strength came from the tough times we faced together and the respect we built through our struggles. I relied on this shaky connection which felt like a flickering candle in the heavy darkness around us. It kept me and everyone else from being swallowed up, lighting a way through the confusion. The choices I made in the upcoming conflict felt really important. I knew that these decisions would not only affect my future but also change the world for generations to come. I felt the huge responsibility weighing on me just like the heavy black stones that gave my enemy their dark strength. It was a constant reminder of how much was at stake. With every beat of my heart I felt the urgency of our mission grow stronger. I knew that we couldn't fail and that made me even more determined. In the face of overwhelming odds, they would either rise as beacons of hope or succumb to the darkness forever lost in the annals of history.

The candle flame, a sputtering, malevolent eye, threw grotesque shadows that writhed and pulsed across the scarred oak table. My fingers, slick with a film of cold sweat, clutched the lukewarm water, its tepidity a mockery of the burning ice that clawed at my throat. The phantom ache, a familiar demon, throbbed with the rhythm of my cursed heart, a constant, brutal reminder of my vampiric existence, a life purchased with the very soul of my humanity. Caspian's blood, a fleeting balm, had offered only a reprieve. Now, the hunger returned, a ravenous beast tearing at my insides, a gnawing, visceral emptiness that left me weak and trembling. It was a torment, this dependence on him, this reliance on his lifeblood to stave off the monstrous hunger that threatened to consume me. The bitter taste of it, the humiliation of it, was a poison more potent than any mortal draught. My pride, once a fortress, lay shattered beneath the relentless onslaught of my insatiable need.

The rap on the door, a bone-jarring percussion against the suffocating stillness, ripped through me. My breath hitched, a metallic tang of fear coating my tongue. Fingers, slick with a cold sweat, instinctively tightened around the wickedly curved hilt of the dagger, its polished surface a chilling mirror to the grim determination in my eyes. This life, a tapestry woven with betrayal and blood, had taught me the bitter truth: trust was a phantom limb, a cruel mockery of a feeling I could no longer afford. The scent of dust and ozone, the ghost of a recent thunderstorm, hung heavy in the air, a suffocating shroud mirroring the weight of my secrets. Each muscle coiled, a spring poised to unleash years of honed savagery. The floorboards groaned beneath my weight, a traitorous whisper in the expectant silence, as I moved, a phantom, a wraith, guided by the hyper-awareness that was both my curse and my salvation. The air itself crackled with the anticipation of violence, a palpable energy humming against my skin.

Caspian burst in, the heavy oak door groaning a protest against the raw force of his entrance. His usual brooding intensity wasn't merely amplified; it crackled, a tangible storm of barely contained fury and dread. The scent of wood smoke and something acrid, metallic, clung to him, a phantom echo of whatever horrors he'd just witnessed. His aqua eyes, usually pools of captivating, hypnotic blue, were now blazed with a feverish light, the fear within them a stark, icy contrast to the inferno raging beneath the surface. It wasn't merely a flicker; it was a wildfire threatening to consume him whole. His normally impeccable attire, the crisp linen, the perfectly tailored coat, was wreckage, torn and stained, mirroring the devastation within him. The controlled precision that usually defined his every move was shattered, replaced by a tension so thick, you could taste the bitterness on your tongue, feel the icy grip of it constricting your breath. His very presence thrummed with raw, desperate energy, a silent scream trapped behind a mask of barely contained violence.

"*They found us,*" the words rasped from him, a sound like stones grinding against bone, a stark betrayal of the silken voice he usually wielded like a weapon. The air itself seemed to thicken, heavy with the metallic tang of fear and the cloying sweetness of impending doom. His usually immaculate linen shirt, now clinging damply to his chest, hinted at a sweat-slicked with terror that ran deeper than mere apprehension. *"The Obsidian Covenant,"* he hissed, the name a venomous whisper that tasted of ash and betrayal on his tongue. *"They know. They know we're unravelling their meticulously crafted lies, picking at the threads of their suffocating control. And they won't tolerate it."* The tremor in his voice, barely perceptible, spoke of desperation that belied his outwardly composed facade, a crack in the icy mask of a man who had spent a lifetime mastering the art of deception, only to find himself facing the ultimate deception, his mortality.

Ice clawed its way into my marrow, a frigid dread that solidified my blood. The Obsidian Covenant wasn't just formidable; it was a cancer, a black rot gnawing at the very foundations of the world. Their resources weren't vast, they were bottomless, a subterranean ocean of ill-gotten gains fueling their insatiable hunger. Their efficiency wasn't ruthless; it was surgical, and precise, leaving behind only the echoes of shattered lives and whispered rumours. The air itself seemed to thicken, heavy with the scent of ozone and the metallic tang of blood, a perfume only the Covenant could wear. Their spies weren't merely present; they were everywhere, phantom limbs brushing against my skin, their eyes burning holes in the darkness, their whispers slithering into my dreams.

The revelation wasn't a chill; it was a seismic tremor that cracked the very earth beneath my feet, the shattering confirmation of fears so deep they'd become a part of my DNA, a genetic inheritance of impending doom. My heart hammered a frantic tattoo against my ribs, a desperate rhythm against the encroaching silence of absolute terror. They were coming. And I knew, with a certainty that tasted like ash and despair, that I was utterly, irrevocably alone.

"How?" The word tore from my throat, a raw, guttural rasp that echoed in the cavernous space. Caspian's face, a granite mask sculpted by years of shadowed secrets and brutal truths, loomed, distorted by the flickering torchlight, the flames dancing like mocking spirits in his cold, unwavering eyes. The coppery taste of my own blood, thick and metallic, was a vile tide flooding my mouth; the ragged edges of the wound screamed in protest against every shuddering breath. His words, a venomous hiss, precise as a surgeon's blade, weren't just accusations; they were a calculated evisceration, ripping away the meticulously crafted facade I'd spent a lifetime building.

I'd foreseen this, a nightmare etched into the marrow of my bones, yet the reality was a crushing weight, a vice around my heart squeezing the air from my lungs. This wasn't mere discovery; it was a ritualistic humiliation, a public flaying that left me exposed, naked to their scorn, the ground itself vibrating under the seismic force of their judgment. The reek of ozone, sharp and acrid, was the stench of a thousand broken oaths, a suffocating pall of betrayal clinging to the air, thick and inescapable as the darkness closed in around me. The chilling whisper of his name, a curse on my lips, tasted like ashes.

A viper in our midst, Caspian rasped, the words tasting like ash in his mouth. The flickering torchlight painted his face in harsh shadows, highlighting the icy glint in his eyes, eyes that had seen too much death, too much betrayal. *"Someone we embraced as kin... someone who shared our bread, our blood, our dreams... someone close enough to whisper secrets into the very heart of our rebellion."* The air crackled with unspoken accusations, thick with the scent of fear and the metallic tang of blood, a phantom taste lingering from a thousand battles fought and won, only to be potentially undone by this insidious treachery. His voice, raw with barely suppressed rage, vibrated with a chilling intensity. The weight of his unspoken grief, a suffocating cloak woven from shattered trust and agonizing loss, hung heavy in the air between them.

The betrayal pressed down, a physical weight crushing the breath from my lungs. The metallic tang of blood, not my own, but the phantom taste of the Obsidian Covenant's treachery, coated my tongue. It clung, a bitter film mirroring the icy dread that coiled in my gut. Each shadow seemed to writhe with menace, each whispered word a potential blade aimed at my heart. The air itself crackled with suspicion, a palpable tension that vibrated in my bones, a constant, gnawing fear that festered beneath my skin. My closest allies, their faces once familiar, were now masks, their eyes shimmering with a deceptive light I couldn't decipher. Was their loyalty a fragile facade, ready to shatter under the slightest pressure? Every smile felt like a calculated risk, every handshake a potential death warrant. Paranoia wasn't just a companion; it was the poisoned chalice I was forced to drink, a necessary evil in this viper's nest of a world. My survival depended on it, yet the price was a soul slowly devoured by its mistrust.

"Who?!" I snarled, the word a ragged claw tearing through the suffocating silence. The metallic tang of blood, my own, a trickle from a split lip, filled my mouth, a bitter counterpoint to the bile rising in my throat. Fear, raw and visceral, clawed at my chest, a frantic beast struggling for release, but it was a snarling, potent rage that fueled my voice, a venomous hiss that vibrated in the air, thick with the scent of ozone and fear. This wasn't a question; it was a demand etched in the cold steel of a blade poised at their throats. The answer held not just the fate of their pathetic rebellion, but the very soul of my fractured world, hanging precariously in the balance, a single, fragile thread swaying in the storm of their deceit. My eyes, narrowed slits of burning ice, bore into them, searching for the tremor of a lie, the flicker of a hidden truth, before the storm broke.

Caspian's head shot up, the coarse wool of his coat a brutal rasp against his stubbled jaw. A primal tremor, a visceral earthquake deep in his gut, resonated with the low, guttural thrum that pulsed through the ancient stones, a heartbeat of impending doom. The air itself seemed to crackle with a malevolent energy. *"We don't know yet,"* he snarled, the words a guttural growl, tasting of iron and bile, the metallic tang clinging to the back of his throat like a phantom wound. *"But the first blow… it shattered the fragile peace. I can smell it, the coppery reek of death, acrid and sickening, staining the very wind itself. Can't you taste it? The blood… the fear…"* His eyes, haunted and shadowed, burned with a cold fury, a chilling blend of grief and righteous rage. The weight of centuries seemed to press down on his broad shoulders, a burden etched into the lines of his ravaged face, a testament to battles fought and betrayals endured.

Before I could respond, the air crackled with dark energy, a tangible weight pressing down on me. I heard the sounds of battle echoing from outside, growing closer with each terrifying second. The building trembled violently beneath my feet as if some monstrous fist were shaking it to its foundations. Fear clawed at my throat as the sounds of chaos and destruction, screams, explosions, and the shattering of something immense, surrounded us, painting a grim and terrifying picture of the carnage unfolding just beyond those walls. I felt a cold dread seep into my bones.

The next few moments were a blur. I remember the searing heat of my magic as I launched a blast, the impact throwing me off balance. Caspian's roar followed a guttural sound that resonated in my chest as he hefted his weapon. I barely saw the strike, but I felt the wind of it. We fought back to back, a whirlwind of motion. I could feel Caspian's demonic strength beside me, a palpable force, his movements honed by years of brutal combat. My fiery abilities answered his strength, a perfect counterpoint. We moved with a terrifying grace, our movements perfectly synchronized, each of our actions anticipating the other's with a terrifying intimacy, a closeness that felt almost... sexual. I knew, even in the heat of the battle, that we were a team, a weapon unlike any other.

The battle was intense and relentless. Demons and warriors clashed in a brutal melee, my weapon clashing against theirs, my roars joining the cacophony that echoed through the night. I fought with a ferocity born of desperation, fueled by the burning memory of my lost village, and by the bitter injustice of the Covenant's actions. Each strike was precise, each movement calculated a testament to my years of gruelling training. I tasted blood, my own, I think, but in the chaos, it was hard to tell. Fear clawed at me, a cold hand gripping my heart, but I pushed it down and channelled it into the next blow. I saw my friend fall, a scream ripped from his throat before silence claimed him. Rage, raw and potent, flooded my veins. I would avenge him. I would avenge my village. I would not fall.

The enemy surged, a relentless tide of steel and fury, each wave crashing over us, bone-jarring impacts echoing in our bruised ribs. The stench of blood, my own and theirs, thick in the air, stung my nostrils with the metallic tang of death. My muscles screamed, a symphony of agony, each fibre screaming for respite, yet the tremors in my hands weren't just from exhaustion; fear, cold and sharp, clawed at my insides. Jax, his face a mask of grim determination, stumbled, a crimson stain blooming on his already ragged tunic. His eyes, usually alight with mischief, burned with a fierce, desperate light. We were ghosts, driven by a hunger deeper than any physical need, the desperate howl of survival, a primal scream against the oblivion threatening to swallow us whole.

For the rebellion? Perhaps. But more, for the fragile hope flickering in Elara's eyes, the hope that burned brighter than any torch in that maelstrom of death, the hope that fueled us all, even as the ground ran red, even as the very air crackled with the promise of annihilation. That, and the bitter knowledge that surrender meant not just death, but a death without meaning, a death that would let the monsters win. We were broken, battered, bleeding, but unbroken. We would not yield.

The tide shattered, not with a gentle ebb, but with a cataclysmic roar of steel and screams. From the vortex of carnage, he rose. Not merely a demon, but Azrael, his name a venomous whisper on the wind, a name that clawed at the sanity already fraying at the edges of my mind. His presence wasn't just felt, it was a physical blow, the air itself crackling with the ozone tang of raw, unholy power. The stench of brimstone and decay clung to him, a suffocating miasma that choked the lungs and curdled the blood. His eyes, twin pits of molten gold, bored into me, searing through the paltry defences of my soul, revealing the cold, bleak terror that festered within. Caspian, his face ashen, stumbled back, a whimper lost in the cacophony of battle, the very air vibrating with the demon's silent, sneering triumph. This wasn't mere power; it was a nihilistic force, a crushing weight of absolute annihilation that threatened to snuff out the flickering flame of our defiance, leaving only ashes and despair in its wake. My fear, sharp and visceral, tasted like iron on my tongue, a bitter prelude to the inevitable.

The ground trembled, a sickening pulse that vibrated through my very bones, heralding its arrival not with a fanfare, but a guttural scream that clawed at the sanity fraying at my edges. This wasn't merely a stronger foe; it was a harbinger of oblivion, a chasm yawning open to swallow the world whole. The air itself crackled, thick with the stench of brimstone and something older, something primal, a nauseating sweetness that promised only death. Its presence choked the light, casting long, skeletal shadows that writhed like tormented things.

This wasn't some demon lord, some petty prince of darkness. This… this was something beyond comprehension, something that sneered at the very concept of power as we knew it. I saw it reflected in the eyes of my comrades, the stark, cold terror that mirrored my own, a reflection of our shared, hopeless doom. The fear wasn't just of death; it was the chilling realization of utter insignificance facing this cosmic horror. A searing pain, not physical, but spiritual, pierced me, the gut-wrenching knowledge that all our struggles, all our sacrifices, had led to this: the unveiling of a true apocalypse, a cosmic malignancy that had finally broken free from its ancient prison. The taste of ash and despair filled my mouth. We were not soldiers facing an enemy; we were insects before a god of annihilation, its shadow stretching across the dying sun.

A mutual glance passed between Caspian and me, a silent pact forged in the shadow of overwhelming peril. Our continued existence hinged upon seamless cooperation, a fusion of our capabilities to surmount this unprecedented challenge. Previous discord and suspicion dissolved into insignificance, eclipsed by the immediacy of our predicament; preservation became paramount. The shared threat welded them together in a crucible of shared purpose, birthing an unexpected camaraderie and collaborative spirit against the backdrop of impending doom.

A cataclysmic assault erupted from the demon, a maelstrom of malevolent energy threatening to annihilate us. Caspian and I steeled against the impending doom, and understood this confrontation would push us to the precipice of our capabilities; the consequences would seal not just our destinies, but the rebellion's very existence. This clash would be the ultimate crucible, forging our combined might and showcasing our unwavering fortitude against impossible odds. It was a brutal ballet of annihilation, a symphony of chaos and ruin where survival itself became the most precious prize.

The grinding, bone-jarring fight chewed at us, a relentless maelstrom of pain that clawed at our very souls. The stench of blood, thick and metallic, filled my nostrils, a grim perfume to the symphony of screams and shattering bone. Each ragged breath scraped against raw lungs, a fire in my chest that mirrored the burning fury in my heart. Survival wasn't just a need, it was a primal scream tearing through the wreckage of my being, a desperate, incandescent howl against the encroaching darkness. My muscles screamed in protest, every fibre ripped and torn, yet I moved, a ghost driven by a vengeance as cold and sharp as shattered glass. The taste of grit and blood coated my tongue, a bitter reminder of the price of defiance. My vision blurred, the edges of reality fraying, yet in the heart of that chaos, a cold, unwavering core remained. We were broken, bleeding, barely human, yet we pushed on, a testament to something beyond mere endurance, a furious, magnificent, and terrifying will to live. We were not merely fighting; we were carving a path through hell, leaving our scars on every inch of that infernal landscape. This was not about survival anymore; this was about transcending it.

The air, thick with the stench of brimstone and the coppery tang of blood, clawed at our throats. Each demonic shriek, a physical blow, tore at our sanity as their relentless assault hammered against our defences. Our once impregnable line, forged in a crucible of sweat, blood, and the screams of the dying, crumbled inch by agonizing inch. I tasted the grit of fear, a metallic, bitter dust coating my tongue, as the monstrous forms, their eyes burning with malevolent glee pressed closer. Their power, a palpable force, a suffocating weight, threatened to crush the very breath from our lungs. We were not merely facing insurmountable odds; we were wrestling with the very fabric of oblivion.

This wasn't survival; it was a desperate, agonizing ballet danced on the razor's edge of annihilation. Seraphina, her face streaked with grime and tears, fought with a ferocity that belied her frail frame, each swing of her blade a testament to a spirit broken and reforged a thousand times. Kael, his eyes hollow yet burning with unwavering resolve, roared defiance against the tide, his every muscle screaming in protest, yet his will remained unbroken, a monument to stubborn hope amidst the carnage. And I, haunted by the ghosts of those we'd lost, fueled by a rage that burned hotter than any hellfire, fought on, knowing that surrender was not an option, that victory, however improbable, was the only path to redemption. This was not mere survival; this was a testament to the defiant, unyielding heart of humanity, a scream of defiance in the face of utter annihilation.

A primal scream tore from my throat, mirroring the raw fury in Caspian's eyes, eyes that burned with a desperate, haunted light I'd never seen before. We were a maelstrom of motion, a whirlwind of honed muscle and crackling power, our combined might a physical manifestation of our hatred. The air itself thrummed, a tangible pressure building in my chest, a nauseating sweetness of ozone stinging my nostrils as we unleashed it, a cataclysmic wave of energy that slammed into the demon with the force of a collapsing star.

The creature roared, unleashing a sound that ripped through the very fabric of reality itself—a guttural symphony of pain and rage that reverberated within my bones seeping into my very soul. I watched in awe and horror as its monstrous form staggered, the infernal glow in its eyes flickering and dimming as a telltale sign of its faltering strength. Its obsidian skin cracked under the strain of our relentless assault revealing glimpses of something dark and turbulent beneath. The stench of burning sulfur mixed with an ancient aroma—something wickedly alive—filled my mouth, coating my tongue with an unsettling taste, a horrifying cocktail of fear and triumph swirling together. It was as if the air itself trembled in response to the creature's wrath. Its formidable power once an overwhelming force began to visibly crumble under the relentless pressure of our desperate unified attack. Each strike we delivered seemed to chip away at its essence peeling back the layers of its malevolence. We fought not just for survival but for the very hope of existence against such darkness. With every ounce of strength we summoned we pressed on, determined to vanquish the embodiment of nightmares before us.

This wasn't just a victory; it was a brutal, agonizing extraction. The demon's retreat wasn't a hasty flight; it was a convulsive, shuddering collapse, a shameful, agonizing expulsion from our world. The echoing silence that followed was thick with the lingering scent of brimstone and the palpable relief, so profound it bordered on agony, that finally, finally, we had survived. Caspian's hand found mine, his grip raw and bone deep. In that shared moment, amidst the ruins of our battle, we found something more profound than victory, we found the fragile, hard-won solace of shared trauma and an understanding forged in the crucible of infernal fire.

Drained and triumphant, Caspian and I slumped to the ground, our muscles screaming, our lungs burning. Survival had come at a terrible cost. The confrontation laid bare the horrifying immensity of the looming danger—a menace far exceeding our wildest fears. This newly revealed, formidable demon, coupled with the Covenant's awareness of our defiance, altered the very fabric of our struggle. The road ahead, previously arduous, now presented an abyss of peril, a landscape far more perilous than any we had previously navigated.

The battle clawed at them, leaving behind a tapestry of ragged flesh and shattered spirits. The stench of blood, acrid and clinging, mingled with the metallic tang of fear, still clinging to their ravaged minds. The conflict's brutal dance had stripped away every pretense, every carefully constructed mask, exposing the raw, bleeding heart of their shared trauma. Their defiance, a snarling defiance against the monstrosity that had stalked them, wasn't just survival; it was a baptism in fire, forging a connection as potent as a venomous cocktail. Each was a reflection of the other's hell, their interdependence a desperate, visceral dance of mutual preservation. This wasn't respect, it was something far deeper, a grim recognition of shared savagery and the terrible beauty of their survival.

This fragile truce, forged in the white-hot crucible of combat, was no longer fragile. It was a hardened, obsidian shard, a testament not just to their grit but to the sheer, unyielding fury of their will to live. They weren't bound by circumstance; they were welded together by the searing heat of admiration born not of heroism, but of raw, bloody necessity. A comprehension forged not in polite conversation, but in the shared agony of near death, the chilling whisper of mortality brushing against their ears. Their bond wasn't just trust, it was an unshakeable certainty, a reliance that reached beyond the mundane, extending its gnarled fingers into the very fabric of their souls.

This wasn't a bond forged in the crucible of shared trauma; it was a monstrous thing, writhing from the blackest depths of their souls, a terrifying symphony of twisted loyalty and raw, primal need. The stench of scorched earth and burnt flesh clung to it, a phantom limb of their shared nightmare. It promised not merely a future beyond the fragile ceasefire, it promised dominion. A legacy painted in crimson, a testament to their resilience born not of hope, but of a ferocious, desperate will to survive, a future clawed from the very marrow of their agonizing past. This was no mere beginning; this was the cataclysmic eruption of a legend, etched not just in scars, visible, weeping wounds that mapped the topography of their suffering, but in the chilling silence that followed each scream, in the haunted gleam of their eyes, a legend whispered on the wind that carried the acrid tang of blood and ash across their shared hellscape. Their faces, etched with the grim beauty of survival, bore witness to a pact sealed in agony, a pact that tasted of vengeance and promised a reign of fire.

FIFTEEN

Rekindled Flames

Lungs screaming bodies a tapestry of bruises and broken bones, minds fractured by the relentless maelstrom of combat. Each gasp for air is a battle of its own, a desperate plea for relief amidst the chaos. Silence falls like a suffocating blanket pressing down heavily upon the weary souls who remain punctuated only by the rasping guttural breaths of the survivors echoing the struggle for life in a world that has become unrecognizable. The eerie stillness that follows the tempest of violence hangs in the air, a stark contrast to the cacophony of destruction that just moments ago enveloped us.

The atmosphere is thick and cloying reeking of blood—its metallic coppery tang stinging the nostrils and lingering long after the battle has ceased. It mingles grotesquely with the acrid bite of burnt ozone, a visceral testament to our brush with oblivion. Each inhalation serves as a grim reminder of what transpired a haunting echo of the lives lost and the innocence shattered. The ground beneath us is littered with the remnants of conflict, a grim mosaic of humanity's darkest impulses laid bare. It is a landscape marred by violence where the echoes of laughter and joy have been replaced by the whispers of ghosts. In this desolate aftermath we are left to grapple with the weight of our survival questioning what it means to endure in a world so irrevocably altered. The shadows of our experiences loom large and in the silence we find ourselves grappling with the echoes of the past as we attempt to forge a path forward through the wreckage.

Caspian, his sapphire eyes glacial, a predator assessing its prey, examined the ragged gash across his arm. Blood pulsed, a crimson tide against the fading light, but the pain was a whisper compared to the chilling dread that coiled in his gut. He tasted blood, metallic and bitter, a familiar tang that spoke of countless battles fought, each scar a testament to his unwavering resolve, each victory purchased in agony. This wound, though deep, was merely an inconvenience, a fleeting distraction from the colossal shadow that threatened to engulf them all. The weight of responsibility, the burden of command, etched lines of exhaustion around his steely gaze. He was a man forged in the crucible of war, his heart a storm of controlled fury, his mind a razor's edge, calculating, relentless. The survival of his comrades rested upon the precision of his next move, a gamble played out under the chilling gaze of an uncertain future.

My body felt broken like the wall I was leaning against. Each painful breath I took felt like a scream. The fire inside me which usually brings me comfort and warmth had faded to a weak flicker with sparks flying like dying stars. The constant need for blood like a hungry monster inside me finally quieted down. It was overwhelmed by my extreme tiredness and the bitter taste of adrenaline leaving a metallic flavor in my mouth. This taste reminded me of the chaos we had just gone through.

My gaze snagged on Caspian, his jaw a granite cliff etched with pain, his hand trembling faintly as he dabbed at a wound that bled a slow, crimson river, a testament to our shared brutality. The stench of burnt flesh and ozone hung heavy in the air, a suffocating perfume of our mutual carnage. He, the enigmatic Caspian, a man sculpted from shadows and secrets, his eyes, usually icy pools of calculation, now held a flicker of something akin to... vulnerability?

Our differences, the chasm that had always separated us, felt insignificant against the backdrop of our shared ordeal. This fragile truce, forged in the crucible of blood and fire, was a pact sealed not with words, but with the raw, shared agony etched onto our faces, a bond precarious as a spider's thread yet strong as the steel of our mutual survival. The air itself throbbed with the unspoken understanding, a volatile mix of exhaustion, dread, and the fragile ghost of something like... hope.

"They'll be back," Caspian rasped, the sound of a guttural growl that ripped through the fragile silence like shattered glass. The scent of ozone, a metallic tang clinging to the air, mingled with the coppery taste of blood still ghosting on his tongue, a visceral reminder of their last encounter. He didn't need to name the Obsidian Covenant; the icy dread that gripped his heart, the phantom pressure of their blades against his skin, spoke volumes. Their relentless pursuit was a venomous serpent coiled around their existence, its scales slick with malice, its fangs poised to strike. The unspoken understanding between them wasn't merely a weight; it was a suffocating pressure in the air, thick and acrid, a miasma of fear and simmering rage, heavy enough to bend the very knees of the bravest. Caspian, his eyes burning with a fierce, unwavering resolve born of countless near deaths, felt the familiar tremor of adrenaline, a thrilling, terrifying cocktail, course through his veins. He tasted ash and victory, defeat and defiance, all at once, the bitter tang a potent reminder that this wasn't a fight for survival, but a war for their very souls.

A constricted throat prevented a reply; my silent affirmation spoke volumes. Their imminent resurgence hung heavy in the unnerving hush that descended. The battle had brutally exposed the enemy's terrifying power, the Covenant's insidious grasp, and our desperate fragility. This brief reprieve felt agonizingly fragile, a deceptive calm before the inevitable maelstrom.

A violent fracture ripped through the decaying structure echoing ominously in the stillness. Instantly alert we braced ourselves, our muscles taut and ready poised to react to whatever threat lay ahead. The thunder of numerous ponderous boots reverberated through the air confirming our worst suspicions; the brief reprieve we had experienced was now over. The Covenant's return was upon us and we knew that it was time to steel ourselves for the impending confrontation that awaited us in the shadows.

Preparedness, not surprise, defined this encounter. Our actions were a balletic choreography of lethal expertise. Caspian, a panther in motion, his gaze a laser beam dissecting the darkness, his senses finely tuned to the faintest whisper. Within me, my innate abilities surged, reigniting the dormant flames of my inner strength, bracing me for the imminent, savage clash.

From the abyss, they clawed their way into existence, not merely demons, but abominations sculpted from shadow and screaming agony. Their forms, a grotesque mockery of flesh and bone, writhed with a sickening, internal luminescence. Eyes, not eyes, but burning coals of hatred, bored into my soul, each a searing brand promising oblivion. The stench, Sulfur and something far older, something sickeningly sweet like decaying lilies, choked me. Their numbers, a legion untold, a tide of horror far exceeding any previous incursion, a testament not merely to the Covenant's resolve, but to their terrifying, almost godlike, power. This wasn't an escalation; it was a cataclysm.

The air didn't merely crackle; it screamed, a symphony of dark energy that vibrated in my very bones, a physical manifestation of dread. The ground itself trembled under the weight of their malice, a palpable pressure threatening to crush me, to grind me into the very dust from which they seemed to have risen. This was not the threat of violence; it was violence, raw and unfiltered, a suffocating blanket of pure, malevolent intent. I tasted fear, a metallic tang on my tongue, and knew, with a certainty that chilled me to the marrow, that this was the end.

The air crackled a stench of Sulfur and scorched flesh thick in my nostrils. A maelstrom of fire and shadow erupted around us, a brutal, visceral dance of death. Caspian, a whirlwind of obsidian muscle and unnatural grace, his eyes burning with a cold, demonic fire that mirrored the hellish flames I wielded, moved with a terrifying elegance. Each strike of his obsidian blade sang a death knell, a counterpoint to the agonizing screams of the demons he carved apart. My attacks were a furious countermelody, searing bolts of hellfire that incinerated the creatures, leaving behind only the acrid scent of burning sinew and the unsettling crunch of pulverized bone.

Back to back, we formed an impenetrable bulwark against the tide of encroaching shadows. Years of brutal training, and a shared history etched in blood and sweat, forged a synchronicity that defied comprehension. It wasn't just trust that bound us; it was a desperate, primal understanding, a ferocious bond forged in the crucible of countless battles. The fear, the raw, visceral terror of facing annihilation, sharpened our senses, and intensified our focus, making us more than the sum of our parts. Each breath was a prayer, each heartbeat a drumbeat against the symphony of destruction. We fought not just for survival, but for something darker, something older, something that burned within the very core of our being. A relentless, terrifying beauty pulsed within the chaos, the defiant heartbeat of two souls clinging to the precipice of oblivion.

The sheer, suffocating weight of their numbers crushed me. A tide of snarling, clawed faces, a legion of eyes burning with unholy glee, surrounded, engulfed. The stench of their decay, acrid and cloying, filled my nostrils, a miasma clinging to my throat, choking the already ragged breaths from my lungs. The ground trembled beneath the thunder of their assault; each blow was a physical blow, a psychic hammer shattering the fragile remnants of my will. My muscles screamed, lactic acid a burning inferno in my veins; the familiar throb of exhaustion pulsed in time with the sickening rhythm of their advance.

This wasn't mere fatigue; it was the gnawing hollowness of a life spent battling shadows, of a past that clawed at my soul with icy fingers. The hunger, a beast always tethered, strained at its leash, its low growl a counterpoint to the battle cries of my foes. The memories, the blood soaked fields, the faces of those I'd failed, these ghosts were as real, as relentless, as the horde itself. Each swing of my blade, each desperate parry, was a fight against not only them but the crushing weight of my cursed existence. My resolve, once a blazing inferno, now flickered like a dying ember, threatened to be snuffed out by the unrelenting darkness.

The stench of ozone and scorched earth filled my nostrils as Caspian, his obsidian eyes blazing with a furious, inner light, lumbered to my side. His demonic form, usually a terrifying spectacle of power, now trembled with exhaustion; the raw, animalistic power that had been a wall of defiance was thinning, the air itself shimmering with the fading heat of his aura. Each bone jarring impact from the relentless assault echoed through me, a symphony of pain that resonated in my very marrow. His protective presence, usually a comforting weight, was now a fragile shield against a storm of hellfire. This wasn't just a battle for survival; it was a desperate, agonizing dance on the precipice of oblivion, each ragged breath a testament to our fading hope. The taste of blood, metallic and bitter, filled my mouth as the very fabric of our existence threatened to unravel. We were broken, yet defiant, clinging to the slimmest thread of survival in the face of unimaginable destruction.

My lungs screamed, a raw, burning agony mirroring the inferno I'd birthed. Every fibre of my being, stretched taut and trembling, convulsed as I unleashed it, a tidal wave of incandescent fury, not merely fire, but a roaring torrent of molten rage that licked at the attackers with the hiss of a thousand vipers and the stench of Sulfurous death. The heat seared my skin, the roar hammered my eardrums, and the taste of ash filled my mouth. That brief respite? A stolen heartbeat, a cruel illusion of safety in the face of annihilation. The air itself crackled with the desperate energy of their struggle, a symphony of clashing steel and ragged breaths, punctuated by the sickening thud of falling bodies. Their screams, choked and broken, were the mournful dirge of a lost battle. This wasn't just a retreat; it was a slow, agonizing descent into the abyss, each staggering step a testament to our waning strength, a grim reminder that we were bleeding out, our defiant blaze a flickering candle against the encroaching darkness.

The onslaught was a maelstrom of bone jarring impacts and screams, a symphony of pain that clawed at our sanity. Sweat sting my eyes, the coppery tang of blood thick in the air, a metallic counterpoint to the stench of Sulfur that blossomed with the creature's arrival. It wasn't merely a figure emerging from the shadows; it burst forth, a colossus of writhing muscle and shadow, its grotesque form eclipsing the dying light. Larger than any nightmare, stronger than the combined might of our weary band, it was a demon sculpted from pure, malignant energy. The ground trembled beneath its weight, a low, guttural growl vibrating through my very bones, a sound that resonated not just in my ears, but in the marrow of my being. Its eyes, twin pits of incandescent malice, burned with a hatred so ancient, so absolute, it threatened to consume our souls. Fear, raw and primal, wasn't just a feeling; it was a physical force, a crushing weight pressing down on our chests, stealing our breath, leaving us gasping for air in a suffocating tide of dread. This was no mere foe; this was the embodiment of annihilation, a horror born from the deepest, darkest recesses of a broken world. The very air crackled with its power; a palpable, sickening energy that tasted of ash and despair. We were facing not just death, but oblivion.

The monstrosity before us, a coiling mass of shadow and sharpened bone, its very breath a reeking miasma, clawed at my sanity. Terror, cold and visceral, seized me, a premonition of utter annihilation that tasted like ash and bile on my tongue. But Caspian, his eyes twin embers blazing defiance against the encroaching darkness, moved with a speed that defied belief. He was a wall of granite, a shield against the horror, his very presence a counterpoint to the foe's vile essence. I pressed close, the rough wool of his tunic scratching my skin as my heart hammered a frantic tattoo against his back, the heat of his body a desperate comfort against the icy dread radiating from the beast. His scent, leather and wood smoke and something primal, something fierce, filled my nostrils, grounding me in the terrifying reality. He knew. This wasn't just another battle; it was a poisoned arrow aimed at the heart of everything we held dear. This demon was a harbinger of their utter ruthlessness, a testament to the war's escalating madness, a chilling promise of the unimaginable horrors to come. The air itself thrummed with the weight of it.

"We need to retreat, " Caspian said, his voice strained but resolute. *"This is beyond what we can handle alone. "* His fingers rough against my skin tightened on my waist, a possessive brand seared into my flesh. The scent of his cologne—dark musky intoxicatingly familiar—filled my nostrils creating a stark contrast to the metallic tang of fear that clung to the back of my throat. For a heartbeat we were suspended between the storm raging within us and the tempest brewing outside. In that moment there was only the raw electric hum of his touch, a sensation that sent shivers down my spine. It wasn't just protection; it was a claim—a desperate reckless gamble played against the backdrop of our fractured volatile history.

His eyes the color of a winter storm bore into mine with an intensity that made my heart race. Those eyes held a glacial depth concealing a fire I knew could consume us both if we weren't careful. We stood on the precipice of something monumental teetering between desire and dread love and betrayal. This fleeting vulnerability, this shared tremor on the fault line of our obsession, felt like a terrifyingly beautiful lie—a fragile truce in a war neither of us knew how to end.

The world around us faded into a blur the chaotic sounds of the storm outside lost in the cacophony of our emotions. I could feel the weight of our decisions pressing down on us heavy like the storm clouds overhead. Was this retreat truly the answer? Or was it just another way of running from the inevitable? I searched his face for answers but all I found was the same turmoil reflected back at me. In that moment I realized that no matter where we chose to go the battle within our hearts would continue to rage on with no clear victor in sight. The only certainty was that we were in this together for better or for worse.

Through sheer force of will and coordinated expertise, we carved a precarious path through the constricted passage. Our retreat, a calculated maneuver, wasn't born of surrender, but of the urgent need for respite; a chance to reconstitute our ranks and forge a counteroffensive. This harrowing flight was a frantic sprint against the relentless march of time, a valiant defiance against insurmountable adversity. Each brutal engagement left our bodies ravaged, yet our resolve remained unshaken, fueled by a primal instinct for survival. The escape felt like a final, desperate gamble, a last ditch attempt to salvage our mission, regroup our forces, and prepare for the inevitable, brutal confrontation to come.

Exhaustion clung to us like a shroud as we stumbled, at last, into Willowshade's protective forest fringe. The damp ground received our weight; ragged breaths rasped from our chests, our bodies quivering with the aftermath of relentless pursuit. The terrifying ordeal had shattered our composure, leaving us profoundly unnerved. Our fortitude was severely strained; our determination was tested to its absolute limits.

Compelled into proximity, we confronted the brutal reality of our struggle: the enemy's overwhelming might and our perilous predicament. Our discord remained, a palpable chasm of distrust, yet the crucible of shared trauma, the brush with oblivion, had unexpectedly welded us together. A fragile, uneasy pact had been forged, not merely through circumstance, but by a cruel destiny and the looming shadow of a common foe intent on our annihilation. We were no longer simply comrades; our destinies were inextricably entwined, a Gordian knot of shared fate forcing us to confront not only the adversary but the turbulent undercurrents of our own complicated emotions. The path forward was treacherous, a gauntlet of peril, but at least we would navigate it shoulder to shoulder.

The forest's edge, a mockery of sanctuary, offered only a fleeting breath before the hunt resumed. The silence, a suffocating blanket woven from the rasping, ragged breaths that hitched in their chests and the whispering malice of the leaves, pressed down with the weight of their unspoken terror. The adrenaline, a fleeting demon, abandoned them, leaving behind a bone deep exhaustion that clawed at their muscles, a vice around their hearts. Caspian, his blue eyes, the colour of a winter sky just before a blizzard, mirrored the encroaching twilight, reflecting the grim understanding in their depths.

He glared at his wound, a crimson river carved into his arm, each throb a brutal reminder of their brush with oblivion; a testament to the predator's relentless hunger still hot on their heels. The metallic tang of blood filled the air, mingling with the earthy scent of decaying leaves and the feral musk of their pursuer, an invisible presence that pricked their skin with a primal fear far deeper than simple exhaustion. The silence, finally, was broken not by sound, but by a shared, chilling certainty: this reprieve was but a deceptive pause before the final, desperate struggle.

My wounds, a tapestry of ragged flesh and searing agony screamed in protest as I slumped against the gnarled, iron hard bark. The ancient tree, a silent sentinel of centuries, offered no solace. My aura, once a blazing inferno, sputtered like a dying ember, the heat a cruel mockery of the icy dread that gripped me. The vampiric hunger, a beast caged but not broken, clawed at my insides, a ravenous tide threatening to breach the fragile dams of my self control. It wasn't just hunger; it was a primal scream, a desperate, guttural yearning that resonated in my very bones, each pulse a hammer blow against my sanity.

The phantom scent of Caspian's blood, coppery, metallic, intoxicatingly him, clung to the air, a phantom limb of the battle, a cruel, exquisite torture. It whispered promises of oblivion, of the sweet release only his lifeblood could provide. His scent, a seductive siren song, played upon my deepest instincts, a constant reminder that this fragile truce, this uneasy alliance forged in the crucible of battle, could shatter at any moment. The taste of his blood, still vivid on my ravaged tongue, a haunting echo of his near death, fueled the torment. He'd paid dearly; I was prepared to pay the same price, and even more, if this insatiable hunger overwhelmed me. This dance with darkness, this precarious balance we walked—each step a gamble with eternity.

"More than a retreat?" Caspian's voice, a dry rasp like stones grinding together, cut through the suffocating silence. His eyes, the colour of a stormy sea, held a chilling stillness that belied the tremors in his jaw. The stench of sweat and fear clung to him, a tangible testament to the brutal fight they'd just endured; yet, his resolve stood unyielding, a granite cliff against the crashing waves of exhaustion. He saw the stark white of my face, the frantic twitch in my hand—a mirror of my desperate fragility—and a grim satisfaction flickered in his gaze. The taste of ash and blood still coated my tongue, a bitter reminder of our near demise. *"A plan,"* he ground out, each syllable a heavy blow. *"Not some half baked, desperate scramble. A plan, forged in the fires of what we've survived. This time, it will be perfect."*

My head bobbed, a single, jerky movement against the thrumming chaos in my skull. The metallic tang of blood, my own, I think, filled my nostrils, mingling with the acrid stench of burnt flesh and ozone. That frantic ballet of death, the desperate scramble for life... a necessary evil, they called it. Bullshit. It was a death rattle disguised as a strategy. We needed something more, a vice-like grip, a crushing blow, a plan forged in the fires of hell itself to break the Obsidian Covenant's spine. Their insidious power, a creeping shadow against the pale dawn of hope, demanded more than a fragile, stitched together alliance of convenience.

This wasn't merely survival; it was a profound quest for vengeance. Each ragged breath we took burned with the intensity of our shared fury. The terror we experienced together—the taste of oblivion lingering on our tongues like bitter ash—had fused us into an unbreakable bond, a twisted and grotesque sculpture of mutual respect forged in the crucible of near annihilation. Yet respect alone was a frail and fragile thing easily shattered by the harsh realities we faced. What we truly needed was something harder, something more resilient, something that would not bend or break under pressure. We craved the kind of strength that was ruthless that would empower us to reclaim what was lost and exact the vengeance that coursed through our veins.

"Whispering Wind," I rasped, the name of a bitter prayer lost in the wind's feral howl, a symphony of rustling leaves and snapping branches that clawed at my sanity. The stench of damp earth and decaying leaves filled my nostrils, a grim counterpoint to the icy dread gripping my heart. That clandestine organization, once a viper's nest of whispers and betrayals, a source of gnawing suspicion that tasted like ash in my mouth, now felt like our only sanctuary, a flickering candle in the encroaching darkness. Caspian, that enigmatic enigma, his connection to them once a festering wound between us, a chasm of mistrust carved by years of unspoken accusations, now loomed as our potential salvation, a lifeline thinner than a spider's silk, yet the only one we had. The weight of it pressed down, a suffocating burden on my chest, each laboured breath a testament to the desperate gamble we were taking.

Caspian's jaw clenched, the muscles corded like iron beneath his skin. The flickering torchlight glinted off the steel in his eyes, mirroring the cold fury that had seized him. *"Trust?"* he spat, the word tasting like ash in the dry air. *"Their promises are whispers on a venomous wind, their smiles like daggers hidden beneath velvet. The stench of their treachery clings to them, a miasma you can almost taste."* He ran a hand through his sweat slicked hair, the gesture betraying a simmering frustration that threatened to boil over. *"Their motives are blacker than the deepest abyss, their loyalties as fickle as the desert sands. They shift and change with every gust of power, every shift in the wind."* A heavy silence descended, broken only by the crackle of the fire, a sound that seemed to mimic the brittle tension in the air. *"But,"* he ground out, each syllable a hammer blow, *"they hold the keys, the infernal, cursed keys, to break the Covenant's grip. We dance with devils, yes. But we dance, or we are consumed."*

The weight of that alliance pressed down, a physical thing, a miasma of unspoken dread clinging to the air, thick and cloying like the scent of stale blood. Each breath tasted of ash and betrayal. We weren't just facing a Covenant horde; we were staring into the abyss of our souls. Their eyes, haunted and weary, reflected the same fear that gnawed at my gut, a cold, visceral dread that twisted with the bitter taste of anticipated failure. They scarred veterans of a thousand unseen battles, carried the burden of past atrocities; the ghosts of their fallen comrades whispering warnings in their ears, a chorus of doubt echoing the demons that clawed at my sanity. This wouldn't be a simple war; it would be a slow, agonizing descent into the darkness within, a brutal struggle against the ingrained distrust that tasted like rust on the tongue, the corrosive skepticism that burned like acid in the throat. The path ahead, choked with the shadows of our own making, promised only pain, a symphony of agonizing choices played out against the backdrop of a war that threatened to consume us all.

"How do we reach them?" I rasped, the words a gritty echo in the suffocating air. My voice, though steeled, trembled with a fatigue that gnawed at my bones. This wasn't some dry logistical exercise; it was a chess match played with lives, a dance on the razor's edge of betrayal. The taste of fear, metallic and bitter, coated my tongue. Each shadow held a hidden blade, each smiled at a potential ambush. We weren't just colleagues; we were gladiators in a coliseum of whispers and deceit, our survival hinging on a fragile, almost obscene, level of trust. To cooperate meant baring our scars, revealing the vulnerabilities that could be our undoing. This wasn't a mere shift in tactics; it was a seismic upheaval, a desperate gamble fueled by necessity and a grudging, hard won respect that tasted like ash in my mouth. The air crackled with unspoken anxieties, a palpable tension that vibrated through the very floor beneath our feet.

Caspian's gaze, a hawk's honed by years of shadowed dealings, raked the oppressive forest. The scent of damp earth and decaying leaves clung to him, a tangible weight mirroring the gravity of our predicament. His silence stretched, punctuated only by the whisper of wind through the gnarled, ancient oaks, each rustling a potential enemy, a hidden threat. Then, his voice, low and gravelly, a sound forged in the fires of countless betrayals, cut through the stillness. *"Forget pretty speeches,"* he rasped, the words tasting of bitter ash on my tongue. *"We start with what we know, the cold, hard facts. We bleed information from every crack in their defences, expose their rotten core, their hidden fears. We become the shadows they dread, the whispers in their nightmares. We exploit their weaknesses, not with clumsy force, but with surgical precision, a serpent's coil around their throats. Then, and only then, do we offer them a choice: surrender, or be utterly crushed beneath the weight of our combined might. They'll see we're not pawns, but the masters of this bloody game."*

The sheer scale of it choked me, a monstrous task reeking of sweat, blood, and the metallic tang of fear. Peril wasn't just a word; it was the rasping breath of shadows, the chilling weight of a thousand unseen eyes. But the alternative, a slow, agonizing death by a thousand cuts, the relentless gnawing of pursuit, the bitter taste of inevitable defeat, that was a hell I wouldn't willingly choose. We'd stared into the abyss, felt the icy fingers of death clutch at our throats, and tasted the ash of near annihilation. And in that crucible, forged in the fires of shared desperation, we found something…unexpected. A resilience born not of bravado, but of bone deep terror and a flickering ember of defiance. It was a twisted alchemy, transforming our scars into a weapon, forging a bond tighter than any oath, hotter than any inferno. We were broken, yes, but broken men can build something beautiful from the wreckage.

The days blend into each other, a fever dream of whispered anxieties and shadowed rendezvous. The air hung thick with the cloying scent of incense and fear, each clandestine meeting a gamble played in the flickering candlelight, the taste of ash and betrayal clinging to my tongue. Caspian, a viper in velvet, his eyes burning with cold intelligence, slithered through his network of demon informants, a tapestry woven from lies and dark promises. He unearthed secrets with the brutal efficiency of a predator, each piece of information a shard of obsidian reflecting the chilling truth of Whispering Wind's depravity.

Meanwhile, I was a crucible, forging myself anew in the white hot furnace of my own self loathing. The raw power pulsed beneath my skin, a scorching tide threatening to consume me, the vampiric hunger a constant, gnawing beast clawing at the edges of my sanity. Each agonizing exercise was a battle against my nature, a desperate struggle to master the elemental fury that threatened to obliterate everything in its path.

Our findings coalesced into a horrifying mosaic: a labyrinthine conspiracy of shifting allegiances, and vicious betrayals stained with the blood of those who dared to oppose them. The stench of corruption reached even the highest echelons of power, a sickening sweetness coating the bitter truth. Every thread we uncovered only deepened the darkness, tightening the noose around the heart of Whispering Wind, and around our own.

The truth clawed its way out like a viper slithering from the heart of Whispering Wind. It wasn't a single cohesive entity—not a unified breath of wind sweeping through the trees—but rather a venomous nest of factions, each a viper with its own scaled ambition, their hisses of conflicting interests echoing ominously in the poisoned air. The very ground felt treacherous beneath our feet each step a gamble in a macabre game of alliances and betrayals where trust was a fleeting shadow. The stench of deceit hung heavy in the atmosphere, a miasma clinging to the silken promises that had been whispered in hushed tones and the razor-sharp betrayals that cut deeper than any blade. I could taste the fear metallic and bitter on my tongue, a reminder of the danger lurking just beneath the surface. Each gaze exchanged was a silent negotiation, a dance of caution and suspicion as we navigated this treacherous landscape. In this world rife with duplicity, allies could quickly become enemies and the truth elusive and serpentine eluded our grasp like smoke slipping through our fingers. The air was thick with tension and we were all players in this perilous game uncertain of who might strike next.

My gut churned with the weight of it, the labyrinthine complexity, the sheer, chilling scale of the deception. We needed more than strategy; we needed surgical precision, a cold calculation of which factions to court, and which to crush. The scent of opportunity mingled with the reek of blood, a heady mix that demanded ruthless efficiency. We had to identify those whose venomous fangs could be turned, whose ambitions could be subtly manipulated to align with ours, while simultaneously dismantling those whose poison threatened to overwhelm us. The whispers of their secrets slithered into my ears, a chorus of lies and half truths, testing the very limits of my resolve. Each heartbeat hammered against my ribs, a frantic drumbeat against the backdrop of this deadly dance. The stakes were higher than any mountain peak, the fall far more devastating than any chasm.

Caspian's gut churned, a viper coiled tight against the icy knowledge that Whispering Wind, with her eyes like chips of obsidian and a smile that promised both ruin and rapture, was his only hope. His distrust, a physical weight pressing down on his chest, a bitter taste on his tongue, was a monumental barrier, but the Obsidian Covenant's shadow, a suffocating pall of dread, the stench of brimstone and death heavy in the air, forced a reluctant alliance. He swallowed the acrid taste of betrayal mingling with the metallic tang of fear.

My own heart hammered a frantic rhythm against my ribs, a frantic drumbeat mirroring the escalating terror. Learning to trust Caspian, a man carved from granite and shadowed by secrets, was a wrenching process, a slow, agonizing thaw of my guarded affections. The heat of his gaze, even now, felt like a brand, a searing reminder of the dangerous dance we had played. The raw, electric charge of our past encounters, a maelstrom of sexual tension and the bitter clash of wills, had been eclipsed, but not erased, by the immediacy of our shared plight. The scent of his leather, usually a provocation, now mingled with the reek of sweat and fear, a brutal reminder of our desperate circumstances. We were bound not by desire alone, but by the cold, unyielding grip of survival.

The pact wasn't forged in shared ambition alone; it was hammered out on an anvil of grudging respect, each of us acutely aware of the other's lethal potential, the predatory glint in their eyes a constant, unsettling reminder. We learned to anticipate each other's moves not with mere tactical awareness but with a visceral understanding, a dark symphony of coordinated brutality. The metallic tang of blood, the acrid bite of gunpowder smoke, these became the perfume of our unholy alliance. Our combined strength wasn't merely seamless; it was a maelstrom, a terrifying dance of death.

The raw, electric charge between us remained, a wildfire banked but never extinguished. It crackled beneath the surface of our pragmatic partnership, a dangerous undercurrent. But now, woven through the simmering lust was something else: a desperate, hard won camaraderie. Survival wasn't merely an objective; it was a shared, visceral craving, a desperate gasp for air in the suffocating darkness we inhabited. Our lives, bound together in this brutal embrace, were more intertwined, more precious than either of us would ever admit.

The plan was a viper coiled tight in my gut, each scale a treacherous maneuver, each sinuous curve a clandestine operation. The taste of ash, the lingering memory of my village's fiery demise, coated my tongue, a bitter counterpoint to the metallic tang of bloodlust. I could practically feel the Obsidian Covenant's insidious web, its threads of power woven through Whispering Wind like the chilling breath of a glacier. To expose their weaknesses, I had to slither into their trust, a viper among vipers, charming the most influential factions, their avarice and ambition my venomous tools. The risk? A chasm yawning beneath my feet, a fall that promised oblivion. But the reward? A symphony of vengeance. The roar of a united front, the satisfying crack of the Covenant's edifice crumbling, the sweet, sweet taste of justice, the chance to finally cleanse the earth of their vile presence and lay my village's ghosts to rest. Their destruction would be my redemption, their blood my atonement.

The air hung thick with the stench of ozone and fear, a miasma clinging to the obsidian walls of the Covenant stronghold. My heart hammered a brutal tattoo against my ribs, a counterpoint to the rhythmic thrum of their energy shields, a sound that vibrated not just in my ears, but deep in my bones. We moved like wraiths, shadows stitched from the very darkness itself, our combined skills a symphony of silent death. Each creak of our armour, each ragged breath, was a gamble against the abyss. Bypassing the outer defences felt less like a strategic maneuver and more like a desperate dance with fate, a hair's breadth away from annihilation.

Inside the heart of the beast pulsed with a malevolent energy that seemed to vibrate through the very ground beneath our feet. The air tasted metallic, a bitter tang that lingered on our tongues while the reek of burning promethium hung heavily around us, a constant reminder of the violence that throbbed beneath the surface like a looming storm. I saw the fear in the eyes of my teammates, each gaze filled with a grim understanding that mirrored my own; this was no mere raid, no simple extraction. This was a suicide mission dressed in the silks of false hope a desperate gamble that could cost us everything. We gathered the intel with trembling hands, each piece a jagged shard of terrifying truth that cut deeper into our resolve. Their plans vast and chillingly efficient stretched across continents intertwining like a spider's web ensnaring all in its path. Their resources were a bottomless pit of arcane technology and unimaginable power, a dark well from which they drew strength leaving devastation in their wake. As we prepared to move deeper into the heart of darkness the weight of our task pressed heavily upon us, each heartbeat echoing the urgency of our mission.

Their leadership... a viper's nest of cunning strategists and cold blooded killers, each more ruthless than the last. This wasn't some pack of mindless demons. This was a meticulously crafted machine of destruction, oiled by decades of calculated malice, its gears grinding towards a future painted in shades of blood and ash. And we, the few, the ragged remnants of a shattered resistance, held the key to its dismantling, a key forged in blood and shadowed by our inevitable mortality. The weight of it pressed down, heavy as the gravity of a collapsing star.

The raw intel, smelling faintly of fear and betrayal, lay before Whispering Wind's council. Their faces, etched with the canyons of suspicion, were barely illuminated by the flickering candlelight. Initially, their skepticism felt like a physical weight, pressing down on me, a suffocating blanket of doubt. But the data—blood soaked maps, intercepted whispers crackling with static, the chilling glint of obsidian in the captured artifacts—spoke volumes. The desperation in their eyes, mirrored in my own, finally pierced the icy shell of distrust.

The ensuing negotiations were a viper's nest of political maneuvering. Each word is a calculated risk, each concession a tremor in the fragile foundation of our nascent alliance. The air crackled with unspoken accusations, the silence punctuated by the rasp of shifting blades concealed beneath robes. My own hands, slick with sweat, clenched and unclenched as Caspian, his eyes burning with a cold, calculating fire, subtly shifted the balance of power with a whispered word, a chillingly precise gesture. We were walking a tightrope stretched across an abyss of treachery.

This alliance wasn't forged in trust; it was hammered out in the fires of mutual annihilation. Whispering Wind, scarred by decades of betrayal, clung to their secrets like life rafts. And Caspian... Caspian, a man whose ambition was a bottomless pit, a shadow in the corners of every room, saw his salvation mirrored in the destruction of the Obsidian Covenant. This wasn't about faith; it was about survival. Our combined forces, a grotesque tapestry woven from necessity and dark desires, held the power to shatter the Covenant. And the chilling thought of that potential power, that brutal, glorious reckoning, settled over us like a shroud.

The alliance, forged not merely in adversity's fires, but in the white hot crucible of shared agony, tasted like blood and ash on our tongues. Each scar, a testament not just to resilience, but to the brutal poetry of our shared sacrifice, pulsed with a dark, electric energy. Their eyes, twin pools reflecting the infernal glow of our mutual struggle, held a haunted beauty, a fierce, unwavering determination that mirrored my own. The bond between us, once fragile, now thrummed with a power that vibrated through the very marrow of my bones—a symphony of pain, loyalty, and something akin to... understanding.

The road ahead, a chasm choked with shadows and the stench of decay, promised only more bloodshed. But this time, the cold dread was tempered by the iron heat of companionship. We found common ground not in polite agreement, but in the shared stench of sweat and fear, in the ragged breaths after a brutal fight, and in the unspoken acknowledgment of the darkness that lived within us all. Our purpose pulsed, a feverish heartbeat driving us forward. It transcended mere survival; it was a desperate, ravenous hunger for a future forged in defiance of fate itself. Vengeance, once a solitary, bitter pursuit, is now entwined with a love born in the crucible of shared trauma, a desperate, ferocious love as raw and untamed as the wilderness surrounding us.

Survival, no longer a bleak, solitary goal, became a tapestry woven with threads of passion, both scorching and heartbreaking. Each breath was a gamble; each touch was a charged current. Their story, far from a simple battle for revenge, was a symphony of darkness and desire, a complex and dangerous ballad played out on the razor's edge of existence. The fight for survival had become something far grander, far more terrifying, and far more beautiful: a desperate, glorious dance with death itself.

CHAPTER

SIXTEEN

Ascent of the Inferno

T he candle flame, a sputtering, malevolent eye, cast skeletal
shadows that writhed and danced across the scarred oak
table. The stench of stale ale and something else, something
acrid and faintly Sulfurous, clung to the air, a miasma mirroring the
grim determination etched onto our faces, faces lined with years of
hardship, betrayal, and the chilling knowledge of what we were about to
undertake. My knuckles, white knuckled around the chipped tankard,
throbbed with a nervous energy that mirrored the crackle of raw power
in the air, a palpable tension thick enough to choke on. Outside, the
wind wasn't merely howling; it screamed, a banshee wail that tore at
the very fabric of the night, a symphony of impending doom perfectly
complementing the icy dread that gripped my heart.

Spread across the table the maps weren't simply charts; they were
battle plans stained with the blood of countless fallen heroes. Each
demonic stronghold, each Whisperwind encampment marked not just
territory but the graves of comrades who had fought bravely and paid
the ultimate price. The echoes of their agonized screams still lingered
in my ears haunting me like a distant sorrowful melody. The parchment
felt brittle beneath my fingertips as fragile as the hope we clung to
with all our might. Every inked line on those maps was a potential
bloodbath, a harbinger of the violence that lay ahead. Each circled
symbol represented a life waged by a soul sacrificed in this high-stakes

game with the very devil himself, a struggle that seemed to stretch into eternity.

My gaze snagged on a particular mark—a crimson blotch where Elara had fallen, her loss still tasted like ash and regret on my tongue, a bitter reminder of the cost of our fight. This wasn't just a mission; it was vengeance whispered in the wind, a desperate quest to reclaim what we had lost and to honor those who had given their all. As I traced the contours of the maps with my eyes I felt the weight of responsibility settle heavily on my shoulders. Each decision I made could alter the fate of our cause and the specter of Elara's sacrifice loomed large fueling my resolve. It was time to act to summon the strength buried deep within and to confront the darkness that awaited us. In this intricate dance of strategy and blood we would either rise victorious or fall into the abyss together.

The chill of the mountain air bit at Caspian's exposed cheeks, a stark contrast to the inferno burning in his icy blue eyes. His usual glacial detachment had shattered, replaced by a grim resolve that etched itself into the sharp angles of his face. A finger, calloused and scarred, traced the crimson line of the enemy stronghold on the worn map, the parchment brittle beneath his touch. The scent of old leather and wood smoke hung heavy in the air, mingling with the metallic tang of blood, a phantom smell, a memory clinging to the fabric of the war. His voice, a low growl that scraped against the silence, vibrated with suppressed fury. *"Their fortress,"* he rasped, each word a carefully weighed stone, *"is a viper's nest, jaws dripping poison. A frontal assault... a death sentence. We'll dance with shadows. We need a whisper, not a roar. Something... unseen."* The unspoken threat in his words hung heavier than any battleaxe. His gaze, cold and piercing, held the weight of countless lost battles and the bitter taste of betrayal. This wasn't just a military strategy; it was a personal vendetta etched in the lines of his face, a dance with death for a future he wasn't sure he deserved.

The embers of my rage banked but were not extinguished glowing faintly beneath a skin slick with sweat. Leaning so far forward that the rough-hewn table dug painfully into my ribs I glared intently at the blood-stained map before me. Its parchment worn and tattered smelled faintly of mildew and death, a testament to the countless battles that had been fought over this cursed land. Recent conflicts had etched themselves into my very bones leaving behind a symphony of aches in every joint a relentless reminder of the price of survival. A phantom pressure throbbed behind my eyes a constant companion that only served to amplify my resolve. Yet curiously the profound weariness that enveloped me only sharpened my focus, honing my mind to a razor's edge ready to slice through the fog of despair. My breath hitched in my throat tasting bitter and metallic, a blend of copper and fear. In this moment of tension I felt alive; a sense of purpose surged through me igniting the dormant embers of my fury into a smoldering blaze that would not be easily quelled.

Her voice, a low, silken counterpoint to the throbbing in my temples, sliced through the silence. *"We exploit their weaknesses,"* she hissed, each word a viper striking. *"Their pathetic reliance on those butchered sacrifices, the stench of their faith clinging to the very air. Their arrogant belief in their invincibility is a festering wound I intend to probe. And their blind faith... their utter, pathetic dependence on that dark, sputtering magic, a faith that will be their undoing."* The glint in her eyes, cold and calculating, mirrored the icy glint of a blade drawn in the shadowed heart of a storm.

The air crackled, a palpable tension mirroring the volatile synergy between us. Caspian, his eyes like chips of obsidian reflecting the hellish glow of his infernal contacts, possessed a chilling intimacy with the demon underworld. Whispering Wind's treacherous politics were his playground; he smelled their fear, tasted their betrayals, and felt the tremors of their rivalries course through the very stones beneath his feet. He'd deliver not just intelligence, but the raw, agonizing screams of their impending doom.

My power, a maelstrom of incandescent fury, roared within me. The Covenant's tactics, their meticulously crafted defences, were an open book, I knew their rhythms, felt the heat of their arrogance, tasted the ash of their coming defeat. I'd paint their strongholds with fire, not just disrupt their operations, but obliterate them, a crimson tide of chaos drowning their hollow pride.

Together we weren't merely a sum of our parts; we were a cataclysm, an unstoppable force of nature. A storm of infernal knowledge and incandescent wrath swirled around us ready to unleash chaos and shatter the very foundations of their world. The mere thought of our combined power ignited a shiver of exquisite terrifying anticipation down my spine as visions of upheaval danced in my mind. We were destined to change everything and I could hardly contain the exhilaration of it all.

"We'll break them," Caspian hissed, the words tasting like ice in the frigid air. The scent of pine and wood smoke, a deceptive calm, couldn't mask the raw fury burning in his eyes, eyes that had seen too much, known too much loss. *"We'll sever their arteries, their supply lines, a slow, agonizing bleed. We'll shatter their whispers, their communication networks, plunging them into a chaos of fear and uncertainty. And their morale? That, we'll crush, bit by agonizing bit, until their spirit is a broken thing, a pathetic echo of its former strength."* A cruel smile touched his lips, a predator's satisfaction. *"We will dismantle them, piece by piece. Weaken their defences until their very bones tremble at the thought of our approach. Only then... only then will we deliver the killing blow."* A low, guttural growl ripped from his throat, a vibration that resonated not just in my ears, but deep in my chest, a primal tremor that mirrored the frantic thump of my own heart. The scent of him, dark, musky, and utterly intoxicating, filled my senses, a heady perfume that overwhelmed the stale air. God, the raw, untamed power in that sound... it wasn't just sexy; it was a visceral assault, a delicious violation that left me breathless, exposed, utterly at his mercy. He wasn't just some man; he was a force of nature, a dangerous storm brewing behind those smouldering eyes, and I was drowning in the tempestuous beauty of it all.

Our plan unspooled, a viper's coil of deceit, infiltration, and calculated risk, each strand slick with the sweat of our palms. The air crackled with the promise of blood, a metallic tang already coating my tongue. Phase one: a surgical strike against Covenant outposts, not glorious battles, but meticulously planned assaults, each a poisoned dart aimed at their heart. The stench of burning earth and shattered wood, the screams muffled by the roar of my elemental fury, would be my symphony of chaos. I, a whirlwind of unleashed power, would be the vanguard, leaving a trail of fiery devastation in my wake; a creature of shadow and flame, born from the very heart of the inferno.

Caspian, a viper himself, slithered in the underbelly of their world, his network of informants a venomous nest, weaving a web of information, securing escape routes with the cold efficiency of a predator. These weren't victories, they were carefully orchestrated tremors, each designed to fracture the enemy's resolve, to sow the seeds of paranoia and fear, a prelude to the symphony of their demise, a chilling lullaby sung in blood and fire.

The second phase: a throat constricting plunge into the heart of the Covenant's obsidian fortress. The air itself hung thick with the stench of brimstone and fear, a palpable dread that clawed at my throat. Caspian, a viper in human skin, his eyes burning with a cold, calculating fire, was our key. His knowledge of the demon underworld wasn't just academic; it was a sickening familiarity, a network of whispers and shadows that ran deeper than any mortal could fathom. He'd secure our passage, forged documents, bought with blood and promises whispered in the ears of creatures that revelled in the taste of despair. The weight of those deals pressed down on me, a tangible burden.

Meanwhile my flames born of raw fury and desperate hope would serve as our shield in this tumultuous battle. I could feel the searing heat bloom in my gut, a vivid kaleidoscope of crimson and gold igniting behind my eyelids. I envisioned the inferno that would engulf the outer defenses, a relentless wave of fire consuming everything in its path. The roar, the crackle, the acrid smell of burning flesh and shattered stone—it would not merely be chaos but a symphony of destruction, a deafening curtain that would mask our approach. This wasn't some polite reconnaissance mission where stealth and subtlety ruled the day. No this was war, a visceral clash of wills where every flicker of flame would signal our intent. We would strike hard and fast unleashing the fury I had harnessed turning the battlefield into a canvas of chaos transforming our desperate hope into a blazing reality that would carve our path forward.

This was a desperate gamble, a knife fight in the dark against an enemy that thrived in the shadows. Our goal, a desperate grab for information, to steal the secrets of their power, their hierarchy, their vile strategy before they could crush us like insects. The fate of everything we held dear hung in the balance, a suffocating pressure in the pit of my stomach. Every breath was a prayer. Every step is a dance with death.

The third phase, a knife's edge balanced precariously over an abyss, demanded a surgical precision of intellect. Whispering Wind, a viper's nest of warring factions, was our target. The air itself crackled with the unspoken threat of betrayal, a tangible weight pressing down on us, thick and suffocating as the desert dust. This wasn't mere political maneuvering; this was a fight for survival, a dance with death played out in gilded chambers and shadowed alleyways. Caspian, a chameleon shifting through the ranks, his eyes the cold, calculating gleam of obsidian, would weave his web. He understood power not as a concept, but as a living, breathing entity, a thing to be tamed and ridden. His whispers held the weight of empires, his smiles concealed daggers honed to razor sharpness. He would forge alliances, fragile as spun glass, yet strong enough, he hoped, to withstand the crushing weight of the Covenant's advance. The taste of blood, metaphorical, for now, lingered on my tongue.

My role? To be the storm that shattered their complacency, the earthquake that toppled their carefully constructed walls. I would unleash a symphony of destruction, a visceral ballet of fire and force, a demonstration so terrifying, so undeniably powerful, that even the most stubborn hearts would be forced to kneel before the urgent need for unity. The stench of fear would be my perfume, the screams of the Covenant, my lullaby.

"Whispering Wind " Caspian hissed the words lingering on his lips like ash, their bitterness nearly palpable. *"It is not a sanctuary; it is a viper's nest teeming with danger and deceit. Feel the tremor in the ground beneath us; that is the friction of their relentless rivalries, the constant clash of hidden blades ready to emerge at any moment. Their agendas slither like shadows in the night each one poised to strike when least expected each one more treacherous than the last. We will not merely play their game; we will dance on their graves orchestrating a symphony of chaos in which we are the conductors. We will seduce the wavering souls those who have been poisoned by the Covenant's festering expansion; their venom will become our weapon transforming their despair into our strength. And those who dare to stand against us... they will learn the true meaning of oblivion. Their screams will echo in the darkness a haunting melody that will be the sweetest music to*

our ears. This is not just about survival; it is about power control and the exhilarating thrill of overthrowing those who think themselves untouchable."

Our plan wasn't brute force; it was a symphony of calculated brutality, a ballet of blades and whispers. The taste of blood, metallic and cold, clung to the air alongside the sickly sweet scent of betrayal. We danced on the razor's edge, a precarious waltz between violence, a lover's caress that could just as easily disembowel, and diplomacy as chilling as a winter's frost. Each move was a high stakes gamble, a desperate throw of the dice against the Obsidian Covenant. Their downfall, or ours, hung precariously in the balance, a coin spinning, spinning, defying gravity.

Success? It hinged not merely on strength, but on the chilling premonition of their next move, a precognitive understanding woven into our very bones. We felt the thrumming pulse of the plan, the icy certainty that ran through our veins, a shared madness, a twisted brotherhood forged in the fires of our desperate ambition. We were players in a deadly game, and our resolve, our terrifying, unwavering commitment, was the only weapon that mattered.

The weeks bled into each other, a maelstrom of shadowed rendezvous, the air thick with the coppery tang of blood and the whispered rasp of treacherous bargains. Each clandestine meeting seared itself onto my soul, the clammy grip of a demon lord's hand, the acrid stench of Sulfur clinging to his rotting robes, the chilling gleam in his obsidian eyes promising both power and betrayal. Caspian, his face a granite mask carved with the weariness of a thousand battles, moved like a phantom through the festering heart of the demon world. His silence spoke volumes; a symphony of controlled rage, simmering barely beneath the surface, a predator stalking its prey in the suffocating darkness.

My fiery aura, a tangible weapon, burned a path through Covenant's outposts. I tasted the ash and Sulfur on my tongue, felt the searing heat of the infernos I unleashed, and heard the screams of the dying, a symphony of terror that fueled my resolve. Each infiltration was a dance with death, a ballet of shadows and flame, leaving behind a trail of smouldering ruins and the chilling whisper of my name, a harbinger of doom sown into the very fabric of their ranks. The discord I sowed wasn't just whispered; it was a wildfire consuming their fragile alliances, a plague eating away at their strength from the inside, leaving them broken and vulnerable.

The fire of shared peril, the stench of sweat and cordite still clinging to us, had forged a bond far exceeding mere survival. It was a bond slick with the unspoken, raw sexual tension of a coiled viper beneath our skin, its venom both intoxicating and terrifying, fueling the volatile dance of our partnership. But the heat of lust was only one layer, a thin membrane over a deeper, colder current. Beneath the surface, something ancient stirred, a grudging respect, born not of sentiment but of grim necessity, a chilling awareness of each other's lethal capabilities, our vulnerabilities laid bare and exploited, yet strangely, strangely cherished. Each glance, a silent battle of wills, each touch a calculated risk, an electric shock across the chasm of our mistrust, a tremor that threatened to shatter the precarious truce we had forged in the heart of the storm. The taste of fear, ours and our enemies', still lingered as a bitter aftertaste to the intoxicating blend of passion and primal fear that defined us.

The air crackled around us a palpable force that hung heavily in the space between our bodies charged with the unspoken understanding of what was to come. Each breath we shared carried with it the taste of sweat, a bitter reminder of the tension that suffused the atmosphere and the impending violence that loomed like a dark cloud overhead. It was a metallic tang that lingered on our tongues a harbinger of the chaos that was about to unfold. Our dance was nothing short of a symphony of death; each step we took a carefully calculated risk and intricate choreography of survival. The silence surrounding us was punctuated only by the harsh rasp of steel clashing against steel, the sickening thud of bone meeting bone echoing through the air like a grim drumbeat. My heart, a fiery beast caged within the confines of my ribs, beat a furious rhythm, its wildness barely tempered by the unyielding calm of Caspian's gaze. His eyes a chilling shade of ice blue burned with a predator's intelligence assessing every move with unnerving precision. His cautious approach akin to a sculptor's careful hand shaping the battlefield was ignited by my reckless abandon. The heat of my rage became a furnace transforming his cold strategy into a weapon of devastating power. Together we were an unstoppable force, a fusion of calculated strategy and unbridled fury ready to plunge into the chaos that awaited us with unwavering resolve.

Our alliance was a twisted knot, a paradox woven from threads of fire and ice. The delicate balance—a knife's edge between a passionate embrace and a brutal strangulation. His submission was a calculated risk, a strategic surrender to my untamed power; my dominance a carefully controlled flood, its destructive potential contained only by his unwavering discipline. We were a duality, a chimera of conflicting forces, a storm of violence wrapped in the cloak of cold, calculating diplomacy. The very air around us trembled with the raw, volatile energy of our bond.

The sweat slicked my palms, the acrid stench of ozone and burnt metal thick in the air. We'd done it. Against impossible odds, our ragged team, a tapestry woven from desperation and grim determination, had ripped the Covenant's secrets from their iron grip. The data screamed from the salvaged datapad, a searing white light against the encroaching darkness of their plans. A city, a human city, slated for annihilation. Not a surgical strike, not a raid, but a blitzkrieg, a tidal wave of plasma fire and unholy fury aimed at wiping a million souls from the face of the earth. I could almost taste the ash on my tongue, and feel the tremor of the impending cataclysm in my bones. Their hidden armouries, a network of shadowed hives throbbing with the malevolent energy of a thousand suns, their coordinates etched into the digital ghost of their demise. And the names... the names of the architects of this carnage, each a viper coiled in the heart of the Covenant's command structure, their faces burned into my memory, a grim gallery of ruthless ambition and chilling fanaticism. This wasn't just intel; this was a lifeline, snatched from the jaws of oblivion. It was the key, forged in blood and fire, to our survival, to our vengeance.

The air crackled, a tangible hum of anticipation preceding the storm. Our meticulously planned assault, a symphony of coordinated strikes designed to carve through the Covenant's brittle defences, felt less like strategy and more like a prayer whispered into the teeth of a hurricane. The metallic tang of blood, a phantom scent from past battles, clung to the back of my throat. Caspian, his eyes twin chips of glacial ice burning with a furious internal fire, stood beside me, a coiled viper ready to strike. This wasn't just a battle; it was a reckoning.

The stakes? Not merely our lives, but the agonizing screams of a city consumed by fire, the ghostly echoes of its lost souls haunting the ravaged landscape. Failure tasted like ash and despair, a bitter end to a fight we'd been waging for years, a fight etched onto our very souls. But we weren't merely fighting for survival, that was a paltry prize. We fought for the raw, untamed loyalty that bound us, a bond forged in the crucible of shared trauma and desperate hope, a connection as volatile and incandescent as a supernova.

Our alliance, rekindled in the fires of a thousand betrayals and agonizing losses, pulsed with a fierce, desperate energy. It wasn't hope, not exactly. It was something darker, something more primal: a shared thirst for vengeance, a relentless hunger to crush our enemies beneath the weight of our combined fury. The Covenant, their arrogance a festering wound, would taste the full measure of our wrath. The final confrontation loomed, a monolithic shadow blotting out the sun.

The weight of countless lives, the whispered pleas of the innocent, the silent cries of the fallen, pressed down on us, a crushing burden we carried with grim determination. This wasn't just a battle for the Covenant's dominion; it was a battle for the soul of our relationship, a tempestuous union forged in the fires of conflict, a love story written in blood and fire. And as the first shots rang out, echoing across the ravaged battlefield, I knew, with chilling certainty, that we would either conquer together or be consumed by the flames of our own making.

The air hung thick with the scent of ozone and fear. My stomach is doing somersaults. Is this happening? All those nights spent poring over maps, all those close calls...it all comes down to this. The Obsidian Covenant stronghold loomed before us, a monolithic structure of black obsidian that seemed to drink the light from the sky. It's even more imposing up close. The legends don't do it justice. Or maybe the legends understated it... Around us, the landscape was scarred, a testament to the battles fought and lost. So many lives were lost...and for what? Will we be added to that grim tally? This was it. The culmination of weeks of meticulously planned attacks, covert operations, and treacherous negotiations. Did we miss something? Is there some crucial detail I overlooked? I've replayed every contingency in my head a hundred times, but… The moment of truth. Breathe. Just breathe. Focus. We've come too far to falter now.

The flickering torchlight glinted off Caspian's sapphire eyes, twin chips of ice in a face carved from granite and shadowed by the heavy, obsidian cloak. The air itself crackled with the suppressed power it barely contained; a tangible hum vibrating against my skin. He traced the pulsing, crimson sigils woven into the enchanted fabric, their arcane energy a burning brand against his fingertips. The scent of ozone and brimstone, the stench of hell itself, clung to the cloak, a chilling testament to the demonic essence it masked. *"Ready, Blaze?"* he rasped the words in a gravelly whisper that clawed at the edges of sanity. It wasn't just a storm brewing within him; it was a maelstrom, a raging inferno threatening to consume him whole. The fleeting glimpse of longing in his eyes, buried beneath layers of grim determination and fear that gnawed at the very bones, was a terrifyingly beautiful paradox. A whisper of vulnerability in the heart of a demon.

My crimson hair, a wildfire unbound, lashed in the gale, a frantic dance mirroring the tempest in my soul. I nodded, my eyes, twin embers burning with a ferocity that matched, and yet surpassed, his own. The scars etched across my flesh, a brutal tapestry woven from recent battles, throbbed with a dull, agonizing ache. The hunger, a ravenous beast within, clawed at my throat, a constant, visceral reminder of my cursed nature. But it was a hunger I would master, a threat I would subdue. My spirit? Unbowed. Unshackled.

Caspian's blood, dark, intoxicating nectar, coursed through my veins, a reprieve from the abyss. Each drop was a lifeline, a precarious link to him, a testament to our unholy alliance. But its power was a double edged sword, a seductive poison that strengthened the bond between us, a bond forged not only in necessity but in terrifying, exquisite reciprocity. Its allure whispered promises of power, of shared destinies, a terrifying entanglement that bound us closer with each passing heartbeat. The taste of it, metallic yet sweet, lingered on my tongue, a constant, haunting reminder of our perilous dance on the razor's edge.

The stench of blood and sweat, a metallic tang clinging to the humid air, hung heavy as Caspian lunged, a reckless, desperate thing. My fingers, talons in his tunic, hauled him back with a force that belied their gentleness. His breath hitched, a ragged gasp against my skin as he slammed into me, the frantic beat of his heart a drum against my ribs. My pulse thundered a wild counterpoint. His lips, trembling, found mine, a collision of desperate need, a ferocious hunger that scorched the air between us. The clash of steel, and the screams of the dying, all dissolved into the raw, incandescent pressure of our mouths. His taste was of fear and adrenaline, sharp and electrifying on my tongue. The world narrowed to the searing heat of his body against mine, the rough texture of his armour digging into my back, and the frantic tremor in his hands clutching at my shoulders. This wasn't a kiss, it was a desperate vow, etched not in ink but in the urgent thrum of our combined life force, a silent defiance whispered against the encroaching darkness. A promise not of mere strength and love, but of survival, of shared fury, of defiance born of a love that would consume us both should this storm break.

He pulled away from the kiss and I was still buzzing from the taste of him on my lips—a strange mix of bitter almonds and a wild flavor that sent shivers through me. His eyes the color of a wild ocean were narrowed like a hunter's holding me still as if I were a deer frozen in the headlights. The air around us felt alive with a buzzing energy filled with unspoken tension that you could almost feel in the atmosphere. The strong manly smell of his cologne surrounded me and it was completely captivating. It felt completely different from the sudden intense shiver that ran through my body. "What was that about?" He spoke in a rough voice sounding like a deep growl that echoed in the space between us, strong and commanding. Even now his touch is gone but it still leaves a warm feeling on my skin—a mark that shows I belong to him. The question lingered in the tense atmosphere filled with a mix of blame and uneasy desire as if he was both expecting an answer and challenging me to reply. I felt his intense stare full of hope and I realized that what happened next would change our relationship forever.

My gaze, a desperate plea in the smoky dimness of the bar, snagged on him and in that moment time seemed to stretch. *Just in case* "I rasped the words tasting like ash and regret bitter and heavy in my throat. *"Just in case this all goes to hell... I needed to feel you one last time.* "The scent of his cologne—sharp and musky rich with memories—lingered in the air between us, a phantom reminder of the intoxicating touch I craved more than anything. It was a scent that wrapped around me like a shroud both familiar and haunting. His eyes, dark and bottomless pools that seemed to reflect a storm of his own making, held a flicker of something dangerous, something wild and untamed. It was an echo of the reckless abandon that pulsed through my veins urging me to take a step closer to the edge. This wasn't just lust; it was a primal need, a desperate grasp for a fleeting moment of solace before the inevitable crash. The world outside faded into insignificance as I focused solely on him feeling the weight of unspoken words and shared regrets. I could feel the tension thickening the air, a palpable electricity that made my skin tingle and my heart race. This was our moment fragile yet intense and I was willing to embrace it fully knowing the consequences that loomed just beyond reach.

The plan stank of desperation, a suicide pact veiled in the desperate hope of survival. A full scale assault? That was a death sentence, a screaming, fiery end. No, we'd go for the throat, a surgical strike exploiting a crack in the Covenant's obsidian shell, a vulnerability so subtle, so cunningly hidden, it felt almost obscene to know it. The metallic tang of blood in the air, the phantom echo of a thousand whispered prayers during our clandestine raids, finally yielded its price: tonight, they'd bleed themselves dry. Their ritualistic sacrifice, a grotesque display of faith, would draw their elite, their fangs and claws, to a single point, leaving the rest of their stronghold exposed, a gaping maw waiting to be devoured. This wasn't a window; it was a hairline fracture in a fortress, a chance so fleeting, so razor thin, it felt like holding onto a live wire. And we were going to ride that lightning.

Caspian's viper tongued informants, creatures of the shadowed alleys within Whispering Wind, had secured it: a rat hole of a passage, a festering wound in the city's defences. Not a mere tunnel, but a tomb carved into the very bowels of the earth. Risky? It was suicide dressed in silk, our only prayer a desperate gamble against oblivion. The air, thick with the stench of mildew and something else... something feral, choked me as we plunged into the suffocating darkness. The weight of our desperation wasn't just felt, it clawed at my throat, a physical presence mirroring the icy dread that gripped my soul. Each footfall echoed with a terrifying resonance, a hammer blow against the fragile hope we clung to. The drip, drip, drip of water was a malevolent metronome counting down to our demise; the frantic, hammering pulse in my ears was a dirge for our souls. And the shadows... God, the shadows. They writhed and pulsed, alive with unseen horrors, promising agonizing ends. My breath, ragged and hot against my lips, tasted of fear and the metallic tang of blood that wouldn't be shed... yet.

The tunnel clawed at us, a suffocating labyrinth of twisting, slime slicked passages. Each turn was a gamble, a sickening lurch closer to the Covenant's festering heart, closer to oblivion. The air, thick as a shroud, choked me with the stench of rot and the acrid bite of dark magic; a miasma clinging to the damp stone like a second skin. My heightened senses screamed, a tremor in the earth, a low thrumming of malevolent energy that vibrated in my bones, a taste of ash and fear on my tongue. Sweat plastered my palms to the rough hewn walls. Caspian, his face a mask of grim determination barely concealing the terror I knew gnawed at him, stumbled behind me. *"Faster, damn it, Caspian!"* I hissed, the words a raw rasp against the oppressive silence, the warning a desperate prayer lost in the echoing darkness. The earth itself seemed to breathe, to writhe, and I knew, with chilling certainty, that this maze was not merely a passage, but a living thing, hungry for our souls.

The air hung thick with the stench of mildew and something else... something ancient and unholy. Each footfall echoed in the oppressive silence of the hidden chambers, a thunderclap in the suffocating darkness. Dormant traps, their mechanisms oiled by centuries of dust and decay, whispered threats, a rusted scythe here, a pressure plate barely concealed beneath a mosaic of crumbling bone there. Spectral guardians, their forms shimmering like heat haze on a desert road, materialized from the shadows, their icy breath a tangible chill against my skin.

My flame magic, a raw, visceral thing, burned with the fury of a caged inferno. I felt the pulse of its power thrumming in my veins as I unleashed it, a precise, agonizing dance that incinerated the wards protecting the tunnels, wards humming with malevolent energy that tasted like ash and despair on my tongue. Caspian, his eyes burning with a fanatical gleam, muttered incantations, a guttural, frantic symphony of demonic tongues, deciphering runes that spoke of unimaginable horrors, his voice a knife twisting in the darkness. Each step was a gamble, a heart stopping plunge into the unknown. This was no mere dance; it was a desperate, bloody ballet against oblivion, our skill and experience the only shields between us and a terrifying, eternal sleep.

After what seemed like an eternity we finally reached our destination—a vast cavernous chamber deep beneath the stronghold where the terrifying ritual sacrifice was set to take place. The air was thick with an oppressive atmosphere heavy with the scent of damp earth and ancient stone. Hidden in the deepest shadows we watched with bated breath our hearts pounding like war drums as the demons began their sinister ritual. The flickering torchlight cast eerie shadows on the walls, heightening the tension of the moment.

Their chanting echoed through the darkened night creating a terrifying symphony of death that sent shivers down the spine. The sacrificial victim bound and utterly helpless trembled in fear before the ominous figures surrounding them.

A sickening stench permeated the air, a miasma of fear and impending doom. We knew our time to strike was near, but a plan must be formed before we attacked.

More than a mere ceremony it was an ostentatious exhibition of might a brutal assertion of their supremacy that reverberated through the air leaving an indelible mark on all witnesses. Their callous indifference to life, a savage flexing of their authority, ignited a furious inferno within me, a potent rage threatening to consume and overwhelm me completely. Each display of power felt like a direct affront to my very being, intensifying my desire to resist and rebel against such tyranny fueling a fire of defiance that could no longer be contained.

Caspian, the master tactician, remained serene, his glacial blue eyes meticulously surveying the hall, calculating their precarious situation. A subtle gesture from him designated our objective, the ritual's malevolent core, the sacrificial centrepiece: a relic of immense antiquity, a conduit for the Covenant's baleful sorcery. Our strategy, though deceptively straightforward, was fraught with mortal danger: obliterate the artifact, thereby shattering the ceremony and crippling the Covenant's sinister dominion.

With their final, guttural incantations echoing, the fiends unleashed their demonic power. My response was instantaneous, a volcanic eruption of searing flame from my palms, transforming the chamber into a crucible of fire. Agonized howls pierced the air as the daemons, desperate, retaliated, their wicked sorceries colliding violently with my elemental might. Meanwhile, Caspian, his infernal gifts blazing, conjured a maelstrom of chaos, a bewildering spectacle that shattered the demons' cohesion and bought me the decisive advantage.

My precise strike, a focused inferno, pulverized the relic. The ensuing detonation rocked the cavern, a seismic tremor that violently interrupted the dark rite. The malevolent energy abruptly severed, dispersed like smoke. Pandemonium reigned as the demons, their infernal power fractured, turned on each other in a frenzy of desperate self preservation. Seizing the unforeseen opportunity, they fled, vanishing into the twisting, subterranean passages.

A desperate flight for survival, a harrowing scramble through legions of infernal creatures, our combined might, a tapestry of magic and martial prowess, barely staved off annihilation. My incandescent rage met Caspian's tactical brilliance; our assault, a terrifying ballet of raw power and surgical strikes. We clawed our way from the subterranean labyrinth, bodies ravaged but spirits unbroken. Our audacious maneuver had succeeded, though victory came at a terrible price. The Covenant's fortress lay crippled, its dominion shattered. The inevitable showdown approached; the final act was about to begin.

Our triumph felt hollow, a pyrrhic victory purchased with an exorbitant cost. Exhaustion, both mental and physical, clung to us like a shroud. The brutal conflict had stretched us to the precipice of collapse, near fatal encounters forging between us an unbreakable connection, a bond as incandescent and turbulent as the inferno that had threatened to engulf us.

Dawn's ethereal light sliced through the desolation illuminating the remnants of our hard-fought triumph. The sun, a delicate orb of gold and crimson cast its rays over the shattered landscape revealing the wreckage of what had once been a fierce battlefield. Caspian and I stood amidst the debris, our hearts still racing from the adrenaline of our recent encounter having delivered a crushing blow to the Obsidian Covenant. We had emerged victorious from this clash but even in the aftermath of our triumph an unsettling feeling lingered in the air. This victory felt like a mere prelude; the war's true fury lay ahead lurking just beyond the horizon waiting to unleash its full force upon us.

The Obsidian Covenant was not one to accept defeat lightly. Their defeat would only serve to fuel their incandescent wrath igniting a conflagration of vengeance that we anticipated with a mixture of dread and resolve. We were ready though; our spirits bolstered by the success we had carved from the chaos. The heady sweetness of success, a potent elixir coursed through our veins invigorating us and sharpening our senses. We had tasted victory and though it was bittersweet it was a taste we were eager to savor further.

Our formidable alliance, a tempestuous bond forged in the crucible of combat, was a force to be reckoned with. Caspian and I had been through the fires of battle together each experience weaving us tighter into the fabric of a partnership that transcended mere friendship. We had fought side by side learning to anticipate each other's moves and our instincts honed to a razor's edge. The camaraderie that had developed between us was born not only of shared trials but also of mutual respect and understanding. It had transformed us into a dynamic duo, a pair of warriors who complemented one another in ways that made us nearly unstoppable.

Our audacious gamble had yielded immediate dividends but the victory we had claimed was only a fleeting moment in the grand tapestry of war. As we surveyed the battlefield the horizon remained shrouded in uncertainty, a maelstrom where love retribution and sheer survival clashed in a violent dance. Each new dawn brought fresh challenges, new adversaries to face and deeper depths of despair to navigate. We understood that the journey we had embarked upon was far from concluded; the path ahead was fraught with peril winding through a landscape riddled with shadows of doubt and fear.

Yet amidst the uncertainty the incandescent fire of our partnership blazed ever brighter a beacon of hope in the encroaching darkness. It illuminated our way forward guiding us toward the inescapable final reckoning that awaited us. We knew that the ultimate price of our victory would not come without sacrifice; the cost of our triumph could very well be the lives we cherished and the dreams we held dear. Our inextricably linked fates hung in the balance, a chilling unknown that sent shivers down our spines.

We were warriors yes but we were also dreamers holding on to the flickering flames of hope that refused to be extinguished. As we stood amidst the wreckage we could not help but wonder what lay ahead. Would we emerge from the impending storm unscathed or would we be consumed by the very forces we sought to vanquish? The answer remained elusive shrouded in the mists of fate. Yet one thing was certain: we would face whatever came next together united in our purpose driven by the indomitable spirit that had brought us this far. As dawn broke over the battlefield we steeled ourselves for the trials yet to come ready to confront the shadows that threatened to engulf us.

A desolate quiet descended after our audacious assault, a stark contrast to the preceding chaos. The atmosphere, previously saturated with the noxious fumes of brimstone and terror, now reeked of coppery blood and the harsh scent of scorched volcanic glass. Caspian, his impeccably tailored cloak ravaged and defiled, slumped against a shattered wall, his respiration shallow and laboured. The sapphire blaze in his eyes, normally so intense, was muted, overshadowed by a profound fatigue that hinted at utter depletion and a more grievous affliction—a despair bordering on hopelessness.

My crimson hair, plastered to my dampened flesh, clung to me as I stood beside him, fingers lightly grazing the pommel of my sword. The usual fiery intensity in my gaze was extinguished, supplanted by a profound, weary quietude. The conflict had exacted its brutal price, leaving my muscles screaming and my soul shattered. The triumphant elation of our conquest felt remote, eclipsed by a creeping dread. Only the mournful cries of the injured and the ominous crackle of embers consuming the Covenant's ravaged fortress punctuated the oppressive stillness.

Our crippling blow against the Obsidian Covenant—the disrupted ritual, the shattered artifact that fueled their malevolent might—proved a devastatingly hollow triumph. The price of victory far exceeded our grimest forecasts. Caspian's clandestine network within Whispering Wind, the lifeline that had yielded vital intelligence and access to their hidden sanctuary, lay shattered. The Covenant's vengeful reprisal was immediate and pitiless, obliterating the majority of Caspian's agents. The confirmation of this catastrophic loss arrived with an icy, inescapable finality.

Caspian's countenance, etched with grim resolve, delivered the devastating report. The crushing burden of our losses pressed down on him; the terrible toll is a stark testament to the perilous nature of our struggle. He had gambled everything on my behalf, and his once vast organization now lay shattered. A suffocating silence descended, pregnant with unsaid grief, the shared culpability a leaden weight, the bitter fruit of our sacrifices lingering on our tongues.

Familiar, agonizing remorse constricted my chest. Our bond, born amidst perilous circumstances and intertwined longing, had always been profoundly unstable, teetering precariously between unwavering devotion and stark self interest. Caspian, time and again, had jeopardized his very existence for my sake, valiantly protecting me from harm, offering his lifeblood to quench my insatiable thirst. And now, his extensive network lay in ruins, a catastrophic consequence of my actions.

A familiar constriction gripped my heart, the crushing burden of duty settling upon my shoulders. The fires of retribution, my long held driving force, sputtered and threatened to die, choked by a profound sorrow and the icy grip of remorse. I yearned to roar, to unleash my fury, to utterly annihilate the Obsidian Covenant, to somehow rewind the devastation wrought upon Caspian and his network. Yet, the truth remained unforgiving, stark and desolate. The damage was irreparable; the losses were permanent.

A confession hung heavy in the air, unspoken until Caspian, his voice a strained breath, uttered the words. His gaze locked onto mine, eyes mirroring profound anguish, a steely resolve, and a chilling undercurrent, a sense of surrender that sent icy tendrils crawling down my back.

He alluded to a clandestine haven, a secluded refuge nestled within the labyrinthine depths of the Whispering Wind, a sanctuary for his solitary restoration. Yet, access demanded a terrible price, an excruciating personal toll. To attain this haven, he would embark on a perilous journey, utterly severing his bonds with the Whispering Wind. This meant relinquishing his affiliations, exposing himself to unimaginable peril, and potentially forfeiting his authority and his considerable wealth. It was, in essence, a gamble with his very life.

Giving up his covert operations meant relinquishing his intricate web of contacts and substantial assets, a self imposed disarmament that would leave him exposed and vulnerable. This drastic action, a tactical withdrawal, risked rendering him utterly impotent, his existence teetering on the brink of annihilation. The sanctuary, while offering solace and protection, felt like a gilded cage, a lonely confinement.

The disclosure struck me with the force of a physical assault leaving me breathless in its wake. I grasped the profound implications of what I had just learned—Caspian's sacrifice was absolutely an extraordinary act that defied comprehension. He relinquished not only his security and authority but also his very essence, the core of who he was all for me for their collective purpose and for their precarious hope of survival in a world rife with uncertainty. His self-immolation, a complete forfeiture of his existence, was a choice made with the utmost conviction a testament to his unwavering dedication. The understanding slammed into me like a seismic shockwave paralyzing my voice and rendering me momentarily speechless. This was far more than a strategic withdrawal; it was an act of breathtaking unparalleled altruism. Caspian's decision reverberated within me a haunting reminder of the depths of human sacrifice pushing me to confront the weight of his gift and the responsibility it bestowed upon me.

My vision swam, overwhelmed by a sudden, stinging flood of tears. The usual steely resolve I cultivated crumbled, revealing a raw, aching tenderness I'd long suppressed. His act of selflessness bore down on me, an unbearable burden of profound thankfulness and agonizing remorse. His love, intense and all consuming, had always held a shadowed edge, but his sacrifice illuminated the terrifying, breathtaking magnitude of his devotion.

A choked whisper escaped Caspian's lips, *"It's the sole recourse,"* laden with profound sorrow. To safeguard you, to guarantee your continued existence—that is paramount. My resources can be restored, my forces reconstituted, but you...you must persevere. Deprived of my guidance, they will be utterly lost; and vulnerable. The Covenant will relentlessly hunt you down. His resolve, etched deep within his actions, far surpassed the limitations of language; his sacrifice was a testament to a love both fierce and unwavering.

My hand found his, fingers entwining. A chill emanated from his skin, yet his grip, unwavering, offered a peculiar solace. A faint tremble betrayed the tempest raging within him, a silent struggle etched onto his palm. The words died in my throat, a strangled cry of *"No,"* of desperate pleas against the agony of his impending absence, the sheer dread of confronting the Covenant alone. Unshed tears welled, mirroring the immeasurable cost of his self sacrifice, a sacrifice so profound it threatened to shatter my spirit.

A pregnant stillness hung heavy, thick with unspoken sentiments, with emotions barely contained. Our connection, forged in the crucible of conflict and loss, intensified in this moment of profound selflessness. It was a bond that defied the grim reality of our shared plight, a lifeline that would bolster, perhaps even redeem us, in the trials ahead. The burden of our intertwined fates, previously equally borne, now tilted as Caspian braced himself for his agonizing act of devotion, shouldering a love as ferocious and perilous as the world that threatened to consume us.

Dawn arrived, cloaked in a chilling premonition yet fueled by unwavering resolve. Caspian's departure was a phantom's retreat, swift and soundless, leaving me isolated to confront the morrow. He bequeathed only his indelible memory, his steadfast devotion, and the resounding thrum of his ultimate offering, a sacrifice echoing in my soul, a testament to our profound love, our unbreakable pact, our joint struggle against the encroaching night. The embers, once blazing symbols of our fervent passion, now shone as a guiding light, illuminating my advance toward the inevitable clash, a journey rendered even more treacherous by his absence. But his sacrifice would not be in vain; his valour would be my shield. The price of our love was exorbitant, yet its power was undeniable, an incandescent emblem of our inextricable bond, a connection that defied mortality and the vicissitudes of fortune.

CHAPTER

SEVENTEEN

Whispers of the Past

The biting wind whipped at my face, mirroring the turmoil within. Caspian's departure, the gut wrenching finality of it, the hollow ache in my chest, felt like a physical wound. It echoed the devastation of the battle, the screams still ringing in my ears, a phantom pain alongside the icy wind. I stood on the precipice of that crumbling tower, the Obsidian Covenant's stronghold reduced to rubble beneath me, a mirror image of my shattered world. Each jagged stone seemed to mock my helplessness, a testament to failure. The dawn painted the sky in hues of bruised purple and angry red, mirroring the fury that gnawed at me, a fitting backdrop to the chaos that raged inside. I clenched my fists, the rough stone digging into my palms, a small, insignificant pain compared to the gaping void Caspian left behind. My breath hitched in my throat, a sob catching in the back of my throat, swallowed down. I had to be strong. I had to be. For them.

Caspian's legacy—a timeworn leather journal—rested in my trembling grasp; its weathered cover a testament to the years it had witnessed bearing the scars of both time and turmoil. As I carefully turned its fragile pages I found them inscribed with a delicate almost skeletal script that seemed to dance before my eyes unveiling the intricate saga of the Whispering Wind and their age-old struggle against the Obsidian Covenant. This was no mere dichotomy of righteousness and wickedness; rather it was a labyrinthine narrative filled with treachery avarice and festering resentments. The story unfolded like a complex tapestry intricately embroidered with strands of illicit sorcery and precarious pacts that had been forged in the shadows of desperation and ambition.

Each line of text drew me deeper into a world where heroes and villains blurred into shades of gray, their motivations tangled in a web of betrayal and longing. The Whispering Wind, a band of rebels, fought valiantly for freedom and justice yet their path was fraught with peril as the Obsidian Covenant, a sinister assembly of dark sorcerers wielded their powers with ruthless precision. I could almost hear the whispers of the past echoing through the corridors of my mind urging me to decipher the lessons concealed within these pages. What sacrifices were made in the name of loyalty? What dreams were dashed against the stones of ambition? The journal was more than a mere account of events; it was a portal to understanding the complexities of human nature and the eternal struggle between light and darkness.

Pre Covenant, the journal recounted a bygone era. The Whispering Wind, then not a covert society, but a formidable, potent entity, exerted its influence from the darkness, striving to uphold a precarious equilibrium between the demonic and mortal spheres. Caspian's lineage included its architects—mighty demons who had sworn fealty to shield humanity from an older, more sinister threat. Yet, that delicate balance had shattered eons past.

Centuries past, a chronicle detailed a cataclysmic conflict between the ethereal Whispering Wind and a rebellious cabal of demons. These infernal beings, progenitors of the Obsidian Covenant, yearned for dominion over both mortal and demonic spheres, their ambition fueled by an insatiable hunger for power. A depraved lust for control consumed them, twisting their essence into instruments of malevolence. The war's brutality etched indelible scars onto the world, fracturing the very foundations of reality. Ancient grudges, long buried treachery, and an unrestrained thirst for supremacy obliterated all vestiges of reason, leaving behind a legacy of devastation.

Though wielding terrifying might, the Whispering Wind suffered catastrophic defeats. Their legions shattered, their dominion crumbled, and they were compelled to withdraw into obscurity, their potency ebbing with the relentless march of time. Reduced to custodians of long lost mysteries, they maintained a precarious equilibrium, their once magnificent heritage fading into faint echoes within the infernal abyss.

Caspian's ancestry, chronicled in the journal's pages, was a saga of immense influence and profound loss. A dwindling remnant of a once great dynasty, they carried the crushing weight of ancestral failings, striving to resurrect a heritage reduced to ruins. Their relentless battles against the Obsidian Covenant were consistently undermined by treacherous machinations and the corrosive infighting that plagued the Whispering Wind. Yet, their unwavering struggle embodied the indomitable spirit of hope amidst the bleakest desolation.

Caspian's sacrifice unfolded before me as I delved into the narrative, its profound implications dawning with each page. The relinquishment of his extensive network wasn't a mere strategic withdrawal; it was a high stakes wager, a courageous bid to safeguard his enduring influence and nurture the tenuous possibility of a future unshackled from the Covenant's oppressive reign. This selfless act, forged in the crucible of ancestral struggles and imbued with the echoes of their countless sacrifices, resonated with immense power. I grasped, with a sudden, chilling clarity, that the mantle of his heritage, heavy with responsibility, now fell upon my shoulders.

The journal's brittle pages, smelling faintly of dust and charred wood, the very scent of my village's funeral pyre, spilled forth secrets I'd chained to the bottom of my soul. It wasn't random. The Obsidian Covenant hadn't merely razed my home; they'd snuffed it out, a deliberate act of vengeance. My blood ran cold as I read of my family's shadowed history, a lineage twisted with the Whispering Wind, rebels, ghosts whispering on the wind, their defiance echoing down through generations to haunt the Covenant's nightmares. My parents weren't simple villagers; they were agents, their quiet lives a carefully constructed mask concealing a desperate, decades long campaign against the Covenant. I could taste the ash on my tongue, and feel the phantom sting of fire on my skin, reliving their final, desperate stand. The journal's stark words clawed at my throat, a raw, burning grief igniting in my chest. Their sacrifice, their meticulously planned defiance…it ended not in glory, but in the merciless, agonizing grip of the Covenant's fury. A fury I now inherited.

The revelation slammed into me, a physical gut punch that stole the breath from my lungs. The air itself tasted metallic, the phantom scent of blood and burning ash thick on my tongue, a visceral reminder of the inferno that had consumed my life. My vengeance, a simmering pyre for years, now roared—a wildfire stoked by a searing truth, a brutal understanding of the rot that festered beneath the surface of our conflict. It wasn't just the massacre of my village—the screams still echoing in the charred husks of my memories—that fueled this fire. It was the weight of the fallen, their silent pleas clinging to me like a shroud. I saw their faces in the flickering flames—eyes wide with terror, then a chilling, unwavering resolve. Their sacrifice, their dreams choked by the cold hand of death… that was the fuel. This wasn't about vengeance anymore. This was about inheriting their legacy, a bloody mantle stained with the sweat and sorrow of generations. This fight was for them, for the future they bled and died to buy, a future I would claw from the jaws of oblivion, even if it meant tearing my soul apart in the process.

The blood-soaked journal screamed its secrets, each word a haunting echo of the past. It revealed that the Covenant's insatiable hunger wasn't merely an avarice for power; it was something much darker: a ravenous beast that thrived on an ancient prophecy. This prophecy steeped in ominous foreboding dripped with the sulfurous stench of a rising flame elemental—me. I was the chosen one, the one destined to bring forth a cataclysm that would incinerate their iron grip on the world and bathe it in cleansing fire.

The prophecy's words etched in the brittle parchment seared themselves into my soul leaving behind a chilling premonition of my destiny. As I read each line the weight of my fate pressed heavily upon me an unyielding force that demanded recognition. The flames of my lineage flickered to life within me igniting a fierce determination to break the chains of oppression that bound my people. I could feel the heat rising not just from the elemental power within but from the sheer urgency of the task ahead.

Every flicker of the candlelight around me seemed to dance in anticipation mirroring the growing fire in my heart. I understood then that my journey was not just a quest for liberation but a sacred duty bestowed upon me by the very fabric of the universe. I was not merely a pawn in their game; I was the storm that would sweep them away, the inferno that would cleanse the darkness. As the journal whispered its truths I felt the mantle of my destiny settle upon my shoulders and I knew I had to embrace it no matter the cost.

Their attacks weren't just brutal; they were a symphony of hate, a furious crescendo orchestrated by a primal, burning fear. Each strike, each agonizing pursuit, vibrated with the raw terror of facing their demise. They didn't merely fear my power; they felt the icy breath of oblivion on their necks, the shadow of my incandescent wrath eclipsing their pathetic reign. The very air crackled with the anticipation of their annihilation, a tangible dread that clung to them like the ashes of a thousand fallen empires. I was not just a threat; I was their doom, a living embodiment of their fractured prophecies, a pyre upon which their legacy would burn.

The prophecy crushed me, a physical weight bowing my shoulders, the words a branding iron searing into my soul. With each syllable a hammer blows against my skull, echoing the deafening roar of my impending doom. This wasn't just responsibility; it was a poisoned chalice, a fate woven from shadows and whispered curses, a task so monstrous it threatened to shatter me. Yet, I would not yield. Caspian's sacrifice—the lingering scent of his blood, a phantom warmth clinging to my skin, the gaping wound in my heart mirroring the chasm in the world—was not a testament, but a shackle. His belief in me, a suffocating possessiveness masquerading as love, was a gilded cage, its bars forged from his dying breath, trapping me within the orbit of his desperate, consuming affection. His love, a brutal, possessive storm, howled in my ears, a terrifying symphony of grief and expectation, its lightning illuminating the encroaching abyss. I could taste the bitterness of his sacrifice, a metallic tang on my tongue, a constant reminder of the price I must pay. The darkness was not just approaching; it had already seized hold, its icy fingers tightening around my throat.

The journal's final pages, brittle as bone and smelling faintly of mildew and fear, clawed at my sanity with a cryptic map. It promised a sanctuary, a hidden refuge deep within the Whispering Wind's skeletal remains, a labyrinth of crumbling tunnels that reeked of damp earth and forgotten horrors. This wasn't just a place to rest; it was my last, desperate gamble, a pit stop before the final, soul crushing battle with the Obsidian Covenant, a battle I felt in my very marrow, a chilling premonition that tasted like ash and iron.

The journey? A suicide run. Each step would be a gamble against the unseen, a dance with shadows that writhed with malice. I could feel the icy breath of unseen predators on my neck, the rasp of unseen blades against my skin. But Caspian's ghost, his vibrant, infuriatingly optimistic spirit, now a cold ache in my chest, propelled me forward. His sacrifice wasn't just a loss; it was a molten core of rage, a blinding inferno forging a will of pure, unadulterated vengeance. That void he left... it wasn't empty. It roared with a power I never knew I possessed, a tempest of grief and fury that threatened to consume me, yet simultaneously fueled my every ragged breath. I would not fail him. I would not fail myself.

The sun, a molten eye in the bleached sky, glared down, baking the cracked earth to a bone dry whisper. Dust, tasting of ash and regret, coated my tongue as I slammed the journal shut, its brittle pages whispering secrets of blood and betrayal. The weight of my past, a crushing glacier of guilt and grief, threatened to suffocate me. But I would not break. Vengeance, once a flickering ember, now roared within me, a furnace fueled by more than just hate. I fought for a future cleansed of the Obsidian Covenant's vile reign, a future where the ghosts of the fallen, Caspian's face, etched in my memory, a phantom kiss upon my lips, found their peace. A future worthy of the love that burned hotter than any infernal flame, a love that death itself could not extinguish.

This journey, a pilgrimage through a hell of my own making, would test me to my limits. The air, thick with the stench of decay and the phantom cries of the damned, clawed at my throat. But I would march onward, my spine a steel rod, my heart a crucible of unwavering resolve. This fire in my soul, this ferocious, consuming love, was both my curse and my salvation. It was the echo of Caspian's sacrifice, a symphony of loss and hope, that fueled my every step. The whispers of the dead, once a chilling chorus, now sang a battle hymn. The truth, brutally revealed, was a weapon I would wield with merciless precision.

My vengeance would be a storm, a relentless tempest, a tidal wave of fire that would obliterate the Covenant's tyranny once and for all. I envisioned a world where their oppression crumbled beneath the weight of my wrath reduced to mere whispers in the howling winds of retribution. As the flames consumed their strongholds I could almost hear the echoes of their defeat resonating in the stillness that would follow. And beyond the carnage amidst the ashes of their ruin dawn would break anew—a fragile yet fiercely guarded future emerging from the desolation. This future radiant and hopeful would be bathed in the incandescent light of a love so profound it defied even the shadow of death itself. Love that could thrive in the bleakest of times illuminating the darkness with its unwavering brilliance. It would be a testament to resilience, a beacon of hope rising from the very depths of despair. Those who survived would remember not just the devastation but also the promise of rebirth, the unwavering strength of unity and the unbreakable bonds forged in the crucible of conflict. Through this I would ensure that the sacrifices made were not in vain transforming pain into purpose and vengeance into a vision of peace.

A mournful wind wailed through the ravaged Obsidian Covenant fortress, its desolate frame a chilling counterpoint to the turmoil consuming me. Caspian's diary, a chronicle of triumphs and heartbreaks, rested unnoticed on the frigid stone. I didn't merely peruse its pages; the narrative pierced me, its essence seeping into my very core, leaving an indelible stain of ages old strife upon my spirit. This revelation served as a brutal baptism, a stark confrontation with a past I had stubbornly suppressed.

Learning about my family's clandestine link to the Whispering Wind, and their concealed participation in the protracted conflict against the Covenant, felt like a cruel betrayal. A gaping chasm of sorrow had always haunted me, a void carved by my village's annihilation—a wound far exceeding simple grief. The truth now pierced me: the Obsidian Covenant hadn't just razed my home; they'd ruthlessly extinguished a glorious heritage, a bloodline of valiant fighters who had bravely defied their oppression for centuries. My parents weren't merely casualties; they were heroic figures, selflessly giving their lives for a cause I was now bound to uphold.

A crushing weight of inheritance burdened me, far exceeding any physical strain. I envisioned my parents—valiant, indomitable figures—locked in a clandestine battle, their existence consumed by a grim, unequal fight. These visions seared themselves into my consciousness, a stark contrast to the furious anger that had previously driven my quest for retribution. That fury now yielded to a profound grief, a visceral comprehension of the immeasurable sacrifices offered on my behalf.

The prophecy—the chilling knowledge that I was the Flame Elemental destined to overthrow the tyrannical Covenant—settled upon me like a shroud of ash. It wasn't merely a burden; it was a crushing weight of responsibility, a destiny I couldn't outrun and couldn't ignore no matter how desperately I wished to. The sheer pressure, the expectation to succeed where countless others had perished in fiery defiance threatened to suffocate me. The weight of their failures pressed down like a mountain of despair threatening to bury my nascent hope. Each day I felt the suffocating grip of their lost dreams, their extinguished flames reminding me of the stakes involved in my journey.

I could almost hear their whispered cries echoing in the recesses of my mind—those who had dared to rise against the Covenant only to be snuffed out like flickering candles in a storm. Their stories woven into the very fabric of my existence haunted my thoughts fueling my trepidation. I was the embodiment of their last flicker of hope yet I felt woefully unprepared. Could I truly bear the mantle of the Flame Elemental? The Covenant was a colossal force, its tendrils reaching into every corner of our world stifling rebellion and crushing dissent.

As I walked the path laid before me each step felt like a treacherous dance on hot coals. The flames within me flickered in response to my doubts, a tumultuous firestorm reflecting my inner turmoil. I knew that embracing my power meant embracing the very essence of my fears. Yet amidst the shadows of uncertainty a flicker of resolve ignited within me—a small defiant spark that refused to be extinguished. It whispered promises of strength urging me to rise above the ashes of despair. Perhaps just perhaps I could forge a new destiny not only for myself but for all those who had been silenced. The journey ahead would be perilous but I was ready to embrace my fate to fan the flames of rebellion into an inferno that could consume the Covenant once and for all.

Yet, even within that suffocating darkness, a tiny spark ignited. I was not alone. I carried the unwavering legacy of my parents, their courage a burning ember in my soul. The spirit of the Whispering Wind, a fierce and untamed power, coursed through my veins, a tangible link to the ancient magic that pulsed within me. And Caspian's sacrifice, a searing memory etched into my very being, fueled my resolve, transforming his loss into a potent, driving force. His death would not be in vain.

The memory of Caspian, the ghost of his touch, the phantom of his scent, the brutal, possessive imprint of his love, haunted me with the same relentless, icy grip as the spectres of my past. Our relationship, born in the crucible of violence and forged in the fires of mutual desperation, was a tangled, thorny paradox. His dominance, initially a terrifying storm that threatened to consume me, had unexpectedly given way to a strange, unsettling resonance, a connection that transcended the purely physical. It was more than the sharing of blood to slake my insatiable thirst; it was the sharing of a soul, a glimpse into the hidden vulnerabilities that lay buried deep beneath his formidable, almost impenetrable exterior. The raw, untamed power he possessed was matched only by the unexpected tenderness that flickered, like a fragile flame in a tempest, within his heart. His love, a maelstrom of conflicting emotions, left me both shattered and strangely, inexplicably whole.

Our intimacy had been a perilous dance on the razor's edge of a precipice, a reckless waltz teetering between the intoxicating pull of dominance and the chilling surrender of submission. It was a love born not of gentle blossoms, but of stark desperation, forged in the white hot crucible of battle, tempered and hardened by a shared understanding of the brutal, unforgiving darkness that clung to us like a second skin. Now, the silence of his absence clawed at me, a deafening roar echoing louder than any scream, a constant, agonizing reminder of the profound sacrifice he'd made, a sacrifice not for himself, but for me, for a future we might never share, a future stolen by the very forces that had forged our bond. His abandonment, far from a rejection, felt like a final, selfless act of protection, a desperate, agonizing shield woven from love as profound, as unwavering, and as dark as the abyss itself, a love that now consumed me in its absence.

The journal's cryptic entries hinted at a tempest brewing within the Whispering Wind, a maelstrom of betrayals and power struggles that mirrored the chilling darkness festering within the Obsidian Covenant. The line between righteous fury and unforgivable wickedness was not merely blurred; it was utterly indistinct, a chaotic scribble on the very fabric of reality, fraying at the edges like a tapestry worn thin by time and treachery. This moral ambiguity, a suffocating miasma, clung to me like a second skin, mirroring the agonizing internal conflict that raged within. My rage, a volcanic inferno fueled by past injustices, warred with a burgeoning empathy, a fragile sapling pushing through the hardened earth of my bitterness. The searing desire for revenge, a relentless tide threatening to consume me, clashed with a growing understanding of the intricate, interwoven forces manipulating events from the shadows, forces far more complex and nuanced than simply good versus evil. The journal's revelations were not just a chronicle of events; they were a harrowing reflection of my fractured soul.

The flickering candlelight danced across the brittle parchment, illuminating the cryptic lines etched into the journal's final pages. My fingers, tracing the faded ink, followed the labyrinthine paths that promised to lead me to the Whispering Wind's hidden sanctuary, a place whispered about in hushed tones, a refuge shrouded in legend. The journey wouldn't be merely difficult; it would be a harrowing gauntlet. The Covenant, with their relentless pursuit, would be hunting me like a pack of ravenous wolves, their hounds baying at my heels, their cruel claws extended, eager to tear me down. The path ahead was treacherous, a treacherous tapestry woven with peril, treacherous cliffs, shadowed forests teeming with unseen dangers, and rivers that churned with unseen currents. But the whispers of the past, the echoes of forgotten voices, had instilled in me a burning sense of purpose, a fierce clarity that had been absent before, a guiding star in the encroaching darkness. This quest, this perilous pilgrimage, was no longer a simple search; it was a reclamation, a fight for the legacy of those who had come before.

I rose, brushing away the clinging dust and debris, a gritty film of the recent struggle. The wind still howled, a ferocious banshee's wail, yet its sound had shifted. It was no longer a mournful lament, but a raw, untamed challenge, a summons whispered on the gale. The ghosts of my past, once shadowy spectres that haunted my waking hours and stole the breath from my sleep, were now familiar companions on this arduous path. They walked beside me, their ethereal forms lending a silent strength, guiding my steps with an unseen hand. My parents' sacrifice, a bonfire of love and courage that had consumed them but illuminated my way, burned bright within my heart. Caspian's love, a beacon in the storm, pulsed with a warmth that defied the biting wind. And the weight of the prophecy, once a crushing burden that threatened to suffocate me, now felt like the pressure of a blacksmith's hammer forging me into something stronger, something indomitable. These were not burdens, but the very fuel that ignited the unyielding flames of my determination, a fire that burned brighter with each passing gust of wind, each step I took towards my destiny.

The battle ahead was not merely a fight for vengeance; it was a war for my very soul, a crucible forging my legacy, a desperate struggle for the future of all the realms. I would confront the Obsidian Covenant, not simply as a flame elemental consumed by retribution, but as the rightful heir to a lineage stretching back through millennia, a legacy etched in fire and whispered on the winds of ages past. I was the embodiment of hope, a flickering candle against the encroaching night, in a world consumed by the Obsidian Covenant's suffocating darkness. I would face the ghosts of my past, the betrayals, the losses, the searing agony, not with fear, but with the unyielding resolve forged in the white hot fires of trauma, tempered and refined by a love that burned brighter, fiercer, and more enduring than any hellfire, a love that fueled my very being. My spirit, hardened yet compassionate, would be my shield against their despair, my unwavering purpose, my sword.

The crumbling stones of the ruined city crunched beneath my boots, each step a deliberate counterpoint to the rising sun's fiery embrace. Its rays, elongated and dramatic, stretched behind me like accusing fingers, a stark reminder of the devastation I had witnessed. This journey, I knew with chilling certainty, would be a crucible, a relentless test of endurance forged in the fires of betrayal and loss. But I was ready. The whispers of the fallen, the echoes of their sacrifices, had become inextricably woven into the fabric of my soul. These voices, once faint murmurs, now roared within me, a burning inferno that would consume the Obsidian

Covenant, its wicked tendrils and shadowy power. They would fuel my relentless advance toward a future I would sculpt from the very ashes of the past, a future stained, perhaps, by the ghosts of loved ones lost and those yet to fall, a price I was grimly prepared to pay. The fight had begun. And victory, however costly, would be mine.

The journey to the sanctuary, promised in the journal's cryptic final pages, began under a sky the colour of a bruised plum, bleeding into angry crimson at the horizon. Each footfall resonated with the weight of forgotten empires, the echoes of countless sacrifices whispering in the wind. The landscape was a ravaged tapestry, a brutal testament to the war that had clawed at the very soul of the land, leaving behind a desolate wasteland mirroring the turmoil within my own heart. Twisted, skeletal trees clawed at the bruised sky, their branches like skeletal fingers reaching for mercy that never came. The air itself hung heavy with the scent of ash and decay, a grim perfume clinging to the tattered remnants of a lost civilization. I travelled alone, a solitary figure against the vast, indifferent expanse, trusting only my instincts and the faint, ethereal whispers of ancient magic, a fragile thread guiding me through the desolate, heart wrenching emptiness.

The journey was a relentless crucible, a merciless test of her physical and mental endurance. The terrain itself was an unforgiving enemy: jagged peaks clawed at the sky, while treacherous canyons yawned beneath her feet. She faced blizzards that howled like banshees, their icy breath threatening to freeze her solid, and scorching heat that baked the land, a relentless sun threatening to incinerate her very being. The ever present shadow of the Obsidian Covenant's patrols chilled her to the bone; their watchful eyes, like those of predatory wolves, never strayed far, their movements a silent, menacing whisper across the desolate landscape. Each obstacle overcome, however, served only to harden her resolve, to forge her spirit into something stronger, more resilient. The naïve nineteen year old who had witnessed the brutal destruction of her village was gone, swallowed by the unforgiving wilderness. In her place stood a warrior, tempered not by steel, but by the agonizing pain of loss and the searing fires of vengeance, a warrior driven relentlessly forward by the faint, yet unwavering, echo of love stolen far too soon.

The memory, a burning ember in her heart, fueled her every step, every breath, every desperate struggle for survival.

Night fell, a suffocating blanket of black velvet embroidered with the faintest prickle of distant stars. Darkness pressed in, a tangible weight against my skin, yet I pressed onward, driven by the incandescent memory of Caspian. His image, a phantom limb of warmth in the icy grip of the night, burned in my mind, a beacon in the suffocating void. I relived his touch, the ghost of his strength lingering on my skin like phantom heat, the raw, searing intensity of our connection a bittersweet torment. It was a constant ache, a phantom limb of love, a reminder of what I had lost, yet simultaneously, a testament to the fierce, unwavering strength he had ignited within me. His words echoed in the silence, harsh as the wind off a jagged cliff, his brutal teachings, once a source of pain, now a foundation of resilience. The brutal honesty that had shattered my illusions, leaving me exposed to the harsh, unforgiving realities of my world, had also forged me anew, stronger and more determined than I had ever believed possible.

A shiver, deeper than the autumn chill, snaked down my spine. I stood at the precipice of a forest so dark it seemed to swallow light, the gnarled, skeletal trees contorted into grotesque shapes, their branches clawing at the bruised twilight sky. The air hung heavy, thick with an unnatural stillness—a silence so profound it vibrated, a palpable hum of ancient magic and suppressed dread. The scent of decaying leaves and damp earth mingled with something else, something acrid and faintly metallic like the tang of blood long spilled. I felt them—unseen eyes, cold and ancient, boring into me from the inky depths of the woods. Each rustle of leaves, each snap of a twig, amplified my growing unease, a symphony of impending threat. The ghosts of my past, once faint echoes, were now tangible presences, their spectral forms pressing against me, their icy breath ghosting my skin. I could almost taste the bitter ash of my family's demise, hear the whispers of their lost voices carried on the wind, not urging me forward, but beckoning, a siren's call to a fate I couldn't escape. The forest held its breath, waiting. And so did I.

The forest was a labyrinth of shadows and illusions, a suffocating maze woven from twilight and whispers. I battled spectral creatures born not just from the land, but from its very bones, beings sculpted from despair and fueled by the centuries of bloodshed that had soaked the earth crimson. Their forms shifted and writhed, grotesque parodies of men and beasts, their eyes burning with the malevolent light of a thousand dying suns. They were more than enemies; they were the living embodiments of collective trauma, the dark echoes of a war so brutal it had poisoned the very soul of the land. Each clash of steel, each desperate parry, felt like a struggle against the weight of history itself. I fought not only for my survival but for the cleansing of this cursed land, to wrest it free from the suffocating grip of the past, to break the cycle of violence and finally lay the tormented spirits to rest. The air itself throbbed with the agony of ages, a silent scream that echoed with every spectral shriek and the clang of my blade.

Emerging from the oppressive, emerald gloom of the forest, my limbs heavy with exhaustion but my spirit unbroken, I saw it, a faint, ethereal glimmer in the encroaching darkness, a beacon of hope piercing the suffocating night. The Sanctuary. It wasn't merely a place; it was a hidden haven, cradled within a secluded valley, shielded by ancient wards that hummed with forgotten power and cloaked in an illusion so potent it bent reality itself. This was a place where the spectral horrors of my past could be confronted, not merely endure, and where a future, bright with possibility, could be painstakingly forged from the ashes of my shattered present.

The ghosts that had relentlessly pursued me, their icy whispers once a constant torment, were now behind me, their chilling voices transmuted into a battle cry that resonated deep within my very soul, a symphony of defiance. I had faced them, not only survived but conquered. The fight, I knew, was far from over; the shadows still stretched long and menacing. But I was ready. I was stronger, forged in the crucible of suffering, more resolute in my purpose, more certain of my path, a path illuminated by the hard won wisdom of my trials. The whispers of the past, once a haunting chorus, had become the compass guiding me toward the dawn of a new era, a future where I would finally embrace, not merely confront, my destiny. The Sanctuary awaited its promise with a tangible weight in the air.

No obsidian palace, no fortress of arrogant stone. This sanctuary was a gnawing fist of humble buildings, clawing at the throat of a valley that tasted of secrets, rank and ancient. The waterfall wasn't a cascade; it was a brutal, white torrent, a screaming banshee tearing through the cliff face, its roar a physical blow against my eardrums, drowning out the slithering whispers of the wind that carried the stench of decay and damp earth. Peaceful? It reeked of it. A suffocating peace, thick and cloying like the scent of overripe fruit masking the festering corpse beneath. The shattered calm was a knife against my gut, a stark, brutal contrast to the ravaged landscape I'd crawled through, leaving a trail of my blood and broken will in its dust. But this peace... this fetid tranquillity... It was a lie. A thin, fragile membrane stretched taut over a history slick with betrayal, stained crimson, a tapestry woven with the screams of the dead. I could taste the iron in the air, and feel the ghosts brushing against my skin, their icy fingers tracing the map of my scars. This was no refuge. This was a cage.

The air itself cracked as I drew near, the shimmering mirage exploding like shattered glass. Gone was the deceptive façade; in its place, a cyclopean city pulsed with a guttural, earth shaking hum. It wasn't merely weathered stone; it was flesh, ancient and living, the very stones thrumming a rhythm that vibrated in my bones, a nauseating lullaby of power that clawed at my sanity. A metallic tang, like ozone and blood, filled my nostrils.

Then they came, emerging from the gnarled trees like obsidian statues given horrifying life. Not shadows, but beings of shadow, their forms flickering at the edges of perception, wielding blades that seemed to drink the starlight itself. Their eyes, twin points of glacial fire, bored into me, assessing, judging, promising oblivion. They weren't merely wary; their gaze held the chilling weight of centuries of silent vigil, of countless souls consumed by this forsaken place.

These were no demons, no men. They were something older, something woven from the very fabric of nightmare; creatures born of the valley's poisonous mists and the whispers of forgotten gods, their essence a toxic blend of ethereal grace and brutal, primal savagery. Fear, raw and visceral, choked me, a desperate gasp against the crushing weight of their ancient, unknowable power. This wasn't just a place; it was a tomb, and I was its unwilling guest.

My voice, a tremor in the suffocating silence, clawed its way into the cavernous space. The scent of ancient stone and damp earth clung to my throat, a bitter taste mirroring the dread coiling in my gut. I spoke of Caspian, the name of a rasping whisper against the backdrop of their unwavering scrutiny. His journal, a relic pulsing with forgotten power, became a physical weight in my hands. The prophecy, a venomous serpent coiled around my heart, I dared to unleash its name. The Guardians, figures carved from shadow and moonlight, exchanged glances that crackled with unspoken power.

Their eyes' dark pools of shadowed obsidian captured the flickering torch light in a haunting dance revealing a depth that held centuries of secrets and the weight of betrayals long past as well as broken oaths that echoed through time. Each glance seemed to whisper untold stories of honor lost and trust shattered a testament to the pain that lingered in the air. Then he moved a titan sculpted from granite his form towering and formidable as if he had been hewn from the very mountains themselves. His presence was both awe-inspiring and terrifying a reminder of the raw power that lay within him. Those molten gold eyes flecked with crimson embers burned with an incandescent fury that threatened to consume everything in their path, a fire so intense it felt as though it could scorch my very soul. In that moment I realized I was standing before a being not just of flesh and blood but one forged from the essence of rage and ancient wisdom, a force of nature that could reshape destinies with a single sweep of his hand.

He didn't speak; he intruded. His voice, a psychic hammer blow, shattered the fragile architecture of my mind. The Whispering Wind's history, a tapestry woven with blood and tears, with agonizing sacrifices and desperate gambles, flooded my consciousness. Their mistakes, etched in agony, seared themselves onto my very being. The Covenant, a ravenous beast gnawing at the edges of existence, its shadow stretching across millennia, became terrifyingly real.

His final message, a glacial hand pressing down on my heart, offered forgiveness. But it wasn't the gentle balm of compassion; it was a raw, brutal understanding, an acknowledgement of the immense price to be paid. It tasted of ash and regret, a bitter pill I was forced to swallow, knowing full well the monstrous battle that awaited.

This hallowed space served as a crucible of contemplation, a sanctuary where the past wasn't expunged but grappled with head on. Within its walls resided the legacies of my predecessors—valiant soldiers, gifted healers, shrewd negotiators—all united by a solemn oath to vanquish the Covenant, yet irrevocably scarred by internecine strife and treachery. Immersed in the study of archaic scrolls, I painstakingly deciphered enigmatic prophecies, meticulously reconstructing the fractured narrative of the Whispering Wind. I uncovered the profound sacrifices of my ancestors and their unwavering resolve in the face of seemingly insurmountable adversity. Their internal conflicts, the insidious betrayals that reverberated through the ages, and the catastrophic errors that claimed countless lives and forever reshaped the course of history, were laid bare before me.

Caspian's diary I finally grasped was not merely a collection of thoughts or a casual record of events; it was a profound self-incrimination, a heartfelt supplication for absolution. Each page I turned seemed to pulsate with his inner turmoil revealing a frantic bid to expiate his transgressions and to rectify the grievous errors of his past. The words he penned were drenched in remorse, a testament to the weight of guilt that had been pressing down on him for so long. His deeds I perceived were not born out of malice but rather stemmed from a tangled web of allegiance terror and a desperate yearning to safeguard the Wind.

Within the labyrinth of his mind I began to understand the complexities that had driven him to commit such heinous acts. His pitilessness and autocratic sway which had long been perceived as mere manifestations of power had actually served as a bulwark—an impenetrable façade concealing an abyss of anguish and self-reproach. The mask he wore was a protective shield crafted to keep the world at bay while he wrestled with the demons of his own making. He had manipulated me. It was true but not solely for personal aggrandizement or to fulfill a narcissistic need for control. There was something far deeper at play, a twisted sense of purpose that guided his actions.

His entanglement with me was a perilous maneuver, a calculated gamble intended to cripple the Covenant and advance his aims. Each interaction we shared had been a thread in a larger tapestry of deception, one that he wove with the utmost care. I realized that I had been an unwitting pawn in his game, a piece positioned to further his agenda. Yet the more I delved into his thoughts the more I discerned the fragility of his motives. His ultimate sacrifice was not merely a strategic ploy but rather the bitter fruit of that same warped unwavering devotion to a cause that in his eyes justified the means.

As I continued to read I was struck by the duality of his existence—the juxtaposition of a ruthless leader and a tormented soul seeking redemption. Each entry unfolded like a confession, a plea for understanding and forgiveness that transcended the boundaries of time and consequence. In his reflections I found echoes of my own struggles a shared humanity that bridged the chasm between us Caspian's diary served as a mirror reflecting the complexities of moral choice and the shadows that lingered in the corners of our shared history. It compelled me to confront my own beliefs and the choices I had made, pushing me to question the very nature of loyalty and sacrifice. In this profound narrative I discovered not only the depths of his despair but also the potential for healing and reconciliation, a journey I was now compelled to undertake alongside him.

A crushing weight of comprehension descended, exceeding any previous burden. The distinctions between justice and injustice dissolved, the conflict's ethics spiralling into profound ambiguity. The Whispering Wind proved not a flawless paragon of virtue, but a flawed entity. They had perpetrated atrocities, horrific deeds justified by a purportedly noble purpose. Yet, their motives, at their very heart, resonated with an unwavering conviction. Their battle stemmed from stark desperation, fueled by an unshakeable faith in their cause's ultimate necessity.

I approached the venerable guardians of the hallowed grounds, ancients whose centuries etched fragility upon their forms yet sharpened the acuity of their intellect, their gaze pools reflecting eons of accumulated sagacity. My transgressions—a thirst for retribution, a callous manipulation of others to fulfill my ambitions—weighed heavily on my soul. I laid bare my internal torment: the ceaseless battle between the savage hunger of my vampiric nature and the fragile flicker of compassion within. The spectre of inadequacy haunted me, the fear of proving unworthy of the weighty inheritance I bore.

A profound stillness, far surpassing any verbal expression, emanated from the elders as they absorbed the tale. They dispensed no facile solutions, no glib pronouncements of pardon. The intricate dance of shadow and illumination, the nuanced terrain between virtue and vice, was deeply familiar to them. Their absolution wasn't a casually bestowed boon, but the arduous fruit of self examination and reconciliation, a testament to the individual's journey.

Through weeks of contemplative silence, I battled my inner turmoil. The spectres of my past, instead of haunting adversaries, emerged as insightful mentors, illuminating the path to self comprehension and acceptance. I granted my parents absolution, acknowledging both the selfless sacrifices they offered and the unintentional weight they imposed. I extended forgiveness to Caspian, recognizing his manipulative tactics and blunt pronouncements as manifestations of his profound suffering and apprehension. Ultimately, and most significantly, I offered myself the profound gift of self forgiveness.

Self compassion wasn't a sudden revelation; rather, it was a painstaking ascent from the depths of self condemnation, a slow, arduous journey. The anger and bitterness that had relentlessly gripped me gradually receded, replaced by a painstaking process of self acceptance. This involved confronting my imperfections, my errors, without falling into the mire of self reproach. I had to recognize that my actions, though ethically ambiguous, arose from profound suffering and despair. Ultimately, it demanded embracing the intricate tapestry of my character, the inherent contradictions within my soul.

My advancement was at last recognized by the esteemed Council of Elders, a body revered for its wisdom and insight. Their approval however was not proclaimed with fanfare or extravagant celebrations; rather it manifested subtly revealed through a delicate alteration in their bearing. It was as if an invisible veil had been lifted allowing a tacit comprehension to flow seamlessly between them. This unspoken current of agreement resonated in the air palpable to those present. It was a moment thick with meaning echoing the trials and tribulations I had faced on my journey.

In this atmosphere of quiet acknowledgment a modest silver pendant was bestowed upon me, its surface glinting softly in the dim light. The pendant was intricately inscribed with the glyphs of the Zephyr's breath symbols that spoke of the winds of change and the resilience required to navigate them. As I held it in my palm I felt its weight not as a burden but as a reminder of the hard-won battles I had fought and the sacrifices I had made. This gift served not as absolution for past missteps or challenges but rather as a poignant memento of my arduous path marking the culmination of my efforts and the growth I had achieved along the way. It was a powerful emblem of my fortitude and unwavering spirit, a tangible representation of my journey that would inspire me in the days to come. With this pendant I felt a renewed sense of purpose ready to embrace the future and the responsibilities that awaited me.

A soft, resonant thrum vibrated against my skin, the amulet a palpable link not merely to my heritage, but to a destiny I was actively forging. Though the spectres of my past remained, their oppressive grip had finally loosened. I bore their imprint, not as a crippling weight, but as a powerful symbol of my inner resilience. The echoes of bygone days, once a mournful dirge, now served as a radiant beacon, charting my course toward the horizon.

The sanctuary's restorative power transcended mere physical healing; it forged a sharper, more resilient spirit within me. My resolve, once a flickering ember, now blazed with unwavering intensity. I confronted the Obsidian Covenant not merely with vengeful flames, but with the seasoned insight of a veteran and a purpose crystalline in its clarity. Emerging from that hallowed space, I was transformed. No longer a lone flame elemental consumed by retribution, I stood as a beacon, ready to rally the fragmented legions of the Whispering Wind, to hammer a new alliance against the encroaching shadows. This leader, hardened in the crucible of adversity and guided by the painfully earned absolution of past transgressions, was born anew.

The struggle for the realms persisted in a relentless contest that tested our very essence yet my battle cry underwent a profound transformation. No longer was it solely the raw fury of unbridled rage that fueled my spirit; it was a deep-seated righteous indignation that had taken its place—a fierce fire stoked by the poignant memories of fallen comrades whose sacrifices weighed heavily on my heart. This newfound strength was tempered by the wisdom of our ancestral spirits guiding us through the darkness with their timeless knowledge. I was propelled forward by an unshakeable faith in a future that we believed was truly deserving of our sacrifices. The whispers of bygone sorrows that once haunted us now swelled into the resonant roar of a triumphant tomorrow echoing the promise of hope and resilience.

EIGHTEEN

Unearthly Longing

The air crackled, a tangible dread clinging to the very timbers of the house, thick as the ash settling from the dying fire. The silence wasn't peaceful; it was a suffocating weight, the unspoken screams of our shared nightmare pressing down on us. This sanctuary, once a haven of serenity, now pulsed with raw, volatile energy, a storm raging between Caspian and me, its lightning a silent, searing exchange of unspoken accusations.

He sat hunched beside the hearth, the flickering firelight painting his face in shifting shades of torment. His eyes, usually glacial pools of controlled fury, burned with a feverish intensity, the harsh angles of his jaw etched deeper by some unseen agony. The carefully constructed wall of his detachment had crumbled, revealing not just fragility, but a shattered core, a terrifying vulnerability that made the scars etched onto his soul as visible as the ones marrying his skin. I caught the metallic tang of blood in the air, a phantom scent clinging to the memory of our escape, mingling with the acrid bite of wood smoke and the bitter taste of betrayal lingering on my tongue. His silence was a symphony of unspoken pain, more devastating than any roar. I saw the flicker of desperate hope in his gaze, a fragile thing threatened by the very shadows that danced in the firelight, shadows mirroring the demons we both carried within.

A force, raw and primal, dragged me closer, a desperate, gut wrenching need to bridge the chasm that yawned between them, a chasm carved not just of space, but of lifetimes of unspoken resentments and simmering desires. The pendant, a shard of glacial ice against my skin, throbbed with a life of its own, a brutal pulse mirroring the tempest raging beneath their meticulously composed exteriors. The scent of ozone and impending storm filled the air, a bitter tang that clung to the bitter truth of their fractured connection. I tasted the metallic tang of fear on my tongue, a premonition of the violence simmering just below the surface of their strained civility. Their eyes, haunted pools reflecting a thousand unspoken words, locked across the room; hers, a storm of defiance and aching vulnerability; his, a glacial mask barely concealing the raw agony of a love lost and perhaps, irrevocably, betrayed. The vibration intensified a physical assault, resonating not just in my bones, but deep within my soul, a visceral echo of their fractured, desperate yearning.

Caspian's gaze, a molten sliver of ice blue fire, burned into me. The air itself crackled, a tangible hum vibrating between us before his fingertips, cold as glacier stone yet strangely soft, brushed my skin. The contact ignited a white hot inferno, an unforeseen eruption of something primal and untamed. His touch, usually a command, a king's decree, faltered, a tremor echoing the frantic beat of my own heart. The scent of his leather and storm infused cologne, usually so bracing, now carried the faint, unsettling whisper of fear. His confession, a low growl rumbling from the depths of his soul, shattered the fragile façade of control he'd painstakingly constructed. The silence that followed was deafening, a chasm filled only with the raw, exposed vulnerability that throbbed between us, a wound laid bare under the cruel moonlight. The weight of his unspoken history pressed down, a suffocating burden shared in the suffocating intimacy of that moment.

His confession erupted, a volcanic torrent of unplanned admissions, scorching the air between us. The scent of his fear, sharp and metallic, mingled with the stale dust motes dancing in the single shaft of sunlight. *"Obligation? Restoration? Lies! A calculated, cold strategy,"* he rasped, the words tearing through the silence like shards of glass. Regret, a thick, suffocating miasma, clung to him. His carefully constructed facade, a brittle eggshell, had shattered. His eyes, twin pools reflecting a storm of guilt and something else... a desperate, terrifying hunger, locked onto mine. The pressure of his hand, bone thin and trembling, against mine was a physical manifestation of his turmoil. *"You,"* he whispered, the single word a branding iron searing its mark onto my soul, igniting a firestorm within me. A conflagration I can neither control nor extinguish. It consumes.

The confession ripped through the air, a sonic boom shattering the meticulously constructed ice palace of his self preservation. The centuries of gnawing solitude clawed at him, a phantom limb pain in the marrow of his bones; the crushing weight of his legacy, a physical burden that bowed his spine, a taste of ash and rust on his tongue. The agonizing burden of his deeds, a miasma of guilt, thick and suffocating, clinging to him like the shroud of a thousand damned souls. He confessed his voice to a rasping whisper that betrayed the seismic tremors within, revealing a profound emptiness, a black hole at the heart of his being. This void, a screaming vacuum, he'd tried to fill with the bitter draught of authority, the iron taste of dominion, the fleeting, sickly sweetness of subjugation, each sip only deepening the abyss. But my defiance, a wildfire in his carefully tended garden, my resistance, a venomous serpent coiling in his very heart, had breached his formidable defences, those walls built of obsidian and fear. I saw then, not the terrifying god he projected, but a fragile creature, a wounded animal huddling in the ruins of its own making, its eyes burning with terrible, desperate loneliness. The stench of his despair, sharp and acrid, filled the air, a testament to his fall.

A tidal wave of empathy, cold and brutal as the ocean's heart, crashed over me, shattering the icy shards of my resentment. The bitterness, a festering wound, began to thaw, revealing the raw, pulsing flesh beneath. His confession, a guttural torrent of truth, ripped through the air, a poisoned arrow piercing the armour of my anger. I tasted the metallic tang of his despair, and felt the tremor of his brokenness vibrate through the floorboards, a seismic shift in the very ground beneath my feet. This wasn't just a man; this was a creature sculpted by torment, his soul a landscape ravaged by fire, each scar a testament to battles fought and lost in the shadowed corners of his own mind. His eyes, twin pools reflecting a storm wracked sky, held a haunting beauty. They spoke of nights spent wrestling demons, of a profound weariness that clung to him like the scent of brine and decay. But beneath the exhaustion, a molten core of fierce, incandescent strength pulsed, defiance flickering in the dying embers of his spirit. He was a paradox, a ruin breathtaking in its desolation, yet possessing a terrifying, seductive power.

My voice, a frail tremor, barely escaped my lips. *"And what of me?"* I demanded, the unspoken accusation hanging heavy in the air. *"How dare you manipulate me, subjugate my will?"*

His body shuddered a physical recoil that sent tremors through his very bones. The stench of his own failure clung to him, thick as the remorse that veiled his eyes, twin pools of churning guilt reflecting the flickering candlelight. *"I understand,"* he rasped, the confession tearing from him like a ragged wound. The taste of ash filled his mouth; the bitter residue of his choices. *"My actions... inexcusable. A brutal, callous disregard for your soul, a festering cancer of self righteous cruelty masked as duty. But even in that abyss... even as the icy fingers of depravity gripped my heart... something else stirred. A monstrous, twisted echo of... something akin to love."*

His stare, unwavering and profound, pierced me. A feeling unprecedented, terrifying yet thrilling, washed over him; it shattered his convictions, leaving him adrift in a sea of doubt.

His words hung in the air, thick, cloying as the scent of overripe plums, each syllable a lead weight pressing down on the suffocating silence. The confession clawed its way out of him, a raw, bleeding thing: the icy terror of my leaving, the gut wrenching horror of my return to that desolate, unforgiving path, a path paved with the shards of his broken promises. His voice, a rasping whisper that scraped against my soul, revealed a desperation so profound it vibrated in the very marrow of my bones. He didn't just want to keep me safe; he wanted to cling to me, to press me against him, a desperate shield against the millennia long blizzard of despair, a wasteland of regret so vast it threatened to swallow him whole. The taste of fear was bitter on my tongue, the texture of his frantic plea rough against my skin. His eyes, twin pools of ancient sorrow reflecting the dying light, held a truth darker and deeper than any abyss I'd known. This wasn't mere affection; it was a primal, desperate grasp at survival, a soul bartering with the shadows to avoid annihilation.

My heart ached with a complex mix of anger, hurt, and a burgeoning tenderness. I'd spent weeks confronting my demons, wrestling with my past, and forgiving those who had wronged me. Now, I found myself facing the daunting task of forgiving him, of accepting the complexity of his character, of acknowledging the genuine feelings I sensed beneath his harsh exterior. It was a struggle, I'll admit. The anger still flared sometimes, a hot coal buried deep inside. But I knew, deep down, that I had to try. I had to find a way to let go.

I remembered his sacrifice, the significant and calculated risk he'd taken for me, an act of profound selflessness that belied his otherwise self-serving nature. In those moments I recalled the sheer weight of his choices and the depth of his commitment that often went unnoticed. I also remembered the moments of tenderness we shared the fleeting glimpses of vulnerability that occasionally pierced through his carefully constructed facade revealing a side of him that few ever saw. I felt again the intense physicality of our encounters and the undeniable chemistry that crackled in the air between us. This primal connection we shared transcended the complicated power dynamics at play, an electric force that drew us together despite our conflicting natures. It was a bond that was as exhilarating as it was a complicated dance of desire and conflict that neither of us could ever fully escape.

The fire roared, a ravenous beast gnawing at the ancient stones of the sanctuary, its fangs of flame spitting shadows that writhed and pulsed across the walls. The air, thick and suffocating, clawed at my throat, a brutal assault of wood smoke, acrid and stinging, mingling with the cloying sweetness of Caspian's presence. His demon scent, a feral perfume, overwhelmed me; rich earth, yes, but laced with the metallic tang of blood and the raw, primal musk of something ancient, something utterly terrifying, something that resonated deep within my own shadowed soul. A tremor, a primal fear, coiled in my gut; this wasn't just a scent, it was a promise, a threat whispered in the wind. His very essence, untamed, dangerous, intoxicating, was a physical force, pressing against me, a silent challenge to my will.

"I... I hated you at first, I admitted," my voice trembling slightly. "I hated you for your power, for the way you controlled me, for the way you used my body like it was your own. The violation of it all still burned. But..."

My pulse, a frantic drum solo against my ribs, threatened to shatter them. The air thickened and tasted metallic, each breath a ragged gasp as I fought for control. My emotions weren't a tangled mess; they were a venomous viper coiled tight in my chest, its scales slick with fear and a forbidden, exhilarating lust. The words, brittle shards of glass, scattered and evaded me. I yearned to unleash the tempest raging within, to bear the raw, exquisite agony and incandescent joy, but my tongue, a traitorous thing, stumbled. *"But I... I feel something for you,"* I rasped, the confession a physical violation. *"Something that claws at my sanity, that both terrifies and... ignites me to the very core."*

The confession hung between us, fragile and vulnerable. Did I say too much? God, I sound so... pathetic. He's probably judging me already. Why did I do that? Why did I have to blurt it all out? My heart hammered against my ribs, a frantic drumbeat accompanying the raw, unfiltered words I'd just spoken. It's out there now, in the open air. No turning back. But... maybe that's okay. It was a terrifying, exhilarating release, my emotions laid bare, a testament to the profound impact he'd had on my life. Impact? That's a polite way of saying he completely wrecked me, and I loved every minute of it. I felt exposed and vulnerable, like a stripped down wire humming with raw energy. He can see right through me. And... I don't even care. But also a strange sense of relief, a weight lifting from my chest. Like finally admitting to myself what I've been desperately trying to ignore for months. Years. I saw it in his eyes, too, the recognition of the complex, intertwined nature of our relationship, a relationship I'd never expected, forged in violence and fueled by a simmering, undeniable desire that I couldn't, and wouldn't, deny any longer. Is this... understanding? Or horror? Please, God, let it be understanding. Because if it's horror, I'm not sure I can handle it. But... I have to know.

Caspian's eyes widened, a flicker of disbelief, of a desperate, aching hope, igniting the darkness in their depths. His breath hitched a barely audible sound that vibrated against my skin as he reached out, his fingers brushing my cheek before gently cupping my face. The touch was surprisingly tender, a stark contrast to the raw intensity burning in his gaze. His thumb, calloused but surprisingly soft, traced the delicate line of my jaw, a feather light caress that sent shivers down my spine.

His gaze, intense and questioning, held a silent plea, a promise of something forbidden, something dangerous, and utterly captivating. The air crackled with unspoken desires, a palpable tension hanging heavy between us, thick enough to taste.

"Blaze..." he whispered, his voice thick with emotion.

The chasm between us yawned, a black gulf echoing with unspoken screams, a silence thick enough to choke on. We knew, with a bone deep certainty that chilled us to the marrow, the intricate, lethal dance of our fates. This was no gentle waltz, no summer flirtation. The stench of cordite and burning flesh still clung to our souls, a bitter perfume marking the crucible where our bond was forged. We'd clawed our way through hell together, our survival a desperate, shared gasp in the face of annihilation. It was a hunger, a ravenous, forbidden thirst, born in the shadowed corners of a war torn world, a hunger hardened by its relentless brutality. The taste of blood, and the metallic tang of fear, were the flavours of our intimacy. Yet, from this charnel house, this landscape of ash and despair, a defiant flower pushed through the cracked earth, a fragile, incandescent promise, burning with a light that threatened to consume us both.

A profound stillness settled between us, the hearth's flickering flames mirroring the unspoken emotions that blazed within. He's looking at me... really looking at me. Is this... is this what it feels like? This intensity... I'm terrified and exhilarated all at once. Our clasped hands, a tangible symbol of our unacknowledged intimacy, lay nestled together. My heart is hammering against my ribs. Should I pull away? No... no, I don't want to. This refuge, previously a haven of solace and introspection, had been transformed; it was now a forge where our deepest feelings were tempered, a crucible wherein our shared frailties found exposure, our inherent affinity finally revealed in its radiant truth. He's so close. I can feel the warmth of his skin against mine. This is more than just friendship, isn't it? It's... something else entirely. Something I've never experienced before. Is this what love feels like? Oh God, I hope so. But what if I'm wrong? What if this is just a moment, a fleeting illusion? The silence stretched, heavy with unspoken words, yet somehow... perfect. Perfect. This is perfect.

The whispers of the past had finally given way to the undeniable roar of the present, a present that felt like a physical force pressing down on me, filled with the complexities, the uncertainties, and the exhilarating, terrifying dangers of a love that dared to defy everything I knew. The path ahead felt treacherous, a minefield under my feet; I knew their enemies still lurked, their shadows stretching long and menacing. But hand in hand with him, I felt a strength surge through me. We would face whatever lay ahead, our bond a rope woven from shared understanding, hard won acceptance, and a raw, untamed love that burned between us like wildfire.

The fight for our lives, for our world, continued, but now I fought not just as a warrior, but as a lover. Our destinies were entwined, our hearts beating a single rhythm against the encroaching darkness. I felt the whispers of the past guiding me, illuminating the path towards a future we would build together, a future forged in the white hot fires of our love, a future where even I, with my shadowed past, could find solace and redemption.

I knew this wouldn't be a stroll through sun dappled meadows. The path ahead, a razor edged ridge, slick with blood red rain and the stench of decay, screamed of peril. The battles looming? Mountains of obsidian, each shadow promising a deeper, more agonizing death. But I'd face them. I had to. With him. His love, a burning brand searing away the icy dread, a molten gold sun piercing the storm wracked the sky of my soul. The future? A maelstrom of shattered stars and phosphorescent leviathans, a churning abyss promising to swallow us whole. But the chilling certainty? I was no longer adrift, lost in the echoing silence of my own despair. I had found him, a scarred warrior with eyes the colour of a tempestuous sea, a man who carried the weight of a thousand battles yet held a tenderness that could mend a shattered heart. And in his gaze, in the raw, electric pulse of his touch, I found it, a reason to fight, a primal, roaring need to live, something more brutal and beautiful than any infernal force, more enduring than the cold embrace of the grave itself.

The firelight, a molten heart in the hearth, blazed in Caspian's eyes, twin embers mirroring the inferno still raging within him,, a controlled burn, dangerous and mesmerizing. His touch, a branding iron disguised as a caress, traced the delicate curve of my jaw, the heat of his skin a searing brand against mine. The gesture, deceptively gentle, a predator's feigned tenderness, belied the raw, untamed power coiled within him, a power that thrummed against my skin like a second heartbeat. It sent shivers, not just down my spine, but through every nerve ending, igniting a wildfire that spread from my touchpoint, a bittersweet agony both familiar and unnervingly comforting.

The acrid taste of resentment, the bitter gall of anger, the suffocating pressure of rage that had choked me for so long, it began to crack, to fissure under the weight of something far more potent. The scent of wood smoke and burning oak filled my nostrils, mirroring the slow, agonizing surrender of my defences. Not acceptance, not exactly. But a terrifying, breathtaking understanding, a recognition of the volatile, chaotic force he truly was, a force both capable of destroying me and holding me captive in its incandescent glow. It was terrifying, exhilarating, and utterly inescapable.

The taste of ash filled my mouth, a bitter residue of his betrayal. He'd used me, a puppet on his strings, dancing to a tune of his cruel design. He'd exploited the cracks in my armour, the raw, bleeding wounds I'd desperately tried to hide. There was no denying the icy grip of his control, the phantom weight of his touch still lingering on my skin. But then came his confession, a guttural rasp that sliced through the silence, a confession that clawed at the fortress I'd painstakingly constructed around my shattered heart. It wasn't the slick, practiced remorse of a coward, no hollow apologies or cheap, glittering excuses. No. This was different. This was a visceral unveiling, a stripping bare of his soul, a raw exposure of his festering darkness—a darkness I saw reflected in the haunted depths of his eyes, a darkness that mirrored the abyss I'd been wrestling with within myself. He laid bare his demons, his desperate, clawing need for connection, a need that mirrored my aching loneliness, a need that whispered of a shared vulnerability, a twisted, dangerous kinship forged in the fires of our mutual pain. And in that brutal, unvarnished honesty, in that chilling, heart wrenching vulnerability, I saw a flicker, a fragile spark—a glimmer of something authentic, something desperate, something worthy of…not just forgiveness, but a terrifying, breathtaking understanding.

353

The confession tore from me, a ragged whisper lost in the suffocating velvet of the night. *"It wasn't just... lust,"* I rasped, the words tasting like ash and betrayal on my tongue. My throat, a raw, burning cavern, choked the sound. This admission, this stripping bare of my soul, felt like a physical violation, the scent of my fear sharp and acrid in the air. The taste of his skin, still lingering phantom like on my lips, mocked the inadequacy of the word lust. It was a cataclysm, a seismic shift in the very tectonic plates of my being. *"It was... something more,"* I breathed, the words a desperate prayer, a plea for understanding, a confession of hunger that gnawed at my sanity, a hunger that transcended the mundane and plunged into the terrifying depths of the unknown. The shadowed corners of the room seemed to writhe with the unspoken intensity, the silence a tangible entity, heavy and suffocating.

The rasp of my voice echoed the grit in my throat as I recounted the searing moments of shared agony, the phantom touch of his calloused hand, a fleeting, brutal tenderness that fractured his obsidian shell. I saw it again, the battlefield haze staining the memory crimson, the silent communion between us, a language woven from the stench of blood and the metallic tang of fear. He moved as if an extension of my fractured soul, a rippling muscle of instinct shielding me from the maelstrom of steel. He anticipated, and knew my every desperate twitch, every parry, every desperate lunge, a terrifying, beautiful symphony of destruction, two souls fused against the crushing weight of a thousand enemies.

The blood was a slick, crimson stain, but it was the taste of it, metallic and coppery, lingering on the back of my tongue, that truly sickened me. It wasn't just the sight, but the gut wrenching resonance of it, a phantom limb empathy clawing at my insides. A shared agony, bitter and viscous as bile, pooled between us. We weren't just wounded; we were festering sores, each a testament to the world's ravenous hunger for our obliteration. He, with his eyes, those haunted obsidian pools reflecting a lifetime of unspeakable torment; I, mirrored back in his gaze, a grotesque mockery of strength. We were pariahs, branded, ostracized, the shattered remnants of a mirror reflecting a truth so horrifyingly intimate it threatened to consume us both. A truth we could not, would not, bear alone. The air itself throbbed with the weight of it, thick and suffocating, a tangible pressure on my chest. We were two venomous snakes, intertwined in a death dance of shared damnation.

Caspian leaned in, his breath a hot whisper against my ear, the scent of earth and wildness clinging to him like a second skin. My breath hitched; the proximity ignited a fire in my veins that far surpassed the intoxicating scent. He didn't speak, but the brush of his lips against my temple sent a shiver down my spine, a silent promise echoing the unspoken desires swirling between us. His dark eyes, pools of molten snow, held a possessive intensity that both thrilled and terrified me. It wasn't just a shared journey they acknowledged, but a shared yearning, a raw, untamed hunger woven into the complex, tangled threads of their volatile connection. The air crackled with unspoken words, with the promise of something forbidden, something dangerous, and undeniably thrilling.

He told me of his past, of the centuries of loneliness, the weight of his responsibilities, the burden of his past actions. He spoke of the sacrifices he'd made, the deals he'd struck with forces far older and more sinister than the Obsidian Covenant. He confessed to the guilt that gnawed at his soul, the constant reminder of the lives he'd taken, the innocents he'd harmed in the name of his twisted sense of duty. He revealed the deep seated fear of losing me, of returning to the crushing emptiness that had haunted him for centuries. This was not the cold, ruthless demon she had first encountered; this was a man broken and scarred, desperately seeking redemption.

I listened, my heart aching with a longing that mirrored his pain. The weariness in his eyes, the shadows that hinted at a power both terrifying and alluring, ignited a fire within me. I understood the weight of his burden and felt the darkness clinging to him like a lover's embrace, a dangerous intimacy. And in that understanding, a profound connection sparked, a raw, electric current passing between us, forged not just in shared battles, but in the shared vulnerability that only profound suffering can reveal. The air crackled with unspoken desires, a silent promise hanging between us heavier than any sword.

I remembered the nights of shared intimacy, the moments of raw, untamed passion that had transcended the power dynamics of our relationship, nights that still left me breathless, a tremor echoing in my core. I recalled the way his touch could both ignite a wildfire within me and soothe the simmering embers afterward, the way his presence filled the empty spaces within me, a possession both thrilling and terrifying. His gaze, lingering just a moment too long, saw past my fiery exterior, past the carefully constructed walls, to the vulnerable heart beneath, a vulnerability that both terrified and exhilarated me. The memory of his skin against mine, the scent of him clinging to my clothes days later… it was a brand, a mark of a claim I both craved and feared.

A rasp, barely louder than the graveyard's sigh, clawed its way from my throat: *"I never thought I'd say this… forgive you."* The words tasted like ash and old regret, a bitter metallic tang coating my tongue. Doubt, a venomous serpent coiled tight in my gut, squeezed the air from my lungs. My heart hammered a frantic rhythm against my ribs, a frantic drumbeat echoing the storm raging within. Then, a crack of lightning, a searing realization that sliced through the suffocating darkness. Forgiveness, I realized, wasn't some magical erasure, some neat whitewashing of the past's brutal canvas. No. It was a brutal, beautiful act; embracing the jagged edges of memory, wrestling with the phantom pain, and extracting, drop by agonizing drop, the bitter wisdom from its poisoned chalice.

Caspian's fingers, like burning ice, tightened around mine, a possessive brand seared into my flesh. The unexpected softness woven through his grip felt like a paradox—a whisper of tenderness against the brutal pressure of his claim. It wasn't just understanding that radiated from him, a bone deep empathy pulsed, a raw, visceral acknowledgment of the terrifying grace, the terrifying freedom I'd unleashed. The scent of his skin, sharp and metallic like ozone after a storm, filled my nostrils, mingling with the coppery tang of my own fear. His heart hammered against my palm, a frantic drumbeat mirroring the tempest raging within me—a tempest both sparked and soothed by his brutal, tender understanding.

His admission of self condemnation, the crushing burden of his past transgressions, laid bare his soul. He yearned profoundly for absolution, a pathway to expiate his guilt, to repair the damage inflicted. And in that unflinching disclosure, that profound exposure of his inner turmoil,

I recognized the echoes of my tormented spirit, my desperate longing for solace.

Their acceptance wasn't a simple act of reconciliation; it was so much more. I felt it as a complex, evolving process, a slow, painful peeling back of layers of hurt and betrayal, a gradual unravelling of our tangled pasts. I had to acknowledge my flaws, my imperfections, and the darkness that dwelled within me. It was terrifying, to face that darkness. But finding solace in our shared vulnerability, in the mutual understanding that bloomed between us, that was a revelation. In those quiet moments, I felt a sense of hope, an unspoken promise of a future where we could confront our demons together, not alone. I knew then that it was a journey we were committed to walking, hand in hand.

The air felt electric, full of things I wanted to say but couldn't. I could smell wood smoke and it stuck to my skin. Hours seemed to stretch on forever as I talked. My voice felt rough mixing with others to create a harsh but powerful sound. We weren't weaving a soft story; instead we were creating something sharp and fiery. Every word felt like a piece of broken glass showing the tough realities I had pulled from the mess of my life. These truths were filled with the sour taste of betrayal and the cold feeling of loss. I opened up completely sharing my deepest feelings and wounds. I showed how delicate my hopes and dreams are like frost that can easily break. My fears felt intense like hungry wolves trying to choke me. I felt my weaknesses exposed like raw skin and it sent a shiver of fear through me. The way in front of me wasn't a sunny field; it was a deep gap filled with sharp dangers hiding in the dark. I knew it was going to be tough and would really push me to my limits. In that intense situation I felt a strong and beautiful connection grow between us. We faced our challenges together and that made our bond both exciting and a little scary.

The hearth's inferno painted the sanctuary in a grotesque ballet of shadow and flame, licking at the ancient stones, mirroring the raw, untamed emotions that raged between us. The air thrummed, a taut membrane stretched to the breaking point, vibrating with unspoken accusations, desires as sharp as shards of glass, promises, whispered oaths, clinging to the smoke thick air like phantom kisses. This sanctuary, once a refuge, now a blasted battlefield, reeked of our past, the bitter tang of betrayal mingling with the intoxicating sweetness of forbidden longing. My heart, a caged beast, clawed at its ribs, mirroring the desperate, desperate hope blooming in the ashes of our shattered lives. His gaze, smouldering coal, burned through me, revealing the labyrinthine depths of his soul, a place of both exquisite beauty and terrifying darkness. The heat of his skin against mine, the taste of his fear and his fierce need, seared themselves into my memory, a brand that would never fade. This crucible forged not only love but a searing knowledge of what it truly cost us both.

The spectres of our past, their icy breath, a reeking miasma on our skin, clawed not just at our minds, but tore at the very fabric of our beings. Their fingers, skeletal and sharp as shards of obsidian, raked across the wounds carved deep into our souls, wounds that pulsed with a phantom agony, a burning, searing echo of betrayals long past. But the chilling whispers, once a symphony of self recrimination, now rasped faintly, their power broken. Fear, that venomous serpent, had not merely loosened its grip; it had been slain, it's cold coils flung from our hearts, leaving behind the faint, metallic tang of victory. Guilt, a festering wound that had festered for years, oozing bitterness and self loathing, was finally beginning to scab over, a fragile, painful crust forming over the chasm of our remorse.

We were seen. Not merely through the cursory glance of tolerance that had become so commonplace nor the pitying gaze that had haunted us for far too long but through a searing soul-deep recognition that cut through the facades we had built. Their eyes' dark pools of understanding were marred by shared shadows reflecting the tormented landscapes of our own minds and hearts. This moment transcended mere acceptance; it was a visceral embrace, an unyielding and brutal yet beautiful affirmation that pulsed with the raw ragged rhythm of a second heart violently beating alongside our own. It served as a testament to the brutal beauty of our shared scars, a reminder that we were not alone in our struggles. Together we created a symphony of survival played on the strings of fractured souls each note resonating with the pain and triumph of our journeys. In this fleeting yet profound connection the taste of freedom lingered on our tongues both bitter and sweet like absinthe awakening a longing for liberation that had been suppressed for far too long. It was a moment of awakening where our struggles intertwined and illuminated the path toward healing and understanding.

We were woven into the tapestry of our shared history, each thread a testament to the brutal beauty of our bond. Our love, forged in the crucible of darkness, shimmered with the heat of a thousand shared sunrises and endured through storms that threatened to shatter us. It was a love that tasted of ash and blood, yet bloomed with a fierce, untamed sweetness. The scent of it, a haunting blend of defiance and vulnerability, hung heavy in the air between us, a palpable echo of the sacrifices we'd made.

We were more than survivors; we were warriors, bearing the battle scars of our journey, each mark a testament to our resilience. We understood the labyrinthine depths of each other's hearts, the shadowed corners where doubt and despair still lingered. This understanding wasn't a fragile truce, but a hard won victory, a testament to our unwavering commitment, a love that defied all odds, a love that roared.

Our fingers, mangled and bleeding, locked in a desperate, bone jarring grip. Defiance, raw and ragged, was all that stood between us and the suffocating, fetid darkness that clawed at the edges of our sanity. Her breath, ragged and hot against my ear, whispered of a terror I mirrored in the icy clutch of my own heart. Our love, a searing brand, a molten core of defiance against the encroaching void, pulsed with the frantic rhythm of our shared dread. This wasn't merely arduous; it was a cataclysm brewing, a maelstrom of agony about to rip us asunder, a symphony of shattering bone and strangled cries that would echo through the desolate eternity closing in.

But we'd meet it together, wouldn't we? Our bond was forged not just in trauma, but in the crucible of a thousand shared nightmares, a twisted, unyielding chain of blood and grit. I felt the frantic hammering of her heart, a frantic drumbeat against the thunderous pulse of the approaching storm, a storm both external and internal, a tempest in our souls mirrored in the raging chaos outside. The metallic tang of blood filled my mouth, a bitter counterpoint to the cloying sweetness of her fear, a perfume clinging to the air like a shroud. Her skin, slick with sweat and the phantom touch of the darkness, burned against mine, a searing brand of life against the encroaching cold. Yet, even in this abyss, the scent of her, wild, desperate, incandescent, anchored me, tethering me to this ravaged, broken earth, to her, and to the furious, beautiful fight that lay before us.

This haven, our ravaged embrace, a fragile sanctuary carved from the very bones of our shattered past, pulsed with the ragged rhythm of our desperate hearts. The scent of salt and blood, the tang of our wounds, the metallic tang of defiance, clung to the air, a perverse perfume of our survival. Our love wasn't merely resilience; it was a primal scream against the encroaching void, a brutal, incandescent bloom pushing through the cracked earth of our destruction. It was a victory stained crimson, hard won in a battle fought not on some distant field, but within the echoing chambers of our own fractured souls.

We had peered into the abyss, into the jagged mirrors reflecting our flaws, the ruins of our former selves, and found not mere acceptance, but a searing, white hot understanding. A fusion forged in the crucible of our shared darkness, a terrifying, exquisite knowledge that burned like a brand. This brutal honesty, this naked truth, was our armour, a razor sharp strength that would cleave through the insidious whispers of our enemies, the relentless tide of those who would see us drown. It was a weapon, honed by pain, tempered in fire, and wielded with the cold fury of the damned.

My journey cut deep into my soul leaving a painful wound that hurt with every breath I took. I held tightly to my friend's hand and it was covered in blood. The bright red color reminded me of the fire that was right behind us. I feel this love burning inside me a bright flame that cuts through the heavy darkness around us. It hurts but it also gives me strength to stand up against everything that tries to hold us back. I could still hear the whispers of my past like poisonous snakes moving through the wreckage of my mistakes. Their cold breath smelled of decay and it made me shiver. I could barely hear their voices over the loud noise of our shared future. This future was shaped not only by love but also by the harsh smell of sweat, the sharp taste of blood and the strong feeling that even as everything fell apart around us we would still stand strong. We were two survivors marked by our struggles standing together in the ruins. The taste of iron in my mouth and hers reminded us of how strong we were. Her eyes filled with a mix of fear and strong love were the only guiding light I needed to get through this tough time. In her eyes I saw not only the pain we both felt but also the scary and exciting beauty of our brave fight against everything that was trying to bring us down.

CHAPTER

NINETEEN

The Price of Power

T he air crackled with a venomous hiss that echoed ominously in my ears a sound that seemed to resonate with the very fabric of reality itself. The static taste of ozone thickened on my tongue a metallic tang that heralded the storm brewing on the horizon. Sweat cold and slick plastered my shirt to my back, a constant clammy reminder of the oppressive heat of the moment. Tension enveloped me like a physical weight pressing down with an unrelenting force—a suffocating shroud woven from the threads of fear and the putrid reek of impending doom. The atmosphere was charged, electrified with the anticipation of something dark and terrible about to unfold.

Before me loomed the Covenant's citadel, a jagged obsidian monolith that towered above the landscape scraping the bruised bleeding twilight sky. It wasn't merely rising; it pulsed with a life of its own throbbing with a sinister energy that resonated deep within me. Each pulse of its malevolent force slammed into me like a visceral blow sending shockwaves through my body that echoed in my very bones and rattled the marrow of my soul. Standing before this dark edifice I felt small and insignificant dwarfed by its overwhelming presence. This was no mere fortress; it was something far more insidious. It was a cancerous growth, a festering wound upon the world's heart oozing corruption and the fetid stench of a thousand broken wills.

As I stared at the citadel I could almost hear the whispers of the countless souls it had devoured, each voice a haunting echo of despair.

They lingered in the air a chorus of lamentation that clawed at my resolve threatening to pull me down into the depths of hopelessness. The very ground beneath me seemed to pulse in rhythm with the citadel, a dark symphony of destruction that played out in the shadows. I could see the tendrils of darkness creeping outward snaking around the remnants of what once was—a vibrant world now dimmed by the encroaching darkness.

The citadel's architecture was a grotesque mockery of beauty; sharp angles and cruel silhouettes combined to create a structure that seemed to mock the light daring it to approach. Each shadow cast by its towering presence seemed alive writhing with a malevolent intelligence as if the very stone beneath my feet conspired against me. I could feel the weight of its gaze, a thousand unseen eyes boring into my very being, judging, measuring and calculating my worth as I stood there frozen in place.

In that moment I understood that this was more than just a battleground; it was the epicenter of a war that had raged for eons, a clash of wills that would determine the fate of everything I held dear. The air was thick with the promise of conflict and as I took a deep breath I steeled myself. Whatever horrors lay ahead I would face them; I had no other choice. The battle for the soul of the world was about to begin.

The stones themselves seemed to writhe, whispering promises of agony in a language older than time, a language my blood understood with chilling clarity. My hand, trembling despite my desperate attempt at control, tightened on the hilt of my blade; a blade I knew, with bone deep certainty, wouldn't be enough. But what choice did I have? To run was to invite a fate far worse than the obsidian hell that awaited.

The chill wind bit at my exposed skin, a stark counterpoint to the heat radiating from Caspian. Gone was his usual glacial detachment; in its place, a raw, volcanic fury simmered, visible in the blazing intensity of his eyes, twin embers reflecting the inferno consuming him. The scent of ozone and blood, faint but undeniable, clung to him, a grim perfume of impending violence. His movements weren't merely graceful; they were a terrifying ballet of controlled power, each muscle coiled like a viper ready to unleash its venom.

The whisper of his dark armour, a seamless sheath of obsidian swallowing the fading light, sent shivers down my spine. It wasn't just armour; it was a second skin, a carapace forged in the fires of a thousand battles, resonating with the weight of his unspoken rage. His hand, gnarled and powerful as a blacksmith's, trembled ever so slightly on the obsidian hilt, a tremor not of fear, but of barely contained, lethal energy. The blade itself, a shard of midnight, hummed with a silent, predatory song, promising a swift, agonizing end. I saw not a man, but a storm given form, a terrifying embodiment of vengeance poised to unleash itself upon the world.

The tremor wasn't apprehension; it was a gut wrenching, primal scream, a beast of terror clawing its way up from the pit of my stomach, choking me with the acrid taste of ash and bile, the metallic tang of blood already blooming on my tongue. But steel, colder than a winter's grave, colder than the dead eyes staring up from the battlefield, solidified my spine. Death? I stared into its abyss, wrestled it bare handed, felt its icy fingers not just around my heart, but squeezing the very breath from my lungs, the bitter, coppery reek of my own defeat, a burning brand on my soul. I'd risen from that charnel house, a grotesque parody of resurrection, each scar a testament to battles fought, a map etched onto my flesh in agony and blood. Reborn, yes, but forged in the crucible of hellfire, my spirit was not merely a weapon, but a volcanic eruption of rage and grief, tempered in the infernal fires of loss, sharper than any blade, more relentless than any storm.

This hunger... it wasn't a mere gnawing. It was a feast of shadows, a ravenous beast clawing at the insides of my skull, its teeth a chorus of agonizing whispers behind my eyes. My temples throbbed, a brutal percussion against the iron clang of decay that permanently coated my tongue, and choked my nostrils, a miasma of rot clinging to the very fabric of my being. Caspian's blood, oh, that devil's bargain, that crimson lie, offered only a fleeting, mocking respite, a thin, brittle ice sheet against the volcanic eruption of my cursed nature. The taste, metallic and fleetingly sweet, was a cruel reminder of the abyss waiting to swallow me whole.

The debt... It wasn't just a weight. It was a noose tightening around my throat, each second a rasping breath, each tick of the damned clock a hammer blow shattering the fragile remnants of my soul. The guillotine loomed, not a physical threat, but the chilling certainty of my fate, a slow, agonizing descent into the monstrous reality I'd embraced. And Caspian? He wasn't just a source of blood; he was a shard of my own damnation, his eyes holding a knowing glint of my inevitable fall, a silent accomplice in my slow self destruction. The price of his lifeblood? My humanity, draining away drop by agonizing drop, leaving behind only the insatiable hunger, the chilling void.

My fingers, calloused and scarred, tightened around the worn leather straps, each groove a familiar comfort. The runes on my armour pulsed with searing heat, a tangible hum against my skin, a living magic that throbbed in time with my own frantic heart. Grandmother's amulet, a cold, heavy weight against my chest, radiated a surprisingly warm pulse, a ghostly echo of her love, a pathetically small solace against the encroaching darkness. The odds? They were a monstrous, snarling beast, and tonight, I faced it alone.

Hellfire detonated. Not a battle, but a cosmic laceration, tearing existence asunder with a shriek that clawed at the soul. The air, thick with the metallic tang of blood, my blood, slick and hot on my lips, choked with the sulfurous stench of oblivion. It vibrated, a skull splitting cacophony of screaming steel, a symphony of agony conducted by a death god himself. Each clang, a hammer blows against my sanity; each groan of the dying, a dirge for a world already lost. The ground bucked and heaved beneath a tempest of unimaginable power; fire, the incandescent vomit of some hellish god, rained down, each blast a gaping maw swallowing men, their screams extinguished in a heartbeat. I tasted ash and felt the heat sear my skin even through the scorched plates of my armour. This wasn't merely fighting; it was drowning in a sea of fire and fury, the screams of the damned my only companions. The faces of the fallen, contorted in silent agony, haunted the edges of my vision. Their fear, their pain, it became mine, weaving itself into the tapestry of my hatred, fueling the burning rage that pulsed in my veins, driving me onward into the heart of the infernal maelstrom. I would not fall. Not here. Not now. Not until every last one of these demons felt the sting of my blade.

From the obsidian maw of the citadel, they poured Covenant demons, abominations sculpted from nightmare and fueled by pure malice. Their eyes, twin embers in the gloom, burned with a hatred that chilled the soul to its core. These weren't just soldiers; they were twisted parodies of life itself, each scarred and mutated body a testament to the horrors they had endured, and inflicted. Their weapons, dripping with ichor and whispering with malevolent energy, felt alive in their hands, extensions of their depraved will. They moved with a terrifying, unnatural speed; a grotesque ballet of slaughter. Their numbers were a suffocating tide, a relentless, unstoppable wave of darkness. Against this horror, the Whispering Wind warriors stood defiant.

Their faces, grim and set with the weight of countless battles, were etched with fierce, unwavering loyalty. Their blades, honed to razor sharpness, danced in a whirlwind of controlled fury, a breathtaking spectacle of precision and lethality. Each strike was a testament to decades spent honing their skills, each parry a testament to the unbreakable bond that held them together. Their magic, unleashed with agonizing precision, tore through the demonic ranks like a vengeful storm, carving pathways of destruction through the relentless tide. But even their skill, their discipline, and their unwavering brotherhood felt like a thin shield against an ocean of unending darkness. Despair, cold and sharp, gnawed at their resolve, a venomous serpent coiled around their hearts. Victory felt less like a possibility, and more like a desperate prayer whispered into the teeth of a storm.

I was a hurricane of fire, a maelstrom of searing agony unleashed. My movements, fluid as molten gold, were a death knell whispered in the wind. Each strike, a precise, agonizing symphony of destruction, each burst of flame a branding iron kiss of oblivion. The acrid stench of burning flesh choked me, mingling with the coppery tang of blood blooming across the ravaged earth. My elemental fury, a volcanic eruption fueled by the molten core of my rage, grief, and the insatiable hunger for vengeance, roared within me.

My blade, a crimson stained whisper in the infernal din, danced a macabre ballet of destruction. I carved a path through the writhing, demonic horde, leaving behind a pyre of smouldering corpses, their screams a fading echo swallowed by the inferno. A grim, savage satisfaction, a bitter taste of fleeting triumph, coated my tongue as I watched them fall, each a minuscule victory in a war that threatened to consume my very soul. But they surged forward, an endless tide of writhing shadows, their numbers a mockery of my desperate struggle.

The ground, slick and unforgiving beneath my boots, squelched with each step, a gruesome testament to the carnage. The air, thick and heavy, vibrated with the guttural roars of the demons and the agonizing rasps of the dying, a symphony of suffering that clawed at the edges of my sanity. Then came the sickening thud. The earth trembled as Kael, my brother in arms, his face a mask of stunned betrayal, crumpled to the earth. His eyes, wide and accusing, mirrored my despair, a reflection of my failing strength, a harbinger of the bleak future that awaited.

The cold dread that gripped my heart was far colder than any inferno, a chilling premonition of the coming defeat that loomed over me like a storm cloud. Each fleeting moment brought with it a sense of impending doom tightening its grip around my soul. My vengeance felt like ashes in my mouth leaving only bitterness and a gnawing emptiness that consumed me from within. The war raged on relentlessly, each clash echoing the futility of our struggle. I knew with a sickening certainty that I was not merely fighting for survival but for the agonizing privilege of succumbing to the endless darkness that awaited us all. Hope had become a distant memory overshadowed by the despair that enveloped me leaving me to grapple with the haunting reality of inevitable defeat.

Caspian, a whirlwind of obsidian steel and shadow slicked fury, fought at my side. The stench of brimstone and scorched flesh clung to the air, thick and acrid, a counterpoint to the metallic tang of blood blooming across the ravaged battlefield. His movements weren't merely graceful; they were a predatory dance, each fluid motion a whisper of death before the brutal reality struck. Every strike, a calculated, precise rending, echoed with the sickening thunk of bone meeting steel. His eyes, burning with the cold fire of a thousand dying stars, held the chilling weight of ages, of countless battles fought and won in the shadowed corners of the world. His blade, a whisper of obsidian, sang a death song, a high, keening wail that sliced through the demonic screams and the thunder of clashing steel. He cleaved demons, their ichor spraying like a black fountain, his movements a terrifying ballet of slaughter.

He moved with the grace of a predator, the precision of a torturer, the merciless efficiency of a vengeful god. The relentless onslaught of hellish creatures washed over him, yet he remained unyielding, an obsidian monolith amidst the crimson tide, a dark god carved from vengeance itself, each heartbeat a drumbeat of ancient sorrow and unquenchable wrath. The very air crackled with the raw power he exuded, a palpable force that both terrified and enthralled. He wasn't merely fighting; he was consuming the darkness, feeding on the despair, his very being a weapon honed to the point of terrifying perfection.

The stench of Sulfur and burnt flesh choked me. Even our combined fury, a maelstrom of steel and desperate prayers, was swallowed by the Covenant tide. They were a legion of nightmares, their obsidian blades glinting under a sky choked with the ash of our failing defences. The despair wasn't a sting; it was a molten brand seared onto my soul, a crushing weight that threatened to shatter my very bones. Caspian, his face a mask of grim determination etched with the sweat of a thousand battles, stumbled. I saw the crimson bloom on his shoulder, the demon's blade a whisper of death that ripped through his armour like tissue paper. His groan was a guttural rasp, a testament to his defiance, to the iron will that refused to yield even as the world crumbled around us. The odds weren't merely overwhelming; they were a monstrous, suffocating presence, a tide of unholy power poised to drown the last embers of our hope, to extinguish the flickering flame of our rebellion in a torrent of demonic blood and fire. The taste of fear mingled with the metallic tang of blood, my own, I realized, as a searing pain lanced through my arm. We were broken, yet we fought on, driven by something beyond simple courage, something primal and desperate, something that echoed in the abyss of our hearts.

Then, the world fractured. A raw, electric jolt, adrenaline, a feral scream of shared purpose, a love so fierce it tasted like blood, ripped through us. Our hands, calloused and trembling, met in a collision of bone and sinew, a fleeting spark igniting in the storm's greasy, Sulfurous breath. In that instant, comprehension wasn't a gentle dawning, it was a brutal, gut wrenching revelation. To fight alone? A pathetic joke whispered on the wind, swallowed by the roaring, incandescent fury of the oncoming tide. No. We had to meld, our very essences intertwining, forging a unity so complete, so terrifyingly potent, it would shatter the foundations of this cursed reality itself.

A shared look, a silent pact forged in the crucible of hate and desperate hope. Then, unleashed. My flames weren't just fire; they were the screaming agony of a thousand dying suns, a searing, crimson tide that engulfed the demons with a roar that ripped through the very fabric of reality. Caspian's shadow magic wasn't mere darkness; it was a tangible, choking entity, a suffocating void that twisted and writhed, binding those vile creatures with icy tendrils, crushing their bones to dust, snuffing out their unholy, Sulfurous breath with a sickening crunch. The earth groaned beneath us, not a tremble, but a convulsive shudder, each heartbeat of the planet echoing the fury of our assault. The air itself shrieked a maelstrom of heat and shadow, thick with the stench of burning flesh and the acrid tang of fear. It wasn't a display, it was a cataclysm. A breathtaking, terrifying symphony of annihilation. The ground, once stone, was now glass, molten and smoking. The citadel, a monument to centuries of evil, groaned, its ancient stones weeping tears of fire under the weight of our combined, unyielding rage. We were a storm, twin forces of wrath, leaving behind only ash and the echoing silence of our victory.

The earth shuddered beneath a maelstrom of screaming agony as demons, legions upon legions crashed down in a rain of fire and corrupted flesh. The air, thick with the coppery tang of blood and ozone, crackled with unbearable energy, a white hot searing that seared the retinas and vibrated in the marrow of my bones. Above, the sky was a canvas of apocalyptic art; violet lightning stabbed through swirling black clouds, illuminating their grotesque forms in a horrifying, flickering strobe. Their screams, a symphony of despair and rage, clawed at the edges of sanity.

For a heart stopping instant, the tide of hell hesitated. Not from fear, exactly, these creatures knew only insatiable hunger, but from the sheer, overwhelming force of our defiance. Their advance stumbled, their ragged ranks momentarily fractured by the raw, untamed power we unleashed, a power born not just from shared trauma, but from the incandescent rage that burned in our hearts, a defiant love forged in the crucible of unimaginable loss. The stench of brimstone fought with the metallic sweetness of our combined magic, a brutal, breathtaking ballet of destruction where every strike was a testament to the sacrifices we made, the horrors we endured, and the unyielding fire of our souls. We were not merely fighting; we were exorcising the very darkness that sought to consume us.

The final confrontation wasn't a duel; it was a maelstrom. This isn't how it was supposed to end. A clean, swift victory. Not this... this chaos. Not a single, clean break, but a brutal, grinding war waged inch by bloody inch across the slick, obsidian floor. My breath hitches, ragged and shallow. I can barely see through the blood. Focus. Just focus. The air, thick with the coppery tang of blood and the acrid bite of ozone from our crackling powers, clawed at our throats. My lungs burn. Is this... is this it? Am I really going to die here? My vision blurred, not just from the sweat stinging my eyes, but from the kaleidoscope of pain blossoming behind my eyelids. No. Not yet. There's still something left. Something... I have to find it. What was it? The plan? Damn it, concentrate! Each blow, each parry, is a gamble. I'm throwing everything I have into each moment and praying to whatever god exists that it's enough. Enough to survive. Enough to... win?

He, he, was a monster sculpted from shadow and spite, his eyes burning with a cold, unholy fire that mirrored the rage twisting my gut. This wasn't just desperation; it was the raw, primal scream of a soul pushed to the absolute brink. Each strike echoed in my bones, the sickening thud of flesh against flesh, the searing crack of bone, the rasping hiss of his blade slicing through my defences. His movements were a grotesque parody of grace, each blow imbued with the weight of centuries of malice, each parry a desperate gamble against oblivion. We danced on the precipice of death, our entwined fates a macabre waltz conducted by the very demons that sought to claim us. The taste of blood, my blood, his blood, was metallic and bitter on my tongue, a grim testament to our relentless struggle.

This wasn't merely about survival; it was about the incandescent blaze of our defiance, a desperate, ferocious love burning brighter than any star. It was the agonizing echo of our stolen years, of the promises whispered in the dead of night, now stained crimson on the cold, unforgiving stone. We fought for the ghost of a future, for the echo of laughter that might never be again, for the fragile, precious flame of a love that dared to defy the very darkness that consumed us. And in that hellish ballet of blood and fury, we found a terrible, beautiful truth: we would not surrender.

The last demon's skull shattered, the silence that followed a crushing weight, a physical thing pressing down on our chests. The air, thick with the coppery tang of blood and the acrid bite of sulfur, vibrated with the unspoken horror of what we'd wrought. The citadel, a skeletal ruin against the bruised twilight sky, groaned under its own wounds; each jagged scar a testament to the infernal fury we'd endured.

Our boots crunched on the frozen ground, a morbid percussion against the symphony of death surrounding us. A grim harvest of twisted limbs and charred flesh lay scattered, a testament to our pyrrhic victory. My own body screamed in protest, each muscle a knot of agony. Caspian, beside me, leaned heavily on my arm, his breath coming in ragged gasps. We were broken, yet our eyes held the unwavering fire of defiance, a defiant spark against the encroaching darkness.

Our love, a twisted, battle hardened vine, had been our shield, our sword, our unwavering north star through the maelstrom. But was it really a north star, or just a stubborn weed clinging to the wreckage? But victory tasted like ash and blood on my tongue. Ash and blood…that's all we're left with? Is this…is this all it was worth? The cost had been exorbitant. I could still feel the phantom burn of the demon's fire across my flesh, the searing pain a constant, pulsing reminder. It's like a brand, a mark of this…this brutal triumph. The wounds, both physical and spiritual, gaped like festering wounds, mirroring the cracks spreading through my soul. Cracks? They're chasms. I'm falling apart. And is he… is he okay? Survival had been purchased with a currency far too dear. Too dear…what did we lose? What part of ourselves did we sacrifice on the altar of victory? And was it even a victory at all?

The path ahead, shrouded in the lingering stench of carnage, felt impossibly long and treacherous. The battle's echoes, the screams, the desperate pleas, the chilling crackle of magic, would haunt our dreams forever. But I clutched Caspian's hand, the rough texture a comfort against the gnawing terror. Our love, bruised but unyielding, was the only promise worth clinging to. We had paid the price of power, etched in the agony of our bodies and the haunting memories of this night. We faced the uncertain future, our hearts heavy, our resolve tempered in the crucible of war, our love a burning ember against the coming cold.

The obsidian citadel, once a monolith of untouchable might, now gaped like a skull, its shattered teeth of black stone scattered across the carnage strewn ground. The air, thick with the coppery tang of blood and the acrid bite of ozone, clawed at my throat, each rasping breath a searing reminder of the battle's obscene violence. Burnt flesh, a grotesque tapestry woven across the ravaged landscape, sent waves of nausea through me. The stench, God, the stench, clung to the very marrow of my bones, a vile perfume of death.

My body, a ruin mirroring the citadel itself, screamed its protest in a symphony of agony. Every muscle throbbed, a brutal counterpoint to the tremors that still shook the shattered earth beneath my feet. I leaned against a splintered pillar, its jagged edges biting into my already ravaged flesh. Fire licked skin, a testament to the infernal heat of the conflict, pulsed with a dull, throbbing ache. Crimson rivers traced trails down my arms, mingling with the dust and ash that coated me like a shroud. The pain, raw and visceral, was a dull roar in my ears, a constant companion to the echoing silence of the battlefield.

The vampiric hunger, that gnawing, ever present beast within, was subdued, but its shadow stretched long and dark across my awareness. A fragile armistice, purchased with the near exhaustion of my very essence. This victory felt hollow, a pyrrhic triumph etched in the agony of my ravaged form. Each heartbeat hammered a grim reminder: survival was a privilege, not a right, and the price had been steep. The lingering taste of ash and blood on my tongue was a bitter testament to that cost. I tasted defeat, yes, but even more so, I tasted survival, and it was far more complicated than victory.

The chaos hadn't touched Caspian, not truly. Or so it seemed. The reek of iron, sharp and acrid, clung to the air around him, a testament to the unseen carnage. A crimson river, thick and sluggish, snaked across his shoulder, a jagged maw tearing through the polished obsidian of his armour. The cold metal bit into his flesh, a chilling contrast to the fiery agony that pulsed beneath. His breath, a ragged, guttural rasp, hitched in his throat, each inhale a searing brand on his lungs. The obsidian blade, still clenched in his hand, felt slick with his dark blood, the weight of it a leaden anchor against his failing strength. A tremor, barely perceptible, ran through his hand, a betrayal whispered only to the watching shadows. His eyes, though, remained pools of glacial fire, reflecting a storm of pain, fury, and a chilling resolve. They burned with the cold light of a dying star, defiant even in the face of oblivion. The intensity in their depths was not merely a testament to his spirit, it was his spirit, unconquerable, unyielding, a terrifying promise of vengeance etched in the obsidian darkness.

The silence clawed at us, a suffocating blanket woven from ash and the stench of brimstone. It pressed down, a physical weight on my chest, broken only by the rasping crackle of the dying pyre, a funeral pyre for demons, yes, but also a chilling echo of the fires that had consumed so much of us. Each groan from the writhing, dying things, a symphony of agony that scraped against the raw edges of my soul, felt like a personal affront, a reminder of the cost. My tongue felt thick and useless, and my throat choked by the dust and the memories. The taste of blood, metallic and bitter, lingered on my lips, a phantom echo of the carnage.

This victory... this hollow, echoing triumph. It tasted like ash. The vastness of the battlefield, now shrouded in an unnatural twilight, pressed in on me, a tangible darkness that amplified the weariness gnawing at my bones. Each breath was labour, each heartbeat a drumbeat of exhaustion and grief. We stood amidst the wreckage of our souls, our shared trauma a festering wound, each scar a testament to losses too numerous to bear. The weight of it, the crushing weight of what we'd endured, of those we'd lost, threatened to collapse us under its unbearable burden. A hard won victory, yes, but purchased at a price that felt infinitely higher than any glory we had earned. This wasn't triumph; it was a grim, silent vigil over the graves we'd dug.

The inferno's dying embers painted Caspian in hues of blood orange and sinister black. Smoke, thick and acrid, clung to his silhouette, tasting of ash and the metallic tang of spilled blood on my tongue. His eyes, usually glacial pools reflecting a distant, uncaring sky, were now burning coals, raw, exposed nerve endings blazing with a vulnerability that both mesmerized and terrified me. It wasn't just pain etched on his face; it was carved, a brutal masterpiece of agony sculpted by fire and steel. His shoulders slumped, the weight of the world crushing him, the exhaustion radiating off him in waves of palpable heat. But even in that broken state, a flicker of obsidian defiance, a grim, feral determination, clung to his gaze, a smouldering ember refusing to be extinguished.

In that heart stopping moment, the carefully constructed masks shattered. Gone was the enigmatic demon who had haunted my dreams, the aloof warrior who commanded armies with a flick of his wrist, the seductive master whose touch could ignite fires within. What remained was a man, broken, bleeding, haunted. The weight of his battles, visible in the tremor of his hand, in the haunted depth of his eyes, felt like a physical pressure against my chest. His losses weren't just abstract casualties; they were etched into the very fabric of his being, a tapestry woven with sorrow and regret, each thread a searing reminder of a life irrevocably changed. The man before me was a ruin, magnificent in its desolation, a testament to a spirit both fiercely defiant and agonizingly broken.

My boots crunched on the shattered bone and grit, each step a measured agony mirroring the slow, agonizing crawl of my fear. The coppery tang of blood, thick and cloying, filled my nostrils, a scent that clung to the ravaged air like a shroud. As I drew nearer, the flickering torchlight revealed the true horror, a crimson river tracing a brutal path across his shoulder, the dark stain blooming across the once proud mail like a malevolent flower. His armour, usually gleaming, was dull with the sheen of death, the metal itself seeming to weep rust. A shudder, primal and visceral, ripped through me, a physical echo of the unseen wounds that scored his soul.

My fingers, clumsy and trembling, dared to touch his skin, the rough texture of his tunic beneath, the chilling dampness of his sweat mingling with the sticky, viscous film of his blood. He didn't flinch; he didn't even breathe. Instead, his weight settled into my touch, a heavy, yielding sign of a man broken yet unbroken, a silent testament to the horrors we'd both endured and the terrible victory we'd somehow, against all odds, wrenched from the jaws of oblivion. The silence between us pulsed, a symphony of shared trauma and the unspoken understanding that bound two shattered souls together.

His eyes, the colour of glacial meltwater, locked onto mine, a silent scream passing between us, colder than the arctic wind. The air crackled, thick with the metallic tang of blood, a phantom echo of the carnage we'd both witnessed. It wasn't just shared pain; it was the raw, festering wound of betrayal, of loss that clawed at our souls, a symphony of unspoken horrors played on the strings of our hearts. His gaze burned, a searing brand of understanding, born not merely in the crucible of battle but forged in the white hot inferno of our hells, each a landscape of shattered trust and brutalized innocence. Our dependency wasn't just mutual; it was a desperate, clinging vine wrapped around a crumbling precipice, fueled by a desperate, forbidden desire that tasted of ashes and bitter regret, a longing born from the shared abyss we'd both stared into and the chilling certainty that only we could truly understand the darkness within each other.

"We won," he rasped, the sound of a guttural growl that vibrated from his chest, a tremor barely louder than the dying embers' hiss. Cinders, like fallen stars, dusted his calloused fingers, mirroring the ash settling on his soul. His eyes, twin pools of shadowed granite, burned with a fierce, unsettling light; a raw, primal triumph warred with the ghost of agony etched deep into their depths. The scent of wood smoke and something else, the metallic tang of blood, perhaps, still clinging to the air, clawed at my throat. This victory, purchased with the marrow of our bones and the very breath in our lungs, felt less like a celebration and more like a chilling, hollow echo in the desolate aftermath. He knew it. I knew it. The unspoken understanding hung heavy, a suffocating weight woven from shared trauma and the bitter knowledge that what we'd gained came at a price too terrible to ever truly repay.

My head bobbed, a strangled gasp catching in my throat, the muscles seizing like a viper's coil. The words—a poisoned dart I couldn't release—clawed at my windpipe, a brutal, silent scream. This victory, forged in the crucible of blood and bone, tasted like ash. The pyrrhic triumph felt cheap, a grotesque mockery against the panorama of carnage. The stench of death clung to me, a suffocating shroud woven from the reek of burnt flesh and pulverized earth. The cost? Not merely immense, but a gaping wound torn through the very fabric of my soul. I had sacrificed everything; my innocence, my comrades, my hope. The ground trembled beneath me, still vibrating with the phantom thunder of explosions. The screams of the dying—a symphony of agony—haunted my ears, a relentless chorus drowning out the faint whisper of relief. I saw their faces in the flickering shadows—each a testament to a life stolen, a future erased, a debt I could never repay. The weight of it, the crushing weight of their sacrifice, threatened to break me. This wasn't a victory. This was a graveyard.

We stood there, ages bleeding into each other, the reek of blood and burnt metal thick in the air, a cloying sweetness that coated my tongue. The silence screamed a deafening roar punctuated only by the ragged rasp of our breaths, each inhaling a burning brand in my chest. Our shared wounds, the raw, gaping holes in flesh and spirit, pulsed with a silent understanding that transcended words. Victory? It clung to us like a shroud, a suffocating weight woven from the threads of our losses, a burden that pressed down, heavy as the shattered stones beneath our boots. Caspian's stoicism, that impenetrable mask he usually wore, a shield forged in years of brutal battles, finally cracked. A low, guttural moan escaped him, a sound of pure, agonizing pain that scraped against the raw edges of my torment. The metallic tang of his blood, staining the cracked earth, mirrored the bitter taste of despair in my mouth. His wince was a betrayal, a glimpse into the fathomless depths of his suffering, a vulnerability that both terrified and strangely connected us in this wasteland of our making.

The icy fingers of the night clawed deeper, a brutal wind slicing through me, sharper than any blade. The embers, dying whispers of a pyrrhic victory, cast grotesque, skeletal shadows that danced with macabre glee. This wasn't triumph; it was a hollow echo in the cavern of my chest, a bitter taste of ash and regret coating my tongue. The losses... God, the losses. Each fallen comrade has a searing brand on my soul.

The air throbbed, a sickening hum that resonated in my bones, a symphony of raw arcane power, still buzzing with the fury of the conflict. It tasted of ozone and blood, a metallic tang clinging to the back of my throat. The ground beneath my boots, still slick with the residue of unimaginable violence, radiated a chilling coldness, a stark contrast to the searing heat that had consumed it only hours ago. The dawn, a cruel mockery of hope, crept in, painting the ravaged landscape in the ghastly hues of a butchered sunrise. My heart, a leaden weight, mirrored the stillness of this killing ground, a battlefield steeped in the silence of death and the bitter knowledge that we had paid too high a price. The victory felt like defeat.

As the first rays of dawn pierced through the smoke filled sky, casting a pale light upon the ruined citadel, we began to tend to our wounds. My hands, though trembling with exhaustion, moved with practiced skill as I cleaned and bandaged Caspian's shoulder, my touch lingering a moment longer than necessary, a feather light brush against his skin that sent a shiver through him—and me. The silence that surrounded us thrummed with unspoken desires, punctuated only by the soft sounds of our actions, the rustling of cloth, the low murmurs of pain barely concealing a ragged breath, the quiet determination to survive interwoven with a raw, burgeoning need. His gaze, dark and intense, met mine over the bandage, a silent conversation passing between us that spoke of more than survival. It was a fragile peace, hard won and tenuous, born of mutual respect and a shared understanding of our connection—a connection that pulsed with a dangerous, unspoken heat. The air crackled with it, a tangible energy that promised something far more potent than survival.

The healing process, both physical and emotional, would be long and arduous. But we faced it together, our bodies pressed close, the phantom aches of our wounds a shared testament to our strength. Each shared breath, each silent understanding, sparked a heat that lingered long after the physical contact ended. The price of power, we knew, extended far beyond the battlefield, into the depths of our souls, a profound and enduring reminder of the sacrifices made, and the intoxicating intimacy forged in the crucible of shared trauma. The battle was won, but the war, both against the Covenant and within ourselves, a war fought in stolen glances and lingering touches, was far from over. The scars we carried, both visible and invisible, mapped a landscape of shared vulnerability, a constant reminder of the price we had paid, and the exquisite pleasure in finding solace in each other's arms. But hand in hand, fingers intertwined, our bodies humming with unspoken desires, we would face the uncertain future, our love a defiant bonfire burning bright against the ever present darkness, promising a warmth that reached far beyond the surface.

CHAPTER

TWENTY

A Shard of Darkness

blood orange sun, a malevolent eye in a bruised, grey sky, clawed its way over the horizon, staining the ravaged earth with the crimson residue of our pyrrhic triumph. The air, thick and acrid, choked me with the stench of burnt metal and something far worse, the metallic tang of death itself, a scent that clung to my throat like a shroud. The Obsidian Covenant was broken, splintered like a shattered mirror reflecting a thousand agonies, yet the hollow victory tasted like ash in my mouth. This wasn't triumph; it was a butchered peace, bought with a currency far exceeding the body count. The simple tally of fallen soldiers placed beside the deeper losses, losses that gnawed at the edges of my soul.

Caspian and I stood amidst the wreckage, the silence between us a suffocating thing, heavier than the leaden exhaustion dragging at my limbs. His gaze, usually sharp as a flint, was dulled, haunted by shadows that mirrored my own. The weight of our grief pressed down, a physical burden, but beneath it simmered something else, a chilling certainty that we had unleashed something far more terrifying than the Obsidian Covenant, a monstrous consequence that stalked us in the ruins of our hard won battle. His jaw was clenched tight enough to shatter stone, and I saw, in the stark light of the dawn, the flicker of a fear far deeper, a fear that whispered of a darkness beyond the pyre, a darkness we had ignited.

My fingers, slick with his dark, viscous blood, blood that refused to clot, a midnight tide staining the bandages, pressed against the ragged edges of Caspian's wounds. They throbbed, not with the simple pain of flesh torn, but with malevolent energy, a pulsating darkness that resonated deep in my bones, a discordant hum that vibrated against my very teeth. The obsidian of his armour, usually a mirror to his cold, unwavering gaze, now seemed to breathe, each faint throb a whispered promise of something terrible. He'd scoffed at it initially, which cursed him, blaming battle magic, but the metallic tang of fear clung to his breath now, a stark contrast to the usual iron will that dominated him. The ache, a deep, visceral throbbing in his very marrow, was no mere discomfort; it was a gnawing beast consuming him from the inside.

The scent of ozone, sharp and acrid, clung to the air, mingling with the coppery reek of blood. His usually glacial gaze was clouded, haunted by something ancient and profoundly unsettling. The iron in his demeanour was fractured, replaced by a terrifying vulnerability that chilled me to the core. This wasn't just a physical weakening; it was a shattering of his very essence. The raw power that once crackled around him, the storm he wielded so effortlessly, was now a flickering ember, choked by an unseen force, a vital link to his strength severed, leaving him adrift in a sea of agonizing weakness. His breaths came ragged, shallow, each one a desperate gasp against the encroaching darkness. He was a king brought low, his majesty stained crimson, his very soul under siege.

The battle's stench, a coppery tang clinging to my ravaged clothes, mirrored the taste of blood, Caspian's blood, a fleeting balm against the ravenous hunger that clawed at my gut. It wasn't a simple thirst; it was a gnawing, consuming fire that threatened to incinerate my very being. The physical wounds, raw and weeping, were mere scratches compared to the abyss that opened within me. A weariness, black and suffocating, settled in my bones, a leaden weight crushing my spirit. It wasn't just fatigue; it was the crushing weight of a thousand souls, their screams echoing in the hollow chambers of my heart.

I saw their faces, friends, twisted and broken beneath the brutal weight of steel; enemies, their eyes mirroring the same terror that had gripped me. Their anguished breaths, still audible in my memory, choked the air around me, leaving me gasping for something that no longer existed: peace. The feral joy of battle, the blood soaked dance of death that once thrilled me, now tasted like ash and bile on my tongue. The metallic tang of blood, my own and others clung to my hands like a curse, a constant, sickening reminder of my savagery. This victory... this pyrrhic triumph... it was a poisoned chalice, a bitter mockery, leaving behind only the cloying sweetness of despair and the gnawing guilt of a thousand broken lives. The price had been far too steep. And I, a monster forged in the crucible of war, felt the chilling, desolate emptiness of a soul left for dead on a battlefield of my own making.

The destruction wasn't limited to the battlefield. The arcane energies unleashed during the confrontation had rippled outwards, disrupting the delicate balance of the land. The very earth seemed to groan under the strain, tremors shaking the ground at unpredictable intervals. Strange, unnatural flora began to sprout in the aftermath of the battle, twisted, thorny vines laced with an unnatural luminescence, their leaves dripping with a viscous, black sap. The air itself felt thick with malevolent energy, a chilling reminder of the power they had unleashed and the potential for unforeseen consequences.

Blood red sun bled across a sky the colour of a bruise, its dying light stretching the corpses into grotesque, clawing shadows across the churned earth. The wind, a razor edged banshee, tore across the battlefield, not whistling, but snarling, a guttural symphony of death that clawed at Caspian's ears and rattled the teeth in his skull. It carried the stench of decay, thick and cloying, mingling with the coppery tang of blood still warm on the ground. These weren't whispers; they were the rasping breaths of something ancient, something malevolent, a chorus of hate that vibrated in his very marrow.

Caspian, his scarred face a roadmap of past battles, felt the hairs on his neck stand on end. It wasn't a prickling; it was a full body convulsion, a primal scream trapped beneath his skin. The premonition wasn't a shiver; it was a seismic tremor, ripping through his soul. He tasted ash and fear, the metallic tang of dread coating his tongue. The air itself throbbed, a tangible malignancy pressing down, heavy as a tombstone, suffocating. He could feel the unseen energies, malevolent currents writhing in the darkness, a palpable tide of annihilation threatening to drag them under. This wasn't just danger; this was the final, agonizing breath of a dying world.

That night, under the watchful gaze of a blood red moon, a new horror emerged. I watched, frozen with fear, as the fallen demons, instead of dissolving into dust as they should have, began to writhe and contort. Their bodies, mangled and broken, reformed before my eyes, their flesh knitting itself together with an unnatural speed that made my stomach churn. Their eyes, once extinguished, ignited with an infernal glow, burning with a hateful intensity that seemed to bore into my soul. I felt a cold dread seep into my bones as they rose, not as the defeated, but as something far more terrifying, grotesque parodies of their former selves, animated by a dark, malevolent energy I could almost feel radiating from them. The battlefield, once silent save for the occasional groan of the dying, erupted in a chorus of unholy shrieks and guttural roars that tore through the night, a sound that will forever haunt my nightmares. My heart hammered against my ribs, a frantic drumbeat against the rising tide of terror.

The stench of brimstone and decaying flesh clawed at my throat as Caspian and I met them, not merely foes, but abominations, far exceeding the Obsidian Covenant's vile legions. These weren't resurrected demons; they were twisted beyond resurrection, their forms bloated and glistening with an unnatural ichor that pulsed with chaotic energy, the very essence of the ravaged land made flesh. The air crackled with it, a palpable horror that signed the skin and chilled the soul.

Their strength was a physical violation, a brutal, unrelenting tide of muscle and bone augmented beyond mortal limits. Each blow landed with the sickening thud of a collapsing building, each roared a guttural scream that tore through the night, a symphony of hate that echoed the desolate screams of the damned. Caspian, his face a mask of grim determination etched with the weariness of countless battles, fought with the desperation of a cornered wolf, his blade a blur against the demonic onslaught. The crimson moon, a malevolent eye in the bruised, blood red sky, cast long, dancing shadows that mocked our desperate struggle. Fear, cold and sharp as shattered glass, pierced the haze of adrenaline, a chilling whisper against the cacophony of battle. This wasn't just a fight for survival; it was a desperate, agonizing clawing against oblivion, against a malevolence so profound, so ancient, it defied comprehension. We were drowning in a sea of hate, and the waves threatened to consume us whole.

Agony clawed at Caspian, each ragged breath a searing brand across his ravaged lungs. The stench of ozone and decay, the reek of his corrupted blood, filled his nostrils, a bitter counterpoint to the metallic tang of his obsidian blade, now leaden in his trembling hand. It had sung a song of death a thousand times, but tonight, the song was choked, a dying whisper against the howling crescendo of the demonic energy. This wasn't mere exhaustion; it was a ravenous hunger, gnawing at his very soul, a malevolent tide pulling him under. The dark energy pulsed, a throbbing second heart beneath his ribs, its rhythm a brutal tattoo against his shattered bones. Each pulse was a fresh wave of searing fire, not just pain, but a sickening knowing, a horrifying intimacy with the encroaching darkness. He tasted ash and despair; his vision swam with the ghastly green luminescence that writhed around him, a mocking parody of the power he once commanded, a power now leaking away like sand through his fractured fingers. He was a king betrayed, his dominion crumbling not just around him, but within, leaving behind only the cold terror of annihilation.

The hunger clawed at me, a ravenous beast gnawing at my insides, its icy breath mingling with the scalding fury that roared in my veins. Each pulse hammered a primal rhythm against my skull, a frantic tattoo accompanying the visceral shriek of battle. The air, thick with the coppery tang of blood and the acrid stench of burning flesh, choked me. My fire, usually a dancer of controlled flames, now erupted in a chaotic maelstrom, a crimson tempest reflecting the madness that consumed me. It tasted of ash and agony, a bitter symphony on my tongue.

Caspian, his face pale as bone beneath the flickering firelight, stumbled back, his breath hitching in ragged gasps. His eyes, usually bright with a mischievous glint, were now wide with a terror that mirrored my own. He was more than a comrade; he was the last tether to my humanity, the fragile thread holding me back from the abyss. Our bond, forged in blood and shared sacrifice, was the only thing preventing the utter collapse of everything we held dear. It was a bond tested not merely to its limits, but strained to the very breaking point,

each ragged breath a testament to its precarious strength. To lose him...
to lose him...the thought itself sent a fresh wave of icy dread through
me, sharper than any blade. I fought not just for survival, but for the
preservation of that desperate, precious connection; a desperate prayer
etched in fire and blood.

The night bled into a dawn choked with ash and the stench of
burning flesh. The battle wasn't a dance; it was a brutal, grinding
maelstrom where life and death wrestled in a crimson tide. Each
shriek of a dying man, each sickening thwack of the blade on bone,
fed the insatiable hunger of the resurrected demons. Their eyes, pits
of incandescent hate, burned into mine, promising oblivion with every
pulse of their corrupted hearts. This wasn't some noble fight; it was a
desperate, clawing struggle against the very fabric of existence. Caspian,
his face a mask of grim determination etched with the grime of battle,
staggered beside me. The familiar coppery tang of blood filled my
nostrils, mixing with the acrid reek of Sulfur and fear. My wounds
screamed a symphony of agony that echoed the despair gnawing at my
soul. Each ragged breath felt like tearing a hole in my lungs, each throb
of pain a hammer blow against my shattered spirit. We were broken,
bleeding, yet somehow, impossibly, still clinging to the precipice of
oblivion. The demons' power, palpable and suffocating, pressed down
upon us, a tangible weight that threatened to crush the last flickering
embers of our defiance.

Our triumph yielded unforeseen and catastrophic repercussions. The
battle's carnage spawned a horrifying new epoch, a malevolent surge
threatening utter annihilation. We discovered, to our dismay, that the
path to victory was paved with unintended cataclysms, a grim testament
to power's capricious nature and the exorbitant cost of our hard won
success. The war, it became tragically clear, was far from concluded. A
chilling silence, broken only by the mournful wind's lament and the
ominous whispers that clung to the air, presaged impending doom. The
struggle for existence, against a revitalized and augmented adversary,
raged on. Our pyrrhic victory left a bitter residue, poisoned by the
shadows our might inadvertently conjure. The price of dominance, we
learned with agonizing clarity, transcended mere physical sacrifice. It

was a debt resonating through the very core of existence, a burden we would bear for eternity.

A blood red sunrise, a ghastly parody of dawn, stained the heavens, mirroring the butchery of the preceding night. The battlefield, already a desolate expanse, now resembled a hellish panorama, forged from fractured obsidian and the gruesome vestiges of corrupted flesh. A miasma of decay and the lingering whispers of infernal energies choked the air. Caspian, leaning against a jagged obsidian splinter, was drenched in sweat and gore. The malignant energy that consumed him surged, a wicked pulse throbbing through his veins. Each gasp felt like inhaling splintered glass. His obsidian armour, once the emblem of his invincible might, was shattered and defaced, a grim reflection of the profound physical and spiritual wounds he had endured.

My knees hit the cold, damp earth beside him, the taste of blood, my own, thick and metallic, a bitter reminder of the carnage. My fire magic, usually a roaring inferno within me, was a flickering ember, choked by exhaustion so profound it felt like physical pressure in my chest. The vampiric hunger gnawed at my insides, a ravenous beast clawing at my throat, its desperation a nauseating tide threatening to pull me under. But Caspian... to drink from him now, to steal what little life remained, would be an unforgivable act of betrayal. The guilt was a physical blow, a fist clenching in my gut.

My fingers, trembling despite my iron will, worked meticulously, cleaning his wounds. The rough texture of the linen against his pale skin sent a shiver down my spine; the scent of his blood, faint but sharp, pierced the metallic tang of my own. The dark energy thrumming from him wasn't just foreign, it was a vile corruption, a creeping shadow that felt both utterly alien and terrifyingly intimate, a parasitic stain slowly dissolving the very core of the man I loved. The weight of it, of him — his near death, his vulnerability, the monstrous attack — pressed down on me, a crushing burden. This wasn't just a fight; it was a violation. And I, his protector, had failed.

The stench of brimstone and decay clawed at my throat, a physical manifestation of the resurrected horrors before me. Their forms weren't merely twisted; they were grotesque parodies of life, limbs contorted at impossible angles, skin a tapestry of festering wounds and charred flesh. The air itself crackled with the malevolent energy that pulsed from their corrupted hearts, a palpable dread that chilled me to the bone, a taste of ash and ruin on my tongue. These weren't the undead; they were abominations, twisted beyond comprehension, each a monument to the obscene power they craved. Their eyes, pits of burning hatred and ancient malice, held the weight of eons, reflecting darkness deeper than any abyss.

This wasn't a battle; it was a sacrilegious violation of all that is holy, a desperate, bloody dance on the precipice of oblivion. The very ground trembled beneath the onslaught of their power, the air screaming with the agony of a dying world. We fought not for survival, but for the soul of existence itself, a desperate struggle against the unravelling of reality, each blow a desperate prayer against the encroaching void. The screams of the dying, my own included, were swallowed by the maelstrom of chaos, a symphony of despair echoing through the fracturing planes of existence. We were pawns in a cosmic game played by entities beyond human comprehension, a sacrifice to their ravenous hunger for oblivion. The price of power? It was the annihilation of everything we held dear.

The sun, a malevolent eye in the blood red sky, clawed its way higher, stretching the battlefield's agony into elongated shadows. Then it came. Not a rise, not a slow emergence, but a rupture of earth, a volcanic birth of nightmare. From the festering wounds of the land, it heaved itself into existence, a colossus of pure, suffocating darkness, a grotesque symphony of shadow and writhing, corrupted flesh. The stench of decay and brimstone choked the air, a palpable wave of nausea washing over the survivors. Its form shifted, a horrifying ballet of impossible angles and pulsating, obscene growths, a vision so nightmarish it etched itself onto the very soul. Immense, it dwarfed even the fallen giants of the Obsidian Covenant, its presence a crushing weight, an eclipse that devoured the last fragile tendrils of dawn. This wasn't merely a being; it was a wound in reality, a manifestation of the unleashed chaos, its very essence a scream of raw, unbridled power. This was the architect of their resurgence, the puppeteer pulling the strings of the resurrected demons, and the chilling certainty of their annihilation settled like ice on every heart. The stench of its breath, a burning, acrid wind, promised only oblivion.

Agony lanced through Caspian, a searing brand across his shattered ribs, yet even the screaming pain couldn't hold him back. His muscles, screaming in protest, bunched, straining against the dark tide that choked his power. He needed to unleash it, a tempest of raw, elemental fury, to obliterate the vile things that dared to defile this sacred ground. But the abyss within, a cold, black heart of shadow, clamped down, crushing the very spark of his essence. The taste of blood, metallic and coppery, filled his mouth, mingling with the acrid tang of corruption clinging to the air. His obsidian blade, usually a living extension of his wrath, felt like a leaden tombstone in his hand, the polished surface slick with his sweat, a testament to his desperate, failing strength. The weight of it, the crushing inertia, mirrored the despair gnawing at his soul. He, Caspian, the storm that had shattered armies, was reduced to this, a quivering husk, his godlike power stolen, his very lifeblood tainted by the insidious darkness. The fear, a chilling wind, whispered promises of utter annihilation. But even in the face of oblivion, a flicker of defiance, a stubborn member of his untamed spirit, refused to be extinguished.

The stench of decay, acrid and cloying, clawed at my throat as I watched him fight. Not just fight, but tear himself apart, piece by agonizing piece, against that...thing. A desperate, white hot fury, born of pure, visceral terror, ignited within me. This wasn't just power I saw; it was a malignant bloom, a festering wound upon reality itself, the very essence of rot given flesh and terrible, writhing movement. It pulsed with a vile, inner light that seared my eyes, a nauseating symphony of corruption played on the strings of my soul.

We had unleashed it. The weight of that realization, a physical blow to my chest, crushed the breath from my lungs. The guilt, a venomous serpent, coiled in my gut, its fangs already sunk deep into my heart. This wasn't some noble sacrifice; this was the bitter fruit of our arrogance, our blind ambition, and the blood price we were now forced to pay, drop by agonizing drop. My reflection in the thing's malevolent glow showed me a face etched with the terror of a condemned man, yet fueled by the stubborn, defiant flicker of a will that refused to break. We were damned, yes, but we would not go down easily. Not while I still drew breath.

My reserves screamed, a bone deep agony as I clawed at the last embers of my fire magic. It felt…thin, a pathetic wisp compared to the inferno I could once unleash. The air itself choked me, a suffocating weight of shadow pressing down, a tangible, viscous darkness that leached the very power from my veins. The taste of ash and fear coated my tongue; the stench of decay, thick and cloying, filled my nostrils. My magic, once a blazing sun, was reduced to a flickering candle flame, spitting weak, orange sparks against a tide of absolute black. Each feeble gesture, each desperate invocation, was met with a mocking silence, the monstrous entity's laughter a silent, crushing pressure against my will. This wasn't a battle; it was a slow, agonizing suffocation, a final, humiliating extinguishing of my light against its unyielding, monstrous power. The despair was a physical thing, icy fingers gripping my heart, while the rage, a molten core within, threatened to consume me utterly.

The stench of ozone and decay choked us, a tangible manifestation of our despair. Our power, the very lifeblood of our being, had been leached away, a cruel mockery of our former strength. This wasn't a battle; it was an annihilation, a slow, agonizing descent into the abyss. Time, a dwindling ember, threatened to extinguish us before we could even strike a meaningful blow. The monstrous thing advanced, I felt the chill of its shadow before I saw it, a wave of icy dread washing over me, the reek of Sulfurous ash stinging my nostrils. Its tendrils, thicker than oak trees, writhed like colossal pythons, their oily blackness glistening under the sickly green luminescence of its eyes, eyes that burned with an ancient, malevolent hunger, promising not merely destruction, but oblivion.

Caspian, his once proud bearing shattered, hauled himself upright, each strained muscle screaming in protest. His breath hitched in ragged gasps, his face a ghastly canvas of bone white skin stretched taut over ravaged features. The gleaming obsidian of his sword, usually an extension of his will, lay discarded, a shameful testament to his utter helplessness, a chilling symbol of our impending doom. The taste of ash and terror was thick on my tongue. We were trapped, cornered, and utterly, irrevocably broken. And the monster was smiling.

"*Time,*" Caspian rasped, the word a strangled cry torn from his ravaged lungs, each syllable snatched by the teeth of the wind. The icy bite of the gale clawed at his exposed skin, a searing pain that mirrored the agony twisting his gut. He tasted blood, his own, a coppery tang mixing with the bitter tang of fear. *"We need time,"* he repeated, his voice a dry whisper against the elemental roar, the words hanging in the air like fragile, frost laden shards. His eyes, usually sharp and calculating, now held the desperate, hunted gleam of a cornered wolf. The weight of a thousand unspoken failures pressed down on him, a crushing burden that threatened to shatter him completely. *"We have to… find a way, or…"* His voice trailed off, choked by a sob that was swallowed by the storm, a silent scream swallowed by the infinite, indifferent wilderness. The unspoken horror hung heavier than the blizzard itself.

His voice choked, a ragged whisper swallowed by the encroaching blackness. The dizzy spell wasn't a wave; it was a tidal surge, dragging him under a sea of nausea, the metallic tang of blood blooming on his tongue. The darkness wasn't just energy; it was a sentient malignancy, a ravenous beast gnawing at his very soul, its icy grip tightening around his heart, each beating a muffled drum against the encroaching void. He tasted ash and felt the chilling caress of its corruption along his spine, a burning brand searing its mark upon his flesh. His vision blurred, the vibrant world fracturing into jagged shards of crimson and obsidian. This wasn't merely fading; it was disintegration, a slow, agonizing unravelling of his being, the stolen breath catching in his throat like a strangled cry. The fear, raw and visceral, was a physical force, crushing him, leaving him a broken husk, consumed by the abyss.

The chilling implication sliced through me, sharper than any blade. A distraction. He wasn't suggesting a mere diversion; he was talking about a bloodbath, a pyre of chaos to shield our desperate scramble against the thing, it, that was their grotesque handiwork. The stench of its creation still clung to the air, a cloying sweetness masking the metallic tang of blood. I could almost taste it, a bitter aftertaste on my tongue, mirroring the bitterness festering in my gut.

This wasn't some abstract moral dilemma; this was our monster, born from their hubris, their insatiable thirst for power. The weight of responsibility, a physical entity pressing against my chest, stealing my breath, constricting my heart, felt like the crushing grip of a titan.

I could feel the icy dread crawling up my spine, the hairs on my arms prickling with a primal fear.

The price of their arrogance, of their victory, had been laid bare. Not in some tidy, metaphorical sense, but in the horrifying reality of it. Its very existence was a testament to their failure, a festering wound laid open for all to see. We were drowning in the consequences, a suffocating tide of our own making.

Escape? It felt impossible, a ludicrous fantasy that danced at the edges of my mind like a fleeting dream. Yet we had to fight; we had to find a way out of this suffocating nightmare even if the path led through the fires of hell itself. We were driven by an unyielding determination, a primal instinct to survive even if it meant sacrificing everything we held dear—our sanity, our souls and perhaps even our very lives. Each moment pressed down on us like a heavy shroud suffocating and relentless. The taste of ash was already on my lips a bitter reminder of the destruction surrounding us and it fueled an urgency within. We could not remain passive resigned to our fate. With every heartbeat the flames of despair flickered closer threatening to consume us entirely. We needed a plan, a glimmer of hope to cling to as we navigated through the chaos that enveloped us. It was a daunting challenge but we could not allow fear to paralyze us. We had to summon every ounce of courage, every scrap of resolve to push forward. We would carve our own path however treacherous and emerge from the shadows into the light once more.

The realization slammed into me, a bone jarring impact that ripped the breath from my lungs. Sacrifice. The word tasted like ash and iron in my mouth; it wasn't a whispered suggestion, it was a brutal, inescapable truth. We were lambs to the slaughter, outmatched, outgunned, our defences crumbling like sandcastles against a tidal wave. Something had to be done, a desperate, sickening gamble to tilt the scales, however infinitesimally.

My gaze locked onto Caspian. His face, usually a mask of wry amusement, was a ravaged landscape of pain, etched with the grim reality of his fading life force. The air throbbed with the stench of decay as the dark energy leached from him, a viscous, unholy tide. I saw the flicker of defiance in his eyes, a stubborn refusal to surrender even as the darkness consumed him. The thought of losing him, of failing him, clawed at my throat, a physical agony that mirrored the gaping wound in his side. It wasn't just unbearable; it was a violation of everything I held sacred.

But the monstrosity loomed, an obsidian behemoth pulsating with malevolent energy. Its shadow, a suffocating blanket of icy dread, pressed down on us, the air itself crackling with anticipation of its unholy embrace. The rasping of its approach, a sound like grinding bones and shattered glass, vibrated through my very being, a symphony of impending doom. I had to choose. And the choice tasted like bitter regret, laced with the metallic tang of blood.

The decision clawed its way up from the pit of my despair, a bitter fruit born of love and a stark, gnawing hunger for survival. My power, the very essence of my being, tasted like ash in my mouth as I prepared to surrender it, to feed the insatiable maw of the beast. For Caspian. For that flickering ember of hope in his haunted eyes, a hope I clung to like a lifeline in a storm tossed sea. This sacrifice, this desperate act of self immolation, was our last, best chance against odds so insurmountable they pressed down on me, a physical weight crushing the breath from my lungs. The air itself crackled with the foreboding, a metallic tang staining the back of my throat. I knew—knew with a chilling certainty—that there was no promise of success, only the stark, brutal gamble. A desperate, reckless throw of the dice against a foe whose power dwarfed even the sun, leaving behind only the bitter taste of dust and the certainty of my impending ruin, but it was the only path, the only damn option.

With a deep breath, I closed my eyes, focusing my remaining energy. A single tear escaped, tracing a cold path down my cheek, mirroring the icy dread creeping into my heart. I drew upon the deep well of my power, the core of my being, the very essence of my flame elemental nature. It hurt, it pained me intensely, a searing agony that ripped through me, leaving behind a hollow ache. But even this unbearable pain was preferable to the thought of Caspian's suffering, the image of a world consumed by darkness etching itself onto my soul. I did it willingly, offering myself as a sacrifice to buy time for Caspian, and possibly even save the world. The price was immense, I knew, a crushing weight settling on my chest. I was giving up my strength, potentially my very life, feeling the vibrant life force within me slowly, agonizingly ebb away. A profound loneliness washed over me, a stark awareness of the emptiness that would follow. It wasn't just the loss of power; it was the loss of hope, the slow, agonizing extinguishing of my future, a future I had so desperately envisioned with him. For Caspian, for our future—a future now stolen from me—for everything we had fought to protect, and now, tragically, had to sacrifice for. As my power flowed towards the entity, I felt my energy deplete, a gradual fading of the essence of myself, a chilling premonition of my mortality settling like a shroud. A silent sob escaped my lips, a testament to the unbearable grief and despair consuming me.

The monstrous entity paused, a tremor of something akin to sadness, a vast, echoing loneliness, rippling through its colossal form. The sudden surge of energy, instead of fueling its wrath, only served to highlight the desolate emptiness within its being. It recoiled, not just from the power, but from a phantom touch of something it hadn't felt in millennia: hope, a cruel mockery in its unending despair. The opportunity to escape was now a fleeting chance for a freedom it no longer believed it deserved, a freedom that felt as distant and cold as the void from which it was born. The weight of its countless failures, its endless sorrow, pressed down on it, a crushing burden far heavier than any physical restraint. Escape offered only a reprieve from a grief so profound it threatened to shatter its very essence.

Caspian, a wraith of a man clinging to the precipice of oblivion, saw his aperture. His lungs screamed, a ragged symphony of pain, yet he hauled himself to his feet, every fibre of his being screaming in protest. The air crackled with the desperate, feral energy he summoned, a final, incandescent flicker before the snuffing of his light. It tasted of iron and ash in his mouth, a bitter tang mirroring the despair that clawed at his soul. The very air vibrated with the raw power he unleashed, a wave of obsidian magic that ripped through the suffocating silence, a targeted strike aimed at the heart of the monstrous entity. This wasn't just a gamble; it was a suicidal plunge into the abyss, our only prayer against annihilation. The scent of ozone and impending doom hung heavy in the air, a palpable omen of the battle's climax. His defiance was a tempest, born of a soul both broken and unbowed, a testament to the resilience of a spirit forged in the fires of countless betrayals and unimaginable loss.

A guttural shriek, a sound like grinding tectonic plates and shattering obsidian, ripped through the air as Caspian's blade found its mark. The monstrous entity, a coiling vortex of shadow and screaming starlight, reeled, its form flickering like a dying candle flame in a hurricane. The air itself crackled with the raw, sickening power of its collapse; the very ground trembled beneath Caspian's weary feet, tasting of ash and ozone. This was it. Their one, blood soaked chance. Victory, or oblivion.

But even as the darkness faltered, a primal dread tightened Caspian's chest. The entity's demise wasn't an ending, but a horrifying metamorphosis. The malevolent energy, a vile essence clinging to the very fabric of reality, pulsed with renewed, amplified fury. It writhed, a sentient storm of corrupted light and shadow, coalescing into a new horror, a grotesque parody of its predecessor, even more terrifying, more hungry. A wave of nausea, the cold sweat of impending doom, washed over Caspian. This wasn't a cycle of destruction; it was an endless, agonizing descent into a hell of their own making. The fight, it seemed, had only just begun. And Caspian, his soul scarred by a thousand battles, felt the chilling certainty that this time, even he might not survive.

The air crackled, a stench of ozone and burnt flesh stinging my nostrils as the monstrosity lunged. It wasn't just a fight; it was a maelstrom of chaos, a symphony of screams and shattering bones echoing in my ears. Reality itself fractured around us, a kaleidoscope of twisting colours and impossible geometries that threatened to swallow us whole. The taste of blood, my own, mostly, was metallic on my tongue, a bitter counterpoint to the acrid tang of fear that choked me. This wasn't just power's price; it was a debt exacted in the currency of souls, a debt Is paid in full, watching loved ones consumed by the very force I wielded.

My hands, scarred and trembling, still clutched the weapon, a testament to the choices that carved my soul into something jagged and unforgiving. This world, this brutal, unforgiving hellscape, had stripped me bare, leaving only the raw, throbbing nerve of survival. It whispered promises of oblivion in the wind, a constant reminder that victory wasn't a certainty, only a fleeting possibility snatched from the jaws of inevitable loss. Every breath was a gamble, every heartbeat a defiance against the encroaching void. This wasn't just a fight; it was a testament to the unrelenting will to endure, a desperate, bloody dance with death.

The abomination unravelled, not into oblivion, but a maelstrom of screaming energy, violet and incandescent, thrashing like a dying god. The air didn't merely crackle; it seethed, a palpable force that burned the nostrils with ozone and the raw tang of something ancient and unholy. Silence descended, a suffocating blanket woven from dread, far heavier than the symphony of destruction that had preceded it, a silence that tasted of ash and despair, that pressed against my eardrums like a physical weight. Then, a groan, not merely echoing, but rippling across the blasted earth, a sound that clawed at the soul, a lament of titanic agony so profound it threatened to shatter the very fabric of reality. It was the death rattle of something that had tasted power, something that had known dominion, and now... now knew only the exquisite torment of its undoing.

Caspian crumpled, his knees hitting the unforgiving stone with a dull thud that echoed the hollow ache in his bones. The stench of ozone, a lingering ghost of the dark energy that had clawed at his soul, filled his nostrils, a bitter counterpoint to the coppery tang of blood on his cracked lips. His breath, a ragged, wheezing symphony of pain, tore through him, each gasping a wrenching reminder of the battle fought and barely won. Gone, yes, the insidious darkness was gone, but it had left behind a wasteland. He felt not merely drained, but eviscerated, a husk of the man he once was. His very being felt like sun baked clay, brittle and cracked, the lifeblood leached out, leaving only the dust of his former self.

He looked at me then, not simply looking but saw me, his gaze piercing, ancient, holding the weight of centuries of sorrow and a thousand unspoken battles. His eyes, once blazing with fierce defiance, were now twin pools of shadowed amethyst, reflecting a profound grief that went beyond words, a despair so vast it threatened to swallow him whole. Relief flickered there, a fragile ember struggling against the encroaching darkness, a testament to his will, but it was overshadowed, utterly consumed by sorrow so raw, so utterly heartbreaking, it stole the breath from my lungs.

My bones vibrated, a frantic hummingbird trapped beneath my skin. The hollow ache where my power used to roar was a physical wound, a gaping chasm that sucked the very air from my lungs. The taste of ash filled my mouth, the acrid tang a grim reminder of the inferno that had been my soul, now reduced to a pathetic whisper of embers, a dying star sputtering its last breaths. The scent of ozone, sharp and metallic, clung to me, the stench of power lost, of a god fallen. My vision blurred, the world wavering like heat rising from scorched earth. This fragile shell, this… thing… that housed the remnants of me was a pathetic imitation of the storm forged elemental I once was. The obsidian shard that had been my heart ached with a dull, throbbing agony. The sacrifice… the price… it gnawed at me, a relentless tide eroding the last vestiges of my strength. But Caspian… his desperate, haunted face flashed before my eyes. He had the time he needed. That cold, brutal comfort was my only solace. For now. But the darkness, hungry and patient, waited. And I felt, with a chilling certainty, it wouldn't wait forever.

Our hard won success felt hollow, a bitter triumph purchased at an exorbitant price. The immediate danger was neutralized, yes, but the devastation was profound: a ravaged environment, a toxic atmosphere, and a palpable sense of foreboding clinging to everything. The toll exacted was catastrophic, a dreadful accounting of sacrifice etched in agony and grief.

A scene of utter destruction unfolded before us. The earth was strewn with the shattered remnants of our foes, their contorted, vile bodies a stark testament to the savagery of the conflict. Where vibrant life once flourished, a barren expanse now stretched, a chilling epitaph to the atrocities we had endured. A palpable miasma hung heavy in the air, the lingering stench of infernal energies leaving an indelible mark of dread upon our souls.

Exhaustion bowed Caspian, his ascent to a standing position a laborious effort, the obsidian blade his weary crutch. Muscles screamed in protest, his keen perceptions clouded by a profound fatigue. The brutal conflict had plundered him, leaving him defenceless, a raw nerve exposed to the world. Still, unyielding resolve smouldered in his gaze, a defiant ember against the encroaching darkness.

His rasping breath barely formed the words, a grim determination etched on his face: *"The conflict remains unresolved. This... this is far from concluded."*

A slow understanding blossomed. Our improbable triumph felt like ash in the mouth, the sweetness overwhelmed by bitter losses. The respite was deceptive; a more sinister enemy, perhaps already gestating in the darkness, loomed. This conflict, a ceaseless, brutal dance of destruction and despair, offered no promise of resolution.

High noon's sun, merciless in its ascent, stretched grotesque shadows across the devastated field of carnage. The vanquished demons, though subdued, had etched their infernal presence into the very fabric of the earth; a festering wound upon the land. A noxious atmosphere, thick with malevolent energy, permeated all things, a miasma clinging like a shroud. Even the breeze whispered of mortality, a chilling dirge carried on the wind's lament.

The silence was broken only by the occasional groan of the dying, a morbid symphony of suffering. The weight of our victory pressed down on us, an invisible burden that threatened to crush us. We had won the battle, but at what cost? The question hung in the air, unanswered, a chilling reminder of the dark reality we inhabited.

Caspian's gaze burned into me, a molten brand searing through the layers of grime and despair clinging to my skin. I tasted the metallic tang of blood, phantom pain echoing the wounds I carried, both seen and unseen. His eyes, the colour of a stormy sea, mirrored the devastation within me, the hollowness of a black abyss reflecting the endless night of my soul. He knew. He saw the cracks spider webbing across my spirit, each one a testament to the agonizing choices I'd made, the lifeblood I'd spilled to drag him from the jaws of oblivion, to snatch us both from the clutches of fate.

The weight of it, the crushing weight of our shared survival, pressed down on him, a physical force I could almost feel radiating from him, a palpable ache that resonated with the deep thrumming grief in my chest. This wasn't just a bond forged in the heat of desire; it was a pact sealed in the fires of hell, forged in the crucible of blood and shadowed desperation, now fused inextricably by the searing agony of our mutual sacrifice, the bitter taste of loss forever clinging to our tongues. Our souls, scarred and broken, were bound together in a communion of shared trauma, a terrifying intimacy born from the depths of our shared nightmare.

His fingers, calloused yet surprisingly soft, closed over mine. The contact wasn't just a touch; it was a searing brand, a jolt that resonated from my hand up my arm, igniting a phantom ache where my power once pulsed, a power bled dry, sacrificed on the altar of our survival. I tasted the metallic tang of blood, a ghost of old wounds, on my tongue. His eyes, the colour of a storm-wracked sea, held mine captive. He saw it all: the ashes of my strength, the flickering embers of a spirit barely clinging to life, the hollowness that gnawed at my soul. This wasn't the gentle respect of a bystander; this was the knowing gaze of a warrior who had fought beside me, who had witnessed my sacrifice, who understood the cost of our victories.

He saw not just weakness, not just vulnerability, but the ruins of a supernova, a testament to my desperate, relentless fight. He sensed the tremor in my hand, the frantic beat of my heart against my ribs, a drum solo of exhaustion and defiance. But in the depths of those storm grey eyes, I saw it mirrored, the same fierce, unyielding resolve, hardened by blood and loss, a resolve that had dragged us both from the jaws of oblivion and that burned with a fire that refused to be extinguished, even now, in the face of utter devastation.

"*We will find a way*," Caspian murmured, his voice low but firm. "*We always do.*"

My fingers crushed his, bone grinding against bone, the resurgence of strength not a fiery blaze, but a cold, hard knot of will in my gut. His words rasped like stones against stones, carried the weight of lifetimes, a fragile solace in the echoing silence. We'd stared into the abyss, and clawed our way back from the precipice of oblivion—victory tasted like ash and blood on my tongue. The burden of our triumph pressed down, a mountain of grief and exhaustion, but beneath it, a shared defiance throbbed, a frantic heartbeat against the encroaching dark. The scent of ozone and something else... something ancient and feral... still clung to our clothes. Whatever hell awaited, we would meet it not as heroes, but as survivors — scarred, broken, and utterly, terrifyingly, together.

The hours that followed were a sombre vigil, a grim process of patching our shattered bodies. Caspian's grievous wounds were a tapestry of pain, yet he bore them with stoic resilience, his suffering a silent testament to his fortitude. Exhausted though I was, my ministries were fervent, a desperate bid to secure his survival. Our efforts transcended mere collaboration; they were a sacred choreography of unspoken empathy, a language born of shared trauma, whispered in the desolate silence of our brutal experience.

Darkness descended, and we sought sanctuary within a shadowed cavern, a meagre haven against the stark, unforgiving terrain. The cave's interior offered a chilling respite from the sun's relentless, fiery assault. Exhausted and battered, we clung together, our bodies aching, our spirits ravaged by the ghastly visions that haunted our memories.

Our hard fought triumph yielded not elation, but a gnawing disquiet. Though one enemy fell, a palpable gloom persisted, a suffocating shroud hinting at further, deeper perils. The cost of dominance, we grimly discovered, was far steeper than imagined, a terrible toll exacted not merely in physical wounds and magical depletion, but in the insidious corruption of our very spirits, a slow, agonizing erosion of our humanity.

Insomnia held us captive, the nocturnal stillness broken only by the mournful cries of phantom beasts and the sibilant secrets of the wind. Our minds, adrift in a sea of contemplation, wrestled with the profound consequences of our triumph. We had peered into the chasm of oblivion, and its gaze, chilling and unwavering, etched itself permanently upon our spirits.

Our struggle wasn't against some external malevolence; it mirrored the insidious shadows dwelling within, the primal darkness inherent in all existence. We bravely confronted our deepest anxieties, laid bare our frailties, and ultimately triumphed, forged anew in the crucible of adversity. Yet, the battle's wounds linger, a stark testament to the formidable cost of dominion.

Days melted into a chaotic whirlwind. Across the devastated terrain, we relentlessly hunted for the living, soothed the injured, and laid the fallen to rest. The work was gruelling, a relentless assault on our spirits, but vital. We functioned as a single organism, our unity forged in the crucible of shared suffering.

Day by day, the weight of our conquest bore down. We had vanquished a formidable foe, yet emerged irrevocably altered, scarred by the terrible cost of our triumph. The elation of success was eclipsed by an agonizing grief, a profound sorrow for those we had lost. The dominion we had won came at an exorbitant price.

Amidst the stillness, we contemplated the unfolding drama, our choices, and their bitter aftermath. We had clawed for existence, for retribution, for a tomorrow shrouded in doubt. We discovered, painfully, that unchecked authority was a malevolent blight, a ruinous and catastrophic affliction.

Our odyssey pressed onward, a treacherous trail riddled with peril, treachery, and the chilling unknown. A single skirmish won, yet the conflict raged, a maelstrom far from its conclusion. The toll of dominion was exorbitant, but our resolve remained unshaken, a unified commitment. We were champions, devoted companions, and resilient souls, tempered in the crucible of a grim, fantastical realm, our destinies inextricably intertwined. We would persevere, to cherish, to endure, even if the expenditure exceeded all comprehension. The struggle for existence relentlessly continued; our hearts, though triumphant, ached under the crushing weight of our collective sacrifice. The awesome burden of our authority bore down upon us, a stark reminder of the immense cost we would continuously bear, both for ourselves and for the realm we valiantly defended.

TWENTY ONE

Embracing the Darkness

The cavern offered no solace, only a suffocating embrace. The air, a fetid miasma, clung to him like a shroud, damp earth rotted in his nostrils, a coppery tang, acrid and metallic, the screaming ghost of blood newly spilled, clawing at the back of his throat. Each breath Caspian choked down was a ragged, searing torment, a rasping shriek swallowed back into the suffocating darkness. His ebony blade, usually an extension of his very soul, lay abandoned, a slick obsidian mirror reflecting the feeble, dying light struggling through the cave mouth. It mocked him, a silent testament to his failure. His face, usually a mask of aristocratic pallor, was now a horrifying tapestry of crimson gashes and blistered, weeping flesh, a brutal testament to the infernal power he'd unleashed, the terrible, agonizing price he'd paid.

The taste of his blood, metallic and bitter, mingled with the stench of decay on his tongue, a grim reminder of his mortality. He felt the raw agony bloom in his ravaged flesh, a searing brand that marked him not as a hero, but as a broken instrument, shattered by the very force he wielded. His heart, a trapped bird beating against his ribs, hammered out a frantic rhythm of despair. This was not victory; this was damnation.

My bones ground against the rough hewn timber of the bench, Caspian's warmth a stark contrast to the icy chill that had settled deep in my marrow. He's so warm... I haven't felt this... safe... in centuries. But that warmth only highlights the cold inside me. The fire, once a roaring furnace within me, was reduced to a pathetic flicker, a dying ember whispering secrets of fading power. Fading... It's fading. Is this it? Is this the end of... everything? Its absence left a void, a black hole sucking the very air from my lungs, each breath a ragged gasp against the suffocating emptiness. I can't breathe. Not really. It's not just the air, it's... hope. The air is thick with the absence of hope. The vampiric thirst, usually a ravenous beast clawing at my throat, was a subdued growl, a simmering volcano threatening to erupt. Even the hunger's weak.

Pathetic. I'm pathetic. It wasn't the physical pain that threatened to overwhelm me—the sting of a dozen shallow cuts barely registered against the agony of powerlessness. These cuts? I've survived worse. A thousand times worse. But this... this emptiness... this is a new kind of hell. It was the emptiness, a profound hollowness that echoed the desolate landscape of my soul. Is this what death feels like? Not the oblivion, but the... fading? The slow extinguishing of... me? No. I won't let it happen. I have to find a way... a way to rekindle the flame... but how...

This... this wasn't exhaustion. It was the crushing, soul rending weight of a thousand defeats, each one a fresh wound reopening in my gut. The screams of the fallen, a chorus of agony, clawed at my sanity, a symphony of despair ringing in my ears. Caspian's hand, rough as granite, a testament to countless brutal clashes, gripped mine—a silent pact forged in the crucible of shared horror. I felt his tremors, a seismic shudder mirroring my internal collapse. The coppery tang of his blood, thick and acrid, mingled with the metallic reek of my wounds; a grim bouquet of carnage. The taste of defeat, bitter bile, ash and rust, clung to my tongue, a sickening reminder of our sacrifice, a victory so dearly bought it felt like annihilation. Each heartbeat was a sledgehammer blow, a brutal percussion against the shattered ribs of my hope. With every pulse, the abyss within me yawned wider, a ravenous maw promising oblivion. The flickering torchlight painted his face in shades of grey, a mask of stoic suffering that betrayed the tempest raging within him. His eyes, usually blazing with a fierce, unwavering resolve, now held the cold, desolate gleam of a conquered land. This wasn't just defeat; it was the slow, agonizing death of hope.

My fingers, trembling despite myself, snaked out, charting the brutal gash across his cheekbone. The raw, ragged edges bit into my skin, a chilling contrast to the unnerving stillness of his flesh beneath. Ice, that's what it felt like; a deathly, porcelain chill that sent a shiver, a primal fear, skittering down my spine. He didn't react, not a muscle twitching, not even a breath hitching. The silence screamed louder than any shout, a suffocating vacuum pressing down on me. His eyes, though, those were burning coals, locked onto something far beyond the stifling walls of our prison, something that held him captive in a way far more dreadful than these four walls. The metallic tang of blood, faint but undeniable, filled my nostrils, mingling with the cloying stench of stale sweat and fear that clung to the air, thick as a shroud. His silence was a defiance, a chilling testament to a soul already lost, yet his gaze...his gaze held a flicker of something else, something unreadable, something terrifyingly captivating.

"Caspian?" The word, a strangled rasp born of ice and desperation, clawed its way from my throat, a pathetic whisper against the banshee wail of the storm. Salt spray, stinging like a thousand needles, lashed my face, the taste of fear a bitter, metallic tang on my tongue, mingling with the coppery sweetness of my blood, a gash on my lip, a crimson testament to my fraying control. My breath hitched, a trapped bird's frantic flutter against the cage of my ribs, as the wind, a brutal, unseen hand, tore at my cloak, threatening to rip me from the unsteady deck and fling me into the churning, grey abyss. The sea, a ravenous beast, gaped before me, its maw a frothing vortex of death. Panic, a venomous serpent, coiled in my gut, its icy scales slick against my skin, a betrayal of the brittle composure I'd painstakingly forged, a dam holding back the flood of terror. This wasn't merely a name; it was a poisoned dart, a desperate, prayer-like invocation, a fraying lifeline tethering me to the edge of oblivion, a precipice where sanity shattered and only the raw, howling wind remained. The name Caspian, a brand seared into the very core of my being, a promise, a threat, a chilling echo of everything I'd lost and everything I desperately sought to reclaim.

His head, a glacial weight on his spine, creaked around. The stench of stale fear, clinging to him like a shroud, hit me before his gaze did. His eyes weren't merely pools of obsidian; they were fathomless chasms, blacker than a moonless night, reflecting the flickering candlelight in fractured, malevolent gleams. Each flicker seemed to pulse with a silent scream, mirroring the jagged edges of the unspoken horrors that twisted between us, a shared tapestry woven from nightmares, stained with the bitter crimson of our past. The air crackled, thick with the unspoken accusations, the ghost of screams still echoing in the desolate space between us. His eyes, those ancient, haunted wells, held the crushing weight of it all; a lifetime of betrayals and broken promises, etched onto his soul with a merciless hand. I tasted the metallic tang of dread on my tongue, a grim premonition settling in my gut. This wasn't just a meeting of gazes; it was a collision of worlds, a confrontation with the ghosts we both carried.

"*It's... quieter now,*" he said, his voice rough, barely a breath.

"*Yes,*" I replied, my throat tight with emotion. "*Too quiet.*"

The silence clawed, a vice of tension squeezing the air from our lungs. The taste of dust and fear coated my tongue; the scent of ozone, sharp and metallic, clung to the sweat plastering my skin. We sat, two predators wounded but not broken, companionable only in the shared agony etched onto our faces, a silent communion of scars. His eyes, the colour of a storm wracked sea, held mine, reflecting not just the flickering candlelight, but the abyss of loss we both stared into. That unspoken understanding wasn't just heavy; it pressed down, a physical weight, a suffocating blanket woven from the threads of our harrowing fight. It was a bond forged not in the fleeting heat of desire, but in the white hot furnace of mutual sacrifice, a pact sealed in blood and whispered oaths, born from the ashes of our near destruction, the echoes of screams still ringing phantom like in the cavernous silence.

The days blend together, a fever dream of grit and blood. The air, thick with the coppery tang of Caspian's wounds and the acrid stench of decay from our meagre rations, clung to us like a shroud. His recovery was a slow, agonizing crawl from the jaws of death; each rasping breath, each flinch of his ravaged body, a fresh stab of agony. The phantom limb pain, I knew, gnawed at him even in his sleep, his moans a low, guttural symphony of suffering that echoed the desolation around us. My own body screamed in protest, muscles screamed, bones ached, yet I wouldn't allow myself respite. I became a shadow, tending to him, a relentless guardian against the encroaching darkness. My hands, raw and trembling, worked with grim determination, cleansing the festering wounds, the rough cloth a constant abrasion against his skin.

Each dressing was a renewed pact with survival, a whispered defiance hurled at the cruel indifference of fate. His near lifelessness stoked a fierce protectiveness within me, a desperate, ferocious love born of shared trauma and the stark reality of our isolation. The silence between us, heavy with unspoken understanding, was not peace, but a taut, desperate vigil, a silent dance on the precipice of despair, performed in the grim, unforgiving theatre of our ruined world.

The raw flesh gaped, a testament to the blades, but it was the unseen wounds that truly bled. A corrosive acid of grief gnawed at our souls, a relentless tide threatening to pull us under, to shatter the fragile remnants of who we were. The stench of death clung to us, a phantom limb of the carnage we'd witnessed, each breath a ragged rasp against the phantom pressure of Obsidian Covenant's gaze. The screams of the fallen echoed in the hollow spaces between our ribs, a symphony of sorrow only we could hear. The taste of ash and fear coated my tongue, a bitter reminder of the pyre of our hopes. We were broken things, clinging to one another, our very sanity a flickering candle in the storm of our shared trauma. The Obsidian Covenant's shadow stretched long and dark over our future, promising a return that tasted of cold steel and an unending nightmare. We were marked, irrevocably, and the mark burned.

The sun bled crimson and gold, a molten explosion across the horizon. The air itself vibrated with the heat, a tangible wave of dying light washing over us, thick with the scent of salt and wood smoke. I turned, and Caspian's eyes, the colour of a storm tossed sea, flecked with the green of submerged kelp, were burning with the same incandescent fury as the sky. Not just gratitude, no. Something darker, wilder flickered there, a yearning so profound it ached, mirroring the raw, untamed beauty of the spectacle before us. His gaze, heavy with unspoken promises and buried regrets, held me captive. The sunset's fire burned not just on the horizon, but in the depths of his soul, a reflection of the chaotic, breathtaking landscape of his heart.

The sky bled orange, a molten fire licking at the bruised purple of twilight. The air itself vibrated with the heat of the dying sun, a thick, cloying sweetness clinging to my tongue, the scent of wood smoke and overripe plums mingling with the sharp tang of Caspian's fear, barely masked beneath a veneer of something else... something desperate. His eyes, the color of storm tossed seas, reflected not just the fiery canvas above, but a maelstrom of emotions, gratitude, yes, a fragile thing clinging to the precipice of something darker, a raw, gnawing need that mirrored the hunger in my soul. The silence between us hummed, a palpable thing, as thick and heavy as the approaching night, broken only by the frantic beat of my own heart, a frantic drum against the backdrop of this breathtaking, terrifying beauty. We were bound not just by the spectacle, but by the shared weight of unspoken truths, our gazes locked in a silent acknowledgment of the precariousness of this moment, a fragile truce forged in the heart of the dying light.

"You saved me," he rasped, the words a guttural whisper clawing its way from a throat scorched raw by terror and near death. The metallic tang of blood still clung to the air, a phantom taste on his tongue, a grim reminder of the carnage. His eyes, the colour of bruised plums, were shadowed hollows, reflecting the flickering candlelight like trapped starlight in a bottomless well. *"I should be dead,"* he repeated, each syllable a heavy stone dropped into the silent chasm of his trauma. Several times over. I felt the icy grip of oblivion. Saw the pearly gates, and tasted the dust of the grave... and each time, the taste was different. Bitter, then sweet, then just... nothing. A void that craved to swallow me whole.

My shoulders hitched, a tremor running through me despite the chill wind whipping at my coat. God, it's cold. Just like...like everything feels now. The dying light, a bruised purple bleeding into the inky black, mirrored the ache blossoming in my chest. A dull, throbbing ache, spreading from my heart like a poison. Is this what grief feels like? This hollow emptiness? The taste of ash and regret coated my tongue. Ash... like the funeral pyre. Did he even want that? Or did I...did I condemn him to it? *"I didn't want you to die,"* I rasped, the words catching on the bitter tang of unshed tears.

A Lie.

A pathetic, desperate lie. Did I? Or did my inaction, my...my cowardice...seal his fate? *"Not yet. Not like this."* Like this? What other way is there? There's no other way. There never was. My gaze, burning with desperate, frantic hope, clung to the fading sun, a silent plea lost in the gathering shadows. Please...let this be a nightmare. Let me wake up and find him beside me, alive and breathing. Anything but this... this emptiness. The air itself throbbed with the unspoken weight of our shared history, a tapestry woven from betrayal and love too fierce to kill. Betrayal...mine. Mostly mine. And yet, the love...the love was real. Is it too late to make amends? Too late to undo what I've done?

"Why?" He asked, his voice a mere whisper.

The silence stretched, a taut wire humming between us. My throat constricted, a knot of raw, visceral emotion choking off the words. I couldn't just say it. The reasons were a tangled, thorny vine, each barb a shared memory, the bitter taste of betrayal on my tongue, the phantom pressure of his hand on my arm, a heat that lingered even now, a ghost of a touch that ignited a wildfire in my core. Respect? A thin veneer over simmering resentment, a fragile truce masking the brutal, beautiful truth. Affection? It had bloomed in the shadow of our conflict, a poisonous, intoxicating flower. And desire...God, the desire. It pulsed, a relentless, throbbing ache, a primal need that transcended reason, that dwarfed everything else. This wasn't some fleeting pact; it was a lifeline, a desperate, clinging embrace forged in the crucible of shared hardship, a bond woven from blood and sweat and something darker, something...more.

The words clawed at my throat, jagged shards of ice tearing through flesh. *"We need each other,"* I croaked, the confession a guttural rasp, tasting of rust and the metallic tang of old blood. The air between us vibrated, a tangible hum of suppressed lust and lethal attraction, thick with the cloying sweetness of decaying lilies, the scent clinging to the damp earth where our fates were sealed, a pact forged in the shadow of death. *"More than we can bear,"* I whispered, the admission of a tremor that shattered the fragile bones of my composure, a cataclysmic rupture in the meticulously constructed façade of our lives. My eyes locked onto his twin vortexes of shadowed desire and desperate, ravenous hunger mirroring the tempest that ravaged my soul. He was a maelstrom, a breathtaking, annihilating storm, and I was sinking, willingly, exulting in the intoxicating, terrifying pull of his abyss. The taste of his danger was a dark wine, heady and addictive, and I was already lost, irrevocably his.

He reached out, his hand gently brushing against mine. The contact was a spark, a tiny explosion igniting a fire in my belly. His touch, feather light yet intensely aware, sent a shiver down my spine, a primal jolt that had nothing to do with the chill in the air. It was more than comfort; it was a promise whispered on the breeze, a silent acknowledgment of a desire simmering beneath the surface. The air thickened, charged with an unspoken longing, a silent question hanging between us, heavy and vibrant as the unspoken words that threatened to erupt. Despite everything, we were not alone, and the knowledge of our shared secret hummed between us, a palpable current.

The air hung thick, a cloying sweetness tinged with the metallic tang of old blood, a phantom scent clinging to our shared silence. We didn't merely surrender our anxieties; we immolated them, casting our uncertainties and shattered aspirations into the heart of that suffocating quiet. It wasn't emptiness that pulsed between us, but a raw, visceral hum, a symphony of unspoken betrayals, ghosts of laughter echoing from happier times, and the bitter, searing knowledge of what we'd survived. The bond forged in the crucible of that infernal conflict wasn't mere rapport; it was a scarred, pulsing artery, a lifeblood of shared trauma and hard won resilience.

The shadows of the war still clung to us like grasping claws, icy fingers on our skin, but their reign was shattered. Not simply broken, but obliterated. Our weaknesses, the cracks in our souls laid bare by the ordeal, were dwarfed by the incandescent strength we'd discovered together. A strength forged in the fires of hell, a force that defied logic, that whispered of the unwavering, almost terrifying power we now possessed. We were changed, irrevocably, hauntingly beautiful in our shared scars. We were survivors, and the world would tremble before us.

The weeks crawled by, each one a poisoned drop in a slow, agonizing drip of months. My skin, a canvas of sickly pallor, bore the faint, whispering etchings of what had been done to us, ghostly white lines, a cruel mockery of healing. The phantom touch of the fire still burned, a searing heat beneath the surface. I could almost taste the metallic tang of blood, long dried, even as the scent of smoke clung to my clothes, a suffocating shroud. But the wounds that truly ached were invisible, festering sores in the soul, resistant to every balm of comfort. We were haunted, my companions and I, each of us bearing the unbearable burden of memory, a symphony of screams and shattered trust playing on repeat in the silent chambers of our hearts. The losses, immeasurable, were a gaping chasm we could never fully cross, a constant reminder of the brutal, exquisite savagery we'd survived. We were survivors, yes, but our souls bore the marks of those who'd stared into the abyss and found only a reflection of their broken selves. We were changed, irrevocably, the price of our endurance, a heavy toll etched not just on flesh, but on the very fabric of our being.

The coppery tang of his blood, sharp and metallic, filled my nostrils as I patched the gash on Caspian's forearm. It was a superficial wound, barely a scratch, yet a tremor, a seismic shudder in his usually iron steady hand, snagged my attention. The cool, smooth surface of his skin, usually a testament to his unnerving control, now throbbed with a frantic energy. His fingers, normally instruments of precise, almost balletic movement, fumbled, the delicate dance replaced by a clumsy, desperate struggle for stillness. He tried to mask it, to bury the tremor beneath a façade of nonchalance, but the lie was etched in the sweat beading on his brow, the stark pallor of his face a stark contrast to the crimson blooming on his skin. His eyes, usually glacial pools of calculation, now held a flicker of something primal, something broken and terrifyingly vulnerable. The scent of fear, acrid and potent, mingled with the metallic tang of blood, whispering a story far more unsettling than any superficial cut.

"*Caspian,*" I murmured, concerned about lacing my tone, "*What troubles you?*"

He looked away, his eyes averted, his usual composure wavering. "*It's nothing,*" he muttered. "*Just... exhaustion.*"

The meticulously crafted mask of his resilience shattered, splintering under the relentless pressure of my gaze. The air itself seemed to crackle with the static of his suppressed agony. I saw it etched not just in the canyons of weariness around his eyes, a landscape ravaged by sleepless nights and silent screams, but felt it in the taut, corded muscles of his shoulders, a coiled spring threatening to snap under the weight of his burden. The metallic tang of blood, though unseen, hung heavy in the space between us, a phantom scent of recent wounds, both physical and those far deeper, festering in the shadowed recesses of his soul. His very breath hitched, a ragged sob choked back, revealing the raw, bleeding heart beneath the carefully constructed façade. This wasn't merely suffering; it was a slow, agonizing crucifix of the spirit, a conflict that had carved its brutal signature into the very fabric of his being, leaving him a ruin of breathtaking, terrifying beauty.

I moved closer, the scent of his skin, warm, musky, filling my senses. My hand rested on his arm, the hard contours of his muscles a thrilling promise beneath my fingertips. I gently kneaded the tension from his bicep, feeling the ripple of his breath against my skin as my fingers traced the line of his forearm. He leaned into my touch, a low groan escaping his lips, the heat radiating from his body igniting a fire in my own. His stillness was deceptive; the barely contained tremor in his hand, the quickened pulse beneath my fingers, spoke volumes of the unspoken desire simmering between us.

The air hung thick with the metallic tang of blood and the cloying sweetness of fear. My voice, a low growl vibrating from the pit of my gut, barely registered above the ragged gasps of the injured. My empathy wasn't some airy sentiment; it was a physical ache, a mirroring of their pain that clawed at my insides. *"Our recovery,"* I rasped, the words catching in my throat, each syllable a testament to the brutal reality we faced, *"won't be a journey. It will be a war. And we will fight it together, or we will bleed out alone."* The glint of unshed tears in my eyes, a reflection of the flickering candlelight, betrayed the chilling calm of my voice. My past, a tapestry woven from betrayal and loss, fueled this grim determination. They wouldn't see the cracks in my armor. Not yet.

Our recuperation unfolded gradually, a painstaking odyssey through shadows, toward the fragile dawn of convalescence. Mutual comfort became our refuge, the shared wound forging a connection exceeding all expectations. Physical and emotional mending were inextricably linked; each advance drew us closer, weaving our fates into an unbreakable tapestry. Uncertain challenges still lay ahead, and the darkness persisted, but we confronted them as one, empowered by the trials we'd endured and the unyielding solidarity born from the depths of our suffering.

A laborious convalescence unfolded in the weeks that followed. What had been a haven transformed into a sacred space, a mute echo of our shared ordeal and burgeoning empathy. Caspian's healing was a gruelling process. His physical injuries mended, leaving a delicate tracery of scars, a palimpsest of our struggles. Yet, the profound wounds, the unseen gashes on his spirit, proved intractable, impervious to the relentless march of time. He retreated into himself, his customary brilliance dimmed, replaced by a sombre contemplation that enveloped him, a chilling cloak.

My eyes burned into him, a raw, visceral sorrow clawing at my throat. The stench of his despair, a bitter blend of ash and sweat, filled my nostrils, mirroring the acrid taste of my unending grief. His anguish wasn't just a sound; it was a physical blow, a tremor that vibrated through the very stones beneath my feet. The phantom touch of burning timbers still seared my skin, the rasp of my parched throat a constant, agonizing reminder of our lost home. The Obsidian Covenant's shadow, a suffocating blanket of dread woven from nightmares and whispers, clung to me, its icy fingers probing the deepest recesses of my soul. Each heartbeat was a hammer blow against the ribs of my memory, each breath a ragged gasp against the suffocating weight of the past. But Caspian... his silence was a wall of obsidian, taller and more impenetrable than any fortress I'd ever faced. A chasm yawned between us, a black void promising only further isolation, and the desperate need to cross it gnawed at me, a hunger more potent than thirst.

I discovered him at the cavern's entrance, one evening, his gaze fixed on the fiery descent of the sun. Age seemed to have etched premature lines upon his face, leaving him drained, exhausted beyond his years. The once brilliant, black depths of his eyes were clouded, devoid of their former spark. A profound, oppressive quiet emanated from him; days had passed since he'd uttered a syllable, his very presence a weighty, suffocating stillness in the confined space.

The cave's icy breath permeated my very being as I settled beside him. His silence, a wall of impenetrable stone, remained unbroken by my attempts at intrusion. I remained a steadfast sentinel of unspoken support. Yet, this shared stillness was profoundly altered. It lacked the balm of restorative quiet; instead, it pressed down, a suffocating weight of unvoiced remorse and self reproach.

After a long while, Caspian finally spoke, his voice a low rasp. *"I betrayed them,"* he confessed, his gaze fixed on the distant horizon. *"The Whispering Wind. I swore an oath to them, yet I risked everything for you, an elemental, an enemy."*

My resolve remains unshaken. I perceived the crushing weight of his remorse, the heavy toll his actions had exacted. A gentle murmur escaped my lips: *"They will comprehend,"* I reassured him. *"Their understanding extends to your deeds, to the profound selflessness you've demonstrated."* His allegiance to the Whispering Wind was profound, a fierce devotion cultivated over countless years within their secretive society. Yet, the bond between us, forged in the crucible of combat and shared suffering, possessed an equal, unwavering strength.

Caspian's head snapped back, the harsh movement jarring loose a strand of sweat slicked hair. *"No,"* he rasped, the word a guttural growl ripped from a throat choked with bile. The air hung thick with the metallic tang of fear, the scent of his terror a suffocating presence in the suffocating silence. *"They won't understand,"* he hissed, his voice a venomous whisper that scraped against the raw edges of his despair. *"Their methods… their methods are a festering wound, a violation of everything I thought was sacred. Obedience? It's not a virtue to them, it's a cage, forged in the fires of blind, unquestioning loyalty, a cage they built for me, and now they'll lock me in and throw away the key. My actions… they weren't a mere violation of their trust. They were a defiance, a shattering of the gilded bonds that choked the life from my soul, a betrayal, yes, but a betrayal born of necessity, a desperate gasp for freedom from their suffocating control."*

"But you saved my life," I pointed out. *"Multiple times. You risked your own life, your very soul, for me. Surely, that counts for something."*

Hope, a tenuous ember in the abyss of his gaze, ignited as he looked at me. A barely audible question, laden with desperation, escaped his lips: *"It is, isn't it?"*

The reconciliation with the Whispering Wind was far from easy. It demanded a perilous journey to their hidden sanctuary, a place shrouded in an ethereal mist that clung to the ancient, gnarled trees like a shroud. These skeletal giants clawed at the bruised twilight sky, their branches twisted into grotesque shapes by centuries of wind and weather. Caspian, his every movement a hesitant step, led the way, the fear of betrayal a palpable thing etched not only onto his face but etched deep into the very lines of his weary body. The air crackled with unspoken tension.

The members of the Whispering Wind, cloaked in shadows that seemed to shift and writhe, emerged from the gloom like phantoms. Their faces, partially obscured, were watchful, their eyes sharp and assessing, glinting with cold, ancient wisdom that hinted at centuries of secrets and betrayals. The silence, broken only by the mournful whisper of the wind through the skeletal branches, pressed down, heavy and suffocating, a silent testament to the weight of mistrust that hung between us. The scent of damp earth and decaying leaves filled the air, mingling with a strange, almost metallic tang that spoke of something ancient and powerful.

Lyra, their leader, a formidable woman whose eyes, like molten silver poured into glacial pools, held the glint of ages past, listened patiently to Caspian's confession. My gaze flickered nervously between Caspian's contrite face and Lyra's impassive one; her expression a carefully constructed mask, betraying nothing of her thoughts. The air thrummed with unspoken accusations, a palpable tension that vibrated in the very roots of the ancient trees surrounding us. The silence, broken only by the whisper of leaves and the mournful groan of branches straining under the weight of centuries, pressed down on us, heavy and suffocating. The weight of Caspian's fate, of his unspoken plea for mercy, hung between us, a tangible thing, almost visible in the shimmering heat rising from the forest floor.

Lyra finally spoke, her voice a low hum that resonated with an ancient power. *"Your actions were reckless, Caspian,"* she said, her voice devoid of emotion. *"You violated the sacred oaths you swore. But we also see the depth of your sacrifice. You risked everything for this... elemental."* Her silence hung heavy, a tangible thing pressing down on me. The air crackled with unspoken things, the scent of ozone sharp in my nostrils as her eyes, glacial blue and unnervingly deep, bored into mine. Each second stretched, an eternity of scrutiny. Then, a whisper, laced with

411

the chilling weight of a thousand untold secrets, slithered from her lips: *"And she, in turn… saved your life. Everything. She staked it all on you."* The rasp of her voice, the icy tremor in it, spoke of sacrifices far beyond comprehension, a debt of such magnitude it threatened to shatter my very bones.

Lyra's declaration echoed, a fragile span bridging the gulf of treachery and pardon. The Whispering Wind, initially skeptical, ultimately conceded to Caspian's account, reluctantly admitting the exceptional nature of events. Their assent wasn't unqualified absolution; rather, it stemmed from a profound appreciation of the unshakeable link between Caspian and me—a connection forged in the inferno of shared suffering and steadfast devotion. This hard won acceptance, a testament to the Wind's shrewd grasp of their principles and the formidable alliance now forged, was a victory hard earned.

Caspian's guilt, a heavy cloak he'd worn for ages, finally shed its oppressive weight. A profound tranquillity settled over him, a liberation long yearned for. His gaze met mine, brimming with heartfelt appreciation and tenderness. This reprieve, this second opportunity, was a precious boon, forged in the crucible of love and selflessness. The absolution granted wasn't solely his; it extended to me, a hesitant but genuine acceptance that infused my soul with a soothing balm of tranquillity. The peace that enveloped me was the exquisite reward of belonging.

A buoyant spirit infused our return to the cavern; the oppressive weight of shared culpability lifted, supplanted by a resolute unity and invigorated resolve. Our alliance, tempered in the crucible of conflict, refined by treachery, and solidified by absolution, shone brighter than ever. We had confronted the abyss together and emerged into the fragile dawn of mutual comprehension. Our intertwined history, an unbreakable chain, would forever shape our destinies as we braced for imminent conflicts and unforeseen perils. The Obsidian Covenant, a persistent menace, no longer held us in its solitary grasp; we possessed the unwavering support of one another, our pact reinforced by a transformative odyssey—a pilgrimage of deceit, pardon, and a burgeoning, profound affection. Our bond was indissoluble, fueled by a potent force that would vanquish any shadow that dared to obstruct our path.

The cave's silence clawed at us, a suffocating weight pressing down, heavy with the reek of damp earth and the metallic tang of blood, our blood, spilled in sacrifice. This was no mere sanctuary; it was a tomb carved from the very heart of despair, a monument to our shattered hopes, painstakingly rebuilt brick by bloody brick. Each drip of water echoing in the oppressive darkness was a hammer blow against our resolve, a relentless reminder of the tempest raging outside, the boundless, gnawing darkness that threatened to swallow us whole. Yet, it was also a beacon. The faintest glimmer of a fire, reflecting in sweat slicked eyes, cast dancing shadows that whispered of enduring devotion, a testament to the unwavering fury in our hearts.

Uncertainty, a venomous serpent, coiled in the pit of our stomachs. We tasted fear, bitter and sharp, but we would not yield. We, the scarred, the broken, the haunted, would face that future, a ragged, defiant line against the encroaching void. Each calloused hand, each trembling limb, a testament to our shared ordeal, our unwavering will. The future was a gaping maw, but we would march into it, shoulder to shoulder, a storm of defiance in the face of oblivion.

CHAPTER

TWENTY TWO

Shadows of Obsidian

The cave, once a sanctuary of healing, now became a haven of hope. The lingering scent of wood smoke and damp earth mingled with the faint, sweet aroma of Caspian's blood, a constant reminder of their shared vulnerability and the unlikely bond they forged. Life settled into a rhythm, a delicate balance between quiet intimacy and the ever present threat of the Obsidian Covenant. They spent their days honing their skills, practicing their fighting techniques, the rhythmic clash of steel against steel a counterpoint to the quiet moments of shared laughter and whispered secrets.

The crushing weight of guilt lifted, and Caspian, reborn, unleashed a torrent of wit sharper than shattered obsidian. His eyes, once pools of despair reflecting a dying sun, now blazed with a feral vitality, mirroring the incandescent fury of my elemental power, a power that tasted of Sulfur and scorched earth on my tongue. The scent of ozone crackled in the air as he moved, a predator unbound. His fighting style was a lethal ballet, each precise movement a whispered threat, a promise of exquisite pain. The rasp of his voice in my ear, low and hypnotic, revealed the secrets of the Whispering Wind: a conspiracy woven from ancient lore and forbidden magic, a tapestry of shadows stitched with the lives of spies and assassins, their cold, calculating breaths on my neck. He showed me techniques to control the ravenous hunger within, a dark, burning thirst, far beyond the desperate, brutal methods I'd scavenged for survival. Those techniques felt like ice against fevered skin, a desperate, welcome relief.

In return, I offered him the inferno that pulsed within my veins, the raw, untamed power of flame magic. The taste of fire, acrid, bitter, intoxicating, clung to my lips as I showed him its true extent. The searing heat of my touch, the very essence of fire's volatile heart, coursed between us, a searing current that shocked and exhilarated. Our lessons were a brutal, beautiful exchange, a desperate dance of power and knowledge, each strike, each revelation forging an unbreakable, terrifying bond between us, a bond forged in the crucible of shared darkness.

The cave air hung thick and cold, a miasma clinging to our skin even as the press of our bodies generated a fragile, desperate heat. The rough stone bit into my back, a constant reminder of our precarious existence, but the warmth of Caspian's breath on my neck was a searing counterpoint. We spoke in hushed whispers, our voices echoing the cavern's vastness, each word a shard of memory. My idyllic childhood, a tapestry of sun drenched fields and laughter, was ripped to shreds by the Obsidian Covenant's crimson tide. I tasted the metallic tang of blood again, saw the flickering flames that consumed my village, and felt the phantom ache of loss claw at my soul. The desire for vengeance, a white hot brand, seared my very being.

Caspian, his eyes the colour of a storm wracked sea, spoke of the Whispering Wind—a brotherhood forged in shadow and blood, where loyalty was a razor's edge and betrayal a swift death. The rasp of his voice painted vivid images of brutal training, the chilling whisper of secrets learned in the dead of night, and the weight of his clandestine oaths. His words were a chilling wind, mirroring the icy grip of the cave itself, yet hinting at a heart that burned as fiercely as my own.

Our stories twisted together, a macabre dance of shared trauma, a dark waltz of sorrow and yearning. Our love, born in the heart of desolation, bloomed not with delicate petals but with savage thorns, as fierce and untamed as the wilderness itself. Our nights were a desperate communion, the scent of damp earth and the acrid tang of fear mingling with the raw, animal heat of our bodies pressed together. Our passion was a tempest, a terrifying beauty forged in the crucible of our shared pain; a testament not just to trust, but to a defiant refusal to be broken.

It was a fragile flame flickering in the face of a brutal world, a defiant act of love against the encroaching darkness.

Our relationship transcended mere romance; we were comrades, perfectly matched in our defiance of the encroaching shadows. A profound interdependence blossomed, our actions anticipating each other with uncanny precision, our intertwined forms a potent fusion of infernal might and incandescent energy. Strategic discussions consumed us, our minds razor sharp, our resolve adamantine as we meticulously crafted our next assault. The Obsidian Covenant, a malevolent spectre perpetually at our heels, could not deter us; we were ready. Our unity, forged in the crucible of conflict and refined by shared suffering, rendered us indomitable.

Challenges shadowed their nascent existence. The Obsidian Covenant loomed, a palpable menace constantly testing their resolve. Intelligence trickled in, painting a grim picture of escalating Covenant operations—sinister rites and clandestine meetings. The wind itself seemed to murmur of a burgeoning malevolence, a gathering tempest poised to break. They braced themselves, sharpening their blades, refining their techniques, stealing their hearts for the unavoidable clash. Yet, even amidst these preparations, pockets of tranquillity bloomed— fleeting moments of shared elation and profound serenity.

We ventured out of the obsidian cave, its mouth a jagged tear in the cliff face overlooking the Whisperwind Valley. The air, thick with the scent of pine and damp earth, was a welcome change from the stale, mineral heavy atmosphere of our underground refuge. The waterfalls, cascading down moss covered cliffs carved from a pale, rose hued stone, fed a river that snaked through the valley floor, its waters impossibly clear, reflecting the vibrant green of the surrounding Xylos forest. These trees, with their luminous, silver leaves that shimmered even in shadow, were unique to this region, their sap a valuable resource used in healing balms, a resource we desperately needed.

The ancient ruins, partially swallowed by the relentless embrace of the jungle, were those of the Sunstone civilization, a people who thrived in this valley centuries ago, their mastery of light and energy evident in the intricate carvings that adorned the remaining structures. We deciphered fragments of their history from the glyphs etched into the stone, tales of a great conflict, a cataclysm that plunged the land into darkness before the Whisperwind Valley emerged as a refuge. Our exploration wasn't just a physical journey; it was a pilgrimage to their forgotten legacy, a search for answers in the echoes of their past.

The sun, a rare and precious visitor in the perpetually twilight drenched valley, felt almost alien on our skin, its warmth a stark contrast to the chill that clung to the cave. The wind, carrying the scent of Xylos blossoms, whispered secrets through our hair, a subtle melody that momentarily drowned out the constant, low hum of the energy fields that pulsed beneath the earth, a constant reminder of the ever present danger lurking beneath the surface. These moments of peace, these stolen breaths of beauty amidst the ruins of a forgotten world, were not just a respite; they were a lifeline, a fragile reaffirmation of our hope for a future free from the darkness that had pursued us for so long. They were a testament to the resilience of the human spirit, capable of finding beauty even in the shadow of despair.

One evening, we sat by the whispering reeds of Lake Aethelred, its surface a mirror reflecting the myriad stars scattered across the inky velvet of the Aethel night sky. The air, crisp with the scent of pine and damp earth, held the faintest tremor of magic, the residual hum of the nearby Whisperwood, a forest said to hold secrets older than the kingdom itself. I traced patterns in the silver sand, the grains cool and fine beneath my fingers, my gaze lost in the celestial tapestry above. The moon, a sliver of polished pearl in the vast expanse, cast long shadows that danced with the swaying reeds.

Caspian, his Blond hair catching the moonlight, watched me, his heart mirroring the lake's tranquil surface, a deep, still pool reflecting his profound love. He reached out, his hand calloused but gentle, covering mine. His touch, a familiar warmth against my skin, was a silent pledge, a promise etched not only in his eyes but in the very fabric of his being, woven from the threads of loyalty forged in the fires of our shared past. He knew the path ahead, leading towards the shadowed peaks of the Dragon's Teeth mountains, would be treacherous. Whispers of betrayal snaked through the taverns of Porthaven, and the loss of the Sunstone, a relic of untold power, loomed like a storm cloud on the horizon. But he also knew, felt it in the very core of his soul, that he had found something worth fighting for, something worth sacrificing everything, even his life, for. The love we shared was a beacon in the encroaching darkness, a light brighter than any star in the Aethel sky.

He leaned in, his breath ghosting over my lips, the air thick with unspoken desire. The kiss that followed was a slow burn, a gentle exploration that ignited a wildfire within. The taste of my lips, sweet nectar, was a heady drug, leaving him breathless and wanting more. Our bodies, pressed together, spoke a language far older than words; the rhythm of our hearts was a frantic drumbeat against the silence of the cave. It wasn't just resilience or love that bound us; it was a raw, primal need, a desperate clinging to each other in the face of overwhelming darkness. Our intertwined limbs felt like a desperate plea, a silent promise of solace in the aftermath of battle. The cave, once a sanctuary, became a crucible, the heat of our bodies radiating against the cold stone. Each touch, each breath, heightened the tension, a palpable energy humming between us. We had faced demons and flames, but the fire burning between us was far more potent, more consuming. This wasn't just hope for a new beginning; it was the urgent, breathtaking promise of a future filled with a passion that burned brighter than any flame elemental. The darkness outside felt insignificant compared to the incandescent heat of our shared intimacy.

Our connection intensified with each shared ordeal, each conflict surmounted, and each obstacle conquered. Facing the unknown, we felt not trepidation, but an unshakeable resolve, our pact forged in the crucible of mutual hardship and the pledge of a future intertwined. Our affection, tempered in the furnace of adversity, became our bedrock, a radiant beacon illuminating our perpetual struggle. Though shadows still threatened, we stood defiantly, side by side, our hearts pulsing in perfect rhythm, our love a formidable shield against the impending trials. The wind's lamentations bore witness to our tenacity, our devotion, our indomitable spirit. The Obsidian Covenant's shadow stretched toward us, but we awaited its arrival, prepared. We had discovered a fresh dawn, a renewed existence, a love impervious even to the deepest gloom. Together, we embraced whatever destiny held in store.

The wind screamed the prophecy, a rasping whisper of obsidian dust and death: the Covenant was gathering. No mere skirmishes this time, no gentle dance of blades. This was a symphony of slaughter, a meticulously orchestrated crescendo of annihilation, conducted by the very void itself. The stench of sulfur and burnt offerings clung heavy in the air, a miasma that choked the breath from my lungs and clawed at the sanity that still clung to me, a fragile thing. I tasted blood, not my own, but the metallic tang of a thousand sacrifices carried on the wind from those unholy crimson moons, moons that bled a sickly light onto the warped, groaning landscape. The earth itself trembled, a fevered pulse beneath my feet, a palpable distortion of reality, a premonition of the final, shattering collapse.

Our sanctuary, once a haven of stolen peace, a fragile bubble of tranquility, now vibrated with a terror so profound it cracked the very stones beneath our feet. The hope we held, a flickering candle flame against the encroaching darkness, was snuffed out by the icy breath of impending doom. It wasn't just hope; it was the memory of laughter, the ghost of warmth, now crushed beneath the heel of a power so ancient, so vast, it defied comprehension. And I, haunted by the faces of those I swore to protect, felt the chilling weight of responsibility, a crushing burden that threatened to shatter me as surely as the Obsidian Covenant would shatter our world.

The dust motes danced in the flickering candlelight, each a tiny, mocking spectre as Caspian, his eyes burning with a feverish intensity, traced the crumbling glyphs of an ancient scroll. The parchment smelled of decay and secrets, the ink a viscous stain whispering forgotten prophecies of the Covenant's malevolent designs. His fingers, stained with the dust of ages, ached with the weight of the knowledge he unearthed: cryptic maps, pulsing with malevolent energy that pricked his skin, revealed the location of hidden strongholds, fortresses carved into the very bones of the earth. Intercepted messages, snatched from the wind's cruel caress by the Whispering Wind's shadowy agents, crackled with a chilling clarity in his mind, a terrifying symphony of coded commands leading to a single, horrifying crescendo: the unleashing of a primordial evil, a darkness so profound it tasted of ash and despair on his tongue.

My training was a brutal baptism. The taste of blood, a constant siren song, throbbed behind my teeth. Each suppressed urge felt like a razor blade against my soul. I wrestled with the chaotic energy within me, my very veins singing with the power of the elements, fire that scorched my throat, earth that clawed at my bones, air that choked my lungs. The agony was exquisite, a relentless hammering against the walls of my sanity. Yet, with every agonizing breath, I saw their faces, the villagers, their eyes wide with terror, their screams echoing in the shadowed corners of my heart. Their blood spilled upon the ravaged earth, fueled my fury, my relentless drive to forge a weapon from my darkness, to meet the coming storm with a strength that would shatter the very foundations of the Covenant's reign of terror. This was not merely survival; this was vengeance. This was redemption.

Each dawn bled into a relentless cycle of preparation, a rhythm as familiar as the sun rising over the horizon. The metallic tang of ancient steel filled our nostrils, awakening memories of battles long lost and victories that had turned to ash. The gritty texture of forgotten battlefields clung to our skin, remnants of histories etched into the earth reminding us of the countless struggles that had taken place on this cursed soil. With every passing moment the gnawing dread in our gut became a constant agonizing companion whispering dark prophecies of what lay ahead. The fight—the world's fight—hung over us like a suffocating weight pressing down on our shoulders a shadow cast by the looming apocalypse that seemed ever closer taunting us with its inevitability.

In our desperate quest for survival we scavenged the graves of fallen empires picking through the remnants of a time long past when glory and honor were once in abundance. The whispers of their dead echoed in the rusting weaponry we unearthed each clang of metal against stone reverberating with the stories of those who had wielded these instruments of war. It was as if the spirits of the fallen were urging us to remember their sacrifices to learn from their triumphs and failures. Our arsenal grew a collection of arcane horrors that defied understanding each artifact pulsing with a malevolent energy that singed our very souls sending shivers of foreboding down our spines.

We were no longer merely scavengers; we had become the custodians of a dark legacy tasked with wielding the remnants of a world teetering on the brink of collapse. Each weapon and each relic held a fragment of the past, a reminder of the fierce battles that had shaped the course of human history. As we prepared for what was to come we felt the weight of our choices pressing down upon us. Would we rise as the phoenix from the ashes of despair or would we be consumed by the very darkness we sought to combat? The air was thick with uncertainty but we steeled ourselves ready to face whatever horrors awaited us in the shadows.

Caspian, a demon sculpted from shadow and rage, his eyes burning with infernal light, pushed us to the brink. His strength, a raw, terrifying power that left the air crackling with ozone, was a brutal test of our endurance, a trial by fire and fury. I, in turn, unleashed the blistering inferno within me, a searing torrent of hellfire that consumed everything in its path, proving our readiness. His demonic might, my fiery wrath, they weren't just complementary forces, they were a symphony of annihilation, a meticulously choreographed ballet of destruction. Each movement a deadly grace, each strike precise and merciless. We were a storm of dark magic and elemental fury, a cataclysm unbound, a force that made the very earth tremble beneath our feet. And they knew it. They felt it.

The acrid bite of burnt gunpowder, a metallic tang clinging to the sheets like a shroud, mocked the phantom sweetness of our stolen kisses, a sweetness now soured, a bitter parody of what we'd lost. Nights, once sanctuaries of whispered promises and limbs entwined in a desperate dance of passion, now throbbed with a silent, venomous energy, a crackling static that threatened to ignite the very air we breathed. Our conversations, once a lover's murmur, were now a chilling ballet of calculated words, a symphony of barely suppressed rage conducted by the ghosts of our shattered trust. Each syllable, a poisoned dart aimed at the heart of our fragile truce.

The unspoken accusations hung heavy, thick as the smoke from a battlefield, each potential betrayal a razor blade twisting, not just in my gut, but in the very marrow of my bones. I could taste the weight of their innocence, a suffocating, metallic pressure on my chest, a bitter tang of blood and betrayal. The guilt, a physical entity, pressed against me, cold and heavy as a tombstone. Their eyes, once pools of luminous desire, now held a chilling intelligence, a calculating ruthlessness that both terrified and strangely fascinated me. This wasn't just a war; it was a slow, agonizing dance of destruction, a waltz with the devil played on the strings of our shattered souls.

He, with eyes the colour of a storm wracked sea, traced the lines of our plan on the sweat slicked table, his touch sending a shiver that had nothing to do with the cold. She, a wildfire in a silken cage, her breath a ragged whisper against my ear, spoke of sacrifices, her voice laced with a steely resolve that both terrified and exhilarated me. Our love, once a refuge, a sun drenched meadow, had become a crucible, forging us in the fires of desperation. It was a bond forged not in tenderness, but in the searing heat of shared danger, a dark and incandescent passion that burned away everything but the raw, essential core of who we were. The fierceness of our desire was tempered, yes, but not extinguished. It fueled our resolve, a burning engine driving us toward a future uncertain, yet painted in the desperate hope of survival.

That night, firelight danced on our faces, a flickering reflection of the anxieties churning within us. Caspian's confession hung heavy in the air, not the dread of mortality, for he'd stared into its abyss countless times, but the agonizing terror of inadequacy. The weight of his lineage, the crushing expectations, the countless souls dependent on his triumph, it all threatened to overwhelm him. My response, though gentle, carried unwavering conviction. I spoke of our intertwined destinies, our resolute determination, and the profound affection binding us, a love potent enough to shatter any obstacle. I gently reminded him of our shared journey, of the unbreakable bond between us; that in our mutual support, true strength resided.

Shared fragility forged a profound connection between us. Was this really happening? Was I being too vulnerable? No, no, it felt right, a necessary shedding of the armor I'd worn for so long. We bared our souls, confessing anxieties, uncertainties, and self doubts. He's listening, really listening. I haven't felt this safe to be this…me…in ages. Is this what love feels like? This terrifying, exhilarating plunge into the unknown? This openness wasn't a sign of frailty; rather, it showcased the resilience of our bond. He's sharing too, mirroring my fears and doubts. It's not just me. We're in this together. In those intimate moments of apprehension and precariousness, our love blossomed, a radiant flame against the encroaching shadows. This is it. This is the real thing. The fear is still there, a low hum beneath the warmth, but it's manageable now, somehow lessened by the sheer intensity of the connection. It's beautiful, terrifying, and utterly, completely worth it.

This battle, we understood, would push us to the precipice, demanding both treachery and profound selflessness. Can we really do this? Treachery? My hands... they've never been stained with such a thing. Yet, our interwoven histories, our collective suffering, So much loss... I can still see their faces... and the unbreakable bonds of affection forged an indissoluble unity. But for them... for them I can do anything. Bound together by destiny, we recognized our amplified strength, a power born from shared experience. This feeling... it's not just courage, it's something... ancient. Like the earth itself rising up to meet the storm. We had confronted the abyss, but its shadows would not claim us. Not this time. Not ever again. We're stronger together. We're going to survive this.

With preparations finalized, we plunged into the Covenant's domain. We were phantoms, gliding through the nocturnal landscape, each movement a calculated risk in a perilous odyssey. Covenant patrols—abominations birthed from the abyss, fiendish soldiers with malevolent eyes—assailed us repeatedly. Yet, my fiery might and Caspian's infernal power formed an indomitable alliance. Every clash was a lethal ballet, a maelstrom of annihilation and resilience. We fought with savage precision, an unstoppable tide shattering the enemy's formations. Caspian's tactical genius, combined with my untamed strength, guaranteed our triumph.

Unveiling hidden crypts, we unearthed ancient relics thrumming with malevolent energy, stark evidence of the Covenant's depraved rites. Each layer of the abyss revealed a terrifying escalation of the looming peril. The Covenant, we learned, was far more than a military force; it was a fanatical sect, driven by a maniacal desire to unleash unimaginable devastation upon the world. We endured harrowing ordeals, our bodies battered, our souls strained, yet our determination remained unyielding. Our profound love, a steadfast flame in the tempest, ignited our every courageous act. We were fierce combatants, devoted partners, steadfast comrades, inextricably linked by a fate we could not, would not, evade.

The Covenant's formidable citadel loomed before us, a harbinger of the ultimate showdown. A palpable aura of malevolent energy crackled in the air, a sinister force menacing not only us, but all existence. We stood at the brink of annihilation, a cataclysmic struggle that would determine the destiny of worlds. The road ahead was treacherous and unknown, yet we advanced as one, our hands intertwined, our spirits unified. Our love, though not a bulwark against the encroaching shadows, served as a potent catalyst, fortifying our determination, amplifying our might, and steering us toward the unavoidable clash. The morrow was veiled in ominous uncertainty, fearsome and daunting. But united, we would confront it. Our love, a tenacious spark in the abyssal darkness, vowed to persist, blazing even more fiercely against the gathering tempest. Our arduous pilgrimage had culminated at this perilous juncture, and we were prepared. Together.

The obsidian gates weren't merely black; they pulsed with an inner, malevolent light, like a dying star crammed into a cage of volcanic glass. Runes, etched in a language older than recorded history, snaked across their surface, glowing faintly with an infernal luminescence. These weren't just gates; they were a solidified scream of primordial chaos, guarding a chasm that had swallowed entire armies in ages past. The air itself crackled with arcane energy, the scent of Sulfur and ozone mixing with the cloying sweetness of nightshade blooms that inexplicably thrived in the barren, rocky landscape surrounding the gates. These blooms, Caspian had learned, were harbingers of the Shadowfell, their perfume a subtle but potent neurotoxin.

The dread wasn't simply atmospheric; it was a tangible entity, a pressure pressing down on their chests, squeezing the air from their lungs. Caspian, his usually stoic face drawn and pale, gripped his ancestral scimitar, its obsidian blade mirroring the gates in a chilling symmetry. His armour, forged from the heart of a fallen meteor, hummed faintly in response to the ambient magic, a low thrum that resonated with the power emanating from me. My elemental magic, the gift of the Sunstone Clan, manifested as a shimmering, golden aura, a defiant beacon against the encroaching darkness. It wasn't merely a counterpoint; it was a living shield, a testament to the ancient pact between my ancestors and the sun god, Solara. The ground beneath our feet vibrated with a low, rhythmic pulse, a heartbeat of the monstrous entity imprisoned beyond the gates, a pulse that mirrored the frantic pounding of my own heart. The task ahead wasn't merely to open the gates; it was to confront a power that threatened to unravel the very fabric of reality.

Our odyssey had been an arduous and relentless trial that welded our connection into an indomitable force surpassing even the limitations of our natures. We had confronted innumerable horrors both tangible and imagined and emerged triumphant, our unwavering devotion serving as a bulwark against the encroaching abyss that sought to claim us. Each step of our journey had tested the very fabric of our resolve shaping us into something greater than we had ever anticipated. Yet this… this was unparalleled. This was the very core of the malevolence, the genesis of the terror that had long pursued us like a shadow in the night.

As we stood before the source of our darkest fears a chilling realization washed over us. It was not merely a physical manifestation of evil that we faced but rather a reflection of all the trials we had endured. The air was thick with an oppressive dread and the ground beneath our feet seemed to pulse with a malevolent energy as if alive and aware of our presence. This was not just a culmination of our struggles; it was the embodiment of our greatest nightmares, the culmination of every whispered fear and every sleepless night spent in torment. We had come so far yet now as we confronted this ultimate adversary our hearts raced with a mixture of dread and determination knowing that the outcome of this confrontation would determine not only our fate but the very essence of our souls.

The earth shuddered beneath us as we drew near the gates, a tremor that resonated in our very bones. An aura of malevolent power crackled in the air, the ancient stones themselves seeming to vibrate with ominous prophecies. From within the Covenant's stronghold, a terrifying chorus assaulted our ears, a savage litany of incantations, the clang of brutal combat, and the monstrous bellows of hellish entities. This symphony of annihilation foreshadowed the cataclysm to come. A glacial terror, a primordial instinct of self preservation, seized my soul, a fear I'd long subjugated, yet the sheer magnitude of the encroaching wickedness threatened to shatter my composure.

Caspian's grip on my hand—a silent testament to his understanding of my fear—tightened with an intensity that spoke volumes. His touch which usually offered a comforting blend of solace and thrilling excitement now bore the weight of a profound burden reflecting the gravity of our situation and the peril we faced together. The imminent threat loomed large, an ominous shadow that darkened our thoughts while the stark possibility of catastrophic failure lay just a heartbeat away palpable in the air around us. Yet despite the overwhelming anxiety that threatened to engulf us his unwavering resolve shone through like a beacon in the darkness fierce and unyielding. Retreat was unthinkable; it was not an option we could afford to entertain. The destiny of all humankind hung in the balance fragile and uncertain and our own survival intertwined intricately with the outcome of this perilous endeavor. We stood on the edge of a precipice both literally and metaphorically with the weight of our choices pressing heavily on our shoulders. The stakes had never been higher and the responsibility felt like a heavy mantle draped around us. I could feel the pulse of adrenaline coursing through my veins matching the rhythm of our racing hearts as we prepared to face whatever lay ahead. Together we were bound by a shared sense of purpose, a fierce determination to confront the unknown. In that moment I knew that whatever challenges awaited us we would face them side by side unwavering in our commitment to protect not only ourselves but also the future of humanity.

Unnoticed, we infiltrated the fortress through a gap in the gate, our passage as quiet as death itself. Within, a nightmarish maze of gloom and hushed menace unfolded—a grotesque mockery of order. Fiendish creatures patrolled the echoing halls, their malevolent gaze burning like hellfire, their very being a suffocating dread. The atmosphere was saturated with the acrid tang of brimstone and carnage, a horrifying testament to the Covenant's depraved ceremonies. With lethal grace, we navigated the labyrinth, evading sentinels, and circumventing deadly contrivances; our actions were a flawless dance of intuition and calculated risk.

Within those desecrated chambers I witnessed unspeakable abominations that clawed at the very fabric of my sanity. The air was thick with the stench of despair and the chilling echoes of vile sacrifices of the innocent reverberated through the stone walls offered to bolster the Covenant's malevolent authority. Each drop of blood spilled upon the cold hard ground was a testament to the grotesque rituals that took place in that accursed place, a reminder of the lives extinguished for the sake of dark ambitions. The depravity ignited within me a volcanic wrath, a righteous inferno that consumed my being, fueling a fire that would not be easily quenched. The anguish etched upon the faces of the victims haunted my thoughts, their silent screams a battle cry that resonated in my soul.

I had borne witness to atrocities before yet these surpassed all others in their horrific grandeur etching themselves into my memory like a cursed brand. The torment and suffering I observed were not merely the acts of a twisted few but the very essence of the wicked Covenant that thrived on chaos and destruction. This was the heart of the shadow that had ravaged my village, the source of the devastation that shattered my existence leaving me adrift in a sea of grief and rage. The echoes of laughter from the tormentors rang in my ears a grotesque symphony that spurred me further along the path of retribution. My quest for vengeance will find no rest until this wickedness is utterly eradicated until the very roots of this malevolence are torn from the earth. I will not rest; I will not falter. The time for reckoning draws near and I will be the harbinger of justice wielding my wrath like a blade to carve a path through the darkness. Each step I take is a promise—no more innocent blood will be shed in vain.

Caspian ever the realist meticulously charted their advance with a keen eye for detail plotting potential avenues of escape while discerning vulnerabilities in the Covenant's formidable fortifications. Every move he made was calculated and deliberate, reflecting his deep understanding of the battlefield. A creature of darkness yet a master of strategy he wielded his tactical genius like a weapon repeatedly snatching victory from the jaws of defeat even when the odds seemed insurmountable. His ability to anticipate the enemy's next move was almost supernatural as he could read the unfolding chaos around him with an uncanny clarity. He was not just a warrior; he was my confidant, my beloved and my unwavering support in times of despair. Together we flowed as one our physical forms harmonizing instinctively as if choreographed by some unseen force. Our minds were interwoven in a silent communion, a bond forged in shared trauma and absolute faith in one another. In the midst of turmoil he was my anchor grounding me when the world threatened to spiral out of control. The synergy between us was palpable allowing us to navigate the treacherous landscape of war with an almost preternatural grace. Every glance exchanged spoke volumes, every decision made was a testament to our collective resilience. We stood united against the onslaught of the Covenant, our hearts beating in synchrony driven by a shared purpose. In the darkest of times it was our connection that illuminated the path forward instilling hope where despair sought to reign and together we forged a destiny that defied the shadows.

Proceeding further into the fortress's core, they arrived at an immense hall. There, amidst his fiercely devoted retinue, resided the Covenant's supreme commander—a figure of awesome, almost incomprehensible might. His followers' eyes blazed with unwavering zeal. A palpable energy thrummed in the chamber, the atmosphere itself pregnant with impending conflict.

The battle was inevitable, a clash of titans, a fight for survival that erupted in a cacophony of screams and shattering bone. I unleashed my elemental fury, a maelstrom of fire that erupted from my fingertips, scorching the demons in a searing wave. Their leathery hides crackled and blackened, the air thick with the stench of burning flesh and Sulfur as they shrieked in agony, their forms consumed in a torrent of fiery destruction. One particularly large demon, its skin a patchwork of obsidian and festering wounds, lunged at me, its claws dripping with venom. I met its attack with a blast of concentrated flame, vaporizing its arm in a flash of incandescent light.

Meanwhile, Caspian, a whirlwind of obsidian muscle and demonic rage, met the Covenant's warriors head on. Their steel weapons shattered against his impenetrable hide as he moved with a blur of deadly precision, each strike a calculated blow that sent their bodies tumbling. He cleaved through their ranks with a massive demonic greatsword, its edge dripping with the blood of a dozen fallen foes. The ground trembled with each of his earth shattering blows, the very air vibrating with the force of his attacks. One warrior, attempting a desperate flanking maneuver, found himself impaled on Caspian's horns, his lifeblood staining the already crimson battlefield.

We fought as one, a devastating whirlwind of destruction. My flames danced and weaved amongst Caspian's brutal strikes, creating a devastating inferno that consumed the enemy. The ground beneath our feet became a charnel house, littered with broken weapons and the charred remains of the Covenant's warriors. Our combined power was a force to be reckoned with, a testament to our unwavering resolve and unyielding fury. Yet, even with our strength, the tide of battle seemed relentless, the demons' numbers seemingly inexhaustible.

A savage, unrelenting struggle pushed us to the precipice of oblivion. This is it, I thought, the bitter taste of fear coating my tongue. Is this how it ends? Alone, broken, with the taste of ash in my mouth? My breath hitched, a ragged gasp in the suffocating pressure. We endured a relentless barrage of life threatening encounters, our bodies ravaged, God, the pain…is this even real? My muscles screamed in protest, each movement a searing agony. Just one more step…one more breath… Our resolve fractured. He's faltering, I can see it in his eyes. And I'm not far behind. A wave of despair threatened to pull me under. Can we even do this? Are we strong enough? Yet, the unwavering strength of our love, That's it. That's the anchor. His hand in mine… his face…his trust. Our inextricable bond, We're not just two people. We're a single entity fighting for a common purpose. and our shared, sacred mission, The memory of why we started, of what we're fighting for. That will get us through. held us fast. It served as our unwavering refuge, A tiny island in this tempest, but it's enough. our indomitable power, We're stronger together than we could ever be alone. the bedrock of our unyielding determination. We will survive. We must.

A maelstrom of destruction and creation engulfed us, a cataclysmic clash of opposing forces. This was a battle for existence itself, a titanic struggle where virtue and wickedness, affection and animosity, optimism and desolation warred for supremacy. Our combat forged us anew, pushing each of us beyond the confines of our perceived capabilities. Our devotion wasn't merely sanctuary; it served as an invincible weapon, a wellspring of energy that fortified our unwavering commitment.

The final blow ripped through the silence, a soundless scream swallowed by the sudden, suffocating stillness. My ears rang, a metallic clang echoing the bone jarring impact that had sent tremors through my very core. The air throbbed, not just with residual energy, but with the stench of blood, hot and coppery on my tongue, the acrid bite of gunpowder stinging my nostrils. This victory, bought with the price of our shattered bodies and the ghosts of fallen comrades, tasted like ash.

My lungs burned, each rasping inhale a branding iron against my raw insides, a searing testament to the unholy waltz we'd just endured. The exhaustion wasn't just a feeling; it was a physical weight, a suffocating shroud woven from the sweat clinging to my skin, the metallic tang of blood thick on my tongue. Pain, my old, familiar lover, throbbed in a grotesque symphony. The dull, sickening grind of fractured ribs resonated with each ragged breath, a counterpoint to the sharp, exquisite agony where the blade had carved its kiss, a searing brand that pulsed with a life of its own. The taste of it, acrid and metallic, lingered, a grim memento mori. Alive. We were alive. But barely. This victory felt less like triumph and more like a reprieve from the executioner's blade, a momentary pause before the inevitable next round. The grit in my teeth tasted like ashes, the taste of survival, the bitter knowledge that the darkness, the hunger that drove us to this, still lurked in the shadows, waiting.

A twisted grin stretched my lips. We stared into the abyss of our uncertain destiny and spat defiance in its face. We had wrestled with fate itself and emerged, bleeding, broken, but undeniably triumphant. The victory felt less like a triumph and more like a brutal reprieve, a testament to the darkness we had both endured and conquered, leaving us scarred and changed forever. It was a victory etched in blood, sweat, and the chilling certainty of the horrors we had witnessed.

Victory tasted like ash and blood. The Obsidian Covenant lay shattered, its obsidian shards glittering like malevolent stars under a bruised, violet sky. But the air, thick with the stench of Sulfur and the lingering phantom cries of the fallen, held no true triumph. A bone deep chill, colder than any winter, settled over us. The world, fractured and bleeding, was a precarious thing, balanced on a knife's edge above an abyss teeming with unseen horrors.

My heart, a frantic drum against my ribs, echoed the unspoken terror. We had stared into the heart of darkness, and though we emerged scarred, bearing the brand of battle on our flesh and souls, the wounds ran deeper than skin. The whispers of uncertainty gnawed at the edges of our hard won peace. Our love, a fiercely burning brand in the suffocating darkness, was our only anchor in this maelstrom. It was a love forged in fire, tested by blood, tempered by the very brink of oblivion. A love that tasted of salt and fear, of desperate hope and quiet defiance.

This was not an ending but a terrifying beginning. The future, an uncharted wasteland stretching before us, was a canvas painted in shades of dread and the faint uncertain glimmer of hope. Each horizon we glimpsed was marred by the scars of past conflicts, reminders of what had been and an ominous forecast of what was still to come. The path ahead remained a treacherous labyrinth shrouded in a suffocating mist each step fraught with peril whispering secrets of danger that lingered just beyond our sight. The air was thick with tension and the ground beneath our feet felt unstable as if it too was unsure of what lay ahead. Yet hand clasped in hand our fingers intertwined like the roots of an ancient tree we would face it together. Our love, a defiant beacon burning against the encroaching night, would light our way even as the shadows stretched and clawed at our heels desperate to pull us into the abyss.

In this stark new reality we were no longer mere survivors; we had become warriors equipped not with swords or shields but with an unyielding bond that fortified us against despair. The final battle might have been won but the war—the true war for our very survival—had only just begun. Each encounter with the remnants of a broken world felt like a test of our resolve, a challenge that sought to unravel the very fabric of our connection. Yet we stood firm drawing strength from one another, our hearts beating in sync with a shared rhythm of courage.

As we ventured deeper into the unknown the landscape morphed into an eerie tapestry of desolation. Crumbling ruins towered like sentinels, remnants of lives once lived echoing with the whispers of those who had fought their own battles. The skies above mirrored our turmoil swirling with dark clouds that threatened to unleash their fury at any moment. But amidst this chaos we found solace in fleeting moments—a shared smile, a gentle squeeze of the hand or a soft laugh that pierced through the gloom.

These small acts of defiance became our rallying cries reminding us that even in the darkest of times there existed the potential for light. We envisioned a future where hope could flourish, a place where love could thrive despite the ashes of our past. With every step we engraved our resolve into the earth beneath us determined to carve a path through the uncertainty that lay ahead. Together we would rise not just to survive but to reclaim our existence in a world that seemed determined to strip it away. In the face of adversity we would forge our own destiny lighting the way for others who wandered lost in the shadows.

CHAPTER

TWENTY THREE

Forged in Fire

Black obsidian fangs, jagged as shattered souls, clawed at the bruised, smoke hazed sky, a sky the colour of a dying god's eye. Our victory? A mockery. A pyrrhic triumph brought with the screams of the damned, their agonizing cries still ringing in my ears, a symphony of agony conducted by the crackling flames. The fortress, once a symbol of unyielding power, now lay a smouldering mausoleum, reeking of incinerated flesh and the bitter, metallic tang of ozone, a taste of ash and betrayal coating my ravaged tongue. The sweetness of their blood, a perversely lingering perfume, clung to the cracked paving stones, a grim testament to the butchery. It stained my hands, a crimson stain that mirrored the stain on my soul.

This rain... this pathetic drizzle hissing against the embers like a coward's whimper each drop a futile mocking tear that falls from the sky taunting me in my moment of despair. It couldn't wash away the stench of smoke and death nor the memories that haunt me like restless ghosts nor the weight of a thousand shattered lives that cling to me like the cursed shroud of a battlefield god. I tasted the ash that lingered in the air, felt the heat still searing my flesh as if the flames had etched their pain into my very being and I sensed the chilling certainty that even this hollow victory wouldn't bring me the peace I so desperately sought. Instead it left me with the gnawing emptiness of a heart hardened by the fires of war, a heart that once knew love and laughter but now only echoes with despair. The screams of the fallen, the blood staining the earth, the ash that chokes the air, they were a part of me now woven into the very fabric of my existence, a grim tattoo on my soul that I could never erase. In the shadows of this relentless rain I stood alone burdened by memories that would not fade.

Caspian's grip, a vice of iron and shattered bone, crushed the air from my lungs. The stench of blood, my own and God knows whose else, filled my nostrils, a coppery tang clinging to the back of my throat. My body, a ravaged landscape of pulsing, screaming wounds, throbbed with the dull, relentless hammer of a thousand tiny deaths. The incandescent rage that had fueled me, a wildfire in my veins, was now a dying spark, choked by the suffocating blanket of exhaustion. My vision swam, the world blurring into a hazy crimson. Yet, even through the pain, a grim satisfaction, cold as grave dirt, settled in my soul. We'd done it. We'd clawed our way from the jaws of hell.

But the price... the price was etched onto every fibre of my being. The victory felt hollow, a bitter pill swallowed down with the metallic taste of my blood. A serpent, not of venom, but of corrosive regret, gnawed at my insides, its icy coils tightening around my heart. It whispered of the faces I'd seen lost to the carnage, the screams that still echoed in my ears, the irrevocable choices made in that infernal crucible. The cost was immeasurable. And in the silence left by the storm, that brutal truth, heavier than Caspian's crushing grip, threatened to shatter me.

The stench of Sulfur and burnt flesh clung to Caspian like a shroud, a grim testament to his demonic resilience finally cracking. His usually hawk-like features, etched with the arrogance of a conqueror, were now slack, the sharp angles softened by a bone deep weariness that tasted like ash on my tongue. His eyes, usually blazing embers, were now dull coals, reflecting not just the pyrrhic victory, but the crushing weight of the future—a future as bleak and unforgiving as the obsidian wasteland we'd left behind.

The Obsidian Covenant's shattering wasn't an ending, it was a goddamn earthquake, leaving the ground trembling beneath our feet. A new dawn, yes, but one painted in the blood red hues of a merciless sunrise. We would shape it, we would control it, but the price... The price was already bleeding into the very air we breathed. Consolidating this power wouldn't be a stroll through a sun drenched meadow. It would demand a cold, calculating ruthlessness, a strategic precision honed to a razor's edge, a cunning so sharp it would draw blood before the first blow fell. And neither he, nor I, had truly tasted that blood before. The game had changed, and the stakes... oh god, the stakes were impossibly high.

Our first strike wasn't a roar, but a viper's hiss, a campaign so subtle, it slithered through the veins of the kingdom. Caspian, a man whose smile could curdle milk and whose eyes held the cold gleam of a winter moon, unleashed his network, the Whispering Wind, a plague of whispers. He didn't just spread rumours; he sculpted them, each carefully chosen word a chisel carving a new reality. The Covenant, once feared, became, in his hands, pathetically heroic figures, their demise a necessary sacrifice, a grim but glorious dawn. The taste of fear was on his tongue, and the scent of panic clung to his fingertips as he orchestrated this symphony of deception. He planted evidence, a bloody sigil here, a shattered sword there, each piece a venomous barb, festering in the minds of the populace. His touch was absolute, his influence a suffocating blanket, smothering the truth under a mountain of carefully crafted lies. He was more than a puppeteer; he was the architect of a nightmare, weaving a tapestry of deceit and carefully calibrated half truths so exquisitely spun that even the most discerning eye could not unravel the threads. The bittersweetness of his success clung to the air, thick and cloying, a testament to his chilling mastery.

The wind, a raw, icy breath against my skin, whispered secrets only I could understand. I felt the earth tremble beneath my feet, a heartbeat echoing the fury simmering in my soul. I didn't merely influence the weather; I wrestled it into submission, a tempestuous dance of lightning and rain orchestrated to blind our enemies, to drown their defences in a deluge of my making. The flames... ah, the flames were a different kind of song. They crackled and roared, a symphony of destruction and rebirth, licking at my fingertips with a searing familiarity. I tasted the acrid smoke, a bitter tang on my tongue, a testament to the power I wielded. These weren't just spirits I allied with; they were ancient, scarred beings, their essence interwoven with the very fabric of the shattered land, drawn to my ruthless ambition, to my promise of a world remade in fire and shadow. They saw not mere manipulation, but a shared vision, a chance to rise from the ashes, to rewrite the rules of this broken world, to exact vengeance upon those who had dared to defile it. I was not merely a force of nature; I was the storm, the fire, the earth itself, a tempest of will and power, shaping the very landscape to my cruel, exquisite design.

The tide turned, not with a gentle shift, but a brutal, seismic upheaval. The air crackled with a newly forged power, a tangible hum that vibrated in our bones, Caspian's, sharp and icy, and mine, a molten core of furious ambition. Smaller demonic factions, those viperous slivers that had once danced to the Obsidian Covenant's deadly tune, began to crumble, their allegiance to the broken god shattering like brittle glass. The stench of fear, sharp and cloying, mingled with the metallic tang of blood, a testament to the Covenant's reign of terror. They crawled to us, these former enemies, drawn not by some hollow promise, but by the raw, terrifying force that pulsed between Caspian and me. They saw in us not mere stability, but the promise of absolute dominion, a terrifying order forged in the crucible of their defeat. Each newly sworn allegiance was a fresh wound inflicted on the Covenant's corpse, feeding the insatiable hunger for our growing power, a power that tasted of Sulfur and victory, a power that whispered promises of utter annihilation.

Their ascension was a blood soaked baptism. The Covenant's collapse didn't create a vacuum; it unleashed a maelstrom. From the channel reeking shadows, things stirred. Not mere rivals, but demon lords whose very names curdled the blood, their laughter, a rasping echo in the wind, felt like icy claws on the soul. Ambitious sorcerers, their eyes burning with unholy ambition, weaved spells that crackled with the stench of brimstone and the taste of ash. And from the deepest, darkest trenches of time, ancient beings awoke, their presence a crushing weight, a palpable dread that choked the very air. Each clawed for dominion over the shattered land, their hunger a palpable thing, a miasma of malice clinging to the fractured earth.

Caspian and I were adrift in that storm. His stoicism, a mask barely concealing the icy terror in his heart, grated against my simmering rage. The threats weren't subtle; they were a constant barrage, a symphony of betrayal, the sting of a poisoned blade, the chilling whisper of a false friend, the agonizing slow burn of treachery. Open warfare was merely the overture to a deeper, more insidious conflict, a dance of shadows fought in the stench of death and the echoing screams of the damned. Each sunrise brought a new battle, each sunset the bitter taste of ashes and the chilling certainty that our reign, bought at such terrible cost, might end in the same bloody chaos that birthed it.

The alliances, forged in the fires of ambition, cracked under the strain. Some, the supposed friends, betrayed us with the cold kiss of Judas, their smiles a venomous mask hiding daggers. Others, I discovered, were true steel, tested and tempered in the crucible of our brutal struggle. The taste of ash and blood was ever present, a bitter reminder of the price of trust. I learned to read the subtle tremor in a hand, the flicker of deceit in an eye, lessons etched into my very soul with the searing brand of betrayal. My touch, once naïve, now held the chilling weight of calculated deception; the art of the lie, a honed weapon in my arsenal.

Caspian, his gaze as sharp as a winter wind, was a figure of unwavering resolve and relentless pragmatism. His ruthlessness akin to the bitter chill of a frosty evening was only equaled by the icy calm that enveloped him in the heat of chaos. He possessed an uncanny ability to see the rot before it blossomed into something more malignant. With an instinct honed by years of experience he anticipated the strikes of our adversaries; he felt the tremors of treachery in the very earth beneath us sensing the shifting tectonic plates of loyalty and betrayal long before the ground would inevitably give way beneath our feet.

The scent of fear—of impending doom—was something he could smell a noxious perfume that lingered in the air and he could taste it bitter and acrid on his tongue. With surgical precision he wielded his intellect like a scalpel deftly cutting the cancers from our organization before they had the chance to metastasize. No one could deny the effectiveness of his methods though some might argue they bordered on ruthless. Yet in the world we navigated where survival often hinged on the ability to eliminate threats swiftly and decisively his approach was not only practical but necessary.

His mind, a labyrinth of strategy and counter-strategy, was a fortress impenetrable to the insidious whispers of our enemies. Every move he made was calculated, every decision meticulously weighed against the potential consequences. He was always three steps ahead anticipating the next play of our foes who lurked in the shadows waiting for a moment of weakness to strike. In a world fraught with deception and danger Caspian stood as a bulwark against chaos, his icy demeanor instilling both fear and respect in those who dared to challenge him. His presence was a chilling reminder that in our line of work hesitation could lead to ruin and decisiveness was the key to survival.

Together, our skills formed a storm, a maelstrom of power. His foresight, damn, he always saw the next move before it happened, a chess master playing against children, and my calculated ruthlessness. Another life ruined, another pawn sacrifice. Is this what I truly want? No, this is what I need. Survival demands it. A dance on the edge of the precipice, a terrifying ballet of survival. One wrong step and the fall will be absolute. But there is no other path, is there? We were not just powerful; we were terrifying. They fear us. Good. Fear is a useful tool. It keeps them in line. Our combined force was a legend whispered in hushed tones, a chilling warning to all who dared to challenge our dominion. Let them whisper. Let them fear. Their fear is our shield, our power... and perhaps, my damnation.

The stench of ash still clung to the ravaged earth, a bitter perfume clinging to our sleeves as we rebuilt. Each hammered nail, each carefully placed timber, was a defiant act against the ruin. We fed the starving, the raw hunger in their eyes, a burning brand on our consciences, supplying not just sustenance, but the fragile hope that bloomed in the face of despair. The taste of salt spray and the reek of sweat mingled with the earthy scent of freshly turned soil as we forged our trade networks, ruthless bargains struck in the shadow of shattered towers. These alliances, born in the fires of chaos, were bonds forged in blood and grit, each handshake a silent acknowledgment of our shared strength.

The screams of the lawless, once a constant chorus, were slowly silenced. Not by brute force, but by the iron fist concealed within a velvet glove. The chilling precision of our justice, meticulously crafted, instilled not fear, but a grudging respect, a desperate yearning for the stability our laws provided. The fragile peace we established was a knife's edge, a precarious balance hanging over the abyss of utter annihilation. Yet, it held.

Our dominion wasn't built on fear but on the chilling calculated understanding of power. We were the architects of influence, the puppeteers pulling strings in the dark. Our every move was a masterstroke of manipulation and cunning. With a deft touch we whispered promises that danced on the edge of truth and we wielded threats like sharpened blades ready to cut through any opposition. We traded favours like deadly weapons, each agreement a calculated risk, each alliance a strategic maneuver in the grand game of dominance. All of this was executed with precision all to forge a kingdom from the ashes of our adversaries a testament to our ruthless ambition and unwavering will.

In the shadows we constructed a realm where loyalty was bought and sold where trust was a luxury few could afford. Our network of influence spread like a web ensnaring those who dared to defy us while elevating those who understood the delicate balance of power. We played our adversaries against one another sowing discord and confusion ensuring that they were too preoccupied with their own struggles to challenge our supremacy. The taste of victory was bitter yes but undeniably sweet leaving a lingering satisfaction that only those who have clawed their way to the top can truly appreciate. Every triumph was a reminder of our unyielding resolve, a beacon of our strategic genius.

In the end we crafted not just a kingdom but a legacy forged in the fires of ambition and tempered by the trials of power. Our story is one of relentless pursuit and calculated risk, a journey marked by shadows and whispers where every moment was a testament to the strength of our resolve and the depth of our cunning.

Our fiery bond, already forged in the white heat of adversity, now faced the ultimate trial: the corrosive power of shared dominion. The incandescent passion that had ignited our union was refined, tempered by the responsibilities of our elevated positions. Our ambitions, once intertwined in a dance of desire, now bore the heavy burden of leadership. The simmering eroticism that had always pulsed beneath the surface deepened into an unbreakable connection, forged in the crucible of shared victories and the resilience born of conquered obstacles.

Grief's consuming grip had loosened its hold. I, once a wrathful maiden, discovered the potency of my gifts, wielding them to sculpt a brighter tomorrow. Retribution, I realized, was a siren song, a deceptive mirage leading only to ruin. Even Caspian, hardened by ages of cynical practicality, transformed. A flicker of empathy pierced his centuries forged armour. We remained ethnically ambiguous, our deeds occasionally brutal, yet a shared objective elevated our actions, imbuing them with profound significance.

Our pact, a venomous bloom grown from the rot of ambition, the sweat of lust, and a grudging respect that tasted like ash in the mouth, swayed constantly on the razor's edge of annihilation. Treachery, a serpent coiled in the heart of our enterprise, struck with the swiftness of a viper, met only by the brutal, cold certainty of retaliation. Disputes, some settled with the chilling grace of a practiced assassin, others with the raw, thunderous violence of a collapsing mountain, etched themselves into the very bone of our uneasy alliance.

The air crackled with the volatile energy of our bond, a suffocating blend of possessive affection and brutal domination that tasted like blood and iron on the tongue. Each stolen kiss burned with the heat of a thousand betrayals, and each shared victory left a bitter residue of fear in its wake. Death, that skeletal hand ever hovering at the edge of our opulent feast, reeked of decay and whispered promises of oblivion in every shadowed corner of our reign. The stench of it clung to our silks, to our skin, a constant, chilling reminder of our tenuous grasp on power. We were architects of our destruction, each of us a masterpiece of depravity, bound together by a shared thirst for dominance and haunted by the chilling certainty that the next blade might be aimed at our hearts.

The empire's shadow stretched, a greasy stain across the land, yet the whispers of defiance grew louder, sharper, tasting of blood and rebellion. Each victory—the sickening thud of a conquered city, the acrid smoke of burning banners—birthed a hydra of new enemies, their fangs bared, eyes glittering with hatred. Every step forward sent shockwaves through the fragile tapestry of allegiances, a kaleidoscope of shifting betrayals, a maelstrom of fear and desperate hope. We were forging a new world from the shattered bones of the old, a kingdom not built on the iron fist of some crazed tyrant, but on a razor's edge of precarious balance—a fragile equilibrium held between two beings, bound by a venomous intimacy, a shared understanding of power's brutal, exquisite price. The taste of it lingered, metallic and bitter, on our tongues. We knew the cost. We felt it in the hollow ache of our bones, in the cold dread that snaked through our veins. And still, we dared to build.

The undertaking remained unfinished, the nascent regime precarious, its pillars still unformed. Yet, Caspian and I united and stood defiant against the morrow. Our odyssey, etched in bloodshed, conflagration, and fervent devotion, was far from concluded. We had mastered the perilous currents of dominion and learned the arts of cunning, subterfuge, and sovereign command. Before us stretched a future of unpredictable challenges, a course riddled with peril and promise. But together, hand clasped in hand, we would confront it; our love, an impenetrable bulwark; our power, a keen edged blade; our destiny, inextricably intertwined.

Caspian's ascent to dominance wasn't a crude exertion of might; it was a masterful orchestration of influence and strategic partnerships. Through his far reaching connections within the shadowy Whispering Wind, he meticulously convened a series of clandestine summits with the leaders of lesser demonic entities. These weren't hostile encounters, but intricately planned negotiations, each subtly laced with veiled menaces and captivating inducements. His ultimatum was stark: forge an alliance with him, and partake in the rich rewards of conquest; or be utterly eradicated as pathetic vestiges of the defunct Obsidian Covenant. He painted a vision of a revitalized era, promising unprecedented stability and opulence, a stark improvement over the tyrannical rule of their former overlords. Caspian's mesmerizing eloquence, refined through eons of manipulating the demonic aristocracy, proved overwhelmingly persuasive. The allure of his offered safeguards, substantial provisions, and a stake in the newly formed commercial arteries proved irresistible to factions clinging to survival.

My strategy diverged. Instead of courting the openly malevolent, I cultivated alliances with entities of a less infernal nature. My inherent might, coupled with the palpable sincerity of my regret for the Obsidian Covenant's devastation, gradually swayed them. I eschewed demands for fealty, instead proposing collaboration—a pact founded on mutual esteem and a collective yearning to heal the scarred earth. Our joint ventures—rehabilitating decimated woodlands, cleansing tainted waterways, and reactivating derelict mines—were not mere displays; they were calculated advancements, fortifying my influence and extending my reach. The very flames responded to my command, unveiling hidden reserves and providing sustenance for the burgeoning settlements, a testament to the transformative power of atonement and shared purpose.

A pivotal pact was established with the Sylvani, venerable arboreal beings dwelling within the mystical Whispering Woods. Their chieftain, Elderwood, a colossal, ageless oak, wielded formidable arcane power and commanded immense sway. Initially, he spurned both demonic and human overtures, harbouring profound suspicion towards both. Yet, through a display of my elemental mastery, I showcased my restorative capabilities. I purged the Obsidian Covenant's vile magic from the ravaged Whispering Woods, repairing the blighted landscape and rejuvenating the decimated vegetation. This act of altruistic regeneration, a stark antithesis to the demons' inherent destructiveness, finally softened Elderwood's resolute heart. He conceded to a fragile alliance, bestowing upon me Sylvani's intimate knowledge of the terrain, their formidable magic, and their unwavering fealty; in return securing my guardianship and a solemn oath to defend the sanctity of the Whispering Woods.

Building these alliances proved a treacherous undertaking. Deception and perfidy were endemic in this shattered realm. A cabal of renegade demons, initially sworn to our cause, launched a covert attempt on Caspian's life. My acute perception and Caspian's proactive defences prevented this heinous act. This harrowing incident highlighted the imperative for unwavering vigilance and ruthless pragmatism. Caspian and I subsequently constructed a formidable intelligence apparatus, ensuring our enemies remain perpetually outmaneuvered. We cultivated an uncanny ability to detect the insidious whispers of treason, preempting and dismantling threats before their fruition. Our already intense partnership deepened through these shared ordeals; our mutual reliance was absolute, our bond forged in the crucible of unrelenting peril.

Strategic trade networks formed a cornerstone of Caspian's dominion. His masterful diplomacy forged pacts with diverse groups, unlocking vibrant commerce and resource exchange. This economic prosperity wasn't merely a byproduct; it served as the bedrock of strengthened political bonds. The resulting interdependence, a carefully woven tapestry of goods and services, inextricably linked these factions to Caspian's authority. Resource allocation was meticulously orchestrated, ensuring equitable distribution and preempting dissent, thus cultivating unwavering allegiance.

A sophisticated framework of trade accords, meticulously calibrated to prevent any single power from dominating, was implemented. Maintaining this precarious equilibrium demanded constant vigilance and shrewd recalibration—a testament to Caspian's unparalleled diplomatic finesse and his masterful command of the complex political landscape.

Caspian and I, through decisive action, imposed a framework of order upon the previously anarchic realm. Our enacted statutes, though stringent, proved essential for the preservation of tranquillity and societal cohesion. A robust judicial apparatus was constructed, ensuring equitable resolution of conflicts and swift retribution for transgressions.

Strategic investments in infrastructure—rehabilitating vital arteries of commerce—facilitated the seamless flow of goods and people. These undertakings were not altruistic gestures; rather, they were calculated maneuvers to fortify our dominion and solidify our reign. We recognized that a stable society, even under a demanding leadership, served our ambitions far better than unrestrained pandemonium. True power, we understood, transcended mere subjugation; it resided in the capacity for effective governance, the fostering of unwavering allegiance, and the precarious maintenance of hard won peace.

The journey was a raw, visceral hell. Obstacles weren't mere bumps in the road; they were jagged mountains clawing at our throats, the air thick with the stench of betrayal and the metallic tang of blood. Clashes weren't mere disagreements; they were eruptions of primal fury, a maelstrom of screams and shattering glass, the taste of fear bitter on our tongues. Our alliances, spun from threads finer than spider silk, frayed and snapped, each rupture a searing pain. We stood on the precipice of annihilation, the wind a chilling whisper of oblivion.

But through gritted teeth, through the blinding flash of steel and the suffocating weight of responsibility, we fought. Painstaking diplomacy became a brutal dance, a delicate waltz on the edge of a knife, each concession a drop of blood squeezed from our very souls. Compromises were carved from the raw flesh of our ambitions, each scar a testament to our resilience. And when diplomacy failed, when the stench of treachery hung heavy in the air, we unleashed hell. The decisive deployment of strength wasn't a calculated maneuver; it was a righteous fury, a tempest of raw power that left our enemies broken and gasping for air.

We emerged, scarred but unbroken. Our bond, forged in the crucible of fire, was no longer fragile. It was a coiled viper, a deadly dance of dominance and subservience, a fierce, incandescent passion that burned brighter than any star. The fervour was a wildfire consuming us both, a terrifying, exhilarating embrace. Beneath it all, a grudging, hard won respect, a bitter understanding born of shared trauma and agonizing sacrifice, bloomed, a fragile flower pushing through the ashes. It was a respect earned not through affection, but through the crucible of utter destruction and desperate survival.

Initially, a raw, primal magnetism ignited our bond. Yet, this volatile spark gradually yielded to a profound comprehension, a shared weight of duty, and a profound reverence for each other's inherent fortitude. Our triumph hinged not merely on individual prowess, but upon the unbreakable strength of our pact—our capacity for seamless collaboration, for preemptive action against threats, and for preserving the precarious equilibrium we had meticulously established. Our dominion remained precarious, our adversary's legion, but Caspian and I, united, stood poised to confront any impending adversity. Our alliance, forged in the crucible of conflict, formed the bedrock of our authority and held the promise of a future yet unwritten, a destiny we would shape together.

The truce between Caspian and me, a brittle pact forged in the fires of necessity and shadowed ambition, splintered. The taste of ashes lingered bitter on my tongue, a constant reminder of the precarious balance we maintained. Our outwardly invincible alliance was a façade, a shimmering mirage built on shifting dunes of lust, power, and a venomous distrust that coiled in our very souls. The stench of our mutual deception hung heavy in the air, a miasma clinging to the opulent tapestries of our shared chambers. The Obsidian Covenant, once our singular focus, now seemed a distant thunderclap, dwarfed by the cataclysmic storm brewing within our hearts. His gaze, cold as glacial ice, yet burning with a feverish intensity, sent shivers down my spine, a silent promise of the inevitable clash to come. Each strained smile, each carefully chosen word, was a razor's edge, threatening to sever the already frayed threads of our uneasy partnership. The blood of our mutual enemies, staining the very ground beneath our feet, felt strangely insignificant compared to the simmering, volcanic rage that threatened to consume us both.

The stench of charred wood and the acrid bite of smoke still clung to me, a phantom echo of my village's annihilation. The vampiric hunger, a gnawing beast within, clawed at my gut, a constant, agonizing reminder of my loss. But it was the power, oh, the power… It surged through me, a molten torrent igniting my veins, a symphony of searing heat and crackling energy. The taste of it, metallic, sharp, exhilarating, was a drug, a forbidden elixir that whispered promises of oblivion. Each flicker of flame I commanded, each dance of the inferno, was a perverse act of creation, a twisted reflection of the life violently stolen from me.

The power, a venomous nectar coursing through my veins, was a goddamned symphony of destruction. This pyromantic mastery, this obscene control over the very breath of hell, sang its siren song, a seductive whisper of annihilation that scorched the last vestiges of my conscience. Their faces, twisted masks of agony, etched in the flickering flames, were branded onto my retinas, the stench of burning flesh a constant companion, their screams a cacophony that clawed at the fragile edges of my sanity. The taste of their terror, acrid and metallic, clung to my tongue, a bitter ash coating every stolen breath.

These alliances, forged in the crucible of blood and lies, felt less like shackles and more like the iron grip of a thousand vipers, each coil tightening, each bite injecting a fresh dose of despair. Their whispered promises, slick with deceit, echoed in the cavernous emptiness of my soul. Was this freedom? Or merely a gilded cage, a more exquisite torment, where the bars were wrought of ambition and the warden was my insatiable hunger for power? The price of this infernal throne? A soul already charred to a cinder.

Was this vengeance? This pyre of destruction, this reign of fire, did it truly satiate the beast within? Or did it only feed its insatiable hunger, leaving me more hollow, more lost, than ever before? Doubt, a venomous serpent, not merely coiled, but squeezed, its fangs embedded in my heart, its venom coursing through my soul. The world I craved, a world free from the darkness that consumed my village, felt further away than ever. A bitter mockery of all I hoped to achieve.

The stench of Sulfur clung to Caspian like a shroud, a fitting aroma for a creature forged in the fires of demonic politics. His smile, a predator's lure, felt cold against my skin, a calculated charm that scraped away the veneer of his centuries old cynicism. Behind those captivating eyes, I glimpsed the abyss, the chilling weight of eons spent navigating the treacherous currents of hellish power. My idealistic prattle about justice and cooperation? He found it laughable, a pathetic melody against the harsh discord of our reality. His amusement was a venomous cocktail, laced with contempt that stung like a viper's bite.

The alliance, a strategic necessity, was a fragile truce built on shifting sands. He saw my naïve hope, my unwavering belief in the possibility of good, as a crippling weakness, a blatant disregard for the brutal truth: survival demanded ruthless pragmatism, a blood soaked baptism into the reality of our world. His frustration, a simmering cauldron of suppressed rage, threatened to boil over. He masked it, of course, with his sardonic wit, a polished blade slicing through the air, each carefully chosen word a calculated strike.

The loyalty he demanded, a suffocating pressure, felt hollow, a charade echoing in the vast emptiness of his soul. My unpredictability, my defiant refusal to embrace his cold, calculating world, grated against him like nails on a chalkboard. It was a clash of titans: his centuries of honed ruthlessness against my untamed, idealistic fire. He couldn't comprehend my stubborn refusal to bow before the inevitable darkness. And in the silent, tense moments between our words, I felt the tremor of his fear, a fear not of me, but of the fragile façade he had meticulously crafted, a fear that my unwavering light might just shatter the carefully constructed prison of his demonic heart.

The raw power of our coupling, a tempest of tangled limbs and desperate gasps, had birthed a battlefield. The scent of his skin, once intoxicating, now clung to me like a shroud, a bitter reminder of the shifting tides of dominance. My strength, a coiled serpent within, throbbed against the subtle pressure of his control, a silken rope, tightening, constricting. His touch, once a searing brand, now felt like the icy grip of a master puppeteer, manipulating my every move. The taste of betrayal, acrid and metallic, coated my tongue; I tasted ashes where passion once burned.

His casual disregard wasn't mere carelessness; it was a calculated annihilation, a deliberate branding of my worthlessness. The scent of his cologne, usually a familiar comfort, now reeked of betrayal, a suffocating perfume clinging to the air like a venomous mist. He didn't see me as a partner, not even as a human being, but as a pathetic insect beneath his heel, a thing to be crushed with contemptuous ease. The glint in his eyes, a predatory gleam like polished obsidian, sent a shiver down my spine, a visceral tremor that resonated with the icy dread seizing my heart. This wasn't injustice; it was a brutal violation, a searing brand seared into my soul. The raw, ragged wound pulsed with a fury that transcended mere anger, it was a primal scream trapped behind gritted teeth. I craved more than recognition; I craved retribution, a reckoning so complete it would shatter his smug facade, exposing the hollow, venomous core that masked his cruel mastery. The taste of bile rose in my throat, bitter and acrid, a mirror of the poison he'd injected into my life. His victory wouldn't be swift; my fight would be a slow, agonizing, exquisitely agonizing death for his complacency.

Our intimacy, once a breathtaking dance of fire and fury, was now a charade. Each touch, each stolen breath, was steeped in the bitter tang of resentment, a silent scream trapped between us. The air crackled with unspoken accusations, the weight of them, a physical burden pressing down, suffocating. I yearned for the flames, but all that remained were the smouldering embers of a love consumed by his poisonous ambition.

The air crackled between us, a palpable tension thick enough to taste, bitter and metallic on my tongue. His words, barbed and sharp

as shards of ice, sliced through me. I felt the weight of his gaze, a cold, predatory stare that burned into my skin, leaving trails of icy fire in its wake. His deliberate omission at that crucial meeting, the way he'd let the crucial piece of intel slip through his fingers, a calculated betrayal, tasted like ash in my mouth, the phantom burn of his treachery a constant reminder. These weren't minor incidents; they were carefully orchestrated acts of war, each a tiny explosion in the silent battle for dominance.

Caspian's guidance, his suffocating protection, felt like a silken noose tightening around my throat, each whispered suggestion of a poisoned caress. The rebellion wasn't a conscious decision, it was a wildfire sparked by his insidious control. I didn't simply flout his orders; I shattered them, a defiant dance on the edge of a precipice. My choices weren't born of spite, but of a desperate craving for freedom, a primal scream against his suffocating authority. I forged my alliances, a network woven from defiance and simmering rage, each contact a venomous whisper against his suffocating grip. I wasn't just challenging him; I was eviscerating his control, piece by agonizing piece, savouring the sweet taste of his slow, agonizing decline.

During tense parleys with a formidable elven cabal, Caspian, the consummate pragmatist, advocated a pact of mutual advantage, stressing lucrative commerce and political expediency. My perspective, however, resonated with the vampires' plight; I perceived their fragility and our intertwined past. Caspian, observing my empathy, experienced a sharp twinge of envy, a chink in his meticulously crafted façade of manipulative prowess. This fundamental disagreement, stemming from our disparate temperaments and underlying aims, generated a chasm threatening to shatter our precarious partnership.

The knives weren't just political; they were plunged into the very marrow of our souls. The stench of death, a cloying sweetness mixed with the coppery tang of blood, clung to us, a constant reminder of our mortality. Our relentless pursuers, shadows in the flickering lamplight, whispered promises of oblivion in the wind's chilling sigh. The weight of command wasn't a burden; it was a suffocating iron crown, pressing down on my skull, grinding my teeth to dust. Shared suffering didn't unite us; it twisted our already fractured loyalties into venomous vipers, each strike aimed at the heart of the other.

Sleep? A luxury denied. My nights were a maelstrom of screams, the ghostly echoes of fallen comrades mingling with the guttural roars of the beasts I'd faced, their burning eyes seared into my mind. These nightmares bled into the waking world, erupting in violent fits of rage, my actions as unpredictable as a storm at sea. Caspian, his usually composed face etched with a weariness that mirrored my despair, bore the brunt of my unravelling. He, who saw me as an unbreakable god, a bastion of unwavering strength, now witnessed my shattered reflection: a broken man, consumed by fear and haunted by the ghosts of my victories. His patience, once boundless, was fraying, a thin thread threatening to snap under the strain of my escalating instability. The chasm between his perception and the agonizing reality of my being yawned wider with each passing day, a chasm filled with the bitter taste of betrayal, not by another, but by myself.

My confinement simmered beneath a veneer of benevolent guardianship. Caspian, cloaked in the guise of protection, subtly curtailed my access to knowledge, orchestrating events to serve his designs. His methods were insidious: veiled pronouncements that dripped with thinly disguised menace, a subtle choreography of manipulation. This wasn't malevolence but sprang from a profound, crippling terror. He feared my unpredictable spirit would shatter our meticulously constructed edifice, and that my unwavering idealism would precipitate our ruin. Yet, his suffocating control only ignited my defiance and nurtured a bitter resentment. Doubts gnawed at the foundations of our pact; I grappled with the agonizing question: was the illusory safety Caspian provided a sufficient recompense for the forfeiture of my autonomy?

Our internal discord cast a long shadow over the external landscape. The fragile alliances we had painstakingly built crumbled under the relentless assault of treachery and unforeseen adversity. Whispers of disloyalty, stoked by rumours of our internal strife, poisoned the well of our partnerships. Opportunistic rivals, sensing our vulnerability, launched brazen challenges to our authority. The hard won stability of our world teetered on the brink of collapse. Caspian and I found ourselves embroiled not only in a desperate struggle against our enemies but also in a desperate fight to preserve our precarious union, besieged by both without and within. The very passion that had ignited our bond now threatened to incinerate us both. The fate of our alliance, indeed the world itself, hung in the delicate balance, a knife's edge separating triumph from utter ruin. Our relationship, a volatile interplay of power and affection, strained under immense pressure, nearing its breaking point. Would our love endure the crucible of conflict, or succumb to its searing heat? The answer depended not merely on our willingness to compromise and understand each other, but on our capacity to conquer our deepest, most personal afflictions. The path forward was treacherous, our inner demons proving as lethal as any external foe.

TWENTY FOUR

Tenuous Truce

A brittle calm, thin as a spider's silk strung across a chasm of boiling shadow, held its breath. Maintaining this precarious peace felt like wrestling a hydra, a task exceeding even Caspian's grim, calculating patience and my weary cynicism. Our supposedly invincible legions, a terrifying spectacle from a distance, were a festering wound up close, gnawed by internal dissent and the constant, gnawing pressure of external threats. The stench of fear and betrayal hung heavy in the air, a miasma thicker than the dust kicked up by marching boots. The Obsidian Covenant, their silence a venomous caress, slithered in the darkness, vipers in human skin, their poison seeping into the very marrow of our alliances. I could taste the acrid metallic tang of their treachery, and feel the icy dread of their manipulations coil around my heart like a serpent. Caspian, his steely gaze betraying nothing of the turmoil within, was a fortress built on a foundation of shattered trust, his every carefully measured word a testament to the burden he carried. Even in this fragile truce, the weight of impending doom pressed down on us, a suffocating blanket woven from betrayal and blood.

The rot festered a malignant bloom at the heart of the Whispering Wind. I tasted the metallic tang of fear, the acrid reek of betrayal thick in the air. Caspian's iron grip, once absolute, was shattered. Years of calculated cruelty, of pragmatic bloodshed, had spawned a viper's nest, not of whispers, but of snarling venomous ambition. The ground trembled beneath the weight of Valerius's shadow; a rebellion, not a rumour, coiled and struck. This wasn't just ambition, it was a predator's hunger, honed over centuries of darkness.

His placid facade, a mask of chilling calm, belied the storm raging within. His eyes, pools of glacial ice, held a glint of something far older than this war, something terrifyingly cold and calculating. He didn't merely defy Caspian; he eviscerated him in public, his voice, a silken blade, dissecting Caspian's strategies with icy precision, branding them relics of a bygone age. He demanded blood, a scorched earth campaign against the Covenant, a symphony of destruction. And his insidious whispers, laced with venom, poisoned the minds of my allies.

He painted Caspian as a weakling, a broken man, a puppet swayed by my naïve, idealistic drivel, my 'unsophisticated utopianism,' a phrase dripping with contempt, a brand seared onto my soul. I felt the icy tendrils of his influence tightening, the chilling certainty that the very foundations of our army were crumbling under the weight of his insidious charm and merciless ambition. The air crackled with the promise of violence; the stench of impending doom suffocated me.

The Caspian mud clung to my boots, a greasy, suffocating weight mirroring the dread that coiled in my gut. Initially, I'd recoiled from Caspian's internal bleeding, a festering wound of rebellion. But the stench of Valerius's ambition, far from repulsing me, was intoxicating; a heady perfume of power. His ruthlessness, a razor's edge slicing through the chaos, hummed with a terrifying brilliance. I saw it then, a weapon forged in the fires of his merciless efficiency, a tool to shatter the Covenant, if I could control the beast. This devilish bargain, this whisper of alliance, ignited a wildfire between Caspian and me.

The air crackled with the silent fury of his betrayal, a tension that hung heavy and palpable wrapping around us like a dense fog. His eyes which were usually pools of glacial calm now blazed with a volcanic rage, a fierce storm brewing beneath the surface. My *"contemplation "* he spat with venom was not just an innocent moment of reflection; it was a treasonous act in his eyes, a dangerous flirtation with the abyss that threatened to crumble everything we had painstakingly built together brick by agonizing brick. Each structure we had erected was now at risk teetering on the precipice of destruction due to the very thoughts I dared to entertain. The ensuing clash wasn't merely a confrontation; it was a maelstrom, a whirlwind of emotions that engulfed us both leaving no room for reason or compromise.

The air crackled with unspoken words, each syllable hanging precariously between us waiting for the right moment to ignite. In that charged atmosphere the shadows of our past danced ominously reminding us of the fragile threads that bound our lives together. This was not just a disagreement; it was an existential battle, a defining moment that would either forge a new understanding or shatter everything into irreparable fragments. The stakes had never felt higher and the outcome remained uncertain swathed in a thick layer of tension that neither of us could ignore.

The taste of blood, his, mine, or perhaps only the metallic tang of fear, filled my mouth as our wills collided. His accusations, like shards of ice, pierced the fragile shield of my resolve. The bitter recriminations, echoing in the cavernous silence, clawed at my soul, each word a venomous viper striking at the heart of our fragile trust. This was no mere struggle for power; it was a battle for the very essence of our souls, a tempest of raw, agonizing emotion that left us both bleeding, broken, and utterly transformed.

Caspian's hiss like a snake striking in the air broke the heavy silence around him. The smell of ozone and his own fear sharp and intense filled my nose.. *"Blaze,"* the name rasped from Caspian's lips, each syllable a shard of ice. His eyes like two icy flames pierced through me burning away any remaining doubt. The air buzzed with the strong energy of his anger. *"You imbecile,"* Caspian snarled, the word dripping with contempt, laced with the bitter taste of betrayal. *"Valerius, that viper, that coiled malignancy, you've invited him, invited him into our sacred fold, into our very hearts. Your recklessness is a cancer, gnawing at our very existence."*

"Caspian," I spat, the word a venomous dart, my voice a razor scraping against the granite of his unwavering stare. The chill of his eyes, like glacial ice, seeped into my bones, mirroring the icy grip of the truth he held, a truth as bitter and unforgiving as the charnel house this conflict had become. A calculated disruption? No, a calculated demolition. That's what we needed, a seismic upheaval to shatter this

suffocating status quo, to rip the rotten foundations from beneath his meticulously crafted empire.

A wildfire of defiance, a brutal, glorious rebellion, roared through me, consuming the last vestiges of my weary compliance. The metallic taste of betrayal coated my tongue; the phantom touch of his manipulative tendrils still clung to my skin, a grotesque reminder of my past servitude. I was no longer his pawn, his puppet dancing to his icy tune. I was the storm, and he would feel the full force of my wrath.

The simmering resentment, a venomous serpent coiled in the heart of our alliance, finally struck. It wasn't a mere eruption; it was a volcanic explosion of icy fury, a silent scream of clashing wills that ripped the very fabric of our world. The air crackled, thick with the metallic tang of betrayal and the bitter taste of ash. Our erstwhile partners, vultures circling a carcass, didn't choose allegiances, they snatched them, their greed a blinding flash against the encroaching darkness. The elegant, fragile balance we'd painstakingly woven, a tapestry of trust and shared ambition, shattered. Not merely disintegrated; it imploded, crushed beneath the weight of our venomous infighting, the echoes of our broken oaths ringing like a death knell in the chilling silence.

The taste of blood, both literal and metaphorical, filled my mouth. I could feel the tremor in my bones, a physical manifestation of the seismic shift that had swallowed our carefully constructed paradise whole. Their perfidy stung, a scorpion's kiss, leaving behind a poisonous legacy of doubt and despair. And in the ruins of our broken pact, I saw only the stark, unforgiving landscape of a war that would claim us all.

The chasm yawned beneath my feet, the stench of impending blood already thick in the air. Valerius's simmering rage, a palpable heat against my skin, pressed against Caspian's icy disdain, a chilling wind that cut to the bone. I saw it all, the ravaged fields, the pyres of burning homes, if their feud wasn't quenched. My solution? A venomous concoction, a gamble born of desperation. A spectacle. A contest of brutal, glorious might, played out before the judgmental eyes of all. Valerius, the lion, muscles rippling with barely contained fury, his gaze burning with a cruel intelligence that both terrified and fascinated. Caspian, the serpent, coiled and watchful, his elegance masking a heart of glacial calculation, a master of manipulation who wielded words like daggers.

They would clash, their dominance a feast for the senses, the clang of steel, the roar of the crowd, the sickening thud of flesh meeting bone. The victor, however fleeting, would claim the Whispering Wind, its treacherous power a prize bought with blood and sweat. It was madness, a dance on the edge of oblivion, but a dance I had to lead, for the only alternative was a holocaust that would consume us all.

The air itself screamed. A fetid stench of ozone and decay clawed at my throat as Valerius, a coiling tempest of shadow given flesh, unleashed his fury. Not merely sorcery, but a visceral eruption of raw, malevolent power; each blast of corrupted energy seared the very air, leaving trails of sizzling, black ichor that writhed like dying serpents. The ground trembled, a bass thrumming through my bones that resonated with the sickening crackle of his power. I tasted blood, my own, I think, from a lip I'd bitten raw in terror.

Caspian, his face a mask of chilling calm beneath a cascade of silver hair slicked with sweat, met this onslaught not with brute force, but with a shimmering, razor sharp intellect. His illusions weren't mere tricks; they were living, breathing nightmares, woven from moonlight and deceit, a labyrinthine cage of shifting mirrors and phantom blades that deflected Valerius's attacks with a sickening thunk that echoed the bone deep dread in my own heart. The scent of ozone warred with the faint, metallic tang of blood, his, perhaps? Or mine, again?

This wasn't a duel; it was a cataclysm, a maelstrom of shadow and light, of hate and cunning, tearing the very fabric of reality asunder. Valerius, a creature born of some forgotten abyss, his eyes burning with the cold fire of a dying star, possessed a power that threatened to consume all. Caspian, however, Caspian, the enigmatic manipulator, whose smile held the icy glint of a predator, fought not only with skill but with a desperate, burning hope that reflected in the desperate flicker of his silver eyes. My own heart, a trapped bird beating against my ribs, hammered out a frantic rhythm against the deafening symphony of destruction; a symphony that could easily drown my soul, leaving behind only the cold, echoing silence of oblivion.

The arena reeked of sweat, ozone, and the metallic tang of blood, a grim perfume clinging to the shattered remnants of their battle. My lungs burned, a furnace stoked by exhaustion, each ragged breath a testament to the brutal deadlock. Caspian, his face a mask of grime and barely suppressed fury mirrored my own ravaged state. We were broken instruments, our strings snapped, our melodies silenced. The bitter truth, a cold fist in the gut, slammed home: neither of us had won. Victory, that shimmering prize, lay shattered like the obsidian shards scattered across the pitted floor. A pact, they called it.

A pathetic, whimpering truce born not of respect, but of a shared, gut wrenching terror. The Obsidian Covenant, a name that tasted like ash and despair on my tongue, loomed over us, a monstrous shadow promising oblivion. We stood, two wounded predators, sharing a precarious peace, bound together by fear and the bitter knowledge of our mutual weakness. His eyes, though, held a flicker of something more, a chilling calculation, perhaps, or the icy glint of a soul already plotting our next confrontation. The agreement felt like a poisoned chalice, its sweetness laced with the bile of defeat. It left me hollow, a gnawing emptiness echoing the emptiness of this pyrrhic stalemate. This... truce. It was a mockery, a festering wound upon the landscape of my soul.

Terra's agony clawed at me, a visceral, burning pain that drowned out Caspian's thunderous pronouncements. His orders, a viper's hiss in my ear, were shattered against the granite of my defiance. For a second time, I spat in the face of his authority, the taste of rebellion bitter and metallic on my tongue. Forget the clash of steel and the reek of blood; I chose the desperate gamble of diplomacy, the suffocating weight of hope pressing down on my chest. I saw Terra's inherent justice, a flickering candle in the storm ravaged landscape of war, and I pleaded with it, my voice a raw rasp against the howling wind. I offered a pact, a lifeline woven from mutual gain, a compromise that would protect both the obsidian fangs of the vampire kingdom and the wind whipped pride of the Whispering Wind. But my audacious defiance, my desperate clinging to mercy, only fueled Caspian's incandescent rage. His hatred, a palpable force, solidified into a grim certainty: compassion, in his eyes, was the harbinger of our doom, a fatal flaw etched onto my very soul.

Caspian's betrayal, a viper's strike disguised as diplomacy, poisoned the air between him and Terra. The very scent of him, a cloying perfume of deceit, sparked a firestorm in her eyes, a raw, incandescent rage that threatened to consume the fragile peace talks. Her refusal to yield, a granite wall against his smooth, oily words, was palpable. The air crackled with unspoken accusations, each silence a thunderclap in the suffocating tension. I saw the tremor in her jaw and felt the chill of her distrust like a phantom touch on my skin. But beneath the fury, a flicker of wounded pride, a yearning for justice, burned bright. It was a perilous game, this dance on the edge of a precipice, but I played it with the ferocity of a cornered wolf, using every ounce of my cunning, every shred of my empathy. I saw past the armour of her anger, past the bitter taste of betrayal, to the vulnerability hidden within. I offered not platitudes, but understanding, a balm to her wounds, and slowly, painstakingly, the ice began to melt. The hard won agreement, a fragile truce carved from the very bedrock of their animosity, tasted like ash and victory. It was a testament, not just to my skill, but to the brutal, beautiful dance of reconciliation.

The peace was a razor's edge, bought with blood and the bitter taste of ash. Caspian, his power a shattered mirror reflecting a diminished self, clung to the remnants of his authority. The Whispering Wind, once a unified storm, now howled with the dissonance of fracturing loyalties, a mirror to the cracks spider webbing through the fragile pact between us. The very fire that had forged our bond, once a sun blazing with passion, now threatened to consume us in its infernal embrace. The acrid scent of betrayal clung to the air, a constant reminder of our precarious position.

Maintaining this uneasy calm felt less like a strategy and more like wrestling a viper. It wasn't merely a test of military prowess or political cunning; it was a visceral struggle against our demons, a desperate fight against the encroaching darkness that clawed at our souls. Each breath was a gamble, each glance a silent negotiation across the chasm that yawned between us. Our relationship, a precarious dance on the precipice of oblivion, stank of desperation and simmered with a volatile chemistry that could explode at any moment. Our love, a grotesque parody of serenity, was a festering wound, throbbing with pain both exquisite and agonizing. It cast a chilling shadow over our truce, a testament to the monstrous sacrifices we'd both made.

The world hung suspended, our fragile power a thin veil against the ravenous hunger of our enemies. The fate of our kingdoms, our very beings, teetered precariously, a macabre ballet played out under the looming shadow of annihilation. Every heartbeat echoed the imminent threat, a chilling reminder of our stolen peace and the terrifying price of our survival.

A precarious truce, forged in the crucible of mutual exhaustion and the icy grip of impending annihilation, offered no genuine reconciliation, only a fleeting reprieve from the inevitable. Within the clandestine headquarters of the Whispering Wind, a palpable tension thrummed, a silent symphony of simmering resentments barely held in check by the fragile peace. The air itself crackled with unspoken accusations. Caspian, his usually glacial composure fractured into a thousand jagged shards, prowled the dimly lit corridors like a cornered wolf, his gaze a relentless searchlight for treachery. He saw it everywhere—in the furtive glances exchanged between his subordinates, their eyes darting like trapped birds; in the subtle shifts of allegiance, like tectonic plates grinding against each other beneath the surface; in the insidious rumours that slithered through the shadowy halls like venomous vipers, their poison seeping into the cracks of the fragile peace, threatening to shatter it completely. The scent of betrayal hung heavy in the air, a miasma clinging to the opulent tapestries and the cold, polished stone. Even the flickering candlelight seemed to dance with a malevolent glee, casting grotesque shadows that mimicked the twisting anxieties within. The silence itself felt weighted, a suffocating blanket woven from suspicion and fear.

A crushing weight descended, not merely upon my shoulders, but upon my very soul. My precarious peace, a fragile truce woven from reluctant compromises and a shared, gnawing fear, teetered on the brink of collapse, threatened by the slightest misstep, the faintest whisper of dissent. I had appeased Terra and her ravenous, bloodthirsty followers, their insatiable hunger momentarily sated, but my appeasement had come at a terrible cost. Caspian, his pride wounded, his trust shattered, seethed with a resentment so profound it vibrated in the very air between us, widening the already chasm-like rift that separated us. The furtive glances, once charged with unspoken passion, now held only suspicion and cold calculation. The lingering touches, once tender and reassuring, were replaced by the deliberate avoidance of contact. The implicit vows that had bound us together, the unspoken promises whispered in the dark, were buried under a suffocating silence, a glacial estrangement more potent, more damning, than any shouted accusation or bitter recrimination. The very air crackled with unspoken anger, a palpable tension that threatened to consume us both.

The tempestuous nights of our love, once a raging inferno of desire and barely controlled passion, now lay buried beneath a chilling, suffocating stillness. Our physical union, a battlefield where wills once clashed in a volatile dance of dominance and submission, had dwindled to infrequent, sterile encounters—pale imitations of the fiery intensity that had defined us. His absence gnawed at my soul, a void deeper and more agonizing than any physical wound could ever inflict. I ached for the forceful possessiveness of his hands, the sharp, thrilling bite of his teeth on my skin, and the intoxicating, perilous dance of power and surrender that had forged the very essence of our bond. But his infrequent caresses were hesitant, apologetic ghosts of their former selves, lacking the potent, electrifying energy that once ignited my spirit and set my blood ablaze. The embers of our passion, once a roaring bonfire, were now reduced to a few pathetic sparks, threatening to extinguish altogether, leaving me adrift in the desolate landscape of our fading love.

The firelight, a flickering ghost in the hearth, cast long, dancing shadows that mocked our dwindling hope. A stark, chilling realization settled upon me like the first frost of autumn: our position was not merely precarious, it was desperate. The Obsidian Covenant, a palpable weight of menace, hung over us like a shroud woven from shadows and whispers. Their insidious influence slithered through the very stones of our fortress, their spies weaving a tapestry of discord, nurturing suspicion and distrust with the cold precision of assassins. But the true danger, I knew with a sickening certainty, lay not in the external threat, however formidable, but in the festering rot within our hearts. The fragile alliance between the Whispering Wind clan and my loyalists, once a bulwark against the encroaching darkness, was crumbling into dust, eroded not by the enemy's blade, but by the corrosive acids of mutual animosity and a deep, festering wound of mistrust. Each whispered accusation, each furtive glance, each carefully planted seed of doubt, chipped away at the foundation of our unity, leaving us vulnerable, exposed, and ripe for the taking.

The candle, a guttering wick spitting defiance against the encroaching dark, threw skeletal fingers across the desk, a chaotic dance of shadows that transformed my secluded study into a tomb. Caspian, hunched like a gargoyle over a battlefield of charts and documents, each stamped with the Crown's malevolent sigil, was drowning in classified secrets. His brow, a roadmap of worry etched deep into his flesh, was slick with sweat. His expression wasn't just concentration; it was a mask of agonizing, soul crushing obsession. The air, thick and cloying, reeked of aged parchment and something else... the acrid bite of blood, faint but undeniable, clinging to the back of my throat. Twilight, a malevolent entity, clawed at the tall, narrow windows, its icy fingers seeping into the room, intensifying the suffocating gloom. He remained oblivious to my presence, his gaze locked onto the cryptic symbols, swirling in a vortex of dread before him; a prisoner held captive not by chains, but by the crushing weight of the truth they concealed.

The silence, punctuated only by the frantic whisper of the dying flame, pressed down with the crushing weight of impending doom. The fragile peace wasn't just precarious; it was a thin sheet of ice, poised to shatter under the weight of his discovery. Each crackle of the flame was a heartbeat, my own, pounding in my ears, mirroring the frantic rhythm of his despair. The metallic tang sharpened a phantom taste of betrayal and impending violence. This wasn't just information; it was a viper coiled, ready to strike at the heart of the kingdom. And Caspian, lost in his feverish quest, was dancing ever closer to its fangs.

A tremor ran through me as I whispered, *"Caspian,"* the name of a fragile, precious thing on my lips.

His gaze, a glacial shard moments before, now lifted, revealing not fatigue, but a chasm of despair so profound it sucked the very air from the room. The chill wasn't just in his eyes, it radiated from his pores, a bone deep frost that whispered of a soul bled dry. The sorrow wasn't etched, it was carved, a brutal relief map of sleepless nights and burdens that would crush the strongest ox. I could taste the metallic tang of his anguish, a bitter iron clinging to the back of my throat. His eyes, once flint, were now the dull embers of a funeral pyre, reflecting not just emptiness, but the horrifying abyss of a spirit shattered, its fragments scattered like dust in the wind. The air hung heavy with the scent of decay, the cloying sweetness of death clinging to him like a shroud woven from nightmares. He wasn't just old; age was a predator that had feasted on him, leaving behind only the skeletal remains of a man, his frame bowed under the unbearable weight of unspoken horrors. Each tremor of his hand, each ragged breath, was a testament to the silent screams trapped within, a symphony of suffering conducted by the cruel hand of fate. The very air around him throbbed with the palpable presence of loss, a suffocating blanket woven from the ashes of a life consumed by grief, a life he couldn't, wouldn't, let go of.

A rasping inquiry escaped his lips: *"Blaze, what do you need?"*

"We need to talk, "I said, approaching him cautiously, my heart racing with uncertainty. *"About us. About everything that has been happening and the feelings we've been avoiding for so long."*

The worn leather map snapped shut, the sound of a pistol shot in the suffocating stillness. His fingers, long and scarred, moved with predatory grace, each gesture a calculated strike, a dance of deadly precision masking the tempest brewing within his icy gaze. The scent of pine and damp earth, usually comforting, now felt cloying, thick as the unspoken hatred that coiled between us, a venomous serpent ready to strike. He didn't need words; the invitation, a curt jerk of his chin towards the moss slicked log, was etched in the cruel lines of his face, a face I knew held the secrets of a thousand buried betrayals.

We sat in silence, a physical weight, pressing down on us like a tomb. The shared past, a tapestry woven with blood and broken promises, hung heavy in the air, each thread a fresh wound. His eyes, the colour of glacial ice, held mine, accusing, judging, daring me to speak the truth that festered between us, a truth I knew would shatter the fragile peace and unleash the storm that raged within him. The air crackled with a tension so fierce, that it tasted like ash and fear on my tongue, a silent scream clawing its way out of our suffocated souls. The very forest seemed to hold its breath, anticipating the inevitable explosion.

"There's a storm brewing Blaze "he finally said, his gaze fixed intently on my face. His expression was grave, filled with a mix of concern and urgency. *"Not just out there in the chaotic world around us but within us deep*

in our hearts and minds. We're tearing ourselves apart caught in a whirlwind of emotions and unresolved conflicts. The turbulence we feel inside reflects the turmoil outside and if we don't address it it will only grow stronger. We need to confront these feelings and find a way to calm the storm before it consumes us entirely. Otherwise we risk losing everything we hold dear."

"*I know,*" I replied, my voice choking with emotion. "*But I don't want to lose us. Not to Valerius, not to the Covenant, not to ourselves.*"

His fingers, ghost light and ice cold, sketched the bone of my jaw, a touch so subtle it was almost a phantom limb. The memory of his brutal possession, a brand seared onto my soul, flickered, replaced by this... reverence. A reverence so profound it choked the air from my lungs, leaving me gasping, tasting the metallic tang of fear mingled with a desperate, forbidden sweetness. The raw power, the volcanic eruption of our past, had been extinguished. In its place: a fragile ember, flickering on the edge of oblivion. A devastating beauty, a heartbreak so exquisite it felt like a knife twisting slowly, deliberately, in my chest. That single touch, a seismic tremor through my very being, vibrated with the unspoken weight of years, a silent scream of regret woven with a longing so intense it was physically painful. The scent of him, wood smoke and something else, something dark and achingly familiar, haunted the air between us. I was trapped, suspended between the ruins of our passion and the phantom promise of something... impossible.

"*Then we need to find a way to bridge this chasm,*" he said, his voice thick with emotion. "*To rebuild the trust that we've lost.*"

The air hung thick, a miasma of stale sweat and fear, as our words became weapons. Each syllable, was a poisoned dart aimed at the festering sores of our shared past. The taste of bile rose in my throat; I could almost smell the decay of our relationship, a rancid perfume of betrayal and unspoken accusations. His eyes, usually pools of deceptive calm, now burned with a feverish intensity, reflecting the inferno raging within us both. His voice, a low growl that vibrated in my chest, tore into the fragile fabric of our pretense.

He didn't just recount the hurts; he savoured them, each detail a meticulous torture, designed to flay the raw nerves of my soul. The ghosts of past lovers, whispered betrayals, the phantom touch of a hand that should never have been mine, it was a vivisection of my deepest fears, each cut precise and excruciating. I retaliated with a venom I didn't know I possessed, my words sharpened by years of simmering resentment, honed to a deadly edge by the chilling realization that this man, this monster, had known all along. The lies, meticulously constructed, crumbled like ash under the glare of our brutal honesty.

The silence between our guttural pronouncements was a physical thing, a suffocating pressure, a void filled with the ghosts of unspoken promises and shattered dreams. The tremor in my hands mirrored the seismic shift in the earth beneath our feet. This wasn't just a fight; it was a seismic rupture, ripping apart years of carefully constructed facades, leaving us exposed, bleeding, and utterly alone in the wreckage. The scent of impending doom was heavy, a premonition of something irreparable hanging in the air like a shroud. Each breath felt like a final gasp, each heartbeat a frantic drum against the encroaching darkness. This wasn't just the end of a relationship; it was the death of something sacred, something irretrievable.

The night clawed at us, offering no resolution, only a brittle truce, a peace treaty scrawled in blood on the battlefield of our souls. It wasn't some Hollywood reconciliation, no soaring declarations or saccharine promises of forever. Hell, no. It was a bone deep weariness settling between us, a raw, desperate hunger for calm in the maelstrom of our being. The air, thick with the metallic tang of unspoken resentments and the phantom scent of past betrayals, crackled with a tension that vibrated in my teeth. This fragile peace, this tentative reunion, felt as thin as a razor's edge, ready to shatter under the weight of a single, careless word.

His eyes, dark pools reflecting the storm raging within him, held a flicker of something akin to remorse—or was it merely exhaustion? I couldn't tell. The taste of ash lingered on my tongue, a bitter reminder of the fires we'd stoked. The touch of his hand, a ghost on my arm, sent a shiver down my spine, a fragile bridge across a chasm of pain. Brighter days? A ludicrous fantasy. Hope, a pathetic firefly battling a hurricane, clung to the precipice of oblivion. The sea churned beneath us, a tempest mirroring the turmoil in our hearts, threatening to swallow us whole.

The peace was a lie, a brittle shard of ice clinging to a knife's edge. The slightest tremor, the faintest shift in the wind, threatened to shatter it completely. The Obsidian Covenant's shadow wasn't just a looming presence; it was a suffocating weight, the stench of sulfur and decay clinging to the very air, a taste of ash and betrayal on our tongues. Their menace pulsed, a venomous heartbeat resonating through our desperate, fevered plans, a constant, icy dread that clawed at the edges of our fragile alliance.

The Whispering Wind, once a symbol of unity, now groaned under the strain, a chasm ripped through its heart. Caspian, his eyes burning with a cold, calculating ambition, his smile a venomous caress played his game with the precision of a viper. Valerius, a whirlwind of volatile passion and shadowed secrets, countered with a fury that scorched the earth. Their rivalry wasn't just bitter; it was a plague, a festering wound that poisoned every breath, every whispered word, every desperate hope. I could taste the blood of our broken trust, and feel the tremor of their hatred vibrating through the very ground beneath my feet. The air itself crackled with the unspoken threat of their imminent, brutal clash. Our tenuous alliance clung to life, a wounded bird fluttering in the teeth of a storm, its death rattle echoing in the silence between our strained smiles.

The air crackled a tangible thrum of their unresolved fury, venomous energy threatening to rip apart our fragile alliance, shattering us like brittle glass. The taste of fear was metallic on my tongue; I could almost feel the vibrations of their simmering hatred, a physical pressure against my chest. Yet, even as shadows clawed at the edges of our world, Caspian and I, two scarred survivors, discovered a resilience forged in the white hot heart of the inferno. His eyes, pools of shadowed midnight reflecting a lifetime of secrets and battle, locked with mine. There was no spoken word, only a raw, visceral understanding; a mutual pact sealed not in ink, but in the shared tremor of our near obliteration. We were bound, not by flimsy promises, but by the brutal, unforgiving truth of survival. And yet... the embers of our once ravaging passion, a tempest that had scorched the earth, now flickered weakly, a dying star, threatened to sink into the icy grave of ash, leaving only the bitter taste of what we had lost. The scent of it hung heavy, betrayal, regret, a haunting sweetness tinged with poison.

The final curtain didn't fall with a triumphant fanfare, but with a gut wrenching silence, a void thick enough to taste, a metallic tang of dread coating my tongue. Our odyssey? It was a charnel house of shattered hopes, a relentless, gnawing hunger in the belly of the beast. Survival wasn't a game anymore; it was a desperate scramble across a field of broken glass, each shard a memory of what we'd lost, each cut a fresh wound bleeding hope.

Our love? A tempest, yes, but not of gentle waves. It was a maelstrom, a furious hurricane of doubt and desire, tearing at us, exposing the raw, bleeding nerves of our souls. His eyes, usually pools of molten gold, were now shadowed, haunted by the ghosts of what might be, the agonizing weight of our uncertain future. My own heart, a trapped bird beating against the bars of its cage, echoed the frantic rhythm of our doomed dance.

And the world? It hung by a thread, frayed and thin as a spider's silk, swaying precariously over the abyss. The stench of impending doom clung to the air, a suffocating miasma of fear and regret, heavy in my lungs, making each breath a struggle, a desperate gasp for air in a vacuum of despair. This wasn't just a battle; it was a war waged on every front, a fight for our lives, our love, our very existence, a fight we might very well lose.

The hard won peace, tenuous as a spider's silk, hinted at a future both breathtakingly beautiful and terrifyingly unpredictable. A future where the radiant promise of dawn held the chilling potential to be extinguished by a storm of unimaginable proportions. Our love, our strength, our very fortitude, stood poised on the precipice, ready to face their ultimate trial, a cataclysmic conflict that would decide not only our fate but the fate of the world itself. The faint, flickering glow of our passion, a testament to an unwavering connection forged in the fires of shared tribulation, served as a solitary beacon against the encroaching, suffocating gloom. A last, desperate hope in the face of overwhelming odds.

CHAPTER

TWENTY FIVE

Whispers of Rebellion

The peace, a brittle truce forged in the acrid stench of burning betrayal and the rasping coughs of the dying, clung to the shattered remnants of our world like frost on a crumbling tombstone. It was a peace held together not by hope, but by the icy grip of terror, the Obsidian Covenant's shadow, a tangible weight pressing down on our chests, the taste of ash and fear coating our tongues. That fear, though, proved a flimsy curtain, barely masking the festering hatred that pulsed within the Whispering Wind like a venomous serpent coiled to strike. I felt it in the gut, a cold, sickening dread, the simmering resentment, thick as clotted blood, the whispers of vengeance sharper than any blade. This fragile peace, delicate as a spider's silk spun across a chasm, snapped with the dawn, not with a bang, but with a sickening, drawn out crack that echoed the splintering of our souls. The first light revealed not the promise of a new day, but the brutal, crimson sunrise of war.

The tremors that had rattled the foundations of power, subtle as the shift of tectonic plates, exploded. Valerius, Caspian's viperous second, a man whose smile was a predatory mask concealing the icy glint of ambition in his eyes, eyes that held the chill of a glacier and the calculating gleam of polished obsidian, launched his attack during the council meeting. His words, slithering with venom masked as solicitude, were poisoned darts, each syllable a precise strike aimed at Caspian's heart. He didn't merely dissent; he carved Caspian's authority to pieces, his voice a rasping saw tearing through the wood of the King's legitimacy. His counter proposals, reeking of self serving ambition, were meticulously crafted to eclipse my own, my painstakingly researched strategies reduced to dust, my meticulously crafted plans relegated to the ignominious footnotes of his grandiose pronouncements.

The air crackled with the palpable energy of a thousand unspoken death threats; the stench of betrayal, thick and suffocating, coated the very tongue. The fragile peace wasn't just shattering; it was imploding in a maelstrom of avarice and malice, the sound of its demise a deafening roar that drowned out the whimpers of reason. The taste of ash filled my mouth, the bitter metallic tang of impending war. This wasn't a challenge; it was a coup, a brutal, swift, and exquisitely planned assassination of Caspian's reign, and I, foolishly, had become a pawn in Valerius's deadly game.

The mahogany table, slick with the sheen of a thousand polished lies, felt less like a battlefield and more like a tomb. Unspoken accusations clawed at the air, a venomous miasma clinging to the ornate ceiling like the suffocating grip of a dying man. Each word, a poisoned dart honed to a razor's edge, hissed from their lips, landing with the precise impact of a viper's strike. Caspian, his glacial composure shattered into a million icy shards, snarled his rebuttals, his voice a low, guttural growl that vibrated in my very bones, a tremor of barely suppressed rage. The tension was a physical entity, a suffocating shroud woven from decades of festering hatred and venomous rivalry, threatening to tear the fragile truce to bloody shreds.

Trapped between them, I tasted the metallic tang of fear, a coppery film coating my tongue. The pressure wasn't just on my chest; it was a vice crushing my very soul, the weight of their conflict a leaden tombstone on my spirit. I was a pawn, yes, but a pawn imbued with a desperate awareness of the game's lethal stakes. Caspian, his ruthlessness masked by a veneer of icy elegance, was a man driven by a hunger for power as bottomless as the abyss itself. And Valerius... Valerius, with eyes like chips of obsidian and a smile that promised only ruin, was a predator, his grace a cruel mockery of the carnage he craved. He circled, a hawk poised to strike, his gaze dissecting our bond with the cold precision of a surgeon, sensing the tremor of doubt, the faintest crack in our armour.

The air crackled, not just with threats, but with the crackling static of raw, primal animosity, the silence punctuated only by the agonizing tick tock of the grandfather clock, each second a hammer blow to the rapidly disintegrating peace. The scent of aged leather and potent, masculine colognes was overwhelmed by the acrid stench of betrayal, a bitter creek clinging to the very fabric of the room, a chilling premonition of the violence to come. The polished surface of the table reflected their distorted images, two men locked in a silent, deadly ballet, and I, caught in the crossfire, braced for the inevitable collision.

The afternoon sun, a molten gold through the palace windows, mocked the chill that had settled in my bones. The gilded cage, once a haven, now felt like a vice, its opulence a suffocating weight. I was trapped, a solitary pawn on a chessboard of polished marble, encircled by Valerius's viperous court. Their smiles, stretched thin as painted smiles on a funerary mask tasted of dust and deceit. The cloying sweetness of their perfume, lilies, I think, but with an undercurrent of something acrid, something like fear, stung my nostrils. Each bow was a precise, almost theatrical gesture, a grotesque parody of respect, the calculated grace a flimsy veil over the simmering malice I felt radiating from them like heat from a forge. Their eyes, though, held the truth: cold, glittering shards of ambition, reflecting the glint of the daggers I knew were hidden beneath their silken robes. The air itself thrummed with unspoken threats, a silent symphony of impending doom.

A palpable tension, thick as the cloying perfume clinging to the silks of these vipers, choked the air. Their words, slick as serpent's scales and laced with the bitter tang of betrayal, slithered into my ears. Each honeyed syllable was a poisoned dart aimed at the heart of my dwindling power. Caspian, they hissed, his name a dirge whispered on the wind, his reign a fading echo, a flickering candle in the encroaching storm. I tasted the metallic edge of fear in the back of my throat as they meticulously chipped away at my authority, each phrase a carefully placed stone in a mausoleum built for my legacy.

The air crackled with the unspoken threat of Valerius, his name a brand seared onto their tongues. *"The Whispering Wind,"* they purred, the title itself a venomous caress. This rising star, this charismatic predator, promised a flood of resources, a tidal wave of influence, a fortress of protection—all shimmering baubles draped over the cold, hard steel of his ambition. I felt the icy grip of his ambition even before the offer was fully formed, a chilling premonition settling deep in my bones. His power, a burgeoning darkness, felt tangible, a physical presence that pressed against my own, a palpable challenge to my very existence. The choice: surrender to the slow, agonizing erosion of my power, or face the storm of his rising might. The scent of betrayal hung heavy, acrid and suffocating, a harbinger of the coming war.

Their words were honeyed poison, but the venom resided not in the syllables themselves, but in the chilling silences that clawed between them. I felt it, a physical pressure, a tightening in my chest mirroring the barely perceptible tremor in Caspian's jaw. Their eyes, like chips of glacial ice, bore into me, their gazes shifting with the predatory grace of wolves circling a wounded stag. The air itself crackled with unspoken threats; not whispers, but a suffocating weight, a palpable dread that tasted like ash and iron on my tongue. My skin prickled, not just with fear, but with the cold certainty of impending doom.

It wasn't their overt threats that cut deepest; those were blunt instruments. No, their insinuations were scalpels, dissecting my defences, exposing the raw, bleeding heart of my vulnerability. Caspian, usually a fortress of unwavering resolve, seemed... diminished. His usual iron control, the shield that had protected us, was fraying at the edges. I saw the exhaustion etched into the lines of his face, the flicker of doubt in his usually steely gaze. He fought it, this erosion of power, but the fight itself spoke volumes.

Their pronouncements weren't just idle pronouncements; they were pronouncements carved in ice, chilling me to the bone. They spoke of the inevitable tide, a relentless wave of Valerius's power, crashing over Caspian's weakening defences. Each carefully dropped word painted a canvas of impending ruin: me, exposed, utterly vulnerable to Valerius's cruel machinations. The unspoken hung in the air, thick and suffocating, a choice, stark and brutal: submit to Valerius, or face oblivion. The taste of that oblivion, cold and metallic, already coated my tongue.

Their smiles, painted on like grotesque masks, cracked under the strain, revealing the icy terror that haunted their eyes, a terror I could taste, a metallic tang on my tongue, a visceral chill that seeped into my

bones. This wasn't a game; it was a meticulously orchestrated dance of vipers, each movement a calculated strike aimed at the heart of another. A tapestry woven not of suspicion, but of venomous lies, slithering threads of deceit that choked the air with their rancid perfume. Their gamble, a brazen wager against fate itself, exploded in their faces with the brutal force of a collapsing star. I, forged in the crucible of unimaginable nightmares, scarred by the echoing screams of the damned, and clawing my way back from the very brink of nothingness, found their threats as hollow as empty skulls, as pathetic as the whimpering of newborn pups. Their fear, I savoured it, a dark wine on my palate, potent and intoxicating.

The days that followed were a crucible of tension, the air thick with unspoken anxieties. Rumours of dissent, like wildfire through dry brush, consumed the Whispering Wind, igniting a conflagration of suspicion and fear. Subtle acts of sabotage, meticulously timed delays in crucial supplies, vital intelligence reports vanishing like phantoms, contradictory orders deliberately issued, became almost commonplace, a chilling demonstration of the growing rebellion. What had begun as a faint, almost imperceptible murmur of discontent swelled into a deafening roar, a chorus of defiance that echoed through the ranks. The delicate balance Caspian had so painstakingly constructed, a fragile edifice of trust and loyalty, teetered precariously on the brink of collapse. He, visibly burdened by the crushing weight of command and the betrayal he perceived, retreated further into himself, a fortress of sorrow and isolation. The fiery passion that had once blazed between us, a beacon in the storm, was extinguished, replaced by a cautious, chilling distance, a chasm of mistrust that yawned between us, threatening to swallow our already fragile relationship, leaving only the bitter ashes of what had been.

One evening, I found Caspian in the armoury, the air thick with the scent of oil and old leather. He stood before a workbench bathed in the ethereal glow of the moon, meticulously cleaning his ancient obsidian blade. The rhythmic scrape of steel on a whetstone, a low, almost hypnotic whisper, was a stark counterpoint to the rising tumult outside, the distant clang of alarms, the muffled shouts of panicked voices. He didn't look up as I approached, his movements were fluid and precise, each stroke a testament to years of practiced skill, a silent ritual performed with unwavering concentration.

The moonlight, filtering through the high, arched windows, painted his face in sharp, dramatic relief, highlighting the grim set of his jaw and the intensity in his dark eyes. Dust motes danced in the beam, illuminating the intricate carvings along the blade's obsidian surface, each one a tiny testament to a forgotten battle, a whispered story of blood and steel. The silence around him felt heavy, charged with an unspoken urgency, a palpable sense of impending doom.

"It's getting worse," I said, my voice low.

He finally looked up, his eyes dark and shadowed, the pupils dilated like twin pools reflecting a storm wracked sky. *"Worse than you think,"* he rasped, his voice a husky whisper that barely carried above the frantic drumming of his own heart. The weariness in his eyes was etched deep, a network of fine lines radiating outwards like cracks in the parched earth, a stark contrast to his usual icy, impenetrable demeanour. The tension, the constant, gnawing vigilance, had begun to take its brutal toll; it had carved gaunt hollows into his cheeks, sharpened the angles of his jaw, and left him trembling on the precipice of something... unravelling. His shoulders slumped, the weight of unspoken burdens pressing down on him like a physical force.

"Valerius," I said. The name had a bitter taste in my mouth. *"He's mobilizing his forces."*

Caspian nodded, his gaze fixed on the blade he was sharpening. *"He's playing a dangerous game, Blaze. A game that could destroy us all."*

"Then we need to stop him," I said, my voice firm.

His eyes, pools of desperate inquiry, lifted to mine. *"Blaze,"* he breathed, the question a raw, agonizing plea, *"How can we quell this insidious insurrection?"*

Success, I understood, hinged not merely on tactical partnerships and military tactics, but on the collective psyche of the populace. Could I truly manipulate that? Is it even possible to control such a chaotic, unpredictable force? Valerius's insurrection wasn't a naked power play; it stemmed from profound societal unrest, a festering dissatisfaction born of long suppressed injustices. He tapped into something real, something I ignored in my pursuit of cold, hard strategy. Did I underestimate the power of emotion? Of righteous anger? The Whispering Wind, like all clandestine organizations built on deceit and concealment, proved susceptible to the insidious internal corrosion that now jeopardized its very existence. My carefully constructed network, crumbling from within. The whispers are louder now, aren't they? The betrayals... were they inevitable? Or did I create the conditions for them? This wasn't just a failure of strategy; it was a failure of understanding. A failure of empathy. Perhaps victory requires more than just cunning. Perhaps it demands... compassion?

Over the ensuing days, I discreetly investigated the unrest within the Whispering Wind, engaging in conversations with numerous adherents. I listened intently to their complaints, aspirations, and anxieties. My inquiries revealed that Valerius's burgeoning support stemmed not from unthinking allegiance, but from a profound dissatisfaction with Caspian's governance. Many felt Caspian's leadership was enervated, irresolute, and demonstrably ineffective against the encroaching Obsidian Covenant. They perceived themselves as marginalized, disregarded, and silenced. Their commitment to Valerius wasn't blind faith, but a fervent yearning for decisive direction—a leader who demonstrably understood their plight.

A gnawing frustration, rooted in the organization's rigid hierarchy and the opaque nature of its decision making process, festered within me. A palpable sense of injustice permeated the air, exacerbated by the widening gulf between Caspian and his increasingly disillusioned commanders. This growing distrust, a chasm between Caspian and myself, was being skillfully manipulated by the ever scheming Valerius. What had begun as a barely perceptible undercurrent of discontent, a hushed whisper in the corridors of power, had swelled into a cacophony of complaints, a tidal wave of rebellion threatening to consume the Whispering Wind entirely. The very foundations of the organization trembled under the weight of this burgeoning dissent.

My investigation unveiled a complex web of alliances and clandestine agendas, a treacherous landscape where loyalties shifted like desert sands. I uncovered evidence that Valerius had been subtly cultivating a power base among the marginalized and overlooked, whispering promises of influence and empowerment, expertly manipulating their hopes and fears. He painted a vivid picture of a brighter future, a future where their grievances would be addressed, and their contributions valued. However, my findings also revealed a critical vulnerability: Valerius's forces, while seemingly formidable, were built on a foundation of discontent, not unwavering loyalty. Many of his supporters, driven by resentment and a yearning for change, lacked the ruthless ambition and single minded dedication that characterized their leader. This internal fragility, a chasm between the charismatic leader and his followers, presented a crucial weakness exploitable by those seeking to thwart his ambitions. The veneer of strength, carefully crafted by Valerius, concealed a deeply fractured and ultimately unreliable power structure.

Armed with this hard won knowledge, I devised a plan, not merely to quell the rebellion, but to excise the very roots of Valerius's discontent. My strategy eschewed brute force, opting instead for a subtle dance of manipulation, a campaign to win hearts and minds. I would turn Valerius's tactics against him, a mirror reflecting his insidious methods upon himself, exploiting the fatal flaws in his seemingly impenetrable strategy. I would weaponized the Whispering Wind's simmering resentments, turning their internal conflicts into a raging inferno that consumed his power base. It was a gamble, a high stakes game played on the knife edge of utter chaos, a desperate bid to preserve the fragile peace and forge a united front against the encroaching, obsidian shadow of the Covenant. My plan, meticulously crafted, involved a carefully orchestrated exposure of Valerius's carefully constructed lies, his concealed vulnerabilities laid bare for all to see, thereby swaying the wavering loyalties of the undecided and turning the tide of the conflict irrevocably in our favour.

Victory remained elusive. A simmering revolt, a persistent hum of dissent, resonated within the shadowed halls of Whispering Wind, starkly highlighting the fragility of our pact. The Obsidian Covenant's looming threat was substantial, yet the struggle to secure the loyalty of Whispering Wind proved equally formidable; a trial not merely of martial prowess, but of our capacity to mend the treacherous fissures threatening to shatter their unity. The precarious equilibrium between fervent ideology and raw authority, between profound affection and brutal conflict, trembled under relentless strain. Our collective destiny, and our survival, hung by a thread. The approaching night promised protracted strife, impenetrable darkness, and imminent peril. But Caspian and I, steadfast in our resolve, would confront the tempest. The insidious murmurings, however, persisted, a haunting echo of our precarious truce and the ever present menace lurking just beneath the placid surface.

The following days were a blur of clandestine meetings, whispered conversations held in the hushed shadows of moonless nights, and maneuvers so subtle they were barely perceptible, yet pregnant with consequence. I moved like a phantom, a wraith in the labyrinthine corridors of the Whispering Wind's headquarters, a gothic masterpiece of echoing halls and secret passageways, gathering intelligence with the practiced ease of a seasoned spy. I spoke to the forgotten, the overlooked; those whose loyalty had been not merely taken for granted, but actively exploited and disregarded; those whose voices had been deliberately silenced, strangled by the suffocating hierarchical structure of the organization, a structure as rigid and unforgiving as a steel cage. Their grievances weren't mere complaints; they were the simmering embers of discontent, the kindling that fueled the wildfire of Valerius's rebellion, each whispered resentment a drop of gasoline poured onto the flames. Their anger, their despair, their yearning for justice, these were the potent ingredients of revolution.

One such encounter was with Cascade, a healer whose mastery of water magic was surpassed only by the weariness etched deep into her face. A weariness that spoke not merely of long hours, but of disillusionment, of a spirit slowly crushed beneath the weight of Valerius's blatant favouritism. Her confession, a barely audible whisper against the hushed backdrop of the healing wing, revealed a network of simmering discontent, a rebellion brewing beneath the surface of placid professionalism. *"They promised us better resources, better recognition,"* she breathed, her voice raspy with suppressed anger, *"a future where our skills wouldn't be squandered, our contributions ignored. But Caspian, they said... Caspian didn't care. We're expendable."*

Cascade's revelations were chillingly specific. She detailed Valerius's subtle manipulations, the insidious drip drip drip of diverted supplies, and the calculated starvation of the healing wing to bolster his forces, leaving them vulnerable, understaffed, and perpetually short of crucial medicines and tools. He'd painted a seductive picture of a brighter future, a future where their skills would finally be valued, where their dedication would be rewarded. A future that, in reality, was merely a gilded cage designed to keep them compliant while he exploited their talents for his nefarious purposes. The unspoken threat in her words hung heavy in the air, a potent mixture of despair and simmering defiance.

I listened patiently, my gaze sharp and unwavering, absorbing every nuance, every subtle shift in expression. The allure of Valerius's promises was palpable, a seductive whisper weaving its way through the discontent simmering beneath the surface. Caspian, weighed down by the crushing burden of leadership and the ghosts of his past, had unwittingly created a power vacuum, a void Valerius expertly exploited with his silver tongue and carefully crafted illusions. This wasn't merely a power struggle; it ran far deeper. It was a festering wound of miscommunication, a profound sense of neglect and undervaluation that had poisoned the hearts of the people. The air crackled with suppressed resentment, a volatile mixture ripe for the kindling of rebellion; a perfect storm brewing on the horizon.

The flickering torchlight cast long shadows across Rhys's grim face, accentuating the hollows beneath his eyes. His usually vibrant blue gaze, the colour of a stormy sea, was now dull, clouded with a weariness that mirrored the kingdom itself. This was not the Rhys who had roared onto the battlefield, a whirlwind of steel and fury; this was a man broken, his loyalty to Caspian frayed like a worn banner. He spoke in a low, gravelly voice, the words catching in his throat, each syllable a testament to the internal conflict raging within him.

Rhys's voice, gravelly with a lifetime of harsh experience, grated, *"Caspian falters. His legendary, swift attacks are now tentative jabs. He shrinks from confrontation, prioritizing prudence over valour. Valerius, naturally, presents a contrasting narrative—a portrait of decisive engagement, of unyielding fury unleashed upon the Obsidian Covenant. He recounts rivers of blood, triumphs achieved not through calculated strategy, but via audacious, unrelenting assaults."*

Valerius, the serpent in the grass, had not merely persuaded; he had meticulously dissected Caspian's vulnerabilities. He had exploited Caspian's fatigue, the weight of a thousand burdens pressing down on his shoulders, twisting his natural prudence into a perceived weakness. He had whispered insinuations of inadequacy, painting Caspian as a hesitant shepherd leading his flock towards slaughter, while Valerius himself offered the promise of a ruthless, victorious wolf. The contrast was stark, the deception insidious, and Rhys, like so many others, found himself wavering on the precipice of betrayal.

I realized then that Valerius's strategy transcended mere brute force; it was a symphony of psychological warfare, a meticulously orchestrated campaign to subtly undermine Caspian's authority and erode the bedrock of loyalty amongst his followers. Valerius was a master manipulator, a puppeteer adept at exploiting the existing fissures and simmering resentments within Caspian's ranks. He didn't simply offer an alternative; he painted a vivid, seductive portrait of himself as a bold, decisive leader, a stark contrast to Caspian's increasingly wary and cautious demeanour. This image resonated deeply with those who yearned for a more aggressive, decisive approach to vanquishing the Obsidian Covenant, those who felt Caspian's careful strategy was nothing more than a slow, agonizing march towards defeat. Valerius's whispers of strength and swift victory were a potent antidote to Caspian's perceived weakness and timidity, cleverly turning the tide of allegiance through a masterful campaign of perception management.

My investigation unearthed a startling vulnerability at the heart of Valerius's rebellion: a profound absence of unwavering commitment. While Valerius commanded a sizable following, a closer examination revealed a disconcerting truth: many flocked to his banner not out of genuine allegiance, but from a wellspring of simmering discontent. Years of internecine strife, punctuated by relentless backstabbing and a pervasive atmosphere of mistrust, had eroded the very fabric of their society. They were weary, not merely of the existing power structure, but of the constant betrayals and the suffocating lack of faith in their leaders. Their desperation for change, for a leader who appeared to understand their plight, proved a far shakier foundation than Valerius had perceived. This yearning for respite, however, masked a fundamental lack of conviction in his cause itself; their allegiance was conditional, easily swayed by shifting winds of fortune and the slightest hint of a more promising alternative.

Armed with this hard won knowledge, I meticulously formulated my counter strategy. It wouldn't involve the messy brutality of a coup d'état, nor the perilous risk of confrontation. My fight would be a subtle battle of perception, a clandestine war of whispers designed to neutralize Valerius's insidious campaign of lies and manipulation. I needed to address the festering wounds of discontent, to delicately expose the root causes of the Whispering Wind's wavering loyalty, and ultimately, to demonstrate to those hesitant members that Caspian, despite the weariness etched upon his face, remained a leader whose strength and vision were worthy of our unwavering trust, a leader who deserved their steadfast allegiance.

The first step was to mend the fractured communication. With Caspian's grudging consent, I orchestrated a series of town hall style meetings, carefully designed to foster open dialogue. Members of the Whispering Wind were finally given a platform to air their grievances directly to Caspian, a risky proposition indeed. Caspian, deeply uncomfortable with public vulnerability and accustomed to a more autocratic style of leadership, initially balked at the idea. His resistance was palpable, a simmering tension in the air. However, I persevered, emphasizing that genuine transparency was not merely desirable, but crucial for rebuilding the shattered trust. It was the only path toward healing the deep wounds within the community, and I argued passionately for its necessity.

The forums crackled with a volatile energy, a digital tempest of accusations and recriminations. Long dormant resentments, like venomous snakes, slithered out from the shadows, their fangs bared. Caspian, initially rigid and guarded, a fortress under siege, slowly began to dismantle his defences. He spoke not with polished rhetoric, but with the raw honesty of a man confronting his failings. He admitted his exhaustion, a weariness etched onto his very soul, confessed to past errors of judgment, and owned his reluctance to embrace change. He offered no empty platitudes, no facile promises; instead, genuine, palpable remorse radiated from his words, a sincere apology for the wounds he'd inflicted. But his actions spoke louder than his words.

He publicly invested Cascade, the unsung healer, with the leadership of the healing wing, bestowing upon her the authority and resources cruelly withheld for so long. This was more than symbolic; it was a tangible demonstration of his commitment. Further, he spearheaded sweeping reforms, tackling the ingrained inequalities and opaque practices that had festered within the organization. These weren't merely cosmetic changes; they were systemic overhauls, designed to foster true fairness and cultivate a culture of transparency and inclusivity. The air, thick with suspicion moments before, began to slowly clear, the scent of reconciliation replacing the acrid stench of conflict.

These seemingly minor adjustments proved profoundly impactful, subtly yet decisively altering the very fabric of Caspian's leadership. They signaled not merely a shift, but a fundamental transformation—a bold embrace of adaptability and a genuine willingness to listen to the concerns of his people. The once deafening chorus of discontent, a cacophony that threatened to shatter his reign, gradually faded to a mere murmur, then to silence. Valerius's meticulously crafted narrative, a carefully constructed edifice of perceived weakness and indecisiveness, began to crumble, its foundations eroded by the palpable evidence of Caspian's newfound strength and resolve. The whispers of doubt, once potent weapons wielded against him, now fell harmlessly to the ground.

Simultaneously, I subtly undermine Valerius's propaganda campaign, a clandestine war fought with whispers and carefully placed truths. Leveraging my influence within the court, I subtly shifted the narrative, highlighting Caspian's past triumphs—not merely as facts, but as shining examples of his unwavering commitment to our shared cause. I showcased his selflessness, and his willingness to sacrifice personal gain for the collective good, painting a picture of a leader whose dedication ran deeper than Valerius's shallow ambition. Through carefully chosen leaks and strategically positioned allies, I exposed Valerius's manipulative tactics, revealing his lies not as accusations, but as irrefutable consequences of his self-serving machinations. My efforts were tireless, a meticulous weaving of a counter narrative that emphasized not only Caspian's strength but the vital necessity of unity and cooperation against the encroaching shadows of Valerius's divisive influence. The campaign was a delicate dance, a slow erosion of Valerius's power, accomplished not through force, but through the patient construction of a more compelling truth.

One moonless night, under a sky choked with inky blackness, I and Caspian confronted Valerius. The air crackled with unspoken threats, not of steel on steel, but of the far more perilous clash of wills. It wasn't a brawl; it was a meticulously orchestrated dismantling. My voice, a honed blade of precision, dissected Valerius's betrayals, each carefully chosen word a scalpel exposing the festering wounds of his lies and his naked, self serving ambition. I laid bare the hollowness of his promises, the pathetic shallowness of his grand pronouncements, and the glittering veneer of his ambition revealed as nothing more than tarnished tinsel.

Valerius, his meticulously constructed façade of power crumbling like ancient sandstone, sputtered justifications, his carefully rehearsed arguments falling flat, lifeless things against the unwavering force of truth. He was outmaneuvered, outwitted, his rebellion unravelling thread by agonizing thread, his carefully cultivated support base melting away like snow in the spring sun. The once confident rebel leader, his posture slumping, his eyes betraying the hollow ache of defeat, stood exposed, a pathetic figure stripped bare of his power and influence. The weight of his treachery, amplified by the unwavering unity of those he had sought to manipulate, finally crushed him. His reign of deception was over.

The storm's fury didn't simply fade; it clawed back, a slow, agonizing retreat of the sea after a maelstrom ripped the very foundations from the earth. The air, thick with the metallic tang of blood and the acrid bite of burnt dreams, still vibrated with the ghost of screams. What was a deafening roar of rebellion now hissed, a venomous undercurrent slithering beneath the fragile surface of peace.

The Whispering Wind, its very soul shattered by betrayal and bloodshed, gasped, a wounded beast licking its wounds. A truce, brittle as ice in a thaw, clung precariously to the ravaged land. It was forged not in the heat of battle alone, but in the chilling realization that the only alternative to this uneasy armistice was annihilation. Each breath held a tremor of fear; the taste of ash lingered on every tongue; the sight of scarred earth and empty eyes was a constant, nauseating reminder of the price of conflict. We were bound, not by trust—that was a luxury we had squandered—but by the sheer, bone deep terror of the encroaching darkness. The shadows, vast and hungry, stretched their claws towards us, a constant threat against which our fragile unity was the only shield, a shield hammered from the shards of our shattered selves. And even then, the whispers of doubt, sharp as shards of obsidian, echoed in the still night.

Caspian and I, forged in the crucible of a war that tasted of blood and burned with the stench of cordite, emerged scarred but indivisible. Our bond, a raw nerve thrumming with the unspoken threat of his ambition and the white hot agony of a forbidden desire, had hardened into something brutal and beautiful. It was more than fondness; it was a visceral ache, a phantom limb where trust and betrayal wrestled for dominance. Our victory, bought with the blood of innocents and the ghosts of our pasts, was not just a pact sealed in blood, it was a sacrament of our love, a defiant bloom in the shadow of a peace that felt like a lie. The lingering bitterness of unresolved conflict only intensified the hunger in our eyes, the tremor in our touch, and the desperate promise we made to each other amidst the wreckage of our shattered world.

But the shadow of the Obsidian Covenant, vast and implacable as a looming mountain range, continued to cast its ominous pall. It served as a stark reminder that the fight for survival was far from over; that the hard won peace was but a fleeting respite in a long and brutal war. The whispers, once harbingers of division, now acted as a vital warning system, a constant, chilling reminder of the dangers that lurked just beyond the fragile veil of peace. They were a testament not only to the precarious nature of their hard won tranquillity, but to the tenacious resilience of their love, a love that had blossomed amidst the ashes of conflict, and which now stood poised to face the coming storm.

CHAPTER

TWENTY SIX

Whispering Veil of Unity

The fragile peace in the Whispering Wind was a deceptive calm, a thin veneer over smouldering embers. Valerius's rebellion, though seemingly quelled, lingered like a phantom limb, its potential for resurgence a constant, gnawing anxiety. Caspian, despite the relief of averted catastrophe, felt the crushing weight of his responsibilities, a burden heavier than any crown. The organization, fractured by years of infighting and suspicion, was not merely wounded; it was shattered. A simple reprieve was insufficient; it craved a deep, transformative healing. Trust, eroded by betrayal and bloodshed, needed to be painstakingly rebuilt, brick by painstaking brick, a process far exceeding mere pronouncements and superficial reforms. The whispers of dissent still echoed in the shadowed corners, and Caspian knew that true stability lay not in the absence of conflict, but in the forging of a new unity, born from shared sacrifice and a hard won understanding.

My mind, a razor honed by years of dissecting deceit, sliced through the problem's veneer of normalcy. The cacophony of the open forums, a tidal wave of keyboard clicks and flashing screens, was a nauseatingly sweet placebo. Their shrill cries of outrage, a thin layer of frosting over a rancid cake. Beneath, the festering sores of mistrust pulsed with a venomous life, a serpent coiled around the heart of our endeavor, ready to strike. I could taste the bitterness of it, a metallic tang on my tongue, the chilling certainty that the entire enterprise teetered on the precipice of ruin.

We had to confront the rot, to rip it out root and branch, even if it meant wading through a mire of betrayal, making choices that would scar us, choices that would leave us bleeding. The screams of those we'd inevitably hurt echoed in my ears, a phantom chorus of pain. Yet, the silence of inaction, the suffocating weight of a world consumed by its poison, was an unbearable agony far exceeding any sacrifice.

Rhys loomed, a wraith in rusted armour, the stench of stale blood and betrayal clinging to him like a shroud. His once bright eyes, now chips of obsidian, held the cold weight of a thousand slaughtered foes, but Valerius's poison had dulled the steel in them, twisting loyalty into a grotesque parody. Caspian's pleas, desperate cries echoing in the cavernous space of Rhys's soul, were met only by the rasping silence of a broken man. He felt the phantom sting of Caspian's outstretched hand, a gesture of forgiveness so pathetically inadequate against the crushing weight of Valerius's whispered promises, promises of power, of vengeance, of sweet, intoxicating oblivion that drowned out the gnawing doubt.

That doubt, a viper coiled not just within him, but in the very marrow of his bones, poisoned his every breath, every strike. The taste of it was ash and bile. His skills, honed in a lifetime of carnage, felt like shackles now, binding him to this festering resentment. Each perfectly executed maneuver, each devastating blow he might deliver, carried the bitter tang of betrayal. He was a blade poised to strike, but the target was uncertain: the enemy, or the alliance itself. The fragile pact, already strained to its breaking point, shuddered under the weight of his potential treachery. His very presence was a crack in the foundation, a fracture threatening to shatter their already desperate campaign, leaving them exposed, vulnerable, and bleeding out onto the unforgiving earth. He was a volcano, simmering with the potential for a cataclysmic eruption, capable of burying them all under an avalanche of bitterness and bloodshed.

The flickering lamplight cast long shadows across Caspian's face, etching the lines of his worry deeper still. He leaned heavily against the rough hewn table, the weight of his decision pressing down on him like a physical burden. *"I can't afford to have him in the ranks,"* he confessed, his voice a low rumble, barely audible above the crackling fire, *"not if his heart isn't fully committed. His lack of dedication... it's a liability we simply can't risk."* He paused, running a hand through his already dishevelled hair, the gesture betraying the turmoil within. *"But to banish him... to cast him out after all he's done... It feels like a gut wrenching betrayal. The sacrifices he's made for this organization... they're immeasurable. It feels like I'm tearing apart a piece of myself."* His gaze drifted to the flames, a silent plea for solace in their dancing light.

My gaze, unwavering and sharp as a winter hawk's, pierced the suffocating tension. The dilemma clawed at me, a brutal beast with teeth of doubt. Rhys's continued presence, a viper coiled in our midst, represented a palpable threat, a potential fifth column ready to strike at our most vulnerable points. Yet, banishment, the cold, brutal severing of ties, would send a chilling message across the fragile landscape of our alliance, a stark confirmation of the very distrust Caspian, with his desperate, almost frantic efforts, was striving so valiantly to dismantle. The weight of this decision, a crushing burden of responsibility, settled heavily on my shoulders.

"There's a third path," I suggested in my voice a low murmur, each word carefully chosen. *"We can offer him a different role, one that leverages his considerable skills without exposing him to the brutal realities of direct combat."* A beat of silence hung in the air before I continued, the proposal carefully unfolding like a meticulously planned maneuver. *"I propose creating a specialized scouting unit, led by Rhys, whose sole purpose is the gathering of intelligence on the Obsidian Covenant. This would allow him to remain engaged, to contribute meaningfully to our efforts, while simultaneously mitigating the significant risk his... potential treachery presents."* I paused, letting the weight of the unspoken hang heavy between us. *"It's a gamble, yes, but a calculated one, a risk I believe is worth taking given the alternatives."*

The decision, agonizing as it was, cleaved through the tense silence like a shard of obsidian. Rhys, his jaw clenched, his usual boisterous defiance muted to a simmering unease, finally nodded. The offer, a compromise born of necessity, hung heavy in the air, a fragile bridge across a chasm of mistrust. He understood the stark logic—his unique skills, honed over years of unwavering loyalty, were crucial to their survival, a lifeline they couldn't afford to sever, even if it meant compromising the security they both so fiercely guarded. It wasn't a complete restoration, not a sweeping erasure of the rift that had fractured their bond, but rather a tentative, painstaking first step towards healing the deep wounds that separated Caspian from his most trusted, yet most profoundly skeptical, follower. The weight of responsibility settled upon Rhys's shoulders, a heavy cloak woven from unspoken hopes and lingering doubts.

A grim dilemma clawed at the heart of the Whispering Wind's leadership. The relentless war against the Obsidian Covenant devoured resources at an alarming rate. Manpower thinned, supplies dwindled to a perilous trickle, leaving the council facing a stark, agonizing choice. To curtail military operations meant surrendering hard won ground, inviting further incursions from the obsidian armoured hordes and jeopardizing the fragile peace painstakingly achieved. Yet, to persist meant courting disaster from within, famine gnawing at the bellies of their soldiers, disease festering in the cramped, resource starved camps, threatening to inflict a far more insidious defeat than any battlefield loss. The very survival of the Whispering Wind hung precariously in the balance, dependent on a decision that could either secure their future or condemn them to oblivion.

Caspian, ever mindful of preserving their already strained fighting force, cautiously suggested rationing supplies. But I vehemently opposed the idea. *"Rationing,"* I countered, my voice sharp with urgency, *"will not simply reduce consumption; it will ignite a wildfire of resentment and paranoia among our already weary troops. Mistrust, born of hunger and perceived inequity, will fester, eroding morale and potentially fracturing our already fragile unity. It will sow the seeds of chaos, leaving us vulnerable at a time when we need every ounce of strength and cohesion. We need a far more sustainable, and equitable, solution, one that addresses the root cause of our shortages, not merely the symptoms."*

Our solution was audacious, a radical departure from conventional warfare. We dared to temporarily suspend offensive operations against the Obsidian Covenant, a decision that redirected our finite resources toward a crucial internal transformation: bolstering our defences and fortifying our infrastructure. It was a high stakes gamble, a calculated risk that exposed us to the very real threat of a devastating counterattack from our formidable foes. The Obsidian Covenant, with its brutal efficiency and seemingly limitless power, could easily crush us. Yet, this bold strategy, this necessary sacrifice, prioritized the long term survival, indeed the very existence, of the Whispering Wind above any short sighted pursuit of immediate advantage. It was a bet on our resilience, a testament to our unwavering commitment to enduring the storm and ultimately emerging stronger.

This decision ignited a firestorm of dissent, particularly among those clamouring for immediate, brutal retribution against the Obsidian Covenant. Their cries echoed through the ranks, a chorus of outrage interpreting the choice as a craven display of weakness, a shameful retreat before a relentless enemy. The air crackled with accusations of cowardice and betrayal. Yet I, unlike them, understood that true strength resided not in the reckless fury of blind aggression, but in the steely resolve of strategic resilience; a fortitude forged not in the heat of battle, but in the cold crucible of calculated planning and unwavering patience. The path to victory, I knew, lay not in a desperate charge, but in a meticulously crafted campaign of attrition and calculated strikes.

To overcome the entrenched resistance, Caspian and I spearheaded a comprehensive program of training and infrastructure revitalization. This involved significant investment in fortifying our defences, modernizing our communication networks with cutting edge technology, and expanding our medical facilities to provide superior care. We relentlessly pursued the rebuilding of morale, fostering a renewed sense of unity and shared purpose shattered by Valerius's treacherous rebellion. Our efforts included targeted initiatives to address the specific grievances that fueled the dissent, coupled with transparent and open communication to rebuild trust and foster collaboration. We sought not merely to suppress the rebellion's aftermath, but to create a more resilient and equitable society, one that would be less susceptible to future upheaval.

The months that followed were a taut, breathless vigil. We lived beneath a perpetual shadow, the ever present threat of an Obsidian Covenant attacking a chilling weight on our shoulders. Each sunrise brought a fresh wave of apprehension, each sunset a fragile reprieve. Yet, this uneasy calm, this tense interlude between storms, proved unexpectedly fertile. It allowed us to rebuild, not merely our strength, but the very foundations of our organization. Fractured alliances mended, and internal conflicts, once bitter and divisive, subsided into a shared understanding forged in the crucible of shared adversity. A renewed sense of purpose, sharp and clear as tempered steel, galvanized us, binding us together with a commitment to our common goal that was both unwavering and deeply felt. We emerged stronger, more unified, and far more dangerous than before.

During this time, my relationship with Caspian deepened, evolving far beyond the initial blaze of passion. Shared trials, the agonizing choices we wrestled with together, the weight of our decisions borne equally, forged a bond stronger than any fleeting infatuation. While the potent current of desire still flowed beneath the surface, our connection transmuted into something richer, more enduring. A profound understanding bloomed, rooted in mutual respect and a hard won trust that had been tested and proven in the fires of our shared experiences. The power dynamics, once so prominent, now subtly informed a complex tapestry of intimacy, woven with threads of both dominance and vulnerability. We discovered a depth of connection that transcended mere physical attraction, revealing a shared soul forged in the crucible of our journey.

Our love, a fragile bloom pushing through cracked asphalt, was never far from the shadow of our battles. The fierce intimacy we shared, a whispered secret in a hurricane, stood in stark contrast to the brutal, unforgiving reality of our fight for survival. It was a sanctuary carved from the heart of relentless chaos, a defiant haven built on stolen moments and desperate clinging. We sought solace in each other's arms, finding strength not in the absence of vulnerability, but in its shared embrace; our weaknesses woven together into an unbreakable cord. The very act of loving, of holding on, became a rebellion against the odds, a testament to the enduring power of the human heart in the face of annihilation.

One moonlit night, as we lay entwined, Caspian confessed his fears. *"What if we fail?"* he whispered, his voice barely audible. *"What if we can't defeat the Obsidian Covenant?"*

The moonlight caught the silver threads in his hair as my fingers traced their path, a silent promise woven into the gesture. Our eyes locked, his deep well reflecting the turmoil within, mine resolute, mirroring a stubborn hope. *"We will find a way,"* I whispered, the words a balm against the storm raging around us. My voice, though soft, held the unwavering strength of granite, the conviction born of shared desperation and unshakeable love. *"We'll fight until the very end,"* I vowed, the final words hanging in the air like a battle cry, *"together."*

My words, ringing with unwavering conviction, were more than a declaration of defiance; they were a testament to the incandescent power of our love—a love forged in the white hot fires of adversity, tempered in the crucible of agonizing decisions, and ultimately strengthened by the shared burden of our responsibilities. Our love story, a vibrant tapestry woven with the darkest threads of violence and betrayal, shone as a resilient beacon in the war torn heart of a world consumed by shadow. It stood as unwavering proof of our enduring strength, a testament to the indomitable power of love flourishing against overwhelming odds.

The whispers of rebellion, once vibrant, had faded to a hushed murmur, but the war raged on, its brutal symphony far from silenced. The path ahead remained treacherous, a jagged, unforgiving landscape fraught with peril. Yet, we would face it together, our love a shimmering shield against the encroaching darkness, a fortress against the storm, our intertwined fates bound by an unbreakable cord of shared purpose and unwavering devotion. The future held uncertainty, but our love, hardened and refined by the trials we had endured, would be our unwavering guide, our constant light in the encroaching night.

The suppression of Valerius's rebellion wasn't a swift, clean victory. It was a brutal, protracted affair, a nightmarish dance of blood and betrayal played out under the grim light of a perpetually overcast sky, a sky the colour of bruised plums, mirroring the mood of the land. The initial wave of defiance, quelled by Caspian's decisive action at the Battle of the Bloodsoaked Mire, a name whispered with dread even now, had left a trail of bodies in its wake, a grim testament to the ferocity of the conflict. Thousands perished, their bones bleaching white against the ever wet, moss covered stones of the battlefield.

The air still hung heavy with the metallic tang of blood, a lingering scent that clung to the very stones of the Whispering Wind's fortress, a colossal structure carved from obsidian like rock, its towers piercing the perpetually gloomy sky like skeletal fingers. Whispers spoke of unnatural storms brewing around the fortress, a consequence of the dark magic Valerius had wielded, magic that still pulsed faintly in the earth, staining the very water that ran from the surrounding mountains a sickly green. The rebellion hadn't simply been a fight for power; Valerius had promised his followers a return to the Age of Whispers, a time of potent magic and unchecked power, a promise that had resonated with those disillusioned by Caspian's iron fisted, technologically driven reign.

Even now, months after the final battle, patrols of Caspian's stormtroopers, clad in polished chrome armour that gleamed eerily in the dim light, patrolled the countryside, hunting down stragglers and rooting out pockets of lingering resistance. The landscape itself bore the scars of war: scorched earth, shattered villages, and the ever present, chilling silence that followed the storm of violence. The scent of blood was only one of the grim reminders; the cries of ravens circling the battlefield were another, their constant cawing a mournful dirge for the fallen.

The aftermath was a scene of grim, visceral devastation. The training grounds, once vibrant with the clashing clang of steel and the shouts of exertion, were now a scarred and broken wasteland, littered with discarded weapons, splintered spears, twisted swords, and the shattered remnants of shields that lay like fallen sentinels. A thick dust, tinged with the coppery scent of blood, hung heavy in the air, clinging to the ragged uniforms of the survivors. The uneasy silence was a palpable thing, broken only by the ragged whimpers of the wounded, the rhythmic thud of medics' hammers against bone, and the occasional, strangled sob escaping cracked lips. A chilling wind whistled through the ravaged landscape, carrying with it the whispers of death and the ghostly echoes of the cheers that would never be. The anticipated celebratory atmosphere was a cruel mockery, replaced by profound, gut wrenching sorrow. This victory, hard won and brutally achieved, felt like defeat; a pyrrhic triumph bought at a price too high, a cost measured not just in lives lost, but in the shattering of hopes and dreams.

Caspian, his normally impassive face a mask of bone deep weariness and grief, surveyed the devastation. The ravaged landscape stretched before him, a grim tapestry woven with the threads of shattered lives.

He moved through the carnage, his boots crunching on the broken remnants of what had once been a vibrant city, his gaze lingering on each fallen soldier. Familiar faces, once alight with the fire of hope and the warmth of comradeship, now lay still and lifeless, their eyes glazed over, staring blankly at the merciless, indifferent sky.

The air hung heavy with the stench of blood and smoke, a suffocating reminder of the brutal conflict. Each lifeless form was a testament to the terrible price exacted for crushing Valerius's rebellion, a price measured not in numbers, but in the irreplaceable loss of cherished friends, loyal companions, and brothers in arms. The victory, hard won and costly, felt hollow, bitter ash clinging to the back of his throat; the taste of triumph soured by the overwhelming bitterness of profound loss. The silence was broken only by the mournful whisper of the wind, carrying with it the echoes of dying screams and the weight of countless shattered dreams.

I stood beside him, my face a mirror reflecting his grief, the stark lines etched deep by sorrow. My fiery spirit, usually a vibrant, untamed blaze, was banked, its fierce energy subdued by the grim, chilling reality of the carnage. I had fought alongside Caspian, my flame elemental powers a raging inferno, a tempest of fire that scorched the rebellious forces. Yet, even the searing heat of my magic couldn't incinerate the haunting images of the fallen, the twisted metal, the still forms, the lingering stench of smoke and blood. The rebellion's suppression, a pyrrhic victory bought with a terrible price, had left a gaping void in our ranks, a chasm of loss far deeper and more enduring than any physical wound. The silence, heavy with unspoken grief, pressed down upon us, a tangible weight more suffocating than the smoke that still clung to the ravaged battlefield.

The whispers of dissent, though carefully muted, still clung to the air like the scent of wood smoke after a fire. Many within the Whispering Wind, once ardent supporters, now privately questioned Caspian's ruthlessness, his casual disregard for the lives sacrificed in the brutal suppression of Valerius's rebellion. Accusations of tyranny, once muttered in hushed tones, now echoed in the shadowed corners of their meeting places; a leader who had traded the organization's founding principles, principles of liberation and justice, for the cold comfort of absolute power. The violence had not merely extinguished Valerius's rebellion; it had scorched the very soul of the Whispering Wind, leaving behind a landscape of distrust and suspicion. The price of victory? A unity shattered, leaving behind only the fragile shards of what once was a powerful, cohesive force. Caspian's iron fist had not forged a stronger organization; it had fractured its heart, leaving its future uncertain and its members deeply divided.

Rhys, despite the gilded cage of his new command, remained a potent source of anxiety. His scouting reports, though undeniably invaluable, were delivered with a chilling undercurrent of resentment towards Caspian, a palpable animosity that served as a constant, gnawing reminder of the fissures fracturing our unity. I sensed, keenly, that Rhys's loyalty, even in this elevated position, was a precarious thing, a fragile raft bobbing precariously on a turbulent sea of uncertainty and simmering mistrust. His obedience felt less like a pledge of allegiance and more like a temporary truce, easily broken by the next capricious wave of his volatile emotions.

The aftermath was a wasteland not just of shattered buildings and broken bodies, but of shattered trust and eroded morale. A chilling certainty settled over the land: violence, like a self replicating plague, had spawned its monstrous offspring. Even the hard won victories tasted like ash, leaving behind a bitterness that gnawed at the soul, a festering wound threatening to metastasize into a societal cancer. The whispers of peace, once a hopeful murmur within Whispering Wind, were now barely audible, lost in the cacophony of grief and resentment. The path to unity felt impossibly distant, a treacherous climb up a mountain of despair.

The weeks that followed were a relentless, agonizing cycle: tending to the wounded, their cries a mournful counterpoint to the rhythmic thud of shovels burying the dead in hastily dug graves. The air, thick with the stench of decay and despair, hung heavy over the ravaged landscape. Attempts to restore order felt futile, a Sisyphean struggle against the overwhelming tide of grief and destruction. The planned celebration, a vibrant tapestry of joy and hope, was shredded, replaced by a sombre, hushed observance, each silent prayer a testament to lives lost. The victory, hard won and costly, felt hollow, a bitter fruit plucked from the jaws of defeat, its sweetness overwhelmed by the pervasive bitterness of sorrow and the gnawing weight of regret. The echoes of gunfire were replaced by the quieter, but no less devastating, sobs of the bereaved.

The Obsidian Covenant, sensing our weakened state like vultures circling a carcass, intensified their attacks with ruthless efficiency. A brutal series of raids, each more devastating than the last, rained down upon the Whispering Wind, exploiting not only the internal divisions down by the recent rebellion but also the festering wounds of betrayal and mistrust. The organization, already strained to its breaking point by the rebellion's bitter aftermath and the lingering scars of dissent, struggled to mount a coherent defence. Its once proud warriors, weary and demoralized, fought with the grim desperation of cornered animals. The respite, a fleeting phantom born of desperate tactical maneuvers and bloody sacrifices, proved cruelly ephemeral; the reprieve bought with such a terrible cost was insufficient to stem the tide of the Obsidian Covenant's relentless onslaught.

I, along with Caspian, felt the bone deep weariness settle into our souls, yet a stubborn resolve burned brighter. We were locked in a brutal double bind: the relentless onslaught of the Obsidian Covenant pressed from without, while the festering wounds of the rebellion's brutal suppression gnawed at us from within. Our relationship, forged in the crucible of unimaginable stress, became a precarious lifeline in the maelstrom. A shared, unwavering dedication to our cause fueled us, a flickering flame against the encroaching darkness, propelling us forward despite the seemingly insurmountable odds. But even the fierce strength of our love couldn't entirely banish the chilling spectre of fear and doubt that clung to us like a shroud. We were trapped in a vicious cycle of bloodshed, each hard won victory only buying us a fleeting respite before plunging us deeper into the conflict, the cost escalating with each passing battle. The weight of it all, the casualties, the betrayals, the relentless pressure, threatened to crush us, leaving us questioning whether the price of our fight was worth the uncertain promise of a future we couldn't guarantee.

The cost of suppressing the rebellion transcended the purely physical. The emotional toll was cataclysmic, etching indelible scars onto the souls of every participant. The stench of violence, the screams,

the faces contorted in agony, these memories clung like phantom limbs, haunting our waking hours and poisoning our dreams long after the last shot was fired. It was a darkness that festered within, a self inflicted wound far more insidious and debilitating than any inflicted by the rebels themselves; a corrosive poison that gnawed at our camaraderie, our faith, and our very humanity. The battleground, once silent, echoed with the ghosts of our shared trauma, a constant, chilling reminder of the brutal price of victory.

The battle was won, but victory tasted like ash. The Whispering Wind, though alive, was a shattered husk, its once proud form scarred and broken. The organization stretched taut like a threadbare tapestry, clung precariously to the fragile unity forged in the crucible of war. The future, a treacherous landscape of uncertainty, loomed before us, the past's brutal harvest, a field of blood soaked earth, heavy upon our shoulders. The whispers of rebellion might be stilled, but the echoes of violence resonated within the organization's very core, a chilling testament to the intoxicating allure of power and the enduring, agonizing consequences of its pursuit.

The healing, a slow, agonizing crawl across a vast wasteland of grief, had barely begun. Even the solace of Caspian's love, a fragile flame in the encroaching darkness, couldn't fully dispel the brutal, sombre truth of our pyrrhic triumph. This war, far from concluded, had merely entered a new, equally perilous chapter, a chapter promising even greater bloodshed, and a heavier toll on our hearts and souls. The silence following the rebellion's demise was more terrifying than the battle's fury itself; a chilling void pregnant with unspoken losses and the ominous uncertainty of the path ahead. A path that twisted and turned, beckoning us towards a future as uncertain as it was fraught with peril. The scars remained, etched not only on our bodies but deep within our very being, a constant, aching reminder of the price we paid.

The silence following the suppression of Valerius's rebellion was a heavier burden than the roar of battle ever had been. It was a silence thick with the stench of blood and the chill of betrayal, a pregnant pause teeming with unspoken accusations that hung heavy in the air like a shroud. The weight of lost lives, shattered dreams and broken oaths, pressed down on every member of the Whispering Wind, a crushing weight that threatened to suffocate them. Even Caspian, his stoicism a carefully constructed mask, felt the insidious cracks spreading through the very foundation of his organization, a creeping decay that undermined their strength from within.

The victory, bought with the blood of so many loyal warriors, had come at a price far steeper than he'd anticipated, a price measured not just in the grim tally of bodies, but in the insidious erosion of trust, the fracturing of their once unbreakable unity, and the gnawing fear that their hard won peace was but a fragile illusion, poised to shatter at any moment. The whispers, once the lifeblood of their clandestine operations, now carried a new, chilling tone, a murmur of doubt and distrust that threatened to unravel everything he had fought so hard to build.

I, ever perceptive, detected the subtle tectonic shifts in the organization's dynamics. The once ubiquitous easy camaraderie, a comfortable blanket of familiarity, had been brutally stripped away, replaced by a chilling landscape of wary glances and hushed, conspiratorial conversations. Rhys, despite his veneer of compliant behaviour, a carefully constructed mask of obedience, seethed with a simmering resentment, a volcanic pressure building beneath the surface, threatening to erupt at any moment. His eyes, when they locked with Caspian's, held a glacial intensity, a stark, unforgiving landscape reflecting a chasm of unspoken grievances, each unspoken word a shard of ice in the heart of their fragile peace. He was a constant, unsettling reminder of the precarious balance holding the Whispering Wind together, a fragile peace hanging by a thread, easily severed. His loyalty, though outwardly professed with practiced ease, felt conditional, a finely honed blade poised to fall, its weight a constant, ominous presence. The air itself crackled with the unspoken tension, a palpable energy that vibrated with the potential for explosive conflict.

Caspian convened a succession of summits, striving to quell the simmering unrest. His addresses, normally vibrant with his inherent magnetism and steadfast determination, now sounded forced, devoid of their accustomed conviction. The burden of his decisions, the carnage inflicted under his authority, shadowed him like a pall. He laboured to justify his actions, to articulate the strategic urgency of quashing the insurgency before it swelled, but his pleas resonated as empty pronouncements, lost on audiences numbed by sorrow and suspicion.

Amidst the carnage, the tireless physicians, ministering to the injured, unknowingly became conduits for discontent. Rumours of Caspian's brutality, stoked by accounts of gratuitous violence and a chilling indifference to human suffering, spread like wildfire amongst them. Observing them closely, I absorbed their murmured grievances, their frustrated sighs—a symphony of quiet outrage. These healers, their hands grimly marked by the blood of friend and foe alike, stood as sombre emblems of the rebellion's devastating toll.

Caspian understood that restoring faith demanded tangible steps, not mere pronouncements. He, therefore, launched a sweeping program of reforms, designed to quell the deep seated discontent roiling beneath the veneer of tranquillity. To temper his power, he convened a venerable council of elders, drawing its members from the diverse and often conflicting elements of the Whispering Wind. This assembly, though initially greeted with distrust, unexpectedly became a forum for frank discourse and vigorous debate, empowering previously marginalized voices to finally resonate.

Progress was glacial, each step agonizing. Every charge, each echo of past suffering, tore open festering grievances. Council sessions were charged with a palpable tension, erupting periodically in furious displays of rage and sorrow. Yet, from this crucible of animosity, a tentative exchange began to form—a slender lifeline spanning the abyss of suspicion.

My contribution to this undertaking proved indispensable. Unwavering devotion to Caspian, coupled with a profound capacity for understanding, transformed me into a pivotal conciliator. I absorbed the outpourings of discontent, acknowledging the depth of suffering and legitimizing our collective concerns. I confronted the stark realities without flinching, yet simultaneously highlighted the unifying objective that held us together. My passionate nature, usually reserved for confronting adversaries, now manifested as a tender empathy, skillfully mending the broken spirits of my fellow soldiers.

Rhys, initially steadfast in his opposition to rapprochement, underwent a subtle transformation. His participation in the council's deliberations, though initially marked by curt pronouncements and ingrained skepticism, blossomed into insightful proposals. He came to appreciate the agonizing dilemmas Caspian had faced, comprehending the strategic imperative underlying the ruthless quelling of Valerius's insurrection. The perilous nature of the Obsidian Covenant's threat became undeniably clear to him, revealing their internal divisions as a critical vulnerability. A profound shift occurred in his perspective; he grasped the overriding importance of our collective strength, recognizing its vital necessity amidst the prevailing adversity.

Trust, fractured by conflict, was meticulously restored not merely within the confines of official gatherings. It blossomed in shared intimacies—quiet suppers, the hushed attentiveness lavished upon the injured. Caspian and I, through exemplary actions, diligently repaired shattered bonds, soothing the lingering trauma of the insurrection. Our intertwined sorrow, profound admiration, and fervent love became a potent emblem of reconciliation, a radiant star piercing the oppressive gloom.

Through shared hardship and triumph, we forged a profound partnership. Mutual understanding blossomed as we came to appreciate each other's unique capabilities, skillfully mitigating individual shortcomings. Our bond, tempered in the crucible of conflict, flourished amidst the rebellion's ruins—a powerful symbol of our enduring resilience and unwavering devotion.

Fueled by the Whispering Wind's internal discord, the Obsidian Covenant pressed their relentless assault. Yet, from the ashes of the rebellion, a unified front emerged. The shared agony of that struggle had welded us together, forging an unbreakable alliance. We countered their aggression with ferocious determination, our renewed resolve born from a common goal: the unwavering defence of our hard won solidarity.

Though the peace was tenuous, a fragile truce etched upon the landscape of lingering resentments, Whispering Wind, once near annihilation, showed signs of robust recovery. The rebellion's wounds, a stark testament to the volatile nature of authority and the precariousness of harmony, remained. Yet, from the ashes of conflict, a profound metamorphosis emerged. The subversive murmurs that threatened our very survival became a crucible of self examination—a harrowing but vital journey that solidified our unity and deepened the bonds between us. We were stronger, forged in the fires of discord.

Danger lurked around every corner. The Obsidian Covenant's implacable menace persisted, a shadow hanging heavy over our fragile peace; the spectre of internal strife still haunted us. Yet, the Whispering Wind, under Caspian's and my command, had discovered an indomitable spirit, a tenacity forged in the crucible of rebellion. Rekindling trust proved a laborious, agonizing undertaking. However, with each deliberate stride forward, each carefully constructed alliance, we inched closer to a destiny where our mutual purpose and profound affection would illuminate our path to ultimate triumph—a victory not merely on the battlefield, but in crafting a future deserving of the immense sacrifices rendered.

The battle was not won; deep seated animosities remained, injuries festered, and the looming menace of the Obsidian Covenant cast a long shadow. However, as Caspian and I surveyed our weary but resolute companions, a spark of optimism ignited within us—a revitalized commitment that had nearly vanished amidst the rebellion's chaotic aftermath. The insidious murmurings of discord had yielded to a silent, steely resolve, a unified pledge to confront the formidable obstacles ahead. We had endured, but our enduring wounds bore stark witness to the heavy price of triumph and the vital need for concord. This precarious peace, hard won and fragile, stood as a testament to our indomitable spirit, our steadfast dedication, and our capacity to pave a path toward reconciliation, and finally, enduring confidence. The arduous trek toward genuine unity was fraught with danger, yet under our guidance, the Whispering Wind at last embarked upon its healing journey.

CHAPTER

TWENTY SEVEN

Shadows of the Past Return

The flickering torchlight, a desperate sun in the cavernous hall, cast long, dancing shadows across the grim faces of the Whispering Wind. Each shadow writhed and pulsed with the intensity of the unspoken anxieties that filled the air, a chilling weight heavier than the recent conflict itself. The uneasy peace, a fragile truce painstakingly forged in the blood soaked aftermath of Valerius's brutal rebellion, hung precariously, a gossamer thread threatened by the encroaching darkness. It had begun subtly, like a venomous serpent slithering into their midst: a patrol vanished without a trace, swallowed by the unforgiving wilderness; a vital supply line severed, leaving them vulnerable and exposed; a series of increasingly brazen attacks on outlying settlements, each more brutal than the last, leaving behind a trail of carnage and whispered terror.

Then came the unmistakable sigils, carved deep into the flesh of the victims, the grotesque, obsidian runes of the Covenant, branding their prey with a mark of utter depravity. The chilling certainty settled upon them like a shroud: they were back. The Obsidian Covenant, their reign of terror seemingly extinguished, had re-emerged from the abyss, and the Whispering Wind stood at the precipice of another, perhaps final, war.

Caspian, his jaw a granite vice, surveyed the grim, sweat slicked faces around him. The tentative trust, painstakingly cultivated over weeks of shared hardship and whispered confidences, disintegrated like ash in a sudden wind, scattering their fragile alliance. Rhys, his gaze a honed obsidian shard, stood a significant pace from Caspian, the subtle shift in his posture a stark betrayal of the uneasy truce. His shoulders were rigidly squared, a silent declaration of defensive readiness. Even I, typically a bastion of unwavering resolve, felt a cold tendril of dread slither down my spine, its icy fingers clutching at my heart. The familiar phantom scent of smoke and char, the visceral memory of fire's incandescent wrath and the sickening crunch of collapsing timbers, threatened to engulf me, to drag me under the suffocating weight of past horrors. The air itself seemed to crackle with unspoken anxieties, a palpable tension hanging heavy as a shroud.

A lone raven, its feathers singed and broken, was the first messenger. It arrived at the Obsidian Keep, its frantic circling a prelude to the horror it carried. The message, scrawled in blood on a fragment of scorched parchment, spoke of a scouting party annihilated near the Whisperwind's southern border, reduced to nothing more than scattered remnants and the stench of brimstone. The sole survivor, a man named Kael, his body a tapestry of wounds both physical and spiritual, clung to life, his whispers painting a nightmarish scene. Not merely a return, he gasped, but a cataclysmic arrival. An unstoppable tide of obsidian shadows, figures whose eyes burned with the malevolent light of a dying star, wielded weapons that cracked the earth itself. Their armour, polished to a mirror sheen, reflected not light, but the abyss itself. They moved with a chilling grace, a horrifying choreography of death, leaving behind a trail of destruction that defied description. The Obsidian Covenant's return was not a resurgence; it was an invasion, a dark storm consuming all in its path. Their vengeance promised to be absolute.

The whispers of our return, insidious and swift as a prairie fire, ignited the smouldering embers of ancient grudges and fanned the flames of fresh anxieties. Council chambers, once hallowed halls of reconciliation, now echoed with the cacophony of heated debate, a maelstrom of clashing strategies and desperate pleas for dwindling resources. The air, thick with the stench of betrayal and fear, crackled with unspoken accusations. Caspian's name, a poisoned dart, was flung across the chamber, each syllable a fresh wound reopening the festering sores of the Valerius rebellion, its heavy losses a constant, agonizing reminder of his perceived failures. The whispers of blame, once muted murmurs, had swelled into a roar, drowning out the fragile hope of unity and threatening to shatter the uneasy peace. Even the flickering lamp light seemed to cast long, accusing shadows.

I, sensing the rising tide of fear that threatened to swamp us all, intervened. My voice, usually vibrant and confident, now carried the steely glint of a honed blade. *"We squabble amongst ourselves,"* I stated, my gaze a sharp, unwavering sweep across the assembled members, each face etched with apprehension, *"while our enemies, like vultures circling a carcass, regroup, sharpening their talons and readying their strike."* The silence that followed hung heavy, thick with the unspoken dread of betrayal. *"Months we spent painstakingly rebuilding the trust Valerius shattered, brick by agonizing brick,"* I continued, my voice resonating with the weight of that shared struggle, *"and now, they, they, threaten to tear it all down again, to reduce our hard won gains to dust."* My words struck a chord, a deep, resonant note that vibrated through the room, reminding each one present of the precariousness of their position, the razor's edge on which they teetered. The fragility of their unity, so recently forged, hung palpable in the air.

Caspian's gaze, sharp and assessing, held mine. A familiar warmth, tinged with a profound worry, flickered in his usually stoic eyes. My resolve, a burning ember in the tempest of uncertainty, seemed to resonate with him; my capacity for empathy, a bridge spanning the chasm of our differences, offered a much needed haven. He rose, his imposing figure commanding attention, his voice a deep baritone that resonated with the authority of a seasoned leader, yet carried the weight of genuine concern. *"Blaze is right,"* he declared, his words cutting through the tension like a honed blade. *"We cannot afford the luxury of division. The Covenant's resurgence is an existential threat, a shadow looming over all of us, regardless of past betrayals or lingering resentments. We must forge a unity, a bulwark against this darkness, or we will surely fall, and the consequences will be catastrophic."*

The veneer of unity shattered, a brittle mask concealing the festering rot beneath. Rhys, a viper in silken robes, his smile a rictus over a heart choked with bile, feigned compliance. Each word he offered in those strategy sessions, ostensibly helpful, a honeyed poison, dripped with the venom of his contempt. Caspian's past mistakes etched onto his memory like branding irons, became Rhys's weapons. His suggestions, precise as surgeon's incisions, carved into Caspian's confidence, leaving bleeding wounds of doubt.

The air thrummed, a tangible thing, thick with the stench of betrayal and the metallic tang of blood, not spilled yet, but poised to erupt. It wasn't a silent war; it was a symphony of hate, a cacophony of unspoken accusations that clawed at the throat. Icy glares, sharp as shards of glass, met across the table. Pointed silences hung heavy, pregnant with the unspoken threats. Whispers, slithering like venomous snakes through the suffocating stillness, carried the weight of years of simmering resentment, each word a poisoned dart aimed directly at the heart. The very floor seemed to tremble under the weight of their mutual loathing, a seismic tremor beneath a façade of strained civility. Caspian tasted ash and fear; Rhys, the taste of victory, a bitter, fleeting triumph laced with the knowledge that his revenge was far from over.

The attacks intensified, a relentless hammer blow against the fragile peace. Smaller settlements, once idyllic havens nestled in the valleys and clinging to the hillsides, fell prey to the Covenant's merciless assault. Homes, once filled with laughter and the scent of wood smoke, were reduced to smouldering ruins, a testament to the invaders' brutal efficiency.

The Whispering Wind, once a formidable force, now stretched thin and fractured by internal strife, fought a desperate rearguard action. Their ranks, depleted by relentless skirmishes and ambushes, struggled to contain the tide of invasion. The air itself crackled with the fear of imminent death; casualties mounted, each fallen warrior a grim addition to a growing pyre of despair, fueling a vicious cycle of fear and mistrust that threatened to consume the land entirely.

Caspian, the weight of command pressing down on him like a physical burden, immersed himself in the grim task of intelligence gathering. He unearthed a chilling pattern in the seemingly random attacks: a calculated orchestration of violence, meticulously placed to sever vital supply lines and cripple communications networks. Each strike, a precisely aimed blow, was part of a larger, insidious campaign designed not merely to inflict damage, but to systematically weaken their defenses, exploiting existing internal divisions with the cold precision of a surgeon. The enemy wasn't merely fighting them; they were dissecting their vulnerabilities, picking them apart piece by agonizing piece.

Meanwhile, I dedicated myself to bolstering the morale of our beleaguered troops. Countless hours were spent at the makeshift hospital, tending to the wounded, not just with bandages and antiseptic, but with a soothing presence and unwavering encouragement. My empathy, a burning ember in the suffocating despair, served as a bridge, connecting the fractured spirits of my comrades. I reminded them of our shared cause, the righteous fury that fueled our resistance, and I acknowledged the vulnerability we all felt, the raw, exposed nerve of our shared mortality. But I also reminded them of the Covenant's atrocities: the villages reduced to ash, the innocent lives brutally extinguished, and the chilling, calculated efficiency of their genocidal campaign. I painted vivid pictures of the horrors they had witnessed, not to dwell on the past, but to reignite the fire of their resolve, to transform grief and fear into righteous anger and unwavering determination. The memories, though grim, served as a potent reminder of the stakes, of why we fought, and why surrender was never an option.

The flickering torchlight cast long, dancing shadows across the damp cavern walls as Caspian and I crouched over the captured Covenant messenger. His ragged breaths hitched in his chest, a stark contrast to the icy terror in his eyes. The interrogation had been brutal, but necessary. What he revealed that night shattered our carefully constructed assumptions, chilling us to the bone. It wasn't just the Obsidian Covenant's relentless advance that we had to contend with; it was a horrifying, unforeseen alliance, a pact forged in the shadows with the very viper we thought we had slain: the remnants of Valerius's treacherous cult.

The rebellion, we had believed extinguished, was not merely dormant; it had metastasized, slithering beneath the surface like a venomous serpent, re emerging now as a far more potent and insidious threat than we could have ever imagined. The weight of this revelation pressed down on us, heavier than any physical burden, as the implications of this unholy union unfolded in the grim silence of the cavern.

The news detonated in the Whispering Wind, a seismic shock that shattered the fragile peace. Years of painstaking diplomacy, a truce built on shifting sands and whispered promises, crumbled in an instant. The betrayal was a venomous strike, a poisoned dart aimed directly at the heart of their precarious unity. Trust, already a thin thread, snapped with a sickening sound, leaving behind only suspicion and recrimination. Whispers of blame, once a muted murmur against Caspian, now swelled into a furious torrent directed at Rhys and the die hard remnants of the Valerius faction. Their faces, etched with betrayal and fear, reflected the widening rift, a chasm opening not just between individuals, but between ideologies, threatening to consume the very fabric of their society, leaving behind only the wreckage of broken alliances and shattered dreams.

The weight of a thousand unspoken regrets pressed down on Caspian, a physical burden mirroring the looming threat that had driven him to this confrontation with Rhys. The air crackled with animosity, a palpable tension that vibrated between them like a taut wire strung across a chasm of years. Caspian's usually regal bearing was fractured, his jaw tight, his eyes shadowed with a weariness that spoke of sleepless nights and the crushing weight of his past. Rhys, his face a mask of hardened defiance, met Caspian's gaze with a cold, unwavering stare. His voice, sharp as shattered glass, cut through the suffocating silence.

He didn't merely refuse to apologize; he launched a scathing counterattack, each accusation a meticulously aimed dart, striking at the very core of Caspian's carefully constructed composure. The whispers of Caspian's ruthlessness, amplified by Rhys's bitter pronouncements, echoed in the cavernous space between them, each word a poisoned barb, threatening to unravel the already precarious threads of their fragile alliance. The scent of betrayal hung heavy in the air, a suffocating perfume mingling with the acrid tang of unspoken resentments.

The clash erupted before me, a brutal ballet of rage and sorrow. I saw it all, the raw, bleeding wounds, both physical and emotional, the haunted eyes reflecting years of accumulated grief. The very air thrummed with the lingering psychic trauma that fueled their animosity, a palpable tension thick enough to choke on. I stepped between them, the silence that followed my intervention heavy with unspoken accusations. Then,

I spoke, my voice cutting through the charged atmosphere. I didn't preach unity; I painted a picture, a stark and terrifying vision of the Obsidian Covenant's encroaching shadow, its tendrils already reaching for them, for everyone.

I spoke of shared vulnerability, of the common enemy that dwarfed their petty squabbles, weaving my narrative of loss and betrayal into the tapestry of their conflict. The pain in my voice mirrored their own, a shared language of suffering that transcended words. It wasn't blame I offered, but a bridge, a precarious path towards reconciliation built on empathy and the shared understanding that only those who have tasted bitterness can truly grasp. My words, born from the crucible of my own experiences, found fertile ground in their wounded hearts.

The path to unity was a jagged, treacherous climb. The scars of the past ran deep, festering wounds left by betrayals that felt like freshly inflicted blades. Yet, under the unwavering leadership of Caspian and myself, the Whispering Wind, battered and bruised but unbroken, began to regroup. The shared threat, the horrifying, palpable resurgence of the Obsidian Covenant and their newly revealed alliance with the remnants of Valerius's treacherous forces, forced us to confront our internal conflicts with brutal honesty. The encroaching darkness, a palpable entity pressing against the very walls of our haven, threatened to consume us all unless we stood united. Slowly, painstakingly, like mending a shattered tapestry, the fragile threads of trust began to knit back together. Each tentative step towards reconciliation was fraught with the risk of relapse, yet the shared peril spurred them onward.

The fight was far from over; the obsidian shadow stretched long and menacing over their future. But for the first time since the devastating rebellion, a fragile ember of hope flickered in the eyes of the Whispering Wind, a beacon against the encroaching darkness. Though the shadows of the past loomed large, threatening to engulf them, they would face them together, united at last, in a desperate, defiant fight for survival. Their unity, hard won and precious, was their only weapon against the looming annihilation.

The fragile peace of the Whispering Wind, a truce stained crimson by Valerius's brutal rebellion, exploded. Not a shattering, but a rending, a visceral tearing of flesh and bone as the Obsidian Covenant's resurgence slammed into it like a siege ram driven by a hellish engine. The air itself crackled, thick with the metallic tang of blood and the acrid stench of betrayal. Valerius's remaining followers, vipers I'd foolishly embraced, their venom masked by promises as hollow as their eyes, struck with the speed and precision of assassins. Their alliance, a venomous lie whispered in the shadows, felt like a blade twisting, not just in my gut, but in the very soul of our fragile alliance.

The tentative unity, once held together by threads of fear and begrudging respect, dissolved into a maelstrom of accusations and hate. The whispers, once venomous slithers in the darkness, became roars, echoing off the jagged cliffs and searing my ears with their fury. I tasted the ash of shattered trust on my tongue and felt the icy grip of paranoia constricting my throat, each breath a ragged gasp against the suffocating wave of treachery. Theirs wasn't just a betrayal; it was a calculated evisceration, a symphony of malice orchestrated by shadows I hadn't even begun to see. And now, I'm left to face the storm, the bitter taste of their treachery a constant reminder of my fatal mistake.

Rhys, his face a mask of simmering resentment etched with the lines of a thousand betrayals, launched a blistering attack on Caspian's leadership. His accusations, barbed and precise, stung with the bitter venom of past grievances, dredging up long buried resentments and fueling the flames of dissent. The whispers of doubt once muted murmurs in the shadows, now echoed through the ranks like the tolling of a death knell, a cacophony threatening to unravel everything Caspian had painstakingly built, brick by agonizing brick. The very foundations of their precarious alliance crumbled, leaving behind only the bitter dust of shattered trust and the chilling promise of all out war.

Caspian, shoulders bowed beneath the weight of his past failures and the precipice of utter chaos, knew decisive action was his only recourse. The internal conflict, a festering wound threatening to consume the kingdom, demanded immediate intervention. He sought out Serenity, a sorceress of formidable power, an elf whose ethereal beauty belied the steely resolve in her eyes.

One of the few remaining neutral members of the fractured council, Serenity possessed an uncanny ability to pierce the facades of deceit, her gaze a chillingly accurate instrument that dissected the swirling currents of ambition and treachery. She was a silent oracle, a weaver of intricate prophecies, who observed the tangled web of alliances and betrayals with an unsettling prescience. Her wisdom, however, was a precious commodity, dispensed only to those who earned her unwavering loyalty through deeds, not empty promises. The price of her counsel was high, demanding a sacrifice of pride and perhaps even more.

Our clandestine meeting unfolded beneath the velvet cloak of night, within the shadowed sanctuary of Serenity's private chambers. The air thrummed with unspoken tension, a palpable energy crackling between us like a storm about to break. The scent of ancient herbs, potent and strangely sweet, mingled with the sharp, almost metallic tang of raw magic, clinging to the very tapestries that draped the walls. Caspian, his face etched with grim determination, laid out the situation with the precision of a seasoned strategist.

He detailed the Covenant's renewed assaults, each strike more brutal and calculated than the last, their devastating alliance with the remnants of Valerius's shattered army a chilling testament to their growing power. His voice, low and urgent, painted a bleak picture: the Whispering Wind, once a united force, now fractured by bitter accusations and simmering resentment, teetered on the precipice of complete disintegration. The very air seemed to hold its breath, heavy with the weight of impending doom.

Serenity listened patiently, her expression a carefully constructed mask of serenity. The flickering candlelight danced in her dark eyes, revealing nothing of the thoughts churning beneath. When he finished his breathless account, she simply nodded, the movement almost imperceptible. A single, perfectly formed curl escaped her meticulously braided hair, swaying gently in the draught. *"The Obsidian Covenant,"* she said, her voice a silken whisper that carried the weight of centuries, *"has always thrived on chaos. Exploiting vulnerabilities, whispering insidious doubts into the hearts of men, it is their very lifeblood. This... this is merely the predictable culmination of their meticulously laid plans. A carefully orchestrated crescendo of deceit."*

"But how do we counter it?" Caspian asked, his voice edged with desperation. *"The trust is shattered. The Whispering Wind is fracturing."*

Serenity's smile was a shard of ice, a cruel, thin crescent moon that never touched the glacial depths of her eyes. The air around her crackled with silent, lethal energy, a palpable chill that seeped into the very marrow of your bones. *"There are others,"* she hissed, the word a viper's caress, slithering across the air, laced with the scent of ozone and blood. *"Others nursing wounds so deep, they fester with the venom of the Covenant's treachery. Their hatred, a ravenous beast gnawing at their souls, mirrors our own, a burning inferno stoked by years of unimaginable suffering. They crave... yearn... for an alliance, a convergence of vengeance so potent it will shatter the very foundations of the Covenant's power. A symphony of retribution, a blood soaked requiem for their loss, a chance to finally... collect."* The final word hung heavy, dripping with the weight of centuries of unforgiven wrongs, a promise whispered in the wind, a death knell for those who stood against them.

Caspian frowned. *"You speak of... outsiders?"*

"Indeed," Serenity confirmed, her voice a low murmur that held the weight of centuries of conflict. *"The Blood Moon Clan. Their hatred for the Covenant isn't simply a political disagreement; it's a venomous legacy, woven from the threads of ancient blood feuds and losses so profound they've become a chilling part of their very identity. They are brutal, yes, ruthless beyond comprehension, and their methods... unorthodox is far too gentle a term. Think of rituals steeped in shadow magic, tactics that defy logic, and savagery that leaves even hardened warriors trembling. But their hatred fuels them, sharpening their already unmatched fighting skills to a razor's edge. And their resources? Let's just say they command power far exceeding their apparent numbers, a power drawn from sources both earthly and... otherwise."*

The idea was audacious, a gamble on the precipice of oblivion. The Bloodmoon Clan, infamous for their savagery, were a storm of violence and treachery, their loyalty as fleeting and unpredictable as the moon's phases. Their reputation preceded them like a chilling wind, a tempest forged in bloodshed and betrayal, whispered in hushed tones across the land. Caspian, however, felt the icy grip of desperation. The Whispering Wind, once a proud and unified tribe, was hemorrhaging from a thousand internal wounds; their simmering conflicts threatened to shatter them, leaving them vulnerable to the ravenous jaws of their enemies. The very air crackled with the tension of their impending collapse, a silence broken only by the whispers of dissent and the ever present threat of betrayal. Caspian's choice was stark: forge an unlikely alliance with the Blood Moon Clan, or watch his people crumble into dust. The risk was monumental, but the alternative was unthinkable.

He sought me out, his gaze earnest beneath the flickering torchlight. He spoke of the Serenity proposal, his voice a low hum that belied the gravity of the situation. He detailed the potential benefits, a fragile alliance, a tenuous peace, painting a picture of a future where the Blood Moon Clan, with their volatile magic and untamed fury, could become unexpected allies. But then the shadows deepened in his eyes as he laid bare the inherent dangers, the risks of a reckless gamble. My usual fiery spirit, a tempest usually quick to ignite, was tempered by a cautious pragmatism. The Bloodmoon Clan were indeed a wild card, an unpredictable force capable of both breathtaking loyalty and brutal betrayal. Yet, the escalating threat from the Obsidian Covenant, a relentless tide of darkness, left them with few palatable choices. The alternative, a slow, agonizing implosion, a descent into internecine conflict, was a far more perilous path to ruin, a certain death compared to the uncertain hope offered by the Serenity proposal.

"It's a gamble," I admitted, my eyes mirroring the flickering, amber flames dancing in the hearth. A gamble? More like a leap of faith into the abyss. Is this the best we can do? What if it all goes wrong? The faces of everyone depending on me flashed through my mind. I can't let them down. A shiver, born less of cold and more of apprehension, traced a path down my spine. This icy dread…it's familiar. It's the feeling I get right before a battle, before a crucial decision. But this…this is different. This feels final. *"A desperate one, perhaps. But one we might have to take. The odds are stacked against us, I won't lie, but we need every conceivable advantage, every sliver of hope we can grasp."* Every sliver? Is that even enough? It feels like grasping at straws in a hurricane. But what choice do we have? We've already lost so much. This is our last stand. And if it fails… I can't even think about that right now. Just focus. Just hope.

The air in the Bloodmoon Clan's cavern hung thick with the scent of wood smoke and something else, something primal and faintly metallic, like dried blood. Negotiations were a charade, a tense dance on the precipice of war. Lyra, their leader, a woman etched by harsh winters and countless battles, regarded Caspian with eyes the colour of glacial ice. Her silence was a weapon, more terrifying than any shout. Each carefully chosen word from Caspian's proposal felt like a pebble dropped into a still pool, sending ripples of suspicion and barely concealed hostility across her impassive features. The flickering torchlight danced on the intricate carvings adorning the cavern walls, ancient symbols hinting at a history of bloodshed and betrayal, a legacy that weighed heavily on the tense atmosphere. The silence between them pulsed with the unspoken threats, the accumulated grievances of generations a palpable force pressing down on both parties like a suffocating shroud. Even the crackling fire seemed to hold its breath, anticipating the spark that could ignite a conflict centuries in the making.

Lyra's demands were exorbitant. She didn't merely request access to the Whispering Wind's resources; she insisted on unfettered access to their vast, meticulously guarded stores. A mere share of the spoils wasn't enough; she demanded a significant portion, a king's ransom carved from the heart of their future plunder. And autonomy? It wasn't a simple request for independence; she demanded complete sovereignty, a self governing fiefdom within their already precarious alliance. Caspian, his kingdom teetering on the brink of collapse, desperate for their formidable military might and arcane knowledge, found himself agreeing to almost every unreasonable condition. The alliance, therefore, was born not of mutual respect or trust, but of stark, desperate necessity; a fragile pact forged in the white hot crucible of shared peril, cemented not by loyalty, but by the cold, hard logic of survival. The very air crackled with unspoken resentments, a volatile truce masking the simmering potential for betrayal.

The combined might of the Whispering Wind and the Bloodmoon Clan slammed against the Obsidian Covenant like a tidal wave of shadow and steel. The Covenant's meticulously crafted offensive, once a tide of disciplined advance, was thrown into disarray, its carefully laid plans dissolving into panicked improvisation. The Bloodmoon Clan's savagery, a brutal symphony of unorthodox tactics, proved devastatingly effective. Their guerrilla warfare was a masterpiece of chaos; swift, silent strikes from the impenetrable darkness bled the Covenant's strength, sapping their morale with every expertly placed ambush. Fear, a chilling wind whispering through the ranks of the once proud Covenant, replaced the steely resolve that had fueled their advance. Each fallen soldier was a testament to the Clan's uncanny ability to strike from the shadows, leaving behind only whispers of terror and the chilling crimson stain of the Blood Moon. The Covenant's meticulously forged order was crumbling under the relentless pressure, replaced by the agonizing disarray of a broken army.

However, the uneasy alliance, forged in the crucible of necessity, was far from perfect. A chasm yawned between the Bloodmoon Clan's brutal, visceral fighting style, a whirlwind of crimson fury and unchecked aggression, and the Whispering Wind's meticulous, calculated approach, favouring strategic maneuvers and controlled warfare. These fundamental differences ignited frequent clashes, sparks of conflict flaring into raging infernos of mistrust. Caspian and I found ourselves perpetually mediating, navigating the treacherous, ever shifting currents of resentment that threatened to shatter our fragile pact. Each negotiation felt like walking a tightrope strung high above a chasm of bloodshed, the slightest misstep capable of plunging us all into ruin. Yet, the looming shadow of the Obsidian Covenant, and the shared, incandescent hatred burning for that malevolent force, served as the precarious glue binding our disparate factions together, a fragile unity forged in the fires of a common enemy.

The culmination of our combined might resulted in a pyrrhic victory. A decisive battle fought beneath the baleful glare of a blood red moon, cleaved the Obsidian Covenant's ranks asunder. Their meticulously formed lines shattered like brittle glass under the relentless assault, their advance crippled, their retreat a desperate, chaotic scramble. Yet, this triumph, hard won and brutally earned, came at a terrible cost. The field ran red with the blood of friend and foe alike; a grim testament to the ferocity of the conflict. The fragile peace, painstakingly forged within our alliance, shuddered violently, threatening to unravel entirely.

The Blood Moon Clan, their insatiable thirst for blood temporarily quenched but far from extinguished, stirred with a restless energy. Their guttural battle cries, barely suppressed, echoed the simmering discontent within their ranks. Lyra, her gaze previously fixed with unwavering resolve, now held a chilling ambiguity, her eyes shimmering with unspoken intentions, hinting at a deeper, more sinister agenda that cast long shadows over our hard fought victory. The air crackled with unspoken tensions, a volatile mix of triumph and trepidation hanging heavy in the aftermath of the crimson moon's descent.

The unexpected alliance, a fragile pact forged in the crucible of desperate necessity, had gifted them a crucial advantage against the Obsidian Covenant. But this hard won victory was a pyrrhic one, ushering in a new era of challenges, far more insidious than the overt threats they'd faced before. The clash of steel and sorcery against the Covenant was over, for now, yet in the smouldering ruins, a different war ignited, a simmering conflict within their ranks, a struggle for power amongst uneasy allies whose loyalties were as brittle as frost.

The shadows of the past, though seemingly receding, cast long, menacing fingers across their present, giving birth to new and unpredictable dangers. Whispers of betrayal slithered through their camp like venomous snakes, fueling mistrust and paranoia. The path to ultimate victory, if such a thing even remained attainable, was a treacherous labyrinth, a winding road paved with uncertainty, fraught with the constant threat of annihilation, not just at the hands of their enemies, but from the daggers plunged by those they once called comrades. Survival itself became a brutal, daily struggle, fought not only against the Obsidian Covenant's remnants but against the insidious erosion of trust and the ever present spectre of internal conflict.

The blood red orb, a malevolent eye burning holes in the suffocating black, bled its crimson light onto their desperate struggle. The stench of fear, sharp and metallic like old blood, mingled with the acrid tang of gunpowder clinging to the damp earth. Each ragged breath rasped in their chests, a counterpoint to the silent, chilling gaze of the moon, a constant, mocking reminder of their fragility, a celestial judge pronouncing their precarious existence. This wasn't merely a fight; it was a gnawing, visceral war waged against the very fabric of their hope. A war where every shadow held a threat, every rustle of leaves a potential ambush, and the chilling wind whispered prophecies of further, unimaginable horrors. Their faces, etched with the grim determination of the hunted, held a haunted beauty, the reflection of a shared trauma that bound them closer than any oath could ever hope to achieve. This wasn't just another battle; it was the heart stopping plunge into a hell they had only dared to imagine, a descent into the abyss where survival itself was a cruel, bitter jest. The fight was far from over; it was just beginning to claw at their souls.

A cloying atmosphere of dread, sweat, and burning wood permeated the war room. Across the crude table, meticulously detailed maps, marred by the grim choreography of conflict, lay scattered. Caspian, his countenance ravaged by sleepless nights and relentless planning, followed the Obsidian Covenant's inexorable advance with a weary finger. Beside him, I stood, my normally incandescent spirit shrouded by the looming battle. Candlelight flickered in my fiery eyes, mirroring the resolute grimness of my expression. Opposite, Lyra, matriarch of the Bloodmoon Clan, sat impassively, her fingers lightly resting on the wicked curve of her dagger. The crackling hearth offered meagre respite from the suffocating silence, a pressure far exceeding any bellowed order.

"*Their numbers... they swell, like a tide of blood rising against the shore,*" Caspian rasped, the words tasting of ash and iron in his mouth. The flickering torchlight glinted off the steel in his eyes, mirroring the cold dread churning in his gut. "*Valerius's curse... they're not remnants. They're a viper's nest, reborn and far more venomous than we imagined. I can feel it, the pressure, a physical weight pressing down on our lines. They slither through the cracks, the weaknesses in this... fragile alliance we cobbled together. The stench of their betrayal hangs heavy in the air, a sickening sweetness masking the metallic tang of spilled blood.*" He slammed a fist on the rough hewn table, the sound echoing the frantic beat of his own heart. "*They're not just attacking our defences; they're consuming them. And soon, they'll consume us all.*"

A cruel smirk twisted Lyra's mouth. "*Flaws?*" she scoffed, her voice a glacial whisper. "*Caspian, the universe is merely a tapestry woven from power imbalances. The dominant devours the vulnerable; it's the immutable law.*" Her gaze, sharp as shattered ice, held him captive, the predatory calm radiating an unsettling aura of cold calculation.

"*We need a coordinated strategy,*" I interjected, my voice sharp. "*We can't afford to be caught off guard again. The Bloodmoon Clan's guerilla tactics are effective, but we need to integrate them with the Whispering Wind's more structured approach."*

"Integration?" Lyra scoffed. *"Your precious strategies are far too slow, too...civilized. We strike swiftly and hard, leaving no survivors. We are the storm, not the carefully constructed dam."* The subtle shift in her tone hinted at the simmering impatience beneath her calm surface.

Caspian sighed, rubbing his temples. *"Lyra, we understand your methods are effective. But our goal is not just to inflict casualties; it's to dismantle the Obsidian Covenant's power structure. We need a long term strategy, not just a series of bloody skirmishes."*

A protracted debate, a stark clash of military doctrines, consumed the afternoon. Caspian's proposals, a labyrinthine web of calculated maneuvers—diversions, deceptive feints, and precisely synchronized offensives—aimed for surgical precision, minimizing bloodshed while maximizing battlefield gains. In stark contrast, Lyra advocated for brutal, unexpected attacks, a scorched earth policy of unrelenting aggression; her vision relied on the paralyzing power of terror and the swift efficiency of unbridled chaos.

Again, I served as an intermediary, bridging the chasm between Caspian's methodical practicality and Lyra's ruthless effectiveness. I possessed intimate knowledge of both perspectives; I'd endured the harsh crucible of survival, yet also grasped the profound importance of foresight and tactical maneuvering. The undertaking proved immensely taxing, and utterly debilitating, demanding an almost preternatural comprehension of the intellects locked in conflict and the brutal exigencies of war.

A bitter dispute erupted over resource distribution. Caspian advocated for a meticulous rationing of provisions, arms, and troops, focusing on fortifying key positions and essential defences. Lyra, however, whose methods were notoriously unrestrained, derided these limitations. She vehemently insisted on a larger portion of the plunder, claiming her elite units deserved the most advanced and devastating arsenal.

"We need to strike a balance," Caspian argued patiently, *"between supporting your unconventional warfare and ensuring we have enough resources to support our main defences."*

"A balance?" Lyra's voice dripped with sarcasm. *"There is no balance. There is only strength and weakness. My warriors bleed for this war, and they deserve the best tools to do their job effectively."*

Beneath the surface of a furious, acrimonious debate, laced with barely concealed intimidation and festering animosity, a clandestine power play unfolded. A perilous, slow burning conflict of attrition simmered among ostensibly allied factions.

A reluctant pact emerged from the deepening shadows of night. Lyra secured a substantial share of the coveted arms and provisions, yielding only to the imperative of unified action under Caspian's command. This agreement forged not in fellowship but in the chilling awareness of annihilation, was a precarious truce. Bound together by a venomous shared enmity toward their mutual foe, their desperate alliance would meet its ultimate test against the encroaching abyss.

A frenetic pace consumed the subsequent days. The Whispering Wind and the Bloodmoon Clan, a volatile alliance forged in necessity, toiled relentlessly. Their partnership, however, was a tempestuous dance between methodical strategy and unrestrained ferocity, a discordant symphony of conflicting styles that sparked perpetual bickering. But a shared, implacable resolve bound them, a grim unity born of the Obsidian Covenant's ominous shadow.

Steel shrieked against steel, and a cacophony of battle cries and simulated death cries resonated across the training grounds. Caspian, a hawk eyed observer, orchestrated the tactical maneuvers, his commands crisp and unwavering. Meanwhile, Lyra, the Bloodmoon Clan's merciless instructor, forged her warriors through a brutal regimen, demanding lightning fast reflexes and cold blooded lethality. Blaze, a tireless peacemaker, navigated the volatile tension between the factions, mediating conflicts, bridging chasms of discord, and harmonizing their efforts into a unified, potent force.

Intense, meticulous preparations consumed us. We amassed resources, reinforced our defences, and honed our battle plans to razor sharpness. The burden of the approaching war pressed heavily on every soldier in both factions; the dreadful cost of this imminent clash was acutely felt. More than land and dominion hung in the balance; our very existence was at stake. Our survival was the ultimate prize.

Caspian, though powerful, bore the immense weight of his people's fate. His every choice dictated the survival of his kingdom and the tenuous stability of their fragile alliance. I, however, battled my inner torments, the gnawing hunger of my vampiric nature a constant, chilling reminder of my fleeting existence. Lyra, her steely eyes betraying no fear, remained an island of icy resolve, a merciless hunter poised to unleash her wrath upon the Obsidian Covenant.

In the predawn gloom of the war room, Caspian and I were utterly isolated. The meagre candle flame painted their weary features with shifting, spectral light, betraying the profound weariness and steely resolve burning within.

"We've done all we can," Caspian said, his voice a low murmur. *"Now, it's up to fate."*

I nodded, my hand resting on the hilt of her blade. *"We fight together, Caspian. Or we fall together."*

An unspoken pact sealed our destinies, forged in the crucible of shared hardship; a testament to our indomitable spirits and profound empathy. With the first light of dawn, the finality arrived. Hostilities commenced. Our existence, indeed the fate of all creation, teetered precariously. This impending conflict would determine everything. Every action, every decision, held the world's future in its trembling balance. The ensuing struggle for survival would be a brutal power play, a clash of ruthless effectiveness and cunning strategy; the ultimate, apocalyptic ballet of a world consumed by darkness.

TWENTY EIGHT

Blood Soaked Dawn

C rimson bled into bruised purple, a venomous sunrise staining the pre-dawn sky, a butcher's palette foreshadowing the carnage to come. The air, thick and cloying, tasted not just of ash and iron, but of something acrid and wrong, a metallic tang coating the back of my throat like the lingering memory of a scream. This ravaged land, a graveyard stretching to the blood red horizon, stank of death and despair. Each crater, a gaping maw carved into the earth by sky fire, whispered tales of the Great Sundering, the cataclysm that had ripped the world asunder, leaving us in this perpetual twilight, a suffocating blanket woven from smoke and sorrow.

My gut churned, a knot of dread tighter than the Obsidian Covenant's iron grip. The tension wasn't just palpable; it was a physical force, a weight pressing down on my chest, heavy as the mountains of charred bone that littered the landscape. The smoke from a thousand burning villages, their villages, choked the air, a miasma of fear and desperation. The Covenant's pyres weren't merely for the dead; they were a grotesque spectacle, a perverse ballet of power, their efficiency a chilling testament to their cold, calculating hearts. I could almost taste the bitter triumph on their lips, the same chilling satisfaction that had stolen the sun and left us to cower in its shadow. The screams of the innocent still echoed in the cracks of the ravaged earth, even now, I could feel the heat of their fear clinging to my skin. Their sacrifice wouldn't be forgotten.

High in the shattered remnants of the watchtower, built from the fused stones of a long dead civilization, the Obsidian Covenant's approach unfolded before me. The tower itself leans precariously, held together by rusted iron braces and sheer stubbornness. From this vantage, I could see the details, the intricate, almost ritualistic carvings adorning their iron armour, depicting grotesque figures fused with warped, obsidian like wings; symbols of their twisted faith in the Shadow God, a deity worshipped through suffering and conquest.

A sea of black, an inexorable tide of warriors clad in iron, their banners rippling like the predatory wings of colossal vultures, vultures whose eyes burned with a malevolent, crimson glow thanks to embedded, hellfire infused gems. These weren't merely warriors; they were fanatics, driven by a faith that demanded bloodshed. Their numbers dwarfed our expectations, a horrifying legion, easily ten thousand strong, poised to overwhelm our painstakingly erected fortifications, built from salvaged metal and hastily felled timber, a pathetic bulwark against such a tide. Beyond the main force, I spotted smaller contingents, monstrous siege engines, their twisted metal limbs hinting at the horrors they were capable of unleashing, and riders mounted on grotesque, obsidian skinned steeds, their eyes gleaming with the same unsettling crimson light. This wasn't just an army; it was a plague, a creeping shadow engulfing our last bastion of hope.

Beside me, Caspian, a granite statue etched with the weariness of a hundred battles, stood unyielding. The stench of sweat and wood smoke clung to him, a familiar perfume of impending carnage. His jaw, usually sharp as a hawk's beak, was slack with exhaustion, yet his eyes—God, those eyes—burned with a glacial fire, defiance that chilled me to the bone. He wasn't merely a strategist; he was a storm of honed steel and raw fury, a chieftain who tasted blood as readily as mead, a man who would meet the enemy's blade with his own, not from behind some gilded throne. His hand, calloused and strong as a vice, clamped onto my arm, the pressure a searing brand against my skin. It wasn't comforting; it was a jolt, a raw, electric current that pulsed through me, a primal connection that even the monstrous shadow of annihilation couldn't entirely eclipse. The air crackled with a silent scream, a symphony of fear and unwavering resolve.

"They're using Valerius's old tactics," Caspian observed, his voice barely a whisper against the rising wind. *"The flanking maneuver. Lyra's scouts confirmed it."*

My head bowed, not in submission, but in a grim acknowledgment of the butchery. The stench of blood, thick and cloying, choked me. My eyes, burning with furious grief, devoured the crimson tapestry spread across the field. The Obsidian Covenant's slaughter wasn't just effective; it was a symphony of calculated brutality, a perverse ballet of death orchestrated by a general whose cold heart was a black hole at the center of the galaxy. They'd carved through our hastily thrown together ranks like a scythe through the wheat, exploiting every weakness with a chilling precision that chilled me to the bone. I tasted the metallic tang of blood, my own, I suspected, from a graze on my cheek, and the grit of the ravaged earth beneath my boots.

Our response? It wouldn't be pretty. It would be a brutal, bloody pincer, a vice squeezing the life from their exposed flanks. We'd pulverize their wings, and shatter their confidence, before unleashing a storm upon their fortified heart, a whirlwind of steel and fury designed to tear down their meticulously constructed defences before they could even draw a proper breath. A desperate gamble, a last ditch effort fueled by hate and the bitter taste of betrayal. But it was our only hope. And in the fire of that desperate hope, I found a chilling calm, the cold certainty of a man who'd stared into the abyss and found only the burning desire for revenge.

Lyra materialized beside us, a glacial shard erupting from the very fabric of the storm. The wind, a mere zephyr moments before, now howled a pathetic counterpoint to the icy tempest radiating from her. It wasn't just cold; it was the chilling breath of death, a palpable absence of warmth that stole the very oxygen from my lungs. Her silence was a weapon, sharper than any blade, a vow etched in the frozen silence, a promise of annihilation. Her eyes, usually glittering with calculating brilliance, were now twin points of glacial fire, boring into the enemy's movements with the predatory grace of a snow leopard stalking its prey. The air crackled with the barely contained fury within her; I could feel the tremor in her fingers, a thrumming vibration that echoed the pulse of a coiled viper ready to strike. The polished obsidian of her dagger felt cold even through my trembling hand as she shifted her grip, a whisper of movement that spoke volumes of lethal intent. Fear, raw and visceral, seized me, not for my own life, but for the utter devastation she was about to unleash.

The earth shuddered as the Covenant's advance crashed down, not merely a wave, but a tidal tsunami of steel and fire, obliterating our defenses in a heartbeat. The stench of burnt flesh and ozone filled my nostrils, a sickening perfume accompanying the death cries, screams swallowed by the monstrous cacophony of clashing blades and the guttural roars of their grotesque war beasts. Their armour, slick with the blood of my brothers, reflected the infernal glow of their weapons, a horrifying mirror to my burning rage. Years of meticulous planning, of strategic brilliance honed to a razor's edge, crumbled like dust before the brute, bestial force of their onslaught.

I was flung into the maelstrom, a tiny spark in a volcano of carnage. The taste of blood, my own, I think, mingled with the acrid tang of smoke. My fiery abilities, normally a precise dance of destruction, erupted in a chaotic, incandescent fury. Each pulse of searing heat was a prayer, a scream, a desperate attempt to stave off the encroaching darkness. Grief, raw and visceral, clawed at my throat, a suffocating weight, fueling a vengeance so potent it felt like it would consume me, too. My village...reduced to ash, a memory choked by dust and smoke. Every blow I landed, a searing brand upon their flesh, a furious, desperate ballet of retribution fueled by the ashes of my home and the ghosts of my people. Their deaths were insufficient payment, a mere drop in the ocean of my sorrow.

The air, thick with the stench of blood and burning flesh, screamed. A maelstrom of violence, a crimson tide, consumed the battlefield. Death wasn't merely a harvest; it was a frenzied feast, its icy breath chilling the very marrow of the survivors. Each guttural cry, each bone shattering impact, was a hammer blow against the soul. Caspian, a whirlwind of honed muscle and lethal instinct, felt the hot spray of blood bloom across his face as his scimitar, a whisper of death carved from obsidian, ripped through the enemy ranks. The weight of each swing, the satisfying thunk of steel meeting bone, a brutal symphony of slaughter. He tasted the metallic tang, a grim reward for his merciless efficiency. He wasn't merely fighting; he was exorcising the demons that clawed at his sanity.

Lyra, a phantom forged in the fires of a broken heart, moved with the grace of a predator, her eyes twin pools of icy fury. She didn't see men; she saw obstacles, impediments to her grim purpose. Each precise thrust of her dagger, a venomous kiss leaving behind a trail of agonizing screams and spilled entrails, was a testament to her cold, calculated rage. The chilling silence of her passage was broken only by the ragged breaths of the dying and the echoing clang of her blade, the counterpoint to the battlefield's cacophony. The weight of countless deaths rested on her shoulders, a burden she carried with an unsettling calm, her vengeance a burning inferno consuming all in its path. She wasn't simply killing; she was consuming. She was the embodiment of the conflict's brutal, unforgiving heart.

The battlefield reeked of blood and scorched earth, a maelstrom of carnage so visceral it clawed at my throat. Hours bled into an eternity of screaming metal and shattered bone, a symphony of death conducted by a furious god. Caspian and I, a whirlwind of steel and shadow, danced a macabre waltz amidst the chaos. The air crackled with the unholy energy of our synergy, a terrifying spectacle that left even hardened veterans staring, mouths agape, their eyes glazed with a mixture of awe and horror. We were a storm, a tempest of coordinated fury, our unlikely alliance forged in the fires of necessity, a fragile truce cemented by mutual desperation and a shared thirst for survival. But even our hellish dance, our meticulously honed combat ballet, wasn't enough.

The Obsidian Covenant's legions, a tide of black armour and cold, implacable fury, crashed over us, wave after wave. I tasted the metallic tang of blood, my own, or another's, it didn't matter. The ground trembled beneath the thunder of their advance, a physical manifestation of their relentless will. Their numbers seemed infinite, their resolve unyielding, a chilling testament to the fanaticism that burned in their hearts, a fire far more dangerous than any blade. The stench of death thickened, a suffocating blanket woven from fear and despair, and I knew, with a chilling certainty that settled deep in my bones, that our fragile truce, and perhaps even our lives, were about to be shattered.

The sun, a molten fist, hammered the battlefield. Blood, thick as honey and the colour of sunset's dying breath, glazed the parched earth. The air, a cloying miasma of copper and decay, burned in my nostrils, each ragged gasp a testament to the butchery. My tongue, thick with the metallic tang of death, tasted the ash of shattered hopes. Around me, the remnants of our legions, haunted figures etched with exhaustion and despair, clung to life with the desperate tenacity of drowning men. Their eyes, hollowed pits reflecting the crimson horror, held not fear, but a chilling, cold fury. Even amongst the shattered stones of our failing defences, a grim resolve held sway; a war forged brotherhood bound by the shared agony of a thousand mortal wounds. Across the field, their ranks, those merciless bastards, stood defiant, their faces grim masks of implacable hatred, their eyes burning with a righteous zeal as twisted as our own. There would be no quarter given, no peace brokered. Only the silence of utter annihilation, or the deafening roar of a victory brought in blood and bone. This wasn't a battle; it was the raw, unyielding struggle for the very soul of our existence.

The battlefield shrieked. A maelstrom of blood and screaming metal, a symphony of death conducted by the obsidian clad colossus himself: Valerius. The stench of burning flesh and pulverized bone clawed at my throat, a bitter counterpoint to the metallic tang of blood in my mouth. From the very heart of that infernal chaos, he surveyed his legions, a god of destruction carved from shadow and polished malice. His obsidian armour, slick with the gore of my people, reflected the flickering torch light in a thousand malevolent gleams. His eyes, twin chips of glacial fury, bored into me, a cold promise etched in the very ice of their depths. This butcher, this architect of my village's obliteration, the screams of my family still echoing in the charred ruins, had kindled in me a fire hotter than any forge, a vengeance so absolute it eclipsed even the sun. The taste of ashes, and the phantom touch of my mother's hand... fueled the inferno consuming me. He would pay. He would pay.

A crimson fury choked me, a molten tide surging through my veins as I hurled myself at him. The air tasted of ozone and blood, a metallic tang that burned my nostrils. My heart hammered a frantic tattoo against my ribs, a savage rhythm echoing the primal scream trapped in my throat. Caspian, his eyes twin chips of obsidian, and Lyra, her face a mask of grim determination, shadowed me, their weapons—a wickedly curved scimitar and a staff crackling with arcane energy—a silent promise of death at my back. This wasn't a mere assault; it was a suicidal charge, a desperate wager against an eternity of torment. The odds were astronomical, a mountain of despair looming over us, but retreat meant oblivion. Our very souls, raw and exposed, clung to the razor's edge of this gamble, our existence a fragile thread spun from defiance and a burning hatred for the monster before us.

Valerius's smile, a rictus of bone white against the bruised purple of his twilight hued skin, met our charge like a physical blow. The air itself cracked, a palpable stench of ozone and decay preceding the surge. It wasn't just power; it was a malevolent tide, a shadow storm erupting from his hand, a clawed fist of darkness that slammed into me with the force of a collapsing star. The agony wasn't just pain; it was a shattering of my very being, a thousand icy needles piercing my soul, the taste of blood blooming coppery and acrid on my tongue. My vision fractured into jagged shards of black, the screams of the wind howling in my ears.

Caspian, his usually jovial face contorted in a mask of grim determination, roared his blade a silver flash against the encroaching darkness. Lyra, her eyes burning with a fierce, desperate courage that belied her slight frame, met the onslaught with a whirlwind of motion, her whispered incantations a desperate counterpoint to the oppressive silence that had swallowed the battlefield. But even their combined might, usually a storm unto itself, buckled under Valerius's weight. He was not merely strong; he was an abyss, a living embodiment of dread, his power a suffocating blanket woven from nightmares and the screams of forgotten gods. This wasn't a battle; it was an execution, and we were mere insects pinned beneath his heel.

As Valerius, poised for a devastating blow, launched another assault, a spectral figure materialized from the inky blackness. A woman, shrouded in impenetrable shadows, her features obscured by a concealing hood, materialized. From the staff she wielded, a searing torrent of incandescent light erupted, striking Valerius with the force of a thunderbolt. He staggered back, momentarily stunned. This unexpected intervention from the enigmatic woman provided Caspian, Lyra, and me with the vital opening we desperately craved.

Our unified assault, a trinity of might, shattered Valerius's defences. A perfectly synchronized onslaught, our combined powers overwhelmed him, his fall echoing the demise of his tyrannical reign. Witnessing their leader's destruction, the Obsidian Covenant fractured; their previously unwavering resolve crumbled into panicked disarray. Fear replaced their former ferocity. Overwhelmed by our irresistible advance, the remaining warriors instantly capitulated, their rebellion extinguished. The victory was ours; the battle decisively won.

The air, thick with the coppery tang of blood and the acrid stench of burnt flesh, hung heavy. A pyrrhic victory, it was, a triumph stained crimson, bought with the very marrow of our souls. The Obsidian Covenant's advance, a tide of obsidian and rage, had been stemmed, but only at a cost that clawed at the throat. Victory tasted like ash in my mouth; a fleeting reprieve in a war that gnawed at the edges of eternity.

The ground trembled beneath my boots, still warm from the inferno of the battle. Shattered obsidian, like the jagged teeth of some monstrous beast, littered the landscape. Each shard reflected the dying light, a macabre mosaic of our suffering. The silence, broken only by the mournful keening of the wind through skeletal trees, was a more chilling torment than any battle cry. For we had awakened them, ancient, slumbering evils, their eyes burning with the cold fire of millennia.

Their torpor shattered, they now watched, patient predators, from the shadows of the ravaged earth. This scarred world, a testament to our brutal dance with oblivion, felt irrevocably changed. The very stones seemed to weep. And the coming peace? It was a bitter jest, a cruel mirage shimmering on the horizon, a promise bought with a sacrifice far exceeding any we had anticipated. The weight of it, the crushing burden of what we'd done and what we'd yet to face, pressed down, a suffocating blanket of dread. The silence screamed.

The crimson tide, a demonic reflux, had finally ebbed, leaving behind a charnel house that scraped the very definition of hell. My lungs burned, not just from the acrid bite of roasting flesh, but from the sheer, suffocating weight of it all. The stench, a blasphemous perfume distilled from death itself, clung to me, a visceral coating of burnt sugar and iron filings coating my tongue, a taste of annihilation.

The sun drenched earth, once vibrant, now writhed under a grotesque tapestry of mud and gore, a macabre mosaic where shattered bone and twisted, groaning metal mocked the remnants of human ambition. Each crunch of my boot, a sickening percussion of pulverized bone and churned earth, echoed the fracturing of my sanity. The screams, though silenced, still clawed at the edges of my mind, a phantom chorus of agony that only amplified the deafening silence. I tasted bile, the metallic tang a bitter counterpoint to the sweetness of blood still clinging to the air, a sweetness that was the last gasp of life, now a chilling reminder of what had been. This wasn't just death; it was the obscene, deliberate dismantling of everything human. And I, a witness, was irrevocably stained.

Silence. Not the peaceful kind, but a suffocating, malevolent silence, a tangible weight pressing down, silencing the desperate gasps of the wounded, smothering the last whispered prayers of the dead. It pressed against my eardrums, a physical pain amplifying the ragged rasp of a dying man nearby, a soldier whose face I recognized, a man who'd laughed with me just hours ago. His eyes, glazed and vacant, held a horrifying understanding of his demise. His final breath, a rattling whisper stolen by the night, echoed the hollow hollowness in my soul.

The flames, a pyre of screaming crimson and infernal gold, danced a macabre jig amongst the charred remains, their grotesque shadows, writhing, pulsating phantoms, mimicking the agonized contortions of the dead. The very air crackled with the heat, a suffocating blanket laced with the acrid bite of burnt flesh and the coppery tang of blood, thick enough to taste, to choke on. Even the wind, a cowardly thing, cowered, its silence a more chilling accomplice than any roar. This wasn't just slaughter; it was a ritual of annihilation, a testament to a depravity so profound it etched itself onto my very soul.

The weight of it pressed down, a physical burden crushing my chest. Each heartbeat hammered a relentless rhythm against my ribs, a morbid drum solo to the symphony of my despair. The battle replayed in my mind, not as a hazy recollection, but as a visceral, agonizing flashback: the screams, the pleading eyes of men I'd fought alongside, the cold certainty in the eyes of my enemy as he met his end, my end. The choices... God, the choices! Each one a brand seared onto my conscience, a testament to my capacity for brutality, for survival at any cost. Were they justified? That question, a venomous serpent, coiled and struck again and again, leaving me drowning in the bitter, inescapable currents of guilt and grief. The faces of the fallen, their silent accusation haunted me, their vacant eyes promising a hell far more terrifying than this pyre of bodies. I, their silent witness, was as damned as they were.

My knees hit the cold, damp earth beside Caspian. The stench of blood, acrid and metallic, filled my nostrils as my fingers, trembling despite myself, explored the ragged chasm in his arm. It wasn't just a wound; it was a gaping maw, a black hole pulsing with malevolent energy that clawed at my very soul, a physical violation that resonated with a sickening thrum against my bones. Valerius's dark magic, I tasted it, a bitter ash on my tongue, a creeping paralysis in my limbs. I felt the corruption, a gnawing frost, eating away at Caspian's flesh, turning vibrant life into a horrifying mockery of decay.

His skin, once sun kissed, was now an unnatural shade of grey, the colour of a corpse slowly thawing. This wasn't merely a testament to Valerius's power; it was a grotesque masterpiece of annihilation. My magic, usually a comforting fire within, felt choked, a sluggish, dying ember burdened by the exhaustion of the battle, and the lingering poison of that cursed Covenant leader. Despair, cold and sharp as shattered glass, pierced my heart. Caspian's life, his very essence, was draining away, stolen by the shadow of Valerius, and I, his supposed protector, felt the chilling weight of my inadequacy.

"It's deep," I rasped, the words a choked prayer escaping my lips, my forehead slick with sweat, the coppery tang of blood thick in the air. My own heart hammered a frantic rhythm against my ribs as I funnelled the raw, searing power of the flame elementals, a white hot inferno burning in my gut, into Caspian's gaping wound. The stench of burning flesh, acrid and sickening, filled my nostrils. Agony contorted Caspian's face, muscles bunching and straining under the searing heat, his jaw clenched tight enough to crack. Yet, he remained utterly still, a statue carved from granite and pain. His gaze, however, held mine with a chilling intensity; those steel grey eyes, usually twinkling with mischievous defiance, now burned with a desperate, shared knowledge of the precipice we teetered on—a silent pact forged in blood and the

chilling certainty of our impending doom. The weight of it pressed down on me, heavy as a tombstone.

Blood slicked the cobblestones, a crimson tide reflecting the sickly yellow gaslight. Lyra, her pragmatic heart a lead weight in her chest, moved through it all like a wraith, efficient, merciless. The stench of burnt flesh and iron filled my nostrils, a brutal symphony accompanying the ragged moans of the wounded. Each touch, each swift assessment, was a testament to the icy calm she wore as a mask, a mask that couldn't entirely conceal the tremor in her hand as she checked a shattered leg, the haunted look in her eyes that spoke of a deeper, far more brutal war waged within. This wasn't victory; it was a reprieve snatched from the jaws of hell, a fleeting breath before the next wave crashed over us, more ferocious, more unforgiving than the last. The taste of ash and fear was thick on my tongue, the bitter promise of what was to come. Lyra, pragmatic as ever, maybe too pragmatic, maybe hiding a desperate hope behind those chilling eyes… She was a casualty, marked by the same cold dread that clawed at my soul, a dread that whispered of our inevitable, bloody end.

Blood stained the crimson sunset, a malevolent smear across the dying light. The sun's final, agonizing plunge left behind a landscape of broken bodies, each a grotesque testament to the day's carnage. The air, thick with the coppery tang of blood and the acrid bite of burnt flesh, clawed at my throat. Silence? There was no silence. Only the rasping breath of the dying, the frantic scrabble of rats amongst the corpses, and the whispers, oh God, the whispers, slithering from the shadowed earth, a chorus of the damned. Victory? This wasn't a victory. This was a charnel house, a testament to our hubris. We'd butchered the Obsidian Covenant, true, but the ground itself seemed to weep their dark essence. I tasted it, the bitterness of their magic, a lingering phantom on my tongue, a chilling promise of retribution. Their leader, Malkor, a broken god whose eyes still held the cold fire of defiance even in death, haunted my every waking moment, and even my dreams were now choked with his icy gaze. This wasn't the end. It was merely the beginning of a far deeper, far darker night.

Caspian, his face the colour of bone, a stark contrast to the furious crimson blooming across his torn sleeve, heaved himself upright. The stench of blood, acrid and thick, filled his nostrils, a familiar perfume of death. Each ragged breath scraped against his shredded lungs, a counterpoint to the dull, throbbing thrum of pain in his arm, a pain I could only marginally dull. He didn't flinch, didn't acknowledge the agony. His gaze, cold and sharp as shattered obsidian, sliced across the ravaged landscape. The battlefield reeked: a symphony of groaning men, the metallic tang of blood mingling with the coppery sweetness of spilled ale, the earth slick and dark under a sky choked with smoke. He saw them, each fallen comrade a testament to their shared failure, a harsh judgment etched in the mud and gore. A smile, devoid of mirth, twisted his lips, a predatory grin that spoke of hardened resolve, of a vengeance yet to be unleashed. The broken man stood defiant, his spirit a flickering flame against the encroaching darkness, and in his eyes, a terrifying promise burned.

"We won," he said, his voice rough but resolute, *"but at what cost?"*

My windpipe seized a single, bitter jerk of my head, the only defiance I could muster. The silence wasn't just silenced; it was a predator, a monstrous thing woven from unspoken accusations, the coppery tang of blood thick on my tongue, acrid and metallic, coating my teeth like a gruesome sacrament. Victory? It tasted of ash and rust, the metallic tang a bitter mockery. The air itself vibrated, a phantom orchestra of screams, the agonized keening of the fallen, a chorus of death echoing in the marrow of my bones, a percussion of shattered lives pounding against my skull. Crimson painted the earth, a visceral stain not just on the soil, but seeping into the very soul of this ravaged land, staining the fabric of my being.

Countless lives, extinguished like fragile flames in a hurricane; each a lost sun in a sky choked with the greasy black smoke of despair, the acrid stench burning my nostrils, a symphony of destruction. And this... this wasn't an end. This was the yawning maw of damnation. A shift, yes, but into a deeper, blacker hell, a descent into an abyss that promised no redemption. A war without end, fought in the fetid shadows where only the pitiless, the utterly broken, the utterly ruthless, survive. My soul, already fractured, felt the chill of that unending night settle over it, a cold, implacable certainty that this was just the beginning of a far greater torment.

The days blend into each other, a gruesome tapestry woven with the stench of decay and the metallic tang of blood. Each sunrise brought a fresh wave of gut wrenching labour: the rasping breaths of the wounded, their eyes, haunted pools reflecting the horrors they'd witnessed; the cold, clammy earth swallowing the newly dead, their faces frozen in silent screams; the splintered remnants of what had once been home, whispering of violence that had ripped through their lives like a vengeful god. Grief wasn't just felt; it was a physical weight, pressing down, choking the air itself with the bitter taste of ash and despair.

The Whispering Wind's headquarters, its proud banners now tattered and stained crimson, had become a charnel house masquerading as a sanctuary. The air throbbed with the ragged rhythm of suffering, the frantic prayers of the dying, punctuated by the sharp cries of those clinging to life by a thread. Here, amongst the flickering lamplight and the shadows that danced with the dying breath, Commander Lyra, her face etched with the grim determination born of countless battles, fought not just for the survival of her people, but also against the creeping despair that threatened to consume her soul. Her lieutenant, the scarred but stoic Ronan, moved through the carnage with a quiet efficiency that masked the turmoil within; his steely gaze betraying the crushing weight of responsibility he carried on his broad shoulders. Their resilience, forged in the crucible of this brutal war, was a testament to the indomitable spirit that flickered, stubbornly refusing to be extinguished, even in the face of such profound loss.

The celebrations, subdued and sombre, were a stark contrast to the fierce battles that had preceded them. There was no jubilation, no triumphant cries of victory. Only a quiet, respectful acknowledgment of the losses suffered and the challenges that lay ahead. The scars of the battle, both physical and emotional, would remain long after the last embers of the fires had died.

The air, thick with the coppery tang of blood and the acrid bite of smoke, hung heavy between frantic bandages and whispered strategies. In those stolen moments, between the screams and the thudding of my own racing heart, Caspian's gaze, usually guarded, shattered. His eyes, the colour of a storm wracked sea, held the ghost of a terror that mirrored my own. Mortality, a brushstroke across his face, had peeled away the polished veneer of his usual composure, revealing a raw, bleeding vulnerability that clawed at my soul. The bone jarring impact of our shared nightmare, the taste of fear thick on my tongue, forged a bond stronger than any vow. A silent understanding, deeper than words could plumb, passed between us, a terrifying, exhilarating intimacy born in the heart of chaos. His touch, when it brushed mine, sent a jolt of raw electricity through me, a stark contrast to the chilling dampness clinging to our clothes. He was both a beacon and a tempest, a man shattered and reborn in the crucible of our desperate struggle.

Secret looks, brief, charged touches, and unspoken longings punctuated our every encounter. The boundary between our partnership and a deeper, more potent connection dissolved with each sunrise, our physical closeness mirroring the shared trauma and burgeoning admiration that bound us. The fervour of our fight against the Obsidian Covenant ignited a passionate inferno within us, twisting our already intricate relationship into a perilous game of forbidden desires, a dangerous waltz on the edge of a precipice we couldn't resist.

Our fleeting reprieve shattered. Whispers, borne on chilling winds and shrouded in darkness, revealed a grim truth: the Obsidian Covenant, far from vanquished, was consolidating its power, preparing a final, ferocious onslaught. Our triumph had been but a momentary interruption, a trifling impediment to their sinister ambitions. The poignant memories of our fallen, their spectral forms haunting us, spurred us to immediate action. The looming confrontation was inescapable. The conflict, we knew, was far from its bloody culmination.

Disturbing tidings emerged from the Shadowlands: a malevolent pact was brewing, a confluence of sinister entities poised to plunge their realm into unending darkness. Though battered, the Obsidian Covenant remained unbroken. Their wounded, yet tenacious leader, Valerius, lived. Reports detailed furtive gatherings, unholy ceremonies, and a burgeoning power eclipsing all previous threats. The ominous murmurs intensified, escalating their profound anxieties into a terrifying crescendo.

Our impending clash wouldn't be a mere skirmish; it would be an existential struggle, a cataclysmic war that would shatter our pacts, expose our vulnerabilities, and relentlessly challenge our survival instincts. The consequences were unprecedented, the risks insurmountable. Capitulation was unthinkable. The crushing burden of global responsibility pressed down upon us, the destiny of our civilization precariously poised on the knife's edge.

War's relentless clamour shattered the precarious truce; preparations recommenced with grim determination. Caspian, Lyra, and I toiled ceaselessly, fortifying our defences, augmenting our depleted legions, and bracing for the imminent invasion. Our previously diffident and dispersed allies, galvanized by shared peril and a resolute purpose, now flocked to our standard, a formidable coalition forged in the crucible of impending doom.

Caspian, a tapestry of blood and grit, stumbled forth, not merely a leader, but a ravaged god carved from the battlefield. His strategic mind, a viper coiled and ready to strike, pulsed with a feverish brilliance that scorched the very air around him. The stench of iron and sweat clung to him, mirroring the unwavering resolve etched onto his face, a mask of pain, yet radiating an authority that silenced even the groaning of the wounded. Lyra, a whirlwind of controlled chaos, her movements precise and lethal as a viper's strike, kept the war machine churning. The rhythmic clang of metal, the greasy sheen of gears, the acrid bite of smoke, all were orchestrated by her cold, efficient hand. She was a predator, elegant and merciless, ensuring every cog turned towards the coming slaughter.

I, consumed by a vengeance so fierce it tasted of ash and bile, felt the heat of my elemental power throb within me, a molten core of rage and loyalty to Caspian. The air crackled with anticipation, each sparks a testament to my burning hatred, a prelude to the inferno I would unleash. My very bones ached with the thrill of impending battle, the taste of blood already thick on my tongue. The screams of the damned echoed in my ears, fueling the inferno within, preparing me for the brutal, beautiful dance of death that awaited.

The air crackled, a tangible dread replacing the sun's warmth. Dust, tasting like ash and fear, coated our tongues. Silence, thick as grave dirt, pressed down, broken only by the wind's keen wail, a dirge for the lives soon to be lost. Each heartbeat hammered against our ribs, a frantic drumbeat against the encroaching darkness. This wasn't merely the approach of a storm; it was the apocalypse, a tempest of fire and blood birthed from centuries of bloodshed.

The ghosts of fallen comrades clawed at our memories, their icy touch a chilling reminder of the price of defiance. Their spectral screams fueled the fire in our bellies, a white hot rage that burned away doubt. We were scarred veterans, our souls etched with the brutal poetry of past battles, each scar a testament to our unwavering resolve, a badge of honour in this final, desperate stand. Anya, her eyes the colour of a storm wracked sea, gripped her sword tighter, her knuckles bone white. Kael, his face a mask of grim determination, checked the whetstone, the rhythmic rasp a counterpoint to the rising terror. And I, haunted by the faces of those I'd failed, felt the cold steel of my blade a comfort against the icy grip of despair.

This wasn't merely a battle; it was a crucible forged in the heart of hell. We wouldn't simply face the inevitable; we would defy it. The shadows of the past, monstrous and malevolent, stretched long fingers towards us, but we would meet their onslaught with burning defiance, the clash of steel a furious symphony against the coming night. We were not merely soldiers; we were the storm, the fury, the unyielding heart of rebellion. Our bond, forged in blood, sweat, and countless shared near deaths, was a weapon sharper than any blade, stronger than any wall of steel. Tonight, we would show them the true meaning of unwavering defiance, or die trying. The darkness came, and we charged into its maw, our hearts aflame, our battle cry a howl of rage against the dying of the light.

CHAPTER

TWENTY NINE

Embers of Defiance

T he air crackled, a venomous hiss in my ears, the tension a
physical weight crushing my chest, heavier than the iron
grey storm clouds pregnant with lethal rain. The battlefield,
a festering wound on the earth, crimson stains still weeping into the
dust like ancient blood, lay rearranged, a macabre chessboard reflecting
Caspian's cold genius and Lyra's ruthless efficiency. Their defensive
lines, a labyrinth of sharpened stakes and coiled magic, writhed across
the ravaged land, a venomous serpent poised to strike. I, at the heart
of the Whispering Wind's fury, felt the elemental power surge within
me, not a mere thrum, but a volcanic eruption of raw, incandescent
rage, mirroring the bitter taste of betrayal that still clung to my tongue.
The metallic tang of blood, a phantom memory from past skirmishes,
fought for dominance with the acrid scent of ozone cracking around us.
This wasn't just a battle; it was a reckoning, a final, desperate gamble
against the encroaching shadows, fueled by hatred so profound it tasted
like ash and defiance. Caspian, with his eyes like chips of glacial ice
and a mind sharper than any blade, wouldn't falter. Lyra, her beauty, a
deceptive mask for an iron will and cunning that would make a viper
proud, wouldn't flinch. And I? I would unleash hell itself.

The earth groaned, a guttural scream swallowed by the obsidian
tide that engulfed us. Not just a wave, but a tsunami of friends, their
eyes, burning coals in sockets rimmed with shadow, fixed on me with a
hatred that tasted of ash and sulfur on my tongue. The stench of their

ichor, thick and acrid, choked me; a reeking perfume of death and decay that clung to the air, a miasma clinging to my skin. Their weapons, dripping with that foul fluid, screamed as they tore through the air, a symphony of death, a discordant chorus of screaming metal and crackling malevolent magic. The ground buckled and fractured beneath the onslaught, the very fabric of reality tearing apart in a maelstrom of fire and fury.

I was no longer a warrior, but a crucible of incandescent rage, a living furnace blazing against the demonic onslaught. Years of brutal training, a lifetime etched in scars both visible and unseen, fueled my every move. Each strike was a calculated masterpiece of violence; the precise, lethal dance of a predator honed by countless battles against such horrors, a balletic slaughter performed with a chilling, almost artistic precision. I felt the heat of the inferno searing my flesh, tasted the metallic tang of blood, and yet I pressed on, driven by a desperate, primal need to survive, to inflict retribution upon these foul spawn of the abyss, each fallen fiend screaming a silent testament to my skill and fury. The weight of their demise settled upon me, a heavy cloak woven from the threads of a thousand shattered lives, but it was a weight I willingly bore, a grim burden born from a war waged for the very soul of existence itself.

Valerius's curse, a searing brand on Caspian's flesh, pulsed with agonizing heat. But the pain fueled him, a wildfire igniting his rage against the Covenant. The stench of blood, thick and coppery, clung to his cruelly curved scimitar, a crimson stained crescent moon that tasted of death. Each swing was a brutal symphony of steel, a shriek of defiance tearing through the enemy ranks. He wasn't just fighting; he was a maelstrom of fury, a whirlwind of death, his every bone screaming a testament to his unyielding will. The very air crackled with the ferocity of his assault; the ground trembled beneath his relentless advance. He tasted the grit of the battlefield on his lips, felt the sting of sweat in his eyes, and smelled the fear of his enemies.

Lyra, however, remained a study in chilling contrast. Her eyes, the colour of glacial ice, never wavered. The air around her hummed with arcane power, a palpable shield woven from whispers and starlight, repelling the enemy's onslaught with an icy grace that bordered on the supernatural. Her commands, clipped and precise, were the subtle, deadly pulse that guided the Whispering Wind's legions. She felt the weight of command, a burden of responsibility as heavy as the ancient stones of her ancestors' tombs; yet, she moved with a ruthless efficiency that belied her outwardly serene demeanour. The screams of the dying were a grim lullaby to her sharp intellect, a testament to her strategic brilliance. Her every calculated move was a dance with death, a masterpiece of lethal strategy.

The tempest of carnage wasn't merely furious; it was a screaming maelstrom of blood and bone, a visceral symphony of screams and the sickening thunk of steel meeting flesh. Hours bled into an eternity of slaughter. The air, thick with the coppery tang of blood and the acrid stench of burning flesh, choked me. The ground, a churning morass of mud and gore, wasn't just a charnel pit; it was a grotesque tapestry woven with the mangled remnants of both fiend and hero, a testament to war's obscene, insatiable hunger. Their strategy, flawless in its conception, crumbled beneath the relentless, seemingly endless tide of Covenant shadows. These weren't just legions; they were a suffocating, hellish swarm, their obsidian forms blotting out the already fading light, each a harbinger of oblivion.

Despair wasn't a whisper; it was a physical blow, a crushing weight on my chest, threatening to extinguish the flickering ember of my will. The taste of fear, metallic and bitter, coated my tongue. I could feel the icy tendrils of annihilation snaking around my heart, yet...I wouldn't yield. No. The chilling dread was met not just with defiance, but with a white hot, incandescent rage that burned away the fear, leaving only a burning core of unwavering resolve. This wasn't some abstract battle; it was a fight for the very soul of existence, a testament to the unwavering spirit forged in the crucible of this unimaginable horror. My weariness, my grief, my fear... they were fuel. They would feed the fire of my vengeance.

From the heart of the demonic maelstrom, a vortex of writhing shadows and sulfurous stench, he erupted. Valerius. Not merely a colossus, but a mountain of corrupted flesh, each scar a testament to a thousand brutal victories, each ravaged muscle a pulsing conduit of infernal power that choked the very air around him. The reek of brimstone and decaying flesh clawed at my throat, a physical manifestation of his dread aura. His eyes, twin embers burning with the cold fire of a dying star, locked onto mine, piercing the flimsy veil of my courage. They held not just rancour, but the chilling weight of ages of betrayal, a simmering rage fueled by the screams of the damned, a rage I tasted, bitter and metallic, on my tongue. This was no mere warrior; this was the embodiment of annihilation, his presence a crushing weight that threatened to shatter my soul, to snuff out the last flickering spark of hope like a careless god extinguishing a candle. He was the storm, the earthquake, the very apocalypse made flesh, and I was caught in his eye.

Valerius. The name itself tasted like ash and brimstone on my tongue. Our battle wasn't a struggle; it was a maelstrom of incandescent rage, a visceral ballet performed on the precipice of oblivion. The air crackled, a palpable symphony of raw power that scorched my lungs and vibrated in my very bones. My attacks, fueled by a fury born of years of simmering resentment and righteous anger, were a hurricane of fire, a desperate, chaotic dance aimed at obliterating him from existence. But he... he met my elemental onslaught with a chilling, contemptuous grace. Each party, each deflection, a casual flick of his wrist, sent shivers down my spine, a terrifying display of effortless mastery over forces that would shatter lesser men. His eyes, glacial pools reflecting the abyss, held a chilling amusement, a cruel awareness of my impending doom.

The ground trembled beneath the weight of our cataclysmic clash, a seismic pulse that threatened to rip the very fabric of reality. The ambient energy throbbed, a malignant heartbeat resonating with the potential to unravel the cosmos itself; I could taste the metallic tang of destruction on the wind. And through it all, I heard their screams. Caspian, his face contorted in grim determination, a whirlwind of steel and sweat. Lyra, her ethereal beauty marred by the desperate ferocity in her eyes, a storm of arcane energy shielding me from the tide of infernal horrors that surged towards us, a tide of writhing shadows and guttural roars, each monster a testament to Valerius's unspeakable power. Their combined defence, though valiant, felt as fragile as a butterfly's wing against the onslaught of a storm. My survival hung by a thread, a thread spun from their courage and my burning, desperate will to overcome the cold, calculating horror that was Valerius.

The infernal symphony of battle, the shriek of rending steel, a banshee wail that tore through my skull, the guttural death rattles of men drowning in their blood, the acrid stench of ozone and burning flesh choking my lungs, hammered at my senses, a brutal assault on every fibre of my being. My power, once a raging inferno that could scorch the very earth, was reduced to a pathetic ember, a dying spark within me. I shivered, not merely from exhaustion, but from a terror so profound it gnawed at my very bones, a primal fear that tasted of ash and despair. The coppery tang of my blood filled my mouth, thick and hot, a bitter tide rising with each ragged breath. The crimson stain blooming across my tunic felt like a branding iron pressed against my flesh, a testament to Valerius's victory. That serpent, Valerius, his eyes glittering with the cold fire of triumph, a cruel amusement twisting his lips, savoured my decline. His laughter, a venomous hiss that scraped against my soul, was a tangible weapon, as potent as his dark magic. That magic, a palpable wave of searing heat, tore through my defences, each strike a white hot brand, not just upon my body, but a searing incision into the very core of my being; each blow a twisted mockery of the power I once wielded. He revelled in my pain, his dark glee a palpable thing, suffocating me more surely than his magic. The knowledge of my impending defeat, the cold, brutal certainty of it, chilled me to the marrow.

The world fractured a jagged mosaic of searing pain that ripped through me, each shard a fresh agony. The stench, acrid, metallic, the reek of incinerated muscle and corrupted sorcery, clawed at my throat, a suffocating perfume heralding my annihilation. My legs, two useless weights of lead, threatened to betray me, to crumple beneath the crushing burden of despair. This was beyond exhaustion; it was the suffocating grip of nihilism, a freezing shroud that choked the last flickering sparks of defiance within me. His laughter, a venomous serpent slithering through the wreckage of my senses, echoed the inevitable. He wasn't merely going to break me; he would pulverize me, a meticulous dismantling of body and soul, each shattering blow a perverse symphony of my destruction. The certainty of it was a brand seared onto my very being, a visceral torment that dwarfed any physical wound, a gnawing, insatiable hunger in the pit of my soul. The taste of blood, metallic and bitter, mingled with the acrid tang of fear, coating my tongue like ashes.

Caspian erupted into being, a raw, visceral force slamming against Valerius's next blow, a blow that tasted of iron and reeked of death. His gaze, molten obsidian burning into mine, seared a promise into my very being; not just safety, but defiance, desperate, beautiful defiance etched in the stark lines of his face, etched in the tremor of his jaw. Then, hell itself unleashed. Shadow, thick and choking like the breath of a dying star, erupted from him, a screaming, searing torrent that slammed into Valerius's attack with the thunderous crash of a collapsing mountain. The air crackled, the very ground trembled under the impact; the stench of ozone filled my nostrils, stinging my eyes. The effort wracked him; a coppery tang, sharp and metallic, stained his lips, his skin the pallid grey of a corpse, sweat slicking his temples, yet he stood, an unyielding monolith, his will a burning, incandescent thing that refused to yield.

Lyra's lightning fast move, a stroke of sheer, incandescent genius, unleashed a cataclysmic spell, a maelstrom of raw magical power that roared and shrieked, a tangible thing clawing at the air. The stench of ozone and burnt earth filled my nostrils as Valerius, his eyes wide with a terror I savoured, was momentarily paralyzed, a statue caught in the heart of a storm. That breathless pause, that stolen moment, was our lifeline. My own heart hammered a frantic rhythm against my ribs, a drumbeat of grief and burning rage. The bitter taste of loss, the phantom weight of my dead brother clinging to me, fueled my assault. It wasn't just a spell, it was a scream, a raw, guttural expulsion of my soul's fury.

A volcanic eruption of fire, a searing inferno that tasted of brimstone and despair, ripped from my very being, engulfing Valerius in a tidal wave of incandescent destruction. The heat blasted against my face, the air itself cracking and shimmering. His desperate retreat was a pathetic scramble, a frantic dance of agony amidst the maelstrom of my power. We had bought ourselves a reprieve, snatched from the jaws of defeat, but the victory felt tainted, ash and blood clinging to the hard won advantage. The cost...the cost remained a bitter knot in my gut.

The raw fury in Caspian's eyes, a storm mirroring the tempest in Lyra's heart, crackled through the Whispering Wind. Their defiance, a searing brand against the twilight sky, wasn't just bravery; it was a visceral rejection of the Covenant's suffocating grip. The air itself thrummed, a symphony of steel clashing, guttural war cries, and the stench of sweat, blood, and burning earth filling their nostrils. Lyra, her silver braid whipping like a viper, screamed a battle cry that tore through the din, a sound that echoed the agonizing loss she carried within her fierce spirit. Caspian, his scarred face a roadmap of past battles, met the Covenant's advance not with mere courage, but with a cold, calculating rage that chilled the very marrow of their bones.

They fought with the desperate energy of cornered wolves, each parrying a testament to their unwavering bond, each blowing a testament to their lost loved ones. The Covenant's relentless tide recoiled, their meticulously planned assault shattered by the sheer, incandescent force of Caspian and Lyra's defiance. Their retreat was not a strategic maneuver; it was a panicked flight, a desperate scramble into the fetid abyss from whence they crawled, the taste of defeat bitter on their lips. Victory? It wasn't a shimmer on the horizon; it roared, a primal scream tearing through the night, a taste of blood and hard won freedom.

The world fractured. A cataclysmic roar, a symphony of shattering bone and screaming metal, ripped through the very fabric of reality. Each blow, a supernova of incandescent fury, seared my retinas, the stench of ozone and burnt flesh thick in the air. My heart, a frantic drum against my ribs, echoed the thunderous clash of titans. Caspian, his face a mask of grim determination etched with the scars of a thousand battles, battles I'd witnessed him fight with a cold, ruthless efficiency that both terrified and inspired me, fought beside me, his blade a silver comet spitting fire. Lyra, her eyes burning with a righteous fire that belied the fragility of her frame, unleashed a torrent of raw magic, the very air crackling and spitting with arcane energy, a taste of sulfur coating my tongue.

Fueled by a power that felt both ancient and alien, a power that surged through me like a tidal wave of molten gold, we were a maelstrom of defiance. Our combined might, a terrifying, incandescent tempest, smashed against the encroaching darkness. Their shadowy claws tore at our defences, icy tendrils of fear snaking into my soul, a chilling whisper of annihilation. But even as the shadows clawed at our very being, the taste of blood metallic on my lips, a primal scream ripped from my throat, mirroring the ferocious howl of cornered wolves. We would not yield. We would not break. We would fight until our last ragged breath until our shattered bodies mingled with the dust of a dying world. Our defiance, a defiant beacon in the encroaching void.

Even broken, Valerius was a nightmare given flesh, his eyes burning with the cold fire of a dying star. His final attack wasn't a mere assault; it was a convulsive eruption of shadow, a sickeningly sweet stench of decay blooming in the air as a wave of obsidian darkness crashed over me. The taste of annihilation, bitter ash and corrupted ozone, filled my mouth. I braced for oblivion, but Lyra, a defiant angel of light against that encroaching night, threw herself before me. The impact ripped through her, a searing shriek tearing from her lips as the malevolent energy, a tangible weight of despair and death, tore at her very soul. I saw the vibrant life drain from her eyes, the sweet scent of her skin replaced by the acrid reek of the encroaching darkness, her body convulsing in a symphony of agony that echoed the shattering of a thousand hearts.

A guttural rasp, the air ripped from her lungs in a final, convulsive shudder, sent me sprawling. Her touch, a searing brand on my skin, flung me back from the precipice of oblivion, a chasm of teeth and shadow that still gnawed at the edges of my vision. Her eyes, twin pools reflecting a lifetime of unshed tears and fierce, untamed defiance, met mine. In that fleeting, incandescent moment, before the darkness claimed her, I saw not just camaraderie, but a desperate, ferocious pact forged in the crucible of our shared despair. The whisper that escaped her cracked lips was a command, a guttural prayer, a venom laced promise: "Get him." The scent of copper and ozone filled the air as her lifeblood drained away, a crimson tide ebbing into the unforgiving stone. Then, only silence, and the chilling certainty of her irrevocable absence, a hollowness that echoed the abyss I'd narrowly escaped.

Lyra's broken body, a porcelain doll shattered by a god's cruel hand, ignited in me a fury so raw it tasted like ash and bile. The stench of scorched flesh and her spilled lifeblood choked me, a bitter perfume clinging to the reeking air. My roar wasn't just a sound; it was a physical blow, a tremor that ripped through the earth, shaking the very marrow in my bones. Valerius, that viper, his smug face etched in a rictus of disbelief, felt the first tendrils of my wrath, a searing heat that stripped the flesh from his bones, leaving behind only the screaming ghost of his arrogance.

No mere inferno, this was a maelstrom of pure, unadulterated vengeance. Crimson fire, laced with the agonizing screams of his Covenant, pathetic insects writhing in a sea of molten rock and shadow, consumed them. The ground buckled and groaned, a monstrous beast in agony, spewing forth rivers of fire that reflected the incandescent rage in my eyes. The sky itself cracked open, weeping not water, but a torrential downpour of black, viscous ichor, mirroring the darkness that now possessed my soul. Each dying breath of Valerius's men was a note in a symphony of annihilation, a twisted lullaby to the tormented ghost of Lyra. My heart, a charred husk mirroring the destruction around me, knew only the cold satisfaction of complete and utter retribution.

Desolation clawed at me, a charnel house built on the shattered bones of a battle beyond imagining. The air, thick with acrid smoke and the cloying sweetness of death, choked my lungs. The taste of ash and blood was metallic on my tongue. My knees buckled, the earth a cold, unforgiving embrace as I collapsed beside Lyra. Her stillness, the finality of it, hammered a brutal rhythm against my ribs. Our pact, a desperate gamble whispered amidst the screaming maelstrom of fire and steel, had been brutally, cruelly violated. It was a pact forged in the searing heat of chaos, sealed not by ink but by the shared taste of fear, the mutual agony of near death. Lyra, her eyes, usually blazing with defiance that matched my own, now vacant pools mirroring the lifeless sky, were gone. But the friendship, forged in that crucible of unimaginable horror, tempered by our shared sacrifices, the near sacrifices, the sacrifices we had made, that remained, a phantom limb, a searing, agonizing reminder of her absence, a testament to the fire that still burned, however faintly, within my ravaged soul.

The taste of victory was bile, bitter ash clinging to the back of my throat, a hollow echo in the cavern of my chest. The Obsidian Covenant, once a monolith of obsidian power, lay shattered, its proud spires reduced to jagged teeth gnawing at the ravaged earth. The air, thick with the stench of cordite and decay, rasped in my lungs, each breath a reminder of the unimaginable cost. The ground, slick with blood, crimson mirroring the sunset's dying embers, vibrated faintly under my boots, a silent symphony of death. I could almost taste the iron tang, feel the phantom tremors of the earth's convulsive shudders. This wasn't a triumph.

This was a mausoleum. The rising sun, a malevolent eye peering through the smoke choked sky, cast long, accusing shadows across the field of carnage. It illuminated not just the broken remnants of a fallen empire, but the gaping wounds in my soul. The faces of my fallen brothers, etched in my memory with the brutality of a sculptor's chisel, haunted me, their silence a deafening roar. Their laughter, once a vibrant chorus, was now a ghostly whisper on the wind.

This wasn't peace. This was a fragile truce, held together by the sheer weight of exhaustion and grief. A grief that clawed at my insides, a constant, gnawing ache that mirrored the landscape itself. Each sunrise would be a cruel reminder, each sunset a slow, agonizing descent into the memory of their sacrifice, a sacrifice offered at the altar of a victory stained crimson with their lifeblood, a victory that tasted of ashes and despair. This new dawn, birthed in the fires of hell, would forever bear the scars of their unwavering loyalty, their ferocious courage... and the unbearable, gut wrenching weight of their absence. A weight I would carry to my grave.

A thunderous hush descended, a horrifying antithesis to the preceding chaos. Smoke, a malevolent serpent, uncoiled sluggishly from the ravaged land, its acrid stench, a blend of charred flesh and extinguished sorcery, clinging to my lungs. I knelt beside Lyra, her stillness a stark betrayal; the residual warmth on her fingers was a macabre reminder of life's fleeting nature. Her normally resolute features, etched with the hardships of countless battles, were now softened into unsettling tranquillity. A solitary tear, a conduit of unbearable sorrow, cut a path through the grime staining my face, a testament to grief so immense it threatened to shatter me.

My fingers followed the graceful arc of her scimitar, resting beside her still form. Lyra... so still. Like a fallen statue carved from moonlight and shadow. The wickedly curved blade, though blunted, retained a ghostly luminescence in the dim light filtering through the smoke laden air. That glow... it almost seems to pulse. Like a faint heartbeat echoing the end of hers. This weapon, a silent testament to countless skirmishes, stained with the ichor of fallen friends, now lay inert, its grim duty discharged. Each stains a story, a life lost. And now… hers is added to their number. A bitter taste filled my mouth, the metallic tang of blood and ash. Should I have done more? Could I have done more?

Lyra, too, was still—a valiant fighter who had surrendered all, paying the ultimate toll. Her eyes… they're so peaceful now. A stark contrast to the fire I saw in them moments before. Yet her sacrifice was not futile. The Obsidian Covenant, that seemingly invincible shadow legion, was vanquished, its dominion shattered, and its reign of terror irrevocably concluded. Vanquished… The words feel hollow. A victory stained crimson. So many lives… for this. A wave of exhaustion, heavier than any armour, washed over me. It's over. But a part of me… a vital part… is gone with her.

Caspian crumpled, ash grey and bone thin, the dust clinging to his ragged clothes like a shroud. The stench of cordite and death still clung to him, a phantom limb of the carnage. His knees hit the ravaged earth with a dull thud that echoed the crushing weight of his grief, a tempest not merely suppressed, but violently caged within his ravaged frame. The screams of the dying, the metallic tang of blood, the suffocating heat of the pyres, all these haunted his eyes, a kaleidoscope of horror etched into his soul. He tasted the bitterness of ashes on his tongue, a bitter counterpoint to the metallic tang of blood still clinging to his lips.

The annihilation, a million shattered lives, a million agonizing deaths, pressed down on him, a physical burden threatening to crush him entirely. Yet, even amidst this abyss of despair, a glacial shard of resolve pierced the gloom. His gaze, though shadowed, held a flicker of icy fire, the ghost of the ruthless strategist, the merciless pragmatist, still burning low within the ruins of his being. The war had carved its name into his flesh, leaving him a ruin as desolate as the battlefields he'd traversed. His spirit, however, shattered and remained a defiant, unyielding ember, fiercely focused on the terrible task that lay before him, a task that demanded a sacrifice even greater than the one he had already made.

Caspian's whisper, a rasping breath against the tomb like silence, clawed at the air. *"Lyra rescued you, Blaze. She sacrificed everything—for this."* The word, this, hung heavy, poisoned with the metallic tang of blood and the bitter ash of betrayal. His attempt at comfort felt like a branding iron against my raw nerves. The crushing weight of her act, a gaping black hole where my soul used to reside, slammed into me, a physical blow. I tasted the dust of her absence, the phantom scent of her hair, a cruel mockery on the wind. This grief, a ravenous beast, would feast on my marrow, forevermore. The triumph felt like a pyrrhic victory, a gilded cage built on the bones of my love.

The air itself cracked with the weight of their grief. Whispering Wind, those wraiths forged in a crucible of years long war, their faces etched not just with the lines of battle, but with the raw, bleeding agony of loss. Each one a monument to brutal efficiency, now warped by sorrow so profound it tasted like ash in the back of my throat. Their eyes, usually flint hard and calculating, were bottomless pits of despair, reflecting the flickering torchlight like trapped souls. The scent of wood smoke and something else, a metallic tang of blood, old and new, mingling with the cloying sweetness of unshed tears, hung heavy in the air, a suffocating shroud woven from their collective agony. This wasn't merely silent anguish; it was a palpable force, a storm of grief that threatened to crush us beneath its terrible weight. Their stillness was more terrifying than any attack; each rigid posture was a testament to the chasm ripped through their brotherhood, a wound that festered, refusing the balm of time. I saw in their haunted gazes the echoes of comrades lost, a legion of ghosts marching alongside them, whispering promises of vengeance that vibrated with chilling intensity.

Lyra's demise was a relentless, agonizing film reel playing on the dark screen of my eyelids. Not again, I thought, the familiar icy grip of grief tightening around my chest. I'd pushed it down so carefully, buried it under layers of... what? Denial? Busywork? The desperation clawed at me, a frantic animal trying to break free. Despite my desperate attempt to extinguish the cacophony of sorrow and anguish, her death remained a searing, unforgettable vision. Her laugh... the way the sunlight caught her hair... The memories stabbed, sharp and precise, each one a fresh wound. Why couldn't I have done more? Was there anything I could have done? No, no, stop it. Don't go there. It won't help. But the questions, insistent and venomous, gnawed at the edges of my consciousness. The image of her, still and lifeless, burned itself into my mind's eye, a grotesque mockery of the vibrant life she'd led. This isn't real. It can't be. Wake up. Wake up. But the darkness held fast, a suffocating blanket woven from loss and regret.

Her resilience surprised me, a quiet fortitude matched only by her unwavering devotion. I recalled her meticulous preparations, the strategic brilliance masked by a seemingly callous exterior. Beneath that shield of indifference lay a wellspring of empathy, profound compassion only fully unveiled in the fiery trials we face together. Lyra's genuine nature, a gentle soul cloaked in steely resolve, blossomed only amidst our shared adversity.

The engine of my life, a vendetta so ravenous it had consumed me for decades, sputtered and died, a choked sob tearing through me. The acrid stench of betrayal, sharp as shattered obsidian, filled my nostrils. The taste of ashes, bitter and metallic, coated my tongue, the Pyrrhic victory of the Obsidian Covenant, a hollow triumph echoing in the cavernous silence of my soul. Her absence... a physical wound, raw and bleeding, a gaping maw in the fabric of my being. The vibrant pulse of her spirit, once a sun blazing against the bleakness, was extinguished, leaving only the suffocating chill of an endless night. My fingers, still stained crimson from the final battle, trembled, tracing phantom lines where her hand once rested on mine, the ghost of her warmth a searing torment. The world, once a tapestry woven with her laughter and fire, had crumbled to dust, leaving me adrift in a desolate wasteland, haunted by the echoes of her laughter, a cruel mockery of my desolation. This victory...this thing... It tasted of nothing but the bitter, metallic tang of my despair.

Sunrise painted elongated silhouettes across the devastated field, a chilling wind whispering through the barren expanse. The air, thick with the stench of mortality and the lingering ghost of fallen comrades, carried the bitter residue of a prematurely extinguished bond. A new day broke, yet its light was dimmed by grief, its victory tainted, its wounds, both bodily and spiritual, indelible.

A melancholic haze enveloped the subsequent days, a period punctuated by sombre ceremonies and hushed sorrow. We struggled amidst the wreckage, striving to piece together a fractured existence. Caspian's unwavering practicality guided my efforts as I coordinated the aid and comfort for those who remained, a necessary task amidst the devastation. He oversaw the interment of both fallen combatants and vanquished demons, a sombre duty underscoring the terrible toll exacted by the conflict.

Gutted, but not broken. The Whispering Wind, a shadow clan forged in the crucible of secrets and whispered oaths, staggered on. The stench of betrayal still clung to them, a bitter tang on their parched tongues, mirroring the hollowness in their hearts. Lyra's absence, the ghost of her laughter, a cruel phantom in the echoing chambers of their hidden sanctuary, was a wound that bled crimson onto the cold stone floor, a wound that refused to clot. Each ragged breath was a testament to their shared agony, the weight of her sacrifice pressing down like a tombstone on their souls.

Lyra, the Serpent's Kiss they called her, a master strategist with eyes like glacial ice and a smile that could disarm a tyrant, yet held the fury of a storm within. Her death, a brutal symphony of steel and screams still ringing in their ears, had shattered their fragile unity. But even as the icy grip of despair threatened to consume them, a flicker of defiance ignited in their ravaged hearts. Lyra's memory, a burning ember against the encroaching darkness, fueled their rage and sharpened their resolve. Her sacrifice would not be a whisper lost to the wind; it would become a hurricane, a storm of vengeance that would obliterate the threats that loomed. They would carry her fire within them, a searing brand on their souls, burning away doubt and forging their commitment to an unyielding, incandescent purpose.

At Lyra's grave, I would often pause, my eyelids shut, the fleeting span of our camaraderie replaying vividly in my mind. The grim struggles, the harrowing conflicts, the explosions of shared mirth—all indelibly imprinted on my soul. The war against the Obsidian Covenant irrevocably altered the world, but Lyra's unwavering loyalty had reshaped me most profoundly, leaving an enduring scar upon my spirit.

Reconstruction was a clawing, agonizing crawl through the mud and bone dust, a stark, festering wound mirroring the one ripped across my soul. The air, thick with the stench of decay and the ghosts of screams, clung to me like a shroud. The land, scarred and bleeding, a testament to the victory's obscene cost, moaned beneath a sky the colour of bruised plums. Each splintered rail, each shattered brick, each vacant eye socket of a ruined building was a fresh stab of grief. The taste of ash lingered on my tongue, a phantom echo of the pyres that consumed everything.

Moments of fragile calm snatched between the nightmares that clawed at my sleep, were like fleeting breaths in a drowning sea. Caspian, his unwavering gaze both a comfort and a condemnation of my weakness, held my hand, his calloused touch a grounding force against the trembling earth of my grief. Even the resolute faces of the surviving Whispering Wind, haunted, scarred, but unbowed, were etched with a shared trauma that mirrored my own, a silent chorus of suffering. Their strength, a flickering candle in the encroaching darkness, offered only the barest sliver of solace amidst the ruins of everything I knew.

The Obsidian Covenant's annihilation did not extinguish the encroaching darkness. Instead, insidious whispers of nascent, malevolent factions slithered into existence, their motives veiled in impenetrable secrecy. Another shadow war? Just when I thought I could finally breathe... I understood—the struggle was far from concluded; this new age ushered in unprecedented trials, perilous threats, and crushing responsibilities. Lyra... her face, her smile... the way she looked at the sunrise... Yet, I remained resolute, propelled by the incandescent memory of Lyra, her indomitable spirit, her ultimate sacrifice. It can't have been for nothing. All that sacrifice... I vowed her death would not be in vain, that the world she valiantly defended would remain unshackled from demonic tyranny. They will not win. Not this time. Not ever. Victory had been achieved, but the war raged on. A pyrrhic victory, at best. But a victory nonetheless. Shouldering the sorrow of our loss and fortified by her legacy, I braced myself for whatever the future might unleash. What horrors await? What new sacrifices will be demanded? As the sun rose on this new day, I, the fiery elemental, would persist, an unwavering symbol of defiance against the encroaching night. For Lyra. For the world. For the hope that still flickers, however faintly.

CHAPTER

THIRTY

Epilogue: A New Dawn

Reconstruction was a laborious, agonizing crawl, a stark
monument to the war's utter destruction. Another year wasted,
I thought, staring at the skeletal remains of the city. Will
we ever truly recover? Entire kingdoms lay pulverized, their villages
transformed into smouldering embers; the earth itself was a tapestry
of countless conflicts. So much blood spilled... for what? Was it all
worth it? However, from this devastation, a tenacious hope emerged.
Hope? It's a fragile thing, easily snuffed out by the next gust of wind.
But maybe... maybe this time it's different. The Obsidian Covenant,
that seemingly invincible shadow, had been vanquished. Vanquished?
The whispers still linger. Are they truly gone? Or simply biding their
time, gathering strength in the shadows? Their tyrannical rule, their
malevolent grasp, was irrevocably shattered. Shattered? Or merely...
fractured? A single crack can bring down an entire empire. And the
cracks are still there, I can feel them.

Caspian's methodical approach was the bedrock of the reconstruction.
His acute mind and steadfast dedication proved indispensable in the
monumental undertaking of restoring shattered lives and ravaged
settlements. He established provisional havens for the displaced populace,
meticulously managing the allocation of sustenance and provisions,
and harmonizing the contributions of the resilient Whispering Wind
survivors and their allies. Beneath his typically frigid exterior, a
wellspring of compassion, previously concealed by pragmatic stoicism,

emerged. Lyra's demise, though profoundly unsettling, unexpectedly ignited within me a profound empathy for the collective suffering. Fueled by a resolute commitment, I laboured relentlessly, striving to forge a future that honoured the immense sacrifices borne.

Lyra's death—the stench of decay still clinging to the air, a phantom pressure on my chest—clawed at the edges of my sanity, choking the reconstruction efforts in their nascent stages. Grief, a physical weight, a suffocating blanket woven from the threads of shattered memories, pressed down, a stark monument to life's brutal fragility. The taste of ash and dust coated my tongue, a bitter reminder of everything lost. My once vibrant pulse, a raging torrent, now trickled, a sluggish stream choked with sorrow so profound it felt like a physical wound. The devastated landscape, a symphony of shattered stone and twisted metal, mirrored the wreckage within me. I wandered those ruins, the chilling wind whispering through the empty sockets of buildings, each gusting a mournful sigh. Lyra's face, hauntingly beautiful even in death, burned behind my eyelids, a searing brand that refused to fade, a torment both exquisite and agonizing. Her ghost, a spectral caress, a chilling touch, haunted every corner of my ravaged soul.

Though the physical injuries of the conflict gradually faded over time Lyra's absence continued to gnaw at the heart leaving behind a festering wound that refused to heal. The vivid recollection of her serene fortitude, her unwavering strength in moments of despair and her unshakeable devotion to those she loved—these were a bittersweet solace, a source of comfort interwoven with a poignant agony that lingered long after the battles had ceased. Each memory served as both a balm and a reminder of the void she left behind.

The phantom pains of the battlefield, dull aches in the bone, were nothing compared to the gnawing emptiness where Lyra had been. Her absence was a physical thing, a cold fist clenching around my heart, each beat a painful echo of her loss. The scent of wood smoke and rain, once a comfort, now only sharpened the memory of her, the ghost of her laughter on the wind, the taste of fear clinging to my tongue like ash from the pyre of our shared past. Her serenity, a fragile porcelain doll shattered on the jagged rocks of war, haunted me. That unwavering devotion, a beacon in the storm, now mocked me with its absence, a cruel reminder of the strength I'd failed to protect. It was a bittersweet symphony of sorrow, a piercing lament played on the strings of my soul; a constant, agonizing ache that carved itself deeper with each passing sunrise.

Though greatly weakened, the clandestine activities of the Whispering Wind persisted. Caspian, their unwavering leader, steered them with iron resolve, upholding Lyra's memory by maintaining their relentless watchfulness. The looming darkness, while seemingly subdued, had not been eradicated. Rival groups were rising, sinister threats festering in the unseen corners of the world. A deceptive calm veiled a precarious global balance, perpetually poised on the precipice of utter pandemonium.

Lyra's death—a gaping maw of agony that ripped through me, leaving a raw, bleeding wound where my heart used to be—ignited a firestorm of purpose. Her ghost, a searing brand seared into my very soul, pulsed with a white hot pain that refused to fade, a constant, agonizing reminder fueling my every breath. The metallic tang of blood, still fresh on my lips from the battle, mingled with the acrid scent of burning flesh and the chilling whisper of her name. It wouldn't be a footnote. Never.

My training became a frenzy, a relentless, self flagellating pursuit of perfection. The raw power of the flame elementals throbbed within me, a burning inferno mirroring the rage that consumed me, a stark contrast to the icy grip of my vampiric hunger. I wrestled that beast into submission, shattering its claws against the unyielding rock of my grief, forging myself into a weapon of unimaginable fury—a whirlwind of fire and shadow, a nightmare given flesh and bone.

The Obsidian Covenant's collapse, their shattered remnants screaming beneath the incandescent heat of my wrath, was a pyrrhic victory—an ephemeral moment of respite in the suffocating darkness that envelops us. The taste of ash lingered in my mouth bitter and acrid while the distant screams echoed hauntingly in my ears, a stark reminder of the chaos that had just unfolded. Yet this fleeting triumph feels like merely a single drop in the blood-soaked ocean of war that looms ominously on the horizon. The coming storm gathers strength, its ominous clouds swirling with an electric fury and its winds carry the chilling promise of far greater sacrifice. With each passing moment the weight of the impending conflict grows heavier, foreshadowing a reckoning that will test the very limits of our resolve and humanity.

Healing, a slow, deliberate process, mirrored my tentative recovery. From the devastation, structures ascended, fields were sown anew, and a fragile community coalesced. Life, irrevocably transformed, gradually revived. Evenings grew less severe, and the wind's lament softened to a murmur. Yet, the wounds endured were etched upon the earth and the souls of those who had survived the conflict. These persistent marks served as stark reminders: of peace's profound cost, and the agonizing burden of triumph.

The ghosts of that butchered age clawed at me, dragging me towards Lyra's tomb, a jagged scar on the earth. The air hung thick, a cloying blend of dust and the metallic tang of dried blood, centuries old yet still potent. I stood there, writing to myself, the nascent sun a molten fist bursting through the bruised purple of the dawn. Its heat, a cruel mockery of warmth, seared my skin, a branding iron against the icy grip of grief that constricted my chest. The beauty was a torment; each vibrant stroke of crimson and gold across the sky was a fresh wound, reopening the chasm Lyra's death had carved in my soul. My fingers, numb with sorrow yet burning with a fury that defied reason, traced the cold, unforgiving stone of her marker. She, a whirlwind of defiance and grace, reduced to this silent monument. I, her cursed shadow, bound to this place, this lingering echo of her brilliance, forever haunted by the echoes of our shared battle and the agonizing silence of her absence.

Lyra's passing, a devastating blow, unexpectedly became a crucible of transformation. Her absence propelled me into uncharted territories, obligating me to grapple with my inner shadows and acknowledge my inherent frailties. Through this crucible, I discovered the profound essence of selflessness, the unwavering strength of camaraderie, and the remarkable resilience of remembrance. The echo of Lyra's life remains indelibly etched within me, a beacon illuminating my path through adversity, a wellspring of both poignant grief and unwavering fortitude.

Hope, tentative yet vibrant, illuminated the nascent era. A precarious peace reigned, the morrow shrouded in ambiguity. Yet, I, and my fellow resilient souls, were resolute in our commitment to forge a superior world—a testament to those we had lost. We would immortalize their memory by persevering in our struggle, guaranteeing that their ultimate sacrifice would not be in vain.

A fragile hope, incandescent yet shivering like a candle flame in a gale, pierced the newborn darkness of the era. The peace was a razor's edge, a precarious balance teetering on the abyss of tomorrow's unknown. The taste of ash still clung to my tongue, a bitter reminder of the pyre that had consumed so much. But I, scarred and battle worn, felt the steel of resolve harden within me, a counterpoint to the tremor in my hands. My fellow survivors, their eyes, haunted yet burning with the same fierce light, stood beside me, ghosts of past battles etched onto their faces. We were a tapestry woven from grief and defiance, each thread a testament to the fallen. We would not let their blood stain the earth without purpose. We would raise a monument to their memory, not of marble and stone, but of a world forged in the crucible of their sacrifice, a world worthy of their ultimate, agonizing gift. We would ensure their deaths were not echoes in the wind, but the thunder that shattered the old order.

Reconstruction blossomed, encompassing not only shattered settlements and realms, but also the fractured spirits of a ravaged land. A profound connection, surpassing the initial fiery intensity of our romance, steadily grew between Caspian and me. Our collaborative efforts, and talents interwoven like threads in a rich tapestry, cemented our alliance. A silent accord existed, a mutual esteem forged in the crucible of shared bereavement and unyielding commitment. Caspian, once an impenetrable fortress, revealed a fragility I'd never before glimpsed, a tender heart laid bare.

Ominous murmurs persisted, the spectre of peril still clung to the edges of existence. Yet, I stood prepared. My strength had deepened, my resolve hardened, and my concentration honed to an unparalleled sharpness. I had confronted her deepest anxieties, survived inconceivable devastation, and emerged profoundly altered. The fire within me blazed with unprecedented intensity, stoked by sorrow, devotion, and an unbreakable commitment to safeguarding the world Lyra had valiantly preserved. This new age presented formidable obstacles, but I, the incandescent elemental, stood defiantly, my heart burdened by grief, yet my spirit indomitable.

The sunrise marked a fresh commencement, a powerful symbol of hope's enduring resilience in the face of adversity. Victory had been achieved, but the struggle for lasting tranquillity had only just commenced. And I, bearing the weight of cherished memories and fortified by the strength of my love, would lead this charge. The path ahead remained shrouded in uncertainty, but one truth remained immutable: my steadfast determination to protect this world, now so precious to me, a world eternally marked by Lyra's legacy.

A wind, sharp and mournful, sighed through the skeletal framework of a city devoured by time, carrying the scent of petrichor and the ghost of wood smoke, a phantom perfume clinging to the dust choked air. I perched precariously on a crumbling parapet, the setting sun igniting the ravaged landscape in a fiery spectacle of bruised orange and deep violet. Crimson bled into the horizon, mirroring the unspoken tragedies etched into the very stones beneath my feet. The silence was absolute, a heavy blanket woven from centuries of sorrow, punctuated only by the whisper of wind blown leaves or the lonely, far off cry of a hawk circling a desolate spire. It was a silence pregnant with the echoes of forgotten battles, the lament of lost lives, the weight of countless vanished dreams. Yet, in the heart of this desolate beauty, in the embrace of this profound stillness, she found a strange, unexpected peace; a solace born from the stark and haunting grandeur of ruin.

The rough ridge of the scar on my forearm, a jagged map of countless battles against the Obsidian Covenant, felt cool beneath my fingertips. It was more than just a line of discoloured skin; it was a palimpsest of pain, a testament etched in flesh to the agonizing trials I'd endured, the sacrifices that had bled into the very fabric of my being. Each jagged edge whispered of near death experiences, of desperate struggles against overwhelming odds. But the scar wasn't merely a chronicle of suffering; it was also a blazing emblem of my resilience, a defiant mark of survival. I had stared into the abyss countless times, felt the icy breath of death on my neck, and each time, I had not only survived but emerged reforged, stronger, more resolute, burning with a fiercer, more incandescent life. This wasn't just a physical hardening; it was a profound deepening of my soul, a visceral understanding of the untamed power that surged within me, a power that resonated not only in the strength of my body but in the unwavering fortitude of my spirit. The scar was a badge of honour, a symbol of my triumph over oblivion.

I closed my eyes, and Lyra's face bloomed in my mind's eye, vivid and sharp as a freshly struck coin. I saw the mischievous glint in her dark, expressive eyes, a spark of rebellion that even death couldn't extinguish. I recalled her laughter, a rare, precious thing, a deep, resonant sound that vibrated through me, a warmth spreading from my chest to fill even the bleakest corners of my soul. It wasn't just a sound; it was a memory, a tangible echo of her spirit. Her death, though a wound that tore through me, wasn't a meaningless end. It was a sacrifice, a testament to her unwavering faith in our cause, a beacon of courage burning brightly even in the face of oblivion. Her sacrifice, a price paid willingly, with a fierce, unwavering loyalty that shamed my doubts, now illuminated the path ahead, guiding me forward with a strength born of her memory.

I realized then that our friendship had been far more profound than a mere whirlwind of shared laughter and good times. It had been a crucible, a journey of intense self discovery forged in the fires of shared experience. She hadn't just been a companion; she'd been a catalyst, pushing me relentlessly to my limits, forcing a confrontation with my deepest insecurities and hidden strengths. This journey of mutual growth and transformation had reshaped me, revealing facets of myself I never knew existed, and strengthening those I'd long underestimated. Her influence had been a transformative force, unlocking potential I hadn't dared to believe I possessed.

My eyes snapped open to a sunrise that wasn't a gentle awakening, but a goddamn hammer blow of light. Not celestial, it felt sacrilegious, a divine intervention ripped from some ancient, furious god. Golden lances, thick as my arm and burning with the heat of a thousand infernos, splintered the bruised purple of the storm clouds. The air, thick with the metallic tang of blood and the acrid bite of ozone, vibrated with the raw power of. Each ray felt like a physical caress, searing my skin, and leaving a trail of fire across my ravaged flesh.

This wasn't just the end of the storm; it was a battle cry, a primal scream tearing through the silence. The ravaged earth, churned mud and twisted metal groaning under a sky that still bled storm, was a mirror to the wreckage inside me. This breathtaking rebirth wasn't just etched across the landscape; it clawed its way into my soul, leaving me raw, reborn, and irrevocably changed. The taste of ash and the ghost of fear lingered, a bitter reminder of what had been lost. But the sunrise? That was a promise, a brutal, beautiful promise of something more. Something stronger. Something…mine.

The war might be over, but the echoes of conflict reverberated, a stark reminder that the fight for peace was far from finished. The world, wounded and broken, lay before me, a vast tapestry woven with loss and suffering, desperately in need of healing. And I, bearing my share of invisible wounds, felt a surge of unwavering resolve. I would play my part. The scars that mapped my body—both visible and those etched upon my soul—were not badges of defeat, but rather, glorious battle honours, testaments to our collective strength and the indomitable spirit that had borne us through unimaginable hardship. They were a living chronicle of our survival, a vibrant reminder that even from the ashes of devastation, the human spirit could rise, phoenix like, its wings ablaze with hope and the unwavering promise of a brighter future.

My relationship with Caspian had undergone a profound transformation, deepened by the shared crucible of loss and forged in the relentless fires of our collective struggle. His leadership, once steely and rigidly impersonal, now possessed a subtle, almost imperceptible, undercurrent of compassion, a poignant testament to the war's brutal reshaping of his character and the lingering shadow of Lyra's death. We were more than a team; we were a unified force, our diverse strengths interwoven like threads in a finely woven tapestry, each complementing and supporting the other. Our bond transcended the purely professional; it was an intimacy forged in the heart of the conflict, a silent, unspoken understanding that blossomed from the ashes of our shared trauma, a silent language spoken only between those who have stared into the abyss and emerged, changed, but together.

The whispers of new threats, insidious and chilling, slithered through the shadowed corners of the world, a constant, unsettling hum beneath the surface of normalcy. Yet within me, a profound shift had taken place, a metamorphosis that transcended mere physical strength.

It was a hard won maturity, forged in the crucible of loss, tempered by the fires of bitter experience. The flame elemental that burned within me pulsed with a potent, almost incandescent energy—a fusion not solely of rage, but of grief, a fierce, unwavering love, and an unshakeable determination. I had plumbed the deepest, darkest depths of despair, wrestled with the gnawing void of loss, and emerged, phoenix like, with a strength that even I found astonishing. I was more than a warrior; I was a survivor, a testament to resilience, a beacon of hope illuminating a world still struggling to mend its shattered physical and emotional landscapes. The scars remained, etched deep, but they were now badges of honour, testaments to the battles fought and won, a map of my journey from the abyss to this newfound, incandescent strength.

The reconstruction was a breathtaking physical manifestation of our collective resolve. From the rubble, kingdoms weren't merely rising; they were blossoming, their structures gaining strength with each meticulously placed stone, each carefully tilled furrow. Farms, once scarred and barren, were bursting forth with life, vibrant green shoots reaching for a sun that seemed to shine a little brighter now. More than just physical rebuilding, a palpable sense of community, forged in the crucible of shared trauma, was emerging, a resilient tapestry woven from threads of empathy and mutual support. I saw the resilience etched not just in the eyes of the survivors, but in the very set of their shoulders, a quiet strength born of shared hardship. Their faces, though lined with the passage of suffering, reflected a shared purpose, a luminous commitment to building not just a brighter future, but a future worthy of the sacrifices made, a future brimming with hope and the promise of enduring peace.

I understood that the journey ahead would be an arduous path to lasting peace paved not with roses but instead with the jagged stones of countless challenges and trials. The road stretched before me long and unforgiving its stark landscape, a relentless reflection of the depth and darkness of the Obsidian Covenant's tyranny. Each step I took echoed with the weight of history reminding me of the struggles endured by those who came before. Yet I was not alone in this daunting endeavor. At my side stood Caspian the unwavering leader of the Whispering Wind, his presence a beacon of hope. His gaze was as steadfast and unwavering as the northern star guiding us through the impending storms. Around me rallied a diverse community of survivors, individuals forged in the crucible of suffering yet bound together by an unbreakable spirit and a shared vision. Together we envisioned a world finally free from the Covenant's oppressive shadow, a world bathed in the radiant light of genuine peace and harmony. With every passing day our resolve deepened and the flicker of hope ignited within our hearts grew into a blazing fire. We were determined to reclaim our future to carve out a destiny defined not by fear but by resilience and unity.

As the sun ascended, its molten gold spilling across the rejuvenated landscape, a profound peace settled over me. The past, once a relentless storm, had been weathered; I had embraced the present with open arms, and the future stretched before me, not as a daunting unknown, but as a canvas waiting to be painted. This new dawn wasn't merely a promise of brighter days; it was a triumphant testament to the enduring power of love, a defiant assertion of resilience, and a blazing affirmation of the indomitable human spirit. The world remained fragile, the peace delicately balanced, a fragile butterfly on the wind. Yet, within the heart of the flame elemental, a core of incandescent energy, a new hope ignited, brighter, stronger, and more fiercely determined than ever before. The fight for lasting peace was far from over; it was a marathon, not a sprint. But as the first rays kissed my face, I knew, with a certainty that resonated deep within my soul, that I was ready. Ready to face whatever challenges lay ahead, armed with the unwavering strength forged in the crucible of the past and fueled by the boundless hope of this reborn day.

The sun, a molten orb of fire and gold, heaved itself over the horizon, its incandescent light painting the sky in strokes of fiery orange and rose. Long, skeletal shadows, cast by the newly planted saplings and the skeletal remains of burned out buildings, stretched across the fields like accusing fingers. The air, still thick with the acrid tang of yesterday's smoke and the lingering ghost of ash, now blended with the surprisingly sweet, earthy perfume of freshly turned soil, a scent both fragile and tenacious. The ravaged land, a scarred tapestry of charcoal and churned earth, once a brutal testament to the Obsidian Covenant's reign of terror, was slowly, painstakingly, breathing again. Each carefully planted seed, each painstakingly repaired irrigation ditch, was a tiny victory, a defiant whisper against the encroaching darkness. It was a testament not merely to the resilience of the human spirit, but to its unwavering hope, a silent, yet powerful rebellion against the devastation that had threatened to extinguish their very flame. The fields, though bearing the marks of war, hummed with a quiet, determined energy, a promise of a future blossoming from the ashes.

The air, thick with the cloying sweetness of fecund earth and the metallic tang of blood still clinging to my ravaged skin, filled my lungs. A grotesque parody of paradise. Around me, life exploded in a riot of emerald green, a mockery of the bone white wasteland I'd crawled from, a wasteland etched into my very soul, as surely as the crimson rivers that traced the map of my survival across my body. Silver scars, like moonlight on frozen blood, overlaid the angry red, each a jagged monument to a fight fought to the death, each a testament to the brutal price of this hard won freedom.

But a fragile, gossamer thing, lighter than the breath of a dying man, settled on my shoulders, hope. Not the absence of Lyra's ghost, the phantom weight of her absence still crushing my ribs like a vice, the emptiness where my heart should be a hollow, echoing chamber, but something beyond. The grief remained, a dull, throbbing ember deep in my chest, a phantom limb where joy used to sing, a constant, gnawing reminder of what I'd lost. Yet, it no longer owned me. No longer chained me to the icy tomb of despair.

The vibrant, almost obscene, green shoots clawing their way through the ravaged earth mirrored the stubborn, feral hope that pulsed within me, a defiant flower blooming in the poisoned soil of my memories. The taste of it, bitter and sweet, like ash and wildflowers, rose on my tongue, a promise whispered in the wind, a fragile, defiant whisper against the howling silence of my past.

Caspian, his face a roadmap of quiet determination mirroring my own, approached with the measured, purposeful tread of a seasoned warrior. The steely gaze that once commanded the Whispering Wind was now softened, etched with the hard won lines of a man who had stared into the abyss of unimaginable loss and returned, bearing not bitterness, but a profound and unexpected compassion. The shared weight of our grief had forged between us a bond stronger than any sworn alliance, a silent understanding woven from the threads of our sorrow, a language that transcended the limitations of words. His presence, a quiet strength in the face of devastation, was a balm to my wounded soul.

"They've found it," Caspain croaked, the words a guttural rasp that clawed its way from a throat choked with dust and the metallic tang of fear. His eyes, usually flint hard and calculating, were shadowed hollows, reflecting the flickering torchlight like trapped embers. The air hung thick with the scent of decay, damp earth, crumbling mortar, and something else... something ancient and subtly sickening. My weariness wasn't just bone deep; it was a soul deep ache, a leaden weight crushing the breath from my lungs. *"Deep in the Covenant's festering heart,"* he whispered, his voice trembling in the oppressive silence, *"buried beneath tons of rubble, beneath centuries of lies and forgotten horrors... something... unspeakable."* The weight of his revelation pressed down on me, a physical force, the implications of a chilling vortex threatening to pull me into its abyss.

My breath hitched, a strangled gasp in the chilling air. The Obsidian Covenant, though vanquished, their shattered remnants scattered like dust across the ravaged landscape, still clutched secrets deep within the earth's cold embrace. These weren't mere whispers of forgotten lore; these were secrets potent enough to rewrite the very fabric of history, to unravel the tapestry of time and offer a terrifyingly seductive glimpse into futures yet unborn, futures that could shatter the present with their brutal revelations.

Caspian continued his gaze fixed on the distant hills as if he could see beyond the horizon into a time long forgotten. *"An ancient prophecy "* he murmured the weight of the words hanging in the air. *"It speaks of others like you Blaze. Other elementals scattered across the land each one holding a unique power that has remained dormant for centuries waiting to be awakened. These beings are not just figments of legend; they are tied to the very essence of our world. Once united they could restore balance and harmony but first they must be found. The journey ahead will be perilous and the fate of our realm may depend on it. You Blaze may hold the key to unlocking their potential."*

The ancient prophecy, etched in glyphs older than the mountains themselves, spoke of a cataclysm, a maelstrom of elemental fury that would either forge a golden age of unparalleled harmony or shatter the world into a million jagged fragments of despair. It foretold the rise of the Elementals, chosen souls imbued with the raw, untamed power of earth, air, fire, and water; individuals destined to wrestle with the forces of creation and destruction, their every decision shaping the fate of existence. But the prophecy hinted at a far greater menace, a creeping shadow from the abyss, a malevolent entity immeasurably more potent than the dreaded Obsidian Covenant, whose reign of terror still echoed in the whispers of terrified elders. This looming darkness, shrouded in an aura of chilling anticipation, threatened to consume all, leaving behind only an echoing silence in the heart of a broken world. The balance, precarious and fragile, rested solely on the shoulders of these chosen few.

The weight of the prophecy crushed me, a physical burden settling on my shoulders, bowing my spine. The war against the Covenant had been a relentless, grinding campaign, a brutal tapestry woven from countless skirmishes, desperate sieges, and agonizing losses. We had fought on scorched battlefields, in the biting chill of frozen wastelands, and beneath the suffocating heat of alien suns. But this... this transcended the mere struggle for territory or power. This was a battle for existence itself, a fight for the very soul of the world, a last stand against the encroaching darkness threatening to extinguish the fragile flame of life.

The prophecy's unveiling ignited within me a fire, a renewed purpose that burned brighter than any sun. Lyra's death, a wound that still bled fresh with sorrow, was not a meaningless end. It had been the crucible in which my spirit was forged anew, tempered in the fires of grief and loss, emerging stronger, and more resilient than I ever thought possible. The prophecy, a whispered promise and a battle cry echoed Lyra's memory, fueling my resolve. Countless times I'd stared into the abyss of death, felt its icy breath on my neck; this was merely another trial, another fight in a war I was determined to win, not for myself, but for Lyra, for the memory of her unwavering spirit, and for the future that she would never see.

The days that followed were a maelstrom of relentless activity. Caspian, leveraging the painstakingly rebuilt intelligence network of the Whispering Wind, a delicate web of informants and whispers now humming with renewed purpose, embarked on the arduous, near impossible task of locating the scattered elementals. Each clue was a shard of glass, each leading a treacherous path potentially leading to dead ends or worse. Meanwhile, I immersed myself in a brutal regimen of training, pushing my already formidable skills to their absolute breaking point. My body screamed in protest, muscles quivering with exhaustion, yet I relentlessly honed my abilities, striving to tame the tempestuous, untamed energy that surged within me, a raw power that threatened to consume as much as it empowered. Each sweat soaked session was a battle fought not against an external foe, but against the very essence of my being, a desperate struggle for mastery over a force both magnificent and terrifying.

The training was a brutal crucible pushing me to the very edge of collapse. Each day felt like an unrelenting storm with my muscles screaming in protest, my lungs burning as if filled with fire and exhaustion gnawing at my resolve like a relentless predator. I often found myself teetering on the brink of surrender grappling with the overwhelming urge to give in to the fatigue that threatened to consume me. Yet amid this chaos and suffering the image of Caspian emerged as a radiant beacon of hope. His unwavering faith shone like a lighthouse in the suffocating darkness guiding me through the treacherous waters of despair and doubt.

His face etched in my memory shimmered vividly in the erratic dance of the flames that flickered around me casting shadows that played tricks on my weary mind. I saw reflections of him in the swirling dust devils whipped up by the gusty winds and even in the turbulent rush of the nearby river where the water seemed to embody the very essence of his strength. It wasn't just his faith that inspired me; it was the raw unshakeable power of his love, a potent elixir coursing through my veins invigorating me with each strained breath I took.

Every agonizing step I forced myself to make was fueled by his belief in me transforming the weight of my exhaustion into a newfound endurance. Every moment of pain morphed into a profound sense of purpose reminding me that I was not alone in this fight. His unwavering belief became my own, a shared bond that transcended the physical challenges I faced. I realized that every ounce of struggle was a testament to the strength of our connection, a reminder that love can indeed be a formidable force. As I pushed through the barriers of my own limitations I understood that each drop of sweat and every aching muscle was a step closer to not just surviving but thriving driven by the powerful legacy of Caspian's faith and love.

Weeks bled into months, each sunrise a fragile promise in the war's desolate aftermath. Slowly, painstakingly, like piecing together a shattered mosaic, they began to locate the other elementals. Each discovery was a jolt, a surge of hope that momentarily eclipsed the despair that had threatened to consume them. The earth elemental, Emerald, was a stoic mountain of a woman, her very presence radiating the unwavering strength of the earth itself; she could command the land to rise and fall, to crumble or to bloom, with a mere gesture.

The air elemental, Ophelia, was a whirlwind of mischievous energy, a spritely youth who controlled the winds with an effortless grace that bordered on the magical; she could summon gales that tore through armies or whisper secrets on the gentlest breeze. And then there was Cascade, the water elemental, a serene, ancient woman whose eyes held the wisdom of the deep ocean, whose power over the tides was both awe inspiring and terrifying; she could unleash devastating waves with a flick of her wrist, or soothe the stormiest seas with a calming word. Wait. Cascade? The name sparked a flicker of recognition, a remembered image of a woman—a woman who had vanished months ago, swallowed by the war's chaos, leaving behind only a lingering echo of her presence. The coincidence was unsettling, a shiver of unease snaking through the growing sense of hope.

As I trained my focus on the prophecy its deeper significance unfurled before us like a breathtaking yet terrifying panorama revealing layers of meaning that we had scarcely begun to comprehend. It wasn't merely a prediction of future calamities awaiting us around the corner; it was a clarion call, a desperate summons urging us to rally the fractured elements of nature against the encroaching shadow that threatened to envelop our world. The ancient words resonated with a power that transcended mere foretelling; they transformed into a battle cry—a desperate plea echoing across the ages reverberating through the very fabric of time itself.

This sacred text served as a reminder that even when the world teetered on the brink of oblivion, hope—fierce incandescent and unwavering hope—could still ignite within us a flame of resilience. This hope burned brighter than the despair that threatened to engulf us all shining forth like a beacon in the encroaching night. It was as if the prophecy beckoned us to awaken from our slumber to rise from the ashes of our complacency and to take our rightful place as stewards of the Earth. In this moment of clarity we understood that we were not mere bystanders in a grand cosmic play; we were active participants in a struggle that spanned generations.

As we delved deeper into the meaning of those ancient words we began to see the interconnectedness of all things. The prophecy illustrated that the well-being of humanity was intricately tied to the health of the natural world. The forests, rivers and mountains were not just backdrops to our existence; they were living entities pulsating with energy and deserving of our reverence and care. Each line of the prophecy illuminated the urgency of our mission compelling us to unite against the forces that sought to divide us.

We realized that the shadows creeping into our lives were not insurmountable; they were challenges that could be faced and overcome. It was in this shared understanding that our spirits were ignited and we found strength in camaraderie. Together we could harness the elemental forces of nature, align our intentions and drive back the darkness. The prophecy's message was clear: we were not alone in this fight. In unity we could forge a path toward a brighter future, one where hope reigns supreme and the light of our collective spirit illuminates even the darkest of nights.

The path ahead remained treacherous, a jagged scar across the landscape, fraught with unseen dangers that whispered from the shadows. But I, armed with the ancient prophecy, its cryptic verses etched upon my soul, and my loyal allies at my side, felt a surge of strength unlike any I had known. It coursed through me, a revitalizing current, replacing the bitter tide of rage and vengeance that had once consumed me. This new energy, born from the crucible of love and loss, burned with a brighter, more potent flame, a beacon of unwavering hope for a better future.

Blood red dawn, a brutal smear across the bruised horizon, promised not rebirth, but vengeance. The air, thick with the scent of scorched earth and the metallic tang of blood, vibrated with the raw, untamed fury of nature, a symphony of wind howled rage, a chorus of earth shattering tremors, a cacophony unleashed against the encroaching, suffocating darkness. My scarred hands, calloused and raw, ached with the memory of battles fought, and losses mourned. These weren't mere scars, they were maps etched onto my flesh, charting the devastation, the butchery, the annihilation. Each one a testament to the price exacted by the darkness, each a whispered promise of retribution.

But even amidst the ruins a flicker of a defiant spark ignited in the ashes of our broken world. Hope wasn't merely some gentle seed waiting for rain; it was a wildfire, a roaring inferno fueled by the bitter bile of our collective grief and pain ignited by the searing heat of our unrelenting resolve and determination to change our fate. It tasted of ash and iron carrying with it the memory of struggles past and smelled of burning defiance a testament to our refusal to fade away. This hope pulsed with the raw throbbing power of a heart that would not surrender resolutely beating against the silence of despair. We would not be broken or defeated. We would rise from the wreckage not reborn into a fragile existence but reforged in the furnace of our trials emerging sharper, stronger and utterly unstoppable. Each step forward was a declaration that we would reclaim our future transforming our scars into symbols of resilience and our pain into a powerful anthem of survival. Together we would forge a new path unyielding and fierce.

A new era was not merely dawning; it was breaking through the oppressive night, a radiant sunrise pushing back the shadows. The fight was far from over; the battle lines were still drawn, and the enemy was still formidable. But for the first time, a profound optimism filled me, a conviction so deep it resonated in my very bones, a belief that we would not merely survive, but thrive, rebuilding a world worthy of Lyra's memory. The echoes of Lyra's laughter, once a haunting reminder of our devastating loss, now resonated as a promise, a testament to the enduring power of love, a guiding beacon illuminating the path ahead.

The future was a jagged cliff, plunging into an abyss of unknown horrors. But the dawn, a brutal, bloody sunrise, clawed its way across the sky, staining the clouds with the bruised purple of a dying god and the sickly yellow of festering wounds. This false hope, a cruel mockery, burned in my gut, acrid and bitter, as potent as the dust that choked my lungs. Leaving Caspian, that viper coiled around our hard won peace, to his petty games, I embarked on my quest. His charming smile, a mask I'd grown weary of seeing, felt like a brand on my soul. I tasted the metallic tang of blood, mine, perhaps, spilled soon, and the grit of the scorched earth under my boots. Each step was a defiance, a testament to the prophecy's burning certainty. The wildflowers, tenacious bastards clinging to life amidst the desolation, mirrored my desperate resolve. For the remaining elements, each a shard of ancient power, each felt like a knife twisting in my ribs, demanded my obedience. Failure meant annihilation; success was a pyrrhic victory at best. The prophecy's promise, a venomous sweetness, was now a curse I was determined to fulfill.

www.ingramcontent.com/pod-product-compliance
Lightning Source LLC
Chambersburg PA
CBHW030029030726
47500CB00001B/15